LIBRARY OF SELECT NOVELS.

ALICE LORRAINE.

A Tale of the South Downs.

By R. D. BLACKMORE,

AUTHOR OF

"CRADOCK NOWELL," "MAID OF SKER," "LORNA DOONE," &c.

NEW YORK:
HARPER & BROTHERS, PUBLISHERS,
FRANKLIN SQUARE.
1875.

Novels are sweets. All people with healthy literary appetites love them—almost all women; a vast number of clever, hard-headed men. Judges, bishops, chancellors, mathematicians, are notorious novel readers, as well as young boys and sweet girls, and their kind, tender mothers.—W. M. Thackeray, in *Roundabout Papers.*

HARPER'S LIBRARY
OF
SELECT NOVELS.

Harper's Select Library of Fiction rarely includes a work which has not a decided charm, either from the clearness of the story, the significance of the theme, or the charm of the execution; so that on setting out upon a journey, or providing for the recreation of a solitary evening, one is wise and safe in procuring the later numbers of this attractive series.—*Boston Transcript.*

No.	Title	Price
1.	Pelham. By Bulwer	$ 75
2.	The Disowned. By Bulwer	75
3.	Devereux. By Bulwer	50
4.	Paul Clifford. By Bulwer	50
5.	Eugene Aram. By Bulwer	50
6.	The Last Days of Pompeii. By Bulwer	50
7.	The Czarina. By Mrs. Hofland	50
8.	Rienzi. By Bulwer	75
9.	Self-Devotion. By Miss Campbell	50
10.	The Nabob at Home	50
11.	Ernest Maltravers. By Bulwer	50
12.	Alice; or, The Mysteries. By Bulwer	50
13.	The Last of the Barons. By Bulwer	1 00
14.	Forest Days. By James	50
15.	Adam Brown, the Merchant. By H. Smith	50
16.	Pilgrims of the Rhine. By Bulwer	25
17.	The Home. By Miss Bremer	50
18.	The Lost Ship. By Captain Neale	75
19.	The False Heir. By James	50
20.	The Neighbors. By Miss Bremer	50
21.	Nina. By Miss Bremer	50
22.	The President's Daughters. By Miss Bremer	25
23.	The Banker's Wife. By Mrs. Gore	50
24.	The Birthright. By Mrs. Gore	25
25.	New Sketches of Every-day Life. By Miss Bremer	50
26.	Arabella Stuart. By James	50
27.	The Grumbler. By Miss Pickering	50
28.	The Unloved One. By Mrs. Hofland	50
29.	Jack of the Mill. By William Howitt	25
30.	The Heretic. By Lajetchnikoff	50
31.	The Jew. By Spindler	75
32.	Arthur. By Sue	75
33.	Chatsworth. By Ward	50
34.	The Prairie Bird. By C. A. Murray	1 00
35.	Amy Herbert. By Miss Sewell	50
36.	Rose d'Albret. By James	50
37.	The Triumphs of Time. By Mrs. Marsh	75
38.	The H—— Family. By Miss Bremer	50
39.	The Grandfather. By Miss Pickering	50
40.	Arrah Neil. By James	50
41.	The Jilt	50
42.	Tales from the German	50
43.	Arthur Arundel. By H. Smith	50
44.	Agincourt. By James	50
45.	The Regent's Daughter	50
46.	The Maid of Honor	50
47.	Safia. By De Beauvoir	50
48.	Look to the End. By Mrs. Ellis	50
49.	The Improvisatore. By Andersen	50
50.	The Gambler's Wife. By Mrs. Grey	50
51.	Veronica. By Zschokke	50
52.	Zoe. By Miss Jewsbury	50
53.	Wyoming	$ 50
54.	De Rohan. By Sue	50
55.	Self. By the Author of "Cecil"	75
56.	The Smuggler. By James	75
57.	The Breach of Promise	50
58.	Parsonage of Mora. By Miss Bremer	25
59.	A Chance Medley. By T. C. Grattan	50
60.	The White Slave	1 00
61.	The Bosom Friend. By Mrs. Grey	50
62.	Amaury. By Dumas	50
63.	The Author's Daughter. By Mary Howitt	25
64.	Only a Fiddler! &c. By Andersen	50
65.	The Whiteboy. By Mrs. Hall	50
66.	The Foster-Brother. Edited by Leigh Hunt	50
67.	Love and Mesmerism. By H. Smith	75
68.	Ascanio. By Dumas	75
69.	Lady of Milan. Edited by Mrs. Thomson	75
70.	The Citizen of Prague	1 00
71.	The Royal Favorite. By Mrs. Gore	50
72.	The Queen of Denmark. By Mrs. Gore	50
73.	The Elves, &c. By Tieck	50
74, 75.	The Step-Mother. By James	1 25
76.	Jessie's Flirtations	50
77.	Chevalier d'Harmental. By Dumas	50
78.	Peers and Parvenus. By Mrs. Gore	50
79.	The Commander of Malta. By Sue	50
80.	The Female Minister	50
81.	Emilia Wyndham. By Mrs. Marsh	75
82.	The Bush-Ranger. By Charles Rowcroft	50
83.	The Chronicles of Clovernook	25
84.	Genevieve. By Lamartine	25
85.	Livonian Tales	25
86.	Lettice Arnold. By Ms. Marsh	25
87.	Father Darcy. By Mrs. Marsh	75
88.	Leontine. By Mrs. Maberly	50
89.	Heidelberg. By James	50
90.	Lucretia. By Bulwer	75
91.	Beauchamp. By James	75
92, 94.	Fortescue. By Knowles	1 00
93.	Daniel Dennison, &c. By Mrs. Hofland	50
95.	Cinq-Mars. By De Vigny	50
96.	Woman's Trials. By Mrs. S. C. Hall	75
97.	The Castle of Ehrenstein. By James	50
98.	Marriage. By Miss S. Ferrier	50
99.	Roland Cashel. By Lever	1 25
100.	Martins of Cro' Martin. By Lever	1 25
101.	Russell. By James	50
102.	A Simple Story. By Mrs. Inchbald	50
103.	Norman's Bridge. By Mrs. Marsh	50
104.	Alamance	50
105.	Margaret Graham. By James	25

No.	Title	Price
106.	The Wayside Cross. By E. H. Milman.	$ 25
107.	The Convict. By James	50
108.	Midsummer Eve. By Mrs. S. C. Hall	50
109.	Jane Eyre. By Currer Bell	75
110.	The Last of the Fairies. By James	25
111.	Sir Theodore Broughton. By James	50
112.	Self-Control. By Mary Brunton	75
113, 114.	Harold. By Bulwer	1 00
115.	Brothers and Sisters. By Miss Bremer	50
116.	Gowrie. By James	50
117.	A Whim and its Consequences. By James	50
118.	Three Sisters and Three Fortunes. By G. H. Lewes	75
119.	The Discipline of Life	50
120.	Thirty Years Since. By James	75
121.	Mary Barton. By Mrs. Gaskell	50
122.	The Great Hoggarty Diamond. By Thackeray	25
123.	The Forgery. By James	50
124.	The Midnight Sun. By Miss Bremer	25
125, 126.	The Caxtons. By Bulwer	75
127.	Mordaunt Hall. By Mrs. Marsh	50
128.	My Uncle the Curate	50
129.	The Woodman. By James	75
130.	The Green Hand. A "Short Yarn"	75
131.	Sidonia the Sorceress. By Meinhold	1 00
132.	Shirley. By Currer Bell	1 00
133.	The Ogilvies	50
134.	Constance Lyndsay. By G. C. H.	50
135.	Sir Edward Graham. By Miss Sinclair.	1 00
136.	Hands not Hearts. By Miss Wilkinson.	50
137.	The Wilmingtons. By Mrs. Marsh	50
138.	Ned Allen. By D. Hannay	50
139.	Night and Morning. By Bulwer	75
140.	The Maid of Orleans	75
141.	Antonina. By Wilkie Collins	50
142.	Zanoni. By Bulwer	50
143.	Reginald Hastings. By Warburton	50
144.	Pride and Irresolution	50
145.	The Old Oak Chest. By James	50
146.	Julia Howard. By Mrs. Martin Bell.	50
147.	Adelaide Lindsay. Edited by Mrs. Marsh	50
148.	Petticoat Government. By Mrs. Trollope	50
149.	The Luttrells. By F. Williams	50
150.	Singleton Fontenoy, R. N. By Hannay	50
151.	Olive. By the Author of "The Ogilvies"	50
152.	Henry Smeaton. By James	50
153.	Time, the Avenger. By Mrs. Marsh.	50
154.	The Commissioner. By James	1 00
155.	The Wife's Sister. By Mrs. Hubback	50
156.	The Gold Worshipers	50
157.	The Daughter of Night. By Fullom.	50
158.	Stuart of Dunleath. By Hon. Caroline Norton	50
159.	Arthur Conway. By Capt. E. H. Milman	50
160.	The Fate. By James	50
161.	The Lady and the Priest. By Mrs. Maberly	50
162.	Aims and Obstacles. By James	50
163.	The Tutor's Ward	50
164.	Florence Sackville. By Mrs. Burbury	75
165.	Ravenscliffe. By Mrs. Marsh	50
166.	Maurice Tiernay. By Lever	1 00
167.	The Head of the Family. By Miss Mulock	75
168.	Darien. By Warburton	50
169.	Falkenburg	75
170.	The Daltons. By Lever	1 50
171.	Ivar; or, The Skjuts-Boy. By Miss Carlen	$ 50
172.	Pequinillo. By James	50
173.	Anna Hammer. By Temme	50
174.	A Life of Vicissitudes. By James	50
175.	Henry Esmond. By Thackeray	50
176, 177.	My Novel. By Bulwer	1 50
178.	Katie Stewart	25
179.	Castle Avon. By Mrs. Marsh	50
180.	Agnes Sorel. By James	50
181.	Agatha's Husband. By the Author of "Olive"	50
182.	Villette. By Currer Bell	75
183.	Lover's Stratagem. By Miss Carlen.	50
184.	Clouded Happiness. By Countess D'Orsay	50
185.	Charles Auchester. A Memorial	75
186.	Lady Lee's Widowhood	50
187.	Dodd Family Abroad. By Lever	1 25
188.	Sir Jasper Carew. By Lever	75
189.	Quiet Heart	25
190.	Aubrey. By Mrs. Marsh	75
191.	Ticonderoga. By James	50
192.	Hard Times. By Dickens	50
193.	The Young Husband. By Mrs. Grey	50
194.	The Mother's Recompense. By Grace Aguilar	75
195.	Avillion, &c. By Miss Mulock	1 25
196.	North and South. By Mrs. Gaskell.	50
197.	Country Neighborhood. By Miss Dupuy	50
198.	Constance Herbert. By Miss Jewsbury.	50
199.	The Heiress of Haughton. By Mrs. Marsh	50
200.	The Old Dominion. By James	50
201.	John Halifax. By the Author of "Olive," &c	75
202.	Evelyn Marston. By Mrs. Marsh	50
203.	Fortunes of Glencore. By Lever	50
204.	Leonora d'Orco. By James	50
205.	Nothing New. By Miss Mulock	50
206.	The Rose of Ashurst. By Mrs. Marsh	50
207.	The Athelings. By Mrs. Oliphant	75
208.	Scenes of Clerical Life	75
209.	My Lady Ludlow. By Mrs. Gaskell.	25
210, 211.	Gerald Fitzgerald. By Lever	50
212.	A Life for a Life. By Miss Mulock	50
213.	Sword and Gown. By Geo. Lawrence	25
214.	Misrepresentation. By Anna H. Drury.	1 00
215.	The Mill on the Floss. By George Eliot	75
216.	One of Them. By Lever	75
217.	A Day's Ride. By Lever	50
218.	Notice to Quit. By Wills	50
219.	A Strange Story	1 00
220.	Brown, Jones, and Robinson. By Trollope	50
221.	Abel Drake's Wife. By John Saunders	75
222.	Olive Blake's Good Work. By J. C. Jeaffreson	75
223.	The Professor's Lady	25
224.	Mistress and Maid. By Miss Mulock	50
225.	Aurora Floyd. By M. E. Braddon	75
226.	Barrington. By Lever	75
227.	Sylvia's Lovers. By Mrs. Gaskell	75
228.	A First Friendship	50
229.	A Dark Night's Work. By Mrs. Gaskell	50
230.	Countess Gisela. By E. Marlitt	25
231.	St. Olave's. By Eliza Tabor	75
232.	A Point of Honor	50
233.	Live it Down. By Jeaffreson	1 00
234.	Martin Pole. By Saunders	50

No.	Title	PRICE
235.	Mary Lyndsay. By Lady Ponsonby.	$ 50
236.	Eleanor's Victory. By M. E. Braddon	75
237.	Rachel Ray. By Trollope	50
238.	John Marchmont's Legacy. By M. E. Braddon	75
239.	Annie Warleigh's Fortunes. By Holme Lee	75
240.	The Wife's Evidence. By Wills	50
241.	Barbara's History. By Amelia B. Edwards	75
242.	Cousin Phillis	25
243.	What Will He Do With It? By Bulwer.	1 50
244.	The Ladder of Life. By Amelia B. Edwards	50
245.	Denis Duval. By Thackeray	50
246.	Maurice Dering. By Geo. Lawrence	50
247.	Margaret Denzil's History	75
248.	Quite Alone. By George Augustus Sala	75
249.	Mattie: a Stray	75
250.	My Brother's Wife. By Amelia B. Edwards	50
251.	Uncle Silas. By J. S. Le Fanu	75
252.	Lovel the Widower. By Thackeray	25
253.	Miss Mackenzie. By Anthony Trollope	50
254.	On Guard. By Annie Thomas	50
255.	Theo Leigh. By Annie Thomas	50
256.	Denis Doone. By Annie Thomas	50
257.	Belial	50
258.	Carry's Confession	75
259.	Miss Carew. By Amelia B. Edwards.	50
260.	Hand and Glove. By Amelia B. Edwards	50
261.	Guy Deverell. By J. S. Le Fanu	50
262.	Half a Million of Money. By Amelia B. Edwards	75
263.	The Belton Estate. By A. Trollope	50
264.	Agnes. By Mrs. Oliphant	75
265.	Walter Goring. By Annie Thomas	75
266.	Maxwell Drewitt. By Mrs. J. H. Riddell	75
267.	The Toilers of the Sea. By Victor Hugo	75
268.	Miss Marjoribanks. By Mrs. Oliphant.	50
269.	True History of a Little Ragamuffin. By James Greenwood	50
270.	Gilbert Rugge. By the Author of "A First Friendship"	1 00
271.	Sans Merci. By Geo. Lawrence	50
272.	Phemie Keller. By Mrs. J. H. Riddell	50
273.	Land at Last. By Edmund Yates	50
274.	Felix Holt, the Radical. By Geo. Eliot.	75
275.	Bound to the Wheel. By John Saunders	75
276.	All in the Dark. By J. S. Le Fanu.	50
277.	Kissing the Rod. By Edmund Yates	75
278.	The Race for Wealth. By Mrs. J. H. Riddell	75
279.	Lizzie Lorton of Greyrigg. By Mrs. Linton	75
280.	The Beauclercs, Father and Son. By C. Clarke	50
281.	Sir Brook Fossbrooke. By Chas. Lever	50
282.	Madonna Mary. By Mrs. Oliphant.	50
283.	Cradock Nowell. By R. D. Blackmore.	75
284.	Bernthal. From the German of L. Muhlbach	50
285.	Rachel's Secret	75
286.	The Claverings. By Anthony Trollope.	50
287.	The Village on the Cliff. By Miss Thackeray	25
288.	Played Out. By Annie Thomas	75
289.	Black Sheep. By Edmund Yates	50
290.	Sowing the Wind. By E. Lynn Linton.	50
291.	Nora and Archibald Lee	50
292.	Raymond's Heroine	$ 50
293.	Mr. Wynyard's Ward. By Holme Lee.	50
294.	Alec Forbes. By George Macdonald	75
295.	No Man's Friend. By F. W. Robinson.	75
296.	Called to Account. By Annie Thomas	50
297.	Caste	50
298.	The Curate's Discipline. By Mrs. Eiloart	50
299.	Circe. By Babington White	50
300.	The Tenants of Malory. By J. S. Le Fanu	50
301.	Carlyon's Year. By James Payn	25
302.	The Waterdale Neighbors	50
303.	Mabel's Progress	50
304.	Guild Court. By Geo. Macdonald	50
305.	The Brothers' Bet. By Miss Carlen.	25
306.	Playing for High Stakes. By Annie Thomas. Illustrated	25
307.	Margaret's Engagement	50
308.	One of the Family. By James Payn.	25
309.	Five Hundred Pounds Reward. By a Barrister	50
310.	Brownlows. By Mrs. Oliphant	38
311.	Charlotte's Inheritance. Sequel to "Birds of Prey." By Miss Braddon	50
312.	Jeanie's Quiet Life. By Eliza Tabor.	50
313.	Poor Humanity. By F. W. Robinson	50
314.	Brakespeare. By Geo. Lawrence	50
315.	A Lost Name. By J. S. Le Fanu	50
316.	Love or Marriage? By W. Black	50
317.	Dead-Sea Fruit. By Miss Braddon. Illustrated	50
318.	The Dower House. By Annie Thomas	50
319.	The Bramleighs of Bishop's Folly. By Lever	50
320.	Mildred. By Georgiana M. Craik	50
321.	Nature's Nobleman. By the Author of "Rachel's Secret"	50
322.	Kathleen. By the Author of "Raymond's Heroine"	50
323.	That Boy of Norcott's. By Chas. Lever	25
324.	In Silk Attire. By W. Black	50
325.	Hetty. By Henry Kingsley	25
326.	False Colors. By Annie Thomas	50
327.	Meta's Faith. By Eliza Tabor	50
328.	Found Dead. By James Payn	50
329.	Wrecked in Port. By Edmund Yates	50
330.	The Minister's Wife. By Mrs. Oliphant	75
331.	A Beggar on Horseback. By Jas. Payn	35
332.	Kitty. By M. Betham Edwards	50
333.	Only Herself. By Annie Thomas	50
334.	Hirell. By John Saunders	50
335.	Under Foot. By Alton Clyde	50
336.	So Runs the World Away. By Mrs. A. C. Steele	50
337.	Baffled. By Julia Goddard	75
338.	Beneath the Wheels	50
339.	Stern Necessity. By F. W. Robinson	50
340.	Gwendoline's Harvest. By James Payn	25
341.	Kilmeny. By William Black	50
342.	John: A Love Story. By Mrs. Oliphant	50
343.	True to Herself. By F. W. Robinson	50
344.	Veronica. By the Author of "Mabel's Progress"	50
345.	A Dangerous Guest. By the Author of "Gilbert Rugge"	50
346.	Estelle Russell	75
347.	The Heir Expectant. By the Author of "Raymond's Heroine"	50
348.	Which is the Heroine?	50
349.	The Vivian Romance. By Mortimer Collins	50

No.	Title	Price
350.	In Duty Bound. Illustrated	$ 50
351.	The Warden and Barchester Towers. By A. Trollope	75
352.	From Thistles — Grapes? By Mrs. Eiloart	50
353.	A Siren. By T. A. Trollope	50
354.	Sir Harry Hotspur of Humblethwaite. By Anthony Trollope. Illustrated	50
355.	Earl's Dene. By R. E. Francillon	50
356.	Daisy Nichol. By Lady Hardy	50
357.	Bred in the Bone. By James Payn	50
358.	Fenton's Quest. By Miss Braddon. Illustrated	50
359.	Monarch of Mincing-Lane. By W. Black. Illustrated	50
360.	A Life's Assize. By Mrs. J. H. Riddell	50
361.	Anteros. By the Author of "Guy Livingstone"	50
362.	Her Lord and Master. By Mrs. Ross Church	50
363.	Won—Not Wooed. By James Payn	50
364.	For Lack of Gold. By Chas. Gibbon	50
365.	Anne Furness	75
366.	A Daughter of Heth. By W. Black.	50
367.	Durnton Abbey. By T. A. Trollope.	50
368.	Joshua Marvel. By B. L. Farjeon	40
369.	Lovels of Arden. By M. E. Braddon. Illustrated	75
370.	Fair to See. By L. W. M. Lockhart.	75
371.	Cecil's Tryst. By James Payn	50
372.	Patty. By Katharine S. Macquoid	50
373.	Maud Mohan. By Annie Thomas	25
374.	Grif. By B. L. Farjeon	40
375.	A Bridge of Glass. By F. W. Robinson	50
376.	Albert Lunel. By Lord Brougham	75
377.	A Good Investment. By Wm. Flagg.	50
378.	A Golden Sorrow. By Mrs. Cashel Hoey	50
379.	Ombra. By Mrs. Oliphant	75
380.	Hope Deferred. By Eliza F. Pollard	50
381.	The Maid of Sker. By R. D. Blackmore	75
382.	For the King. By Charles Gibbon	50
383.	A Girl's Romance, and Other Tales. By F. W. Robinson	50
384.	Dr. Wainwright's Patient. By Edmund Yates	50
385.	A Passion in Tatters. By Annie Thomas	75
386.	A Woman's Vengeance. By Jas. Payn.	50
387.	The Strange Adventures of a Phaeton. By William Black	75
388.	To the Bitter End. By Miss Braddon.	75
389.	Robin Gray. By Charles Gibbon	50
390.	Godolphin. By Bulwer	50
391.	Leila. By Bulwer	50
392.	Kenelm Chillingly. By Lord Lytton.	75
393.	The Hour and the Man. By Harriet Martineau	50
394.	Murphy's Master. By James Payn	25
395.	The New Magdalen. By Wilkie Collins.	$ 50
396.	"'He Cometh Not,' She Said." By Annie Thomas	50
397.	Innocent. By Mrs. Oliphant. Illustrated	75
398.	Too Soon. By Mrs. Macquoid	50
399.	Strangers and Pilgrims. By Miss Braddon	75
400.	A Simpleton. By Charles Reade	50
401.	The Two Widows. By Annie Thomas	50
402.	Joseph the Jew	50
403.	Her Face was Her Fortune. By F. W. Robinson	50
404.	A Princess of Thule. By W. Black.	75
405.	Lottie Darling. By J. C. Jeaffreson.	75
406.	The Blue Ribbon. By Eliza Tabor.	50
407.	Harry Heathcote of Gangoil. By Anthony Trollope	25
408.	Publicans and Sinners. By Miss M. E. Braddon	75
409.	Colonel Dacre. By Author of "Caste"	50
410.	Through Fire and Water. By Frederick Talbot	25
411.	Lady Anna. By Anthony Trollope.	50
412.	Taken at the Flood. By Miss Braddon.	75
413.	At Her Mercy. By James Payn	50
414.	Ninety-Three. By Victor Hugo	25
415.	For Love and Life. By Mrs. Oliphant.	75
416.	Doctor Thorne. By Anthony Trollope.	75
417.	The Best of Husbands. By Jas. Payn.	50
418.	Sylvia's Choice. By Georgiana M. Craik	50
419.	A Sack of Gold. By Miss V. W. Johnson	50
420.	Squire Arden. By Mrs. Oliphant	75
421.	Lorna Doone. By R. D. Blackmore.	75
422.	Treasure Hunters. By Geo. M. Fenn.	40
423.	Lost for Love. By Miss Braddon	75
424.	Jack's Sister. By Miss Dora Havers.	75
425.	Aileen Ferrers. By Susan Morley	50
426.	The Love that Lived. By Mrs. Eiloart.	50
427.	In Honor Bound. By Charles Gibbon.	50
428.	Jessie Trim. By B. L. Farjeon	50
429.	Hagarene. By George A. Lawrence.	75
430.	Old Myddelton's Money. By Mary Cecil Hay	50
431.	At the Sign of the Silver Flagon. By B. L. Farjeon	40
432.	A Strange World. By Miss M. E. Braddon	75
433.	Hope Meredith. By Eliza Tabor	50
434.	The Maid of Killeena, and Other Stories. By William Black	50
435.	The Blossoming of an Aloe. By Mrs. Cashel Hoey	50
436.	Safely Married. By the Author of "Caste"	50
437.	The Story of Valentine; and his Brother	75
438.	Our Detachment. By Katharine King.	50
439.	Love's Victory. By B. L. Farjeon	25

ALICE LORRAINE.

A Tale of the South Downs.

By R. D. BLACKMORE,

AUTHOR OF "CRADOCK NOWELL," "THE MAID OF SKER," "LORNA DOONE," &c.

NEW YORK:
HARPER & BROTHERS, PUBLISHERS,
FRANKLIN SQUARE.
1875.

ALICE LORRAINE.

A TALE OF THE SOUTH DOWNS.

CHAPTER I.

WESTWARD of that old town Steyning, and near Washington and Wiston, the lover of an English landscape may find much to dwell upon. The best way to enjoy it is to follow the path along the meadows, underneath the inland rampart of the Sussex hills. Here is pasture rich enough for the daintiest sheep to dream upon; tones of varied green in stripes (by order of the farmer), trees as for a portrait grouped, with the folding hills behind, and light and shadow making love in play to one another. Also, in the breaks of meadow and the foot-path bendings, stiles where love is made in earnest, at the proper time of year, with the dark-browed hills imposing everlasting constancy.

Here no man, however lame he may be from the road of life, after sitting awhile and gazing, can deny himself to be refreshed and even comforted. Though he hold no commune with the heights so far above him, neither with the trees that stand in quiet audience soothingly, nor even with the flowers still as bright as in his childhood, yet to himself he must say something—better said in silence. Into his mind, and heart, and soul, without any painful knowledge, or the noisy trouble of thinking, pure content with his native land and its claim on his love are entering. The power of the earth is round him with its lavish gifts of life—bounty from the lap of beauty, and that cultivated glory which no other land has earned.

Instead of panting to rush abroad and be lost among jagged obstacles, rather let one stay within a very easy reach of home, and spare an hour to saunter gently down this meadow-path. Here in a broad bold gap of hedge, with bushes inclined to heal the breach, and mallow-leaves hiding the scar of chalk, here is a stile of no high pretense, and comfortable to gaze from. For hath it not a preface of planks, constructed with deep anatomical knowledge, and delicate study of maiden decorum? And lo! in spite of the planks—as if to show what human nature is—in the body of the stile itself, toward the end of the third bar down, are two considerable nicks, where the short-legged children from the village have a sad habit of coming to think. Here, with their fingers in their mouths, they sit and think, and scrape their heels, and stare at one another, broadly taking estimate of life. Then, with a push and scream, the scramble and the rush down hill begin, ending (as all troubles should) in a trackless waste of laughter.

However, it might be too much to say that the cleverest child beneath the hills, or even the man with the license to sell tea, coffee, snuff, and tobacco, who now comes looking after them, finds any conscious pleasure, or feels quickening influence from the scene. To them it is but a spread of meadows under a long curve of hill, green and mixed with trees down here, brown and spotted with furze up there; to the children a play-ground; to their father an acreage, inspected with no other view than glances at its rental.

So it is: and yet with even those who think no more of it, the place, if not the scenery, has its aftermath of influence. In later times, when sickness, absence, or the loss of sight debars them, men will feel a deep impression of a thing to long for. To be longed for with a yearning stronger than mere admiration, or any limner's taste can form. For he, whatever pleasure rises at the beauty of the scene, loses it by thinking of it; even as the joy of all things dies in the enjoying.

But to those who there were born (and never thought about it), in the days of age or ailment, or of better fortune even in a brighter climate, how at the sound of an ancient name, or glimpse of faint resemblance, or even on some turn of thought untraced and unaccountable, again the hills and valleys spread, to aged memory more true than ever to youthful eyesight; again the trees are rustling in the wind as they used to rustle; again the sheep climb up the brown turf in their snowy zigzag. A thousand winks of childhood widen into one clear dream of age.

CHAPTER II.

"How came that old house up there?" is generally the first question put by a Londoner to his Southdown friend leading him through the lowland path. "It must have a noble view; but what a position, and what an aspect!"

"The house has been there long enough to get used to it," is his host's reply; "and it is not built, as they are where you live, of the substance of a hat."

That large old-fashioned house, which looks as if it had been much larger, stands just beneath the crest of a long-backed hill in a deep embrasure. Although it stands so high, and sees much less of the sun than the pole-star, it is not quite so weather-beaten as a stranger would suppose. It has some little protection, and a definite outline for its grounds, because it was built on an old and extensive settlement of the chalk; a thing unheeded in early times, but now very popular and attractive, under the name of "land-slip." Of these there are a good many still to be traced on the sides of the Sussex hills, caused (as the learned say) by the shifting of the greensand, or silt, which generally underlies the more stable chalk. Few, however, of them are so strongly marked and bold as this one, which is known as "Coombe Lorraine." It is no mere depression or irregular subsidence, but a perpendicular fall, which shows as if a broad slice had been cut out from the chine to the base of the highland.

Here, in the time of William Rufus, Roland de Lorraine, having a grant from him, or from the Conqueror, and trusting the soil to slide no more, or ignorant that it had ever slidden, built himself a dwelling-place to keep a lookout on his property. This abode, no doubt, was fitted for warlike domesticity, being founded in the fine old times when every gentleman was bound to build himself a castle.

It may have been that a little jealousy of his friend, De Braose (who had taken a larger grant of land, although he was of newer race, and had killed fewer men than Sir Roland), led this enterprising founder to set up his tower so high. At any rate, he settled his Penates so commandingly, that if Bramber Castle had been in sight, he might have looked down its chimneys as freely as into his villein's sheep-cots. Bramber Castle, however, happened to be round the corner.

This good knight's end, according to the tradition of the family, was not so thoroughly peaceful as a life of war should earn. One gentle autumnal evening, Sir Roland and his friend and neighbor, William de Braose, were riding home to a quiet supper, both in excellent temper and spirits, and pleasant contempt of the country. The harvest-moon was rising over breadths of corn in grant to them, and sheep and cattle tended by their villeins, once the owners. Each congratulated the other upon tranquil seizin, and the good-will of the neighborhood; when suddenly their way was stopped by a score of heavy Englishmen.

These, in their clumsy manner, sued no favor, nor even justice; only to be trodden down with fairness and show of reason.

"Ye shall be trodden all alike," De Braose shouted fiercely, having learned a good deal of English from the place he lived in; "clods are made to be trodden down. Out of my road, or I draw my sword!"

The men turned from him to Sir Roland, who was known to be kind of heart.

"Ye do the wrong thing to meet me thus," he answered, in his utmost English; "the thing—that is to say, I hearken, but not with this violence."

Speaking thus he spurred his horse, and the best of the men made way for him. But one of them had an arrow straining on the cord, with intent to shoot—as he said to the priest at the gallows—De Braose, and him only. As the two knights galloped off, he let his arrow, in the waning of the light, fly after them; and it was so strongly sped that it pierced back-harness, and passed through the reins of Roland de Lorraine. Thus he died; and his descendants like to tell the story.

It is not true, although maintained by descendants of De Braose, that he was the man who was shot, and the knight who ran away Sir Roland. The pious duties rendered by the five brave monks from Fécamp were for the soul of Sir Roland, as surely as the arrow was for the body of De Braose. But after eight hundred years almost, let the benefit go between them.

Whichever way this may have chanced, in an age of unsettled principles, sure it is that the good knight died either then or afterward. Also that a man was hanged at a spot still shown in his behalf, and that he felt it such an outrage on his sense of justice, after missing his proper shot, that even now he is often seen, when the harvest-moon is lonely, straining a long-bow at something, but most careful not to shoot.

These, however, are mere legends, wherewith we have naught to do. And it would have been better not to rouse them up from slumber, if it could have been shown without them how the house was built up there. Also one may fairly fancy that a sweet and gallant knight may have found his own vague pleasure in a fine and ample view. Regarding which matter, we are perhaps a little too hard on our ancestors; presuming that they never owned such eyes as ours for "scenery," because they knew the large impossibility of describing it.

CHAPTER III.

WHETHER his fathers felt, or failed to see, the beauty beneath their eyes, the owner of this house and land, at the time we have to speak of, deserved and had the true respect of all who dwelt below him.

It is often said that no direct descendant, bred from sire to son, still exists, or at any rate can show that he has right to exist, from any knight, or even cook, known to have come with the Conqueror. The question is one of delicacy, and therefore of deep feeling. But it must be owned, in candor, upon almost every side, that there are people, here and there, able to show something. The present Sir Roland Lorraine could show as much in this behalf as any other man in England. Here was the name, and here the place; and here the more fugitive being man, still belonging to both of them.

Whether could be shown or not the strict red line of lineage, Sir Roland Lorraine was the very last man likely to assert it. He had his own opinions on that all-important subject, and his own little touches of feeling when the matter came into bearing. His pride was of so large a nature that he seldom could be proud. He had his pleasant vein of humor about almost every thing, wholly free from scoffing, and most sensitive of its limit. Also, although he laid no claim to any extensive learning or especially accurate scholarship, his reading had been various, and his knowledge of the classics had not been allowed to fade away into misty memory.

Inasmuch as he added to these resources the farther recommendations of a fine appearance and gentle manners, good position and fair estates, it may be supposed that Sir Roland was in strong demand among his neighbors for all social purposes. He, however, through no petty feeling or small exclusiveness, but from his own taste and likings, kept himself more and more at home, and in quietude, as he grew older. So that ere he turned sixty years, the owner of Coombe Lorraine had ceased to appear at any county gatherings, or even at the hospitable meetings of the neighborhood.

His dinner-party consisted only of himself and his daughter Alice. His wife had been dead for many years. His mother, Lady Valeria, was still alive and very active, but having numbered fourscore years, had attained the right of her own way. By right or wrong, she had always contrived to enjoy that special easement; and even now, though she lived apart, little could be done without her in the household management.

Hilary, Sir Roland's only son, was now at the Temple, eating his way to the bar, or feeding for some other mischief; and Alice, the only daughter living, was the baronet's favorite companion, and his darling.

Now whether from purity of descent, or special mode of selection, or from living so long on a hill with northern consequences, or from some other cause to be extracted by philosophers from bestial analogies — anyhow, one thing is certain: these Lorraines were not, and had not for a long time been, at all like the rest of the world around them. It was not pride of race that made them unambitious, and well content, and difficult to get at; neither was it any other ill affection to mankind. They liked a good man, when they saw him; and naturally so much the more as it became harder to find him. Also, they were very kind to all the poor people around them, and kept well in with the church, and did whatever else is comely. But long before Sir Roland's time, all Sussex knew, and was content to know, that, as a general rule, "those Lorraines went nowhere."

Neighbors who were conscious of what we must now begin to call "co-operative origin," felt that though themselves could claim justices of the peace, high sheriffs, and knights of the shire among their kin, yet they could not quite climb over that romantic bar of ages which is so deterrent perhaps because it is so shadowy. Neither did they greatly care to press their company upon people so different from themselves, and so unlikely to admire them. But if any one asked where lay the root of the difference which so long had marked the old family on the hill, perhaps no one, least of all any of the Lorraines themselves, could have given the proper answer. Plenty of other folk there were who held aloof from public life. Simplicity, kindness, and chivalry might be found, by a man with an active horse, in other places also: even a feeling as nearly akin as our nature admits to contempt of money at that time went on somewhere. How, then, differed these Lorraines from other people of equal rank and like habits with them?

Men who differ from their fellows seem, by some law of nature, to resent and disclaim the difference. Those who are proud, and glory in their variance from the common type, seldom vary much from it. So that in the year of grace 1811, the mighty comet that scared the world, spreading its tail over good and bad, overhung no house less conscious of any thing under its roof peculiar than the house of Coombe Lorraine.

With these Lorraines there had been a tradition (ripened, as traditions ripen, into a small religion), that a certain sequence of Christian names must be observed, whenever allowed by Providence, in the heritage. These names in right order were Roland, Hilary, and Roger; and the family had long believed, and so had all their tenants, that a certain sequence of character, and the events which depend upon character, might be expected to coincide with the succession of these names. The Rolands were always kindly proud, fond of home and of all their people, lovers of a quiet life, and rather deep than hot of heart. A Hilary, the next of race, was prone to the opposite extremes, though still of the same root-fibre. Sir Hilary was always showy, affable, and romantic, eager to do something great, pleased to give pleasure to every body, and leaving his children to count the cost. After him there ought to arise a Roger, the savior of the race; beginning to count pence in his cradle, and growing a yard in common sense for every inch of his stature, frowning at every idea that was not either of land or money, and weighing himself and his bride and most of his principles, by Troy-weight.

CHAPTER IV.

Upon a very important day, as it proved to be, in his little world, the 18th of June, 1811, Sir Roland Lorraine had enjoyed his dinner with his daughter Alice. In those days men were not content to feed in the fashion of owls, or wild ducks, who have lain abed all day. In winter or summer, at Coombe Lorraine, the dinner-bell rang at half-past four, for people to dress; and again at five, for all to be down in the drawing-room. And all were sure to be prompt enough; for the air of the Southdown hills is hungry, and Nature knew what the demand would be, before she supplied her best mutton there.

When the worthy old butler was gone at last, and the long dark room lay silent, Alice ran up to her father's side, to wish him, over a sip of wine, the good old wish that sits so lightly on the lips of children.

"Darling papa, I wish you many happy, happy returns of the day, and good health to enjoy them."

Sir Roland was sixty years old that day; and being of a cheerful, even, and pleasant, though shy temperament, he saw no reason why he should not have all the bliss invoked on him. The one great element in that happiness now was looking at him, undeniably present and determined to remain so.

His quick glance told that he felt all this; but he was not wont to show what he felt; and now he had no particular reason to feel more than usual. Nevertheless he did so feel, without knowing any reason, and turned his eyes away from hers, while he tried to answer lightly.

This would not do for his daughter Alice. She was now in that blush of time, when every thing is observed by maidens, but every thing is not hinted at. At least it used to be so then, and still is so in good places. Therefore Alice thought a little before she began to talk again. The only trouble, to her knowledge, which her father had to deal with, was the unstable and romantic character of young Hilary. This he never discussed with her, nor even alluded to it; for that would have been a breach of the law in all duly-entailed conservatism, that the heir of the house, even though a fool, must have his folly kept sacred from the smiles of inferior members. Now Hilary was not at all a fool; only a young man of large mind.

Knowing that her father had not any bad news of Hilary, from whom he had received a very affectionate letter that morning, Alice was sorely puzzled, but scarcely ventured to ask questions; for in this savage island, then, respect was shown and reverence felt by children toward their parents; and she, although such a petted child, was full of these fine sentiments. Also now in her seventeenth year, she knew that she had outgrown the playful freedoms of the babyhood, but was not yet established in the dignity of a maiden, much less the glory of womanhood. So that her sunny smile was fading into the shadow of a sigh, when, instead of laying her pretty head on her father's shoulder, she brought the low chair and favorite cushion of the younger times, and thence looked up at him, hoping fondly once more to be folded back into the love of childhood.

Whatever Sir Roland's trouble was, it did not engross his thoughts so much as to make him neglect his favorite. He answered her wistful gaze with a smile, which she knew to be quite genuine; and then he patted her curly hair, in the old-fashioned way, and kissed her forehead.

"Lallie, you look so profoundly wise, I shall put you into caps after all, in spite of your sighs, and tears, and sobs. A head so mature in its wisdom must conform to the wisdom of the age."

"Papa, they are such hideous things! and you hate them as much as I do. And only the other day you said that even married people had no right to make such frights of themselves."

"Married people have a right to please one another only. A narrow view, perhaps, of justice; but—however, that is different. Alice, you never will attend when I try to teach you any thing."

Sir Roland broke off lamely thus, because his child was attending, more than himself, to what he was talking of. Like other men, he was sometimes given to exceed his meaning; but with his daughter he was always very careful of his words, because she had lost her mother, and none could ever make up the difference.

"Papa!" cried Alice, with that appealing stress upon the paternity which only a pet child can throw, "you are not at all like yourself to-day."

"My dear, most people differ from themselves, with great advantage. But you will never think that of me. Now let me know your opinion as to all this matter, darling."

Her father softened off his ending suddenly thus, because he saw the young girl's eyes begin to glisten, as if for tears, at his strange new way.

"What matter, papa? The caps? Oh no; the way you are now behaving. Very well, then, are you quite sure you can bear to hear all you have done amiss?"

"No, my dear, I am not at all sure. But I will try to endure your most heart-rending exaggerations."

"Then, dear papa, you shall have it all. Only tell me when to stop. In the first place, did you, or did you not, refuse to have Hilary home for your birthday, much as you knew that I wanted him? You confess that you did. And your only reason was something you said about Trinity term, equally incomprehensible. In the next place, when I wanted you to have a little change to-day, Uncle Struan for dinner, and Sir Remnant, and one or two others—"

"My dear, how could I eat all these? Think of your uncle Struan's size."

"Papa, you are only trying now to provoke me, because you can not answer. You know what I mean as well as I do, and perhaps a little better. What I mean is, one or two of the very oldest friends and relations to do what was nice, and help you to get on with your birthday; but you said, with unusual ferocity, 'Darling, I will have none but you!'"

"Upon my word, I believe I did! How wonderfully women—at least I mean how children—astonish one, by the way they touch the very tone of utterance, after one has forgotten it!"

"I don't know what you mean, papa. And your reflection seems to be meant for yourself, as every thing seems to be for at least a week, or I might say—"

"Come, Lallie, come now, have some moderation."

"Well, then, papa, for at least a fortnight. I will let you off with that, though I know it is much too little. And when you have owned to that, papa, what good reason can you give for behaving so to me—me—me, as good a child as ever there was?"

"Can 'me, me, me,' after living through such a fortnight of mortification—the real length of the period being less than four hours, I believe—can she listen to a little story without any excitement?"

"Oh papa, a story, a story! That will make up for every thing. What a lovely pleasure! There is nothing I love half so much as listening to old stories. I seem to be living my old age over, before I come to any age. Papa, I will forgive you every thing, if you tell me a story."

"Alice, you are a little too bad. I know what a very good girl you are; but still you ought to try to think. When you were only two years old, you looked as if you were always thinking."

"So I am now, papa; always thinking—how to please you, and do my best."

Sir Roland was beaten by this, because he knew the perfect truth of it. Alice already thought too much about every thing she could think of. Her father knew how bad it is, when the bright young time is clouded over with unseasonable cares; and often he had sore misgivings, lest he might be keeping his pet child too much alone. But she only laughed whenever he offered to find her new companions, and said that her cousins at the rectory were enough for her.

"If you please, papa," she now broke in upon his thinking, "how long will it be before you begin to tell me this beautiful story?"

"My own darling, I forgot; I was thinking of you, and not of any trumpery stories. But this is the very day of all days to sift our little mystery. You have often heard, of course, about our old astrologer."

"Of course I have, papa—of course! And with all my heart I love him. Every thing the shepherds tell me shows how thoroughly good he was."

"Very well, then, all my story is about him, and his deeds."

"Oh papa, then do try, for once in your life, to be in a hurry. I do love every thing about him; and I have heard so many things."

"No doubt you have, my dear; but perhaps of a somewhat fabulous order. His mind, or his manners, or appearance, or at any rate something seems to have left a lasting impression upon the simple folk hereabouts."

"Better than a pot of money: an old woman told me the other day it was better than a pot of money for any body to dream of him."

"It would do them more good, no doubt. But I have not had a pinch of snuff to-day. You have nearly broken me, Alice; but still you do allow me one pinch when I begin to tell you a good story."

"Three, papa; you shall have three now, and you may take them all at once; because you never told such a story, as I feel sure it is certain to be, in all the whole course of your life before. Now come here, where the sun is setting, so that I may watch the way you are telling every word of it; and if I ask you any questions you must nod your head, but never presume to answer one of them, unless you are sure that it will go on without interrupting the story. Now, papa, no more delay."

CHAPTER V.

THE LEGEND OF THE ASTROLOGER.

Two hundred years before the day when Alice thus sat listening, an ancestor of hers had been renowned in Anatolia. The most accomplished and most learned prince in all lesser Asia was Agasicles Syennesis, descended from Mausolus (made immortal by his mausoleum), and from that celebrated king, Syennesis of Cilicia. There had been, after both these were dead, and much of their repute gone by, creditable and happy marriages in and out their descendants, at a little over, and a little under, twenty-two centuries ago; and the best result and issue of all these was now embodied in Prince Agasicles.

The prince was not a patron only, but also an eager student, of the more recondite arts and science then in cultivation. Especially he had given his mind to chemistry (including alchemy), mineralogy, and astrology. Devoting himself to these fine subjects, and many others, he seems to have neglected anthropology; so that in his fiftieth year he was but a lonesome bachelor. Troubled at this time of life with many expostulations—genuine on the part of his friends, and emphatic on that of his relatives—he held a long interview with the stars, and taking their advice exactly as they gave and meant it, married a wife the next afternoon, and (so far as he could make out) the right one. This turned out well. His wife went off, on the occasion of her first confinement, leaving him with a daughter, born A.D. 1590, and all women pronounced her beautiful.

The prince now spent his leisure time in thought and calculation. He had almost made his mind up that he was sure to have a son; and here was his wife gone; and how could he risk his life again so? Upon the whole, he made up his mind that matters might have been worse, although they ought to have been much better, and that he must thank the stars, and not be too hard upon any one; and so he fell to at his science again, and studied almost every thing.

In that ancient corner of the world, old Caria, the fine original Leleges looked up to the prince, and loved him warmly, and were ready by night or day to serve him, or to rob him. They saw that now was the finest chance (while he was looking at the stars, with no wife to look out for him) for them to do their duty to their families by robbing him; and this they did with honest comfort, and a sense of going home in the proper way to go.

Prince Agasicles, growing older, felt these troubles more and more. As a general rule, a man growing older has a more extensive knowledge that he must be robbed of course; and yet he scarcely ever seems to reconcile himself with maturing wisdom to the process. And so it happened to this good prince; not that he cared so very much about little trifles that might attract the eye of taste and the hand of skill, but that he could not (even with the aid of all the stars) find any thing too valuable to be stolen. Hence, as his daughter, Artemise, grew to the fullness of young beauty, he thought it wise to raise the most substantial barrier he could build betwixt her and the outer world.

There happened to be in that neighborhood then an active supply of villains. Of this by no means singular fact the prince might well assure himself, by casting his eyes down from the stars to the narrow bosom of his mother earth. But whether thus or otherwise forewarned of local mischief, the Carian prince took a very strong measure, and even a sacrilegious one. In or about the year of our reckoning, 1606, he walled off his daughter, and other goods, in a certain peninsula of his own, clearly displayed in our maps, and as clearly forbidden to be either trenched or walled by a Pythia skilled in trimeter tone, who seems to have been a lady of exceptionally clear conservatism.

The prince, as the sage of the neighborhood, knew all about this prohibition, and that it was still in force, and must have acquired twenty-fold power by the lapse of twenty centuries; and as the sea had retreated a little during that short period, it was evident that Jove had been consistent in the matter. "He never meant it for an island, else he would have made it one." Agasicles therefore felt some doubt about the piety of his proceeding, retaining as he did, in common with his neighbors, some respect for the classic gods. His respect, however, for the stars was deeper, and these told him that young Artemise was likely to be run away with by some bold adventurer. A peninsula was the very thing to suit his purpose, and none could be fairer or snugger than this of his own, the very site of ancient Cnidos, whereof Venus once was queen.

Undeterred by this local affection, or even the warnings of Delphi, the learned prince exerted himself, and by means of a tidy hedge of paliure and aspalathus made the five stades of isthmus proof against even thick-trowsered gentlemen, *a fortiori* against the natives all unendowed with pantaloons. Neither might his fence be leaped by any of the roving horsemen — Turks, Cilicians, Pamphylians, Karamanians, or reavers from the chain of Taurus.

This being fixed to his satisfaction, with a couple of sentries at the gate, and one at either end, prompt with matchlocks, and above all, the young lady inside provided with many proverbs, Prince Agasicles set forth on a visit to an Armenian sage reputed to be as wise as himself almost. With him he discussed Alhasen, Vitellio, and their own contemporary, Kepler, and spent so many hours aloft, that on his return to his native place he discovered his own little oversight. This was so very simple that it required at least a sage and great philosopher to commit it. The learned man appears to have forgotten that the sea is navigable. So it chanced that a gay young Englishman, cruising about in an armed speronera among the Ægean islands, and now in the Carpathian sea, hunting after pirates, heard of this Eastern Cynosure, and her walled seclusion. This of course was enough for him. Landing under the promontory where the Cnidian Venus stood, he fell, and falling dragged another, into the wild maze of love.

Mazed they seemed of course, and nearly mad no doubt to other folk. To themselves, however, they were in a new world altogether, far above the level and the intellect of the common world. Artemise forgot her pride, her proverbs, and pretensions; she had lost her own way in the regions of a higher life; and nothing to her was the same as it had been but yesterday. Heart and soul, and height and depth, she trusted herself to the Englishman, and even left her jewels.

Therefore they two launched their bark upon the unknown waters; the damsel with her heart in tempest of the filial duties shattered, and the fatherland cast off, yet for the main part anchored firmly on the gallant fluke of love; the youth in a hurry to fight a giant, if it would elevate him to her.

Artemise, with all her rashness, fared much better than she deserved for leaving an adoring father the wrong side of the quickset hedge. The bold young mariner happened to be a certain Hilary Lorraine, heir of that old house or castle in the Southdown coombe. Possessed with the adventurous spirit of his uncles, the famous Shirley brothers, he had sailed with Raleigh, and made havoc here and there, and seen almost as much of the world as was good for himself or it.

Enlarged by travel, he was enabled to suppress rude curiosity about the wishes of the absent prince; and deferring to a better season the pleasure of his acquaintance, he made all sail with the daughter on board, as set forth already; and those two were made into one, according to the rites of the old Greek Church, in the classic shades of Ida. And to their dying day it never repented either of them—much.

When the prince returned, and found no daughter left to meet him, he failed for a short time to display that self-command upon which he had for years been wont to plume himself. But having improved his condition of mind by a generous bastinado of servants, peasants, and matchlock-men, he found himself reasonably remounting into the sphere of pure intellect. In a night or two an interesting conjunction of heavenly bodies happened, and eclipsed this nebulous world of women.

In a few years' time he began to get presents, eatable, drinkable, and good. Gradually thus he showed his wisdom, by foregoing petty wrath; and when he was summoned to meet a star, militant to his grandson, he could not help ordering his horse.

CHAPTER VI.

THE LEGEND OF THE ASTROLOGER.

ALTHOUGH this prince knew so much more of the heaven above than the earth beneath, he did not quite expect to ride the whole of the way to England. At Smyrna he took ship, and after some difficulties and dangers, landed at Shoreham, full of joy to behold his four grandchildren, who proved to be five by the time he saw them. The Sussex roads were as bad as need be, and worse than could be anywhere else; but the sturdy oxen set their necks to drag through all things, thick or thin; and the prince stuck fast to his coach, as firmly as the coach stuck fast with him. Having never seen any roads before, he thought them a wonderful institution, and though misled by the light of nature to grumble at some of his worst upsets, a little reflection led him softly back into contentment. A mind "irretrievably analytic" at once distinguished wisdom's element in the Sussex reasoners.

"Gin us made thase hyur radds gooder, volk 'ood be radin' down droo 'em avery dai, a'most! The Lard in heaven never made radds as cud ever baide the work, if straunngers cud goo along, wi'out bin vorced to zit down, and mend 'un."

When this was interpreted to his highness, he was so struck with its clear sound sense, and logical sequence, that he fell back, and for the rest of his journey admired the grandeur of English character. This sentiment, so deeply founded, was not likely to be impaired by further acquaintance with our great nation. For more than a twelvemonth Prince Agasicles made his home in England, and many of his quaint remarks abode on Sussex shepherds' tongues for generations afterward, recommended as they were by the vantage of princely wisdom; for he picked up quite enough of the language to say odd things as a child does, and with a like simplicity. With this difference, however, that while the great hits of the little ones, by the proud mother chronicled, are the lucky outbursts of happy inexperience, the old man's sage words were the issue of unhappy experience.

Nevertheless he must have owned a genial nature still at work. For he loved to go down the village-lane, when the wind was cold on the highland, and there to wait at a cottage door till the children came to stare at him. And soon these children had courage to spy that, in spite of his outlandish dress, pockets were about him, and they whispered as much to one another, while their eyes were testing him. At other times when the wind was soft, and shadows of gentle clouds were shed in chase of one another, this great man who had seen the world, and knew all the stars hanging over it—his pleasure was to wander in and out of the ups and downs and nooks of quaintly-plaited hills, and feast his eyes upon their verdure. After that, when the westering light was spreading the upland ridge with gold, and the glades with gray solemnity, this man of declining years was well content to lean on a bank of turf, and watch the quiet ways of sheep. Often thus his mind was carried back to the land of childhood, soothed as in his nurse's arms by nature's peace around him. And if his dreams were interrupted by the crisp fresh sound of browsing, and the ovine tricks as bright as any human exploits, he would turn and do his best to talk with the lonely shepherds.

These, in their simple way, amused him, with their homely saws, and strange content, and independence; and he no less delighted them by unaccustomed modes of speech, and turns of thought beyond their minds, and distant wisdom quite brought home. Thus, and by many other means, this ancient prince, of noble presence, and of flowing snow-white hair, and vesture undisgraced by tailors, left such trace upon these hills, that even his ghost was well believed to know all the sheep-tracks afterward.

Pleased with England, and with English scenery and customs, as well as charmed with having five quite baby stars to ephemerize, this great astrologer settled to stay in our country as long as possible. He sent his trusty servant, Memel, in a merchant-ship from Shoreham to fetch his implements and papers, precious things of many kinds, and curiosities long in store. Memel brought all these quite safe, except one little thing or two, which he accounted trifles; but his master was greatly vexed about them.

The prince unpacked his goods most carefully in his own eight-sided room, allowing none but his daughter to help him, and not too sure about trusting her. Then forth he set for a real campaign among the stars of the Southdowns—and supper-call and breakfast-bell were no more than the bark of a dog to him. And thus he spent his nights, alas! forgetful of the different clime, under the cold stars, when by rights he should have been under the counterpane.

This grew worse and worse, until toward the middle of the month of June, A.D. 1611, his mind was altogether much above its proper temperature. Great things were pending in the heavens, which might be quoted as pious excuse for a little human restlessness. The prince with his implements always ready, either in his lantern-chamber, or at his favorite spot of the hills, according to the weather, grew more and more impatient daily for the sun to be out of the way, and more and more intolerant every night of any cloudiness. Self-perplexed, downcast, and moody (except when for a few brief hours a brighter canopy changed his gloom into a nervous rapture), he wasted and waned away in body, as his mind grew brighter. After the hurried night, he dragged his faint way home in the morning, and his face of exhausted power struck awe into the household. No one dared to ask him what had happened, or why he looked so; and he like a true philosopher kept all explanations to himself. And then he started anew, and strode, with his Samian cloak around him, over the highest and darkest and most lonesome hill, out of people's sight.

One place there was, which beyond all others suited his purposes and his mood. A well-known landmark now, and the scene of many a merry picnic, Chanctonbury Ring was then a lonely spot imbued with terror of a wandering ghost — an ancient ghost with a long white beard, walking even in the afternoon, with its head bowed down in search of something—a vain search of centuries. This long-sought treasure has now been found; not by the ghost, however, but by a lucky stroke of the plowshare; and the spectral owner roves no more. He is supposed, with all the assumption required to make a certainty, to have been a tenant on Chancton Manor, under Earl Gurth, the brother of Harold, and being slain at Hastings, to have forgotten where his treasure lay.

The Ring, as of old, is a height of vantage for searching all the country round with a telescope on a breezy day. It is the salient point and foreland of a long ridge of naked hills, crowned with darker eminence by a circle of storm-huddled trees. But when the astrologer Agasicles made his principal night-haunt here, the Ring was not overhung with trees, but only outlined by them; and the rampart of the British camp (if such it were) was more distinct, and uninvaded by planters. So that here was the very place for a quiet sage to make his home, sweeping a long horizon and secure from interruption. To such a citadel of science, guarded by the fame of ghosts, even his daughter Artemise, or his trusty servant Memel, would scarcely dare to follow him; much less any of the peasants, who, from the lowland, seeing a distant light, crossed themselves; for that fine old custom flourished still among them. Therefore, here his tent was pitched, and here he spent the nights in gazing, and often the days in computation, not for himself but for his descendants; until his frame began to waste, and his great dark eyes grew pale with it.

CHAPTER VII.

THE LEGEND OF THE ASTROLOGER.

ARTEMISE, and all around the prince, had been alarmed of late by many little symptoms. He always had been rashly given to take no heed of his food or clothes; but now he went beyond all that, and would have no one take heed for him, or dare to speak of the matter much. Hence, without listening to any nonsense, all the women were sure of one thing—the prince was wearing himself away.

The country people who knew him, and loved him with a little mystery, said that it was no wonder he should worry himself, for being so long away from home, in manners, and in places also. "Sure it must be a trial for him; out all night in the damp and fog; and he no sense of breeches!"

There was much of truth in this, no doubt, as well as much outside it. Yet none of them could enter into his peculiar state of mind. So that he often reproached himself for having been rude, but could not help it. Every one made allowance for him, as Englishmen do for a foreigner, as being of a somewhat lower order, in many ways, in creation. Yet with a mixture of mind about it, they admired him more and more.

The largeness of his nature still was very conspicuous in this—he never brought his telescope to bear on his own planet. His heart was reaching so far forward into future ages, that he strove to follow downward nine or ten entails of stars. To know what was to become of all that were to be descended from him; a highly interesting, but also a deeply exhausting question. This perpetual effort told very hard upon his constitution, for nothing less than fatal worry could have so impaired his native grace and lofty courtesy.

Yet before his sudden end, a softer and more genial star was culminant one evening. When one's time comes to be certain —whether by earthly senses, or by influence of heaven—of the buoyant balance turning, and the slender span outspun, tender thinkings, and kind wishes, come to the good side of us. Through this power, the petty troubles, and the crooked views of life, and the ambition to make others better than we care to be, and every other little turn of wholesome self-deception — these drop off, and leave us sinking into a sense of having lived and made a humble thing of it.

Whether this be so or not, upon the 18th of June in the year 1611, Prince Agasicles came home rather hot, and very tired, and fain for a little sleep, if such there were, to wear out weariness. But still he had heavy work left for that night; as a mighty comet had lately appeared, and scared the earth abundantly; yet now he had two or three hours to spare, and they might as well be happy ones. Therefore he sent for his daughter to come, and see to his food and such like, and then to sit with him some few minutes, and to watch the sunset.

Artemise, still young and lovely, knew of course, from Eastern wisdom, that woman's right is to do no wrong. So that she came at once when called, and felt as a mother ought to feel, that she multiplied her obedience vastly, by bringing all her children. Being in a soft state of mind, the old man was glad to see them all, and let them play with him as freely as childhood's awe of white hair allowed. Then he laid his hand upon Roger, the heir of the house, and blessed him on his way to bed; and after that he had his supper, waited on by Artemise, who was very grateful for his kindness to her children. So that she brought him the right thing exactly at the right moment without overcrowding him; and then she poured him sparkling wine, and comforted his weary feet, and gave him a delicious pipe of Persian meconopsis (free from the bane of opium, yet more dreamy than tobacco). Also she sprinkled around him delicate attar of the Vervain (sprightlier and less oppressive than the scent of roses), until his white beard ceased to flutter, and the strong lines of his face relaxed into soft drowsiness.

Observing thence the proper time when sweet sleep was encroaching, and haste, and heat, and sudden temper were as far away as can be from a man of Eastern blood, Artemise, his daughter, touched him with the smile which he used to love, when she was two years old and upward; and his thoughts without his knowledge flew back to her mother.

"Father to me, father dearest," she was whispering to him, in the native tongue which charms the old, as having lulled their cradles; "father to me, tell what trouble has together fallen on you in this cold and foreign land."

Melody enough was still remaining in the most melodious of all mortal languages, for a child to move a father into softer memories, at the sound of ancient music thus revived, and left to dwell.

"Child of my breast," the prince replied, in the very best modern Hellenic, "a strong desire to sleep again hath overcome mine intellect."

"Thus is it the more suited, father, for discourse with such as mine. Let your little one share the troubles of paternal wisdom."

Suasion more than this was needed, and at every stage forth-coming, more skillfully than English words or even looks could render, ere ever the paternal wisdom might be coaxed to unfold itself; and even so it was not disposed to be altogether explicit.

"Ask me no more," he said at last; "enough that I foresee great troubles overhanging this sad house."

"Oh father, when, and how, and what? How shall we get over them, and why should we encounter them? And will my husband or my children—"

The prince put up one finger, as if to say, "ask one thing at a time," the while he ceased not to revolve many and sad counsels in his venerable head, and in his gaze deep pity mingled with a father's pride and love. Then he spoke three words in a language which she did not comprehend, but retained their sound, and learned before her death that they meant this—"Knowledge of trouble trebles it."

"Now, best-loved father," she exclaimed, perceiving that his face was set to tell her very little, "behold how many helpless ones depend upon my knowledge of the evils I must shield them from. It is—nay, by your eyes—it is the little daughter whom you always cherished with such love and care, who now is the cause of a mind perplexed, as often she has been to you. Father, let not our affairs lay such burden on your mind, but spread them out and lighten it. Often, as our saying hath it, oftentimes the ear of folly is the purse for wisdom's gems."

"I hesitate not, I doubt no longer. I do not divide my mind in twain. The wisdom of them that come after me carries off and transcends mine own, as a mountain doth a half-peck basket. Wherefore, my daughter Artemise, wife of the noble Englishman, with whom she ran away from Caria, and mother of my five grandchildren, she is worthy to know all that I have learned from heaven; ay, and she shall know it all."

"Father to me dearest, yes! Oh how noble and good of you!"

"She shall know all," continued the prince, with a gaze of ingenuous confidence, and counting on his fingers slowly; "it may be sooner, or it may be later; however, I think one may safely promise a brilliant knowledge of every thing in five years after we have completed the second century from this day. But now the great comet is waiting for me. Let me have my boots again. Uncouth, barbarous, frightful things! But in such a country needful."

His daughter obeyed without a word, and hid her disappointment. "It is only to wait till to-morrow," she thought, "and then to fill him a larger pipe, and coax him a little more perhaps, and pour him more wine of Burgundy."

To-morrow never came for him, except in the way the stars come. In the morning he was missed, and sought for, and found dead and cold at the end of his longest telescope. In Chanctonbury Ring he died, and must have known, for at least a moment, that his death was over him; for among the stars of his jotting-chart was traced, in trembling charcoal, "Sepeli, ubi cecidi"—"Bury me where I have fallen."

CHAPTER VIII.

Alice Lorraine, with no small excitement, heard from her father's lips this story of their common ancestor. Part of it was already known to her, through traditions of the country; but this was the first time the whole had been put into a connected narrative. She wondered, also, what her father's reason could be for thus recounting to her this piece of family history, which had never been (as she felt quite sure) confided to her brother Hilary; and, like a young girl, she was saying to herself as he went on—"Shall I ever be fit to compare with that lovely Artemise, my ever-so-long-back grandmother, as the village people call it? and will that fine old astrologer see that the stars do their duty to us? and was the great comet that killed him the one that frightens me every night so? and why did he make such a point of dying without explaining any thing?"

However, what she asked her father was a different question from all these.

"Oh papa, how kind of you to tell me all that story! But what became of Artemise—'Lady Lorraine' I suppose she was?"

"No, my dear; 'Mistress Lorraine,' or 'Madame Lorraine' perhaps they called her. The old earldom had long been lost, and Roger, her son, who fell at Naseby, was the first baronet of our family. But as for Artemise herself—the daughter of the astrologer, and wife of Hilary Lorraine, she died at the birth of her next infant, within a twelvemonth after her father; and then it was known why he had been so reluctant to tell her any thing."

"Oh, I am so sorry for her! Then she is that beautiful creature hanging third from the door in the gallery, with ruches beautifully picked out and glossy, and wonderful gold lace on her head, and long hair, and lovely emeralds hanging down as if they were nothing."

"Yes," said Sir Roland, smiling at his daughter's style of description, "that of course is the lady; and the portrait is clearly a likeness. At one time we thought of naming you after her—'Artemise Lorraine'—for your nurse discovered that you were like her at the mature age of three days."

"Oh papa, how I wish you had! It would

have sounded so much nicer, and so beautifully romantic."

"Just so, my child; and therefore, in these matter-of-fact times, so deliciously absurd. Moreover, I hope that you will not be like her, either in running away from your father, or in any other way—except her kindness and faithfulness."

He was going to say, "in her early death;" but a sudden touch of our natural superstition stopped him.

"Papa, how dare you speak as if any one ever, in all the world, could be fit to compare with you? But now you must tell me one little thing—why have you chosen this very day, which ought to be such a happy one, for telling me so sad a tale, that a little more would have made me cry?"

"The reason, my Lallie, is simple enough. This happens to be the very day when the two hundred years are over; and the astrologer's will, or whatever the document is, may now be opened."

"His will, papa! Did he leave a will? And none of us ever heard of it!"

"My dear, your acquaintance with his character is, perhaps, not exhaustive. He may have left many wills without wishing to have them published; at any rate you shall have the chance, before it grows dark, to see what there is."

"Me! or I—whichever is right?—me, or I, to do such a thing! Papa, when I was six years old I could stand on my head; but now I have lost the art, alas!"

"Now, Alice, do try to be sensible, if you ever had such an opening. You know that I do not very often act rashly; but you will make me think I have done so now, unless you behave most steadily."

"Papa, I am steadiness itself; but you must make allowance for a little upset at the marvels heaped upon me."

"My dear child, there are no marvels; or, at any rate, none for you to know. All you have to do is to go, and to fetch a certain document. Whether you know any more about it is a question for me to consider."

"Oh papa—to raise me up so, and to cast me down like that! And I was giving you credit for having trusted me so entirely! And very likely you would not even have sent me for this document, if you had your own way about it."

"Alice," Sir Roland answered, smiling at her knowledge of him, "you happen to be particularly right in that conjecture. I should never have thought of sending you to a lonely and forsaken place if I were allowed to send any one else, or to go myself. And I have not been happy at thinking about it ever since the morning."

"My father, do you think that I could help rejoicing in such a job? It is the very thing to suit me. Where are the keys, papa? Do be quick!"

"I have no intention, my dear child, of hurrying either you or myself. There is plenty of time to think of all things. The sun has not set, and that happens to be one of the little things we have to look to."

"Oh how very delightful, papa! That makes it so much more beautiful. And it is the astrologer's room, of course."

"My dear, it strikes me that you look rather pale, in the midst of all your transports. Now, don't go if you are at all afraid."

"Afraid, papa! Now you want to provoke me. You quite forget both my age, it appears, and the family I belong to."

"My pet, you never allow us to be very long forgetful of either of those great facts; but I trust I have borne them both duly in mind, and I fear that I should even enhance, most needlessly, your self-esteem, if I were to read you the directions which I now am following. For, strangely enough, they do contain predictions as to your character such as we can not yet perceive (much as we love you) to have come to pass."

"Oh, but who are the 'we,' papa? If every body knows it—even grandmamma, for instance—what pleasure can I hope to find in ever having been predicted?"

"You may enjoy that pleasure, Alice, as exclusively as you please. Even your grandmother knows nothing of the matter we have now in hand; or else—at least I should say perhaps that, if it were otherwise—"

"She would have been down here, of course, papa, and have marched up to the room herself; but, if the whole thing belongs to one's self, nothing can be more delightful than to have been predicted, especially in glowing terms such as I beg you now, papa, to read in glowing tones to me."

"Alice, I do not like that style of—what shall I call it?—on your part. *Persiflage*, I believe, is the word; and I am glad that there is no English one. It is never graceful in any woman, still less in a young girl like you. Hilary brought it from Oxford first; and perhaps he thought it excellent. Lay it aside now, once and for all. It hopes to seem a clever thing, and it does not even succeed in that."

At these severe words, spoken with a decided attempt at severity, Alice fell back, and could only drop her eyes and wonder what could have made her father so cross upon his birthday. But, after the smart of the moment, she began to acknowledge to herself that her father was right, and she was wrong. This flippant style was foreign to her, and its charms must be foregone.

"I beg your pardon, father dear," she said, looking softly up at him; "I know that I am not clever, and I never meant to seem so."

"Quite right, Alice; never attempt to do any thing impossible." Saying this to her,

Sir Roland said to himself that, after all, he should like to know very much where to find any girl half so clever as Lallie, or any girl even a quarter so good, and so loving, and so beautiful.

"The sun is almost gone behind the curve of the hill, and the scrubby beech, and the nick cut in the gorse-bush. Alice, you know we only see it for just the midsummer week like that."

Alice came, with her eyes already quit of every trace of tears; with vanity and all petty feelings melting into larger thought. The beauty of the world would often come around and overcome her, so that she felt nothing else.

"The sun must always be the same," Sir Roland said, rather doubtfully, after waiting for Alice to begin. "No doubt he must always be the same; but still the great Herschel seems to think that even the sun is changing. If he is fed by comets (as our old astronomers used to say), he ought to be doing very well just now. Alice, the sun is above ground still for people on the hill-top, and there is the comet already kindling!"

"Of course he is, papa; he never waits for the sun's convenience. But I must not say that—I forgot. There would be no English name for it—would there now, papa?"

"You little tyrant, what troubles I would inflict upon you if I studied the stars! But I scarcely know the belt of Orion from the Northern Crown. Astronomy does not appear to have taken deep root in our family; but look, there is part of the sun again emerging under Chancton! In five minutes more he will be quite gone; now is the time for me to read these queer directions, which contain so poetical an account of you."

Alice, warned by his former words, and reduced to proper humility, did not speak while her father opened the small strip of parchment, at which she had so long been peeping curiously.

"It is written in Latin," Sir Roland said, "and has been handed from father to son unsealed, and as you see it, from the time of the prince till our time."

"May I see it, papa? What a very clear hand! but you must translate it for me."

"Then here it is: 'To the father and master of the family of Lorraine, whoever shall be in the year, according to Christian computation, 1811, Agasicles Syennesis, the Carian, bids hail. Do thou, on the 18th day of June, when the sun has well descended, or departed'—*decesserit*, the word is—'send thy eldest daughter, without any companion, to the astronomer's *cœnaculum*'—why, he never ate supper, the poor old fellow, unless it was the one he died of—'and there let her search in a closet or cupboard'—*in secessu muri*, the words are, as far as I can make out—'and she will find a small document, which to me has been in great price. There will also be something else, to be treated *pro re nata*'—that means, according to circumstances—'and according to the orders in the document aforesaid. The virgin will be brave and beautiful, ready to give herself for the house, and of swiftly-growing prudence. If there be no such virgin, then the need for her will not have arisen. It is necessary that no young man should go, and my document must lie hidden for another century. It is not possible that any one of uncertain skill should be certain. But there ought to be a great comet also burning in the sky, of the same complexion as the one that makes my calculations doubtful. Farewell, whosoever thou shalt be, from me descended, and obey me.'"

"Papa, I declare, it quite frightens me. How could he have predicted me, for instance, and this great comet, and even you?"

"Then you think that you answer to your description! My darling, I do believe that you do. But you never shall 'give yourself for the house,' or for fifty thousand houses. Now, will you have any thing to do with this strange affair; or will you not? Much rather would I hear you say that you will have nothing to do with it, and that the old man's book may sleep for at least another century."

"Now, papa, you know how much you would be disappointed in me. And do you think that I could have any self-respect remaining? And besides all that, how could I hope to sleep in my bed with all those secrets ever dangling over me?"

"That last is a very important point. With your excitable nature you had better go always through a thing. It was the same with your dear mother. Here are the keys, my daughter. I really feel ashamed to dwell so long on a mere superstition."

CHAPTER IX.

THE room known as the Astrologer's (by the maids, less reverently entitled the "star-gazer's closet") was that old eight-sided, or lantern, chamber, which has been mentioned in the short account of the Carian sage and his labors. He had used it alternately with his other quarters in the Chancton Ring; for this had outlook of the rising, as the other had of the setting stars. At the eastern end of the house, it stood away from roofs and chimney-tops, commanding the trending face of hill, and the amplitude of the world below, from north-west round the north and east, to the rising point of Fomahault.

To this room Alice now made her way, as if she had no time to spare. With quick, light steps, she passed through the hall, and then the painted library, as it was called from some old stained glass — and at the farther end she entered a little room with double doors, her father's favorite musing-place. In the eastern end of this quiet chamber, and at the eastern end of all, there was a low and narrow door. This was seldom locked, because none of the few who came so far would care to go any farther. For it opened to a small landing-place, dimly lighted, as well as damp, and leading to a newel staircase, narrow, and made of a chalky flint, angular and irregular.

Alice stopped to think a little. All things looked so uninviting that she would rather do without them. Surely, now that the sun had departed—whether well or otherwise—some other time would do as nicely for going on with the business. There was nothing said of any special hurry, so far as she could remember; and what could be a more stupid thing than to try to unlock an ancient door without any light for the key-hole? She had a very great mind to go back, and to come again in the morning.

She turned with a quick turn toward the light, and the comfort, and the company; then suddenly she remembered how she had boasted of her courage; and who would be waiting to laugh at her, if she came back without her errand. Fearing further thought, she ran like a sunset cloud up the stairway.

Fifty or sixty steps went by her before she had time to think of them; a few in the light of loop-holes, but the greater part in governed gloom, or shadowy mixture flickering. Then at the top she stopped to breathe, and recover her wits, for a moment. Here a long black door repelled her—a door whose outside she knew pretty well, but had no idea of the other side. Upon this she began to think again; and her thoughts were almost too much for her.

With a little sigh that would have moved all imaginable enemies, the swiftly sensitive girl called up the inborn spirit of her race, and her own peculiar romance. These in combination scarcely could have availed her to turn the key, unless her father had happened to think of oiling it with a white pigeon's feather.

When she heard the bolt shoot back, she made the best of a bad affair. "In for a penny, in for a pound;" "Faint heart is fain;" "Two bites at a cherry;" and, above all, "Noblesse oblige." With all these thoughts to press her forward, in she walked, quite dauntlessly.

And lo, there was nothing to frighten her. Every thing looked as old and harmless as the man who had loved them all; having made or befriended them. His own little lathe, with its metal bed (cast by himself from a mixture of his own, defying the rust of centuries), wanted nothing more than dusting, and some oil on the bearings. And the speculum he had worked so hard at, for a reflecting telescope—partly his own idea, and partly reflected (as all ideas are) some years ere the time of Gregory—the error in its grinding, which had driven him often to despair, might still be traced by an accurate eye through the depth of two hundred dusty years. Models, patterns, moulds, and castings — many of which would have shown how slowly our boasted discoveries have grown — also favorite tools, and sundry things passed out of their meaning, lay about among their fellows, doomed alike to do no work, because the man who had kept them moving was shorter-lived than they were.

Now young Alice stood among them in a reverential way. They were, of course, no more than other things laid by to rust, according to man's convenience. And yet she could not make up her mind to meddle with any one of them. So that she only looked about, and began to be at home with things.

Her eager mind was always ready to be crowded with a rash, young interest in all things. It was the great fault of her nature that she never could perceive how very far all little things should lie beneath her notice. So that she now had really more than she could contrive to take in all at once.

But while she stood in this surprise, almost forgetting her errand among the multitude of ideas, a cloud above the sunset happened to be packed with gorgeous light. Unbosoming itself to the air in the usual cloudy manner, it managed thereby to shed down some bright memories of the departed one. And hence there came a lovely gleam of daylight's afterthought into the north-western facet of the old eight-sided room. Alice crossed this glance of sunset, wondering what she was to do, until she saw her shadow wavering into a recess of wall. There, between the darker windows to the right hand of the door, a little hover of refraction, striking upon reflection, because it was fugitive, caught her eyes. She saw by means of this a key-hole in a brightened surface, on a heavy turn of wall that seemed to have no meaning. In right of discovery, up she ran, passed her fingers over a plate of polished Sussex iron, and put her key into the hole, of course.

The lock had been properly oiled perhaps, and put into working order sometimes, even within the last hundred years. But still it was so stiff that Alice had to work the key both ways, and with both hands, ere it turned. And even after the bolt went back, she could not open the door at once, perhaps because the jamb was rusty, or the upper hinge had given forward. Whatever the hesitation was, the girl would have no refusal. She set the key crosswise in the lock, and drew one corner of her linen handkerchief through the loop of it, and then tied a knot, and with both hands pulled. Inasmuch as her handkerchief was not made of gauze, or lace, or gossamer, and herself of no feeble material, the heavy door gave way at last, and every thing lay before her.

"Is that all? oh, is that all?" she cried, in breathless disappointment, and yet laughing at herself. "No jewels, no pearls, no brooches or buckles, nor even a gold watch! And the great astrologer must have foreseen how sadly, in this year of our reckoning, I should be longing for a gold watch! Alas! without it, what is the use of being 'brave and beautiful?' Here is nothing more than dust, mouldy old deeds, and a dirty cushion!"

Alice had a great mind at first to run back to her father and tell him that, after all, there was nothing found that would be worth the carrying. And she even turned, and looked round the room, to support this strong conclusion. But the weight of ancient wisdom (pressed on the young imagination by the stamp of mystery) held her under, and made her stop from thinking her own thoughts about it. "He must have known better, of course, than I do. Only look at his clever tools! I am sure I could live in this room for a week, and never be afraid of any thing."

But even while she was saying this to herself, with the mind in command of the heart, and a fine conscientious courage, there came to her ears, or seemed to come, a quiet, low, unaccountable sound. It may have been nothing, as she tried to think, when first she began to recover herself; or it may have been something quite harmless, and most easily traced to its origin. But whatever it was, in a moment it managed to quench her desire to live in that room. With quick hands, now delivered from their usual keen sense of grime, she snatched up whatever she saw in the cupboard, and banged the iron door, and locked it, with a glance of defiant terror over the safer shoulder first, and then over the one that was nearer the noise.

Then she knew that she had done her duty very bravely; and that it would be a cruel thing to expect her to stay any longer. And so, to shut out all further views of any thing she had no right to see, she slipped back the band of her beautiful hair; and, under that cover, retreated.

CHAPTER X.

At this very time there happened to be a boy of no rank, and of unknown order, quietly jogging homeward. He differed but little from other boys, and seemed unworthy of consideration, unless one stopped to consider him; because he was a boy by no means virtuous, or valiant; neither gifted by nature with any inborn way to be wonderful. Having nothing to help him much, he lived among the things that came around him, to his very utmost; and he never refused a bit to eat, because it might have been a better bit. And now and then, if he got the chance (without any more in the background than a distant view of detection), he had been imagined perhaps to lay hand upon a stray trifle that would lie about, and was due, but not paid, to his merits. Nobody knew where this boy came from, or whether he came at all indeed, or was only the produce of earth or sky at some improper conjunction. Nothing was certain about him, except that there he was; and he meant to stay; and people, for the most part, liked him. And many women would have been glad to love him in a protective way, but for the fright by all of them felt, by reason of the magistrates.

These had settled it long ago, at every kind of session, that this boy (though so comparatively honest) must not be encouraged much. He had such a manner of looking about after almost any thing, and of making the most of those happy times when luck embraces art; above all, he had such exhaustive knowledge of apple-trees, and potato-buries, and cows that wanted milking, as well as of ticklish trout, and occasional little ducks that had lost their way—that after long-tried lenience, and allowance for such a neglected child, justice could no longer take a large and wholesome view of "Bonny."

Bonny held small heed of justice (even in the plural number) whenever he could help it. The nature of his birth and nurture had been such as to make him take an outside view of every thing. If people liked him, he liked them, and would be the last to steal from them; or, at any rate, would let them be the last for him to steal from. His inner meaning was so honest, that he almost always waited for some great wrong to be done to him, before he dreamed of making free with almost any body's ducks.

Widely as he was known, and often glanced at from a wrong point of view, even his lowest detractor could not give his etymology. Many attempted to hold that he might have been called, in some generative outburst, "Bonnie," by a Scotchman of imagination. Others laughed this idea to scorn, and were sure that his right name was "Boney," because of his living in spite of all terror of "Bonyparty." But the true solution probably was (as with all analytic inquiries) the third—that his right name was "Bony," because his father, though now quite a shadowy being, must have at some time or other, perhaps, gone about crying, "Rags and Bones, oh!"

These little niceties of origin passed by Bonny as the idle wind. He was proud of his name, and it sounded well; and wherever he went the ladies seemed to like him, as an unknown quantity. Also (which mattered far more to him) the female servants took to him. And, with many of these, he had such a way, that it found him in victuals, perhaps twice in a week.

Nevertheless, he was forced to work as hard as could be, this summer. The dragging weight of a hopeless war (as all, except the stout farmers, now were beginning to consider it) had been tightening, more and more, the strain upon the veins of trade, and the burden of the community.

This good boy lived in the side of a hill, or of a cliff (as some might call it), white and beautiful to look at from a proper distance. Here he had one of those queer old holes, which puzzle the sagest antiquary, and set him in fiercest conflict with the even sager geologist. But in spite of them all, the hole was there; and in that hole lived Bonny.

Without society, what is life? Our tenderest and truest affections were not given us for naught. The grandest of human desires is to have something or other to wallop; and fate (in small matters so hard upon Bonny) had known when to yield, and had granted him this—that is to say, a donkey.

A donkey of such a clever kind, and so set up with reasoning powers and a fine heart of his own, that all his conclusions were almost right, until they were beaten out of him. His name was "Jack," and his nature was of a level and sturdy order, resenting wrongs, accepting favors, with all the teeth of gratitude, and braying (as all clever asses do) at every change of weather. His personal appearance also was noble, striking, and romantic; and his face reminded all beholders of a well-colored pipe-bowl upside down. For all his muzzle and nose were white, as snowy white as if he always wore a nosebag newly floured from the nearest windmill. But just below his eyes, and across the mace of his jaws, was a ring of brown, and above that not a speck of white, but deepening into cloudy blackness throughout all his system. Then (like the crest of Hector) rose a menacing frontlet of thick hair, and warlike ears as long as horns, yet genially revolving; and body and legs, to complete the effect, conceived in the very best taste to match.

These great virtues of the animal found their balance in small foibles. A narrow-minded, self-seeking vein, a too vindictive memory, an obstinacy more than asinine, no sense of honor, and a habit of treating too many questions with the teeth or heels. These had lowered him to his present rank; as may be shown hereafter.

To any worked and troubled mind, escaping into the country, it would have been a treat to happen (round some corner suddenly, when the sun throws shadows long) upon Bonny and his jackass. In the ripe time of the evening, when the sun is at its kindest, and the earth most thankful, and the lines of every shadow now are well accustomed; when the air has summer hope of never feeling frost again; and every bush, and tump, and hillock quite knows how to stand and look; when the creases of yellow grass, and green grass, by the roadside, leave themselves for explanation, till the rain shall settle it; and the thick hedge, in the calm air, can not rustle, unless it holds a rabbit or a hare at play—when all these things, in their quiet way, guide the shadowy lines of evening, and the long lanes of farewell, what can soothe the spirit more than the view of a boy on a donkey?

Bonny, therefore, was in keeping with the world around him (as he always contrived to be) when he came home on Jack, that evening, from a long day's work at Shoreham. The lane was at its best almost, with all the wild flowers that love the chalk, mixed with those that hug the border where the chalk creams into loam. Among them Bonny whistled merrily, as his favorite custom was; to let the Pixies and the Fairies, ere he came under the gloom of the hill, understand that he was coming, and nobody else to frighten them.

Soothed with the beauty of the scene and the majesty of the sunset, Jack drew back his ears and listened drowsily to his master. "Britannia rules the Waves" was then the anthem of the nation; and as she seemed to rule nothing else, though fighting very grandly, all patriotic Britons found main comfort in governing water.

The happiness of this boy and donkey was of that gleeful see-saw chancing, which is the heartiest of all. This has a snugness of its own, which nothing but poverty can afford, and luck rejoice to revel in. As a rich man hugs his shivers, when he has taken a sudden chill, and huddles in over a roaring fire, and boasts that he can not warm himself, so a poor fellow may cuddle his home, and spread his legs as he pleases, for the sake of its very want of comfort, and the things it makes him think of; all to be hoped for by-and-by. And Bonny was so destitute that he had all the world to hope for.

He lived in a hole in the scarp of chalk, at the foot of the gully of Coombe Lorraine; and many of his delightful doings might have been seen from the lofty windows, if any one ever had thought it worth while to slope a long telescope at him. But nobody cared to look at Bonny, and scatter his lowly happiness—than which there is no more fugitive creature, and none more shy of inspection.

Being of a light and dauntless nature, Bonny kept whistling and singing his way, over the grass and through the furze, and in and out the dappled leafage of the summer evening; while Jack with his brightest blinkings, picked the parts of the track that suited him. The setting sun was in their eyes, and made them wink every now and then, and threw the shadow of long ears, and walking legs, and jogging heads, here and there and anywhere. Also a very fine lump of something might in the shadows be loosely taken to hang across Jack in his latter parts, coming after Bonny's legs, and choice things stowed in front of them.

The meaning of this was that they had been making a very lucky long-shore day, at the mouth of the river Adur; and on their way home, had received some pleasing tribute to their many merits in the town of Steyning, and down the road. Jack had no panniers, for his master could not provide such luxuries; but he had what answered as well, or better—a long and trusty meal-sack, strongly stitched at the mouth, and slit for inlet some way down the middle. So that, as it hung well balanced over his sturdy quarters, any thing might be popped in quickly; and all the contents must abide together, and churn up into fine tenderness.

As for Bonny himself, the shadows did him strong injustice, such as he was wont to take from all the world, and make light of. The shadows showed him a ragged figure, flapping and flickering here and there, and random in his outlines. But the true glow of the sunset, full upon his face, presented quite another Bonny; no more to be charged as a vagabond than the earth and the sun himself were; but a little boy who loved his home, such as it was, and knew it, and knew little else. Dirty, perhaps, just here and there, after the long dry weather—but if he had been ugly, could he have brought home all that dripping?

To the little fellow himself as yet the question of costume was more important than that of comeliness. And his dress afforded him many sources of pride and self-satisfaction. For his breeches were possessed of inexhaustible vitality, as well as bold and original color, having been adapted for him by the wife of his great patron, Bottler the Pigman, from a pair of Bottler's leggings, made of his own pig-skin. The skin had belonged, in the first place, to a very remarkable boar, a thorough Caledonian hog, who escaped from a farm-yard, and lived for months a wild life in St. Leonard's Forest. Here he scared all the neighborhood, until at last Bottler was invoked to arise like Meleager, and to bring his pig-knife. Bottler met him in single combat, slew him before he had time to grunt, and claiming him as the spoils of war, pickled his hams at his leisure. Also, he tanned the hide in his own yard, and made himself leggings as everlasting as the fame of his exploit.

With these was Bonny now indued over most of his nether moiety. Shoes and stockings he despised, of course, but his little shanks were clean and red, while his shoulders and chest were lost in the splendor of a coachman's crimson waistcoat. At least they were generally so concealed, when he set forth in the morning, for he picked up plenty of pins, and showed some genius in arranging them; but after a hard day's work, as now, air and light would always re-assert their right of entrance. Still, there remained enough of the mingled charm of blush and plush to recall in soft domestic bosoms by-gone scenes, forever past — but oh, so sweet among the trays!

To judge him, however, without the fallacy of romantic tenderness—the breadth of his mouth, and the turn of his nose, might go a little way against him. Still, he had such a manner of showing bright white teeth in a jocund grin, and of making his frizzly hair stand up, and his sharp blue eyes express amazement, at the proper moment; moreover, his pair of cheeks was such (after coming off the downs), and his laugh so dreadfully infectious, and he had such tales to tell—that several lofty butlers were persuaded to consider him.

Even the butler at Coombe Lorraine—but that will come better hereafter. Only as yet may be fairly said, that Bonny looked up at the house on the hill with a delicate curiosity; and felt that his overtures might have been somewhat ungraceful, or at least ill-timed, when the new young footman (just taken on) took it entirely upon himself to kick him all the way down the hill. This little discourtesy, doubling of course Master Bonny's esteem and regard for the place, at the same time introduced some constraint into his after intercourse. For the moment, indeed, he took no measures to vindicate his honor; although, at a word (as he knew quite well), Bottler the Pigman, would have brought up his whip and seen to it. And even if any of the maids of the house had been told to tell Miss Alice about it, Bonny was sure of obtaining justice, and pity, and even half a crown.

Quick as he was to forget and forgive the many things done amiss to him, the boy, when he came to the mouth of the coombe, looked pretty sharply about him for traces of that dreadful fellow who had proved himself such a footman. With Jack to help him, with jaw and heel, Bonny would not have been so very much afraid of even him; such a "strong-siding champion" had the donkey lately shown himself. Still, on the whole, and after such a long day's work by sea and shore, the rover was much relieved to find his little castle unleaguered.

The portal thereof was a yard in height,

and perhaps fifteen inches wide; not all alike, but in and out, according to the way the things, or the boy himself, went rubbing it. A holy hermit once had lived there, if tradition spoke aright. But if so, he must have been as narrow of body to get in, as wide of mind to stop there. At any rate, Bonny was now the hermit, and less of a saint than a sinner.

The last glance of sunset was being reflected under the eaves of twilight when these two came to their home and comfort in the bay of the quiet land. From the foot of the steep white cliff, the green sward spread itself with a gentle slope, and breaks of roughness here and there, until it met the depth of corn-land, where the feathering bloom appeared—for the summer was a hot one—reared upon its jointed stalk, and softened into a silver-gray by the level touch of evening. The little powdered stars of wheat-bloom could not now be seen, of course; neither the quivering of the awns, nor that hovering radiance, which in the hot day moves among them. Still the scent was on the air, the delicate fragrance of the wheat, only caught by waiting for it, when the hour is genial.

Bonny and Jack were not in the humor now to wait for any thing. The scent of the wheat was nothing to them, but the smell of a loaf was something. And Jack knew, quite as well as Bonny, that let the time be as hard as it would—and it was a very hard time already, though nothing to what came afterward—nevertheless, there were two white loaves, charmed by their united powers out of maids who were under notice to quit their situations. Also on the homeward road, they had not failed entirely of a few fine gristly hocks of pork, and the bottom of a skin of lard, and something unknown, but highly interesting, from a place where a pig had been killed that week, much as the time of year was wrong.

"Now, Jack, tend thee'zell," said Bonny, with the air of a full-grown man almost, while he was working his own little shoulders in betwixt the worn hair on the ribs, and the balanced bag overhanging them. Jack knew what he was meant to do, for he brought his white nose cleverly round, just where it was wanted, and pushed it under one end of the bag, and tossed it carefully over his back, so that it slid down beautifully.

When this great bag lay on the ground (or rather, stood up, in a clumsy way, by virtue of what was inside of it), the first thing every body did was to come and poke and sniff at it. And though the every body was no more than Jack and his donkey, the duty was not badly done, because they were both so hungry.

When the strings were cut, and the bag in relief of tension panted, ever so many things began to ooze and to ease themselves out of it. First of all two great dollops of oar-weed, which had excellently performed their task of keeping every thing tight and sweet with the hungry fragrance of the sea. Then came a mixture of almost any thing which a boy of no daintiness was likely to regard as eatable, or a child of no science whatever to look upon as a rarity. Bonny was a collector of the grandest order—the one who collects every thing. Here was food of the land, and food of the sea, and food of the tidal river, mingled with food for the mind of a boy, who had no mind—to his knowledge. In the humblest way he groped about, and wondered at almost every thing.

Now he had things to wonder at which, in the heat of the day and the work, had been caught and stowed away anyhow. The boy and the donkey had earned their load with such true labor that now they could not remember even half of it. Jack, by hard collar-work at the nets; Bonny, by cheering him up the sand, and tugging himself with his puny shoulders, and then by dancing and treading away, and kicking with naked feet among the wastrel fish, full of thorns and tails shed from the vent of the drag-net by the spent farewell of the shoaling wave.

For on this very day, there had been the great Midsummer haul at Shoreham. It was the old custom of the place; but even custom must follow the tides, and the top of the summer spring-tides (when the fish are always liveliest) happened, for the year 1811, to come on the 18th day of June. Bonny for weeks had been looking forward; and now before him lay his reward.

After many sweet and bitter uses of adversity, this boy, at an early age, had caught the tail of prudence. It had been to his heart, at first, a friendly and a native thing, to feast to the full (when he got the chance), and go empty away till it came again. But now, being grown to riper years, and, after much consideration, declared to be at least twelve years old by the only pork-butcher in Steyning, Bonny began to know what was what, and to salt a good deal of his offal.

For this wise process he now could find a greater call than usual; because, through the heat of the day, he had stuck to his first and firmly-grounded principle—never to refuse refuse. So that many other fine things were mingled, jumbled, and almost churned, among the sundry importations of the flowing tide and net. All of these, now, he well delivered (so far as sappy limbs could do it) upon a cleanish piece of ground, well accustomed to such favors. Then Bonny stood back, with his hands on his knees, and Jack spread his nose at some of it.

Loaves of genuine wheaten bread were getting scarce already. Three or four bad harvests, following long arrears of discontent, and hanging on the heavy arm of desperate taxation, kept the country, and the farmers, and the people that must be fed, in such a condition that we (who can not be now content with any thing) deserve no blame when we smack our lips in our dainty contempt of our grandfathers.

Bonny was always good to Jack, according to the way they had of looking at one another; and so, of the choicest spoils, he gave him a half-peck loaf, of a fibre such as they seldom softened their teeth with. Jack preferred this to any clover, even when that luxury could be won by clever stealing; and now he trotted away with his loaf to the nearest stump where backing power against his strong jaws could be got. Here he laid his loaf against the stump, and went a little way back to think about it, and to be sure that every atom was for him. Then, without scruple or time to spare, he tucked up his lips, and began in a hurry to make a bold dash for the heart of it.

"More haste, less speed" is a proverb that seems, at first sight, one of the last that need be quoted to a donkey. Yet, in the present instance, Jack should have spared himself time to study it; for in less than a moment he ran up to Bonny, with his wide mouth at its widest, snorting with pain, and much yearning to bellow, but by the position disabled. There was something stuck fast in the roof of his mouth, in a groove of the veiny black arches; and work as he might with his wounded tongue, he was only driving it farther in. His great black eyes, as he gasped with fright, and the piteous whine of his quivering nose, and his way altogether so scared poor Bonny, that the chances were he would run away. And so, no doubt, he must have done (being but a little boy as yet), if it had not chanced that a flash of something caught his quick eye suddenly, something richly shining in the cavern of the donkey's mouth.

This was enough, of course, for Bonny. His instinct of scratching and digging and hiding, was up and at work in a moment. He thrust his brown hand betwixt Jack's great jaws, and drew it back quickly enough to escape the snap of their glad reunion. And in his hand was something which he had drawn from the bag of the net that day, but scarcely stopped to look at twice, in the huddle of weeds and the sweeping. It had lain among many fine gifts of the sea—skates, and dog-fish, sea-devils, sting-rays, thornbacks, inky cuttles, and scollops, cockles, whelks, green crabs, jelly-fish, and every thing else that makes fishermen swear, and then grin, and then spit on their palms again. Among these in Bonny's bag had lain manifold boons of the life-giving earth, extracted from her motherly feeling by one or two good butchers.

Bonny made no bones of this. Fish, flesh, fowl, or stale red-herring—he welcomed all the works of charity with a charitable nose, and fingers not of the nicest. So that his judgment could scarcely have been "prejudicially affected by any preconceived opinion"—as our purest writers love to say—when he dropped this thing, and smelled his thumb, and cried, "Lord, how it makes my hands itch!"

After such a strong expression, what can we have to say to him? It is the privilege of our period to put under our feet whatever we would rather not face out; at the same time, to pretend to love it and lift it by education. Nevertheless, one may try to doubt whether poor Bonny's grandchildren (if he ever presumed to have any) thrive on the lesson, as well as he did on the loaf, of charity.

CHAPTER XI.

THERE used to be a row of buildings well within the sacred precincts of the Inner Temple, but still preserving a fair lookout on the wharves and the tidal gut at their back, till the whole view was swallowed by gas-works. Here, for long ages, law had flourished on the excrete things of outlawry, fed by the reek of Whitefriars, as a good nettle enjoys the mixen.

Already, however, some sweeping changes had much improved this neighborhood; and the low attorneys who throve on crime, and of whom we get unpleasant glimpses through our classic novelists, had been succeeded by men of repute and learning and large practice. And among all these there was not one more widely known and respected than Glanvil Malahide, K.C., an eminent equity barrister, who now declined to don the wig in any ordinary cause. He had been obliged, of course, to fight, like the rest of mankind, for celebrity; but as soon as this was well assured, he quitted the noisier sides of it. But his love of the subtleties of the law (spun into fairer and frailer gossamer by the soft spider of equity), as well as the power of habit, kept him to his old profession; so that he took to chamber practice, and had more than he could manage.

Sir Roland Lorraine had known this gentleman by repute at Oxford, when Glanvil Malahide was young, and believed to be one of the best scholars there; in the days when scholarship often ripened (as it seldom does now) to learning. For the scholarship now must be kept quite young, for the smaller needs of tuition.

Hence it came to pass that as soon as Hilary Lorraine was quite acquit of Oxford leading-strings, and had scrambled into some degree, his father, who especially wished (for some reasons of his own) to keep the boy out of the army, entered him gladly among the pupils of Mr. Glanvil Malahide. Not that Hilary was expected ever to wear the horse-hair much (unless an insane desire to do so should find its way into his open soul); but that the excellent goodness of law might drop, like the gentle dew from heaven, and grow him into a justice of the peace.

Hilary looked upon this matter, as he did on too many others, with a sweet indifference. If he could only have had his own way, he would have been a soldier long ago; for that was the time when all the spirit of Britain was roused up to arms. But this young fellow's great fault was, to be compact of so many elements that nothing was settled among them. He had "great gifts," as Mr. Malahide said—"extraordinary talents," we say now—but nobody knew (least of all their owner) how to work them properly. This is one of the most unlucky compositions of human mind—to be applicable to every thing, but applied to nothing. If Hilary had lain under pressure, and been squeezed into one direction, he must have become a man of mark.

This his father could not see. As a general rule a father fails to know what his son is fit for; and after disappointment, fancies (for a little time at least) himself a fool to have taken the boy to be all that the mother said of him. Nevertheless, the poor mother knows how right she was, and the world, how wrong.

But Hilary Lorraine, from childhood, had no mother to help him. What he had to help him was good birth, good looks, good abilities, a very sweet temper, and a kind and truly genial nature. Also a strongish will of his own (whenever his heart was moving), yet ashamed to stand forth boldly in the lesser matters. And here was his fatal error; that he looked upon almost every thing as one of the lesser matters. He had, of course, a host of friends, from the freedom of his manner; and sometimes he would do such things that the best, or even the worst of them, could no longer walk with him. Things not vicious, but a great deal too far gone in the opposite way—such as the snatching up of a truly naked child and caressing it, or any other shameful act, in the face of the noblest Christendom. These things he would do, and worse; such as no toady with self-respect could smile at in broad daylight, and such as often exposed the lad to laughter in good society. One of his best friends used to say that Hilary wanted a vice or two to make his virtues balance. This may have been so; but none the less he had his share of failings.

For a sample of these last he had taken up and made much of one of his fellow-pupils in these well-connected chambers. This was one Gregory Lovejoy, a youth entirely out of his element among fashionable sparks. Steadfast ambition of a conceptive mother sent him, against his stars, to London; and here he became the whetstone for those brilliant blades, his fellow-pupils. Because he had been at no university, nor even so much as a public school, and had no introduction to any body who had never heard of him.

Now the more the rest disdained this fellow, the more Lorraine regarded him; feeling, with a sense too delicate to arise from any thought, that shame was done to good birth by being even conscious of it, except upon great occasions. And so, without giving much offense, or pretending to be a champion, Hilary used to shield young Lovejoy from the blunt shafts of small humor continually leveled at him.

Mr. Malahide's set of chambers was perhaps the best to be found in Equity Walk, Inner Temple. His pupils—ten in number always, because he would accept no more, and his high repute insured no less—these worthy youths had the longest room, facing with three whitey-brown windows into "Numa Square." Hence the view containing all "utilitarian edifices," freely ranged across the garden's classic walks of asphodel to the broad Lethean river on whose wharves we are such weeds. For "Paper Buildings," named from some swift sequence of suggestion, reared no lofty height as yet to mar the sedentary view.

All who have the local key will enter into the scene at once; so far, at least, as necessary change has failed to operate. But Mr. Malahide's pupils scarcely ever looked out of the windows. None, however, should rashly blame them for apathy as to the prospect. They seldom looked out of the windows, because they were very seldom inside them.

In the first place, their attendance there was voluntary and precarious. They paid their money, and they took their choice whether they ever did any thing more. Each of them paid—or his father for him—a fee of a hundred guineas to have the "run of the chambers," and most of them carried out their purpose by a runaway from them. The less they came, the less trouble they caused to Mr. Glanvil Malahide; who always gave them that much to know when they paid their fee of entrance. "If you mean to be a lawyer," he said, "I will do my best to make you one. If you only come for the name of it, I shall say but little more to you." This, of course, was fair enough, and the utmost that could be expected of him: for most of his pupils were young men of birth, or good position in the English counties, to whom in their future condition of life a little smattering of law, or the credit of owning such smattering, would be worth a few hundred guineas. Common Law, of course, was far more likely to avail them in their rubs of the world than equity; but of that fine drug they had generally taken their dose in Pleaders' Chambers, and were come to wash the taste away in the purer shallows of equity.

Hilary, therefore, might be considered, and certainly did consider himself, a remarkably attentive pupil, for he generally was to be found in chambers four or even five days of the week, coming in time to read all the news before the five o'clock dinner in Hall. Whereas the Honorable Robert Gumption and Sir Francis Kickabout, two of his fellow-pupils, had only been seen in chambers once since they paid their respective fees; and the reason of their attendance then was that they found the towels too dirty to use at the billiard-rooms in Fleet Street. The clerks used to say among themselves, that "these young fellows must be dreadful fools to pay one hundred guineas, because any swell with the proper cheek might easy enough have the go of the chambers, and nobody none the wiser; for they wouldn't know him, nor the other young gents, and least of all old "horsewig."

However, there chanced to be two or three men who made something more than a very expensive lounge of these eminent chambers. Of these worthy fellows, Rice Cockles was one (who had been senior wrangler two years before, and from that time knew not one good night's rest, till the Woolsack broke his fall into his grave), and another was Gregory Lovejoy. Cockles was thoroughly conscious — as behooves a senior wrangler—of possessing great abilities; and Lovejoy knew, on his own behalf, that his mother at least was as sure as could be of all the wonders he must do.

Hilary could not bear Rice Cockles, who was of a dry, sarcastic vein; but he liked young Lovejoy more and more, the more he had to defend him. Youths who have not had the fortune to be at a public school or a college, seldom know how to hold their tongues until the world has silenced them. Gregory, therefore, thought no harm to boast opportunely one fine May morning (when some one had seen a tree blossoming somewhere) of the beauty of his father's cherry-trees. How noble and grand they must be just now—one sheet of white, white, white, he said, as big as the Inner and the Middle Temple and Lincoln's Inn all put together! And then how the bees were among them buzzing, knowing which sort first to milk; and the tortoise-shell butterflies quite sure to be out for the first of their summering. But in the moonlight, best of all, when the moon was three days short of full—then was the time an unhappy Londoner must be amazed with happiness. Then to walk among them was like walking in a fairy-land, or being lost in a sky of snow, before a flake begins to fall. A delicate soft world of white, an in and out of fancy lace, a feeling of some white witchery, and almost a fright that little white blossoms have such power over one.

"Where may one find this grand paradise?" asked Rice Cockles, as if he could scarcely refrain his feet from the road to it.

"Five miles the other side of Seven Oaks," Gregory answered, boldly.

"I know the country. Does your father grow cherries for Covent Garden market?"

"Of course he does. Didn't you know that?" Thenceforth in chambers Lovejoy was always known as "Cherry Lovejoy." And he always answered to that name.

It was now the end of June, and the cherries must be getting ripe. The day had been very hot and sultry, and Hilary came into chambers later than his usual time, but fresh as a lark, as he always was. Even Mr. Malahide had felt the weight of the weather, and of his own threescore years and five, and in his own room was dozing. The three clerks in their little den were fit for next to nothing, except to lie far away in some meadow, with sleepy beer, under alder-trees. Even Rice Cockles had struck work with one of those hopeless headaches which are bred by hot weather from satire, a thing that turns sour above freezing-point; and no one was dwelling in the long hot room save the peaceful and steady Gregory.

Even he, with his resolute will to fulfill his mother's prophecies, could scarcely keep his mind from flagging, or his mouth from yawning, as he went through some most elaborate answer to a grand petition in equity — the iniquity being, to a common mind, that the question could have arisen. But Mr. Malahide, of course, regarded things professionally.

"Lovejoy, thy name is 'Love misery,'" cried young Lorraine, who never called his fellow-pupil "Cherry," though perfectly welcome to do so. "I passed an optician's shop just now, and the thermometer stands at 96°. That quill must have come from an ostrich to be able to move in such weather. Even the counselor yields to the elements. Hark how he winds his sultry horn! Is it not a great and true writer who says, 'I tell thee that the quills of the law are the deadliest shafts of the Evil One?' Come, therefore, and try a darting match."

Gregory felt no inclination for so hot a pastime: he had found, however, a habit of yielding to the impulsive and popular Hilary, which led him into a few small scrapes, and one or two that were not small. Lorraine's unusual brightness of nature, and personal beauty and gentle bearing, as well as an inborn readiness to be pleased with every body, insured him a good liking with almost all kinds of people. How then could young Lovejoy, of a fine but unshapen character, and never introduced to the very skirts of good society, help looking up to his champion Hilary as a charming deity? Therefore he made way at once for Hilary's sudden freak for darts. The whole world being at war just then (as happens upon the average in every generation), Cherry Lovejoy slung his target, a legal almanac for the year. Then he took four long quills, and pared them of their plumes, and split the shafts, and fitted each with four paper wings, cut and balanced cleverly. His aptness in the business showed that this was not his first attempt; and it was a hard and cruel thing that he should now have to prepare them. But the clerks had a regular trick of stealing the "young pups'" darts from their unlocked drawers, partly for practice among themselves, but mainly to please their families.

"Capital! Beautifully done!" cried Hilary, as full of life as if the only warmth of the neighborhood were inside him. "We never turned out such a good lot before; I could never do that like you. But now for the tips, my dear fellow!"

"Any fool can do what I have done. But no one can cut the tip at all, to stick in the target, and not bounce back; only you, Mr. Lorraine."

"Mister Lorraine! now Gregory Lovejoy, I thought we liked one another well enough to have dropped that long ago. If you will only vouchsafe to notice, you shall see how I cut the slit, so that the well-sped javelin pierces even a cover of calf-skin." It was done in a moment, by some quick art, inherited, perhaps, from Prince Agasicles, and then they took their stations.

From the farther end of the room they cast (for thirty feet and more perhaps) over two great tables scarred by keen generations of lawyers. Hilary threw the stronger shaft, but Gregory took more careful aim; so that in spite of the stifling heat the contest grew exciting.

"Blest if they young donkeys knows hot from cold!" said the senior clerk, disturbed in his little room by the prodding and walking, and the lively voices.

"Sooner them, than you nor me!" the second clerk muttered sleepily. When the most ungrammatical English is wanted, a copying clerk is the man to supply it.

In spite of unkindly criticism, the brisk acontic strife went on. And every hit was chronicled on a long sheet of draft paper.

"Sixteen to you, eighteen to me!" cried Gregory, poising his long shadowed spear, while his coat and waistcoat lay in the folds of a suit that could never terminate, and his square Kentish face was even redder than a ripe May-duke. At that moment the door was opened, and in came Mr. Malahide.

"Just so!" he said, in his quiet way; "I now understand the origin of a noise which has often puzzled me. Lorraine, what a baby you must be!"

"Can a baby do that?" said Hilary, as he stepped into poor Gregory's place, and sped his dart into the Chancellor's eye, the bull's-eye of their target.

"That was well done," Mr. Malahide answered; "perhaps it is the only good shot you will ever make in your profession."

"I hope not, sir. Under your careful tuition I am laying the foundations of a mighty host of learning."

At this the lawyer was truly pleased. He really did believe that he took some trouble with his pupils; and his very kind heart was always gratified by their praises. And he showed his pleasure in his usual way, by harping on verbal niceties.

"Foundations of a host, Lorraine! Foundations of a pile, you mean; and as yet, *lusisti pilis*. But you may be a credit to me yet. Allowance must be made for this great heat. I will talk to you to-morrow."

With these few words, and a pleasant smile, the eminent lawyer withdrew to his den, feigning to have caught no glimpse of the deeply-blushing Lovejoy. For he knew quite well that Gregory could not afford to play with his schooling; and so (like a proper gentleman) he fell upon the one who could. Hilary saw his motive, and with his usual speed admired him.

"What a fine fellow he is!" he said, as if in pure self-commune: "from the time he becomes Lord Chancellor, I will dart at no legal almanac. But the present fellow—however, the weather is too hot to talk of him. Lovejoy, wilt thou come with me? I must break out into the country."

"What!" cried Gregory, drawing up at the magic word from his stool of repentance, and the desk of his diminished head. "What was that you said, Lorraine?"

"Fair indeed is the thing thou hast said, and fair is the way thou saidest it. Tush! shall I never get wholly out of my ignorant knowledge of Greek plays? Of languages that be, or have been, only two words survive this weather, in the streets of London town; one is 'rus,' and the other 'country.'"

"'It is a sweet and decorous thing to die on behalf of the country.' That line I remember well; you must have seen it somewhere?"

"It is one of my earliest memories, and not a purely happy one. But that is 'patria,' not 'rus.' 'Patria' is the fatherland; 'rus' is a fellow's mother. None can understand this parable till they have lived in London."

"Lorraine," said Gregory, coming up shyly, yet with his brown eyes sparkling, and a steadfast mouth to declare himself, "you are very much above me, of course, I know."

"I am uncommonly proud to hear it," Hilary answered, with his most sweet smile; "because I must be a much finer fellow than I ever could have dreamed of being."

"Now, you know well enough what I mean. I mean, in position of life, and all that—and birth, and breeding, and every thing else."

"To be sure," said Hilary, gravely, making a trumpet of blotting-paper; "any other advantage, Gregory?"

"Fifty, if I could stop to tell them. But I see that you mean to argue it. Now argument is a thing that always—"

"Now, Gregory, just acknowledge me your superior in argument; and I will confess myself your superior in every one of those other things."

"Well, you know, Lorraine, I could scarcely do that. Because it was only the very last time—"

"Exactly," said Hilary; "so it was—the very last time, you left me no more than a shadow caught in a cleft stick. Therefore, friend Gregory, say your say, without any traps for the sole of my foot."

"Well, what I was thinking was no more than this—if you would take it into consideration now—considering what the weather is, and all the great people gone out of London, and the streets like fire almost, and the lawyers frightened by the comet, quite as if, as if, almost—"

"As if it were the devil come for them."

"Exactly so. Bellows's clerk told me, after he saw the comet, that he could prove he had never been articled. And when you come to consider also that there will be a row to-morrow morning—not much, of course, but still a thing to be avoided till the weather cools—I thought; at least, I began to think—"

"My dear fellow, what? Anxiety in this dreadful weather is fever."

"Nothing, nothing at all, Lorraine. But you are the sweetest-tempered fellow I ever came across; and so I thought that you would not mind—at least, not so very much, perhaps—"

"My sweet temper is worn out. I have no mind to mind any thing, Gregory; come and dine with me."

"That is how you stop me always, Lorraine; I can not be for ever coming, and come, to dine with you. I always like it; but you know—"

"To be sure, I know that I like it too. It is high time to see about it. Who could dine in Hall to-day, and drink his bottle of red-hot port?"

"I could, and so could a hundred others. And I mean to do it, unless—"

"Unless what? Mysterious Gregory, by your face I know that you have some very fine thing to propose. Have you the heart to keep me suspended, as well as uncommonly hungry?"

"It is nothing to make a fuss about. Lorraine, you turn upon one so, as if you forget the difference. I was only thinking just by accident, of something that came into my head quite casually."

"Such things have an inspiration. Out with it at last, fair Gregory."

"Well then, if you must have it, how I should like for you to come with me to have a little turn among my father's cherry-trees!"

"What a noble thought!" said Hilary; "a poetic imagination only could have hit on such a thought. The thermometer at 96°—and the cherries—can they be sour now?"

"Such a thing is quite impossible," Gregory answered, gravely; "in a very cold wet summer they are sometimes a little middling. But in such a splendid year as this, there can be no two opinions. Would you like to see them?"

"Now, Lovejoy, I can put up with much; but not with maddening questions."

"You mean, I suppose, that you could enjoy half a dozen cool red cherries, if you had the chance to pick them in among the long green leaves?"

"Half a dozen! Half a peck; and half a bushel afterward. Where have I put my hat? I am off, if it costs my surviving sixpence."

"Lorraine, how very good you are! But you are always in such a hurry. You ought to think a good many times, before you are sure that you ought to do it. Remember that my father's house is very good indeed, and very comfortable, I am sure; still it is very different from what you are accustomed to."

"Such things are not worth thinking about. Custom, and all that, are quite below contempt; I know they are. The greatest mistake of our lives is custom; and the greatest delight is to kick it away. Will your father be glad to see me?"

"He has heard so much of you, Lorraine, that he vowed he would come to London (though he hates it so abominably), to see you and to ask you down; if I were afraid to do so. It is a very old-fashioned place; you must please to bear that in mind. Also, my father, and my mother, and all of us, are old-fashioned people, living in a quiet way. You would carry on more in an hour, than we do in a twelvemonth. We like to go all over things, ever so many times, perhaps (like pushing rings up and down a stick) before we begin to settle them. But, when we have settled them, we never start again; as you seem to do."

"Now, Gregory, Gregory, this is bad. When did you know me to start again? Ready I am to start this once, and to dwell in the orchards forever."

In a few words more, these two young fellows agreed to take their luck of it. There was nothing in chambers for Lovejoy to lose, by going away for a day or two;

and Hilary long had felt uneasy at leaving a holiday overdue. Therefore they made their minds up promptly for an early start next morning, while the drowsy town should be thrusting chimney-pots to catch the dew.

"Gregory," said Lorraine, at last, "your mind is a nest of genius. We two will sit upon bushel-baskets, and watch the sun rise out of sacks. Before he sets, we will challenge him to face our early wagon. Covent Garden is our trysting-spot, and the hour 4 A.M. Oh, day to be marked with white chalk forever!"

"I am sure I can't tell how that may be," answered the less fervent Gregory. "There is not much chalk down our way, and I never saw black chalk anywhere. But can I trust you to be there? If you don't come, I shall not go without you, and the whole affair must be put off."

"No fear, Gregory; no fear of me. The lark shall still be on her nest; but wait, my friend, I will tell the counselor, lest I seem to dread his face."

Lovejoy saw that this was the bounden duty of a gentleman, inasmuch as the learned lawyer had promised his young friend a little remonstrance upon the following morning. The chances were that he would forget it; and this, of course, enhanced the duty of making him remember it. Therefore Hilary gave three taps on the worm-eaten door of his good tutor, according to the scale of precedence. This rule was—inferior clerk, one tap; head-clerk, two taps; pupil (being no clerk at all, and paying, not drawing, salary), as many taps as he might think proper, in a reasonable way.

Hilary, of course, began as he always managed to begin with almost every body.

"I am sorry to disturb you, sir, and I have nothing particular to say."

"In that case, why did you come, Lorraine? It is your usual state of mind."

"Well, sir," said Hilary, laughing at the terse mood of the master, "I thought you had something to say to me—a very unusual state of mind," he was going to say, "on your part;" but stopped, with a well-bred youth's perception of the unbecoming.

"Yes, I have something to say to you. I remember it now, quite clearly. You were playing some childish game with Lovejoy, in the pupil's room. Now, this is all well enough for you, who are fit for nothing else, perhaps. Your father expects no work from you; and if he did, he would never get it. You may do very well, in your careless way, being born to the gift of indifference. But those who can and must work hard—is it honest of you to seduce them? You think that I speak severely. Perhaps I do, because I feel that I am speaking to a gentleman."

"It is uncommonly hard," said Hilary, with his bright blue eyes half conscious of a shameful spring of moisture, "that a fellow always gets it worse for trying to be a gentleman."

"You have touched a great truth," Mr. Malahide answered, laboring bitterly not to smile; "but so it always must be. My boy, I am sorry to vex you; but to be vexed is better than to grieve. You like young Lovejoy—don't make him idle."

"Sir, I will dart at him henceforth, instead of the late lord chancellor, now sitting upon asphodel."

"Lorraine," the great lawyer suddenly asked, in a flush of unusual interest; "you have been at Oxford quite recently. They do all sorts of things there now. Have they settled what asphodel is?"

"No, sir, I fear that they never will. There are several other moot questions still. But with your kind leave, I mean to try to settle that point to-morrow."

CHAPTER XII.

Martin Lovejoy, Gregory's father, owned and worked a pleasant farm in that part of Kent which the natives love to call the "Garden of Eden." In the valley of the upper Medway, a few miles above Maidstone, pretty hamlets follow the soft winding of the river. Here an ancient race of settlers, quiet but intelligent, chose their home, and chose it well, and love it as dearly as ever.

To argue with such people is to fall below their mercy. They stand at their cottage doors, exactly as twelve generations ago they stood. A riotous storm or two may have swept them, but it never lasted long. The bowers of hop and of honeysuckle, trimmed alleys, and rambling roses, the flowering trees by the side of the road, and the truest of true green meadows, the wealth of deep orchards retiring away—as all wealth does—to delight itself; and where the land condescends to wheat, the vast gratitude of the wheat-crop—nobody wonders, after a while, that these men know their value.

The early sun was up and slurring light upon London house-tops, as a task of duty only, having lost all interest in a thing even he can make no hand of. But the brisk air of the morning, after such a night of sweltering, and of strong smells under slates, rode in the perpetual balance of the clime, and spread itself. Fresh, cool draughts of new-born day, as vague as the smile of an infant, roved about; yet were to be caught according to the dew-lines. And of these the best and truest followed into Covent Garden, under the force of attraction toward the green stuff they had begotten.

Here was a wondrous reek of men before the night had quite spent itself. Such a Babel, of a market-morning in the "berry-season," as makes one long to understand the mother-tongue of nobody. Many things are nice and handsome; fruit and flowers are fair and fresh; life is as swift as life can be; and the pulse of price throbs everywhere. Yet, upon the whole, it is wiser not to say much more of it.

Martin Lovejoy scarcely ever ventured into this stormy world. In summer and autumn he was obliged to send some of his fruit to London; but he always sent it under the care of a trusty old retainer, Master John Shorne, whose crusty temper and crisp wit were a puzzle to the Cockney coster-monger. Throughout the market, this man was known familiarly as "Kentish Crust," and the name helped him well in his business.

Now, in the summer morning early, Hilary Lorraine, with his most sprightly walk and manner, sought his way through the crowded alleys and the swarms of those that buy and sell. Even the roughest of rough customers (when both demand and supply are rough), though they would not yield him way, at any rate did not shove him by. "A swell, to buy fruit for his sweetheart," was their conclusion in half a glance at him. "Here, sir, here you are! berries for nothing, and cherries we pays you for eating of them!"

With the help of these generous fellows, Hilary found his way to John Shorne and the wagon. The horses, in unbuckled ease, were munching their well-earned corn close by; for at that time Covent Garden was not squeezed and driven as now it is. The tail-board of the wagon was now hanging upon its hinges, and "Kentish Crust," on his springy rostrum, dealt with the fag-end of his goods. The market, in those days, was not flooded with poor foreign produce, fair to the eye, but a fraud on the belly, and continually ending in dropsy. Englishmen, at that time, did not spend the whole power of their minds upon the newest and speediest measures for robbing their brother Englishmen; and a native would really buy from his neighbor as gladly as from his born enemy.

Master John Shorne had a canvas bag on the right side of his breeches, hanging outside, full in sight, defying every cut-purse. That age was comparatively honest; nevertheless, John kept a club, cut in Mereworth Wood, quite handy. And, at every sale he made, he rang his coin of the realm in his bag, as if he were calling bees all round the wagon. This generally led to another sale. For money has a richly irresistible joy in jingling.

Hilary was delighted to watch these things, so entirely new to him. He had that fatal gift of sliding into other people's minds, and wondering what to do there. Not as a great poet has it, still reserving his own strength, and playing on the smaller nature kindly as he loves it, but simply as a child rejoices to play with other children. So that he entered eagerly into the sudden changes of John's temper, according to the tone, the bidding, and, most of all, the importance of the customers that came to him. By this time the cherries were all sold out, having left no trace except some red splashes, where an over-ripe sieve had been bleeding. But the Kentish man still had some bushels of peas, and new potatoes, and bunches of coleworts, and early carrots, besides five or six dozens of creamy cauliflowers, and several scores of fine-hearted lettuce. Therefore he was dancing with excitement up and down his van, for he could not bear to go home uncleared; and some of his shrewder customers saw that by waiting a little longer they would be likely to get things at half-price. Of course, he was fully alive to this, and had done his best to hide surplus stock by means of sacks, and mats, and empty bushels piled upon full ones.

"Crusty, thou must come down, old fellow," cried a one-eyed coster-monger, winking first at John, and then through the rails, and even at the springs of the van; "half the load will go back to Kent, or else to the cow-keeper, if so be you holds on so almighty dear."

"Ha, then, Joe, are you waiting for that? Go to the cow-yard and take your turn. They always feeds the one-eyed first. Gentlemen, now—while there's any thing left! We've kept all the very best back to the last, 'cos they chanced to be packed by an Irishman. 'First goes in, must first come out.' Paddy, are you there to stick to it?"

"Be jabers, and how could I slip out, when the hape of you was atop of me? And right I was, be the holy poker; there it all is the very first in the bottom of the vhan!"

"Now, are you nearly ready, John?" asked Gregory, suddenly appearing through the laughter of the crowd; "here is the gentleman going with us, and I can't have him kept waiting."

"Come up, Master Greg, and help sell out, if you know the time better than I do." John Shorne was vexed, or he would not so have spoken to his master's son.

To his great surprise, with a bound up came, not Gregory Lovejoy, who was always a little bit shy of the marketing, but Hilary Lorraine, declared by dress and manner (clearly marked, as now they never can be) of an order wholly different from the people round him.

"Let me help you, sir," he said; "I have long been looking on; I am sure that I understand it."

"Forty years have I been at un, and I scarcely knows un now. They takes a deal of mannerin', sir, and the prices will go in and out."

"No doubt; and yet for the sport of it, let me help you, Master Shorne. I will not sell a leaf below the price you whisper to me."

In such height of life and hurry, half a minute is enough to fetch a great crowd anywhere. It was round the market in ten seconds that a grand lord was going to sell out of Grower Lovejoy's wagon. For a great wager, of course it must be; and all who could rush, rushed to see. Hilary let them get ready, and waited till he saw that their money was burning. Meanwhile Crusty John was grinning one of his most experienced grins.

"Don't let him, oh don't let him!" Gregory shouted to the salesman, as Hilary came to the rostrum with a bunch of carrots in one hand and a cauliflower in the other. "What would his friends say if they heard it?"

"Nay, I'll not let un," John Shorne answered, mischievously taking the verb in its (now) provincial sense; "why should I let un? It can't hurt he, and it may do good to we."

In less than ten minutes the van was cleared, and at such prices as Grower Lovejoy's goods had not fetched all through the summer. Such competition arose for the honor of purchasing from a "nobleman," and so enchanted were the dealers' ladies, many of whom came thronging round, with Hilary's bright complexion, gay address, and complaisancy.

"Well done, my lord! well done indeed!" Crusty John, to keep up the fiction, shouted when he had pouched the money, 'Gentlemen and ladies, my lord will sell again next week; he has a heavy bet about it with the Prince Reg—tush, what a fool I am! They will send me to prison if I tell!"

As a general rule, the more suspicious people are in some ways, the more credulous are they in all the rest. Kentish Crust was aware of this, and expected and found for the next two months extraordinary inquiry for his goods.

"Friend Gregory, wherefore art thou glum?" said Hilary to young Lovejoy, while the horses with their bunched-up tails were being buckled to again. Lorraine was radiant with joy, both at his recent triumph in a matter quite unknown to him, and even more because of many little pictures spread before him by his brisk imagination far away from London. Every stamp of a horse's hoof was as good as a beat of the heart to him.

"Lorraine," the sensible Gregory answered, after some hesitation, "I am vexed at the foolish thing you have done. Not that it really is at all a disgrace to you, or your family, but that the world would take it so; and we must think as the world does."

"Must we?" asked Hilary, smiling kindly; "well, if we must, let us think it on springs."

At the word he leaped into the fruit-van so lightly that the strong springs scarcely shook; and Gregory could do no better than climb in calmly after him. "Gee-wugg," cried Master Shorne again; the bright brass harness flashed in the sun, and the horses merrily rang their hoofs on the road to their native land of Kent.

CHAPTER XIII.

Hilary Lorraine enjoyed his sudden delivery from London, and the fresh delight of the dewy country, with such loud approval, and such noisy lightsomeness of heart, that even Crusty John, perched high on the driving-box above him, could not help looking back now and then into the van, and affording the horses the benefit of his opinion. "A right-down hearty one he be, as 'll make some of our maids look alive. And the worst time of year for such work too, when the May-dukes is in and the Hearts a-coloring!"

Hilary was sitting on an empty "half-sieve," and with his usual affability enjoying the converse of "Paddy from Cork," as every body called the old Irishman, who served alike for farm, road, or market, as the "lad of all work." But Gregory Lovejoy, being of a somewhat grave and silent order, was already beginning to doubt his own prudence in bringing their impulsive friend so near to a certain fair cousin of his now staying at the hospitable farm, in whom he felt a tender interest. Poor Lovejoy feared that his chance would be small against this dashing stranger; and he balanced uncomfortably in his mind, whether or not he should drop a hint, at the first opportunity, to Lorraine, concerning his views in that quarter. Often he almost resolved to do so; and then to his diffidence it seemed presumptuous to fancy that any young fellow of Hilary's birth and expectations would entangle himself in their rustic world.

At Bromley they pulled up, to bait "man and beast," three fine horses and four good men eager to know the reason why they should not have their breakfast. Lorraine, although very short of cash (as he always found the means to be), demanded and stood out for leave to pay for every body. This privilege was obtained at last—as it generally is by persistency—and after that it was felt that Hilary could no longer be denied his manifest right to drive the van. He had driven the Brighton four-horse coach, the whole way to London, times and again; and it was perfectly absurd to suppose that he could not manage three horses. Master John Shorne yielded his seat, apparently to this reasoning, but really to his own sure knowledge that the horses after so long a journey would be, on their way to stall, as quiet as lambs in the evening. Therefore he rolled himself up in the van, and slept the sleep of the man who has been up and wide-awake all night for the sake of other people.

The horses well knew the true way home, and offered no cause for bit or whip; and they seemed to be taken sometimes with the pleasure which Hilary found in addressing them. They lifted their tails, and they pricked their ears, at the proper occasions genially; till the heat of the day settled down on their backs, and their creases grew dark and then lathery. And the horse-fly (which generally forbears the pleasure of nuisance till July) in this unusually hot summer was earnest in his vocation already. Therefore, being of a leisurely mind, as behooves all genuine sons of the soil, Master Shorne called a halt, through the blazing time of noon, before battling with the "Backbone of Kent," as the beautiful North Down range is called. Here in a secluded glen they shunned the heats of Canicula under the sign of the "Pig and Whistle."

Thus the afternoon was wearing when they came to Sevenoaks, and passing through that pleasant town, descended into the weald of Kent. No one but Hilary cared for the wonderful beauty and richness of the view, breadth upon breadth of fruit-land, woven in and out with hops and corn; and toward the windings of the Medway, pastures of the deepest green, even now after the heat of the sun, and the thirst of the comet that drank the dew. Turning on the left from the Tonbridge road, they threaded their way along narrow lanes, where the hedges no longer were scarred with chalk, but tapestried with all shades of green, and, even in the broken places, rich with little cascades of loam. Careless dog-rose played above them with its loose abandonment; and honeysuckle was almost ready to release its clustered tongues; but "traveler's joy"—the joy that makes all travelers long to rest in Kent—abode as yet in the hopeful bud, a pendent shower of emerald.

These things were not heeded much, but pleasantly accepted, by the four men and three horses. All felt alike that the world was made for them, and for them to enjoy themselves; and little they cared to go into the reason, when they had the room for it. With this large sense of what ought to be, they came to the gate of Old Applewood Farm, a great white gate with a padlock on it. This stopped the road, and was meant to do so; for Martin Lovejoy, Gregory's father, claimed the soil of the road from this point, and denied all right of way, public or even private, to all claimants of whatsoever kind. On the other hand the parish claimed it as a public thoroughfare, and two farmers farther on vowed that it was an "occupation road;" and what was more, they would use it as such. "Grower Lovejoy," as the neighborhood called him—not that he was likely to grow much more, but because of his cherry-orchards—here was the proper man to hold the gate against all his enemies. When they sawed it down, he very promptly replaced it with cast-iron; and when this was shattered with a fold-pitcher, he stopped their premature triumph by a massive barrier of wrought metal, case-hardened against rasp or cold chisel. Moreover, he painted it white, so that any nocturnal attack might be detected at a greater distance.

When Paddy had opened this gate with a key which he had carried to London, they passed through an orchard of May-duke cherries, with the ripe fruit hanging quite over the road. "No wonder you lock the gate," said Lorraine, as Crusty John, now on the box again, handed him a noble cluster, with the dark juice mantling richly under the ruddy gloss of skin.

"Do you mean that we should get them stolen?" Gregory asked, with some indignation; for his Kentish pride was touched: "oh no, we should never get them stolen. Nobody about here would do such a thing."

"Then they don't know what's good," answered Hilary, jumping at another cluster; "I was born to teach the Kentish public the proper way to steal cherries."

"Well, they do take them sometimes," the truthful Gregory confessed; "but we never call it stealing, any more than we do what the birds take."

"Valued fellow-student, thy strong point will not be the criminal law. But you must have a criminal love of the law, to jump at it out of these cherry-trees."

"It was my mother's work, as you know. Ah, there she is, and my cousin Phyllis!"

For the moment Lovejoy forgot his duty to his friend and particular guest, and slipping down from the tail of the van, made off at full speed through the cherry-trees. Hilary scarcely knew what to do. The last thing that ever occurred to him was that any one had been rude to him; still it was rather unpleasant to drive, or be driven, up to the door of his host, sitting upon a bushel-basket, and with no one to say who he was. Yet to jump out and run after Gregory, and collar him while he saluted his mother, was even a worse alternative. In a very few moments that chance was gone; for the team, with the scent of their corn so nigh, broke into a merry canter, and rattled along with their ears pricked forward, and a pleasant jingling. Neither did they stop until they turned into a large farm-yard, with an oast-house at the farther end of it. The dwelling-house was of the oldest fashion, thatched in the middle, at each end gabled, tiled in some places, and at some parts slabbed. Yet, on the whole, it looked snug, dry, and happy. Here, with one accord, they halted, and shook themselves in their harness, and answered the neighs of their friends in the stables.

Hilary, laughing at his own plight, but feeling uncommonly stiff in the knees, arose from his basket, and looked around; and almost the first thing that met his gaze destroyed all his usual presence of mind. This was a glance of deep surprise, mingled with timid inquiry and doubt, from what Master Hilary felt at once to be the loveliest, sweetest, and most expressive brown eyes in the universe. The young girl blushed as she turned away, through fear of having shown curiosity; but the rich tint of her cheeks was faint, compared with the color of poor Lorraine's. That gay youth was taken aback so utterly by the flash of a moment that he could not find a word to say, but made pretense in a wholesale manner to see nothing at all particular. But the warm blood from his heart belied him, which he turned away to hide, and worked among the baskets briskly, hoping to be looked at, and preparing to have another look as soon as he felt that it could be done.

Meanwhile, that formidable creature, whose glance had produced such a fine effect, recovered more promptly from surprise, and felt perhaps the natural pride of success, and desire to pursue the fugitive. At any rate, she was quite ready to hear whatever he might have to say for himself.

"I must ask you to forgive me," Lorraine began in a nervous manner, lifting his hat, and still blushing freely, "for springing so suddenly out of the earth — or rather, out of this van, I mean; though that can't be right, for I still am in it. I believe that I have the pleasure of speaking to Miss Phyllis Clitherow. Your cousin, Mr. Lovejoy, is a very great friend of mine indeed; and he most kindly asked, or rather, what I mean to say is, invited me to come down for a day or two to this delightful part of the world; and I have enjoyed it so much already, that I am sure—that—that in fact—"

"That I hope you may soon enjoy it more." She did not in the least mean any sarcasm or allusion to Hilary's present state; still he fancied that she did; until the kind look, coming so sweetly from the kind warm heart, convinced him that she never could be so cruel.

"I see the most delightful prospect I ever could imagine of enjoying myself," Lorraine replied, with a glance, imparting to his harmless words the mischief of that which nowadays we call "a most unwarrantable personal allusion." But she did not, or would not, take it so.

"How kind of you to be pleased so lightly! But we do our best in our simple way, when any one kindly comes to see us."

"Why, Miss Clitherow, I thought from what your cousin said to me that you were only staying here for a little time yourself."

"You are quite right as to Miss Clitherow. But I am not my cousin Phyllis. I am only Mabel Lovejoy, Gregory Lovejoy's sister."

"By Jove, how glad I am!" cried Hilary, in his impetuous way; "what a fool I must have been not to know it, after I saw him run to meet his cousin in the orchard! But that treacherous Gregory never told me that he even had a sister. Now, won't I thoroughly give it to him?"

"You must not be angry, Mr. Lorraine, with poor Gregory, because—because Phyllis is such a beautiful girl."

"Don't let me hear about beautiful girls! As if—as if there could be any—"

"Good enough for Gregory," she answered, coming cleverly to his rescue, for he knew that he had gone too far; "but wait till you have seen cousin Phyllis."

"There is one thing I shall not defer for the glory of seeing a thousand Miss Clitherows, and that is the right that I have to shake hands with my dear friend Gregory's sister."

He had leaped from the van some time ago, and now held out his hand (a good strong one, pleasingly veined with cherry-juice), and she, with hospitable readiness, laid her pretty palm therein. He felt that it was a pretty hand, and a soft one, and a hearty one; and he found excuse to hold it longer, while he asked a question.

"Now how did you know my name, if you please, while I made such a stupid mistake about yours?"

"By your bright blue eyes," she was going to answer, with her native truthfulness; but the gaze of those eyes suggested that the downright truth might be dangerous. Therefore, for once, she met a question with a question, warily.

"Was it likely that I should not know you, after all I have heard of you?" This pleased him well in a general way. For Hilary, though too free (if possible) from conceit and arrogance, had his own little share of vanity. Therefore, upon the whole, it was lucky, and showed due attention to his business, that Grower Lovejoy now came up, to know what was doing about the van.

Martin Lovejoy was not a squatter, by seven years stamped into "tenant right," which means for the most part landlord's wrong. Nor was he one of those great tenant farmers who, even then, were beginning to rise, and hold their own with "landed gentry." His farm was small, when compared with some; but it was outright his own, having descended to him through long-buried generations. So that he was one of the ever-dwindling class of "franklins," a class that has done good work for England, neither obtaining nor wanting thanks.

Old Applewood Farm contained altogether about six hundred acres, whereof at least two-thirds lay sweetly in the Vale of Medway, and could show root, stem, or bine against any other land in Kent, and therefore any in England. Here was no fear of the heat of the sun, or the furious winter's rages, such a depth of nature underlay the roots of every thing. Nothing ever suffered from that poverty of blood which makes trees canker on a shallow soil; and no tree rushed into watery strength (which very soon turns to weakness), through having laid hold upon something that suited only a particular part of it.

And not the trees alone, but all things, grew within that proper usage of a regulated power (yet with more of strength to come up, if it should be called for), which has made our land and country fertile over all the world; receiving submissively the manners and the manure of all nations. This is a thing to be proud of; but the opportunity for such pride was not open to the British mind at the poor old time we deal with.

Martin Lovejoy knew no more than that the rest of Europe was amassed against our island; and if England meant to be England, every son of that old country must either fight himself or pay. Martin would rather have fought than paid, if he had only happened to be a score and a half years younger.

Hilary Lorraine knew well (when Martin Lovejoy took his hand, and welcomed him to Old Applewood) that here was a man to be relied on, to make good his words and mind. A man of moderate stature, but of sturdy frame, and some dignity; ready to meet every body pretty much as he was met.

"Glad to see you, sir," he said; "I have often heard of you, Master Lorraine; it is right kind of you to come down. I hope that you are really hungry, sir."

"To the last degree," answered Hilary. "I have been eating off and on, but nothing at all to speak of, in the noble air I have traveled through."

"Our air has suited you, I see by the color of your cheeks and eyes. Aha! the difference begins, as I have seen some scores of times, at ten miles out of London. And we are nearly thirty here, sir, from that miserable place. Excuse me, Master Lorraine, I hope I say nothing to offend you."

"My dear sir, how can you offend me? I hate London heartily. There must be a million people there a great deal too good to live in it. We are counting every body this year; and I hear that when it is made up there will be a million and a quarter!"

"I can't believe it. I can not believe it. There never was such a deal before. And how can there want to be so many now? This numbering of the people is an unholy thing, that leads to plagues. All the parsons around here say that this has brought the comet. And they may show something for it; and they preach of Jerusalem when it was going to be destroyed. They have frightened all our young maids terribly. What is said in London, sir?"

"Scarcely any thing, Mr. Lovejoy; scarcely any thing at all. We only see him every now and then, because of the smoke between us. And when we see him, we have always got our own work to attend to."

"Wonderful, wonderful!" answered the grower; "who can make out them Londoners? About their business they would go if Korah, Dathan, and Abiram were all swallowed up in front of them. For that I like them. I like a man— But come in to our little supper, sir."

CHAPTER XIV.

THE next day was Sunday; and Hilary (having brought a small bag of clothes with him) spent a good deal of the early time in attending to his adornment. For this he had many good reasons to give, if only he had thought about them; but the only self-examination that occurred to him was at the looking-glass. Here he beheld himself looking clean and bright, as he always did look; and yet he was not quite satisfied (as he ought to have been) with his countenance. "There is room for a lot of improvement," he exclaimed at himself, quite bitterly: "how coarse, and how low, I begin to look! But there is not a line in her face that could be changed without spoiling it. There again! Hairs, hairs, coming almost every-where! Beautiful girls have none of that stuff. How they must despise us! All their hair is ornamental, and ours comes so disgracefully!"

When he had no one else to talk to, Hilary always talked to himself. He always believed that he knew himself better than any body else could know him. And so he had a right to do; and so he must have done just now, if doubtful watch of himself and great shaking of his head could help him.

At last he began to be fit to go down, according to his own ideas, though not at all sure that he might not have managed to touch himself up just a little bit more—which might make all the difference. He thought that he looked pretty well; but still he would have liked to ask Gregory before it was too late to make any change and the beautiful eyes fell upon him. But Gregory, and all the rest, were waiting for him in the breakfast-room; and no one allowed him to suspect how much he had tried their patience.

Young Lovejoy showed a great deal of skill in keeping Lorraine to the other side of the table from Phyllis Clitherow; and Hilary was well content to sit at the side of Mabel. Phyllis, in his opinion, was a beautiful girl enough, and clever in her way, and lively; but lovely was the only word to be used at all about Mabel. And she asked him to have just a spoonful of honey, and to share a pat of butter with her, in such a voice, and with such a look, that if she had said, "here are two ounces of cold-drawn castor-oil—if you take one, I'll take the other," he must have opened his mouth for it.

So they went on; and neither knew the deadly sin they were dropping to—that deadly sin of loving when the level and entire landscape of two lives are different.

Through the rich fields, and across a pretty little wandering brook, which had no right to make a quarter of the noise it was making, this snug party went to church. Accurate knowledge of what to do, as well as very pretty manners, and a sound resolve to be overnice (rather than incur the possibility of pushing), led the two young men from London rather to underdo the stiles, and almost go quite away, than to express their feelings by hands, whenever the top-bar made a tangle, according to the usual knot of it. The two girls entered into this, and said to themselves, what a very superior thing it was to have young men from London in comparison with young hop-growers, who stood here and there across them, and made them so blush for each inch of their legs. What made it all the more delicate, and ever so much more delightful, was, that the excellent grower was out of the way, and so was Mrs. Lovejoy. For the latter, being a most kind-hearted woman, had rheumatic pains at the first church-bell, all up the leaders of her back; so that the stiles were too many for her, and Master Lovejoy was compelled to drive her in the one-horse shay.

By the time these staid young men and maidens came to the little church-yard gate every thing was settled between them, as if by deed under hand and seal, although not so much as a wave of the air, much less any positive whisper of the wind, had stirred therein. The import of this unspoken and even undreamed covenant was, that Gregory now must walk with Phyllis, and see to her, and look at her, without her having any second thoughts concerning Hilary. Hilary, on the other hand, was to be acknowledged as the cavalier of Mabel; to help her when she wanted helping, and to talk when she wanted talking; although it might be assumed quite fairly that she could do most of that for herself. Feeling the strength of good management, all of them marched into church accordingly.

In the very same manner they all marched out, after behaving uncommonly well, and scarcely glancing at one another, when the clergyman gave out that the heat of the weather had not allowed him to write a new discourse that week; but as the same cause must have made them forgetful of what he had said last Sunday (when many of them seemed inattentive), he now proposed, with the divine assistance, to read the same sermon again to them.

With the unconverted youthful mind, a spring (like that of Jack-out-of-the-box) at the outer door of the church jumps up, after being so long inside, into that liberal good-will which is one of our noblest sentiments. Any body is glad to see almost every body; and people (though of one parish) in great joy forego their jangling. The sense of a grand relief, and a conscience wiped clean for another week, leads the whole lot to love one another as far as the gate of the church-yard.

But our young people were much inclined to love one another much farther. The more they got into the meadow-land, and the strength of the summer around them, with the sharp stroke of the sun, and the brisk short shadows of one another, the more they were treading a dangerous path, and melting away to each other. Hilary saw with romantic pride that Mabel went on as well as ever, and had not a bead on her clear bright cheeks; while at the same time Phyllis, though stopping to rest every now and then—but Hilary never should have noticed this. Such things are below contempt.

In this old and genial house, the law was that the guest should appoint the time for dinner, whenever the cares of the outer work permitted it. And as there were no such cares on Sunday, Hilary had to choose the time for the greatest event of the human day. This had been talked of and settled, of course, before any body got the prayer-books; and now the result at two o'clock was a highly excellent repast. To escape the power of the sun they observed this festival in the hall of the house, which was deliciously cool even now, being paved with stone, and shaded by a noble and fragrant walnut-tree. Mrs. Lovejoy knew, what many even good housekeepers seem not to know—to wit, that to keep a room cool, it is not necessary to open the windows when the meridian sun bombards. "For goodness sake, let us have some air in such weather as this!" they cry, when they might as well say, "let us cool the kitchen by opening the door of the oven."

Lorraine was one of those clever fellows who make the best of every thing; which is the cleverest thing that can be done by a human being. And he was not yet come to the time of life when nothing is good if the dinner is bad; so that he sat down cheerily, and cheered all the rest by doing so.

Of course there were many things said and done, which never would have been said, or thought of, at the dinner-table of Coombe Lorraine. But Hilary (though of a very sensitive fibre in such matters) neither saw, nor heard, nor felt, a single thing that irked him. There was nothing low about any body; whereas there was something as high as the heavens dining out of the very next plate. He made himself (to the very utmost of his power) agreeable, except at the moments when his power of pleasing quite outran himself. Then he would stop and look at his fork—one of the fine old two-pronged fellows—and almost be afraid to glance, to ask what she was thinking.

She was thinking the very things that she should have known better than to think. But what harm could there possibly be in scarcely thinking, so much as dreaming, things that could have nothing in them? Who was she, a country girl, to set herself up, and behave herself, as if any body meant any thing? And yet his eyes, and the bend of his head, and his choice of that kidney-potato for her (as if he were born a grower), and then the way he poured her beer—if there was nothing in all this, why then there was nothing in all the world, except delusion and breaking of heart.

Hilary, sitting at her knife-hand, felt a whole course of the like emotions, making allowance for gender. How beautifully she played her knife, with a feminine tenderness not to make too strong a slice of any thing! And how round her little wrist was, popping in and out of sleeves, according as the elbow went; and no knob any where to be seen, such as women even of the very latest fashion have. And then her hair was coming toward him (when she got a bit of gristle) so that he could take a handful, if the other people only would have the manners not to look. And oh, what lovely hair it was! so silky, and so rich, and bright, and full of merry dances to the music of her laugh! And he did not think he had ever seen any thing better than her style of eating, without showing it. Clearly enjoying her bit of food, and tempting all to feed their best; yet full of mind at every mouthful, and of heart at every help. But above all, when she looked up, quite forgetting both knife and fork, and looked as if she could look like that into no other eyes but his; with such a gentle flutter, and a timid wish to tell no more, and yet a sudden pulse of glad light from the innocent young heart—nothing could be lovelier than the way in which she raised her eyes, except her way of dropping them.

These precious glances grew more rare and brief the more he sought for them; and he wondered whether any body else ever had been treated so. Then, when he would seem to be doubtful, and too much inclined to stop, a look of surprise, or a turn of the head, would tempt him to go on again. And there would be little moments (both on his side and on hers) of looking about at other people with a stealthy richness; with a sense of some great treasure, made between them, and belonging to themselves in private; a proud demand that the rest of the world should attend to its proper business; and then, with one accord, a meeting of the eyes that were beginning, more and more, to mean alike.

All this was as nice as could be, and a pretty thing to see. Still, in a world that always leaves its loftiest principles to accumulate, at the lowest interest (and once in every generation to be a mere drug in the market), "love" is used, not in games alone, as the briefest form of "nothing." All our lovers (bred as lovers must be under school boards) know what they are after now, and who can pay the ninepence. But in the ancient time, the mothers had to see to most of that.

Mrs. Lovejoy, though she did not speak, or look particularly, had her perception of what was going on close by. And she said to herself, "I will see to this. It is no good interfering now. I shall have Miss Mabel all to myself in three-quarters of an hour."

CHAPTER XV.

Mrs. Lovejoy's lecture to her daughter seemed likely to come just a little too late, as so many excellent lessons do. For as soon as he saw that all had dined, the host proposed an adjournment, which was welcomed with no small delight by all except the hostess.

"Now, Master Lorraine, and my niece Phyllis, what say you, if we gather our fruit for ourselves in the shady places; or rather, if we sit on the bank of the little brook in the orchard, where there is a nice sheltered spot; and there we can have a glass of wine while the maidens pick the fruit for us?"

"Capital," answered Hilary; "what a fine idea, Mr. Lovejoy! But surely we ought to pick for the ladies instead of letting them pick for us."

"No, sir, we will let them have the pleasure of waiting upon us. It is the rule of this neighborhood, and ought to be observed everywhere. We work for the ladies all the week, serve, honor, and obey them. On Sundays they do the like for us, and it is a very pleasant change. Mabel, don't forget the pipes. Do you smoke, Master Lorraine? If so, my daughter will fill a pipe for you."

"That would be enough to tempt me, even if I disliked it, whereas I am very fond of it. However, I never do smoke, because my father has a most inveterate prejudice against it. I promised him some time ago to give it up for a twelvemonth. And the beauty of it is that there is nothing he himself enjoys so much as a good pinch of snuff. Ah, there I am getting my revenge upon him. My sister will do any thing I ask her; and he will do any thing she asks him; and so, without his knowledge, I am breaking him of his snuff-box."

"Aha, well done! I like that. And I like you too, young man, for your obedience to your father. That virtue is becoming very rare; rarer and rarer every year. Why, if my father had knocked me down I should have lain on the ground, if it was a nettle-bed, till he told me to get up. Now, Greg, my boy, what would you do?"

"Well, sir, I think that I should get up as quick as I could, and tell my mother."

"Aha! and I should have the nettles then. Well said, Greg, my boy; I believe it is what all the young fellows nowadays would do. But I don't mean you, of course, Master Lorraine. Come along, come along! Mabel, you know where that old Madeira is that your poor Uncle Ambrose took three times to Calcutta. Ah, poor man, I wish he was here! As fine a fellow as ever shotted a cannon at a Frenchman. Nelson could have done no better. And it did seem uncommonly hard upon him never to go to church-yard. However, the will of the Lord be done! Now mind, the new patent cork-screw."

Mabel was only too glad to get this errand to the cellar. With filial instinct she perceived how likely she was to "catch it," as soon as her mother got the chance. Not that she deserved it. Oh no, not in the least, her conscience told her. Was she to be actually rude to her father's guest, and her brother's friend? And as if she was not old enough now, at eighteen and a quarter, to judge for herself in such childish matters as how to behave at dinner-time!

By the side of a pebbly brook—which ran within stone-throw of the house, sparkling fresh and abundant from deep well-springs of the hill-range—they came to a place which seemed to be made especially for enjoyment. A bend of the grassy banks and rounded hollow of the fruit-land, where cherry and apple and willow tree clubbed their hospitable shade, and fugitive water made much ado to ripple down the zigzag rill. Here, in cool and gentle shelter, the grower set his four legs down; *i. e.*, the four legs of his chair, because, like all that in gardens dwell, he found mother earth too rheumatic for him, especially in hot weather, when deep sluggish fibres radiate. The groweress also had her chair, borne by the sedulous Gregory. All the rest, like nymphs and shepherds, strewed their recumbent forms on turf.

"God Almighty," said Master Lovejoy, fearing that he might be taking it too easy for the Sabbath-day, "really hath made beautiful things for us his creatures to rejoice in, with praise, thanksgiving, and fruitfulness. Mabel, put them two bottles in the brook—not there, you stupid child! can't you see that the sun comes under that old root? In the corner, where that shelf of stone is. Thank you, Master Lorraine. What a thing it is to have a head-piece! But God Almighty never made, among all his wonderful infinite works, the waters and the great whales, and the fruit-tree yielding fruit, whose seed is in itself, and the green herb for meat, which means to come to table with the meat; his mercy endureth forever; and he never showed it as when he made tobacco, and clay for tobacco-pipes—the white clay that he made man of." With this thanksgiving, he began to smoke.

"Now, Martin, I never could see that," answered Mrs. Lovejoy; "the best and greatest work of the Lord ought to have been for the women first."

"Good wife! then it must have been the apple. Ah, Gregory, I had your mother there. However, we won't dispute on a Sunday; it spoils all the goodness of going to church, and never leaves any thing settled. Mabel, ran away now for the fruit, while Gregory feels if the wine is cold. Master Lorraine, I hope that our little way of going on, and being overfree on a Sunday perhaps, does not come amiss to you."

Hilary did not look as if any thing came amiss to him, as now he lay at the feet of Mabel, on the slope of the sweet rich sward, listening only for her voice, more liquid than even the tone of the brook. He listened for it, but not to it; inasmuch as one of those sudden changes, which (at less than half a breath) vapor the glass of the feminine mind was having its turn with the maiden. Mabel felt that she had not kept herself to herself, as she should have done. Who was this gentleman, or what, that she should be taken with him so suddenly as to feel her breath come short every time that she even thought of her mother? A gentleman from London, too, where the whole time of the Court was spent, as Master Shorne brought news every week, in things that only the married women were allowed to hear of. In the present case, of course, she knew how utterly different all things were. How lofty and how grand of heart, how fearful even to look at her much—still, for all that, it would only be wise to show him, or at least to let him see that—that, at any rate, for the present—

"Now, Mabel, when are you going for the cherries? Phyllis—bless my heart alive! Gregory, are you gone to sleep? What are all the young people made of, when a touch of summer makes them only fit to sprawl about?"

"Bring three sorts of cherries, Mabel," Gregory shouted after her; "Mr. Lorraine must be tired of May-dukes, I am sure. The

Black Geans must be ripe, and the Eltons, and the Early Amber. And go and see how the White-hearts are on the old tree against the wall."

"Much he knows about cherries, I believe!" grumbled Mr. Lovejoy; "John Doe and Richard Roe be more to his liking than the finest Griffins. Why, the White-hearts haven't done stoning yet! What can the boy be thinking of?" It was the grower's leading grievance that neither of his two sons seemed likely to take to the business after him. Here was the elder being turned by his mother into a "thieves' counselor," and the younger was away at sea, and whenever he came home told stories of foreign fruit which drove his father into a perfect fury. So that now it was Martin's leading wish to marry his only daughter to some one fitted to succeed him, who might rent the estate from the proper heir, for the land had been disgaveled.

It is a pleasing thing to a young man—ay, and an old one may be pleased—to see a pretty girl make herself useful in pretty and natural attitudes; and that pleasure now might be enjoyed at leisure and in duplicate. For Phyllis Clitherow was a pretty, or rather a beautiful young woman, slender, tall, and fair of hue. Not to be compared with Mabel, according to Hilary's judgment; but infinitely superior to her in the opinion of Gregory. All that depends upon taste, of course; but Mabel's beauty was more likely to outlast the flush of youth, having the keeping qualities of a bright and sweet expression, and the dark lustre of sensible eyes.

These two went among the cherry-trees, with fair knowledge what to do, and having light scarfs on their heads, brought behind their ears and tied under the curves of their single chins. Because they knew that the spurs and sprays would spoil their lovely Sunday hats, even if they should escape the drip of a cherry wounded by some fine thrush. The blackbirds pop them off entire, and so do the starlings; but the thrushes sit and peck at them, with the juice dripping down on their dappled breasts, and a flavor in their throats which they mean to sing about at their leisure. But now the birds that were come among them meant to have them wholesale. Phyllis, being a trifle taller, and less deft of finger, bent the shady branches down for Mabel to pluck the fruit. Mabel knew that she must take the northern side of the tree, of course; and the boughs where the hot sun had not beaten through the leaves and warmed the fruit. Also she knew that she must not touch the fruit with her hand and dim the gloss; but above all things to be careful—as of the goose with the golden eggs—to make no havoc of the young buds forming at the base of every cluster, for the promise of next year's crop.

Hilary longed to go and help them; but his host being very proud of the grandeur of his Madeira wine, would not even hear of it. And Mrs. Lovejoy, for other reasons, showed much skill in holding him; so that he could but sit down and admire the picture he longed to be part of. Hence he beheld in the happy distance, in and out the well-fed trees, skill, and grace, and sprightly movements, tiny baskets lifted high, round arms bent for drawing downward, or thrown up for a jumping catch, and every thing else that is so lovely, and safe to admire at a distance.

By-and-by the maids came back, bearing their juicy treasure, and blithe with some sage mysticism of laughter. They had hit upon some joke between them, or something that chanced to tickle them; and when this happens with girls, they never seem to know when the humor is out of it. And of course they make the deepest mystery of a diminutive jest so harmless, that it hits no one except themselves. Mrs. Lovejoy looked at them strongly. Her time for common sense was come; and she thought they were stealing a march upon her, by some whispers about young men, the last thing they should ever think of.

Whereas the poor girls had no thought of any thing of the kind. Neither would they think one atom more than they could help, of what did not in the least concern them, if their elders, who laid down the law, would only leave them to themselves. And it was not long till this delightful discretion was afforded them. For, after a glass or two of wine, the heat of the day began to tell, through the cool air of the hollow, on that worthy couple, now kindly hand in hand, and calmly going down the slope of life. They hoped they had got a long way to go yet; and each thought so of the other. Neither of them had much age, being well under three-score years; just old enough to begin to look on the generation judiciously. But having attained this right at last, after paying heavily, what good could they have of it, if young people were ever so far above their judgment? Meditating thus they dozed, and youthful voice, and glance, and smile, were drowned in the melody of—nose.

The breeze that comes in the afternoon of every hot day (unless the sky is hushing up for a thunder-storm) began to show the under-side of leaves and the upper gloss of grass, and with feeble puffs to stir the stagnant heat into vibration, like a candle quivering. Every breath at first was hot, and only made the air feel hotter, until there arrived a refreshing current, whether from some water-meadows or the hills where the chalk lay cool.

"The heat is gone," said Martin Lovejoy, waking into the pleasant change; "it will be a glorious afternoon. Pooh, what is this to call hot weather? Only three years ago, in 1808, I remember well—"

"It may have been hotter then, my dear," said Mrs. Lovejoy, placidly; "but it did not make you forget your pipe, and be ungrateful to Providence about me."

"Why, where can the children be?" cried the grower; "I thought they were all here just this moment! It is wonderful how they get away together. I thought young Lorraine and Gregory were as fast asleep as you or I! Oh, there, I hear them in the distance, with the girls, no doubt, all alive and merry!"

"Ay, and a little too merry, I doubt," answered Mrs. Lovejoy; "a little too much alive for me. Why, they must be in the wall garden now! Goodness alive, I believe they are, and nobody to look after them!"

"Well, if they are they can't do much harm. They are welcome to any thing they can find, except the six strawberries I crossed, and Mabel will see that they don't eat those."

"Crossed strawberries, indeed now, Martin!" Mrs. Lovejoy never could be brought to understand cross-breeding. "They'll do something worse than cross your strawberries unless you keep a little sharper lookout. They'll cross your plans, Master Martin Lovejoy, and it's bad luck for any one who does that."

"I don't understand you, wife, any more than you understand the strawberries. How could they cross them at this time of year?"

"Why, don't you see that this gay young Lorraine is falling over head and ears in love with our darling Mabel?"

"Whew! That would be a sad affair," the grower answered, carelessly. "I like the young fellow, and should be sorry to have him so disappointed. For of course he never could have our Mab unless he made up his mind to turn grower. Shorne says that he is a born salesman; perhaps he is also a born grower."

"Now, husband, why do you vex me so? You know as well as I do that he is the only son of a baronet, belonging, as Gregory says, to one of the proudest families in England; though he doesn't show much pride himself, that's certain. Is it likely they would let him have Mabel?"

"Is it likely that we would let Mabel have him? But this is all nonsense, wife; you are always discovering such mare's-nests. Tush! why, I didn't fall in love with you till we fell off a horse three times together."

"I know that, of course. But that was because they wanted us to do it. The very thing is that it happens at once when every body's face is against it. However, you've had your warning, Martin, and you only laugh at it. You have nobody but yourself to thank if it goes against your plots and plans. For my own part, I should be well pleased if Mabel were really fond of him, and if the great people came round in the end, as sooner or later they always do. There are very few families in the kingdom that need be ashamed of my daughter, I think. And he is a most highly accomplished young man. He said last night immediately after prayer-time that I might try for an hour, and he would be most happy to listen to me, but I never, never could persuade him that I was over forty years old. Therefore, husband, see to it yourself. Things may take their own course for me."

"Trust me, trust me, good wife," said Martin; "I can see, as far as most folk can. What stupes boys and girls are, to be sure, to go rushing about after watery fruit, and leave such wine as this here Madeira. Have another glass, my dear good creature, to cheer you up after your prophecies."

Meanwhile, in the large old-fashioned garden, which lay at the east end of the house, farther up the course of the brook, any one sitting among the currant-bushes might have judged which of the two was right, the unromantic franklin, or his more ambitious but sensible wife. Gregory and Phyllis were sitting quietly in a fine old arbor, having a steady little flirt of their own, and attending to nothing in the world besides. Phyllis was often of a pensive cast, and she never looked better than in this mood, when she felt the deepest need of sympathy. This she was receiving now, and pretending of course not to care for it; her fingers played with moss and bark, the fruits of the earth were below her contempt, and she looked too divine for any body.

On the other hand, the rarest work and the most tantalizing tricks were going on at a proper distance between young Mabel and Hilary. They had straggled off into the strawberry-beds where nobody could see them, and there they seemed likely to spend some hours if nobody should come after them. The plants were of the true Carolina, otherwise called the "old scarlet pine," which among all our countless new sorts finds no superior, perhaps no equal, although it is now quite out of vogue, because it fruits so shyly?

What says our chief authority? "Fruit medium-sized, ovate, even, and regular, and with a glossy neck, skin deep red, flesh pale red, very firm and solid, with a fine sprightly and very rich pine flavor." What lovelier fruit could a youth desire to place between little pearly teeth, reserving the right to have a bite, if any of the very firm flesh should be left? What fruit more suggestive of elegant compliments could a maid open her lips to receive, with a dimple in each mantled cheek—lips more bright than the skin of the fruit, cheeks by no means of a pale red now, although very firm and solid?

and as for the sprightly flavor of the whole, it may be imagined, if you please, but is not to be ascertained as yet.

"Now, I must pick a few for you, Mr. Lorraine. You are really giving me all you find. And they are so scarce—no, thank you; I can get up very nicely by myself. And there can't be any brier in my hair. You really do imagine things. Where on earth could it have come from? Well, if you are sure, of course you may remove it. Now I verily believe you put it there. Well, perhaps I am wronging you. It was an unfair thing to say, I confess. Now wait a moment, while I run to get a little cabbage-leaf!"

"A cabbage-leaf! Now you are too bad. I won't taste so much as the tip of a strawberry out of any thing but one. How did you eat your strawberries, pray?"

"With my mouth, of course. But explain your meaning. You won't eat what I pick for you out of what?"

"Out of any thing else in the world except your own little beautiful palm."

"Now, how very absurd you are! Why, my hands are quite hot."

"Let me feel them, and judge for myself. Now the other, if you please. Oh, how lovely and cool they are! How could you tell me such a story, Mabel, beautiful Mabel?"

"I am not at all beautiful, and I won't be called so. And I know not what they may do in London. But I really think, considering—at least when one comes to consider that—"

"To consider what? You make me tremble, you do look so ferocious. Ah, I thought you couldn't do it long. Inconsiderate creature, what is it I am to consider?"

"You can not consider! Well, then remember. Remember it is not twenty-four hours since you saw me for the very first time, and surely it is not right and proper that you should begin to call me 'Mabel,' as if you had known me all your life!"

"I must have known you all my life. And I mean to know you all the rest of my life, and a great deal more than that—"

"It may be because you are Gregory's friend you are allowed to do things. But what would you think of me, Mr. Lorraine, if I were to call you 'Hilary'—a thing I should never dream of?"

"I should think that you were the very kindest darling, and I should ask you to breathe it quite into my ear—'Hilary, Hilary!'—just like that; and then I should answer just like this, 'Mabel, Mabel, sweetest Mabel, how I love you, Mabel!' and then what would you say, if you please?"

"I should have to ask my mother," said the maiden, "what I ought to say. But luckily the whole of this is in your imagination. Mr. Lorraine, you have lost your strawberries by your imagination."

"What do I care for strawberries!" Hilary cried, as the quick girl wisely beat a swift retreat from him. "You never can enter into my feelings, or you never would run away like that. And I can't run after you, you know, because of Phyllis and Gregory. There she goes, and she won't come back. What a fool I was to be in such a hurry! But what could I do to help it? I never know where I am when she turns those deep, rich eyes upon me. She never will show them again, I suppose, but keep the black lashes over them. And I was getting on so well—and here are the stalks of the strawberries!"

Of every strawberry she had eaten from his daring fingers he had kept the stalks and calyx, breathed on by her freshly fragrant breath, and slyly laid them in his pocket; and now he fell to at kissing them. Then he lay down in the Carolinas, where her skirt had moved the leaves, and to him, weary with strong heat, and a rush of new emotions, comfort came in the form of sleep. And when he awoke, in his open palm most delicately laid, he found a little shell-shaped cabbage-leaf piled with the fruit of the glossy neck.

CHAPTER XVI.

These doings of Hilary and his love—for his love he declared her to be forever, whether she would have him for hers or not—seem to have taken more time almost in telling than in befalling. Although it had been a long summer's day, to them it had passed as a rapid dream. So at least they fancied, when they began to look quietly back at it, forgetting the tale of the golden steps so lightly flitted over by the winged feet of love.

Martin Lovejoy watched his daughter at supper-time that Sunday; and he felt quite sure that his wife was wrong. Why, the girl scarcely spoke to Lorraine at all, and even neglected his plate so sadly, that her mother was compelled to remind her sharply of her duties. Upon which the grower dispatched to his wife a smile of extreme sagacity, which (being fetched out of cipher and short-hand by the matrimonial key) contained all this: "Well, you are a silly, as you always are when you want to advise me. The girl is cold-shouldering that young fellow, the same as she does all the young hop-growers. And well she knows how to do it, too. She gets her intellect from her father. Now please not to put in your oar, Mrs. Lovejoy, another time, till it is asked for."

Moreover, he thought that if Mabel took the smallest delight in Hilary, she could not have answered as she had done, when that pious youth, in the early evening, expressed his sincere desire to attend another performance of divine service.

"I had no idea," said the simple Gregory, "that you made a point of going to church at least twice every Sunday. I seldom see you of a Sunday in London. But the very last place I should go to, to find you, would probably be the Temple Church."

"That is quite a different thing, don't you see? A country church, and a church in London, are as different as a meadow and a market-place."

"But surely, Mr. Lorraine, you would find the duty of attending just the same." Thus spoke Mrs. Lovejoy, who seldom missed a chance of discharging her duty toward young people.

"Quite so; of course I do, Mrs. Lovejoy. But then we always perform our duties best when they are pleasures. And besides that, I have a special reason for feeling bound, as one might say, to go to church well in the country."

"I suppose one must not venture to ask you what the reason is, sir."

"Oh yes, to be sure. It is just this. I have an uncle, my mother's brother, who is a country clergyman."

"Well done, Master Lorraine!" said the grower, while the rest were laughing. "You take a very sensible view, sir, of things. It is too much the fashion nowadays to neglect our trade connections. But Gregory will go with you, and Phyllis and Mabel. The old people stay at home to mind the house. For we always let the maid-servants go."

"Oh father," cried Mabel; "poor Phyllis is so overcome by the heat, that she must not go. And I must stop at home to read to her."

So that the good Lorraine took nothing by his sudden religious fervor, except a hot walk with Gregory, and a wearisome doze in a musty pew, with nobody to look at.

With fruit-growers Monday is generally the busiest day of the week, except Friday. After paying all hands on the Saturday night, and stowing away all implements, they rest them well till the Sunday is over, having in the summer-time earned their rest, by night-work as well as day-work, through the weary hours of the week. This is not the case with all, of course. Many of them, especially down in Kent, grow their fruit, or let it grow itself, and then sell it by the acre, or the hundred acres, to dealers, who take all the gathering and marketing off their hands altogether. But for those who work off their own crops, the toil of the week begins before the day-star of the Monday. At least for about six weeks it is so, according to the weather and the length of the "busy season." Before the stars fade out of the sky, the pickers advance through the strawberry quarters, carrying two punnets each, yawning more than chattering even, whisking the gray dew away with their feet, startling the lark from his nest in the row, groping among the crisp leaves for the fruit, and often laying hold of a slug instead.

That is the time for the true fruit-lover to try the taste of a strawberry. It should be one that refused to ripen in the gross heat of yesterday, but has been slowly fostering goodness, with the attestation of the stars. And now (if it has been properly managed, properly picked without touch of hand, and not laid down profanely), when the sun comes over the top of the hedge, the look of that strawberry will be this — at least, if it is of a proper sort: the beard of the footstalk will be stiff, the sepals of the calyx moist and crisp, the neck will show a narrow band of varnish, where the dew could find no hold, the belly of the fruit will be sleek and gentle, firm, however, to accept its fate; but the back that has dealt with the dew, and the sides where the color of the back slopes downward, upon them such a gloss of cold and diamond chastity will lie that the human lips get out of patience with the eyes in no time.

Every body was so busy with the way the work went on, all for their very life pretending scarcely to have time to breathe, whenever the master looked at them, that the "berries" were picked, and packed, and started, long before the sun grew hot—started on the road to London, the cormorant of the universe.

Hilary helped with all his heart; enjoying it, with that triumphant entrance into any novelty, which always truly distinguished him. He carried his punnets, and kept his row (as soon as they had shown him how), as well as the very best of them, dividing his fruit into firsts, and seconds, and keeping the "toppers" separate. Of course he broke off many trusses entire—ripe fruit, green fruit, and barren blossom — until he learned how to "meet his nails," and how much drag to put on the stalks. A clever fellow learns all that from an hour or two of practice.

But one thing there is which the cleverest fellows can learn by no experience—how to carry the head for hours upside down without hurting it. How to make the brain so hard that it can not shift; or else so soft that the top is as good as the bottom. The question is one for a great physician, who, to understand it, must keep his row, and pick by the job. Then let him say if he has learned how to explain the well-established fact that a woman can pick twice as fast as a man; for who could assent to the reason assigned by one of themselves sagaciously —that "they was generally always used to keep their heads turned upside down?"

Leaving such speculative inquiries to go on forever, Hilary (who knew better than to say a word about them) came in for his breakfast at six o'clock, and ate it as thoroughly as he had earned it. The master, a man of true Kentish fibre, obstinate, placable, hearty, and dry, made known to his wife and to every body else, his present opinion of Hilary. Martin Lovejoy never swore. He never went beyond "God knows," or "The Lord in heaven look down on us," or some other good exclamation, sanctioned by the parish vicar. As a general rule—proved by many exceptions—the Kentish men seldom swear very hard.

"Heart alive, young sir!" he exclaimed, piling Hilary's plate, as he spoke, with the jellied delights of cold pigeon-pie; "you have been the best man of the morning. Ah, don't you be in a hurry, good wife. No tea or coffee, our way, thankee. No, nor any 'cask-wash.' We've worked a little too hard for that. Mabel, whatever has come to you, that you keep always out of the way so? And I never saw you anigh the baskets. Now don't pipe your eye, child. I'm not going to scold thee, if thou didst have a little lie-a-bed. Here, take this here key, child. A wink's as good as a nod—ah, she knows pretty well what to do with it."

For Mabel was glad to turn away as quickly as possible, after a little well-managed courtesy to Hilary, whom she had not seen for the morning—certainly through no fault of his—and without a word she went to the dresser (for in these busy times they took their breakfast wisely in the kitchen), and from the wooden crook unhung a quaint little jug, with a narrow mouth and a silver lip and handle. With this she set off down a narrow passage and some steps to a little stone cellar, where the choicest of the home-brewed ale was kept. Although it lay well beneath the level of the ground, and no ray of sun pierced the wired lattice, the careful mistress of the house had the barrels swathed closely with wetted sacks. The girl, with her neat frock gathered up—for she always was cleanliness itself—went carefully to the corner cask, and lifted the wet sack back from the head, lest any dirty water should have the chance of dripping upon her sleeve. Then she turned the tap, and a thin bright thread ran out of it sideways, being checked by some hops in the tube, perhaps, or want of air at the vent-peg. But Mabel held the jug with all patience, although her hand shook just a little.

"Now," said the grower, when she came back and placed the jug at her father's side, without a word to Hilary, "Master Lorraine, let me pour you a drop, not to be matched in Kent, nor yet in all England, I do believe. Home-grown barley, and home-grown hops, and the soft water out of the brook that has taken the air of the sky for seven mile or more; without a drain anigh it. Ah, those brewers can never do that! They must buy their malt, and their musty hops, and pump up their water, and boil it down, to get the flint-stones out of it. But our brook hath cast the flint-stones and the other pebbles all along. That makes a sight of difference, sir. Every water is full of stones, and if you pump it up from the spring, the stones be all alive in it. But let it run seven miles or eight, and then it is fit to brew with."

"Ah, to be sure. Now that explains a great many things I never understood." Hilary would have swallowed a camel rather than argue at this moment.

"Young sir, just let me prove it to you. Just see the color it runs out, and the way the head goes creaming! Lord, ha' mercy, if she has gived us a glass, or a stag's horn from the mantel-piece! Why, Mabel, child —Mabel, art thou gone? Nobody wants to poison thee."

"I think, sir, I saw your daughter go round the corner by the warming-pan, this side of where the broom hangs."

"Then all I can say is, she is daft. She worked very hard last week, poor thing. And yesterday she was a-moving always, when the Lord's day bids us rest. I must beg your pardon, Master Lorraine. Our Kentish maids always look after our guests. When I was at school, I read in the grammar that the moon always managed the women; but now I do believe it is the comet. Let the comet come, say I. When the markets are so bad, I feel that I am ready to face almost any thing. And now we must drink from the jug, I reckon!"

Hilary saw that his host was vexed; but he felt quite certain in his own heart that Mabel could never be so rude, or show such resentment of any little oversweetness on his part, as to go away in that sour earnest, and make the two of them angry. A dozen things might have happened to upset her, or turn her a little askew; and her own father ought to know her better than he seemed to do. And lo, ere the grower had quite finished grumbling, Mabel reached over his shoulder unseen, and set his own pet glass before him; and then round Hilary's side she slid, without ever coming too nigh to him, and the glass of honor of the house, cut in countless facets, twinkled like the Pleiades at him!

"Adorn me!" said the grower. "Now I call that a true good girl! Girls were always made, Master Lorraine, for the good of those around them. If any body treats them any way else, they come to nothing afterward. Mabel, dear, give me a kiss. You deserve it; and there it is for you. Now be off, like a good maid, and see what they be at in Vale Orchard, while Master Lorraine and I think a bit over these here two glasses."

The rest of the day was much too busy, and too much crowded with sharp eyes, for any fair chance of love-making. For they all set to at the cherry-trees, with ladders, crooks, and hanging baskets, and light boys to scale the more difficult antlers, strip them, and drop upon feather-beds. And though the sun broke hot and bright through the dew-cloud of the morning, and quickly drank the beaded freshness off the face of herb and tree, yet they picked, and piled, and packed, (according to their sort and size) the long stalked dancers that fringe the bough, and glance the sun so ruddily.

"You must have had a deal too much of this," young Lovejoy said to Hilary, when the noonday meal had been spread forth and dealt with, in a patch of fern near a breezy clump. "If I had worked as you have done, my fingers would scarcely be fit for a quill this side of next Hilary Term."

"My dear fellow, be not, I pray you, so violently facetious. The brain, when outraged, takes longer to resume its functions than the fingers do. Moreover, I trust that my fingers will hold something nobler than a quill, ere the period of my namesake."

"Sir Hilary charged at Agincourt; I hope you will do nothing of the sort;" said Gregory, with unwitting and unprecedented poetry.

"Lovejoy, my wits are unequal altogether to this encounter. The brilliancy of your native soil has burst out so upon you, that I must go back to the Southdown hills, before I dare point a dart with you. Nevertheless, on your native soil, I beat you at picking cherries."

"That you do, and strawberries, too; and still more so at eating them! But if you please, you must stop a little. My mother begs, as a great favor, to have a little private talk with you."

Hilary's bright face lost its radiance, as his conscience pricked him. Was it about Mabel? Of course it must be. And what the dickens was he to say? He could not say a false thing. That was far below his nature. And he must own that he did love Mabel; and far worse than that—had done his utmost to drag that young and innocent Mabel into love with him. And if he were asked about his father—as of course he must be—on the word of a true man he must confess that his father would never forgive him if he married below his rank in life; also, that though he was the only son, there were very peculiar provisions in the settlement of the Lorraine estates, which might throw him entirely upon his own wits, if his father turned against him; also, that though his father was one of the very best men in the world, and the kindest and loftiest you could find, still there was about him something of a cold and determined substance. And, worst of all (if the whole truth was to be shelled out, as he must unshell it), he knew in his heart that his father loved his sister's little finger more than all the members, put together, of his own too lively frame.

CHAPTER XVII.

Mrs. Lovejoy sat far away from all the worry, and flurry, and fun of picking, and packing, and covering up. She had never entirely given herself to the glories of fruit-growing; and she never could be much convinced that any glory was in it. She belonged to a higher rank of life than any of such sons of Cain. Her father had been a navy captain, and her cousin was attorney-general. This office had always been confounded in the provincial mind, with rank in a less pugnacious profession. Even Mrs. Lovejoy thought, when the land was so full of "militiamen," that her cousin was the general of the "Devil's Own" of the period. Therefore she believed herself to know more than usual about the law; as well as the army, and of course the navy. And this high position in the legal army of so near a relation helped, no doubt, to foster hopes of the elevation of Gregory.

"I beg your pardon, Mr. Lorraine," she began, as Hilary entered the bower, to which she had just retired, "for calling you away from a scene which you enjoy perhaps from its novelty; and where you make yourself, I am sure, so exceedingly active and useful. But I feared, as you must unluckily so very soon return to London, that I might have no other chance of asking what your candid opinion is upon a matter I have very near at heart."

"Deuce and all!" thought Hilary within himself, being even more vexed than relieved by this turn of incidence; "she is much cleverer than I thought. Instead of hauling me over the coals, she is going to give me the sack at once; and I didn't mean to go, for a week at least!" Mrs. Lovejoy enjoyed his surprise, as he stammered that any opinion he could form was entirely at her service.

"I am sure that you know what it is about. You must have guessed at once, of course, when I was rude enough to send for you, what subject is nearest to a mother's heart. I wish to ask you, what they think of my son Gregory, in London."

Lorraine, for the moment, was a little upset. His presence of mind had been worked so hard, that it was beginning to flutter and shift. And much as he liked his fellow-pupil he had not begun to consider him yet as an object of public opinion.

"I think—I really think," he said, while waiting for time to think more about it, "that he is going on as well as ever could be expected, ma'am."

If he had wanted to vex his hostess—which to his kind nature would have been one of the last things wanted—he scarcely could have hit on a phrase more fitted for his purpose.

"Why, Mr. Lorraine, that is exactly what the monthly nurses say! I hope you can say something a little better than that of Gregory."

"I assure you, Mrs. Lovejoy, nothing can be finer than the way he is going on. His attention, punctuality, steadiness, and every thing else, leave nothing to be desired, as all the wine-merchants always say. Mr. Malahide holds him up as a pattern to be avoided, because he works so hard, and I think that he really ought to have country air, at this time of year, and in such weather, for a week; at the very shortest."

"Poor boy! Why should he overwork himself? Then you think that three days' change is scarcely enough to set him up again?"

"He wants at least a fortnight, ma'am. He has a sort of a hacking cough, which he does his best to keep under. And the doctors say that the smell of ink out of a pewter inkstand, and the inhaling of blotting-paper—such as we inhale all day—are almost certain, in hot weather, to root a tussis, or at any rate a pituita, inward."

Mrs. Lovejoy was much impressed, and tenfold so when she tried to think what those maladies might be.

"Dear me!" she said: "it is dreadful to think of. I know too well what those sad complaints are. My dear grandfather died of them both. Do you think now, Mr. Lorraine, that Mr. Malahide could be persuaded to spare you both for the rest of the week?"

"I scarcely think that he could, Mrs. Lovejoy. We are his right hand, and his left. Your son, of course, his dexter hand; and my poor self the weaker member. Still if you were to write to him, nicely (as of course you would be sure to write), he might make an effort to get on, with some of his inferior pupils."

"It shall be done, before the van goes—by the very next mail, I mean. And if they can spare you, do you think that you could put up with your very poor quarters for a few days longer, Mr. Lorraine?"

"I never was in such quarters before. And I never felt so comfortable;" he answered, with a gush of truth, to expiate much small hypocrisy. And thereby he settled himself forever in her very best graces. If Mrs. Lovejoy had any pride—and she always told herself she had none—that pride lay in her best feather-beds.

A smile, quite worthy of her larger husband and of her pleasant homestead, spread itself over her thoughtful face; and Hilary, for the first time, saw that her daughter, after all, was born of her. What can be sweeter than a smile, won from a sensible woman like that?

"Then you give us some hope that we may endeavor to keep you a few days more, sir?"

"The endeavor will be on my part," he answered, with his most elegant bow; "as all the temptation falls on me."

"I do hope that Mr. Malahide will do his best to spare you both. Though to lose both his right hand and his left hand must be very melancholy."

"To a lawyer, Mrs. Lovejoy, that is nothing. We think nothing of such trifles. We are ready to fight when we have no hands, nor even a leg to stand upon."

"Yes, to be sure you live by fighting, as the poor sailors and soldiers do. The general of the attorneys, now, is my first cousin, once removed. Now, can you tell me what opinion he has formed of my Gregory? Of course, there must be a number of people trying to keep my poor boy back—pressing him down, as they always do, with all that narrow jealousy. But his mother's cousin might be trusted to give him fair play, now, don't you think?"

"One never can tell," answered Hilary; "the faster a young fellow goes up the tree, the harder the monkeys pelt him. But if I only had a quarter of your son's ability, I would defy them all at once, from the Lord Chief-Justice downward."

"Oh no, now, Mr. Lorraine; that really would be bad advice. He has not been called to the Bar as yet; and he must remember that there are people many years in front of him. No, no; let Gregory wait for his proper time in its proper course, and steadily rise to the top of the tree. With patience, Mr. Lorraine, you know—with patience all things come to pass. But I must go to the house at once, and write to Mr. Malahide. Do you think that he would be offended, if I asked him to accept a basket of our choicest cherries and strawberries?"

"I scarcely think that he would regard it as a mortal injury; especially if you were to put it as a tribute from his grateful pupil, Hilary Lorraine."

"How kind of you to let me use your name! And you have such influence with him, Gregory is always telling me. No doubt he will accept them so."

However, when she came to consider the matter, Mrs. Lovejoy, with shameful treachery, sent them as a little offering from that grateful pupil, her own son; while she laid upon Hilary all the burden of this lengthened mitching-time; as in the main perhaps was just. Moreover, she took good care that Shorne should have no chance of appearing in chambers, as he was only too eager to do; for her shrewd sense told her that the sharp wits there would find him a joy forever, and an enduring joke against Gregory.

It is scarcely needful to say, perhaps, that throughout the rest of the week Lorraine did his utmost to bring about snug little interviews with Mabel. And she, having made up her mind to keep him henceforth at his distance, felt herself bound by that resolution to afford him a glimpse or two once in a way. For she really had a great deal to do; and it would have been cruel to deny her even the right to talk of it. And Hilary carried a basket so much better than any body else, and his touch was so light, and he stepped here and there so obediently and so cleverly, and he always looked away so nicely, if any thing happened to her frock—as now and then of course must be—that Mabel began every day to think how dreadfully she would miss him.

And then, as if it were not enough to please her ears, and eyes, and mind, he even contrived to conciliate the most grateful part of the human system, as well as the most intelligent. For on the Tuesday afternoon, the turn of the work, and the courses of fruit, led them near a bushy corner where the crafty brook stole through. As clever and snug an ingle as need be, for a pair of young people to drop accidentally out of sight and ear-shot. For here the corner of the orchard fell away, as a quarry does, yet was banked with grass and ridges, so that children might take hands and run. But if they did so, they would be certain to come to grief at the bottom, unless they could clear at a jump three yards, which would puzzle most of them. For here the brook, without any noise, came under a bank of good brown loam, with a gentle shallow slide, and a bottom content to be run over.

"Trout, as I'm a living sinner!" cried Hilary, with a fierce delight, as he fetched up suddenly on the brink, and a dozen streaks darted up the stream, like the throw of a threaded shuttle. "My prophetic soul, if I didn't guess it! But I seem to forget almost every thing. Why, Miss Lovejoy, Miss Mabel Lovejoy, Mabel Miss Lovejoy (or any other form, insisting on the prefix despotically), have I known you for a century or more, and you never told me there were trout in the brook!"

"Oh do let me see them; please to show me where," cried Mabel, coming carefully down the steep, lest her slender feet should slip: "they are such dears, I do assure you. My mother and I are so fond of them. But my father says they are all bones and tail."

"I will show them to you with the greatest pleasure, only you must do just what I order you. They are very shy things, you know, almost as shy as somebody—"

"Mabel, Mabel, Mab, where are you?" came a loud shout over the crest; and then Gregory's square shoulders appeared, a most unwelcome spectacle.

"Why, here I am to be sure," she answered; "where else do you suppose I should be? The people must be looked after, I suppose. And if you won't do it, of course I must."

"I don't see any people to look after here, except indeed—however, you seem to have looked so hard, it has made you quite red in the face, I declare!"

"Now, Greg, my boy," cried Hilary, suddenly coming to the rescue; "I called your sister down here on purpose to tell me what those things in the water are. They look almost like some sort of fish."

"Why, trout, Lorraine! Didn't you know that? I thought that you were a great fisherman. If you like to have a try at them, I can fit you out. Though I don't suppose you could do much in this weather."

"Miss Lovejoy, did you ever taste a trout?" Hilary asked this question as if not a word had yet passed on the subject.

"Oh yes," answered Mabel, no less oblivious; "my brother Charles used to catch a good many. They are such a treat to my dear mother, and so good for her constitution. But I don't think my father appreciates them."

"Allow me to help you up this steep rise. It was most inconsiderate of me to call you down, Miss Lovejoy."

"Pray do not mention it, Mr. Lorraine. Gregory, how rude you are to give Mr. Lorraine all this trouble! But you never were famous for good manners."

"If I meddle with them again," thought Gregory, "may I be adorned, as my father says! However, I must keep a sharp lookout. The girl is getting quite independent; and I—oh, I am to be nobody! I'll just go and see what Phyllis thinks of it."

But Mabel, who had not forgiven him yet for his insolent remarks about her cheeks, deprived him of even that comfort.

"Now, Gregory dear, you have done nothing all day but wander about with Cousin Phyllis. Just stay here for a couple of hours; if you can't work yourself, your looking on will make the other people work. I am quite ashamed of my inattention to Mr. Lorraine all the afternoon. I am sure he must want a glass of ale, after all he has gone through. And while he takes it, I can rout out Charlie's tackle for him. I know where it is, and you do not. And Charlie left it especially under my charge, you remember."

"That is the first I have heard of it. However, if Lorraine wants beer, why so do I. Send Phyllis out with a jug for me."

"Yes, to be sure, dear—to be sure. How delighted she will be to come!"

"As delighted as you are to go," he replied; but she was already out of hearing; and all he took for his answer was an indignant look from Hilary.

An excellent and most patient fisherman

used to say that the greatest pleasure of the gentle art was found in the preparation to fish. In the making of flies, and the knotting of gut, and the softening of collars that have caught fish, and the choosing of what to try this time, and how to treat the river. The treasures of memory glow again, and the sparkling stores of hope awake to a lively emulation.

Hilary's mind had securely landed every fish in the brook at least, and laid it at the feet of Mabel, ere ever his tackle was put to rights, and every thing else made ready. At last he was at the very point of starting, with his ever high spirits at their very loftiest pitch, when Mabel (who was scarcely a whit behind him in the excitement of this great matter) ran in for the fiftieth time at least, but this time wearing her evening frock. That frock was of a delicate buff, and she had a suspicion that it enhanced the clearness of her complexion, and the kind and deep loveliness of her eyes.

"You must be quite tired of seeing me, I am as sure as sure can be. But I am not come now to tie knots, or untie; and you quite understand all I know about trout, and all that my dear brother Charlie said. Ah, Mr. Lorraine, you should see him; Gregory is a genius, of course. But Charlie is not; and that makes him so nice. And his uniform, when he went to church with us—but to understand such things, you must see them. Still, you can understand this now, perhaps."

"I can understand nothing, when I look at you. My intellect seems to be quite absorbed in—in—I can't tell you in what."

"Then go and absorb it in catching trout; though I don't believe you will ever catch one. It requires the greatest skill and patience, when the water is bright, and the weather dry. So Charlie always said, when he could not catch them. Unless you take to a worm, at least, or something a great deal nastier."

"A worm! I would sooner lime them almost. Now you know me better than that, I am sure."

"How should I know all the different degrees of cruelty men have established? But I came to beg you just to take a little bit of food with you; because you must be away some hours, and you are sure to lose your way."

"How wonderfully kind you are! Mabel—you must be Mabel now."

"Well, I suppose I have been Mabel ever since they christened me. But that has nothing at all to do with it. Only I came to make you put this half of cold duck into your basket, and this pinch of salt, and the barley-cake, and a drop of our ale in this stone bottle. To drink it, you must do like this."

"Do you know what I shall be wanting every bit of the time, and forever?"

"Oh, the mustard—how stupid of me! but I hoped that the stuffing would do instead."

"Instead of the cold half duck, I shall want every atom of the whole duck warm."

"Well, there they are, Mr. Lorraine, in the yard; fourteen of them now coming up from the pond. Take one of them, if you can eat it raw. But my mother will make you pay for it."

"I will pay for my duck!" he said, lifting his hat, "if it costs me every farthing I have or shall ever have in this world or another."

And so he went fishing; and she ran up stairs, and softly cried, as she watched him going; and then lay down, with her hand on her heart.

CHAPTER XVIII.

The trout knew nothing of all this. They had not tasted a worm for a month, except when a sod of the bank fell in, through cracks of the sun, and the way cold water has of licking upward. And even the flies had no flavor at all; when they fell on the water, they fell flat, and on the palate they tasted hot, even in under the bushes.

Hilary followed a path through the meadows, with the calm bright sunset casting his shadow over the shorn grass, or up in the hedge-road, or on the brown banks where the drought had struck. On his back he carried a fishing-basket, containing his bits of refreshment; and in his right hand a short springy rod, the absent sailor's favorite. After long council with Mabel, he had made up his mind to walk up stream, as far as the spot where two brooks met, and formed body enough for a fly flipped in very carefully to sail downward. Here he began, and the creak of his reel, and the swish of his rod, were music to him, after the whirl of London life.

The brook was as bright as the best cut glass, and the twinkles of its shifting facets only made it seem more clear. It twisted about a little, here and there; and the brink was fringed now and then with something, a clump of loose-strife, a tuft of avens, or a bed of flowering water-cress, or any other of the many plants that wash and look into the water. But the trout, the main object in view, were most objectionably too much in view. They scudded up the brook, at the shadow of a hair, or even the tremble of a blade of grass; and no pacific assurance could make them even stop to be reasoned with. "This won't do," said Hilary, who very often talked to himself, in lack of a better comrade; "I call this very hard upon me. The beggars won't rise till it is quite dark. I must have the interdict off my tobacco, if this sort of thing is to go on. How I should enjoy a pipe just now! I may just as well sit on a gate and think. No, hang it, I hate thinking now. There are troubles hanging over me, as sure as the tail of that comet grows. How I detest that comet! No wonder the fish won't rise. But if I have to strip, and tickle them in the dark, I won't go back without some for her."

He was lucky enough to escape the weight of such horrible poaching upon his conscience. For suddenly to his ears was borne the most melodious of all sounds, the flop of a heavy fish sweetly jumping after some excellent fly or grub.

"Ha, my friend!" cried Hilary; "so you are up for your supper, are you? I myself will awake right early. Still I behold the ring you made. If my right hand forget not its cunning, you shall form your next ring in the frying-pan."

He gave that fish a little time to think of the beauty of that mouthful, and get ready for another; the while he was putting a white moth on, in lieu of his blue upright. He kept the grizzled palmer still for tail-fly, and he tried his knots, for he knew that this trout was a Triton.

Then, with a delicate sidling and stooping, known only to them that fish for trout in very bright water of the summer-time—compared with which art the coarse work of the salmon-fisher is as that of a scene-painter to Mr. Holman Hunt's—with, or in, and by a careful manner, not to be described to those who have never studied it, Hilary won access of the water, without any doubt in the mind of the fish concerning the prudence of appetite. Then he flipped his short collar in, not with a cast, but a spring of the rod, and let his flies go quietly down a sharpish run into that good trout's hole. The worthy trout looked at them both, and thought; for he had his own favorite spot for watching the world go by, as the rest of us have. So he let the grizzled palmer pass, within an inch of his upper lip; for it struck him that the tail turned up in a manner not wholly natural, or at any rate unwholesome. He looked at the white moth also, and thought that he had never seen one at all like it. So he went down under his root again, hugging himself upon his wisdom, never moving a fin, but oaring and helming his plump, spotted sides with his tail.

"Upon my word, it is too bad!" said Hilary, after three beautiful throws, and exquisite management down stream: "every thing Kentish beats me hollow. Now, if that had been one of our trout, I would have laid my life upon catching him. One more throw, however. How would it be if I sunk my flies? That fellow is worth some patience."

While he was speaking, his flies alit on the glassy ripple, like gnats in their love-dance; and then, by a turn of the wrist, he played them just below the surface, and let them go gliding down the stickle, into the shelfy nook of shadow, where the big trout hovered. Under the surface, floating thus, with the check of ductile influence, the two flies spread their wings, and quivered, like a centiplume moth in a spider's web. Still the old trout, calmly oaring, looked at them both suspiciously. Why should the same flies come so often, and why should they have such crooked tails, and could he be sure that he did not spy the shadow of a human hat about twelve yards up the water? Revolving these things he might have lived to a venerable age—but for that noble ambition to teach, which is fatal to even the wisest. A young fish, an insolent whipper-snapper, jumped in his babyish way at the palmer, and missed it through overeagerness. "I'll show you the way to catch a fly," said the big trout to him; "open your mouth like this, my son."

With that he bolted the palmer, and threw up his tail, and turned to go home again. Alas! his sweet home now shall know him no more. For suddenly he was surprised by a most disagreeable sense of grittiness, and then a keen stab in the roof of his mouth. He jumped, in his wrath, a foot out of the water, and then heavily plunged to the depths of his hole.

"You've got it, my friend," cried Hilary, in a tingle of fine emotions; "I hope the sailor's knots are tied with professional skill and care. You are a big one, and a clever one too. It is much if I ever land you. No net, or gaff, or any thing. I only hope there are no stakes here. Ah, there you go! Now comes the tug."

Away went the big trout down the stream, at a pace very hard to exaggerate, and after him rushed Hilary, knowing that his line was rather short, and that if it ran out all was over. Keeping his eyes on the water only, and the headlong speed of the fugitive, headlong over a stake he fell, and took a deep wound from another stake. Scarcely feeling it, up he jumped, lifting his rod, which had fallen flat, and fearing to find no strain on it. "Aha, he is not gone yet!" he cried, as the rod bowed like a springle-bow.

He was now a good hundred yards down the brook from the corner where the fight began. Through his swiftness of foot, and good management, the fish had never been able to tighten the line beyond yield of endurance. The bank had been free from bushes, or haply no skill could have saved him; but now they were come to a corner where a nut-bush quite overhung the stream.

"I am done for now," said the fisherman; "the villain knows too well what he is about. Here ends this adventure."

Full though he was of despair, he jumped anyhow into the water, kept the point of his rod close down, reeled up a little, as the fish felt weaker, and just cleared the drop of the hazel boughs. The water flapped into the pockets of his coat, and he saw red streaks flow downward. And then he plunged out to an open reach of shallow water and gravel slope.

"I ought to have you now," he said; "though nobody knows what a rogue you are; and a pretty dance you have led me!"

Doubting the strength of his tackle to lift even the dead weight of the fish, and much more to meet his despairing rally, he happily saw a little shallow gut, or backwater, where a small spring ran out. Into this by a dexterous turn he rather led than pulled the fish, who was ready to rest for a minute or two; then he stuck his rod into the bank, ran down stream, and with his hat in both hands appeared at the only exit from the gut. It was all up now with the monarch of the brook. As he skipped and jumped, with his rich yellow belly, and chaste silver sides, in the green of the grass, joy and glory of the highest merit, and gratitude, glowed in the heart of Lorraine. "Two and three-quarters you must weigh. And at your very best you are! How small your head is! And how bright your spots are!" he cried, as he gave him the stroke of grace. "You really have been a brave and fine fellow. I hope they will know how to fry you."

While he cut his fly out of this grand trout's mouth, he felt for the first time a pain in his knee, where the point of the stake had entered it. Under the buckle of his breeches blood was soaking away inside his gaiters; and then he saw how he had dyed the water. After washing the wound and binding it with dock-leaves and a handkerchief, he followed the stream through a few more meadows, for the fish began to sport pretty well as the gloom of the evening deepened; so that by the time the gables of the old farm-house appeared, by the light of a young moon, and the comet, Lorraine had a dozen more trout in his basket, silvery-sided and handsome fellows, though none of them over a pound, perhaps, except his first and redoubtable captive.

Herewith he resolved to be content, for his knee was now very sore and stiff, and the growing darkness baffled him; while having forgotten his food, as behooved him, he was conscious of an agreeable fitness for the supper-table. Here, of course, he had to tell, at least thrice over, his fight with the Triton, who turned the scale at three pounds and a quarter, and was recognized as an old friend and twice conqueror of the absent Charlie. Mrs. Lovejoy (as was to be expected) made a great ado about the gash in the knee—which really was no trifle—while Mabel said nothing, but blamed herself deeply for having equipped him to such misfortune.

For the next few days Master Hilary was compelled to keep his active frame in rest, and quiet, and cosseting. Even the grower, a man of strong manhood, accustomed to scythe-cuts, and chopper-hits, and pole-springs, admitted that this was a case for broth, and low feeding, and things that the women do. For if inflammation set up, the boy might have only one leg left for life. It was high time, however, for the son of the house to return to his beloved law-books; so that he tore himself away from Phyllis, and started in the van, about noon on Friday, having promised to send back by John Shorne all that his fellow-pupil wanted.

Lorraine soon found that his kind and quick hostess loved few things better than a cheerful, dutiful, and wholesome-blooded patient; and therefore he rejected with scorn all suggestions as to his need of a "proper doctor." And herein the grower backed him up.

"Adorn me, if any one of them ever lays finger on me, any more than on my good father before me! They handle us when we are born, of course, and come to no manner of judgment; but if we let them handle us afterward, we deserve to go out of the world with them."

This sound discretion (combined with the plentiful use of cold water and healing herbs) set Hilary on his legs again in about eight or ten days' time. Meanwhile he had seen very little of Mabel, whether through her fault or that of others he could not tell—only that so it was. Whenever his hostess was out of the way, Phyllis Clitherow, or else the house-maid, did their best to supply her place; and very often the grower dropped in to enjoy his pipe, and to cheer his guest. By means of simple truth they showed him that he was no burden to them, even at this busy time.

After all this, it was only natural that Hilary should become much attached as well as grateful to his entertainers. Common formality was dropped, and caste entirely sunk in hearty liking and loving-kindness. And young Lorraine was delighted to find how many pleasant virtues flourished under the thatch of that old house, uncoveted and undisturbed, inasmuch as their absence was not felt in the mansions of great people.

This affection for virtue doubtless made him feel sadly depressed and lonely, when the time at length arrived for quitting so much excellence.

"In the van he came, and in the van he would go," he replied to all remonstrance; and the grower liked him all the better for his loyalty to the fruit-coach. So it was settled when Crusty John was "going up light," for a Thursday morning, that Hilary should have a mattress laid in the body of the vehicle, and a horse-cloth to throw over him, if the night should prove a cold one. For now a good drop of rain had fallen, and the weather seemed on the change a while.

"I must catch you another dish of trout," said Hilary to Mrs. Lovejoy; "when shall I have such a chance again? The brook is in beautiful order now; and thanks to your wonderful skill and kindness, I can walk again quite well now."

"Yes, for a little way you can. But you must be sure not to overdo it. You may fish one meadow, and one only. Let me see. You may fish the long meadow, Hilary; then you will have neither stile nor hedge. The gate at this end unlatches, mind. And I will send Phyllis to let you out at the lower end, and to see that you dare not go one step farther. She shall be there at half-past six. The van goes at eight, you know, and we must sit down to supper at seven exactly."

Upon this understanding he set forth, about five o'clock in the afternoon, and meeting Miss Clitherow in the lane, he begged her, as an especial favor, to keep out of Mrs. Lovejoy's way for the next two hours only. Phyllis, a good-natured girl on the whole, though a little too proud of her beauty perhaps, readily promised what he asked, and retired to a seat in the little ash coppice to read a poem, and meditate upon the absent Gregory.

Lorraine was certainly in luck to-day for he caught a nice basket of fish down the meadow; and toward the last stickle near the corner, where silver threads of water crossed, and the slanting sunshine cast a plaid of soft gold over them, light footsteps came by the side of the hedge, and a pretty shadow fell near him.

"Miss Lovejoy!" cried Hilary; "how you amaze me! Why, I thought it was Phyllis who was coming to fetch me. I may call her Phyllis; oh yes, she allows me. She is not so very ceremonious. But some people are all dignity."

"Now, you want to vex me the very last thing. And they call you so sweet tempered! I am so sorry for your disappointment about your dear friend Phyllis. But I am sure I looked for her everywhere, before I was obliged to come myself. Now, I hope you have not found the poor little trout quite so hard to please as you are."

"At any rate, not so shy of me, as somebody has been for a fortnight. Because I was in trouble, I suppose, and pain, and supposed to be groaning."

"How can you say such bitter things? It shows how very little you care—at least, that is not what I mean at all."

"Then, if you please, what is it that you do mean?"

"I mean that here is the key of the gate. And my father will expect you at seven o'clock."

"But surely you will have a look at my trout? They can not bite, if I can."

He laid his fishing-creel down on the grass, and Mabel stooped over it to hide her eyes; which (in spite of all pride and prudence) were not exactly as she could have wished. But they happened to be exactly as Hilary wished; and catching a glimpse of them unawares, he lost all ideas except of them, and basely compelled them to look at him.

"Now, Mabel Lovejoy," he said slowly, and with some dread of his own voice, "can you look me in the face and tell me you do not care twopence for me?"

"I am not in the habit of being rude," she answered, with a sly glance from under her hat; "that I leave for other people."

"Well, do you like me, or do you not?"

"You do ask the most extraordinary questions. We are bound to like our visitors."

"I will ask a still more extraordinary question. Do you love me, Mabel?"

For a very long time he got no answer, except a little smothered sob, and two great tears that would have their way. "Darling Mabel, look up and tell me. Why should you be ashamed to say? I am very proud of loving you. Lovely Mabel, do you love me?"

"I—I—I am—very—much afraid—I almost do."

She shrank away from his arms and eyes, and longed to be left to herself for a little. And then she thought what a mean thing it was to be taking advantage of his bad leg. With that she came back, and to change his thoughts said, "Show me a trout in the brook now, Hilary."

"You deserve to see fifty for being so good. There you must help me along, you know. Now just stand here, and let me hold you, carefully and most steadily. No, not like that. That will never do. I must at least have one arm round you, or in you go, and I have to answer for your being 'drownded!'"

"Drowned! You take advantage now to make me so ridiculous. The water is scarcely six inches deep. But where are the little troutsies?"

"There! There! Do you see that white stone? Now look at it most steadfastly, and then you are sure not to see them. Now turn your head like that, a little, not too much, whatever you do. Now, what do you see, most clearly?"

"Why, I see nothing, but you and me, in the shadow of that oak-tree, standing over the water, as if we had nothing better in the world to do!"

"We are standing together, though. Don't you think so?"

"Well even the water seems to think so. And what can be more changeable?"

"Now look at me, and not at the water. Mabel, you know what I am."

"Hilary, I wish I did. That is the very thing that takes such a long time to find out."

"Now, did I treat you in such a spirit? Did I look at you, and think, 'Here is a rogue I must find out?'"

"No, of course, you never did. That is not in your nature. At the same time, perhaps, it might not matter so long to you, as it must to me."

She met his glad eyes with a look so wistful, yet of such innocent reliance, to assuage the harm of words, that Hilary might be well excused for keeping the grower's supper waiting, as he did that evening.

CHAPTER XIX.

The excellent people of Coombe Lorraine as yet were in happy ignorance of all these fine doings on Hilary's part. Sir Roland knew only too well, of course, that his son and heir was of a highly romantic, chivalrous and adventurous turn. At Eton and Oxford many little scrapes (which seemed terrible at the time) showed that he was sure to do his best to get into grand scrapes, as the occasion of his youthful world enlarged.

"Happen what will, I can always trust my boy to be a gentleman," his father used to say to himself, and to his only real counselor, old Sir Remnant Chapman. Sir Remnant always shook his head; and then (for fear of having meant too much) said, "Ah, that is the one thing, after all! People begin to talk a great deal too much about Christianity."

At any rate, the last thing they thought of was the most likely thing of all—that Hilary should fall in love with a good, and sweet, and simple girl, who, for his own sake, would love him, and grow to him with all the growth of love. "Morality"—whereby we mean now, truth and right and purity—was then despised in public, even more than now in private life. Sir Remnant thought it a question of shillings, how many maids his son led astray; and he pitied Sir Roland for having a son so much handsomer than his own.

Little as now he meddled with it, Sir Roland knew that the world was so; and the more he saw of it, the less he found such things go down well with him. The broad low stories and practical jokes, and babyish finesse of oaths, invented for the ladies—many of which still survive in the hypocrisy of our good tongue—these had a great deal to do with Sir Roland's love of his own quiet dinner-table, and shelter of his pet child, Alice. And nothing, perhaps, except old custom and the traditions of friendship, could have induced him to bear, as he did, with Sir Remnant's far lower standard. Let a man be what he will, he must be moved one way or another by the folk he deals with. Even Sir Roland (though so different from the people around him) felt their feelings move here and there, and very often come touching him. And he never could altogether help wanting to know what they thought about him. So must the greatest man ever "developed" have desired a million-fold, because he lived in each one of the million.

However, there were but two to whom Sir Roland Lorraine ever yielded a peep of his deeply-treasured anxieties. One was Sir Remnant; and the other (in virtue of office, and against the grain) was the Rev. Struan Hales, his own highly respected brother-in-law.

Struan Hales was a man of mark all about that neighborhood. Every body knew him, and almost every body liked him. Because he was a genial, open-hearted, and sometimes even noisy man; full of life—in his own form of that matter—and full of the love of life, whenever he found other people lively. He hated every kind of humbug, all revolutionary ideas, Methodism, asceticism, enthusiastic humanity, and exceedingly fine language. And though, like every one else, he respected Sir Roland Lorraine for his upright character, lofty honor, and clearness of mind; while he liked him for his generosity, kindness of heart, and gentleness; on the other hand, he despised him a little for his shyness and quietude of life. For the rector of West Lorraine loved nothing better than a good day with the hounds, and a roaring dinner-party afterward. Nothing in the way of sport ever came amiss to him; even though it did—as no true sport does—depend for its joy upon cruelty.

Here, in his snug house on the glebe, under the battlement of the hills, with trees and garden of comfort, and snug places to smoke a pipe in, Mr. Hales was well content to live and do his duty. He liked to hunt twice in a week, and he liked to preach twice every Sunday. Still he could not do either always; and no good people blamed him.

Mrs. Hales was the sweetest creature ever seen almost anywhere. She had plenty to say for herself, and a great deal more to say for others; and if perfection were to be found, she would have been perfection to every mind, except her own, and perhaps her husband's. The rector used to say that his wife was an angel, if ever one there were; and in his heart he felt that truth. Still he did not speak to her always as if he were fully aware of being in colloquy with an angel. He had lived with her "ever so long," and he knew that she was a great deal better than himself; but he had the wisdom not to let her know it; and she often thought that he preached at her. Such a thing he never did. No honest parson would ever do it; of all mean acts it would be the meanest. Yet there are very few parsons' wives who are not prepared for the chance of it. And Mrs. Hales knew that she "had her faults," and that Mr. Hales was quite up to them. At any rate, here they were, and here they meant to live their lives out, having a pretty old place to see to, and kind old neighbors to see to them. Also they had a much better thing—three good children of their own; enough to make work and pleasure for them, but not be a perpetual worry, inasmuch as they all were girls—three very good girls, of their sort—thinking as they were told to think, and sure to make excellent women.

Alice Lorraine liked all these girls. They were so kind, and sweet, and simple; and when they had nothing whatever to say, they always said it so prettily. And they never pretended to interfere with any of her opinions, or to come into competition with her, or to talk to her father, when she was present, more than she well could put up with. For she was a very jealous child; and they were well aware of it. And they might let their father be her mother's brother ten times over, before she would hear of any "Halesy element"—as she once had called it—coming into her family more than it had already entered. And they knew right well, while they thought it too bad, that this young Alice had sadly quenched any hopes any one of them might have cherished of being a Lady Lorraine some day. She had made her poor brother laugh over their tricks, when they were sure that they had no tricks; and she always seemed to put a wrong construction upon any little harmless thing they did. Still they could afford to forget all that; and they did forget it, especially now when Hilary would soon be at home again.

It was now July, and no one had heard for weeks from that same Hilary; but this made no one anxious, because it was the well-known manner of the youth. Sometimes they would hear from him by every post, although the post now came thrice in a week; and then again for weeks together not a line would he vouchsafe. And as a general rule, he was getting on better when he kept strict silence.

Therefore Alice had no load on her mind at all worth speaking of, while she worked in her sloping flower-garden, early of a summer afternoon. It was now getting on for St. Swithin's Day; and the sun was beginning to curtail those brief attentions which he paid to Coombe Lorraine. He still looked fairly at it, as often as clouds allowed in the morning, almost up to eight o'clock; and after that he could still see down it, over the shoulder of the hill. But he felt that his rays made no impression (the land so fell away from him), they seemed to do nothing but dance away downward, like a lasher of glittering water.

Therefore, in this garden grew soft and gently natured plants, and flowers of delicate tint, that sink in the exhaustion of the sun-glare. The sun, in almost every garden, sucks the beauty out of all the flowers: he stains the sweet violet even in March; he spots the primrose and the periwinkle; he takes the down off the heart's-ease blossom; he browns the pure lily of the valley in May; and, after that, he dims the tint of every rose that he opens; and yet, in spite of all his mischief, which of them does not rejoice in him?

The bold chase, cut in the body of the hill, has rugged sides, and a steep descent for a quarter of a mile below the house—the cleft of the chalk on either side growing deeper toward the mouth of the coombe. The main road to the house goes up the coombe, passing under the eastern scarp, but winding away from it here and there to obtain a better footing. The old house, facing down the hill, stands so close to the head of the coombe, that there is not more than an acre or so of land behind and between it and the crest, and this is partly laid out as a court-yard, partly occupied by out-buildings, stables, and so on, and the ruinous keep ingloriously used as a limekiln; while the rest of the space is planted in and out with spruce and birch trees, and any thing that will grow there. Among them winds a narrow outlet to the upper and open Downs—too steep a way for carriage-wheels, but something in appearance between a bridle-path and a timber-track, such as is known in those parts by the old English name, a "bostall."

As this led to no dwelling-house for miles and miles away, but only to the crown of the hills and the desolate track of sheep-walks, ninety-nine visitors out of a hundred to the house came up the coombe, so that Alice from her flower-garden, commanding the course of the drive from the plains, could nearly always foresee the approach of any interruption. Here she had pretty seats under laburnums, and even a bower of jessamine, and a noble view all across the weald, even to the range of the North Downs; so that it was a pleasant place for all who love soft sward and silence, and have time to enjoy that very rare romance of the seasons—a hot English summer.

Only there was one sad drawback. Lady Valeria's windows straightly overlooked this pleasant spot, and Lady Valeria never could see why she should not overlook every thing. Beyond and above all other things, she took it as her own special duty to watch her dear granddaughter Alice; and now in her eighty-second year she was proud of her eyesight, and liked to prove its power.

"Here they come again!" cried Alice, talking to herself or her rake and trowel; "will they never be content? I told them on Monday that I knew nothing, and they will not believe it. I have a great mind to hide myself in my hole, like that poor rag-and-bone boy. It goes beyond my patience quite to be cross-examined and not believed."

Those whom she saw coming up the steep

road at struggling and panting intervals, were her three good cousins from the Rectory—Caroline, Margaret, and Cecil Hales; rather nice-looking and active girls, resembling their father in face and frame, and their excellent mother in their spiritual parts. The decorated period of young ladies, the time of wearing great crosses and starving, and sticking as a thorn in the flesh of mankind, lay as yet in the happy future. A parson's daughters were as yet content to leave the parish to their father, helping him only in the Sunday-school, and for the rest of the week minding their own dresses, or some delicate jobs of pastry, or gossip.

Though Alice had talked so of running away, she knew quite well that she never could do it, unless it were for a childish joke; and swiftly she was leaving now the pretty and petty world of childhood, sinking into that distance whence the failing years recover it. Therefore, instead of running away, she ran down the hill to meet her cousins, for truly she liked them decently.

"Oh, you dear, how are you? How wonderfully good to come to meet us! Madge, I shall be jealous in a moment if you kiss my Alice so. Cecil—what are you thinking of? Why, you never kissed your cousin Alice."

"Oh yes, you have all done it very nicely. What more could I wish?" said Alice; "but what could have made you come up the hill so early in the day, dears?"

"Well, you know what dear mamma is. She really fancied that we might seem (now there is so much going on) really unkind and heartless, unless we came up to see how you were. Papa would have come; but he feels it so steep, unless he is coming up to dinner; and pony, you know— Oh, she did such a thing! The wicked little dear, she got into the garden and devoured £10 worth of the grand new flower just introduced by the Duchess 'Dallia,' or 'Dellia'—I can't spell the name. And mamma was so upset that both of them have been unwell ever since."

"Oh, Dahlias!" answered Alice, whose grapes were rather sour, because her father had refused to buy any; "flaunty things, in my opinion. But Caroline, Madge, and Cecil, have you ever set eyes on my new rose?"

Of course they all ran to behold the new rose; which was no other than the "Persian yellow," a beautiful stranger, not yet at home. The countless petals of brilliant yellow folding inward full of light, and the dimple in the centre, shy of yielding inlet to its virgin gold, and then the delicious fragrance, too refined for random sniffers—these and other delights found entry into the careless beholder's mind.

"It makes one think of astrologers," cried Caroline Hales; "I declare it does! Look at all the little stars! It is quite like a celestial globe."

"So it is, I do declare!" said Madge. But Cecil shook her head. She was the youngest, and much the prettiest, and by many degrees the most elegant of the daughters of the Rectory. Cecil had her own opinion about many things, but waited till it should be valuable.

"It is much more like a cowslip-ball," Alice answered, carelessly. "Come into my bower now; and then we can all of us go to sleep."

The three girls were a little hot and thirsty, after their climb of the chalky road; and a bright spring ran through the bower, as they knew, ready to harmonize with sherbet, sherry wine, or even shrub itself, as had once been proved by Hilary.

"How delicious this is! How truly sweet!" cried the eldest and perhaps most loquacious Miss Hales; "and how nice of you always to keep a glass! A spring is such a rarity on these hills; papa says it comes from a different stratum. What a stratum is, I have no idea. It ought to be straight, one may safely say that; but it always seems to be crooked. Now, can you explain that, darling Alice? You are so highly taught, and so clever!"

"Now, we don't want a lecture," said Madge, the blunt one; "the hill is too steep to have that at the top. Alice knows every thing, no doubt, in the way of science, and all that. But what we are dying to know is what came of that grand old astrologer's business."

"This is the seventh or eighth time now," Alice answered, hard at bay; "that you will keep on about some little thing that the servants are making mountains of. My father best knows what it is. Let us go to his room and ask him."

"Oh no, dear! oh no, dear! How could we do that? What would dear uncle say to us? But come, now tell us. You do know something. Why are you so mysterious? Mystery is a thing altogether belonging to the dark ages now. We have heard such beautiful stories that we can not manage to sleep at night without knowing what they are all about. Now, do tell us every thing. You may just as well tell us every single thing. We are sure to find it all out, you know; and then we shall all be down on you. Among near relations, dear mamma says, there is nothing to compare with candor."

"Don't you see, Alice," Madge broke in, "we are sure to know sooner or later; and how can it matter which it is?"

"To be sure," answered Alice, "it can not matter. And so you shall all know, later."

This made the three sisters look a little at one another, quietly. And then, as a desperate resource, Madge, the rough one, laid eyes upon Alice, and, with a piercing look, exclaimed, "You don't even understand what it means yourself!"

"Of course I do not," answered Alice; "how many times have I told you so, yet you always want farther particulars! Dear cousins, now you must be satisfied with a conclusion of your own."

"I can not at all see that," said Caroline.

"Really, you are too bad," cried Margaret.

"Do you think that this is quite fair?" asked Cecil.

"You are too many for me, all of you," Alice answered, steadfastly. "Suppose I came to your house and pried into some piece of gossip about you that I had picked up in the village. Would you think that I had a right to do it?"

"No, dear, of course not. But nobody dares to gossip about us, you know. Papa would very soon stop all that."

"Of course he would. And because my father is too high-minded to meddle with it, am I to be questioned perpetually? Come in, Caroline; come in, Margaret; come in, dear Cecil; I know where papa is, and then you can ask him all about it."

"I have three little girls at their first sampler, such little sweets!" said Caroline; "I only left them for half an hour, because we felt sure you must want us, darling. It now seems as if you could hold your own in a cross-stitch we must not penetrate. It is nothing to us. What could it be? Only don't come, for goodness' sake, don't come rushing down the hill, dear creature, to implore our confidence suddenly."

"Dear creature!" cried Alice, for the moment borne beyond her young self-possession—"I am not quite accustomed to old women's words. Nobody shall call me a 'dear creature' except my father (who knows better) and poor old Nanny Stilgoe."

"Now, don't be vexed with them," Cecil stopped to say in a quiet manner, while the two other maidens tucked up their skirts, and down the hill went, rapidly; "they never meant to vex you, Alice; only you yourself must feel how dreadfully tantalizing it is to hear such sweet things as really made us afraid of our own shadows; and then to be told not to ask any questions!"

"I am sorry if I have been rude to your sisters," the placable Alice answered; "but it is so vexatious of them that they doubt my word so. Now, tell me what you have heard. It is wonderful how any foolish story spreads."

"We heard, on the very best authority, that the old astrologer appeared to you, descending from the comet in a fire-balloon, and warned you to prepare for the Judgment-day, because the black-death would destroy in one night every soul in Coombe Lorraine; and as soon as you heard it you fainted away, and Sir Roland ran up and found you lying, as white as wax, in a shroud made out of the ancient gentleman's long foreign cloak."

4

"Then, beg Cousin Caroline's pardon for me. No wonder she wanted to hear more. And I must not be touchy about my veracity, after lying in my shroud so long. But truly I can not tell you a word to surpass what you have heard already; nor even to come up to it. There was not one single wonderful thing—not enough to keep up the interest. I was bitterly disappointed; and so, of course, was every one."

"Cousin Alice," Cecil answered, looking at her pleasantly, "you are different from us, or, at any rate, from my sisters. You scarcely seem to know the way to tell the very smallest of small white lies. I am very sorry always; still I must tell some of them."

"No, Cecil, no; you need tell none, if you only make up your mind not to do it. You are but a very little older than I am, and surely you might begin afresh. Suppose you say at your prayers in the morning, 'Lord, let me tell no lie to-day!'"

"Now, Alice, you know that I never could do it. When I know that I mean to tell ever so many, how could I hope to be answered? No doubt I am a story-teller—just the same as the rest of us; and to pray against it, when I mean to do it, would be a very double-faced thing."

"To be sure it would. It never struck me in that particular way before. But Uncle Struan must know best what ought to be done in your case."

"We must not make a fuss of trifles," Cecil answered, prudently; "papa can always speak for himself; and he means to come up the hill to do it, if Mr. Gate's pony is at home. And now I must run after them, or Madge will call me a little traitor. Oh, here papa comes, I do declare. Good-bye, darling, and don't be vexed."

"It does seem a little too bad," thought Alice, as the portly form of the rector, mounted on a borrowed pony, came round the corner at the bottom of the coombe, near poor Bonny's hermitage—"a little too bad that nothing can be done without its being chattered about. And I know how annoyed papa will be if Uncle Struan comes plaguing him again. We can not even tell what it means ourselves; and whatever it means, it concerns us only. I do think curiosity is the worst, though it may be the smallest vice. He expects to catch me, of course, and get it all out of me, as he declared he would. But sharp as his eyes are, I don't believe he can have managed to spy me yet. I will off to my rock-work, and hide myself, till I see the heels of his pony going sedately down the hill again."

With these words, she disappeared; and when the good rector had mounted the hill, "Alice, Alice!" resounded vainly from the drive among the shrubs and flowers, and echoed from the ramparts of the coombe.

CHAPTER XX.

ONE part of Coombe Lorraine is famous for a seven-fold echo, connected by tradition with a tale of gloom and terror. Mr. Hales, being proud of his voice, put this echo through all its peals, or chime of waning resonance. It could not quite answer, "How do you do?" with "Very well, Pat, and the same to you"—and its tone was rather melancholy than sprightly, as some echoes are. But of course a great deal depended on the weather, as well as on the time of day. Echo, for the most part, sleeps by daylight, and strikes her gong as the sun goes down.

Failing of any satisfaction here, the Rev. Struan Hales rode on. "Ride on, ride on!" was his motto always; and he seldom found it fail. Nevertheless, as he rang the bell (which he was at last compelled to do), he felt in the crannies of his heart some wavers as to the job he was come upon. A coarse nature often despises a fine one, and yet is most truly afraid of it. Mr. Hales believed that in knowledge of the world he was entitled to teach Sir Roland; and yet he could not help feeling how calmly any impertinence would be stopped.

The clergyman found his brother-in-law sitting alone, as he was too fond of doing, in his little favorite book-room, walled off from the larger and less comfortable library. Sir Roland was beginning to yield more and more to the gentle allurements of solitude. Some few months back he had lost the only friend with whom he had ever cared to interchange opinions, a learned parson of the neighborhood, an antiquary, and an elegant scholar. And ever since that he had been sinking deeper and deeper into the slough of isolation and privacy. For hours he now would sit alone, with books before him, yet seldom heeded, while he mused and meditated, or indulged in visions mingled of the world he read of and the world he had to deal with. As no less an authority than Dr. Johnson has it—"This invisible riot of the mind, this secret prodigality of being, is secure from detection, and fearless of reproach. The dreamer retires to his apartment, shuts out the cares and interruptions of mankind, and abandons himself to his own fancy." And again—"This captivity it is necessary for every man to break, who has any desire to be wise or useful. To regain liberty, he must find the means of flying from himself; he must, in opposition to the Stoic precept, teach his desires to fix upon external things; he must adopt the joys and the pains of others, and excite in his mind the want of social pleasures and amicable communication."

Sir Roland Lorraine was not quite so bad as the gentleman above depicted; still he was growing so like him that he was truly sorry to see the jovial face of his brother-in-law. For his mind was set out upon a track of thought, which it might have pursued until dinner-time. But, of course, he was much too courteous to show any token of interruption.

"Roland, I must have you out of this. My dear fellow, what are you coming to? Books, books, books! As if you did not know twice too much already! Even I find my flesh falling away from me, the very next day after I begin to punish it with reading."

"That very remark occurs in the book which I have just put down. Struan, let me read it to you."

"I thank you greatly, but would rather not. It is in Latin or Greek, of course. I could not do my duty as I do, if I did it in those dead languages. But I have the rarest treat for you; and I borrowed a pony to come and fetch you. Such a badger you never saw! Sir Remnant is coming to see it and so is old General Jakes, and a dozen more. We allow an hour for that, and then we have a late dinner at six o'clock. My daughters came up the hill to fetch your young Alice, to see the sport. But they had some blaze-up about some trifle, as the chittish creatures are always doing. And so pretty Alice perhaps will lose it. Leave them to their own ways, say I; leave them to their own ways, Sir Roland. They are sure to cheat us, either way; and they may just as well cheat us pleasantly."

"You take a sensible view of it, according to what your daughters are," Sir Roland answered, more sharply than he either meant or could maintain; and immediately he was ashamed of himself. But Mr. Hales was not thin of skin; and he knew that his daughters were true to him. "Well, well," he replied; "as I said before, they are full of tricks. At their age and sex it must be so. But a better and kinder team of maids is not to be found in thirteen parishes. Speak to the contrary who will."

"I know that they are very good girls," Sir Roland answered kindly; "Alice likes them very much; and so does every body."

"That is enough to show what they are. Nobody ever likes any body, without a great deal of cause for it. They must have their faults of course, we know; and they may not be quite butter-lipped, you know—still I should like to see a better lot, take them in and out and altogether. Now you must come and see Fox draw that badger. I have ten good guineas upon it with Jakes; Sir Remnant was too shy to stake. And I want a thoroughly impartial judge. You never would refuse me, Roland, now?"

"Yes, Struan, yes; you know well that I will. You know that I hate and despise cruel sports. And it is no compliment to invite me, when you know that I will not come."

"I wish I had staid at the bottom of the hill, where that young scamp of a boy lives. When will you draw that badger, Sir Roland, the pest of the Downs, and of all the county?"

"Struan, the boy is not half so bad as might be expected of him. I have thought once or twice that I ought to have him taught, and fed, and civilized."

"Send him to me, and I'll civilize him. A born little poacher! I have scared all the other poachers with the comtat; but the little thief never comes to church. Four pair of birds, to my knowledge, nested in John Gate's veitches, and hatched well, too, for I spoke to John—where are they? Can you tell me where they are?"

"Well, Struan, I give you the shooting, of course; but I leave it to you to look after it. But it does seem too cruel to kill the birds, before they can fly, for you to shoot them."

"Cruel! I call it much worse than cruel. Such things would never be dreamed of upon a properly managed property."

"You are going a little too far," said Sir Roland, with one of his very peculiar looks; and his brother-in-law drew back at once, and changed the subject clumsily.

"The shooting will do well enough, Sir Roland. I think, however, that you may be glad of my opinion upon other matters. And that had something to do with my coming."

"Oh, I thought that you came about the badger, Struan. But what are these even more serious matters?"

"Concerning your dealings with the devil, Roland. Of course, I never listen to any thing foolish. Still, for the sake of my parish, I am bound to know what your explanation is. I have not much faith in witchcraft, though in that perhaps I am heterodox; but we are bound to have faith in the devil, I hope."

"Your hope does you credit," Sir Roland answered; "but for the moment I fail to see how I am concerned with this orthodoxy."

"Now, my dear fellow, my dear fellow, you know as well as I do what I mean. Of course there is a great deal of exaggeration; and knowing you so well, I have taken on myself to deny a great part of what people say. But you know the old proverb, 'No smoke without fire;' and I could defend you so much better, if I knew what really has occurred. And besides all that, you must feel, I am sure, that you are not treating me with that candor which our long friendship and close connection entitle me to expect from you."

"Your last argument is the only one requiring any answer. Those based on religious, social, and even parochial grounds, do not apply to this case at all. But I should be sorry to vex you, Struan, or keep from you any thing you claim to know in right of your dear sister. This matter, however, is so entirely confined to those of our name only, at the same time so likely to charm all the gossips who have made such wild guesses about it, and after all it is such a trifle except to a superstitious mind; that I may trust your good sense to be well content to hear no more about it, until it comes into action—if it ever should do so."

"Very well, Sir Roland, of course you know best. I am the last man in the world to intrude into family mysteries. And my very worst enemy (if I have one) would never dream of charging me with the vice of curiosity."

"Of course not; and therefore you will be well pleased that we should drop this subject. Will you take white wine or red wine, Struan? Your kind and good wife was quite ready to scold me, for having forgotten my duty in that, the last time you came up the hill."

"Ah, then I walked. But to-day I am riding. I thank you, I thank you, Sir Roland; but the General and Sir Remnant are waiting for me."

"And, most important of all, the badger. Good-bye, Struan; I shall see you soon."

"I hardly know whether you will or not," the rector answered testily; "this is the time when those cursed poachers scarcely allow me a good night's rest. And to come up this hill, and hear nothing at the top! It is too bad at my time of life! After two services every Sunday, to have to be gamekeeper all the week!"

"At your time of life!" said Sir Roland, kindly: "why, you are the youngest man in the parish, so far as life and spirits go. Today you are not yourself at all. Struan, you have not sworn one good round oath!"

"Well, what can you expect, Roland, with these confounded secrets held over one? I feel myself many pegs down to-day. And that pony trips so abominably. Perhaps, after all, I might take one glass of red wine before I go down the hill."

"It is a duty you owe to the parish. Now come, and let me try to find Alice to wait upon you. Alice is always so glad to see you."

"And I am always so glad to see her. How narrow your doors are in these old houses! Those Normans must have been a skewer-shouldered lot. Now, Roland, if I have said any thing harsh, you will make all allowance for me, of course; because you know the reason."

"You mean that you are a little disappointed—"

"Not a bit of it. Quite the contrary. But after such weather as we have had, and nothing but duty, duty, to do, one is apt to get a little crotchety. What kind of sport can be got anywhere? The landrail-shooting is over, of course, and the rabbits are running in families; the fish are all sulky, and the water low, and the sea-trout not come up yet. There are no young hounds fit to handle yet; and the ground cracks the heels of a decent hack. One's mouth only waters at oiling a gun; all the best of the cocks are beginning to mate; and if one gets up a badger-bait, to lead to a dinner-party, people will come, and look on, and make bets, and then tell the women how cruel it was! And with all the week thus, I am always expected to say something new every Sunday morning!"

"Nay, nay, Struan. Come now; we have never expected that of you. But here comes Alice from her gardening work! Now, she does look well; don't you think she does?"

"Not a rose in June, but a rose in May!" the rector answered gallantly, kissing his hand to his niece, and then with his healthy, bright lips saluting her: "you grow more and more like your mother, darling. And when I think of the by-gone days, before I had any wife, or daughters, things occur to me that never—"

"Go and bait your badger, Struan, after one more glass of wine."

CHAPTER XXI.

Nature appears to have sternly willed that no man shall keep a secret. There is a monster here and there to be discovered capable of not even whispering any thing; but he ought to expect to be put aside in our estimate of humanity. And lest he should be so, the powers above provide him, for the most part, with a wife of truly fecund loquacity.

A word is enough on such parlous themes; and the least said the soonest mended. What one of us is not exceedingly wise, in his own or his wife's opinion? What one of us does not pretend to be as "reticent" as Minerva's owl, and yet in his heart confess that a secret is apt to fly out of his bosom?

Nature is full of rules; and if the above should happen to be one of them, it was illustrated in the third attack upon Sir Roland's secrecy. For scarcely had he succeeded in baffling, without offending, his brother-in-law, when a servant brought him a summons from his mother, Lady Valeria.

According to all modern writers, whether of poetry or prose, in our admirable language, the daughter of an earl is always lovely, graceful, irresistible, almost to as great an extent as she is unattainable. This is but a natural homage on the part of Nature to a power so far above her; so that this daughter of an Earl of Thanet had been, in every outward point, whatever is delightful. Neither had she shown any slackness in turning to the best account these notable things in her favor. In short, she had been a very beautiful woman, and had employed her beauty well, in having her own will and way. She had not married well, it is true, in the opinion of her compeers; but she had pleased herself, and none could say that she had lowered her family. The ancestors of Lord Thanet had held in villeinage of the Lorraines, some three or four hundred years after the Conquest, until from being under so gentle a race they managed to get over them.

Lady Valeria knew all this; and feeling, as all women feel, the ownership of her husband (active or passive, whichever it be), she threw herself into the nest of Lorraine, and having no portion, waived all other obligation to parental ties. This was a noble act on her part, as her husband always said. He, Sir Roger Lorraine, lay under her thumb, as calmly as need be; yet was pleased as the birth of children gave some distribution of pressure. For the lady ruled the house and lands, and all that was therein, as if she had brought them under her settlement.

Although Sir Roger had now been sleeping, for a good many years, with his fathers, his widow, Lady Valeria, showed no sign of any preparation for sleeping with her mothers. Now in her eighty-second year, this lady was as brisk and active, at least in mind if not in body, as half a century ago she had been. Many good stories (and some even true) were told concerning her doings and sayings in the time of her youth and beauty. Doings were always put first, because for these she was more famous, having the wit of ready action more than of rapid words perhaps. And yet in the latter she was not slack, when once she had taken up the quiver of the winged poison. She had seen so much of the world, and of the loftiest people that dwell therein—so far at least as they were to be found at the Court of George the Second—that she sat in an upper stratum now over all she had to deal with. And yet she was not of a narrow mind, when unfolded out of her creases. Her suite of rooms was the best in the house, of all above the ground-floor at least; and now she was waiting to receive her son, with her usual little bit of state. For the last five years she had ceased to appear at the table where once she ruled supreme; and the servants, who never had blessed her before, blessed her and themselves for that happy change. For she would have her due, as firmly and fairly (if not a trifle more so), as and than she gave the same to others, if undemanded.

In her upright seat she was now beginning—not to chafe, for such a thing would have been below her—but rather to feel her sense of right and duty (as owing to herself) becoming more and more grievous to her the longer she was kept waiting. She had learned long ago that she could not govern her son as absolutely as she was wont to rule his father; and having a clearer perception of her own will than of any large principles, whenever she found him immovable, she set the cause down as prejudice. Yet by feeling her way among these prejudices carefully, and working filial duty hard, and flying as a last resort to the stronghold of her many years, she pretty nearly always managed to get her own way in every thing.

But few of those who pride themselves on their knowledge of the human face would have perceived in this lady's features any shape of steadfast will. Perhaps the expression had passed away, while the substance settled inward; but however that may have been, her face was pleasant, calm, and gentle. Her manner also to all around her was courteous, kind, and unpretending; and people believed her to have no fault, until they began to deal with her. Her eyes, not overhung with lid, but delicately set and shaped, were still bright, and of a pale blue tint; her forehead was not remarkably large, but straight and of beautiful outline; while the filaments of fine wrinkles took, in some lights, a cast of silver from snowy silkiness of hair. For still she had abundant hair, that crown of glory to old age; and like a young girl, she still took pleasure in having it drawn through the hands, and done wisely, and tired to the utmost vantage.

Sir Roland came into his mother's room with his usual care and diligence. She with ancient courtesy rose from her straight-backed chair, and offered him one little hand, and smiled at him; and from the manner of that smile he knew that she was not by any means pleased, but thought it as well to conciliate him.

"Roland, you know that I never pay heed," she began, with a voice that shook just a little, "to rumors that reach me through servants, or even allow them to think of telling me."

"Dear mother, of course you never do. Such a thing would be far beneath you."

"Well, well, you might wait till I have spoken, Roland, before you begin to judge me. If I listen to nothing I must be quite unlike all the other women in the world."

"And so you are. How well you express it! At last you begin to perceive, my dear mother, what I perpetually urge in vain—your own superiority."

What man's mother can be expected to endure mild irony, even half so well as his wife would?

"Roland, this manner of speech—I know not what to call it, but I have heard of it among foreign people years ago—whatever it is, I beg you not to catch it from that boy Hilary."

"Poetical justice!" Sir Roland exclaimed; for his temper was always in good control, by virtue of varied humor; "this is the self-same whip wherewith I scourged little Alice quite lately! Only I feel that I was far more just."

"Roland, you are always just. You may not be always wise, of course; but justice you have inherited from your dear father and from me. And this is the reason why I wish to know what is the meaning of the strange reports which almost any one except myself would have been sure to go into, or must have been told of, long ago. Your thorough truthfulness I know. And you have no chance to mislead me now."

"I will imitate, though perhaps I can not equal, your candor, my dear mother, by assuring you that I greatly prefer to keep my own counsel in this matter."

"Roland, is that your answer? You admit that there is something important, and you refuse to let your own mother know it!"

"Excuse me, but I do not remember saying any thing about 'importance.' I am not superstitious enough to suppose that the thing can have any importance."

"Then why should you make such a fuss about it? Really, Roland, you are sometimes very hard to understand."

"I was not aware that I had made a fuss," Sir Roland answered, gravely; "but if I have, I will make no more. Now, my dear mother, what did you think of that extraordinary bill of Bottler's?"

"Bottler the Pigman is a rogue," said her ladyship, peremptorily; "his father was a rogue before him; and those things run in families. But surely you can not suppose that this is the proper way to treat the subject."

"To my mind a most improper way—to condemn a man's bill on the ground that his father transmitted the right to overcharge!"

"Now, my dear son," said Lady Valeria, who never called him her son at all, unless she was put out with him, and her "dear son" only when she was at the extremity of endurance—"my dear son, these are sad attempts to disguise the real truth from me. The truth I am entitled to know, and the truth I am resolved to know. And I think that you might have paid me the compliment of coming for my advice before."

Finding her in this state of mind, and being unable to deny the justice of her claim, Sir Roland was fain at last to make a virtue of necessity, while he marveled (as so many have done) at the craft of people in spying things, and espying them always wrongly.

"Is that all?" said Lady Valeria, after listening carefully; "I thought there must have been something a little better than that to justify you in making it such a mystery. Nothing but a dusty old document, and a strange-looking packet, or case like a squab. However, I do not blame you, my dear Roland, for making so small a discovery. The old astrologer appears to me to have grown a little childish. Now, as I keep to the old-fashioned hours, I will ask you to ring the bell for my tea, and while it is being prepared you can fetch me the case itself and the document to examine."

"To be sure, my dear mother, if you will only promise to obey the commands of the document."

"Roland, I have lived too long ever to promise any thing. You shall read me these orders, and then I can judge."

"I will make no fuss about such a trifle," he answered with a pleasant smile; "of course you will do what is honorable."

Surely men, although they deny so ferociously this impeachment, are open at times to at least a little side eddy of curiosity; Sir Roland, no doubt, was desirous to know what were the contents of that old case, which Alice had taken for a "dirty cushion," as it lay at the back of the cupboard in the wall; while his honor would not allow him comfortably to disobey the testator's wish. At the same time he felt, every now and then, that to treat such a matter in a serious light was a proof of superstition, or even childishness, on his part. And now, if his mother should so regard it, he was not at all sure that he ought to take the unpleasant course of opposing her.

CHAPTER XXII.

Sir Roland smiled at his mother's position, and air of stern attention, as he came back from his book-room with a small but heavy oaken box. This he placed on a chair, and, without any mystery, unlocked it. But no sooner had he flung back the lid and shown the case above described, than he was quite astonished at the expression of Lady Valeria's face. Something more than fear and terror—downright awe, as if at the sight of something supernatural—had taken the pale tint out of her cheeks, and made her fine forehead quiver.

"Dear mother, how foolish I am," he said, "to worry you with these trifles! I wish I had kept to my own opinion—"

"It is no trifle; you would have been wrong to treat it as a trifle. I have lived a long life, and seen many strange things; but this is the strangest of all of them."

For a minute or two she lay back, and was not fit to speak or be spoken to; only she managed to stop her son from ringing for her maid or the housekeeper. He had never beheld her so taken before, and could scarcely make out her signs to him to fasten both doors of the drawing-room.

Like most men who are at all good and just, Sir Roland was prone to think softly and calmly, instead of acting rapidly; and now his mother, so advanced in years, showed less hesitation than he did. Recovering, ere long, from that sudden shock, she managed to smile at herself and at his anxiety about her.

"Now, Roland, I will not meddle with this formidable and clumsy thing. It seems to be closed most jealously. It has kept for two centuries, and may keep for two more, so far as I am concerned. But if it will not be too troublesome to you, I should like to hear what is said about it."

"In this old document, madam? Do you see how strangely it has been folded? Whoever did that knew a great deal more than we know now about folding."

"The writing to me seems more strange than the folding. What a cramped hand! In what language is it written?"

"In Greek, the old Greek character, and the Doric dialect. He seems to have been proud of his classic descent, and perhaps Dorian lineage. But he placed a great deal too much faith in the attainments of his descendants. Poor Sedley would have read it straight off, I dare say; but the contractions, and even some of the characters, puzzled me dreadfully. I have kept up, as you know, dear mother, whatever little Greek I was taught, and perhaps have added to it; but my old Hedericus was needed a great many times, I assure you, before I got through this queer document; and even now I am not quite certain of the meaning of one or two passages. You see at the head a number of what I took at first to be hieroglyphics of some kind or other; but I find that they are astral or sidereal signs, for which I am none the wiser, though perhaps an astronomer would be. This, for instance, appears to mean the conjunction of some two planets, and this—"

"Never mind them, Roland. Read me what you have made out of the writing."

"Very well, mother. But if I am at fault, you must have patience with me, for I am not perfect in my lesson yet. Thus it begins:

"'Behold, ye men, who shall be hereafter, and pay heed to this matter. A certain Carian, noble by birth and of noble character, to whom is the not inglorious name, Agasicles Syennesis, hath lived not in the pursuit of wealth, or power, or reputation, but in the unbroken study of the most excellent arts and philosophies. Especially in the heavenly stars and signs of the everlasting kosmos hath he disciplined his mind, and surpassed all that went before him.' There is nothing like self-praise, is there, now, dear mother?"

"I have no doubt that he speaks the truth," answered the Lady Valeria; "I did not marry into a family accustomed to exaggerate."

"Then what do you think of this? 'Not only in intellect and forethought, but alse in good-will and philanthropy, modesty, and self-forgetfulness, did this man win the prize of excellence; and he it is who now speaks to you. Having lived much time in a barbarous island, cold, and blown over with vaporous air, he is no longer of such a sort as he was in the land of the fair afternoons. And there is when it is to his mind a manifest and established thing, that the gates of Hades are open for him, and the time of being no longer. But he holds this to be of the smallest difference, if only the gods produce his time to the perfect end of all the things lying now before him."

"How good, and how truly pious of him, Roland! Such a man's daughter never could have had any right to run away from him."

"My dear mother, I disagree with you, if he always praised himself in that style. But let him speak for himself again, as he seems to know very well how to do: 'These things have not been said, indeed, for the sake of any boasting, but rather to bring out thoroughly forward the truth in these things lying under, as if it were a pavement of adamant. Now, therefore, know ye, that Agasicles, carefully pondering every thing, has found, so to say the word, an end to accomplish and to abide in. And this is no other thing than to save the generations descended from him from great evil fortunes about to fall, by the ill-will of some divinity, at a destined time upon them. For a man of birth so renowned and lofty has not been made to resemble a hand-worker, or a runaway slave, but has many stars regarding him from many generations. And now he perceives that his skill and wisdom were not given to him to be a mere personal adornment, but that he might protect his descendants to the remote futurity. To him, then—it having been revealed that in the seventh generation hence, as has often come to pass with our house, or haply in the tenth (for the time is misty), a great calamity is bound to happen to those born afar off from Syennesis—the sage has labored many labors, though he can not avert, at least to make it milder, and to lessen it. He has not, indeed, been made to know, at least up to the present time, what this bane will be, or whether after the second or after the third century from this period. But knowing the swiftness of evil chance, he expects it at the earlier time; and whatever its manner or kind may be, Agasicles in all his discoveries has discovered no cure for human evils, save that which he now has shut up in a box. This box has been so constructed that nothing but dust will meet the greedy eyes of any who force it open, in the manner of the tomb of Nitocris. But if it be opened with the proper key, and after the proper interval, when the due need has arisen, there will be a fairer sight than ever broke upon mortal eyes before.'

"There, mother, now, what do you think of all that? I am quite out of breath with my long translation, and I am not quite sure of all of it. For instance, where he says—"

"Roland," his mother answered, quickly, "I am now much older than the prince, according to tradition, can have been. But I make no pretense to his wisdom, and I have reasons of my own for wondering. What have you done with the key of that case?"

"I have never seen it. It was not in the closet. And I meant to have searched throughout his room until I found out the meaning of this very crabbed postscript—'That fool, Memel, hath lost the key. It will cost me months to make another. My hands now tremble, and my eyes are weak. If there be no key found herewith, let it be read that Nature, whom I have vanquished, hath avenged herself. Whether or no have I labored in vain? Be blest now, and bless me, my dear descendants.'"

"That appears to me," said the Lady Valeria, being left in good manners by her son to express the first opinion, "to be of the whole of this strange affair the part that is least satisfactory."

"My dear mother, you have hit the mark. What satisfaction can one find in having a case without a key, and knowing that if we force it open there will be nothing but dust inside? Not a quarter so good as a snuff-box. I must have a pinch, my dear mother, excuse me, while you meditate on this subject. You are far more indulgent in that respect than little Alice ever is."

"All gentlemen take snuff," said the lady; "who is Alice to lay down the law? Your father took a boxful three times in a week. Roland, you let that young girl take very great liberties with you."

"It is not so much that I let her take them. I have no voice in the matter now. She takes them without asking me. Possibly that is the great calamity foretold by the astrologer. If not, what other can it be, do you think?"

"Not so," she answered, with a serious air, for all her experience of the witty world had left her old age quite dry of humor; "the trouble, if any is coming, will not be through Alice, but through Hilary. Alice is certainly a flighty girl, romantic, and full of nonsense, and not at all such as she might have been if left more in my society. However, she never has thought it worth while to associate much with her grandmother, the result of which is that her manners are unformed, and her mind is full of nonsense. But she has plenty, and (if it were possible) too much of that great preservative, pride of birth. Alice may come to affliction herself, but she never will involve her family."

"Any affliction of hers," said Sir Roland, "will involve at least her father."

"Yes, yes, of course. But what I mean is the honor and rank of the family. It is my favorite Hilary, my dear, brave, handsome

Hilary, who is likely to bring care on our heads, or rather upon your head, Roland: my time, of course, will be over then, unless he is very quick about it."

"He will not be so quick as that, I hope," Sir Roland answered, with some little confusion of proper sentiments; "although in that hot-bed of mischief, London, nobody knows when he may begin. However, he is not in London at present, according to your friend Lady De Lampnor. I think you said you had heard so from her."

"To be sure, Mr. Malahide told her himself. The dear boy has overworked himself so that he has gone to some healthy and quiet place to recruit his exhausted energies."

"Dear me," said Sir Roland, "I could never believe it, unless I knew from experience, what a very little work is enough to upset him. To write a letter to his father, for instance, is so severe an exertion that he requires a holiday the next day."

"Now, Roland, don't be so hard upon him. You would apprentice him to that vile law, which is quite unfit for a gentleman. I am not surprised at his being overcome by such odious labor; you would not take my advice, remember, and put him into the only profession fit for one of his birth — the army. Whatever happens, the fault is your own. It is clear, however, that he can not get into much mischief where he is just now—a rural and quiet part of Kent, she says. It shows the innocence of his heart to go there."

"Very likely. But if he wanted change, he might have asked leave to come home, I think. However, we shall have him here soon enough."

"How you speak, Roland! Quite as if you cared not a farthing for your only son! It must be dreadfully galling to him, to see how you prefer that Alice."

"If he is galled, he never winces," answered Sir Roland, with a quiet smile; "he is the most careless fellow in the world."

"And the most good-natured, and the most affectionate," said Lady Valeria, warmly. "Nothing else could keep him from being jealous, as nine out of ten would be. However, I am tired of talking now, and on that subject I might talk forever. Take away that case, if you please, and the writing. On no account would I have them left here. Of course you will lock them away securely, and not think of meddling with them. What is that case made of?"

"I can scarcely make out. Something strong and heavy. A mixture, I think, of shagreen and some metal. But the oddest thing of all is the key-hole. It is at the top of the cone, you see, and of the strangest shape, an irregular heptagon, with some rare complication of points inside. It would be next to impossible to open this case without shattering it altogether."

"I do not wish to examine the case; I wish to have it taken away, my son. There, there, I am very glad not to see it, although I am sure I am not superstitious. We shall do very well, I trust, without it. I think it is a most extraordinary thing that your father never consulted me about the writing handed down to you. He must have been bound by some pledge not to do so. There, Roland, I am tired of the subject."

With these words, the ancient lady waved her delicate hand, and dismissed her son, who kissed her white forehead, according to usage, and then departed with case and parchment locked in the oaken box again. But the more he thought over her behavior, the more he was puzzled about it. He had fully expected a command to open the case, at whatever hazard; and perhaps he had been disappointed at receiving no such order. But above all, he wanted to know why his mother should have been taken aback, as she was, by the sight of these little things. For few people, even in the prime of life, possessed more self-command and courage than Lady Valeria, now advancing into her eighty-second year.

CHAPTER XXIII.

At the top of the hill, these lofty themes were being handled worthily; while, at the bottom, little cares had equal glance of the democrat sun, but no stars allotted to regard them. In plain English, Bonny and Jack were as busy as their betters. They had taken their usual round that morning, seeking the staff of life—if that staff be applicable to a donkey—in village, hamlet, and farmhouse, or among the lanes and hedges. The sympathy and good-will between them daily grew more intimate, and their tastes more similar; so that it scarcely seemed impossible that Bonny in the end might learn to eat clover, and Jack to rejoice in money. Open air and roving life, the ups and downs of want and weal, the freedom of having nothing to lose, and the joyful luck of finding things—these, and perhaps a little spice of unknown sweetness in living at large on their fellow-creatures' labors, combined to make them as happy a pair as the day was long, or the weather good. In the winter—ah! why should we think of such trouble? Perhaps there will never be winter again.

At any rate, Bonny was sitting in front of the door of his castle (or rather in front of the door-way, because he was happy enough not to have a door), as proud and contented as if there could never be any more winter of discontent. He had picked up a hat in a ditch that day, lost by some man going home from his inn; and knowing from his patron, the pigman, Bottler, that the surest token of a blameless life is to be found in the hat of a man, the boy, stirred by the first heave of ambition, had put on this hat, and was practicing hat-craft (having gone with his head as it was born hitherto), to the utter surprise, and with the puzzled protest, of his beloved donkey. It was a most steady church-going hat of the chimney-pot order (then newly imported into benighted regions, but now of the essence of a godly life all over this free country); neither was it such a shocking bad hat as a man would cast away, if his wife were near. For Bonny's young head it was a world too wide, but he had padded it with a blackbird's nest; and though it seemed scarcely in harmony with his rakish waistcoat, and bare red shanks (spread on the grass for exhibition, and starred with myriad furze and bramble), still he was conscious of a distinguished air, and nodded to the donkey to look at him.

While these were gazing at one another, with free interchange of opinion, the rector of the parish, on his little pony, turned the corner suddenly. He was on his way home, at the bottom of the coombe, not in the very best temper perhaps, in spite of the sport in prospect; because Sir Roland had met so unkindly his kind desire to know things.

"What have you got on your lap, boy?" Mr. Hales so strongly shouted that sulky Echo pricked her ears, and "on your lap, boy," went all around.

Bonny knew well what was on his lap—a cleverly plaited hare-wire. Bottler had shown him how to do it, and now he was practicing diligently, under the auspices of his first hat. Mr. Hales was a "beak," of course; and the aquiline beak of the neighborhood. Bonny had the honor of his acquaintance in that fierce respect, and in no other. The little boy knew that there was a church, and that great people went there once a week, for very great people to blow them up. But this only made him the more uneasy to clap his bright eyes on the parson.

"Hold there! whoa!" called the Rev. Struan, as Bonny for his life began to cut away. "Boy, I want to talk to you."

Bonny was by no means touched with this very fine benevolence. Taking, perhaps, a low view of duty, we made the ground hot, to escape what we now call the "sacerdotal office." But Struan Hales (unlike our parsons) knew how to manage the laity. He clapped himself and his pony, in no time, between Master Bonny and his hole, and then in calm dignity called a halt, with his riding-whip ready at his button-hole.

"It is, it is, it is!" cried Bonny, coming back with his head on his chest, and meaning (in the idiom of the land) that now he was beaten, and would hold parley.

"To be sure it is!" the rector answered, keeping a good balance on his pony, and well pleased with his own tactics. He might have chased Bonny for an hour in vain through the furze, and heather, and blackberries; but here he had him at his mercy quite, through his knowledge of human nature. To put it coarsely—as the rector did in his mental process haply—the bigger thief any body is, the more sacred to him is his property. Not that Bonny was a thief at all; still that was how Mr. Hales looked at it. In the flurry of conscience, the boy forgot that a camel might go through the eye of a needle with less exertion than the parish incumbent must use to get into the Bonny castle.

"Oh hoo, oh hoo, oh hoo!" howled Bonny, having no faith in clerical honor, and foreseeing the sack of his palace and home.

"Give me that wire," said Mr. Hales, in a voice from the depth of his waistcoat. "Now, my boy, would you like to be a good boy?"

"No, sir; no, sir; oh no, plaize, sir! Jack nor me couldn't bear it, sir."

"Why not, my boy? It is such a fine thing. Your face shows that you are a sharp boy. Why do you go on living in a hole, and poaching, and picking, and stealing?"

"Plaize, sir, I never steals nothin', without it is somethin' as don't belong to me."

"That may be. But why should you steal even that? Shall I go in, and steal your things now?"

"Oh hoo, oh hoo, oh hoo! Plaize, sir, I han't got nothin' for 'e to steal."

"I am not at all sure of that," said the rector, looking at the hermit's hole longingly; "a thief's den is often as good as the bank. Now, who taught you how to make this snare? I thought I knew them all pretty well; but this wire has a dodge quite new to me. Who taught you, you young scamp?—this moment!"

"Plaize, sir, I can't tell 'e, sir. Nobody taught me, as I knows on."

"You young liar, you couldn't teach yourself. What you mean is that you don't choose to tell me. Know I must, and know I will, if I have to thrash it out of you!" He had seized him now by his gorgeous waistcoat, and held the strong horsewhip over his back. "Now, will you tell, or will you not?"

"I 'ont, I 'ont. If 'e kills me, I 'ont!" the boy cried, wriggling vainly, and with great tears of anticipation rolling down his sunburned cheeks.

The parson admired the pluck of the boy, knowing his own great strength of course, and feeling that if he began to smite, the swing of his arm would increase his own wrath, and carry him perhaps beyond reason. Therefore he offered him one chance more. "Will you tell, sir, or will you not?"

"I 'ont tell; that I 'ont!" screamed Bonny; and at the word the lash descended. But only once, for the smiter in a moment was made aware of a dusty rush, a sharp roar of wrath, and great teeth flashing under mighty jaws. And perhaps he would never have walked again if he had not most suddenly wheeled his pony, and just escaped a tremendous snap, well aimed at his comely and gartered calf.

"Ods bods!" cried the parson, as he saw the jackass (with a stretched-out neck, and crest erect, eyes flashing fire, and a lashing tail, and, worst of all terrors, those cavernous jaws) gathering legs for a second charge, like an Attic trireme, Phormio's own, backing water for the diecplus.

"May I be dashed," the rector shouted, "if I deal any more with such animals! If I had only got my hunting crop; but, kuk, kuk, kuk, pony! Quick, for God's sake! Off with you!"

With a whack of full power on the pony's flanks, away went he at full gallop; while Jack tossed his white nose with high disdain, and then started at a round trot in pursuit, to scatter them more disgracefully, and after them sent a fine flourish of trumpets, to the grand old national air of hee-haw.

While the Rev. Struan Hales was thus in sore discomfiture fleeing away as hard as his pony could be made to go, and casting uneasy glances over one shoulder at his pursuer, behold, he almost rode over a traveler footing it lighly round a sudden corner of the lane.

"Why, Uncle Struan!" exclaimed the latter; "is the dragon of St Leonard's after you? Or is this the usual style of riding of the beneficed clergy?"

"Hilary, my dear boy," answered the rector, "who would have thought of seeing you? You are come just in time to defend your uncle from a ravenous beast of prey. I was going home to bait a badger, but I have had a pretty good bait myself. Ah, you pagan, you may well be ashamed of yourself, to attack your clergyman!"

For Jack, perceiving the re-enforcement, and eying the stout stick which Hilary bore, prudently turned on his tail and departed, well satisfied with his exploit.

"Why, Hilary, what has brought you home?" asked his uncle, when a few words had passed concerning Jack's behavior. "Nobody expects you, that I know of. Your father is a mysterious man; but Alice would have been sure to tell me. Moreover, you must have walked all the way from the stage, by the look of your buckles, or perhaps from Brighton even."

"No; I took the short cut over the hills, and across by way of Beeding. Nobody expects me, as you say. I am come on important business."

"And, of course, I am not to know what it is. For mystery, and for keeping secrets, there never was such a family."

"As if you did not belong to it, uncle!" Hilary answered, good-naturedly. "I never heard of any secrets that I can remember."

"And good reason too," replied the rector; "they would not long have been secrets, my boy, after they came to your ears, I doubt."

"Then let me establish my reputation by keeping my own, at any rate. But, after all, it is no secret, uncle. Only, my father ought to know it first."

"Alas, you rogue, you rogue! Something about money, no doubt. You used to condescend to come to me when you were at school and college. But now you are too grand for the purse of any poor Sussex rector. I could put off our badger for half an hour, if you think you could run down the hill again. I should like you particularly to see young Fox: it will be something grand, my boy. He is the best pup I ever had in all my life."

"I know him, uncle; I know what he is; I chose him first out of the litter, you know. But you must not think of waiting for me. If I come down the hill again, it will only be about eight o'clock for an hour's rabbit-shooting."

Since he first met Mabel Lovejoy, Hilary had been changing much, and in every way, for the better. Her gentleness, and soft regard, and simple love of living things (at a time when cruelty was the rule, and kindness the rare exception), together with her knowledge of a great deal more than he had ever noticed in the world around, made him feel, in his present vein of tender absence from her, as if he never could bear to see the baiting of any badger. Therefore he went on his way to his father, pitying all things that were tormented.

CHAPTER XXIV.

Sir Roland Lorraine, in his little book-room, after that long talk with his mother, had fallen back into the chair of reflection, now growing more and more dear to him. He hoped for at least a good hour of peace, to think of things and to compare them with affairs that he had read of. It was all a trifle, of course, and not to be seriously dwelt upon. No man could have less belief in star, or comet, or even sun, as glancing out of their proper sphere, or orbit, at the dust of earth. No man smiled more disdainfully at the horn-books of seers and astrologers; and no man kept his own firm doubtings to himself more carefully.

And yet he was touched, as nobody now would be in a case of that sort, perhaps, by the real grandeur of that old man in devoting himself (according to his lights) to the stars that might come after him. Of these the brightest now broke in; and the dreamer's peace was done for.

What man has not his own queer little turns? Sir Roland knew quite well the step at the door—for Hilary's walk was beyond mistake; yet what did he do but spread hands on his forehead, and to the utmost of all his ability—sleep?

Hilary looked at his male parent with affectionate sagacity. He had some little doubts about his being asleep, or at any rate quite so heartily as so good a man had a right to repose. Therefore, instead of withdrawing, he spoke.

"My dear father, I hope you are well. I am sorry to disturb you, but—how do you do, sir; how do you do?"

The school-boy's rude answer to this kind inquiry—"None the better for seeing you"—passed through Hilary's mind, at least, if it did not enter his father's. However, they saluted each other as warmly as can be expected reasonably of a British father and a British son; and then they gazed at one another, as if it was the first time either had enjoyed that privilege.

"Hilary, I think you are grown," Sir Roland said, to break the silence, and save his lips from the curve of a yawn. "It is time for you to give up growing."

"I gave it up, sir, two years ago, if the standard measures of the realm are correct. But perhaps you refer to something better than material increase. If so, sir, I am pleased that you think so."

"Of course you are," his father answered; "you would have grown out of yourself, to have grown out of pleasant self-complacency. How did you leave Mr. Malahide? Very well? Ah, I am glad to hear it. The law is the healthiest of professions; and that your countenance vouches. But such a color requires food after fifty miles of traveling. We shall not dine for an hour and a half. Ring the bell, and I will order something while you go and see your grandmother."

"No, thank you, sir. If you can spare the time, I should like to have a little talk with you. It is that which has brought me down from London in this rather unceremonious way."

"Spare me apologies, Hilary, because I am so used to this. It is a great pleasure to see you, of course, especially when you look so well. Quite as if there were no such thing as money—which happens to you continually, and is your panacea for moneyed cares. But would not the usual form have done—a large sheet of paper (with tenpence to pay), and, 'My dear father, I have no ready cash—your dutiful son, H. L.?'"

"No, my dear father," said Hilary, laughing in recognition of his favorite form; "it is a much more important affair this time. Money, of course, I have none; but still I look upon that as nothing. You can not say that I ever show any doubt as to your liberality."

"You are quite right. I have never complained of such diffidence on your part. But what is this matter far more important than money in your estimate?"

"Well, I scarcely seem to know," said Hilary, gathering all his courage, "whether there is in all the world a thing so important as money."

"That is quite a new view for you to take. You have thrown all your money right and left. May I hope that this view will be lasting?"

"Yes, I think, sir, that you may. I am about to do a thing which will make money very scarce with me."

"I can think of nothing," his father answered, with a little impatience at his prologues, "which can make money any scarcer than it always is with you. I know that you are honorable, and that you scorn low vices. When that has been said of you, Hilary, there is very little more to say."

"There might have been something more to say, my dear father, but for you. You have treated me always as a gentleman treats a younger gentleman dependent upon him—and no more. You have exchanged (as you are doing now) little snap-shots with me, as if I were a sharp-shooter, and upon a level with you. I am not upon a level with you. And if it is kind, it is not fair play."

Sir Roland looked at him with great surprise. This was not like Hilary. Hilary, perhaps, had never been under fatherly control as he ought to be; but still, he had taken things easily as yet, and held himself shy of conflict.

"I scarcely understand you, Hilary," Sir Roland answered, quietly. "If you have any grievance, surely there will be time to discuss it calmly, during the long vacation, which you are now beginning so early."

"I fear, sir, that I shall not have the pleasure of spending my long vacation here. I have done a thing which I am not sure that you will at all approve of."

"That is to say, you are quite sure that I shall disapprove of it."

"No, my dear father; I hope not quite so bad as that, at any rate. I shall be quite resigned to leave you to think of it at your leisure. It is simply this—I have made up my mind, if I can obtain your consent, to get married."

"Indeed!" exclaimed his father, with a smile of some contempt. "I will not say that I am surprised; for nothing you do surprises me. But who has inspired this new whim, and how long will it endure?"

"All my life!" the youth replied, with fervor, and some irritation; for his father alone of living beings knew how to irritate him. "All my life, sir, as sure as I live! Can you never believe that I am in earnest?"

"She must be a true enchantress so to have improved your character! May I venture to ask who she is?"

"To be sure, sir. She lives in Kent, and her name is Mabel Lovejoy, the daughter of Mr. Martin Lovejoy."

"Lovejoy! A Danish name, I believe; and an old one, in its proper form. What is Mr. Martin Lovejoy by profession, or otherwise?"

"By profession he is a very worthy and long-established grower."

"A grower! I fail to remember that branch of the liberal professions."

"A grower, sir, is a gentleman who grows the fruits of the earth for the good of others."

"What we should call a 'spade husbandman,' perhaps. A healthful and classic industry—under the towers of Œbalia. I beg to be excused all further discussion, as I never use strong language. Perhaps you will go and enlist your grandmother's sympathy with this loyal attachment to the daughter of the grower."

"But, sir, if you would only allow me—"

"Of course; if I would only allow you to describe her virtues—but that is just what I have not the smallest intention of allowing. Let the wings of imagination spread themselves in a more favorable direction. This interview must close on my part with a suggestive (but perhaps self-evident) proposition. Hilary, the door is open."

CHAPTER XXV.

In the village of West Lorraine, which lies at the foot of the South Down ridge, there lived at this moment, and had lived for three generations of common people, an extraordinary old woman of the name of Nanny Stilgoe. She may have been mentioned before, because it was next to impossible to keep out of her, whenever any body whosoever wanted to speak of the neighborhood. For miles and miles around she was acknowledged to know every thing; and the only complaint about her was concerning her humility. She would not pretend to be a witch; while every body felt that she ought to be, and most people were sure that she was one.

Alice Lorraine was well accustomed to have many talks with Nanny; listening to her queer old sayings, and with young eyes gazing at the wisdom or folly of the by-gone days. Nanny, of course, was pleased with this; still she was too old to make a favorite now of any one. People going slowly upward toward a better region, have a vested interest still in earth, but in mankind a mere shifting remainder.

Therefore all the grace of Alice and her clever ways and sweetness, and even half a pound of tea and an ounce and a half of tobacco, could not tempt old Nanny Stilgoe to say what was not inside of her. Every body made her much more positive in every thing (according as the months went on, and she knew less and less what became of them) by calling upon her at every new moon to declare to them something or other. It was not in her nature to pretend to deceive any body, and she found it harder from day to day to be right in all their trifles.

But her best exertions were always forthcoming on behalf of Coombe Lorraine, both as containing the most conspicuous people of the neighborhood, and also because in her early days she had been a trusty servant under Lady Valeria. Old Nanny's age had become by this time almost an unknown quantity, several years being placed to her credit (as is almost always done) to which she was not entitled. But, at any rate, she looked back upon her former mistress, Lady Valeria, as comparatively a chicken, and felt some contempt for her judgment, because it could not have grown ripe as yet. Therefore the venerable Mrs. Stilgoe (proclaimed by the public voice as having long since completed her century) can not have been much under ninety in the year of grace 1811.

Being of a rather stiff and decided—not to say crabbed—turn of mind, this old woman kept a small cottage to herself at the bend of the road beyond the blacksmith's, close to the Well of St. Hagydor. This cottage was not only free of rent, but her own for the term of her natural life, by deed of gift from Sir Roger Lorraine, in gratitude for a brave thing she had done when Roland was a baby. Having received this desirable cottage, and finding it followed by no others, she naturally felt that she had not been treated altogether well by the family. And her pension of three half-crowns a week, and her Sunday dinner in a basin, made an old woman of her before her time, and only set people talking.

In spite of all this, Nanny was full of good-will to the family, forgiving them all their kindness to her, and even her own dependence upon them; foretelling their troubles plentifully, and never failing to dwell upon them. And now on the very day after young Hilary's conflict with his father, she had the good luck to meet Alice Lorraine, on her way to the rectory, to consult Uncle Struan or beg him to intercede. For the young man had taken his father at his word, concluding that the door, not only of the room, but also of the house, was open for him on the inhospitable side; and, casting off his native dust from his gaiters, he had taken the evening stage to London, after a talk with his favorite Alice.

Old Nanny Stilgoe had just been out to gather a few sticks to boil her kettle, and was hobbling home with the fagot in one hand, and in the other a stout staff chosen from it, which she had taken to help her along. She wore no bonnet or cap on her head, but an old red kerchief tied round it, from which a scanty iron-gray lock escaped, and fluttered now and then across the rugged features and haggard cheeks. Her eyes, though sunken, were bright and keen, and few girls in the parish could thread a fine needle as quickly as she could. But extreme old age was shown in the countless seams and puckers of her face, in the knobby protuberance where bones met, and, above all, in the dull, wan surface of skin whence the life was retiring.

"Now, Nanny, I hope you are well to-day," Alice said, kindly, though by no means eager to hold discourse with her just now; "you are working hard, I see, as usual."

"Ay, ay, working hard, the same as us all be born to, and goes out of the world with the sweat of our brow. Not the likes of you, Miss Alice. All the world be made to fit you, the same as a pudding do to a basin."

"Now, Nanny, you ought to know better than that. There is nobody born to such luck, and to keep it. Shall I carry your fagot for you? How cleverly you do tie them!"

"'Ee may carr the fagot as far as 'ee wool. 'Ee wunt goo very far, I count. The skin of thee isn't thick enow. There, set 'un down now beside of the well. What be all this news about Haylery?"

"News about Hilary, Nanny Stilgoe! Why, who has told you any thing?"

"There's many a thing as comes to my knowledge without no need of telling. He have broken with his father, haven't he? Ho, ho, ho!"

"Nanny, you never should talk like that. As if you thought it a very fine thing, after all you have had to do with us!"

"And all I owes you! Oh yes, yes; no need to be bringing it to my mind, when I gets it in a basin every Sunday."

"Now, Mrs. Stilgoe, you must remember that it was your own wish to have it so. You complained that the gravy was gone into grease, and did we expect you to have a great fire; and you came up and chose a brown basin yourself, and the cloth it was to be tied in; and you said that then you would be satisfied."

"Well, well, you know it all by heart. I never pays heed to them little things. I leaves all of that for the great folk. Howsever, I have a good right to be told what doth not consarn no strangers."

"You said that you knew it all without telling! The story, however, is too true this time. But I hope it may be for a short time only."

"All along of a chield of a girl—warn't it all along of that? Boys thinks they be sugar-plums always, till they knows 'en better."

"Why, Nanny, now, how rude you are! What am I but a child of a girl? Much better, I hope, than a sugar-plum."

"Don't tell me! Now, you see the water in that well. Clear and bright, and not so deep as this here stick of mine is."

"Beautifully cool and sparkling even after the long hot weather. How I wish we had such a well on the hill! What a comfort it must be to you!"

"Holy water they calls it, don't em? Holy water, tino! But it do well enough to boil the kittle when there be no frogs in it. My father told me that his grandfather, or one of his forebears afore him, seed this well in the middle of a great roaring torrent, ten feet over top of this here top step. It came all the way from your hill, he said. It fetched more water that Adur River; and the track of it can be followed now."

"I have heard of it," answered Alice, with a little shiver of superstition; "I have always longed to know more about it."

"The less you knows of it the better for 'ee. Pray to the Lord every night, young woman, that you may never see it."

"Oh, that is all superstition, Nanny. I should like to see it particularly. I never could understand how it came; though it seems to be clear that it does come. It has only come twice in five hundred years, according to what they say of it. I have heard the old rhyme about it ever—oh, ever since I can remember."

"So have I heered. But they never gets things right now; they be so careless. How have you heered of it, Miss Alice?"

"Like this—as near as I can remember:

'When the Woeburn brake the plain,
Ill it boded for Lorraine,
When the Woeburn came again,
Death and dearth it brought Lorraine.
If it ever floweth more,
Reign of the Lorraines is o'er.'

Did I say it right now, Nanny?"

"Yes, child, near enough, leastways. But you haven't said the last verse at all:

'Only this can save Lorraine,
One must plunge to rescue twain.'"

"Why, I never heard those two lines, Nanny!"

"Like enough. They never cares to finish any thing nowadays. But that there verse belongeth to it, as certain as any of the Psalms is. I've heered my father say it scores of times, and he had it from his grandfather. Sit you down on the stone, child, a minute, while I go in and start the fire up. Scarcely a bit of wood fit to burn round any of the hedges now, they thieving children goes everywhere. Makes my poor back stiff, it doth, to get enow to boil a cow's foot or a rind of bakkon."

Old Nanny had her own good reasons for not wanting Alice in her cottage just then. Because she was going to have for dinner a rind of bacon truly, but also as companion thereto a nice young rabbit with onion sauce; a rabbit fee-simple whereof was legally vested in Sir Roland Lorraine. But Bottler the pigman took seizin thereof, *vi et armis*, and conveyed it *habendum*, *coquendum*, *et vorandum*, to Mrs. Nanny Stilgoe, in payment for a pig-charm.

Meanwhile, Alice thought sadly over the many uncomfortable legends concerning her ancient and dwindled race. The first outbreak of the "Woeburn," in the time of Edward the Second, was said to have brought forth deadly poison from the hill-side whence it sprang. It ran for seven months, according to the story to be found in one of their earliest records, confirmed by an inscription in the church; and the Earl of Lorraine and his seven children died of the "black death" within that time. Only a posthumous son was left to carry on the lineage. The fatal water then subsided for about a century and a half, when it broke forth suddenly in greater volume, and ran for three months only. But in that short time the fortune of the family fell from its loftiest to its lowest; and never thenceforth was it restored to the ancient eminence and wealth. On Towton field, in as bloody a battle as ever was fought in England, the Lorraines, though accustomed to driving snow, perished like a snowdrift. The bill of attainder, passed with hot speed by a slavish Parliament, took away family rank and lands, and left the last of them an outcast, with the block prepared for him.

Nanny having set that coney boiling, and carefully latched the cottage door, hobbled at her best pace back to Alice, and resumed her subject.

"Holy water! Oh, ho, ho! Holy to old Nick, I reckon; and that be why her boileth over so. Three wells there be in a row, you know, miss, all from that same spring, I count—the well in parson's garden, and this, and the uppest one, under the foot of your hill, above where that gypsy boy harboreth. That be where the Woeburn breaketh ground."

"You mean where the moss and the cotton-grass is. But you can scarcely call it a well there now."

"It dothn't run much, very like; and I haven't been up that way for a year or more. But only you try to walk over it, child; and you'd walk into your grave, I hold. The time is nigh up for it to come out, according to what they tells of it."

"Very well, Nanny, let it come out. What a treat it would be this hot summer! The Adur is almost dry, and the shepherd-pits everywhere are empty."

"Then you never have heered, child, what is to come of it, if it ever comes out again. Worse than ever comed afore to such a lot as you be."

"I can not well see how it could be worse than death, and dearth, and slaughter, Nanny."

"Now that shows how young girls will talk, without any thought of any thing. To us poor folk it be wise and right to put life afore any thing, according to natur'; and arter that the things as must go inside of us. There let me think, let me think a bit. I forgets things now; but I know there be some'at as you great folk counts more than life, and victuals, and natur', and every thin'. But I forgets the word you uses for it."

"Honor, Nanny, I suppose you mean—the honor, of course, of the family."

"May be, some'at of that sort, as you builds up your mind upon. Well, that be running into danger now, if the old words has any truth in 'em."

"Nonsense, Nanny, I'll not listen to you. Which of us is likely to disgrace our name, pray? I am tired of all these nursery stories. Good-bye, Mrs. Stilgoe."

"It'll not be you, at any rate;" the old woman muttered wrathfully, as Alice, with sparkling eyes and a quick firm step, set off for the rectory: "if ever there was a proud piece of goods—even my bacco her'll never think of in her tantrums now! Ah well! ah well! We lives, and we learns to hold our tongues in the end, no doubt." The old lady's judgment of the world was a little too harsh in this case, however; for Alice Lorraine, on her homeward way, left the usual shilling's-worth of tobacco on old Nanny's window-sill.

CHAPTER XXVI.

"It is worse than useless to talk any more," Sir Roland said to Mr. Hales, who by entreaty of Alice had come to dine there that day and to soften things: "Struan, you know that I have not one atom of obstinacy about me. I often doubt what is right, and wonder at people who are so positive. In this case there is no room for doubt. Were you pleased with your badger yesterday?"

"A capital brock, a most wonderful brock! His teeth were like a rat-trap. Fox, however, was too much for him. The dear little dog, how he did go in! I gave the ten guineas to my three girls. Good girls, thoroughly good girls all. They never fall in love with any body. And when have they had a new dress—although they are getting now quite old enough?"

"I never notice those things much," Sir Roland (who had given them many dresses) answered, most inhumanly; "but they always look very good and pretty. Struan, let us drink their healths, and happy wedlock to them."

The rector looked at Sir Roland with a surprise of geniality. His custom was always to help himself; while his host enjoyed by proxy. This went against his fine feelings sadly. Still it was better to have to help himself, than be unhelped altogether.

"But about that young fellow," Mr. Hales

continued, after the toast had been duly honored; "it is possible to be too hard, you know."

"That sentiment is not new to me. Struan, you like a capeling with your port."

"Better than any olive always. And now there are no olives to be had. Wars everywhere, wars universal! The powers of hell gat hold of me. Antichrist in triumph roaring! Bloodshed weltering everywhere! And I am too old myself; and I have no son to—to fight for Old England."

"A melancholy thought! But you were always pugnacious, Struan."

"Now, Roland, Roland, you know me better. 'To seek peace and to ensue it' is my text and my tactic everywhere. And with them that be of one household, what saith St. Paul the apostle in his Epistle to the Ephesians? You think that I know no theology, Roland, because I can sit a horse and shoot?"

"Nay, nay, Struan, be not thus hurt by imaginary lesions. The great range of your powers is well known to me, as it is to every one. Particularly to that boy whom you shot in the hedge last season."

"No more of that, an you love me. I believe the little rascal peppered himself to get a guinea out of me. But as to Hilary, will you allow me to say a few words without any offense? I am his own mother's brother, as you seem very often to forget, and I can not bear to see a fine young fellow condemned and turned out of house and home for what any young fellow is sure to do. Boys are sure to go falling in love until their whiskers are fully grown. And the very way to turn fools into heroes (in their own opinion) is to be violent with them."

"Perhaps those truths are not new to me. But I was not violent—I never am."

"At any rate you were harsh and stern. And who are you to find fault with him? I care not if I offend you, Roland, until your better sense returns. But did you marry exactly in your own rank of life yourself."

"I married a lady, Struan Hales—your sister—unless I am misinformed."

"To be sure, to be sure! I know well enough what you mean by that; though you have the most infernal way of keeping your temper and hinting things. What you mean is that I am making little of my own sister's memory by saying that she was not your equal."

"I meant nothing of the sort. How very hot your temper is! I showed my respect for your family, Struan, and simply implied that it was not graceful, at any rate, on your part—"

"Graceful be hanged! Sir Roland, I can not express myself as you can—and perhaps I ought to thank God for that—but none the less for all that, I know when I am in the right. I feel when I am in the right, sir, and I snap my fingers at every one."

"That is right. You have an unequaled power of explosion in your thumb-joint—I heard it through three oaken doors the last time you were at all in a passion; and now it will go through a wall at least. Nature has granted you this power to exhibit your contempt of wrong."

"Roland, I have no power at all. I do not pretend to be clever at words; and I know that you laugh at my preaching. I am but a peg in a hole, I know, compared with all your learning, though my church-warden, Gates, won't hear of it. What did he say last Sunday?"

"Something very good, of course. Help yourself, Struan, and out with it."

"Well, it was nothing very wonderful. And as he holds under you, Sir Roland—"

"I will not turn him out for even the most brilliant flash of his bramble-hook."

"You never turn any body out. I wish to goodness you would sometimes. You don't care about your rents. But I do care about my tithes."

"This is deeply disappointing after the wit you were laden with. What was the epigram of Church-warden Gates?"

"Never you mind. That will keep—like some of your own mysteries. You want to know every thing and tell nothing, as the old fox did in the fable."

"It is an ancient aphorism," Sir Roland answered, gently, "that knowledge is tenfold better than speech. Let us endeavor to know things, Struan, and to satisfy ourselves with knowledge."

"Yes, yes, let us know things, Roland. But you never want us to know any thing. That is just the point, you see. Now, as sure as I hold this glass in my hand, you will grieve for what you are doing."

"I am doing nothing, Struan; only wondering at your excitement."

"Doing nothing! Do you call it nothing to drive your only son from your doors, and to exasperate your brother-in-law until he blames the Lord for being the incumbent instead of a curate, to swear more freely? There, there! I will say no more. None but my own people ever seem to know what is inside of me. No more wine, Sir Roland, thank you. Not so much as a single drop more! I will go while there is good light down the hill."

"You will do nothing of the kind, Struan Hales," his host replied, in that clear voice which is so certain to have its own clear way; "you will sit down and take another glass of port, and talk with me in a friendly manner."

"Well, well, any thing to please you. You are marvelous hard to please of late."

"You will find me most easy to please, if only without any further reproaches, or hinting at things which can not concern you, you will favor me with your calm opinion in this foolish affair of poor Hilary."

"The whole thing is one. You so limit me," said the parson, delighted to give advice, but loath to be too cheap with it; "you must perceive, Roland, that all this matter is bound up, so to speak, altogether. You shake your head? Well, then, let us suppose that poor Hilary stands on his own floor only. Every tub on its own bottom. Then what I should do about him would be this: I would not write him a single line, but let him abide in his breaches or breeches—whichever the true version is—and there he will soon have no half-pence to rattle, and therefore must grow penitent. Meanwhile I should send into Kent an envoy, a man of penetration, to see what manner of people it is that he is so taken up with. And according to his report I should act. And thus we might very soon break it off; without any action for damages. You know what those blessed attorneys are."

Sir Roland thought for a little while; and then he answered pleasantly.

"Struan, your advice is good. I had thought of that course before you came. The stupid boy soon will be brought to reason; because he is frightened of credit now; he was so singed at Oxford. And I can trust him to do nothing dishonorable or cold-blooded. But the difficulty of the whole plan is this: whom have I that I can trust to go into Kent, and give a fair report about this mercenary grower and his crafty daughter?"

"Could you trust me, Roland?"

"Of course I could. But, Struan, you never would do such a thing!"

"Why not? I should like to know, why not? I could get to the place in two days' time; and the change would do me a world of good. You laity never can understand what it is to be a parson. A deacon would come for a guinea, and take my Sunday morning duty, and the congregation for the afternoon would rejoice to be disappointed. And when I come back, they will dwell on my words, because the other man will have preached so much worse. Times are hard with me, Roland, just now. If I go, will you pay the piper?"

"Not only that, Struan; but I shall thank you to the uttermost stretch of gratitude."

"There will be no gratitude on either side. I am bound to look after my nephew's affairs: and I sadly want to get away from home. I have heard that there is a nice trout-stream there. If Hilary, who knows all he knows from me, could catch a fine fish, as Alice told me—what am I likely to do, after panting up in this red-hot chalk so long? Roland, I must have a pipe, though you hate it. I let you sneeze; and you must let me blow."

"Well, Struan, you can do what you like, for this once. This is so very kind of you."

"I believe if you had let that boy Hilary smoke," said the rector, warming unto his pipe, "you never would have had all this bother with him about this trumpery love-affair. Cupid hates tobacco."

CHAPTER XXVII.

On the second evening after the above discourse, a solitary horseman might have been seen, or, to put it more indicatively, a single pony-man was seen pricking gallantly over the plains, and into the good town of Tonbridge, in the land of Kent. Behind him, and strapped to his saddle, he bore what used to be called a "vady"—a corruption, perhaps, of "vade mecum"—that is to say, a small leather cylinder, containing change of raiment, and other small comforts of the traveler. The pony he bestrode was black, with a white star on her forehead, a sturdy trudger, of a spirited nature, and proud of the name of "Maggie." She had now recovered entirely from her ten-guinea feast of dahlias, and was as pleased as the rector himself to whisk her tail in a change of air. Her pace was still gallant, and her ears well pricked, especially when she smelled the smell which all country towns have of horses, and of rubbing down, hissing, and bucketing, and (best of all) of good oats jumping in a sieve among the chaff.

Maggie was proud of her master, and thought him the noblest man that ever cracked a whip, having imbibed this opinion from the young smart hunter, who was up to every thing. And it might have fared ill with Jack the donkey, if Maggie had carried her master when that vile assault was perpetrated. But if Maggie was now in good spirits, what lofty flight of words can rise to the elation of her rider?

The rector now, week after week, had been longing for a bit of sport. His open and jovial nature had been shut up, pinched, and almost poisoned, for want of proper outlet. He hated books, and he hated a pen, and he hated doing nothing; and he never would have horsewhipped Bonny, if he had been as he ought to be. Moreover, he had been greatly bothered, although he could not clearly put it, by all those reports about Coombe Lorraine, and Sir Roland's manner of scorning them. But now here he was, in a wayfaring dress, free from the knowledge of any one, able to turn to the right or the left, as either side might predominate; with a bagful of guineas to spend as his own, and yet feel no remorse about them. Tush! that does not express it at all. With a bagful of guineas to spend as he chose, and rejoice in the knowledge that he was spending another man's money, for his own good, and the benefit of humanity. This is a fine feeling, and a rare one to get the luck of. Therefore, whosoever gets it, let him lift up his heart and be joyful.

Whether from that fine diffidence which so surely accompanies merit, or from honorable economy in the distribution of trust-funds, or from whatever other cause it was, —in the face of all the town of Tonbridge, this desirable traveler turned his pony into the quiet yard of that old-fashioned inn, "The Checkers." All the other hostlers grunted disapprobation, and chewed straws; while the one hostler of "The Checkers" rattled his pail with a swing of his elbow, hissed in the most enticing attitude, and made believe to expect it.

Mr. Hales, in the manner of a cattle-jobber (which was his presentment now), lifted his right leg over the mane of the pony, and so came downward. Every body in the yard at once knew thoroughly well what his business was. And nobody attempted to cheat him in the inn, because it is known to be a hopeless thing to cheat a cattle-jobber in any other way than by gambling. So that with little to say, or be said, this unclerkly clerk had a good supper, and smoked a wise pipe with his landlord.

Of course he made earnest inquiries about all the farmers of the neighborhood, and led the conversation gently to the grower and his affairs; and as this chanced to be Master Lovejoy's own "house of call" at Tonbridge, the landlord gave him the highest character, and even the title of "Esquire."

"Ah, yes," he exclaimed, with his rummer in one hand, and waving his pipe with the other; "there be very few in these here parts to compare with Squire Lovejoy. One of the true old Kentish stock, sir; none of your come-and-go bagmen. I have heered say that that land have been a thousand year in the family."

"Lord bless me!" cried Mr. Hales; "why, we get back to the time of the Danes and the Saxons!"

"There now!" said the landlord, giving him a poke of admiration with his pipe; "you knows all about it as well as if I had told 'ee. And his family brought up so respectable! None of your sitting on pillions. A horse for his self, and a horse for his son, and a horse for his pretty darter. Ah, if I were a young man again—but there she be above me altogether! Though 'The Checkers,' to my thinking, is more to the purpose than a bigger inn might be, sir."

"You are right, I believe," replied his guest. "How far may it be to Old Applewood farm?"

"Well, sir, how far? Why, let me see: a matter of about five mile, perhaps. You've heered tell of the Garden of Eden, perhaps?"

"To be sure! Don't I read about it"—he was going to say "every Sunday," but stopped, in time to dissemble the parson.

"And the finest ten mile of turnpike in England. You turns off from it about four mile out. And then you keeps on straight-forrard."

"Thank you, my good friend. I shall ask the way to-morrow. Your excellent punch is as good as a night-cap. But I want to combine a little pleasure with business, if I can, to-morrow. I am a bit of a sportsman in a small way. Would Mr. Lovejoy allow me to cast a fly in his water, think you?"

"Ay, that he will, if you only tell him that you be staying at 'The Checkers' inn."

The rector went to bed that night in a placid humor, with himself, and his landlord, and all the county. And sleeping well after change of air, a long ride, and a good supper, he awoke in the morning, as fresh as a lark, in a good state of mind for his breakfast.

Old Applewood farm was just "taking it easy" in the betwixt and between of hard work. The berry season was over now, and the hay was stacked, and the hops were dressed; John Shorne and his horses were resting freely, and gathering strength for another campaign—to cannonade London with apples and pears. All things had the smell of summer, passing rich, and the smell of autumn, without its weight leaning over the air. The nights were as warm as the days almost, yet soft with a mellow briskness; and any young man who looked out of his window said it was a shame to go to bed. Some people have called this the "saddest time of the whole sad twelvemonth;" the middle or end of July, when all things droop with heavy leafiness. But who be these to find fault with the richest and goodliest prime of nature's strength? Peradventure the fault is in themselves. All seasons of the year are good to those who bring their seasoning. And now, when field, and wood, and hedge stand up in their flush of summering, and every bird, and bat, and insect of our British island is as active as he ought to be (and sometimes much too much so); also, when good people look at one another in hot weather, and feel that they may have worked too hard, or been too snappish when the frosts were on (which they always are except in July), and then begin to wonder whether their children would like to play with the children of one another, because they can not catch cold in such weather; and after that, begin to speak of a rubber in the bower, and a great spread of delightfulness, when all this comes to pass, what right have we to make the worst of it?

That is neither here nor there. Only one thing is certain, that our good parson, looking as unlike a parson as he could—and he had a good deal of capacity in that way—steered his pony Maggie round the corner into the grower's yard, and looked about to see how the land lay. The appearance of every thing pleased him well, for comfort, simplicity, and hospitality shared the good quarters between them. Even a captious man could hardly, if he understood the matter, find much fault with any thing. The parson was not a captious man, and he knew what a good farm-yard should be, and so he said "Capital, capital!" twice, before he handed Maggie's bridle to Paddy from Cork, who of course had run out with a sanguine sense of a shilling arrived.

"Is Squire Lovejoy at home?" asked the visitor, being determined to "spake the biggest," as Paddy described it afterward. For the moment, however, he only stared, while the parson repeated the question.

"Is it the maisther ye mane?" said Paddy; "faix then, I'll go and ax the missus."

But before there was time to do this, the grower appeared with a spud on his shoulder. He had been in the hop-ground; and hearing a horse, came up to know what was toward. The two men looked at one another with mutual approval. The parson, tall, and strong, and lusty, and with that straightforward aspect which is conferred, or at least confirmed, by life in the open air, field sports, good living, and social gatherings. His features, too, were clear and bold, and his jaws just obstinate enough to manage a parish; without that heavy squareness which sets the whole church by the ears. The grower was of moderate height, and sturdy, and thoroughly useful; his face told of many dealings with the world; but his eyes were frank, and his mouth was pleasant. His custom was to let other people have their say before he spoke; and now he saluted Mr. Hales in silence, and waited for him to begin.

"I hope," said his visitor, "you will excuse my freedom in coming to see you thus. I am trying this part of the country for the first time for a holiday. And the landlord of 'The Checkers' inn at Tonbridge, where I am staying for a day or two, told me that you, perhaps, would allow me to try for a fish in your river, sir."

"In our little brook! There be none left, I think. You are kindly welcome to try, sir. But I fear you will have a fool's errand of it. We have had a young gentleman from London here, a wonderful angler, sure enough, and I do believe he hath caught every one."

"Well, sir, with your kind permission, there can be no harm in trying," said the rector, laughing in his sleeve at Hilary's crude art compared with his own. "The day is not very promising, and the water of course is strange to me. But have I your leave to do my best?"

"Ay, ay, as long as you like. My ground goes as far up as there is any water, and down the brook to the turnpike road. We will see to your nag; and if you would like a bit to eat, sir, we dine at one, and we sup at seven, and there be always a bit in the larder 'tween whiles. Wil't come into house before starting?"

"I thank you for the kind offer; but I think I'd better ask you the way, and be off. There is just a nice little coil of cloud now; in an hour it may be gone, and the brook, of course, is very low and clear. Whatever my sport is, I shall call in and thank you when I come back for my pony. My name is Hales, sir, a clerk from Sussex; very much at your service, and obliged to you."

"The same to you, Master Halls; and I wish you more sport than you will get, sir. Your best way is over that stile; and then when you come to the water, go where you will."

"One more question, which I always ask: what size do you allow your fish to be taken?"

"What size? Why, as big, to be sure, as ever you can catch them. The bigger they are, the less bones they have."

With a laugh at this answer, the parson set off, with his old fly-book in his pocket, and a rod in his hand which he had borrowed (by grace of his landlord) in Tonbridge. His step was brisk, and his eyes were bright, and he thought much more of the sport in prospect than of the business that brought him there.

"Aha!" he exclaimed, as he hit on the brook, where an elbow of bank jutted over it, "very fine tackle will be wanted here, and one fly is quite enough for it. It must be fished downward, of course, because it can not be fished upward. It will take all I know to tackle them."

So it did, and a great deal more than he knew. He changed his fly every quarter of an hour, and he tried every dodge of experience; he even tried dapping with the natural fly, and then the blue-bottle and grasshopper, but not a trout could he get to rise, or even to hesitate, or show the very least sign of temptation.

So great was his annoyance (from surety of his own skill, and vain use of it), that after fishing for about ten hours and catching a new-born minnow, the rector vehemently came to a halt, and repented that he had exhausted already his whole stock of strong language. When a good man has done this, a kind of reaction (either of the stomach or conscience) arises, and leads him astray from his usual sign-posts, whether of speech, or deed, or thought.

The Rev. Struan Hales sat down, marveling if he were a clumsy oaf, and gave Hilary no small credit for catching such deeply sagacious and wary trout. Then he dwelt bitterly over his fate for having to go and fetch his pony, and let every yokel look into his basket and grin at its beautiful emptiness. Moreover, he found himself face to face with starvation of the saddest kind; that which a man has challenged, and superciliously talked about, and then has to meet very quietly.

Not to exaggerate—if that were possible—the Rev. Struan found his inner man (thus rashly exposed to new Kentish air) "absolutely barking at him," as he strongly expressed it to his wife, the moment he found himself at home again. But here he was fifty miles from home, with not a fishing-basket only, but a much nearer and dearer receptacle full of the purest vacuity. "This is very sad," he said, and all his system echoed it.

CHAPTER XXVIII.

WHILE the rector still was sitting thus, on the mossy hump of an apple-tree, weary and disconsolate, listening to the murmuring brook, with louder murmurings of his own, he espied a light, well-balanced figure crossing the water on a narrow plank some hundred yards up the stream-way.

"A pretty girl!" said the parson; "I am sure of it, by the way she carries herself. Plain girls never walk like that. Oh that she were coming to my relief! But the place is rather dangerous. I must go and help her. Ah, here she comes! What a quick, light foot! My stars, if she hasn't got a basket! Nothing for me, of course. No such luck on this most luckless of all days."

Meanwhile she was making the best of her way, as straight as the winding stream allowed, toward this ungrateful and skeptical grumbler; and presently she turned full upon him, and looked at him, and he at her.

"What a lovely creature!" thought Mr. Hales, "and how wonderfully her dress becomes her! Why, the mere sight of her hat is enough to drive a young fellow out of his mind almost! Now I should like to make her acquaintance, if I were not starving so. 'Acrior illum cura domat,' as Sir Roland says."

"If you please, sir," the maiden began, with a bright and modestly playful glance, "are you Mr. Halls, who asked my father for leave to fish this morning?"

"Hales, fair mistress, is my name, a poor and unworthy clerk from Sussex."

"Then, Mr. Hales, you must not be angry with me for thinking that you might be hungry."

"And — and thirsty!" gasped the rector. "Goodness me, if you only knew my condition, how you would pity me!"

"It occurred to me that you might be thirsty too," she answered, as she took out of her basket a napkin, a plate, a knife and fork, half a loaf, and something tied up in a cloth whose fragrance went to the bottom of the parson's heart, and then a stone pipkin, and a half-pint horn, and after that a pinch of salt. All these she spread on a natural table of grass, which her clever eyes discovered over against a mossy seat.

"I never was so thankful in all my life—I never was, I never was. My pretty dear, what is your name, that I may bless you every night?"

"My name is Mabel Lovejoy, sir; and I hope that you will excuse me for having nothing better to bring than this. Most fishermen prefer duck, I know; but we happened only to have in the larder this half, or so, of a young roast goose—"

"A goose! An infinitely finer bird. And so much more upon it! Thank God that it wasn't a duck, my dear. Half a duck would scarcely be large enough to set my poor mouth watering. For goodness' sake, give me a drop to drink! What is it—water?"

"No, sir, ale; some of our own brewing. But you must please to eat a mouthful first. I have heard that it is bad to begin with a drink."

"Right speedily will I qualify," said the parson, with his mouth full of goose; "delicious—most delicious! You must be the good Samaritan, my dear; or at any rate you ought to be his wife. Your very best health, Mistress Mabel Lovejoy; may you never do a worse action than you have done this day; and I never shall forget your kindness."

"Oh, I am so glad to see you enjoy it. But you must not talk till you have eaten every mouthful. Why, you ought to be quite famishing."

"In that respect I fulfill my duty. Nay more, I am downright famished."

"There is a little stuffing in here, sir; let me show you; underneath the apron. I put it there myself, and so I know."

"What most noble, most glorious, most transcendent stuffing! Whoever made that was born to benefit, retrieve, and exalt humanity."

"You must not say that, sir; because I made it."

"Oh, Dea, certe! I recover my Latin under such enchantment. But how could you have found me out? And what made you so generously think of me?"

"Well, sir, I take the greatest interest in fishermen, because—oh, because of my brother Charlie; and one of our men passed you this afternoon, and he said he was sure that you had caught nothing, because he heard you—he thought he heard you—"

"No, no, come now, complaining mildly—not 'swearing,' don't say 'swearing.'"

"I was not going to say 'swearing,' sir. What made you think of such a thing? I am sure you never could have done it; could you? And so, when you did not even come to supper, it came into my head that you must want refreshment, especially if you had caught no fish to comfort you for so many hours. And then I thought of a plan for that, which I would tell you, in case I should find you unlucky enough to deserve it."

"I am unlucky enough to deserve it thoroughly; only look here, pretty Mistress Mabel." With these words he lifted the flap of his basket, and showed its piteous emptiness.

"West Lorraine!" she cried—"West Lorraine!" for his name and address were painted on the inside wicker of the lid. "Oh, I beg your pardon, Mr. Hales: I had no right to notice it."

"Yes, you had. But you have no right to turn away your head so. What harm has West Lorraine done you, that you won't even look at its rector?"

"Oh, please not; oh, please don't! I never would have come if I could have only dreamed—"

"If you could have dreamed what? Pretty Mistress Mabel, a parson has a right to an explanation, when he makes a young lady blush so."

"Oh, it was so cruel of you! You said you were a clerk, of the name of 'Halls!'"

"So I am, a clerk in holy orders; but not of the name of 'Halls.' That was your father's mistake. I gave my true name; and here you see me very much at your service, ma'am. The uncle of a fine young fellow, whose name you never heard, I dare say. Have you ever happened to hear of a youth called Hilary Lorraine?"

"Oh, now I know why you are come! oh dear! It was not for the fishing, after all! And perhaps you never fished before. And every thing must be going wrong. And you are come to tell me what they think of me. And very likely you would be glad if you could put me in prison!"

"That would be nice gratitude—would it not? You are wrong in almost every point. It happens that I have fished before, and that I did come for the fishing partly. It happens that nothing is going wrong; and I am not come to say what they think of you, but to see what I think of you—which is a very different thing."

"And what do you think of me?" asked Mabel, casting down her eyes, standing saucily, and yet with such a demure expression, that his first impulse was to kiss her.

"I think that you are rogue enough to turn the head of any body. And I think that you are good enough to make him happy ever afterward."

"I am not at all sure of that," she answered, raising her sweet eyes, and openly blushing; "I only know that I would try. But every one is not like a clergyman, to understand good stuffing. But if I had only known who you were, I would never have brought you any dinner, sir."

"What a disloyal thing to say! Please to tell me why I ought to starve for being Hilary's uncle."

"Because you would think that I wanted to coax you to—to be on my side, at least."

"To make a goose of me, with your goose! Well, you have me at your mercy, Mabel. I shall congratulate Hilary on having won the heart of the loveliest, best, and cleverest girl in the county of Kent."

"Oh no, sir, you must not say that, because I am nothing of the sort, and you must not laugh at me like that. And how do you know that he has done it? And what will every one say, when they hear that he—that he would like to marry the daughter of a grower?"

"What does his father say? That is the point. It matters very little what others say. And I will not conceal from you, pretty Mabel, that his father is bitterly set against it, and turned him out-of-doors when he heard of it."

"Oh, that is why he has never written. He did not know how to break it to me. I was sure there was something bad. But of course I could expect nothing else. Poor, poor sillies, both of us! I must give him up, I see I must. I felt all along that I should have to do it."

"Don't cry so; don't cry, my dear, like that. There is plenty of time to talk of it. Things will come right in the end, no doubt. But what does your father say to it?"

"I scarcely know whether he knows it yet. Hilary wanted to tell him; but I persuaded him to leave it altogether to me. And so I told my mother first; and she thought we had better not disturb my father about it until we heard from Hilary. But I am almost sure sometimes that he knows it, and is not at all pleased about it, for he looks at me very strangely. He is the best and the kindest man living almost; but he has very odd ways sometimes, and it is most difficult to turn him."

"So it is with most men who are worth their salt. I despise a weather-cock. Would you like me to come in and see him; or shall I fish a little more first? I am quite a new man since you fed me so well; and I scarcely can put up with this disgrace."

"If you would like to fish a little longer," said Mabel, following the loving gaze, which (with true angling obstinacy) lingered still on the coy, fair stream; "there is plenty of time to spare. My father rode off to Maidstone as soon as he found that you were not coming in to supper; and he will not be back till it is quite dark. And I should have time for a talk with my mother while you are attempting to catch a trout."

"Now, Mabel, Mabel, you are too disdainful. Because I am not my own nephew (who learned what little he knows altogether from me), and because I have been so unsuccessful, you think that I know nothing; women always judge by the event, having taken the trick from their fathers, perhaps. But you were going to tell me something to make up for my want of skill."

"Yes; but you must promise not to tell any one else, upon any account. My brother Charlie found it out; and I have not told even Hilary of it, because he could catch fish without it."

"You most insulting of all pretty maidens, if you despise my science thus, I will tell Sir Roland that you are vain and haughty."

"Oh dear!"

"Very ill-tempered."

"No, now, you never could say that."

"Clumsy, ill-dressed, and slatternly."

"Well done, well done, Mr. Hales!"

"Yes, and very ugly."

"Oh!"

"Aha! I have taken your breath away with absolute amazement. I wish Hilary could see you now; he'd steal something very delightful, and then knock his excellent uncle down. But now, make it up, like a dear good girl; and tell me this great secret."

"It is the simplest thing in the world. You just take a little bit of this—see here, I have some in my basket; and cut a little delicate strip, and whip it on the lower part of your fly. I have done it for Charlie many a time. I will do one for you, if you like, sir."

"Very well. I will try it, to please you; and for the sake of an experiment. Good-bye, good-bye till dark, my dear. We shall see whether a clerk can catch fish or no."

When Mr. Hales returned at night to the hospitable old farm-house, he carried on his ample back between two and three dozen goodly trout; for many of which he confessed himself indebted to Mabel's clever fingers. Mrs. Lovejoy had been prepared by her daughter to receive him; but the grower was not yet come home from Maidstone; which, on the whole, was a fortunate thing. For thus the rector had time enough to settle with his hostess what should be done on his part and on hers toward the removal, or at any rate the gradual reduction, of the many stumbling-blocks that lay, as usual, upon true-love's course. For both foresaw that if the franklin's pride should once be wounded, he would be certain to bar the way more sternly than even the baronet himself. And even without that, he could hardly be expected to forego all in a moment his favorite scheme above described, that Mabel's husband should carry on the ancestral farm, and the growth of fruit. In his blunt old fashion, he cared very little for baronets, or for Norman blood; and, like a son of Tuscan soil, was well content to lead his life in cleaving paternal fields with the hoe, and nourishing household gods and hearth.

CHAPTER XXIX.

It is a fine thing to have quarters in an English country town, where nobody knows who the sojourner is, and nobody cares who he may be; to begin (at gentle leisure) to feel interest in the place, and quicken up to the vein of humor throbbing through the High Street. The third evening can not go over one's head without a general sense being gained of the politics of the town, and, far more important—the politicians; and if there only is a corporation, wisdom cries in the streets, and nobody can get on with any body. However, when the fights are over, generally speaking, all cool down.

But this is about the last thing that a stranger should exert his intellect to understand. It would be pure waste of time; unless he means to buy a house and settle down, and try to be an alderman in two years' time, and mount ambition's ladder even to the giddy height of mayoralty; till the hand of death comes between the rungs and vertically drags him downward. And even then, for three months shall he be "our deeply lamented townsman."

But if this visitor firmly declines (as, for his health, he is bound to do) these mighty combats, which always have the eyes of the nation fixed on them—if he is satisfied to lounge about, and say "good-morning" here and there, to ascertain public sentiment concerning the state of the weather, and to lay out sixpence judiciously in cultivating good society—then speedily will he get draughts of knowledge enough to quench the most ardent thirst; while the yawn of indolence merges in the quickening smile of interest. Then shall he get an insight into the commerce, fashion, religious feeling, jealousies, and literature of the town, its just and pleasant self-esteem, its tolerance and intolerance (often equally inexplicable), its quiet enjoyments, and, best of all, its elegant flirtations.

These things enabled Mr. Hales to pass an agreeable week at Tonbridge, and to form acquaintance with some of its leading inhabitants; which in pursuit of his object he was resolved, as far as he could, to do. And from all of these he obtained very excellent tidings of the Lovejoys, as being a quiet, well-conducted, and highly respectable family, admitted (whenever they cared to be so) to the best society of the neighborhood, and forgiven for growing cherries, and even for keeping a three-horsed van.

Also, as regarded his own impressions, the more he saw of Old Applewood farm, the more he was pleased with it and with its owners; and calling upon his brother parson, the incumbent of the parish, he found in him a congenial soul, who wanted to get a service out of him. For this Mr. Hales was too wide awake, having taken good care to leave sermons at home, because he had been long enough in holy orders to know what delight all parsons find in spoiling one another's holidays. Moreover, he had promised himself the pleasure of sitting in a pew, for once, repossessing the right to yawn *ad libitum*, and even fall into a murmurous nap, after exhausting the sweetness of the well-known Lucretian sentiment—to gaze in safety at another's labors; or, as the navvy more tersely put it, when asked of his *summum bonum*, to "look on at t'other beggars."

Meanwhile, however, many little things were beginning to go crosswise. For instance, Hilary walked down headlong, being exceedingly short of cash, to comfort Mabel, and to get good quarters, and perhaps to go on about every thing. Luckily, his uncle Struan met him in the street of Sevenoaks (whither he had ridden for a little change), and amazed him with very strong language, and begged him not to make a confounded fool of himself, and so took him into a hostelry. The young man, of course, was astonished to see his uncle carrying on so, dressed as a layman, and roving about without any wife or family.

But when he knew for whose sake it was done, and how strongly his uncle was siding with him, his gratitude and good emotions were such that he scarcely could finish his quart of beer.

"My boy, I am thoroughly ashamed of you," said his uncle, looking queerly at him. "You are most immature for married life, if you give way to your feelings so."

"But, uncle, when a man is down so much, and turned out-of-doors by his own father—"

"When a 'man!' When a 'boy' is what you mean, I suppose. A man would take it differently."

"I am sure I take it very well," said Hilary, trying to smile at it. "There, I will drink up my beer; for I know that sort of thing always vexes you. Now, can you say that I have kicked up a row, or done any thing that I might have done?"

"No, my boy, no; quite the opposite thing; you have taken it most angelically."

"Angelically, without an angelus, uncle, or even a stiver in my pocket! Only the cherub aloft, you know—"

"I don't know any thing about him; and the allusion, to my mind, is profane."

"Now, uncle, you are hyperclerical, because I have caught you dressed as a bagman!"

"I don't understand your big Oxford words. In my days they taught theology."

"And hunting; come now, Uncle Struan, didn't they teach you hunting?"

"Well," said the rector, stroking his chin; "I was a poor young man, of course, and could not afford that sort of thing."

"Yes, but you did, you know, Uncle Struan; I have heard you boast of it fifty times."

"What a plague you are, Hilary! There may have been times—however, you are going on quite as if we were sitting and having a cozy talk after dinner at West Lorraine."

"I wish to goodness we were, my dear uncle. I never shall see such a dinner again."

"My dear boy, my dear boy, to talk like that at your time of life! What a thing love is, to be sure! However, in that state, a dinner is no matter."

"Well, I shall be off now for London again. A bit of bread-and-cheese, after all, is as good as any thing. Good-bye, my dear uncle, I shall always thank you."

"You shall thank me for two things before you start. And you should not start, except that I know it to be at present best for you. You shall thank me for as good a dinner as can be got in a place like this; and after that for five good guineas, just to go on for a bit with."

Thus the rector had his way, and fed his nephew beautifully, and sent him back with a better heart in his breast, to meet the future. Hilary of course was much aggrieved, and inclined to be outrageous, at having walked four-and-twenty miles, with eager proceeding at every step, and then being balked of a sight of his love. However, he saw that it was for the best; and five guineas (feel as you will) is something.

His good uncle paid his fare back by the stage, and saw him go off, and kissed hands to him, feeling greatly relieved as soon as ever he was round the corner; for he must have spoiled every thing at the farm. Therefore this excellent uncle returned to the snug little sanded parlor, to smoke a fresh pipe; and to think, in its influence, how to get on with these new affairs.

Here were heaps of trouble rising; as peaks of volcanoes come out of the sea. And who was to know how to manage things so as to make them all subside again? Hilary might seem easy to deal with, so long as he had no money; but even he was apt to take strange whims into his head, although he might feel that he could not pay for them. And then there was the grower, an obstinate factor in any calculation; and the grower's wife, who might appeal, perhaps, to the attorney-general; also Sir Roland, with his dry, unaccountable manner of regarding things; and last, not least, the rector's own superior part of his household. If he could not manage them, any body at first sight would say that the fault must be altogether his own—that a man who can not lay down the law to his own wife and daughters, really is no man, and deserves to be treated accordingly. Yet this depends upon special gifts. The rector could carry on very well, when he understood the subject, even with his wife and daughters, till it came to crying. Still, in the end (as he knew in his heart), he always got the worst of it.

Now what would all these ladies say if the incumbent of the parish, the rector of the rectory, the very husband or father of all of themselves—as the case might be—were to depart from his sense of right, and the principles he had laid down to them, to such an extent as to cherish Hilary in black rebellion against his own father? Suasion would be lost among them. It is a thing that may be tried, under favorable circumstances, as against one lady, when quite alone; but with four ladies all taking different views of the matter in question, yet ready in a moment to combine against any form of reason, a bachelor must be Quixotic, a husband and father idiotic, if he relies upon any other motive power than that of his legs. But the rector was not the man to run away, even from his own family. So, on the whole, he resolved to let things follow their own course until something new should begin to rise. Except at least upon two little points—one that Hilary should be kept from visiting the farm just now; and the other, that the grower must be told of all this love-affair.

Mr. Hales, as an owner of daughters, felt that it was no more than a father's due to know what his favorite child was about in such important matters; and he thought it the surest way to set him bitterly against any moderation, if he were left to find out by surprise what was going on at his own hearth. It happened, however, that the grower had a shrewd suspicion of the whole of it, and was laughing in his sleeve, and winking (in his own determined way) at his good wife's manœuvres. "I shall stop it all when I please," he said to himself every night at bed-time; "let them have their little game, and make up their minds to astonish me." For he, like almost every man who has attained the age of sixty, looked back upon love as a brief excrescence, of about the same character as a wart.

"Ay, ay, no need to tell me," he answered, when Mrs. Lovejoy, under the parson's advice, and at Mabel's entreaty, broke the matter to him. I don't go about with my eyes shut, wife. A man that knows every pear that grows can tell the color on a maiden's cheek. I have settled to send her away tomorrow to her Uncle Clitherow. The old mare will be ready at ten o'clock. I meant to leave you to guess the reason; you are so clever all of you. Ha, ha! you thought the old grower was as blind as a bat; now, didn't you?"

"Well, at any rate," replied Mrs. Lovejoy, giving her pillow an angry thump, "I think you might have consulted me, Martin; with half her clothes in the wash-tub, and a frayed ribbon on her Sunday hat! Men are so hot and inconsiderate. All to be done in a moment, of course! The least you could have done, I am sure, would have been to tell me beforehand, Martin, and not to pack her off like that."

"To be sure! Just as you told me, good wife, your plan for packing her off for good! Now just go to sleep, and don't beat about so. When I say a thing I do it."

CHAPTER XXX.

When the flaunting and the flouting of the summer-prime are over; when the leaves of tree, and bush, and even of unconsidered weeds, hang on their stalks, instead of standing upright, as they used to do; and very often a convex surface, by the cares of life, is worn into a small concavity, a gradual change, to a like effect, may be expected in the human mind.

A man remembers that his own autumn is once more coming over him; that the light is surely waning, and the darkness gathering in; that more of his plans are shed and scattered, as the sun "draws water" among the clouds, or as the gossamer floats idly over the sear and seeded grass. Therefore it is high time to work, to strengthen the threads of the wavering plan, to tighten the mesh of the woven web, to cast about here and there for completion, if the design shall be ever complete.

So now, as the summer passed, a certain gentleman, of more repute, perhaps, than reputation, began to be anxious about his plans.

Sir Remnant Chapman owned large estates adjoining the dwindled but still fair acreage of the Lorraines in the weald of Sussex. Much as he differed from Sir Roland in tastes and habits and character, he announced himself, wherever he went, as his most intimate friend and ally. And certainly he was received more freely than any other neighbor at Coombe Lorraine, and knew all the doings and ways of the family, and was even consulted now and then. Warm friendship, however, can scarcely thrive without mutual respect; and though Sir Remnant could never escape from a certain unwilling respect for Sir Roland, the latter never could contrive to reciprocate the feeling.

Because he knew that Sir Remnant was a gentleman of a type already even then departing, although to be found, at the present day, in certain parts of England. A man of fixed opinions, and even what might be accounted principles (at any rate by himself) concerning honor, and birth, and betting, and patriotism, and some other matters, included in a very small et cetera. It is hard to despise a man who has so many points settled in his system; but it is harder to respect him when he sees all things with one little eye, and that eye a vicious one. Sir Remnant Chapman had no belief in the goodness of woman, or the truth of man—in the beautiful balance of nature, or even the fatherly kindness that comforts us. Therefore nobody could love him, and very few people paid much attention to his dull hatred of mankind. "Contempt," he always called it; but he had not power to make it that; neither had he any depth of root, to throw up eminence. A "bitter weed" many people called him; and yet he was not altogether that. For he liked to act against his nature, perhaps from its own perversity; and often did kind things, to spite his own spitefulness by doing them. As for sense of right and wrong, he had none outside of his own wishes; and he always expected the rest of the world to move on the same low system. How could such a man get on, even for an hour, with one so different—and more than that, so opposite to him—as the good Sir Roland? Mr. Hales, who was not (as we know) at all a tight-laced man himself, and may perhaps have been a little jealous of Sir Remnant, put that question to himself, as well as to his wife and family; and echo only answered "How?" However, soever, there was the fact; and how many facts can we call to mind ever so much stranger?

Sir Remnant's only son, Stephen Chapman, was now about thirty years of age, and every body said that it was time for him to change his mode of life. Even his father admitted that he had made an unreasonably long job of "sowing his wild oats," and now must take to some better culture. And nothing seemed more likely to lead to this desired result than a speedy engagement to an accomplished, sensible, and attractive girl. Therefore, after a long review and discussion of all the young ladies round, it had been settled that the heir of all the Chapmans should lay close siege to young Alice Lorraine.

"Captain Chapman"—as Stephen was called by courtesy in that neighborhood, having held a commission in a fashionable regiment until it was ordered to the war—this man was better than his father in some ways, and much worse in others. He was better, from weakness; not having the strength to work out works of iniquity; and also from having some touches of kindness, whereof his father was intact. He was worse, because he had no sense of honor, no rudiment of a principle; not even a dubious preference for the truth, at first sight, against a lie. Captain Chapman, however, could do one manly thing, and only one. He could drive, having cultivated the art in the time when it meant something. Horses were broken then, not trained—as nowadays they must be—and skill and nerve were needed for the management of a four-in-hand. Captain Chapman was the first in those parts to drive like Ericthonius, and it took him a very long time to get his father to sit behind him; for the roads were still very bad and perilous, and better suited for postilions than for Stephen Chapman's team.

He durst not drive up Coombe Lorraine, or at any rate he feared the descent as yet, though he meant some day to venture it. And now that he was come upon his wooing, he left his gaudy equipage at the foot of the hill, to be sent back to Steyning and come for him at an appointed time. Then he and his father, with mutual grumblings, took to the steep ascent on foot.

Sir Roland had asked them, a few days ago, to drive over and dine with him, either on Thursday, or any other day that might suit them. They came on the Thursday, with their minds made up to be satisfied with any thing. But they certainly were not very well pleased to find that the fair Mistress Alice had managed to give them the slip entirely. She was always ready to meet Sir Remnant, and discharge the duties of an hostess to him; but from some deep instinctive aversion she could not even bear to sit at table with the captain. She knew not at all what his character was; neither did Sir Roland know a tenth part of his ill repute; otherwise he had never allowed him to approach the maiden. He simply looked upon Captain Chapman as a fashionable man of the day, who might have been a little wild perhaps, but now meant to settle down in the country and attend to his father's large estates.

However, neither of the guests suspected that their visit had fixed the date of another little visit pending long at Horsham; and one girl being as good as another to men of the world of that stamp, they were well content, when the haunch went out, to clink a glass with the rector's daughters, instead of receiving a distant bow from a diffident and very shy young lady.

"Now, Lorraine," began Sir Remnant, after the ladies had left the room, and the captain was gone out to look at something, according to arrangement, and had taken the rector with him, "we have known one another a good many years; and I want a little sensible talk with you."

"Sir Remnant, I hope that our talk is always sensible; so far at least as can be expected on my part."

"There you are again, Lorraine, using some back meaning, such as no one else can enter into. But let that pass. It is your way. Now I want to say something to you."

"I also am smitten with a strong desire to know what it is, Sir Remnant."

"Well, it is neither more nor less than this. You know what dangerous times we live in, with every evil power let loose, and Satan, like a roaring lion, rampant and triumphant. Thank you, yes, I will take a pinch; your snuff is always so delicious. With the arch-enemy prowling about, with democracy, non-conformity, infidelity, and rickburnings—"

"Exactly so. How well you express it! I was greatly struck with it in the *George and Dragon's* report of your speech at the farmer's dinner at Billinghurst."

"Well, well, I may have said it before; but for all that, it is the truth. Can you deny it, Sir Roland Lorraine?"

"Far be it from me to deny the truth. I am listening with the greatest interest."

"No, you are not; you never do. You are always thinking of something to yourself. But what I was going to say was this, that it is high time to cement the union, and draw close the bonds of amity between all good men, all men of any principle—by which I mean—come now, you know."

"To be sure; you mean all stanch Tories."

"Yes, yes; all who hold by Church and State, land and the constitution. I have educated my son carefully in the only right and true principles. Train up a child—you know what I mean. And you, of course, have brought up your daughter upon the same right system."

"Nay, rather, I have left her to form her own political opinions. And to the best of my belief, she has formed none."

"Lorraine, I am heartily glad to hear it. That is how all the girls should be. When I was in London, they turned me sick with asking my opinion. The less they know, the better for them. Knowledge of any thing makes a woman so deucedly contradictory. My poor dear wife could read and write, and that was quite enough for her. She did it on the jam-pots always, and she could spell most of it. Ah, she was a most wonderful woman!"

"She was. I often found much pleasure in her conversation. She knew so many things that never come by way of reading."

"And so does Stephen. You should hear him. He never reads any sort of book. Ah, that is the true learning. Books always make stupid people. Now it struck me that —ah, you know, I see. A wink's as good as a nod, etc. No catching a weasel asleep." Here Sir Remnant screwed up one eye, and gave Sir Roland a poke in the ribs, with the most waggish air imaginable.

"Again and again I assure you," said his host, "that I have not the smallest idea what you mean. Your theory about books has in me the most thorough comfirmation."

"Aha! it is all very well—all very well to pretend, Lorraine. Another pinch of snuff, and that settles it. Let them set up their horses together as soon as ever they please—eh?"

"Who? What horses? Why will you thus visit me with impenetrable enigmas?"

"Visit you! Why, you invited me yourself! Who, indeed? Why, of course, my lad Steenie and your girl Lallie!"

"Captain Chapman and my Alice! Such a thought never entered my mind. Do you know that poor Alice is little more than seventeen years old? And Captain Chapman must be—let me see—"

"Never mind what he is. He is my son and heir, and there'll be fifty thousand to settle on his wife, in hard cash—not so bad nowadays."

"Sir Remnant Chapman, I beg you not to say another word on the subject. Your son must be twice my daughter's age, and he looks even more than that—"

"Dash my wig! Then I am seventy, I suppose. What the dickens have his looks got to do with the matter? I don't call him at all a bad-looking fellow. A chip of the old block, that's what he is. Ah, many a fine woman, I can tell you—"

"Now, if you please," Sir Roland said, with a very clear and determined voice—"if you please, we will drop this subject. Your son may be a very good match, and no doubt he is in external matters; and if Alice, when old enough, should become attached to him, perhaps I might not oppose it. There is nothing more to be said at present; and, above all things, she must not hear of it."

"I see, I see," answered the other baronet, who was rather short of temper. "Missy must be kept to her bread and milk, and good books, and all that, a little longer. By-the-bye, Lorraine, what was it I heard about your son the other day—that he had been making a fool of himself with some grocer's daughter?"

"I have not heard of any grocer's daughter. And as he will shortly leave England, people perhaps will have less to say about him. His commission is promised, as perhaps you know; and he is not likely to quit the army because there is fighting going on."

Sir Remnant felt all the sting of that hit; his face (which showed many signs of good living) flushed to the tint of the claret in his hand, and he was just about to make a very coarse reply, when luckily the rector came back suddenly, followed by the valiant captain. Sir Roland knew that he had allowed himself to be goaded into bad manners for once, and he strove to make up for it by unwonted attention to the warrior.

CHAPTER XXXI.

It was true that Hilary had attained at last the great ambition of his life. He had changed the pen for the sword, the sand for powder, and the ink for blood; and in a few days he would be afloat, on his way to join Lord Wellington. His father's obstinate objections had at last been overcome; for there seemed to be no other way to cut the soft net of enchantment, and throw him into a sterner world.

His uncle Struan had done his best, and tried to the utmost stretch the patience of Sir Roland, with countless words, until the latter exclaimed at last, "Why you seem to to be worse than the boy himself! You went to spy out the nakedness of the land, and you returned in a fortnight with grapes of Eshcol. Truly this Danish Lovejoy is more potent than the great Canute. He turns at his pleasure the tide of opinion."

"Roland, now you go too far. It is not the grower that I indict of, but his charming daughter. If you could but once be persuaded to see her—"

"Of course. Exactly what Hilary said. In him I could laugh at it; but in you—! Well, a great philosopher tells us that every jot of opinion (even that of a babe, I suppose) is to be regarded as an equal item of the 'universal consensus.' And the universal consensus becomes, or forms, or fructifies, or solidifies, into the great homogeneous truth. I may not quote him aright, and I beg his pardon for so lamely rendering him. However, that is a rude sketch of his view, a brick from his house—to mix metaphors—and perhaps you remember it better, Struan."

"God forbid! The only thing I remember out of all my education is the stories—what do you call them?—mythologies. Capital some of them are, capital! Ah, they do so much good to boys—teach them manliness and self-respect!"

"Do they? However, to return to this lovely daughter of the Kentish Alcinous—by-the-way, if his ancestors were Danes who took to gardening, it suggests a rather startling analogy. The old Corycian is believed (though without a particle of evidence) to have been a pirate in early life, and therefore to have taken to pot-herbs. Let that pass. I could never have believed it, except for this instance of Lovejoy."

"And how, if you please," broke in the rector, who was always jealous of "Norman blood," because he had never heard that he had any; "how were the Normans less piratical, if you please, than the Danes, their own grandfathers? Except that they were sick at sea—big rogues, all of them, in my opinion. The Saxons were the only honest fellows. Ay, and they would have thrashed those Normans, but for the leastest little accident. When I hear of those Normans, without any shoulders—don't tell me; they never would have built such a house as this is, otherwise—what do you think I feel ready to do, sir? Why, to get up, and to lift my coat, and—"

"Come, come, Struan, we quite understand all your emotions without that. This makes you a very bigoted ambassador in our case. You meant to bring back all the truth, of course. But when you found the fishing good, and the people roughly hospitable, and above all a Danish smack in their manners, and figures, and even their eyes, which have turned on the Kentish soil, I am told, to a deep and very brilliant brown—"

"Yes, Roland, you are right for once. At any rate, it is so with her."

"Very well. Then you being, as you always are, a sudden man—what did you do but fall in love (in an elderly, fatherly manner, of course) with this—what is her name, now again? I never can recollect it."

"You do. You never forget any thing. Her name is 'Mabel.' And you may be glad to pronounce it pretty often, in your old age, Sir Roland."

"Well it is a pretty name, and deserves a pretty bearer. But, Struan, you are a man of the world. You know what Hilary is; and you know (though we do not give ourselves airs, and drive four horses in a hideous yellow coach, and wear diamond rings worth a thousand pounds), you know what the Lorraines have always been—a little particular in their ways, and a little inclined to, to, perhaps—"

"To look down on the rest of the world, without ever letting them know it, or even knowing it yourselves, perhaps. Have I hit it aright, Sir Roland?"

"Not quite that. Indeed, nothing could be farther from what I was thinking of." Sir Roland Lorraine sighed gently here; and even his brother-in-law had not the least idea why he did so. It was that Sir Roland, like all the more able Lorraines for several centuries, was at heart a fatalist. And this family taint had perhaps been deepened by the infusion of Eastern blood. This was the bar so often fixed between them and the rest of the world—a barrier which must hold good, while every man cares for his neighbor's soul so much more than his own forever.

"Is it any thing in religion, Roland?" the rector whispered kindly. "I know that you are not orthodox, and a good deal puffed up with carnal knowledge. Still, if it is in my line at all; I am not a very high authority—but perhaps I might lift you over it. They are saying all sorts of things now in the world; and I have taken two hours a day, several days—now you need not laugh—in a library we have got up at Horsham, filled with the best divinity, so as to know how to answer them."

"My dear Struan," Sir Roland replied, without so much as the gleam of a smile, "that was really good of you. And you now have so many other things to attend to with young dogs, and that; and the first of September next week, I believe! What a relief that must be to you!"

"Ay, that it is. You can not imagine, of course, with all your many ways of frittering time away indoors, what a wearing thing it is to have nothing better than rabbit-shooting, or teaching a dog to drop to shot. But now about Hilary: you must relent—indeed you must, dear Roland. He is living on sixpence a day, I believe—virtuous fellow, most rare young man! Why, if that dirty Steve Chapman now had been treated as you have served Hilary—note of hand, bill-drawing, post-obits—and you might even think yourself lucky if there were no big forgery to hush up. Ah, his father may think what he likes; but I look on Hilary as a perfect wonder, a Bayard, a Crichton, a pelican!"

"Surely you mean a paragon, Struan? What young can he have to feed from his own breast?"

"I meant what I said, as I always do. And how can you know what young he has, when you never even let him come near you? Ah, if I only had such a son!" Here the rector, who really did complain that he had no son to teach how to shoot, managed to get his eyes a little touched with genial moisture.

"This is grievous," Sir Roland answered; "and a little more than I ever expected, or can have enabled myself to deserve. Now, Struan, will you cease from wailing if I promise one thing?"

"That must depend upon what it is. It will take a good many things, I am afraid, to make me think well of you again."

"To hear such a thing from the head of the parish! Now, Struan, be not vindictive. I ought to have let you get a good day's shooting, and then your terms would have been easier."

"Well, Roland, you know that we can do nothing. The estates are tied up in such a wonderful way, by some lawyer's trick or other, through a whim of that blessed old lady—she can't hear me, can she?—that Hilary has his own sister's life between him and the inheritance, so far as any of us can make out."

"So that you need not have boasted," answered Sir Roland, with a quiet smile, "about his being a Bayard, in refraining from post-obits."

"Well, well; you know what I meant quite well. The Jews are not yet banished from England. And there is reason to fear that they never will be. There are plenty of them to discount his chance; if he did what many other boys would do."

Sir Roland felt the truth of this. And he feared in his heart that he might be pushing his only son a little too hard, in reliance upon his honor.

"Will you come to the point for once?" he asked, with a look of despair, and a voice of the same. "This is my offer—to get Hilary a commission in a foot-regiment, pack him off to the war in Spain; and if in three years after that he sticks to that Danish Nausicaa, and I am alive—why, then, he shall have her."

Mr. Hales threw back his head—for he had a large, deep head, and when it wanted to think it would go back—and then he answered warily.

"It is a very poor offer, Sir Roland. At first sight it seems fair enough. But you, with your knowledge of youth, and especially such a youth as Hilary, rely upon the effects of absence, change, adventures, dangers, Spanish beauties, and, worst of all, wider knowledge of the world, and the company of fighting men, to make him jilt his love, or perhaps take even a worse course than that."

"You are wrong," said Sir Roland, with much contempt. "Sir Remnant Chapman might so have meant it. Struan, you ought to know me better. But I think that I have a right, at least, to try the substance of such a whim before I yield to it, and install, as the future mistress, a—well, what do you want me to call her, Struan?"

"Let it be, Roland; let it be. I am a fair man, if you are not; and I can make every allowance for you. But I think that your heir should at least be entitled to swing his legs over a horse, Sir Roland."

"I, on the other hand, think that it would be his final ruin to do so. He would get among reckless fellows, to whom he is already too much akin. It has happened so with several of my truly respected ancestors. They have gone into cavalry regiments, and ridden full gallop through their estates. I am not a penurious man, as you know, and few think less of money. Can you deny that, even in your vitiated state of mind?"

"I can not deny it," the rector answered; "you never think twice about money, Roland—except, of course, when you are bound to do so."

"Very well; then you can believe that I wish poor Hilary to start afoot solely for his own benefit. There is very hard fighting just now in Spain, or on the confines of Portugal. I hate all fighting, as you are aware. Still it is a thing that must be done."

"Good Lord!" cried the rector, "how you do talk! As if it was so many partridges!"

"No, it is better than that—come, Struan

—because the partridges carry no guns, you know."

"I should be confoundedly sorry if they did," the rector answered, with a shudder. "Fancy letting fly at a bird who might have a long barrel under his tail!"

"It is an appalling imagination. Struan, I give you credit for it. But here we are, as usual, wandering from the matter which we have in hand. Are you content, or are you not, with what I propose about Hilary?"

In this expressly alternative form, there lurks a great deal of vigor. If a man says, "Are you satisfied?" you begin to cast about, and wonder whether you might not win better terms. Many side-issues come in and disturb you, and your way to say "Yes" is dubious. But if he only clench his inquiry with the option of the strong negative, the weakest of all things, human nature that hates to say "no," is tampered with. This being so, Uncle Struan thought for a moment or so; and then said, "Yes, I am."

CHAPTER XXXII.

Is it just, or even honest—fair, of course, it can not be—to deal so much with the heavy people, the eldermost ones and the bittermost, and leave altogether with nothing said of her—or not even let her have her own say—as sweet a young maiden as ever lived, and as true, and brave, and kind a one? Alice was of a different class altogether from Mabel Lovejoy. Mabel was a dear-hearted girl, loving, pure, unselfish, warm, and good enough to marry any man, and be his own wife forever.

But Alice went far beyond all that. Her nature was cast in a different mould. She had not only the depth—which is the common property of women—but she also had the height of loving. Such as a mother has for her children, rather than a wife toward her husband. And yet by no means an imperious or exacting affection, but tender, submissive, and delicate. Inasmuch as her brother stood next to her father, or in some points quite on a level with him, in her true regard and love, it was not possible that her kind heart could escape many pangs of late. In the first place, no loving sister is likely to be altogether elated by the discovery that her only brother has found some one who shall be henceforth more to him than herself is. Alice, moreover, had a very strong sense of the rank and dignity of the Lorraines; and she disliked, even more than her father did, the importation of this "vegetable product," as she rather facetiously called poor Mabel, into their castle of lineage. But now when Hilary was going away, to be drowned on the voyage, perhaps, or at least to be shot, or sabred, or ridden over by those who had horses—while he had none—or, even if he escaped all that, to be starved, or frozen, or sun-struck, for the sake of his country—as our best men are, while their children survive to starve afterward—it came upon Alice as a heavy blow that she never might happen to see him again. Although her father had tried to keep her from the excitement of the times, and the gasp of the public for dreadful news (a gasp which is deeper and wider always, the longer the time of waiting is), still there were too many mouths of rumor for any one to stop them all. Although the old butler turned his cuffs up—to show what an arm he still possessed—and grumbled that all this was nothing, and a bladder of wind in comparison with what he had known forty years agone, and though Mrs. Pipkins, the housekeeper, quite agreed with him and went farther; neither was the cook at all disposed to overdo the thing; it was of no service—they could not stay the torrent of public opinion.

Trotman had been taken on, rashly (as may have been said before), as upper footman in lieu of the old-established and trusty gentleman, who had been compelled by fierce injustice to retire, and take to a public-house—with a hundred pounds to begin upon—being reft of the office of footman for no other reason that he could hear of, except that he was apt to be, toward night-fall, not quite able to "keep his feet."

To him succeeded the headlong Trotman; and one of the very first things he did was —as declared a long time ago, with deep sympathy, in this unvarnished tale—to kick poor Bonny, like a hopping spider, from the brow of the hill to the base thereof.

Trotman may have had good motives for this rather forcible movement; and it is not our place to condemn him. Still, in more than one quarter it was believed that he acted thus through no zeal whatever for virtue or justice, but only because he so loved his perquisites, and suspected that Bonny got smell of them. And the butler quite confirmed this view, and was much surprised at Trotman's conduct; for Bonny was accustomed to laugh at his jokes, and had even sold some of his bottles for him.

In such a crisis, scarcely any one would regard such a trivial matter. And yet none of us ought to kick any body, without knowing what it may lead to. Violence is to be deprecated; for it has to be paid for beyond its value in twelve cases out of every dozen. And so it was now; for, if Coombe Lorraine had been before this, as Mrs. Pipkins declared (having learned French from her cookery-book), "the most Triestest place in the world," it became even duller now that Bonny was induced, by personal considerations, to terminate rather abruptly his overtures to the kitchen-maid. For who brought the tidings of all great events and royal proceedings? Our Bonny. Who knew the young man of every house-maid in the vales of both Adur and Arun? Our Bonny. Who could be trusted to carry a scroll (or, in purer truth, perhaps, a scrawl) that should be treasured through the love-lorn hours of waiting—at table—in a zebra waistcoat? Solely and emphatically, Bonny!

Therefore every tender domestic bosom rejoiced when the heartless Trotman was compelled to tread the track of his violence, lamely and painfully, twice every week, to fetch from Steyning his *George and the Dragon*, which used to be delivered by Bonny. Mr. Trotman, however, was a generous man, and always ready to share as well as enjoy the delights of literature. Nothing pleased him better than to sit on the end of a table among the household, ladies and gentlemen, with Mrs. Pipkins in the chair of honor, and interpret from his beloved journal the chronicles of the county, the country, and the Continent.

"Why, ho!" he shouted out one day, "what's this? Can I believe my heyes? Our Halary going to the wars next week!"

"No, now!" "Never can be!" "Most shameful!" some of his audience exclaimed. But Mrs. Pipkins and the old butler shook their heads at one another, as much as to say, "I knowed it."

"Mr. Trotman," said the senior house-maid, who entertained connubial views, "you are sure to be right in all you reads. You are such a bootiful scholard! Will you obleege us by reading it out?"

"Hem! hem! Ladies all, it is yours to command, it is mine to obey. 'The insatiable despot who sways the Continent seems resolved to sacrifice to his baleful lust of empire all the best and purest and noblest of the blood of Britain. It was only last week that we had to mourn the loss sustained by all Sussex in the most promising cion of a noble house. And now we have it on the best authority that Mr. H. L., the only son of the well-known and widely respected baronet residing not fifty miles from Steyning, has received orders to join his regiment at the seat of war, under Lord Wellington. The gallant young gentleman sails next week from Portsmouth in the troopship *Sandy-legs*, or some such blessed Indian name!"

"The old scrimp!" exclaimed the cook, a warm adherent of Hilary's. "To send him out in a nasty sandy ship, when his birth were to go on horseback, the same as all the gentlefolks do to the wars!"

"But, Mrs. Merryjack, you forget," explained the accomplished Trotman, "that Great Britain is a hisland, ma'am. And no one can't ride from a hisland on horseback; at least it was so when I was a boy."

"Then it must be so now, John Trotman; for what but a boy are you now, I should like to know? And a bad-mannered boy, in my humble opinion, to want to teach his helders their duty. I know that I lives in a hisland, of course, the same as all the Scotchmen does, and goes round the sun like a joint on a spit; and so does nearly all of us. But perhaps John Trotman doesn't."

With this "withering sarcasm," the lady-cook turned away from poor Trotman, and then delivered these memorable words:

"Sir Rowland will repent too late. Sir Rowland will shed the briny tear, the same as might any one of us, even on £3 a year, for sending his only son out in a ship, when he ought to a' sent 'un on horseback."

Mrs. Pipkins nodded assent, and so did the ancient butler; and Trotman felt that public opinion was wholly against him, until such time as it should be further educated. But such a discussion had been aroused, that there was no chance of its stopping here; and Alice, who loved to collect opinions, had many laid before her. She listened to all judiciously, and pretended to do it judicially; and after that she wondered whether she had done what she ought to do. For she knew that she was only very young, with nobody to advise her; and the crushing weight of the world upon her, if she tripped or forgot herself. Most girls of her age would have been at school, and taken childish peeps at the world, and burnished up their selfishness by conflict with one another; but Sir Roland had kept to the family custom, and taught and trained his daughter at home, believing as he did that young women lose some of their best and most charming qualities by what he called "gregarious education." Alice, therefore, had been under care of a good and well-taught governess—for "masters" at that time were proper to boys—until her mind was quite up to the mark, and capable of taking care of itself. For in those days it was not needful for any girl to know a great deal more than was good for her.

Early one September evening, when the day and year hung calmly in the balance of the sun; when sensitive plants and clever beasts were beginning to look around them, and much of the growth of the ground was ready to regret lost opportunities; when the comet was gone for good at last, and the earth was beginning to laugh at her terror (having found him now clearly afraid of her), and when a sense of great deliverance from the power of drought and heat throbbed in the breast of dewy nurture, so that all took breath again, and even man (the last of all things to be pleased or thankful) was ready to acknowledge that there might have been worse moments, at such a time fair Alice sat in her garden thinking of Hilary. The work of the summer was over now, and the fate of the flowers pronounced and settled, for better or worse, till another year; no frost, however, had touched them yet, while the heavy dews of autumnal night and the brisk air flowing from the open downs had gladdened, refreshed, and sweetened them. Among them, and between the shrubs, there spread and sloped a pleasant lawn for all who love soft sward and silence, and the soothing sound of leaves. From the form of the ground and bend of the hills, as well as the northerly aspect, a peculiar cast and tone of color might be found, at different moments, fluctuating differently. Most of all, in a fine sunset of autumn (though now the sun was behind the ridge), from the fullness of the upper sky such gleam and glance fell here and there, that nothing could be sure of looking as it looked only a minute ago. At such times all the glen seemed thrilling like one vast lute of trees and air, drawing fingered light along the chords of trembling shadow. At such a time, no southern slope could be compared with this for depth of beauty and impressive power, for the charm of clear obscurity and suggestive murmuring mystery. A time and scene that might recall the large romance of grander ages; where wandering lovers might shrink and think of lovers whose love was over; and even the sere man of the world might take a fresh breath of the boyish days when fear was a pleasant element.

Suddenly Alice became aware of something moving near her, and, almost before she had time to be frightened, Hilary leaped from behind a laurel. He caught her in his arms and kissed her, and then stepped back to leave plenty of room for contemplative admiration.

"I was resolved to have one more look. We sail to-morrow, they are in such a hurry. I have walked all the way from Portsmouth. At least I got a little lift on the road, on the top of a wagon-load of wheat."

"How wonderfully good of you, Hilary dear!" she exclaimed, with tears in her eyes, and yet a strong inclination to smile, as she watched him. "How tired you must be! Why, when did you leave the dépôt? I thought they kept you at perpetual drill."

"So they did. But I soon got up to all that. I can do it as well as the best of them now. What a provoking child you are! Well, don't you notice any thing?"

For Alice, with true sisterly feeling, was trying his endurance to the utmost, dissembling all her admiration of his fine fresh "uniform." Of course, this was not quite so grand as if he had been (as he had right to be) enrolled as an "*eques auratus;*" still it looked very handsome on his fine straight figure, and set off the brightness of his clear complexion. Moreover, his two months of drilling at the dépôt had given to his active and well-poised form that vigorous firmness which alone was needed to make it perfect. With the quickness of a girl, his sister saw all this in a moment; and yet, for fear of crying, she laughed at him.

"Why, how did you come so 'spick and span?' Have you got a sheaf of wheat inside your waistcoat? It was too cruel to put such clothes on the top of a harvest-wagon. I wonder you did not set it all on fire."

"Much you know about it!" exclaimed the young soldier, with vast chagrin. "You don't deserve to see any thing. I brought my togs in a haversack, and put them on in your bower here, simply to oblige you; and you don't think they are worth looking at!"

"I am looking with all my might, and yet I can not see any thing of a sword. I suppose they won't allow you one yet. But surely you must have a sword in the end."

"Alice, you are enough to wear one out. Could I carry my sword in a haversack? However, if you don't think I look well, somebody else does—that is one comfort."

"You do not mean, I hope," replied Alice, missing his allusion carefully, "to go back to your ship without coming to see papa, dear Hilary?"

"That is exactly what I do mean; and that is why I have watched for you so. I have no intention of knocking under. And so he will find out in the end; and somebody else, I hope, as well. Every body thinks I am such a fool, because I am easy-tempered. Let them wait a bit. They may be proud of that never-do-well, silly Hilary yet. In the last few months, I can assure you, I have been through things—however, I won't talk about them. They never did understand me at home, and I suppose they never will. But it does not matter. Wait a bit."

"Darling Hilary! don't talk so. It makes me ready to cry to hear you. You will go into some battle, and throw your life away, to spite all of us."

"No, no, I won't. Though it would serve you right for considering me such a nincompoop. As if the best, and sweetest, and truest-hearted girl in the universe was below contempt, because her father happens to grow cabbages! What do we grow? Corn, and hay, and sting-nettles, and couch-grass. Or at least our tenants grow them for us, and so we get the money. Well, how are they finer than cabbages?"

"Come in and see father," said Alice, straining her self-control to shun argument. "Do come, and see him before you go."

"I will not," he answered, amazing his sister by his new-born persistency. "He never has asked me, and I will not do it."

No tears, no sobs, nor coaxings moved him; his troubles had given him strength of will, and he went to the war without seeing his father.

CHAPTER XXXIII.

One man there is, or was, who ought to have been brought forward long ago. Every body said the same thing of him—he wanted nothing more than the power of insisting upon his reputation, and of checking his own bashfulness, to make him one of the foremost men anywhere in or near Steyning. His name was Bottler, as every body knew; and through some hereditary veins of thought, they always added "the pig-man"—as if he were a porcine hybrid!

He was nothing of the sort. He was only a man who stuck pigs, when they wanted sticking; and if at such times he showed humanity, how could that identify him with the animal between his knees? He was sensitive upon this point at times, and had been known to say, "I am no pigman; what I am is a master pork-butcher."

However, he could not get over his name, any more than any body else can. And if such a trifle hurt his feelings, he scarcely insisted upon them, until he was getting quite into his fifth quart of ale, and discovering his true value.

A writer of the first eminence, who used to be called "Tully," but now is euphoniously cited as "Kikero," has taught us that to neglect the world's opinion of one's self is a proof not only of an arrogant, but even of a dissolute mind. Bottler could prove himself not of an arrogant, and still less of a dissolute mind; he respected the opinion of the world; and he showed his respect in the most convincing and flattering manner, by his style of dress. He never wore slops, nor an apron even, unless it were at the decease or during the obsequies of a porker. He made it a point of honor to maintain an unbroken succession of legitimate white stockings—a problem of deep and insatiable anxiety to every woman in Steyning town. In the first place, why did he wear them? It took several years to determine this point; but at last it was known, amidst universal applause, that he wore them in memory of his first love. But then there arose a far more difficult and excruciating question—How did he do it? Had he fifty pairs? Did he wash them himself, or did he make his wife? How could he kill pigs and keep his stockings perpetually unsullied? Emphatically and despairingly, why had they never got a hole in them?

He, however, with an even mind, trod the checkered path of life with fustian breeches and white stockings. His coat was of West of England broadcloth, and of a rich imperial blue, except where the color had yielded to time; and all his buttons were of burnished brass. His honest countenance was embellished with a fine candid smile whenever he spoke of the price of pigs or pork, and no one had ever known him to tell a lie—or at any rate he said so.

This good and remarkable man was open to public inspection every morning in his shop, from eight to twelve o'clock. He then retired to his dinner, and customers might thump and thump with a key or knife, or even his own steel, on the counter, but neither Mr. nor Mrs. Bottler would condescend to turn round for them. Nothing less than the chink of a guinea would stir them at this sacred time. But if any one had a guinea to rattle on the board, and did it cleverly, the blind across the glass door was drawn back on its tape, and out peeped Bottler.

When dinner and subsequent facts had been dealt with, this eminent pigman horsed his cart, hoisted his favorite child in over the foot-board, and set forth in quest of pigs, or, as he put it more elegantly, "hanimals german to his profession." That favorite child, his daughter Polly, being of breadth and length almost equal, and gifted with "bow-legs" (as the public had ample means of ascertaining), was now about four years old, and possessed of remarkable gravity even for that age. She would stand by the hour between her father's knees, while he guided the shambling horse, and gaze most intently at nothing at all; as if it were the first time she ever had enjoyed the privilege of inspecting it.

Rags and bones (being typical of the beginning and end of humanity) have an inner meaning of their own, and stimulate all who deal in them. At least it often seems to be so, though one must not be too sure of it. Years of observation lead us to begin to ask how to observe a little.

Bonny had not waited for this perversity of certainty. He had long been taking observations of Polly Bottler—as he could get them—and the more he saw her, the more his finest feelings were drawn forth by her, and the way she stood between her father's legs. Some boys have been known to keep one virtue so enlarged and fattened up, like the liver of a Strasbourg goose, that the flavor of it has been enough to abide—if they died before dissolution—in the rue of pious memory.

Exactly so it was with that Bonny. He never feigned to be an honest boy, because it would have been too bad of him; besides that, he did not know how to do it, and had his own reasons for waiting a bit; yet nothing short of downright starvation could have driven him at any time to steal so much as one pig's trotter from his patron's cart, or shop, or yard. Now this deserves mention, because it proves that there does, or at any rate did, exist a discoverable specimen of a virtue so rare, that its existence escaped all suspicion till after the classic period of the Latin tongue.

A grateful soul, or a grateful spirit—we have no word to express "animus," though we often express it toward one another—such was the Roman form for this virtue, as a concrete rarity. And a couple of thousand years have made it ever so much rarer.

In one little breast it still abode, purely original and native, and growing underneath the soil, shy of light and hard to find, like the truffle of the South Downs. Bonny was called, in one breath every day, a shameful and a shameless boy; and he may have deserved but a middling estimate from a lofty point of view. It must be admitted that he slipped sometimes over the border of right and wrong, when a duck or a rabbit, or a green goose haply, hopped or waddled on the other side of it, in the tempting twilight. But even that he avoided doing, until half-pence were scarce, and the weather hungry.

Now being, as has been said before, of distinguished countenance and costume, he already had made a tender impression upon the heart of Polly Bottler; and when she had been very good and conquered the alphabet up to P the pig—at which point professional feelings always overcame the whole family—the reward of merit selected by herself would sometimes be a little visit to Bonny, as the cart came back from Findon. There is room for suspicion, however, that true-love may not have been the only motive power, or at least that poor Bonny had a very formidable rival in Jack the donkey; inasmuch as the young lady always demanded as the first-fruit of hospitality a prolonged caracole on that quadruped, which she always performed in cavalier fashion, whereto the formation of her lower members afforded especial facility.

Now one afternoon toward All-hallows day, when the air was brisk and the crisp leaves rustled, some underfoot and some overhead, Mr. Bottler, upon his return from Storrington, with four pretty porkers in under his net, received from his taciturn daughter that push on his right knee, whose import he well understood. It meant—"We are going to see Bonny to-day. You must turn on this side, and go over the fields."

"All right, little un," the pigman answered, with his never-failing smile. "Daddy knows as well as you do a'most, though you can't expect him to come up to you."

Polly gave a nod, which was as much as any one ever expected of her all the time she was out-of-doors. At home she could talk any number to the dozen, when the mood was on her; but directly she got into the open air, the size of the world was too much for her. All she could do was to stand, and wonder, and have the whole of it going through her, without her feeling any thing.

After much jolting, and rattling, and squeaking of pigs at the roughness of sod or fallow, they won to the entrance of Coombe Lorraine, and the hermitage of Bonny. That exemplary boy had been all day pursuing his calling with his usual diligence, and was very busy now, blowing up his fire to have some hot savory stew to warm him. All his beggings and his buyings, etc., were cast in together; and none but the cook and consumer could tell how marvelously they always managed to agree among themselves, and with him. A sharp little turn of air had set in, and made every rover of the land sharp set; and the lid of the pot was beginning to lift charily and preciously, when the stubble and bramble crackled much. Bonny ensconced in his kitchen corner, on the right hand outside his main entrance, kept stirring the fire, and warming his hands, and indulging in a preliminary smell. Bearing ever in mind the stern duty of promoting liberal sentiments, he had felt, while passing an old woman's garden, how thoroughly welcome he ought to be to a few sprigs of basil, a handful of onions, and a pinch of lemon-thyme; and how much more polite it was to dispense with the frigid ceremony of asking.

As the cart rattled up in the teeth of the wind, Polly Bottler began to expand her frank ingenuous nostrils; inhaled the breeze, and thus spake with her mouth,

"Dad, I'se yerry hungy."

"No wonder," replied the paternal voice; "what a boy, to be sure, that is to cook! At his time of life, just to taste his stoos! He've got a born knowledge what to put in—ay, and what to keep out; and how long to do it. He deserveth that pot as I gived him out of the bilin' house; now dothn't he? If moother worn't looking for us to home, with chittlings and fried taties, I'd as lief sit down and sup with him. He maketh me in the humor, that he doth."

As soon as he beheld his visitors, Bonny advanced in a graceful manner, as if his supper was of no account. He had long been aware, from the comments of boys at Steyning (who were hostile to him), that his chimney-pot hat was not altogether in strict accord with his character. This had mortified him as deeply as his lightsome heart could feel; because he had trusted to that hat to achieve his restoration into the bosom of society. The words of the incumbent of his parish (ere ever the latter began to thrash him) had sunk into his inner and deeper consciousness and conscience; and therein had stirred up a nascent longing to have something to say to somebody whose fore-legs were not employed for locomotion any longer.

Alas, that ghost of a definition has no leg to stand upon! No two great authorities (perfect as they are, and complete in their own system) can agree with one another concerning the order of a horse's feet, in walking, ambling, or trotting, or even standing on all-fours in stable. The walk of a true-born Briton is surely almost as important a question. Which arm does he swing to keep time with which leg; and bends he his elbows in time with his knees; and do all four occupy the air, or the ground, or himself, in a regulated sequence; and if so, what aberration must ensue from the use of a walking-stick? Œdipus, who knew all about feet (from the tenderness of his own soles), could scarcely be sure of all this before the time of the close of the market.

This is far too important a question to be treated hastily. Only, while one is about it, let Bonny's hat be settled for. Wherever he thought to have made an impression with this really guinea-hat, ridicule and execration followed on his naked heels; till he sold it at last for tenpence-half-penny, and came back to his naked head. Society is not to be carried by storm even with a picked-up hat.

Jack the donkey was always delighted to have Polly Bottler upon his back. Not perhaps from any vaticination of his future mistress, but because she was sure to reward him with a cake, or an apple, or something good; so that when he felt her sturdy little legs, both hands in his mane, and the heels begin to drum, he would prick his long ears, and toss his fine white nose, and would even have arched his neck, if nature had not strictly forbidden him. On the present occasion, however, Polly did not very long witch the world with noble donkeymanship; although Mr. Bottler sat patiently in his cart, smiling as if he could never kill a pig, and with paternal pride stamped on every wrinkle of his nose; while the brief-lived porkers poked their snouts through the net, and watched with little sharp hairy eyes the very last drama perhaps in which they would be spectators only. The lively creatures did not suspect that Bonny's fire, the night after next, would be cooking some of their vital parts, with a truly fine smell of sausages.

Sausages were too dear for Bonny, as even the pigs at a glance were aware; but he earned three-quarters of a pound for nothing, by noble hospitality. To wit, his angel of a Polly had not made more than three or four parades, while he (with his head scarcely reaching up to the mark at the back of the donkey's ears, where the perspiration powdered) shouted and hallooed, and made believe to be very big—as boys must do, for practice toward their manhood—when by some concurrent good-will of air, and fire, and finer elements, the pot-lid arose, to let out a bubble of goodness returning to its native heaven; and the volatile virtue gently hovered to leave a fair memory behind.

The merest corner of this fragrance flipped into Polly Bottler's nose, as a weaker emanation had done, even before she began her ride. And this time her mouth and her voice expressed cessation of hesitation.

"'Et me down, 'et me down," she cried, stretching her fat short arms to Bonny; "I 'ants some; I'se so hungry."

"Stop a bit, miss," said Bonny, as being the pink of politeness to all the fair: "there, your purty little toes is on the blessed ground again. Stop a bit, miss, while I runs into my house for to get the spoon."

For up to this time he had stirred his soup with a forked stick made of dogwood, which helps to flavor every thing; but now as a host he was bound to show his more refined resources. Polly, however, was so rapt out of her usual immobility, that she actually toddled into Bonny's house to make him be quick about the spoon. He, in amazement, turned round and stared, to be sure of his eyes that such a thing could ever have happened to him. The jealousy of the collector strove with the hospitality of the householder and the chivalry of the rover. But the finer feelings conquered, and he showed her round the corner. Mr. Bottler, who could not get in, cracked his whip and whistled at them.

Polly, with great eyes of wonder and fright at her own daring, longed with one breath to go on, and with the next to run back again. But the boy caught hold of her hand, and she stuck to him through the ins and outs of light, until there was something well worth seeing.

What is the sweetest thing in life? Hope, love, gold, fame, pride, revenge, danger—or any thing else, according to the nature of the liver. But with those who own very little, and have "come across" all that little, with risk and much uncertainty, the sweetest thing in life is likely to be the sense of ownership. The mightiest hoarder of gold and silver, Crœsus, Rhampsinitus, or Solomon, never thought half so much of his stores, or at any rate never enjoyed them as much as this rag-and-bone collector his. When he came to his room he held his breath, and watched with the greatest anxiety for corresponding emotion of Polly.

The room was perhaps about twelve feet long, and eight feet wide at its utmost, scooped from the chalk without any sharp corners, but with a grand contempt of shape. The floor went up and down, and so did the roof, according to circumstances; the floor appearing inclined to rise, and the roof to come down if called upon. Much excellent rubbish was here to be found; but the window was the first thing to seize and hold any stranger's attention. It must have been built either by or for the old hermit who once had dwelt there; at any rate, no one could have designed it without a quaint ingenuity. It was cut through a three-foot wall of chalk, the embrasure being about five feet in span, and three feet deep at the crown of the arch.

In the middle a narrow pier of chalk was left to keep the arch up, and the lights on either side were made of horn, stained glass, and pig's bladder. The last were of Bonny's handiwork, to keep out the wind when it blew too cold among the flaws of ages. And now as the evening light fetched round the foot of the hills, and gathered strongly into this western aspect, the richness of colors was such that even Polly's steadfast eyes were dazed.

Without vouchsafing so much as a glance at Bonny's hoarded glories, the child ran across the narrow chamber, and spread out her hands and opened her mouth wider even than her eyes at the tints now streaming in on her. The glass had been brought perhaps from some ruined chapel of the hill-side, and glowed with a depth of color infused by centuries of sunset; not one pane of regular shape was to be found among them; but all, like veins of marble, ran with sweetest harmony of hue, to meet the horn and the pig's bladder. From the outside it looked like a dusty slate traversed with bits of a crusted bottle; it required to be seen from the inside, like an ancient master's painting.

Polly, like the rest of those few children who do not overtalk themselves, spent much of her time in observation, storing the entries inwardly. And young as she was, there might be perhaps a doubt entertained by those who knew her whether she were not of a deeper and more solid cast of mind than Bonny. Her father at any rate declared, and her mother was of the same opinion, that by the time she was ten years old she would buy and sell all Steyning. However, they may have thought this because all their other children were so stupid.

Now, be they right or be they wrong—as may be shown hereafter—Polly possessed at least the first and most essential of all the many endowments needful to approach success. Polly Bottler stuck to her point. And now, even with those fine old colors, like a century of rainbows, puzzling her, Polly remembered the stew in the pot, and pointed with her finger to the window-ledge, where something shone in a rich blue light.

"Here's a 'poon, Bonny!" she exclaimed; "here's a 'poon! 'Et me have it, Bonny."

"No, that's not a spoon, miss; and I can't make out for the life of me whatever it can be. I've a-seed a many queer things, but I never seed the likes of that afore. Ah, take care, miss, or you'll cut your fingers!"

For Polly, with a most resolute air, had scrambled to the top of an old brown jar (the salvage from some shipwreck) which stood beneath the window-sill, and thence with a gallant sprawl she reached and clutched the shining implement, which she wanted to eat her stew with. The boy was surprised to see her lift it with her fat brown fingers, and hold it tightly without being cut or stung, as he expected. For he had a wholesome fear of this thing, and had set it up as a kind of fetish, his mind (like every other) requiring something to bow down to. For the manner of his finding it first, and then its presentment in the mouth of Jack, added to the interest which its unknown meaning won for it.

With a laugh of triumph the bow-legged maiden descended from her dangerous height, and paying no heed to all Bonny's treasures, waddled away with her new toy, either to show it to her father, or to plunge it into the stew-pot, perhaps. But her careful host, with an iron spoon and a saucer in his hands, ran after her, and gently guided her to the crock, whither also Mr. Bottler sped. This was as it should be; and they found it so. For when the boy Bonny, with a hospitable sweep, lifted the cover of his cookery, a sense of that void which all nature protests against rose in the forefront of all three, and forbade them to seek any farther. Bottler himself, in the stress of the moment, let the distant vision fade—of fried potatoes and combed chittlings—and lapsed into that lowest treason to Lares and Penates—a supper abroad, when the supper at home is salted, and peppered, and browning.

But though Polly opened her mouth so wide, and smacked her lips, and made every other gratifying demonstration, not for one moment would she cede possession of the treasure she had found in Bonny's window. Even while most absorbed in absorbing, she nursed it jealously on her lap; and even when her father had lit his pipe from Bonny's bonfire, and was ready to hoist her in again over the foot-board, the child stuck fast to her new delight, and set up a sturdy yell when the owner came to reclaim it from her.

"Now don't 'ee, don't 'ee, that's a dear," began the gentle pork-butcher, as the pigs in the cart caught up the strain, and echo had enough to do; for Polly of course redoubled her wailings, as all little dears must, when coaxed to stop: "here, Bonny, here lad, I'll gie thee sixpence for un, though her an't worth a penny, I doubt. And thou mayst call to-morrow, and the misses 'll gie thee a clot of sassages."

Bonny looked longingly at his fetish; but gratitude and true-love got the better of veneration. Polly, moreover, might well be trusted to preserve this idol, until in the day when he made her his own, it should return into his bosom. And so it came to pass that this Palladium of the hermitage was set up at the head of Polly Bottler's little crib, and installed in the post of her favorite doll.

CHAPTER XXXIV.

THOUGH Coombe Lorraine was so old a mansion, and so full of old customs, the Christmas of the "comet year" was as dull as a Sunday in a warehouse. Hilary (who had always been the life of the place) was far away, fed upon hardships and short rations. Alice, though full sometimes of spirits, at other times would run away, and fret, and blame herself, as if the whole of the fault was on her side. This was of course an absurd idea; but sensitive girls, in moods of dejection, are not good judges of absurdity; and Alice at such times fully believed that if she had not intercepted so much of her father's affection from her brother, things would have been very different. It might have been so; but the answer was that she never had wittingly stood between them, but, on the contrary, had laid herself out, even at the risk of offending both, to bring their widely different natures into kinder unity.

Sir Roland also was becoming more and more reserved and meditative. He would sit for hours in his book-room, immersed in his favorite studies, or rather absorbed in his misty abstractions. And Lady Valeria did not add to the cheer of the household, although, perhaps, she did increase its comfort, by suddenly ceasing to interfere with Mrs. Pipkins and every body else, and sending for the parson of the next parish, because she had no faith in Mr. Hales. That worthy's unprofessional visits, and those of his wife and daughters, were now almost the only pleasant incidents of the day or week. For the country was more and more depressed by the gloomy burden of endless war, the scarcity of the fruits of the earth, and the slaughter of good brave people. So that as the time went on, what with miserable expeditions, pestilence, long campaigns, hard sieges, furious battles, and starvation, there was scarcely any decent family that was not gone into mourning.

Even the Rector, as lucky a man as ever lived, had lost a nephew, or at least a nephew of his dear wife—which, he said, was almost worse to him—slain in battle, fighting hard for his country and constitution. Mr. Hales preached a beautiful sermon, as good as a book, about it; so that all the parish wept, and three young men enlisted.

The sheep were down in the lowlands now, standing up to their knees in litter, and chewing very slowly; or sidling up against one another in the joy of woolliness; or lying down, with their bare grave noses stretched for contemplation's sake, winking with their gentle eyes, and thanking God for the roof above them, and the troughs in front of them. They never regarded themselves as mutton, nor their fleeces as worsted yarn: it was really sad to behold them, and think that the future could not make them miserable.

No snow had fallen; but all the downs were spread with that sombre brown which is the breath or the blast of the wind-frost. But Alice Lorraine took her daily walk, for her father forbade her to ride on the hill-tops in the bleak and bitter wind. Her thoughts were continually of her brother; and as the cold breeze rattled her cloak, or sprayed her soft hands through her gloves, many a time she said to herself, "I suppose there is no frost in Spain; or not like this, at any rate. How could the poor fellow sleep in a tent in such dreadful weather as this is?"

How little she dreamed that he had to sleep (whenever he got such a blissful chance), not in a tent, but an open trench, with a keener wind and a blacker frost preying on his shivering bones, while cannon-balls and fiery shells in a pitiless storm rushed over him! It was no feather-bed fight that was fought in front of Ciudad Rodrigo. About the middle of January, A.D. 1812, desperate work was going on.

For now there was no time to think of life. Within a certain number of days the fort must be taken, or the army lost. The defenses were strong, and the garrison brave, and supplied with artillery far superior to that of the besiegers; the season also, and the bitter weather, fought against the British, and so did the indolence of their allies, and so did British roguery. The sappers could only work in the dark (because of the grape from the ramparts); and working thus, the tools either bent beneath their feet or snapped off short. The contractor had sent out false-grained stuff, instead of good English steel and iron; and if in this world he earned his fortune, he assured his fate in the other.

At length, by stubborn perseverance, most of these troubles were overcome, and the English batteries opened. Roar answered roar, and bullet bullet, and the black air was striped with fire and smoke; and men began to study the faces of the men that shot at them, until, after some days of hard pounding, it was determined to rush in. All who care to read of valor know what a desperate rush it was—how strong men struggled and leaped and climbed, hung and swung, on the crest of the breach, like stormy surges towering, and then leaped down upon spluttering shells, drawn swords, and sparkling bayonets.

Before the signal to storm was given, and while men were talking of it, Hilary Lorraine felt most uncomfortably nervous. He did not possess that stolid phlegm which is found more often in square-built people; neither had he any share of fatalism, cold or hot. He was nothing more than a spirited young Englishman, very fond of life, hating cruelty, and fearing to have any hand in it. Although he had been in the trenches, and exposed to frequent dangers, he had not been in hand-to-hand conflict yet, and he knew not how he might behave. He knew that he was an officer now in the bravest and hardiest army known on earth since the time of the Samnites—although perhaps not the very best behaved, as they proved that self-same night. And not only that, but an officer of the famous Light Division, and the fiercest regiment of that division—everywhere known as the "Fighters;" and he was not sure that he could fight a frog. He was sure that he never could kill any body, at least in his natural state of mind; and worse than that, he was not at all sure that he could endure to be killed himself.

However, he made preparation for it. He brought out the Testament Mabel had given him as a parting keepsake in the moment of true-love's piety; and he opened it at a passage marked with a woven tress of her long rich hair—"Soldiers, do that is commanded of you;" and he wondered whether he could manage it. And while he was trembling, not with fear of the enemy, but of his own young heart, the colonel of that regiment came, and laid his one hand on Hilary's shoulder, and looked into his bright blue eyes. In all the army there was no braver, nobler, or kinder-hearted man than Colonel C——, of that regiment.

Hilary looked at this true veteran with all the reverence, and even awe, which a young subaltern (if fit for any thing) feels for commanding experience. Never a word he spoke, however, but waited to be spoken to.

"You will do, lad. You will do," said the colonel, who had little time to spare. "I would rather see you like that than uproarious, or even as cool as a cucumber. I was just like that before my first action. Lorraine, you will not disgrace your family, your country, or your regiment."

The colonel had lost two sons in battle, younger men than Hilary, otherwise he might not have stopped to enter into an ensign's mind. But every word he spoke struck fire in the heart of this gentle youth. True gratitude chokes common answers, and Hilary made none to him. An hour afterward he made it by saving the life of the colonel.

The Light Division (kept close and low from the sight of the sharp French gunners) were waiting in a hollow curve of the inner parallel, where the ground gave way a little, under San Francisco. There had been no time to do any thing more than breach the stone of the ramparts; all the outer defenses were almost as sound as ever. The Light Division had orders to carry the lesser breach, cost what it might, and then sweep the ramparts as far as the main breach, where the strong assault was. And so well did they do their work, that they turned the auxiliary into the main attack, and bodily carried the fortress.

For, sooth to say, they expected, but could not manage to wait for, the signal to storm. No sooner did they hear the firing on the right than they began to stamp and swear; for the hay-bags they were to throw into the ditch were not at hand, and not to be seen. "Are we horses, to wait for the hay?" cried an Irishman of the Fifty-second; and with that they all set off as fast as ever their legs could carry them. Hilary laughed—for his sense of humor was never very far to seek—at the way in which these men set off, as if it were a game of foot-ball; and at the wonderful mixture of fun and fury in their faces. Also, at this sudden burlesque of the tragedy he expected—with heroes out at heels and elbow, and small-clothes streaming upon the breeze. For the British Government, as usual, left coats, shoes, and breeches to last forever.

"Run, lad, run," said Major Napier, in his quiet Scottish way; "you are bound to be up with them, as one might say, and your legs are unco long. I shall na hoory mysell, but take the short cut over the open."

"May I come with you?" asked Hilary, panting.

"If you have na mither nor wife," said the major; "na wife, of course, by the look of you."

Lorraine had no sense what he was about; for the grape-shot whistled through the air like hornets, and cut off one of his loose fair locks, as he crossed the open with Major Napier, to head their hot men at the crest of the glacis.

Now how things happened after that, or even what things happened at all, that headlong young officer never could tell. As he said in his letter to Gregory Lovejoy—for he was not allowed to write to Mabel, and would not describe such a scene to Alice—"The chief thing I remember is a lot of rushing and stumbling, and swearing and cheering, and staggering and tumbling backward. And I got a tremendous crack on the head from a cannon laid across the top of the breach, but luckily not a loaded one; and I believe there were none of our fellows in front of me, but I can not be certain, because of the smoke, and the row, and the rush, and confusion; and I saw a Crapaud with a dead level at Colonel C——. I suppose I was too small game for him, and I was just in time to slash his trigger-hand off (which I felt justified in doing), and his musket went up in the air and went off, and I just jumped aside from a fine bearded fellow who rushed at me with a bayonet; and before he could have at me again he fell dead, shot by his own friends from behind, who were shooting at me—more shame to them—when our men charged with empty muskets. And when the breach was our own, we were formed on the top of the rampart, and went off at double-quick, to help at the main breach, and so we did; and that is about all I know of it."

But the more experienced warriors knew a great deal more of Hilary's doings, especially Colonel C——, of his regiment, and Major Napier, and Colonel M'Leod. All of these said that "they never saw any young fellow behave so well, for the first time of being under deadly fire; that he might have been 'off his head' for the moment, but that would very soon wear off—or if it did not, all the better, so long as he always did the right thing thus; and (unless he got shot) he would be an honor to the country, the army, and the regiment!"

CHAPTER XXXV.

HAVING no love of bloodshed, and having the luck to know nothing about it, some of us might be glad to turn into the white gate across the lane leading into Old Applewood farm—if only the franklin would unlock it for any body in this war-time. But now he has been getting sharper and sharper month after month; and hearing so much about sieges and battles, he never can be certain when the county of Kent will be invaded. For the last ten years he has expected something of the sort at least, and being of a prudent mind, keeps a duck-gun heavily loaded.

Moreover, Mabel is back again from exile with Uncle Catherow; and though the grower only says that "she is well enough, for aught he knows," when compliments are paid him about her good looks by the neighborhood, he knows well enough that she is more than that; and he believes all the county to be after her. It is utterly useless to deny—though hot indignation would expand his horticultural breast at the thought—that he may have been just a little set up by that trifling affair about Hilary. "It never were the cherries," he says to himself, as the author of a great discovery; "aha, I seed it all along! Wife never guessed of it, but I did"—shame upon thee, grower, for telling thyself such a dreadful "caulker!"—"and now we can see, as plain as a pike-staff, the very thing I seed, when it was that big!" Upon this he shows himself his thumb-nail, and feels that he has earned a glass of his ale.

Mabel, on the other hand, is dreadfully worried by foreign affairs. She wants to know why they must be always fighting; and as nobody can give any other reason, except that they "suppose it is natural," she only can shake her head very sadly, and ask, "How would you like to have to do it?"

They turn up the udders of the cows to think out this great question, and the spurting into the pail stops short, and the cow looks round with great bountiful eyes, and a flat broad nose, and a spotted tongue, desiring to know what they are at with her. Is her milk not worth the milking, pray?

This leads to no satisfaction whatever upon behalf of any one; and Mabel, after a shiver or two, runs back to the broad old fire-place, to sit in the light and the smell of the wood, to spread her pointed fingers forth, and see how clear they are, and think. For Mabel's hands are quite as pretty as if they were of true Norman blood, instead of the elder Danish cast; and she is very particular now not to have any line visible under her nails.

And now in the month of February, 1812, before the witching festival of St. Valentine was prepared for, with cudgeling of brains, and violent rhymes, and criminal assaults upon grammar, this "flower of Kent"—as the gallant hop-growers in toasting moments entitled her—was sitting, or standing, or drooping her head, or whatever suits best to their metaphor, at or near the fire-place in the warm old simple hall. Love, however warm and faithful, is all the better for a good clear fire, ere ever the snow-drops begin to spring. Also it loves to watch the dancing of the flames, and the flickering light, and even in the smoke discovers something to itself akin. Mabel was full of these beautiful dreams, because she was left altogether to herself; and because she remembered so well what had happened along every inch of the dining-table; and, above all, because she was sleepy. Long anxiety, and great worry, and the sense of having no one fit to understand a girl—but every body taking low, and mercenary, and fickle views, and even the most trusty people giving base advice to one, in those odious proverbial forms—"A bird in the hand is worth two in the bush," "Fast find fast bind," "There is better fish in the sea," etc.; Mabel thought there never had been such a selfish world to deal with.

Has not every kind of fame, however pure it may be and exalted, its own special disadvantage, lest poor mortals grow too proud? At any rate, Mabel now reflected, rather with sorrow than with triumph, upon her fame for pancakes—because it was Shrove-Tuesday now, and all her tender thrills and deep anxieties must be discarded for, or at any rate distracted by, the composition of batter. Her father's sense of propriety was so strong, and that of excellence so keen, that pancakes he would have on Shrove-Tuesday, and pancakes only from Mabel's hand. She had pleaded, however, for leave to make them here in the dining-hall, instead of frying at the kitchen fire-place, because she knew what Sally the cook and Susan the maid would be at with her. Those two girls would never leave her the smallest chance of retiring into her deeper nature, and meditating. Although they could understand nothing at all, they would take advantage of her good temper, to enjoy themselves with the most worn-out jokes. Such trumpery was below Mabel now; and some day or other she would let them know it.

Without thinking twice of such low matters, the maiden was now in great trouble of the heart, by reason of sundry rumors. Paddy from Cork had brought home word from Maidstone only yesterday, that a desperate fight had been fought in Spain, and almost every body had been blown up. Both armies had made up their minds to die so, that with the drums beating and the colors flying, they marched into a powder-magazine, and tossed up a pin which should be the one to fire it, and blow up the others. And the English had lost the toss, and no one survived to tell the story.

Mabel doubted most of this, though Paddy vowed that he had known the like, "when wars was wars, and the boys had spirit;" still she felt sure that there had been something, and she longed most sadly to know all about it. Her brother Gregory was in London, keeping his Hilary term, and slaving at his wretched law-books; and she had begged him, if he loved her, to send down all the latest news by John Shorne every market-day—for the post would not carry newspapers. And now, having mixed her batter, she waited, sleepy after sleepless nights, unable to leave her post and go to meet the van, as she longed to do, the while the fire was clearing.

Pensively sitting thus, and longing for somebody to look at her, she glanced at the face of the clock, which was the only face regarding her. And she won from it but the stern frown of time—she must set to at her pancakes. Batter is all the better for standing ready-made for an hour or so, the weaker particles expire, while the good stuff grows the more fit to be fried, and to turn over in the pan properly. With a gentle sigh, the "flower of Kent" put her frying-pan on, just to warm the bottom. No lard for her, but the best fresh butter—at any rate for the first half-dozen, to be set aside for her father and mother; after that she would be more frugal, perhaps.

But just as the butter began to ooze on the bottom of the pan, she heard, or thought that she heard, a sweet distant tinkle coming through the frosty air, and running to the window she caught beyond doubt the sound of the bells at the corner of the lane—the bells that the horses always wore when the nights were dark and long—and a throb of eager hope and fear went to her heart at every tinkle.

"I can not wait; how can I wait?" she cried, with flushing cheeks and eyes twice-laden between smiles and tears; "father's pancakes can wait much better. There, go back," she spoke to the frying-pan, as with the prudent care of a fine young housewife, she lifted it off and laid it on the hob for fear of the butter burning; and then, with quick steps, out she went, not even stopping to find a hat, in her hurry to meet the van, and know the best or the worst of the news of the war. For "crusty John," who would go through fire and water to please Miss Mabel, had orders not to come home without the very latest tidings. There was nothing to go to market now; but the van had been up with a load of straw to some mews where the grower had taken a contract, and, of course, it came loaded back with litter.

While Mabel was all impatience and fright, John Shorne, in the most deliberate manner, descended from the driving-box, and purposely shunning her eager glance, began to unfasten the leader's traces, and pass them through his horny hands, and coil them into elegant spirals, like horns of Jupiter Ammon. Mabel's fear grew worse and worse, because he would not look at her.

"Oh, John, you never could have the heart to keep me waiting like this, unless—"

"What! you there, missie? Lor' now, what can have brought 'ee out this weather?"

"As if you did not see me, John! Why, you must have seen me all along."

"This here be such a dreadful horse to smoke," said John, who always shunned downright fibs, "that railly I never knows what I do see when I be longside of un. Ever since us come out of Sennoaks, he have a-been confusing of me. Not that I blames un for what a can't help. Now there, now! The watter be frozen in trough. Go to the bucket, jackanapes!"

"Oh, John, you never do seem to think—because you have got so many children only fit to go to school, you seem to think—"

"Why, you said as I couldn't think now, missie, in the last breath of your purty mouth. Well, what is it as I ought to think? Whoa there! Stand still, wull 'ee?"

"John, you really are too bad. I have been all the morning making pancakes, and you sha'n't have one, John Shorne, you sha'n't, if you keep me waiting one more second."

"Is it consarning they fighting fellows you gets into such a hurry, miss? Well, they have had a rare fight, sure enough! Four-score officers gone to glory, besides all the others as was not worth counting!"

"Oh, John, you give me such a dreadful pain here! Let me know the worst, I do implore you."

"He an't one of 'em. Now, is that enough?" John Shorne made so little of true-love now, and forgot his early situations so, in the bosom of a hungry family, that he looked upon Mabel's "coorting" as an agreeable play-ground for little jokes. But now he was surprised and frightened at her way of taking them.

"There, don't 'ee cry now, that's a dear," he said, as she leaned on the shaft of the wagon, and sobbed so that the near wheeler began in pure sympathy to sniff at her. "Lord bless 'ee, there be nothing to cry about. He've a been and dooed wonders, that a hath."

"Of course he has, John; he could not help it. He was sure to do wonders, don't you see, if only—if only they did not stop him."

"He hathn't killed Bonyparty yet," said John, recovering his vein of humor, as Mabel began to smile through her tears; "but I b'lieve he wool, if he gooeth on only half so well as he have begun. For my part, I'd sooner kill dree of un than sell out in a bad market, I know. But here, you can take it, and read all about un. Lor' bless me, wherever have I put the papper?"

"Now do be quick, John, for once in your life. Dear John, do try to be quick, now."

"Strornary gallantry of a young hofficer! Could have sworn that it were in my breeches-pocket. I always thought 'gallantry' meant something bad. A running after strange women, and that."

"Oh no, John—oh no, John; it never does. How can you think of such dreadful things? But how long are you going to be, John?"

"Well, it did when I wor a boy, that's certain. But now they changes every thing so—even the words we was born to. It have come to mean killing of strange men, hath it? Wherever now can I have put that papper? I must have dropped un on the road, after all."

"You never can have done such a stupid thing!—such a wicked, cruel thing, John Shorne! If you have, I will never forgive you. Very likely you put it in the crown of your hat."

"Sure enough, and so I did. You must be a witch, Miss Mabel. And here's the very corner I turned down when I read it to the folk at the 'Pig and Whistle.' 'Glorious British victory—capture of Shoedad Rodleygo—eighty British officers killed, and forty great guns taken!' There, there, bless your bright eyes! now will you be content with it?"

"Oh, give it me, give it me! How can I tell until I have read it ten times over?"

Crusty John blessed all the girls of the period (becoming more and more too many for him) as his master's daughter ran away to devour that greasy journal. And by the time he had pulled his coat off, and shouted for Paddy and another man, and stuck his own pitchfork into the litter, as soon as they had backed the wheelers, Mabel was up in her own little room, and down on her knees to thank the Lord for the abstract herself had made of it. Somehow or other, the natural impulse of all good girls at that time was to believe that they had a Creator and Father whom to thank for all mercies. But that idea has been improved since then.

CHAPTER XXXVI.

At Coombe Lorraine these things had been known and entered into some time ago. For Sir Roland had not left his son so wholly uncared for in a foreign land as Hilary in his sore heart believed. In his regiment there was a certain old major, lame, and addicted to violent language, but dry and sensible according to his lights, and truthful, and upright, and quarrelsome. Burning to be first, as he always did in every desperate conflict, Major Clumps saw the young fellows get in front of him, and his temper exploded always. "Come back, come back, you—" condemned offspring of canine lineage, he used to shout; "let an honest man have a fair start with you! Because my feet are—there you go again; no consideration, any of you!"

This Major Clumps was admirably "connected," being the nephew of Lord de Lampnor, the husband of Lady Valeria's friend. So that by this means it was brought round that Hilary's doings should be reported. And Lady Valeria had received a letter in which her grandson's exploits at the storming of Ciudad Rodrigo were so recounted that Alice wept, and the ancient lady smiled with pride; and even Sir Roland said, "Well, after all, that boy can do something."

The following afternoon the master of Coombe Lorraine was sent for, to have a long talk with his mother about matters of dry business. Now Sir Roland particularly hated business; his income was enough for all his wants; his ambition (if ever he had any) was a vague and vaporous element; he left to his lawyers all matters of law; and even the management of his land, but for his mother's strong opposition, he would gladly have left to a steward or agent, although the extent of his property scarcely justified such an appointment. So he entered his mother's room that day with a languid step and reluctant air.

The lady paid very little heed to that. Perhaps she even enjoyed it a little. Holding that every man is bound to attend to his own affairs, she had little patience and no sympathy with such philosophic indifference. On the other hand, Sir Roland could not deny himself a little quiet smile when he saw his mother's great preparations to bring him both to book and deed.

Lady Valeria Lorraine was sitting as upright as she had sat throughout her life, and would sit, until she lay down forever. On the table before her were several thick and portentously dirty documents, arranged and docketed by her own sagacious hand; and beyond these, and opened at pages for reference, lay certain old law-books of a most deterrent guise and attitude. Sheppard's "Touchstone" (before Preston's time), Littleton's "Tenures," Viner's "Abridgment," Comyn's "Digest," Glanville, Plowden, and other great authors, were here prepared to cause delicious confusion in the keenest feminine intellect; and Lady Valeria was quite sure now that they all contradicted one another.

After the formal salutation, which she always insisted upon, the venerable lady began to fuss about a little, and pretend to be at a loss with things. She was always dressed as if she expected a visit from the royal family; and it was as good as a lecture for any slovenly young girls to see how cleverly she avoided soil of dirty book, or dirtier parchment, upon her white cuffs or Flemish lace. Even her delicate pointed fingers, shrunken as they were with age, had a knack of flitting over grime, without attracting it.

"I dare say you are surprised," she said, with her usual soft and courteous smile, "at seeing me employed like this, and turning lawyer in my old age."

Sir Roland said something complimentary, knowing that it was expected of him. The ancient lady had always taught him—however erroneous the doctrine—that no man who is at a loss for the proper compliment to a lady deserves to be thought a gentleman. She always had treated her son as a gentleman, dearer to her than other gentlemen; but still to be regarded in that light mainly. And he, perhaps by inheritance, had been led to behave to his own son thus—a line of behavior warmly resented by the impetuous Hilary.

"Now I beg you to attend—you must try to attend," continued Lady Valeria: "rouse yourself up, if you please, dear Roland. This is not a question of astrologers, or any queer thing of that sort, but a common-sense matter, and, I might say, a difficult point of law, perhaps."

"That being so," Sir Roland answered, with a smile of bright relief, "our course becomes very simple. We have nothing that we need trouble ourselves to be puzzled with uncomfortably. Messrs. Crookson, Hack & Clinker. They know how to keep in arrear, and to charge."

"It is your own fault, my dear Roland, if they overcharge you. Every body will do so, when they know that you mean to put up with it. Your dear father was under my guidance much more than you have ever been, and he never let people overcharge him—more than he could help, I mean."

"I quite perceive the distinction, mother. You have put it very clearly. But how does that bear upon the matter you have now to speak of?"

"In a great many ways. This account of Hilary's desperate behavior, as I must call it upon sound reflection, leads me to consider the great probability of something happening to him. There are many battles yet to be fought, and some of them may be worse than this. You remember what Mr. Malahide said when your dear father would insist upon that resettlement of the entire property in the year 1799."

Sir Roland knew quite well that it was not his dear father at all, but his mother, who had insisted upon that very stringent and ill-advised proceeding, in which he himself had joined reluctantly, and only by dint of her persistence. However he did not remind her of this.

"To be sure," he replied, "I remember it clearly, and I have his very words somewhere. He declined to draw it in accordance with the instructions of our solicitors, until his own opinion upon it had been laid before the family—a most unusual course, he said, for counsel in chambers to adopt; but having some knowledge of the parties concerned, he hoped they would pardon his interference. And then his words were to this effect: 'The operation of such a settlement may be most injurious. The parties will be tying their own hands most completely, without—so far as I can perceive—any adequate reason for doing so. Supposing, for instance, there should be occasion for raising money upon these estates during the joint lives of the grandson and granddaughter, and before the granddaughter is of age, there will be no means of doing it. The limitation to her, which is a most unusual one in such cases, will preclude the possibility of representing the fee-simple. The young lady is now just five years old; and if this extraordinary settlement is made, no marketable title can be deduced for the next sixteen years, except, of course, in the case of her decease.' And many other objections he made, all of which, however, were overruled; and after that protest he prepared the settlement."

"The matter was hurried through your father's state of health; for at that very time he was on his death-bed. But no harm whatever has come of it, which shows that we were right, and Mr. Malahide quite wrong. But I have been looking to see what would happen, in case poor Hilary—ah! it was his own fault that all these restrictions were introduced. Although he was scarcely twelve years old, he had shown himself so thoroughly volatile, so very easy to lead away, and, as it used to be called by vulgar people, so 'happy-go-lucky,' that your dear father wished, while he had the power, to disable him from lessening any further our lessened estates. And but for that settlement, where might we be."

"You know, my dear mother, that I never liked that exceedingly complicated and most mistrustful settlement. And if I had not been so sick of all business, after the loss of my dear wife, even your powers of persuasion would have failed to make me execute it. At any rate, it has had one good effect. It has robbed poor Hilary to a great extent of the charms that he must have possessed for the Jews."

"How can they discover such things? With a firm of trusty and most respectable lawyers—to me it is quite wonderful."

"How many things are wondrous, and nothing more wondrous than man himself—except, of course, a Jew. They do find out; and they never let us find out how they managed it. But do let me ask you, my dear mother, what particular turn of thought has compelled you to be so learned?"

"You mean these books? Well, let me think. I quite forget what it was that I wanted. It is useless to flatter me, Roland, now. My memory is not as it was, nor my sight, nor any other gift. However, I ought to be very thankful; and I often try to be so."

"Take a little time to think," Sir Roland said, in his most gentle tone; "and then, if it does not occur to you, we can talk of it some other time."

"Oh, now I remember! They told me something about the poor boy being smitten with some girl of inferior station. Of course, even he would have a little more sense than ever to dream of marrying her. But young men, although they mean nothing, are apt to say things that cost money. And above all others, Hilary may have given some grounds for damages—he is so inconsiderate! now if that should be so, and they give a large verdict, as a low-born jury always does against a well-born gentleman, several delicate points arise. In the first place, has he any legal right to fall in love under this settlement? And if not, how can any judgment take effect on his interest? And again, if he should fall in battle, would that stay proceedings? And if all these points should be settled against us, have we any power to raise the money? For I know that you have no money, Roland, except what you receive from land; as under my advice every farthing of accumulation has been laid out in buying back, field by field, portions of our lost property."

"Yes, my dear mother; and worse than that; every field so purchased has been declared or assured—or whatever they call it—to follow the trusts of this settlement, so that I verily believe if I wanted £5000 for any urgent family purposes, I must raise it—if at all—upon mere personal security. But surely, dear mother, you can not find fault with the very efficient manner in which your own desires have been carried out."

"Well, my son, I have acted for the best, and according to your dear father's plans. When I married your father," the old lady continued, with a soft quiet pride, which was quite her own, "it was believed, in the very best quarters, that the Duchess Dowager of Chalcorhin, of whom perhaps you may have heard me speak—"

"Truly yes, mother, every other day."

"And, my dear son, I have a right to do so of my own godmother, and great-aunt. The sneering spirit of the present day can not rob us of all our advantages. However, your father (as was right and natural on his part) felt a conviction—as those low Methodists are always saying of themselves—that there would be a hundred thousand pounds, to help him in what he was thinking of. But her Grace was vexed at my marriage; and so, as you know, my dear Roland, I brought the Lorraines nothing."

"Yes, my dear mother, you brought yourself, and your clear mind, and clever management."

"Will you always think that of me, Roland, dear? Whatever happens, when I am gone, will you always believe that I did my best?"

Sir Roland was surprised at his mother's very unusual state of mind. And he saw how her delicate face was softened from its calm composure. And the like emotion moved himself; for he was a man of strong feeling, though he deigned so rarely to let it out, and froze it so often with fatalism.

"My dearest mother," he answered, bowing his silver hair over her snowy locks, "surely you know me well enough to make such a question needless. A more active and devoted mind never worked for one especial purpose—the welfare of those for whose sake you have abandoned show and grandeur. Ay, mother, and with as much success as our hereditary faults allowed. Since your labors began, we must have picked up fifty acres."

"Is that all you know of it, Roland?" asked Lady Valeria, with a short sigh; "all my efforts will be thrown away, I greatly fear, when I am gone. One hundred and fifty-six acres and a half have been brought back into the Lorraine rent-roll, without even counting the hedge-rows. And now there are two things to be done, to carry on this great work well. That interloper, Sir Remnant Chapman, a man of comparatively modern race, holds more than two thousand acres of the best and oldest Lorraine land. He wishes young Alice to marry his son, and proposes a very handsome settlement. Why, Roland, you told me all about it—though not quite so soon as you should have done."

"I do not perceive that I neglected my duty. If I did so, surprise must have 'knocked me out of time,' as our good Struan expresses it."

"Mr. Hales! Mr. Hales, the clergyman! I can not imagine what he could mean. But it must have been something low, of course; either badger-baiting or prize-fighting—though people of really good position have a right to like such things. But now we must let that poor stupid Sir Remnant, who can not even turn a compliment, have his own way about silly Alice, for the sake of more important things."

"My dear mother, you sometimes try me. What can be more important than Alice? And to what overpowering influence is she to be sacrificed?"

"It is useless to talk like that, Sir Roland. She must do her best, like every body else who is not of ignoble family. The girl has plenty of pride, and will be the first to perceive the necessity. 'Twill not be so much for the sake of the settlement, for that of course will go with her; but we must make it a stipulation, and have it set down under hand and seal, that Sir Remnant, and after his time his son, shall sell to us, at a valuation, any pieces of our own land which we may be able to repurchase. Now, Roland, you never would have thought of that. It is a most admirable plan, is it not?"

"It is worthy of your ingenuity, mother. But will Sir Remnant agree to it? He is fond of his acres, like all land-owners."

"One acre is as good as another to a man of modern lineage. Some of that land passed from us at the time of the great confiscation, and some was sold by that reckless man, the last Sir Hilary but one. The Chapmans have held very little of it for even so much as two centuries; how then can they be attached to it? No, no. You must make that condition, Roland, the first and the most essential point. As for the settlement, that is nothing; though of course you will also insist upon it. For a girl of Alice's birth and appearance, we could easily get a larger settlement and a much higher position, by sending her to London for one season, under Lady de Lampnor. But how would that help us toward getting back the land?"

"You look so learned," said Sir Roland, smiling, "with all those books which you seem to have mastered, that surely we may employ you to draw the deed for signature by Sir Remnant."

"I have little doubt that I could do it," replied the ancient lady, who took every thing as in earnest; "but I am not so strong as I was, and therefore I wish you to push things forward. I have given up, as you know, my proper attention to many little matters (which go on very badly without me) simply that all my small abilities might be devoted to this great purpose. I hope to have still a few years left—but two things I must see accomplished before I can leave this world in peace. Alice must marry Captain Chapman, upon the conditions which I have expressed, and Hilary must marry a fortune, with special clauses enabling him to invest it in land upon proper trusts. The boy is handsome enough for any thing; and his fame for courage, and his martial bearing, and above all his regimentals, will make him irresistible. But he must not stay at the wars too long. It is too great a risk to run."

"Well, my dear mother, I must confess that your scheme is a very fine one; supposing, I mean, that the object is worth it, of which I am by no means sure. I have not made it the purpose of my life to recover the Lorraine estates; I have not toiled and schemed for that end; although," he added with dry irony, which quite escaped his mother's sense, "it is of course a far less exertion to sell one's children, with that view. But there are several hitches in your little plan—for instance, Alice hates Captain Chapman, and Hilary loves a girl without a penny—though the grower must have had good markets lately, according to the price of vegetables." Clever as Sir Roland was, he made the mistake of the outer world: there are no such things as "good markets."

"Alice is a mere child," replied her grandmother, smiling placidly; "she can not have the smallest idea yet as to what she likes or dislikes. The captain is much better bred than his father, and he can drive four-in-hand. I wonder that she has shown such presumption as either to like or dislike him. It is your fault, Roland. Perpetual indulgence sets children up to such dreadful things; of which they must be broken painfully, having been encouraged so."

"My dear mother," Sir Roland answered, keeping his own opinions to himself; "you clearly know how to manage young girls a great deal better than I do. Will you talk to Alice (in your own convincing and most eloquent manner) if I send her up to you?"

"With the greatest pleasure," said Lady Valeria, having long expected this; "you may safely leave her to me, I believe. Chits of girls must be taught their place. But I mean to be very quiet with her. Let me see her to-morrow, Roland; I am tired now, and could not manage her without more talking than I am fit for. Therefore I will say 'good-evening.'"

CHAPTER XXXVII.

ALICE had "plenty of spirit of her own," which of course she called "sense of dignity;" but, in spite of it all, she was most unwilling to encounter her valiant grandmother. And she knew that this encounter was announced, the moment she was sent for.

"Is my hair right? Are my bows right? Has the old dog left any paw-marks on me?" she asked herself; but would rather have died—as in her quick way she said to herself—than have confessed her fright by asking any of the maids to tell her. Between herself and her grandmother there was little love lost, and still less kept; for each looked down upon the other from heights of pure affection. "A flighty, romantic, unfledged girl, with no deference toward her superiors"—"A cold-blooded, crafty, plotting old woman, without a bit of faith in any one;"—thus would each have seen the other's image, if she had clearly inspected her own mind, and faced its impressions honestly.

The elder lady, having cares of her own, contrived, for the most part, to do very well without seeing much of her grandchild; who, on the other hand, was quite resigned to the affliction of this absence. But Alice could never perceive the justice of the reproaches wherewith she was met, whenever she came, for not having come more often where she was not wanted.

Now with all her courage ready, and not a sign in eye, face, or bearing, of the disquietude all the while fluttering in the shadow of her heart, the young lady looked at the ancient lady respectfully, and saluted her. Two fairer types of youth and age, of innocence and experience, of maiden grace and matron dignity, scarcely need be sought for; and the resemblance of their features heightened the contrast of age and character. A sculptor might have been pleased to reckon the points of beauty inherited by the maiden from the matron—the slim round neck, the graceful carriage of the well-shaped head, the elliptic arch of brow, the broad yet softly moulded forehead, as well as the straight nose and delicate chin—a strong resemblance of details, but in the expression of the whole an even stronger difference. For Alice, besides the bright play of youth and all its glistening carelessness, was gifted with a kinder and larger nature than her grandmother. And as a kind large-fruited tree, to all who understand it, shows—even by its bark and foliage and the expression of its growth—the vigor of the virtue in it, and liberality of its juice; so a fine sweet human nature breathes and shines in the outer aspect, brightens the glance, and enriches the smile, and makes the whole creature charming.

But Alice, though blessed with this very nice manner of contemplating humanity, was quite unable to bring it to bear upon the countenance of her grandmother. We all know how the very best benevolence perpetually is pulled up short; and even the turn of a word, or a look, or a breath of air with a smell in it, scatters fine ideas into corners out of harmony.

"You may take a chair, my dear, if you please," said Lady Valeria, graciously; "you seem to be rather pale to-day. I hope you have not taken any thing likely to disagree with you. If you have, there is still a little drop left of my famous ginger-cordial. You make a face! That is not becoming. You must get over those childish tricks. You are—let me see how old are you?"

"Seventeen years and a half, madam; about last Wednesday fortnight."

"It is always good to be accurate, Alice. 'About' is a very loose word indeed. It may have been either that day or another."

"It must have been either that day or some other," said Alice, gravely courtesying.

"You inherit this catch-word style from your father. I pass it over, as you are so young. But the sooner you leave it off, the better. There are many things now that you must leave off. For instance, you must not pretend to be witty. It is not in our family."

"I did not suppose that it was, grandmother."

"There used to be some wit when I was young, but none of it has descended. There is nothing more fatal to a young girl's prospects than a sad ambition for jesting. And it is concerning your prospects now that I wish to advise you kindly. I hear from your father a very sad thing—that you receive with ingratitude the plans which we have formed for you."

"My father has not told me of any plans at all about me."

"He may not have told you, but you know them well. Consulting your own welfare and the interest of the family, we have resolved that you should at once receive the addresses of Captain Chapman."

"You can not be so cruel, I am sure. Or, if you are, my father can not. I would sooner die than so degrade myself."

"Young girls always talk like that when their fancy does not happen to be caught. When, however, that is the case, they care not how they degrade themselves. This throws upon their elders the duty of judging and deciding for them as to what will conduce to their happiness."

"To hear Captain Chapman's name alone conduces to my misery."

"I beg you, Alice, to explain what you mean. Your expressions are strong, and I am not sure that they are altogether respectful."

"I mean them to be quite respectful, grandmother and I do not mean them to be too strong. Indeed I should despair of making them so."

"You are very provoking. Will you kindly state your objections to Captain Chapman?"

Alice for the first time dropped her eyes under the old lady's steadfast gaze. She felt that her intuition was right, but she could not put it into words.

"Is it his appearance, may I ask? Is he too short for your ideal? Are his eyes too small and his hair too thin? Does he slouch in walking, and turn his toes in? Is it any trumpery of that sort?" asked Lady Valeria, though in her heart such things were not scored as "trumpery."

"Were such things trumpery when you were young?" her grandchild longed to ask, but duty and good training checked her.

"His appearance is bad enough," she replied, "but I do not attach much importance to that." "As if I believed it!" thought Lady Valeria.

"Then what is it that proves fatal to him, in your sagacious judgment?"

"I beg you as a favor not to ask me, madam. I can not—I can not explain to you."

"Nonsense, child," said the old lady, smiling; "you would not be so absurd if you had only seen a little good society. If you are so bashful, you may look away; but at any rate you must tell me."

"Then it is this," the maiden answered, with her gray eyes full on her grandmother's face, and a rich blush adding to their lustre; "Captain Chapman is not what I call a good man."

"In what way? How? What have you heard against him? If he is not perfect, you can make him so."

"Never, never! He is a very bad man. He despises all women; and he—he looks—he stares quite insolently—even at me!"

"Well, this is a little too good, I declare!" exclaimed her grandmother, with as loud a laugh as good-breeding ever indulges in. "My dear child, you must go to London; you must be presented at Court; you must learn a little of the ways of the world; and see the first gentleman in Europe. How his Royal Highness will laugh, to be sure; I shall send him the story through Lady de Lampnor, that a young lady hates and abhors her intended, because he even ventures to look at her!"

"You can not understand me, madam. And I will not pretend to argue with you."

"I should hope not, indeed. If we spread this story at the beginning of the season, and have you presented while it is fresh, we may save you, even yet, from your monster, perhaps. There will be such eagerness to behold you, simply because you must not be looked at, that every body will be at your feet, all closing their eyes for your sake, I should hope."

Alice was a very sweet-tempered girl; but all the contempt with which in her heart she unconsciously regarded her grandmother was scarcely enough to keep her from flashing forth at this common raillery. Large tears of pride and injured delicacy formed in her eyes, but she held them in; only asking with a courtesy, "May I go now, if you please?"

"To be sure, you may go. You have done quite enough. You have made me laugh, so that I want my tea. Only remember one serious thing—the interest of the family requires that you should soon learn to be looked at. You must begin to take lessons at once. Within six months you must be engaged, and within twelve months you must be married to Captain Stephen Chapman."

"I trow not," said Alice to herself, as with another courtesy, and a shudder, she retreated.

But she had not long been sitting by herself, and feeling the bitterness of defeat, before she determined, with womanly wit, to have a triumph somewhere; so she ran at once to her father's room; and he of course was at home to her.

"If you please, dear papa, you must shut your books, and you must come into this great chair, and you must not shut even one of your eyes, but listen in the most respectful manner to all I have to say to you."

"Well, my dear," Sir Roland answered, "what must be must. You are a thorough tyrant. The days are certainly getting longer; but they scarcely seem to be long enough for you to torment your father."

"No candles, papa, if you please, as yet. What I have to say can be said in the dark, and that will enable you to look at me, papa, which otherwise you could scarcely do. Is it true that you are plotting to marry me to that odious Captain Chapman?"

Sir Roland began to think what to say; for his better nature often told him to wash his hands of this loathsome scheme.

"Are you so tired of me already?" said the quick girl, with sound of tears in her voice; "have I behaved so very badly, and shown so little love for you, that you want to kill me so very soon, father?"

"Alice! come, Alice! you know how I love you, and that all that I care for is your own good."

"And are we so utterly different, papa, in our tastes, and perceptions, and principles, that you can ever dream that it is good for me to marry Mr. Chapman?"

"Well, my dear, he is a very nice man, quiet, and gentle, and kind to every one, and most attentive to his father. He could place you in a very good position, Alice, and you would still be near me. Also, there are other reasons making it desirable."

"What other reasons, papa, may I know? Something about land, I suppose. Land is at the bottom of every mischief."

"You desperate little radical! Well, I will confess that land has a good deal to do with it."

"Papa, am I worth twenty acres to you? Tell the truth now, am I?"

"My darling, you are so very foolish. How can you ask such a question?"

"Well, then, am I worth fifty? Come, now; am I worth as much as fifty? Don't be afraid now, and say that I am, if you really feel that I am not."

"How many fifties—would you like to know? Come to me, and I will tell you."

"No, not yet, papa. There is no kiss for you unless you say I am worth a thousand!"

"You little coquette! You keep all your coquetries for your own old father, I do believe."

"Then tell me that I am worth a thousand, father—a thousand acres of good rich land, with trees and hedges, and cows and sheep—surely I never can be worth all that; or at any rate not to you, papa."

"You are worth to me," said Sir Roland Lorraine, as she fell into his arms, and sobbed, and kissed him, and stroked his white beard, and then sobbed again, "not a thousand acres, but ten thousand—land and hearth, and home and heart!"

"Then, after all, you do love me, father. I call nothing love that loves any thing else. And how much," she asked, with her arms round his neck, and her red lips curving to a crafty whisper, "how much should I be worth if I married a man I despise and dislike? Enough for my grave, and no more, papa, just the size of your small book-table."

Here she fell away, lost in her father's arms, and for the moment could only sigh with her lips and eyelids quivering; and Sir Roland, watching her pale, loving face, was inclined to hate his own mother. "You shall marry no one, my own child," he whispered through her unbraided hair; "no one whom you do not love dearly, and who is not thoroughly worthy of you."

"Then I will not marry any one, papa," she answered, with a smile reviving; "for I do not love any one a bit, papa, except my own father and my own brother; and Uncle Struan of course, and so on, in an outer and milder manner. And as for being worthy of me, I am not worth very much, I know. Still, if I am worth half an acre, I must be too good for that Captain Chapman."

CHAPTER XXXVIII.

The stern and strong will of a single man is a very fine thing for weaker men—and still more so for women—to dwell upon. But the stern strong will of a host of men, set upon one purpose, and resolved to win it or die for it, is a power that conquers the powers of earth and of nature arrayed against them. The British army was resolved to carry by storm Badajos; and their vigorous manner of setting about it, and obstinate way of going on with it, overcame at last the strength of all that tried to stand before them.

This was the more to their credit, because—the worst of all things for a man to get over—even the weather itself was against them. Nothing makes a deeper impression in the human system than long spite of weather does. The sense of luck is still over us all (in spite of philosophy and mathematics), and of all the behavior of fortune, what comes home to our roofs and hats so impressively as the weather does?

Now thoroughly as these British men were resolved to get within the wall, with equal thoroughness very brave Frenchmen were resolved to keep them out. And these had the weather in their favor; for it is an ill wind that blows no one any good; and the rain that rains on the just and unjust seems to have a preference for the latter. Though it must be acknowledged in the present case that, having a view to justice, a man of equal mind might say there was not too much on either side. At any rate, the rain kept raining, for fear of any mistake among them.

Moreover, the moon, between the showers, came out at night, or the sun by day—according to the habits of each of them—exactly when they were wanted by the Frenchmen, and not at all by the Englishmen. If an Englishman wanted to work in the dark, the moon would get up just behind his back; and muskets, rifles, and cannon itself were trained on him, as at a target; and his only chance was to fall flat on his stomach, and shrink back like a toad in a bed of strawberries. And this made us eager to advance, per contra.

And after being shot at for a length of time, almost every man one can meet with desires to have his turn of shooting. Not for the sake of revenge, or any thing low at all in that way; but simply from that love of fairness which lies hidden—too deep sometimes—somewhere or other in all of us. We are anxious to do, one to another, as the other desires to do to us; and till we come to a different condition, men must shoot and be shot at.

All these peaceable distinctions, and regards of right and wrong, were utterly useless, and out of place, in front of the walls of Badajos. Right or wrong, the place must be taken; and this was the third time of trying it. Fury, frenzy, rushing slaughter, and death (that lies still, when the heat is over), who can take and tell them truly; and if he could, who would like to do it, or who would thank him to hear of it?

All the British army knew that the assault was to be made that night; and the Frenchmen, as appeared by-and-by, knew right well what was coming. For when the April sun went down in the brightest azure of all blue skies, a hush of wonder and of waiting fell and lay upon all the scene.

The English now were grown to be what they always grow to be with much fighting—solid in their ways, and (according to the nature of things) hot or cool with discipline, square in their manner of coming up, and hard to be sent back again, certain sure of their strength to conquer, and ready to charge the devil himself if he had the courage to wait for them. They were under a man who knew how to lead them, and trusted them to follow him; their blood was stirred without grand harangues or melodramatic eloquence.

Every man in that solid army knew his own work, and meant to do it, shoulder to shoulder, with rival hardihood and contagious scorn of death.

The walls were higher and the approach much harder than at Ciudad Rodrigo; the garrison stronger, and the captain a strenuous and ingenious warrior. Therefore on the 6th of April, 1812, as the storming-parties watched the sunset fading along the Guadiana, and the sudden fall of night, which scarcely gives a bird time to twitter on his roost, they wanted no prophet to tell them how different their number would be to-morrow. But still, as the proper and comforting law of human nature ordains it, every man thought, or at any rate hoped, that his messmate rather than himself was the one to leave a widow and orphans by midnight.

Hilary Lorraine was now beginning to get used to fighting. At first, in spite of all his talk about his sword and so on, blows and bloodshed went against the grain of his kind and gay nature. He even thought, in his fresh aversion at so many corpses, that war was a worse institution than law. That error, however, he was beginning to abjure, through the power of custom, aided by two sapient reflections. The first of these was that without much slaughter there can be no real glory—an article which the young man had now made up his mind to attain; and his other wise recollection was that a Frenchman is the natural enemy of the human race, and must, at all hazards and at any sacrifice of pious lives, be extirpated. Moreover, he may have begun to share, by virtue of his amiability, the views of his brother-officers, which of course were duly professional. So that this young fellow, upon the whole, was as full of fight as the best of them.

"No man died that night with more glory—yet many died, and there was much glory." So writes the Thucydides of this war; not about Hilary (as good-luck willed it), but one of his senior officers. And that such a sentence should ever have been written is a thing to think about. With all that dash of bright carnage fresh on the page of one who did his duty so grandly both with sword and pen, peaceful writers (knowing more of sandy commons and the farm-house fagot than of fascines and gabions, of capons than of caponnières, and of shot grapes than of grape-shot) wisely may stick to the garden-ing-knife, or, in fiercest moments, the pruning-hook; and have nothing to say to the stark sword-blade.

Such duty becomes tenfold a pleasure when the sword-blades not only swing overhead or glitter at the unarmed breast; but bolted into great beams of wood at the most offensive angles, are flashing in the dark at the stomach of a man, like a vast electric porcupine; while bursting shells and powder-barrels, and blasts of grape-shot thick as hail (drowning curses, shrieks, and wails), sweep the craggy rampart clear, or leave only corpses roasting. Such, and worse by a thousand-fold than words may render or mind conceive, was the struggle of that awful night at the central breach of Badajos; and here was Hilary Lorraine, wounded, spent with fruitless efforts, dashed backward on spikes and on bayonet-points, trampled under foot, and singed by the beard of a smouldering comrade, yet glad even to lie still for a minute in the breathless depths of exhaustion. "All up with me now," he was faintly thinking—"perhaps my father will be satisfied. Good-bye, dear Alice and darling Mabel—and good-night to this poor Hilary!"

And here his career—of fame or of shame—must have been over and done with, if he had not already won good liking among the men of his company. For one of them, with his next step ready to be planted on the young officer's breast, caught a view of his face by the light of a fire-ball, stopped short, and stooped over him.

"Blow me!" he exclaimed, while likely to be blown into a thousand pieces; "if this bain't the very young chap as saved me when I wur a-dropping upon the road. One good turn desarves another. Here, Bob, lend a hand, my boy."

"A hand! I can't lend thee a hinch," cried Bob; "they be squazing me up like a squatting-match."

For while all the front men were thus lying dead, the men from the rear would not stop from shoving, and bodily heaving the others before them, as buffaloes rush when they lose their wits. They thrust, every man his front man, on the *chevaux-de-frise*, as if it were a joke, with that bitter recklessness of life and readiness to take their own turn at death which falls upon men of true British birth, and their cousins across the Atlantic, whenever the strong blood is churned within them. And yet all this time they know what they are about.

And so did these two soldiers now. Neither time nor room had they to lift poor Hilary out of the bed of shattered granite where he lay, with wedged spikes sticking into him. And the two men who wanted to do it were swept by the surge of living bodies upward. But first they did this — which saved his life — they threw two muskets across him. Loaded or empty, they knew not; and of course it could not matter so long as the climbing men (laboring their utmost to be killed) found it readier for their feet to tread on the bridge of these muskets (piered with blocks of granite) than on the ribs of poor Hilary. So the struggle went on; and there he lay, and began to peep under other people's legs.

In this rather difficult position he failed to make out any thing at all to satisfy or to please him. Listeners hear little good of themselves, and lurking gazers have about the same luck. Not that Hilary was to be blamed for lying in this groove, inasmuch as he really had no chance or even time to get out of it. A great hulking Yorkshireman (as he turned out) had fallen obliquely upon Hilary's bridge, and was difficult to push aside, and quite impossible to lift up. He groaned a good deal, but he was not dead —if he had not been a Yorkshireman the one fact might have implied the other, but Yorkshiremen do groan after death: however, he was not dead; and he keeps a mill on the Swale at this minute.

Hilary, under these disadvantages, naturally tried to lessen them; and though he was pretty safe where he lay—unless a shell came through the Yorkshireman, and that would have needed a very strong charge—still he became discontented. What with the pain of his wound or wounds (for he knew to his cost that he had several of them), also the violent thirst which followed, as well as the ache of his cramped position, and a piece of spiked plank that worried him, he began to grow more and more desirous of a little change of air.

"Now, my dear sir," he said, with his usual courtesy, to the Yorkshireman, "you do not mean to be in my way, of course; but the fact is that I can't get out of this hole by reason of your incumbency. If you could only, without inconvenience, give a little roll to the right or left, you would be in quite as good a position yourself; or if you have grown attached to this particular spot, I would try to replace you afterward."

"Grah!" was the Yorkshireman's only reply, a grunt of contempt and of surly temper, which plainly meant, "go to—Halifax."

"This is uncivil of you," answered Hilary; "it is getting so hot in here that I shall be forced to retort, I fear, your discourtesy. I beg your pardon a thousand times for making this sharp suggestion."

With these words he pricked the great son of the North in a sensitive part with a loose spike he had found by the light of a French fire-ball, whereupon, with a curse, the fellow rolled over like one of his father's millstones. Then Hilary crawled from his hole of refuge, and stiffly resting on his hand and knees, surveyed the scene of carnage.

The moon had now risen, and was shining gloomily under a stripe of heavy cloud, over the bastion of the Trinidad into the channel of the fatal breach, down which the sultry night-wind sighed, laden with groans, whenever curses and roar of artillery left room for them. The breach itself was still unstormed, and looked more terrible than ever; for the sword-blades fixed at the top were drenched and reeking to the hilt with red, and three had corpses impaled upon them with scarlet coats, gay in the moonlight. The rest, like the jaws of a gorging crocodile, presented their bloody jagginess, clogged here and there with limbs, or heads, or other parts of soldiers. For the moment the British had fallen back to the other side of the ravelin, and their bugles were sounding for the retreat, while the triumphant French were shooting, and shouting, "Why enter you not at all Badajos, messieurs? It is a good place for the English health. Why enter you not, then, Badajos?"

The sullen Britons answered not, but waited for orders to begin again; recovering breath, and heart, and spirit, and gathering closer to one another, to be sure that any body was alive. For more than two thousand men lay dead or dying in a space of one hundred yards square. Of the survivors, every man felt that every other man had done his best—but how about himself? Could he be sure that he never had flinched, nor even hung back for a foot or so, nor pushed any other man on to the spikes to save himself from going there? And was that cursed fortress never to be taken by any skill or strength? was even Lord Wellington wrong for once in setting them to do it? and was it to be said in every British church-yard that Britons were not of the stuff of their fathers?

Sadly thus thinking, but after the manner of our nation not declaring it, they were surprised by a burst of light, and a flight of glittering streaks in it. And almost before these came down again, they saw that the murderous *cheval-de-frise* had a great gap in its centre. With a true British cheer stirring every British heart, out they rushed from their shelter, and up the dark breach, and into Badajos.

One form, however, passed first into Badajos with undisputed precedence, because it happened to be close by, when the sword-blades rocketed away so. And not only that, but the act of that one had enabled the others to follow—an act of valor inspired by luck and incited by bodily anguish.

It was thus. In the depth of that horrible pause and dejection of the assailants, Hilary, getting relieved of his cramp, rose slowly and stood in a sheltered spot, to recover himself before running away. Every thing seemed much against him, so far as he could discover; and no one with a social turn was there to discuss the position.

Moreover, his wounds were beginning at once to sting him and to stiffen him—a clever arrangement made by nature to teach men not to fight so much. Nearly mad with pain —which is felt tenfold as much by quick-born Normans as by slow-born Dutchmen—he saw a shell fall and roll very kindly just between his dragging feet. It carried a very long fuse, sticking out of it at a handsome curve, and steadily spluttering with fire, like the tail of a rat when bad boys have ignited it.

"For better, for worse," cried Hilary, talking to himself, even in his agony, by the power of habit; "go into that hole, my friend, and do your utmost there." So much had he been knocked about, that the shell (although a light one) was as much as he could stagger with, till he dropped it into a shelfy hole, which he had long been looking at, under the baulk of six-inch beam, into which the swords were riveted. Then down he fell, whether from exhaustion or presence of mind—he could never tell. Through the jags of the riven granite he heard the shell in a smothered way sputtering (like a "devil" in a wasp's nest)—and then with a thunderous roar and whiz, and a rush through the air of wood, stone, and iron, the Frenchman's deadly bar was burst.

For a moment Lorraine was so stunned and shaken that all he could do was to stay on the ground; but the shock made one of his wounds bleed afresh, and this perhaps revived him. At any rate he arose, and feebly tottered in over the crest of the breach. The soldiers of the Forty-third and Fifty-second regiments gave him a cheer as they ran up the steep, while on the part of the enemy not a weapon was leveled at him. This, however, was not from any admiration of his valor—though Frenchmen are often most chivalrous foes—but because these heroic defenders at last were compelled to abandon the breaches. Being taken in the rear by the Fifth Division, which had forced its way in at San Vincente, knowing also that the castle had fallen, and seeing their main defense lie shattered, they retired through the town and across the bridge of the Guadiana.

And now it is an accursed truth that the men who had been such glorious heroes, such good brethren to one another, strong, and grand, and pitiful, turned themselves within half an hour into something lower than the beasts that perish. They proved that the worst of war is not bloodshed, agony, and slow death; nor even trampled freedom, hatred, tyranny, and treachery. On that same night of heroism, patriotism, and grand devotion, the nicest and most amiable vice indulged by those very same heroes and devoted patriots was swinish and wallowing drunkenness. Rapine, arson, fury, murder, and outrages unspeakable—even their own allies the Spaniards, glad to be quit of the French, and to welcome warmly these deliverers, found bitter cause ere sunrise to lament the British victory.

So it came to pass that young Lorraine, weak and weary, and vainly seeking a surgeon to bind up his wounds, was compelled to fight once more that night, before he could lay him down and rest.

CHAPTER XXXIX.

THERE would seem to be times, and scenes, and cases in which human nature falls helpless under sudden contamination—a mental outbreak of black murrain, leprosy, or plague. A panic, a superstitious fervor, a patriotic or loyal rush, a rebellion, a "revival"—all of these drive men in masses, like swine down a precipice; but the sack of a large town bloodily stormed is more maddening than all the rest put together.

Even good and steady soldiers caught the taint of villainy. They confessed (when their headaches began to get better) how thoroughly ashamed they were of themselves for having been led into crime and debauch by the scamps and the scum of the regiment. Still, at the moment, they were as bad as, or even worse than, the general blackguards, because they had more strength to rush astray.

Hilary knew mankind very little, and only from a gentleman's point of view; so that when he found, or lost, his way into the great square of the town, he was quite amazed, in his weak state of mind, by the scene he was breaking into. Here, by the light of a blazing bonfire made of costly furniture, he descried Major Clumps of his regiment, more neatly than pleasantly attached to the front door of a large mansion. Across his breast and arms a couple of musket-straps were tightly strained and pegged with bayonets into the timber so firmly that this active officer could not even put foot to the ground. On his head was a very conspicuous fool's cap made of a copy of a proclamation, with that word in large type above his brows; while a gigantic grenadier, as tipsy as a fiddler, was zealously conducting the exhibition, by swinging him slowly to and fro, to the tune of Margery Daw, even as children swing each other on a farm-yard gate. The major's fury and the violence of his language may be imagined, but must not be reported. He had always been famous for powers of swearing; but in this case he outdid himself, renewing (every moment) and redoubling the grins of all spectators.

"You shall swing for this," he screamed to his showman just as Hilary came up; "you shall swing for this, you," etc., etc.

"You shwing first, old cock, at any rate," the grenadier answered, with a graceful sweep of the door and the pendant major.

"Oh, Lorraine, Lorraine!" cried the latter, as the arc of his revolution brought him face to face with Hilary; "for Heaven's sake, stop those miscreants!—ah, you can do nothing, I see—you are hit badly, my poor boy."

"My friend," said Hilary to the grenadier, with that persuasive grace which even the coster-mongers could not resist; "you are much too good a soldier to make a laughing-stock of a brave British officer. I can not attempt to use force with you, for you are lucky enough to be unwounded. Thank God for that, and release your prisoner; remember that he is not a Frenchman, but a brave and good English major."

With these, and perhaps some more solid persuasions, he obtained the release of his senior officer, who for some moments could scarcely speak, through excitement and exhaustion. But he made signs to Hilary that he had something to say of great importance, and presently led him into a narrow archway.

"There will be vile work done in that house," he contrived at last to tell Hilary; "the men were bad enough at Rodrigo; but they will be ten times worse to-night. We are all so scattered about that no man has his own officer near him, and he don't care a button for any others. It was for trying to restrain some scoundrels of the Fifth Division that I was treated in that cursed way. Only think how we should feel, Lorraine, if our own daughters were exposed so!"

"I haven't got any daughters," said Hilary, groaning with pain, perhaps at the thought. "But I'd drive my sword through any man's heart—that is to say, if I had got any sword, or any arm to drive it with." His sword had been carried away by a grape-shot, and his right arm hung loose in a cluster of blood; for he had nothing to bind it up with.

"You are a man, though a wounded man," the major replied, being touched a little by Hilary's strength of expression, inasmuch as he had some nice pretty daughters, out of harm's way in England; "it is most unlucky that you are hit so hard."

"That is quite my own opinion. However, I can hold out a good bit, major, for any work that requires no strength."

"Do you know where to find any of our own fellows? They would be quite ready to fight these blackguards; they are very sore about the way those scoundrels stole into the town. We have always been the foremost hitherto. Your legs are all right, I suppose, my boy?"

"All right, except that I am a trifle light-headed, and that always flies to the legs—or at least we used to say so at Oxford."

"Never mind what you said at Oxford. Only mind what you say in Badajos. Collect every man you can find of ours. Tell him the Fifth are murdering, robbing, cheating us again, as they did by sneaking in at a corner, and insulting our best officers. Drunk or sober, bring them all. The more our men drink, the more sober they get." It is likely enough that officers of the Fifth Division would have thought the same paradox of their own men.

"I can not get along at my usual pace," said Hilary; "but I will do my best. But will not the mischief be done already?"

"I hope not. I asked Count Zamora, who seems to be the foremost man of the town, which he thought most of—his wine, or his daughters. And he answered, of course, as a gentleman must. His cellars contain about three hundred butts; it will take some time for our men to drink that. And I spread a report of their quality, and a rumor that all the ladies had escaped. The night is hot. All the men will plunge into those vast cellars first. And when they come up, any sober man will be a match for twenty."

"What a pest that I am so knocked about!" cried Hilary, quite forgetting his pain in the chivalry of his nature. "Major, if only for half an hour you can hold back the devilry, I will answer for the safety of the household. But beware of fire."

"You need not tell me about that, young man. I have seen this work before you were born. I shall pick up a cloak and berette, and cork my eyebrows, and be a Spaniard; major-domo, or whatever they call it. I can jabber the tongue a bit; enough to go down with English ears. I will be the steward of the cellars, and show them where the best wine is; and they don't know wine from brandy. And they will not know me, in their cups, till I order them all into custody. Be quick; there is no more time to lose."

Hilary saw that Major Clumps was going to play a very dangerous part; for many of the men had their muskets loaded, and recked not at whom they fired them. However, there was nothing better for it; and so he set out upon his own errand, when he ought to have been in hospital.

At first he was very unfortunate, meeting no men of his own regiment, and few even of his own division; for most of them doubtless were busy in the houses, laying hold of every thing. But after turning many corners, he luckily hit upon Corporal White of his own company, a very steady man, who knew the importance of keeping sober at a time of noble plundering. This man was a martinet in a humble way, but popular in the ranks in spite of that; and when he heard of the outrage to a major of his regiment, and his present danger; and knew that a rich don's family was threatened by rascals of the Fifth Division, he vowed that he would fetch a whole company to the rescue ere a man could say "Jack Robinson."

"And now, sir," he said, "you are not able to go much farther, or do any more. Round the corner there is a fountain of beautiful spring water, worth all the wines and spirits these fellows are disgracing of themselves with. Ah, I wish I had a glass of good English ale—but that is neither here nor there. And for want of that, a thirsty man may be glad of a drop of this water, sir. And when you have drunk, let it play on your arm. You have a nasty place, sir."

With these words he ran off; and Hilary, following his directions, enjoyed the greatest of all the mere bodily joys a man can be blessed with—the slaking of furious thirst with cold, delicious, crystal water. He drank, and drank, and sighed with rapture, and then began to laugh at himself; and yet must have another drink. And then for the moment he was so refreshed that his wounds were not worth heeding. "I will go and see what those villains are about," he said to himself and the pretty Saint Isidore (to whose pure statue bending over the gracious water he lifted hat, as a gentleman ought to do); "I have drank of your water, and thank you, Saint; though I have no idea what your name is. Our family was Catholic for five hundred years; and I don't know why we ever left it off."

Rubadub, dubbledy, dulluby-dub — what vowels and dissonants can set forth the sound of a very drunken drummer, set upon his mettle to drum on a drum, whose head he has been drinking from? Having no glasses, and having no time to study the art of sloping a bottle between the teeth with drainage, they truly had happened on a fine idea. They cracked the bottles on the rim of the drum, and put down their mouths and drunk well of it. The drum was not so much the worse for this proceeding as they were, because they allowed no time for the liquor to soak into the greasy parchment; but as many as could stand round were there, and plenty of others came after them. So that the drum-head never once brimmed over, though so many dozens were cracked on it. No wonder, when such work was toward, that many a musket-shot rang along the fire-lit streets of Badajos, and many a brave man who had baffled the fury of the enemy fell dead in the midst of his frolicking.

Hilary felt that he had been shot enough, and to spare, already; and so, while slowly and painfully plodding his way back to the great square of the town, from corner to corner he worked a traverse, in shelter (wherever the shelter offered) of porch, or pier, or any other shadowy folds of the ancient streets. And thus, without any more damage, he returned to the house of the Count of Zamora.

Here he found the main door closely fastened—by the fellows inside, no doubt, to keep their villainous work to themselves—and as the great bonfire was burning low, he thought that he might have mistaken the house, until with his left hand he felt the holes where the bayonets had pegged up the good major. And while he did this, a great roar from the cellars quickened his eagerness to get in.

"This is a nice thing," he said to himself; "the major inside, and no getting at him! Such a choleric man in the power of those scamps! And they can not take him for a Spaniard long, for he is sure to use strong English. And not only Clumps, but the whole of the household at their will and pleasure!"

But even while calling in question his superior officer's self-control, he did not show himself possessed of very wonderful coolness. For, hearing a rush as of many feet upward from the lower quarters, Hilary made the best of his way to the smouldering bonfire, and seized with his left hand—for his right was useless—a chunk of some fine wood too hard to burn (perhaps of the African blackwood, or the bread-fruit-tree, or brown cassia), and came back with it in a mighty fury, and tried to beat the door in. But the door was of ancient chestnut-wood, and at his best he could not have hurt it. So now, in his weakness, he knocked and knocked; and nobody even heard him.

"This is enough to wear any one out," he said to himself, in his poor condition—for the lower the state of a man is, the more he relapses upon his nature, and Hilary's nature was to talk to himself—"if I can not get in like this, I must do something or other, and get in somehow."

This would have cost him little trouble in his usual strength and activity. For the tipsy rascals had left wide open a window within easy reach from the street to a man sound of limb and vigorous. But Lorraine, in his present condition, had no small pain and difficulty in making his way through the opening. This being done at last, he found himself in a dark passage floored with polished timber, upon which he slipped and fell.

"What an evil omen!" he cried, lightly—little imagining how true his words would prove—"to fall upon entering a strange house, even though it be by the window. However, I am shaken more than hurt. Goodness knows, I can't afford to bleed again."

Fastening again his loosened bandage—for he had bound his arm now with a handkerchief—he listened and heard a great noise moving, somewhere in the distance. Nothing can be less satisfactory than to hear a great noise, and hearken very steadfastly for its meaning, yet not learn what it can be about, or even where it comes from. Hilary listened, and the noise seemed now to come from one way and then from another. For the old house was peopled with indolent echoes, lazily answering one another, from corner to corner of passages, like the clapping of hands at a banquet. Wherefore Lorraine, being puzzled, went onward, as behooves a young Englishman. And herein instinct served him well—at least as the luck of the moment seemed—for it led him into the main hall, whence niches and arches seemed leading away anywhere and everywhere. Hilary here stopped short, and wondered. It was so different from an English house; and he could not tell whether he liked it or not. There was some light of wax, and some of oil, and some of spluttering torches stuck into any thing that would hold them, throwing a fugitive gleam on the floor, where the polish of the marble answered it. In other places there were breadths of shadow, wavering, jumping, and flickering.

"This is a queer sort of place," said Hilary; "what is the proper thing for me to do?"

The proper thing for him to do became all at once quite manifest; for a young girl suddenly sprang into the hall like a hunted butterfly darting.

"They can not catch me," she exclaimed in Spanish—"they are too slow, the intoxicated men. I may always laugh at them. Here I will let them have another chase."

Flitting in and out the shadows, as softly as if she were one of them, she stopped by the side of Hilary Lorraine, in a dark place, without seeing him. And he, without footfall, leaned back in a niche, and trembled at being so close to her. For a gleam of faint light glanced upon her, and suggested strange, wild beauty. For the moment, Hilary could only see glittering abundance of loosened hair, a flash of dark eyes, and raiment quivering from the quick turn of the form inside. And then he heard short breath, sudden sighs, and the soothing sound of a figure settling from a great rush into quietude.

"This beats almost every thing I ever knew," said he to himself, quite silently. "I can't help her. And she seems to want no help, so far as I can judge. I wonder who she is, and what she would be like by daylight?"

Before he could make up his mind what to do in a matter beyond experience, a great shout arose in some up-stair places, and a shriek or two, and a noise of trampling. "Holy Virgin! they have caught Camilla!" cried the young lady at Hilary's side. "She ought to have a little more of wisdom. Must I peril myself to protect her?" Without further halt to consider that question—swifter than the slow old lamps cast shadow, she rushed betwixt pillars, and up a stone stairway. And young Lorraine, with more pain than prudence, followed as fast as he could get along.

At the top of the stairs was a broad stone gallery, leading to the right and left, and lit as badly as a village street. But Hilary was not long in doubt, for he heard on the right hand a clashing noise, and soon descried broken shadows flitting, and felt that roguery was going on. So he made at his best pace toward it. And here he had not far to seek; for in a large room, hung with pictures, and likely to be too full of light, the fate of the house was being settled. In spite of all drunken stupidity, and the time spent in the wine-cellars, the plunderers had found out the inmates, and meant to make prizes of war of them. Small wonder that British intervention was not considered a godsend, when our allies were treated so. But British soldiers, however brutal in the times gone by (especially after furious carnage had stirred the worst elements in a man, and ardent liquor fired them), still had one redeeming point—the national love of fair play and sport. They had stolen this Spanish gentleman's wines, burned his furniture in the square, and done their best to set his house on fire, as long as they thought that he skulked away. But now that they touched his dearer honor, and he came like a man to encounter them, something moved their tipsy hearts to know what he was made of.

Miguel de Montalvan, the Count of Zamora, was made of good stuff, as he ought to be, according to his lineage. He was fighting for his children's honor, and he knew how to use a rapier. Two wounded roysterers on the floor showed that, though his hair was white, his arm was not benumbed with age. And now, with his slender Toledo blade, he was holding his own against the bayonet of his third antagonist, a man of twice his strength and weight—the very same tall grenadier who had pegged Major Clumps to the door of the house, and swung him so despitefully.

At the farther end of the room two young and beautiful ladies stood or knelt, in horrible dread and anguish. It was clear at a glance that they were sisters, although they behaved very differently. For one was kneeling in a helpless manner, with streaming eyes and strained hands clasping the feet of a marble crucifix. She had not the courage to look at the conflict, but started convulsively from her prayers at clash of steel or stamp of foot. The other stood firmly, with her hair thrown back, one hand laid on her sister's head, and the other grasping a weapon, her lips set hard and her pale cheeks rigid, while her black eyes never left the face of the man who was striking at her father. At the first glance Hilary knew her to be the brave girl who had escaped to the hall, and returned to share her sister's fate.

Things can not be always done chivalrously, or in true heroic fashion. From among the legs of the reeling Britons (who, with pipes and bottles and shouts of applause, were watching the central combat) Hilary snatched up with his left hand a good-sized wine-bag, roughly rent at the neck, but still containing a part of its precious charge. The rogues had discovered it in the cellar, and guessed that its contents were good. And now, as the owner of the house, hard pressed and unable to reach his long-armed foe, was forced to give way, with the point of the bayonet almost entering his breast, and bearing him back on his daughters, Lorraine, with a sweep of his left arm, brought the juicy bag down on the back of the head of the noble grenadier. At the blow, the rent opened and discharged a gallon of fine old crusted Port and beeswing down the warrior's locks, and into his eyes, and the nape of his neck. Blinded with wine, and mad with passion, he rushed at his new assailant; but the count, as he turned, passed his rapier neatly between the tendons of his right arm. Down fell his musket, and Hilary seized it, and pointed it at the owner's breast. And now the grenadier remembered what he had quite forgotten throughout his encounter with the Spaniard—his musket was loaded, and on the full-cock! So he dropped (like a grebe or a dabchick diving), having seen smart practice with skirmishers.

However, it must have gone ill with Hilary, as well as the count and his household, if succor had not come speedily. For the wassailers, who had shown wondrous temper—Mars being lulled on the lap of Bacchus—suddenly awoke, with equal reason, to wild fury. With much reviling, and condemnation of themselves and one another, they formed front (having discipline even in their cups), and bore down the long room upon the enemy.

Drunk as they were, this charge possessed so much of their accustomed weight and power, that the don looked on all as lost, and could only stand in front of his daughters. But Hilary, with much presence of mind, faced them, as if he were in command, and cried "Halt!" as their officer.

With one accord they halted, and some of them tumbled down in doing it; and before they could form for another charge, or mutiny against orders, Corporal White, with half a company of his famous regiment, took them in the rear, and smote right and left, and they fled with staggered consciences.

CHAPTER XL.

As soon as the count and his daughters knew how much they owed to Hilary, and saw the weak and wounded plight in which he had labored for their good, without any loss of time they proved that Spaniards are not an ungrateful race. The count took the young man in his arms, as well as he could without hurting him, and kissed him upon either cheek; and though the young ladies could not exactly follow their father's example, they made it clear that it was not want of emotion which deterred them. They kissed the left hand of the wounded youth, and bent over it, and looked at him with eyes so charming and so full of exquisite admiration, that Major Clumps, who was lying on the floor corded—and far worse, actually gagged—longed to rap out a great oath; but failed in his struggle to break the commandment.

"Oh, he is so hurt, my father!" cried the braver and, if possible, the lovelier of the two fair maidens; "you do not heed such things, because you are so free yourself to wound. But the cavalier must be taken to bed. See, he is not capable now of standing!"

For Hilary, now that all danger was past, grew faint; while he scorned himself for doing so in the presence of the ladies.

"It is to death; it is to death!" exclaimed the timid damsel. "What shall we do? Oh holy saints! To save us, and to have slain himself!"

"Be tranquil, Camilla," said the Spanish gentleman, kindly, and without contempt. "You have not shown the spirit of our house; but we can not help our natures. Claudia, you are as brave as a man; seek for the good woman Teresina, she has not run away like the rest; she must be hiding somewhere. Camilla, release that other brave señor. Gentlemen all, pray allow us to pass."

Corporal White drew his men aside, while the count, concealing his own slight wounds, led and supported young Lorraine through a short passage and into a bedroom, dark, and cool, and comfortable. Here he laid him to rest on a couch, and brought cold water, and sponged his face. And presently old Teresina came, and moaned, and invoked the Virgin a little, and then fell to and pulled all his clothes off, as if he were her daughter's baby. And Hilary laughed at her way of working, and soothing him like some little pet kid; so that he almost enjoyed the pain of the clotted places coming off.

For, after all, he had not received—like Brigadier Walker that hot evening—twenty-seven wounds of divers sorts, but only five, and two bad bruises, enough to divert the attention. If a man has only one place of his body to think about and to be full of, he is scarcely better off than a gourmand, or a guest at a lord mayor's dinner. But if he finds himself peppered all over, his attention is not over-concentrated, and he finds a new pleasure in backing one hole of his body against another. In the time of the plague this thing was so, and so it must be in the times of war.

From the crown and climax of human misery, Lorraine (by the grace of the Lord) was spared. No doctor was allowed to come near him. That fatal step in the strongest man's life (the step tempting up to the doctor's bell), happily in his case was not trodden; for the British surgeons were doing their utmost at amputating dead men's legs; while Señor Gines de Passamonte (the only Spanish graduate of medicine in good circles) had been roasted at one of the bonfires to enable him to speak English. This was a well-meant operation, and proved by no means a fatal measure; the jack, however, revolved so well, that he went on no medical rounds for three months.

"Señor, we can no doctor get," said the anxious count to Hilary, having made up his mind to plunge into English, of which he had tried some private practice. "Señor, what is now to do? I can no more speak to please."

"You can speak to please most nobly; I wish that I could speak the grand Hispanic tongue at all, sir."

"Señor, you shall. So brave a gentleman never will find bad to teach. The fine Angles way of speaking is to me very strong and good; in one year, two year, three year, sir. Alas! I behold you laughing."

"Count, it was but a twinge of pain. You possess a great knowledge of my native tongue. But I fear that after such a night as this you will care to cultivate it no more."

"From what cause? I have intelligence of you. But the thing has itself otherwise. The Angles are all very good. They incend my goods, and they intoxicate my wines. They are — what you call — well to come. They make battle with me for the donnas, but fairly, very fairly; and with your valiant assistance I victor them. I have no complaint. Now I make adventure to say that you can speak the French tongue. I can do the very same affair, and so can my daughters two. But in this house it must not be. We will speak the Angles until you have intelligence of the Spanish. With your good indulgence, señor. Does that recommend itself to you?"

"Excellently, count," said Hilary. And then, in spite of pain, he added, with his usual courtesy, "I have often longed to learn your magnificent language. This opportunity is delightful."

"I have, at this time, too prolonged," Don Miguel answered, with such a bow as only a Spaniard can make, and a Spaniard only when highly pleased; "sleep, sir, now. The good Teresina will sit always on your head."

The good Teresina could not speak a word of any tongue but her own, and in that she could do without any answers, if only she might make to herself as many as she pleased of them. She saw that Hilary had no bones broken, nor even a bullet in his body—so far as she could yet make out — but was sadly hacked about, and worn, and weak with drains of bleeding. Therefore what he wanted now was nourishment, cold swathes, and sleep; and all of these he obtained abundantly under the care of that good nurse.

Meanwhile, poor Major Clumps (to whom the count and his daughters owed quite as much as they did to young Lorraine) did not by any means become the object of overpowering gratitude. He was neither wounded nor picturesque; and his services, great as they were, had not been rendered in a striking manner. So that although he did his best—as most old officers are inclined to do —to get his deserts attended to, his reward (like theirs) was the unselfish pleasure of seeing inferior merit preferred.

"Of course," he cried, after a preface too powerful to have justice done to it—"of course this is what one must always expect. I get bruised, and battered, and laughed at, and swung on a door, and gagged and corded, the moment I use a good English word; and then the girls for whose sake I did it, and turned myself into a filthy butler, because I am not a smart young coxcomb, and my wounds are black instead of being red, begad, sir, they treat me as if I had been all my life their father's butler!"

The loss of his laurels was all the more bitter to the brave and choleric major, not only because it was always happening—which multiplied it into itself at every single recurrence—but also because he had been rapidly, even for his time of life, subdued by the tender and timorous glances of the sweet young Donna Camilla. The greater the fright this girl was in, the better it suited her appearance; and when she expected to be immolated (as the least of impending horrors), her face was as that of an angel. The major, although trussed tight with whipcord, and full of an old stocking in his mouth, had enjoyed the privilege of gazing at her while she clasped her crucifix. And that picture would abide upon his retentive, stubborn, and honest brain as long as the brain itself abode. He loved an angelical girl, because his late wife had been slightly demoniac.

Now, by the time that our British soldiers had finished their sack of Badajos—which took them three days, though they did their best—and were beginning to be all laid up (in spite of their iron trim and training) by their own excesses, Lorraine was able to turn in his bed, and to pay a tender heed to things. He began to want some sort of change from the never-wearying, but sometimes wearisome, tendance of old Teresina, whose rugged face and pointed cap would dwell in his dreams forever. Of course he was most grateful to her, and never would forget her kindness. Still he longed for a sight of somebody else; ugly or beautiful, he cared not—only let it be some other face. And his wish was granted, as generally happened, and sometimes only too graciously.

Our very noble public schools and ancient universities know, and always have known, how to educate young people. From long experience, they are well aware that all languages are full of mischief; and a man who desires that element finds it almost wherever he pleases. So that our authorities did well to restrict themselves to the grand old form, and the distance of two thousand years. Hence, as a matter of course, poor Hilary had not learned, either at school or college, even one irregular verb of the fine pervasive and persuasive language of all languages. To put it more simply, he could not speak French. In print he could follow it, off and on (as most men, with Latin to lead them, can); but from live lips it was gibberish to him, as even at this day it is to nine and a half out of ten good Britons.

And now, when suddenly a soft rich voice came over his shoulder (just turned once more in great disgust from the dreary door), and asked, in very good French indeed, "How do you carry yourself, sir?" Hilary was at a pinch to answer, "Most well, a thousand thanks, most well." And after this Anglo-Gallic triumph, he rolled on his bandages very politely (in spite of all orders to the contrary) to see who it was, and to look at her.

Even in the gloom of the shaded windows, and of his own enfeebled sight, he could not help receiving an impression of wondrous beauty—a beauty such as it is not good for any young man to gaze upon, unless he is of a purely steadfast heart, and of iron self-control. And Hilary was not of either of these, as himself and his best friends knew too well.

The Count of Zamora's younger daughter, Claudia de Montalvan, was of Andalusian birth, and more than Andalusian beauty. Form, and bloom, and brilliant change, and harmony, and contrast, with the charm of soft expression, and the mysterious power of large black eyes—to all of these, in perfection, add the subtle grace of high lineage, and the warmth of southern nature, and it must be confessed that the fairest English maid, though present in all her beauty, would find a very dangerous rival.

"I quite forgot," said the señorita, approaching the bed with most graceful movement, and fixing her radiant eyes on poor Hilary—"there is one thing, sir, that I quite forgot. My good father will not allow French to be spoken by any child of his. He is so patriotic! What a pity, since you speak French so well!"

Hilary took some time to make out this. Then, knowing how barbarous his accent was, he weakly endeavored with his languid eyes to pierce the depth of the Spanish maiden's, and learn whether she were laughing at him. Neither then nor afterward, when his sight was as keen again as ever, did he succeed in penetrating the dark profundity of those bright eyes.

"How shall we manage it?" the young lady continued, dropping her long curved lashes, and slightly flushing under his steadfast gaze. "You can not speak the Spanish, I fear, not even so well as the droll old señor, who makes us laugh so much down stairs. On the contrary, I can not speak the English. But, in spite of that, we must hold converse. Otherwise, how shall we ever thank you, and nurse you, and recover you? One thing must be begun at once—can I, without pain, lift your hand?"

Great part of this speech was dark to Hilary; but he understood the question about his hand, and kept the disabled one out of sight, and nodded, and said, "Oui, señora." Whereupon, to his great surprise, beautiful Claudia fell on her knees by the side of the couch, caught his left hand in both of hers, and pressed it in the most rapturous manner, ever so many times, to her sweet, cool lips. And a large tear, such as large eyes should shed, gently trickled on each fair cheek, but was cleverly kept from dripping on his hand, because he might not have liked it. And then, with her face not far from his, she looked at him with a long, soft gaze, and her hair (with the gloss and the color of a filbert over the Guadiana) fell from her snowy forehead forward; and Hilary was done for.

CHAPTER XLI.

A SAD and a sorry task it is to follow the lapse of a fine young fellow, from the straight line of truth and honor into the crooked ways of shame. Hilary loved Mabel still, with all his better heart and soul; her pure and kind and playful glance, and the music of her true voice, never wholly departed from him. In the hot infatuation to which (like many wiser and older men) he could not help but yield himself, from time to time a sudden pang of remorse and of good love seized him. Keenly alive to manly honor, and to the goodness of womankind, he found himself playing false to both, and he hated himself when he thought of it. But the worst of him was that he did not think habitually and steadfastly; he talked to himself, and he thought of himself, but he very seldom examined himself. He felt that he was a very good fellow in the main, and meant no harm; and if he set up for a solid character, who would ever believe him? The world had always insisted upon it that he was only a trifler; and the world's opinion is very apt to create what it anticipates. He offered excuses enough to himself, as soon as he saw what a wrong he was doing. But the only excuse a good man can accept is the bitterness of his punishment.

The British army, having exhausted havoc to the lees and dregs, marched upon its glorious way, in quest of other towns of our allies no less combustible. But many wounded champions were left behind in Badajos, quartered on the grateful townsmen, to recover (if they could) and rejoin as soon as possible. Lieutenant Lorraine was one of these, from the necessity of his case; and Major Clumps managed to be another, from his own necessities. But heavily wounded as he was (by one of Don Miguel's daughters), the fighting major would never have got himself certified on the sick-list, unless he had known, from the course of the war, that no battle now was imminent.

Regardless of his Horace, and too regardful of cruel Glycera, more than too much pined Major Clumps, and would have chanted mournful ditties in a minor key, if nature had only gifted him with any other note than D. Because his junior shone beyond him, with breach of loyal discipline. He might console himself, however, with the solace offered by the sprightly bard — the endless chain of love revolving with links on the wrong cog forever. Major Clumps was in love with Camilla; the saintly Camilla declined from him with a tender slope toward Hilary; Hilary went down hill too fast with violent pangs toward Claudia; and Claudia rose at the back of the wheel, with her eyes on the distant mountains.

Of all Lorraine's pure bodily wounds, the worst (though not the most painful, as yet) was a gash in his left side, made by pike, or sword, or bayonet, or something of a nasty poignancy. Hilary could give no account of it, when he took it, or where, or how: he regretted deeply to have it there; but beyond that he knew nothing. It seemed to have been suggested cleverly, instead of coarsely slashing down, so far as a woman who had not spent her youth in dissecting-rooms could judge. But Major Clumps (too old a warrior to lose his head to any thing less perturbing than a cannon-ball) strenuously refused to believe in Hilary's ignorance about it. He had a bad opinion of young men, and believed that Hilary had fallen into some scrape of which he was now ashamed. At the same time he took care to spread it abroad (for the honor of the regiment) that their young lieutenant had been the first to leap on the sword-blades of the breach, even as afterward he was first to totter through the gap he made. But now it seemed likely that either claim would drop into abeyance, until raked up as a question of history.

For the wound in Hilary's side began to show very ugly tokens. It had seemed to be going on very nicely for about a fortnight, and Teresina praised and thanked the saints, and promised them ten days' wages, in the form of candles. But before her vow was due, or her money getting ready, the saints (whether making too sure of their candles, or having no faith in her promises) suddenly struck work, and left this good woman, rags, bottles, and bones, in a miserable way. For violent inflammation began to kindle beneath the bandages, and smiles were succeeded by sighs and moaning, and happy sleep by weary tossings and light-headed wakefulness.

By way of encouraging the patient, Major Clumps came in one day with a pair of convalescent Britons, and a sheet of paper, and pressed upon him the urgent necessity for making his will; to leave the world with comfort and composure. Hilary smiled, through all his pain, at the thought of his having in the world any thing but itself to leave; and then he contrived to say, pretty clearly,

"Major, I don't mean to leave the world. And if I must, I have nothing but my blessing to leave behind me."

"Then you do more harm than good by going; and none need wish to hurry you. Sergeant Williams, you may go, and so may Private Bodkin. You will get no beer in this house, I know; and you have both had wine enough already. Be off! what are you spying for?"

The two poor soldiers, who had looked forward to getting a trifle for their marks, glanced at one another sadly, and, knowing what the major was, made off. For ever since the tricks played with him by drunken fellows who knew him not, Major Clumps had been dreadful toward every sober man of his own regiment. The course of justice never does run smooth.

This was a thing such as Hilary would have rejoiced to behold, and enter into, if he had been free from pain. But gnawing, wearing, worrying pain sadly dulls the sense of humor and power of observation. Yet even pain, and the fear of the grave with nothing to leave behind him, could not rob him of all perception of a sudden brightness shed softly over all around. Two lovely maidens were come to pray for him, and to scatter his enemies.

Claudia de Montalvan led her gentle and beautiful sister Camilla, to thank, once for all, and perhaps to say farewell to, their preserver. Camilla, with her sad heart beating tremulously, yet controlled by maiden dignity and shame, followed shyly, fearing deeply that her eyes would tell their tale. And thus, even through the more brilliant beauty of her braver sister, the depth of love and pity made her, for the time, more beautiful.

Between the two sisters there was but little, even for the most careful modeler to perceive, of difference. Each had the purely moulded forehead, and the perfect arch of eyebrow, and the large expressive eyes, well set and clearly cut and shaded; also the other features shaped to the best of all nature's experience. This made it very nice to notice how distinct their faces were by inner difference of mind and will.

"Señor," said Claudia to Major Clumps, who could manage to make out Spanish, "we have heard that he is very ill. We are come to do the best for him. Camilla will pray—it is so good—and I will do any thing that may need. But it is not right to detain you longer. The gentlemen can not pray at all till they are in the holy orders."

The major bowed, and grimly smiled at this polite dismissal; and then, with a lingering glance at Camilla, stumped away in silence to a proper swearing distance.

His glance might have lingered till dark night fell, before that young Donna returned it. All her power of thought or feeling, fearing, hoping, or despairing, was gathered into one sad gaze at her guest, her savior, and her love. Carefully as she had watched him through the time when there was no danger, she had not been allowed by the ancient nurse to come near him for the last three days. And even now she had been content to obey Teresina's orders, and to trust in the saints, with her calm sweet faith —the saints who had sent this youth to save her—but for her stronger sister's will.

"Disturb him not, sister, but let him rest," said Claudia, whose fair bosom never was a prey to gratitude; "see you not how well he lies? If we should happen to cause disturbance, he might roll over, and break into bleeding; and then you could pray for his soul alone."

"Sister mine, you do not speak well," Camilla answered, gently; "he has shed so much blood for us, that he is not likely to bleed more. It is now the want of the blood and the fever that will make us mourn forever. Cavalier, brave cavalier, can you not look up and muse?"

Hilary, being thus invoked, though he had no idea what was meant—the language being pure Castilian—certainly did look up, and try with very bad success to muse. His eyes met kind Camilla's first (because she was leaning over him), but, in spite of close resemblance, found not what they wanted in them, and wandered on, and met the eyes of Claudia, and rested there.

Camilla, with the speed of love outwinging all the wings of thought, felt, like a stab, this absence from her and this presence elsewhere. And having plenty of inborn pride, as behooved her and became her well, she turned away to go, and leave her sister (who could not pray at all) to pray for what seemed to be more her own. And her heart was bitter as she turned away.

Claudia (who cared not one half-real for Hilary, or what became of him; and who never prayed for herself, or told her beads, or did any religious thing) was also ready to go, with a mind relieved of a noxious duty; when her softer, and therefore nobler, sister came back, with her small pride conquered.

"It is not a time to dispute," she said, "nor even to give one's self to pray, when violent pain is tearing one. My sister, I have prayed for days, and twice as much by night; and yet every thing grows much worse, alas! Last night I dreamed a dream of great strangeness. It may have come from my birthday saint. The good Teresina is having her dinner; and she always occupies one large hour in that consummation. Do a thing of courage, sister; you always are so rich in courage."

"What do you mean?" asked Claudia, smiling; "you seem to have all the courage now."

"Alas! I have no courage, Claudia. You are laughing at me. But if you would only raise the bandage—I dare not touch the poor cavalier—where the sad inflammation is, that makes him look at you so—it is possible that I could, or perhaps that you could—"

"Could what?" asked Claudia, who was not of a long-enduring temper; "I have no fear to touch him; and he seems to be all bandages. There now, is that what you require?" Camilla shuddered as her sister firmly (as if she were unswathing a mummy of four thousand years) untied Teresina's knots and laid bare the angry wound which was eating Hilary's life away. Then a livid virulent gash appeared, banked with proud flesh upon either side, and Claudia could not look at it.

But Camilla gathered the courage often latent in true gentleness, and heeded only in her heart how the poor young fellow fell away and fainted from the bold exposure, and falling back, thus made his wound open and gape wider.

"I see it! I see it! I shall save him yet!" she cried, in feminine ecstasy; and while Claudia thought her mad, she snatched from the chain at her zone a little steel implement, often carried by Spanish girls for beauty's sake. With dainty skimmings, and the lightest touch, she contrived to get this well inside all the mere outward mischief, and drew out a splinter of rusty iron, and held it up to the light in triumph; and then she went down on her knees and sobbed, but still held fast her trophy.

"What is it? Let me see!" cried Claudia, being accustomed to take the lead: "Saint plague, what is a mere shred like that, to cause so much emotion? It may be something the old nurse put there, and so you have done more harm than good."

"Do nurses put pieces of jagged iron into a wound to heal it? It is part of a cruel Frenchman's sword. Behold the fangs of it, and the venomous rust! What agony to the poor cavalier! Now sponge his forehead with the vinegar; for you are the best and most welcome nurse. And when he revives show him this, and his courage will soon be renewed to him. I can stay here no longer, I feel so faint. I will go to my saint, and thank her."

When old Teresina returned, and found her patient looking up at Claudia, with his wound laid bare, she began to scold and wring her hands, and order her visitor out of the room; but the proud young lady would have none of that.

"A pretty nurse you are," she cried, "to leave this in your patient's wound! Is this your healing instrument, pray? What will the Count of Zamora say when I show him this specimen of your skill? How long will he keep you in this house? Oh blind, demented, gorging, wallowing, and most despicable nurse!"

That last word she pronounced with such a bitterness of irony, that poor Teresina's portly form and well-fed cheeks shook violently. "For the love of all the saints, sweet Donna, do not let my lord know this. The marvelous power of your bright eyes has cast their light on every thing. That poor old I, with these poor members, might have gazed and gazed forever; when lo! the most beautiful and high-born lady under heaven appears, and saves the life of the handsome lord that loves her."

"We will speak no more upon this matter," Claudia answered, magnanimously. And the nurse thenceforth was ready to vow, and Hilary only too glad to believe, that the sorely wounded soldier owed his life to a beautiful maiden. And so he did, but not to Claudia.

CHAPTER XLII.

ALONG the northern brow and bend of the Sussex hills, the winter lingers, and the spring wakes slowly. The children of the southern slope, toward Worthing and West Tarring, have made their cowslip balls, and pranked their hats and hair with blue-bells, before their little Northern cousins have begun to nurse and talk to, and then pull to pieces, their cuckoo-pint, and potentilla, dead-nettle, and meadow crowfoot.

The daffodil, that comes and "takes the winds of March with beauty," here reserves that charming capture for the early breeze of May; for still the "black-thorn winter" buffets the folds of chilly April's cloak, and the hail-fringed mantle of wan sunlight. This is the time when a man may say, "Hurra! Here is summer come at last, I verily do believe. For goodness' sake, wife, give us air, and take those hot things from the children's necks. If you want me, I shall be in the bower, having a jolly pipe at last." And then, by the time all the windows are open, and the little ones are proud to show their necks and the scratches of their pins, in rushes papa, with his coat buttoned over, and his pipe put out by hail.

None the less for all of that, the people who like to see things moving—though it be but slowly—have opportunity now of watching small delights that do them good. How trees, and shrubs, and plants, and even earth and stone, begin to feel the difference coming over them. How little points, all black one day, and as hard as the tip of a rook's bill the next time of looking at them, show a little veiny shining. And then as the people come home from church, and are in their most observant humor, after long confinement, a little child finds a real leaf (most likely of an elder-tree), and many young faces crowd around it, while the old men, having seen too many springs, plod on, and doubt this for a bad one.

Much of this had been done, with slow advance from Sunday to Sunday, and the hedges began to be feathered with green, and the meadows to tuft where the good stuff lay, and the corn in the gloss of the sun to glisten; when every body came out of church one Sunday before Pentecost. The church was that which belonged to the Rev. Struan Hales (in his own opinion), and so did the congregation, and so did every thing, except the sermon. And now the rector remained in the vestry, with his favorite daughter Cecil, to help him off with his "academicals," and to put away his comb.

"I hope your mother will be quick, my dear," said the parson, stooping his broad shoulders, as his daughter tugged at him; "she can not walk as she used, you know; and for the last half-hour I have been shuddering and trembling about our first forequarter."

"I saw that you were uncomfortable, papa, just as you were giving out your text. You seemed to smell something burning, didn't you?"

"Exactly!" said the rector, gazing with surprise at his clever and queer Cecil. "Now how could you tell? I am sure I hope none of the congregation were up to it. But ninepence a pound is no joke for the father of three hungry daughters."

"And with a good appetite of his own, papa. Well, I'll tell you how I knew it. You have a peculiar way of lifting your nose when the meat is too near the fire, as it always is with our new cook; and then you looked out of that round-arched window, as if you expected to see some smoke."

"Lift my nose, indeed!" answered the rector; "I shall lift something else; I shall lift your lips, if you laugh at your poor old father so. And I never shaved this morning, because of Sir Remnant's dinner-party to-morrow. There, what do you think of that, Miss Impudence?"

"Oh papa, what a shameful beard! You preached about the stubble being all burned up; perhaps because you were thinking of our lamb. But I do declare you have got as much left as Farmer Gate's very largest field. But talking about Sir Remnant, did you see who skulked into church in the middle of the anthem, and sat behind the gallery pillar, in one of the laborers' free seats?"

"No, I did not. You ought to be ashamed of looking about in church so, Cecil. Nothing escapes you, except the practical application of my doctrine."

"Well, papa, now, you must have been stupid, or had your whole mind upon our new cook, if you didn't see Captain Chapman!"

"Captain Chapman!" cried the rector, with something which in any other place would have been profane; "why, what in the world could he want here? He never came to hear me; that's certain."

"No, papa; nor to hear any thing at all. He came to stare at poor Alice all the time, and to plague her with his escort home, I fear."

"The poor child, with that ungodly scamp! Who were in the servants' pew? I know pretty well; but you are sure to know better."

"Oh, not even one of the trusty people. Neither the old butler, nor Mrs. Pipkins, nor even Mrs. Merryjack. Only that conceited 'Mister Trotman,' as he calls himself, and his 'under-footman,' as he calls the lad, and three or four flirty house-maids."

"A guinea will send them all around the other way; and then he will pester Alice all the way back. Run home, that's a dear, you are very quick of foot; and put the lamb back yourself nine inches; and tell Jem to saddle Maggie quick as lightning, and put my hunting-crop at the green gate, and have Maggie there; and let your mother know that sudden business calls me away to Coombe Lorraine."

"Why, papa, you quite frighten me! As if Alice could not take care of herself!"

"I have seen more of the world than you have, child. Do as I order you, and don't argue. Stop! take the meadow way, to save making any stir in the village. I shall walk slowly, and be at the gate by the time you have the pony there."

Cecil Hales, without another word, went out of the vestry door to a stile leading from the church-yard into a meadow, and thence by an easy gap in a hedge she got into the Rectory shrubbery.

"Just my luck," said the rector to himself, as he took to the rambling village street, to show himself as usual. "The two things I hate most are a row, and the ruin of a good dinner. Hashes and cold meat ever since Wednesday; and now when a real good joint is browning—oh, confound it all!—I quite forgot the asparagus—the first I have cut, and as thick as my thumb! Now if I only had Mabel Lovejoy here! I do hope they'll have the sense not to put it on; but I can't very well tell Jem about it; it will look so mollyish. Can I send a note in? Yes, I can. The fellow can't read; that is one great comfort."

No sooner said than done; he tore out the fly-leaf of his sermon, and under his text, inculcating the duty of Christian vigilance, wrote in pencil, "Whatever you do, don't put on the asparagus."

This he committed to the care of Jem; and then grasping his hunting-whip steadfastly, he rode up the lane, with Maggie neighing at this unaccustomed excursion. For horses know Sunday as well as men do, and a great deal better.

Struan Hales was a somewhat headlong man; as most men of kind heart, and quick but not very large understanding, are apt to be. Like most people of strong prejudices, he was also of strong impulses; for the lowest form of prejudice is not common—the abstract one, and the negative. His common sense and his knowledge of the world might have assured him that Captain Chapman would do nothing to hurt or even to offend young Alice. And yet, because he regarded Stephen with inveterate dislike, he really did for the moment believe it his duty thus to ride after him.

Meanwhile the gallant and elegant captain had done at least one thing according to the rector's anticipation. By laying a guinea in Trotman's palm, he had sent all the servants home over the hill, and thus secured for himself a private walk with his charmer along the lane that winds so prettily under the high land. Now his dress was enough to win the heart of any rustic damsel, and as he passed the cottage doors, all the children said, "Oh my!" This pleased him greatly, and could not have added less than an inch to his stature and less than a pound to the weight of his heel at each strut. This proves that he was not a thorough villain; for thorough villains attach no importance to the opinion of children.

Unaware of the enemy in advance, Alice walked through the little village, with her aunt and two cousins, as usual; and she said "Good-bye" to them at the Rectory gate; knowing that they wanted to please her uncle with his early Sunday dinner. Country parsons, unless they are of a highly distinguished order, like to dine at half-past one very punctually on a Sunday. Throughout the week (when they shoot or fish, or ride to hounds, etc.) they manage to retard their hunger to five, or even six o'clock. On Sunday it is healthily otherwise. A sinking feeling begins to set in about half-way through the sermon. And why? In an eloquent period, the parson looks round, to infect his congregation. He forgets for the moment that he is but unit, while his hearers are a hundred-fold. What happens? All humanity is, at eloquent moments, contagious, sensitive, impressible. A hundred people in the church have got their dinner coming on at one o'clock; they are thinking of it, they are dwelling on the subject; and the hundred and first, the parson himself (without knowing it, very likely, and even while seven heavens above it), receives the recoil of his own emotions, in epidemic appetite.

That may be all wrong, of course, even unsacerdotal, or unscientific (until the subject is tabulated); but facts have large bones; and the fact stands thus. Alice Lorraine was aware of it, though without any scent of the reason; so she kissed her aunt and cousins two—Cecil being (as hath been seen) in clerical attendance—and lightly went her homeward way. She stopped for a minute at Nanny Stilgoe's, to receive the usual grumbling sauced with the inevitable ingratitude. And then, supposing the servants to be no very great distance before her, she took to the lonely Ashwood lane, with a quick, light step, as usual.

Presently she came to a place where the lane dipped suddenly into the hollow of a dry old water-course—the course of the Woeburn, according to tradition, if any body could believe it. There was now not a thread of open water; but a little dampness, and a crust of mud, as if some under-ground duct were anxious to maintain user of its right of way. By the side of the lane, an old oak-trunk (stretched high above the dip, and furnished with a broken hand-rail), showed that there must have been something to cross; though nobody now could remember it. In this hollow lurked the captain, placid and self-contented, and regarding with much apparent zest a little tuft of forget-me-not.

Alice, though startled for a moment by this unexpected encounter, could not help smiling at the ill-matched brilliance of her suitor's apparel. He looked like a smaller but far more costly edition of Mr. Bottler, except that his waistcoat was of crimson taffeta, with a rolling collar of lace; and instead of white stockings, he displayed gold-buttoned vamplets of orange velvet. Being loath to afford him the encouragement of a smile, the young lady turned away her face as she bowed, and with no other salutation continued her homeward course, at a pace which certainly was not slower. But Stephen Chapman came forth, and met her with that peculiar gaze which would have been insolent from a more powerful man, but as proceeding from a little dandy bore rather the impress of impudence.

"Miss Lorraine, you will not refuse me the honor of escorting you to your home. This road is lonely. There still are highwaymen. One was on the Brighton Road last week. I took the liberty of thinking, or rather, perhaps, I should say of hoping, that you might not altogether object to a military escort."

"Thank you," said Alice; "you are very kind; but I have not the least fear; and our servants are not very far away, I know. They have orders to keep near me."

"They must have mistaken your route, I think. I am rather famous for long sight; and I saw the Lorraine livery just now going up the footpath that crosses the hill."

Alice was much perplexed at this. She by no means enjoyed the prospect of a long and secluded walk in the company of this gallant officer. And yet her courage would not allow her to retrace her steps, and cross the hill; neither could she well affront him so; for much as she disliked this man, she must treat him as any other lady would.

"I am much obliged to you, Captain Chapman," she answered, as graciously as she could; "but really no kind of escort is wanted, either military or civilian, in a quiet country road like this, where every body knows me. And perhaps it will be more convenient for you to call on my father in the afternoon. He is always glad when you can stay to dinner."

"No, thank you; I must dine at home to-day. I wish to see Sir Roland this morning, if I may. And surely I may accompany you on your way home; now, may I not?"

"Oh yes," she answered with a little sigh, as there seemed to be no help for it; but she determined to make the captain walk at a speed which should be quite a novelty to him.

"Dear me, Miss Lorraine! I had no idea that you were such a walker. Why, this must be what we call in the army 'double-quick march' almost. Too fast almost to keep the ranks unbroken, when we charge the enemy."

"How very dreadful!" cried Alice, with a little grimace, which greatly charmed the captain. "May I ask you one particular favor?"

"You can ask none," he replied, with his hand laid on his crimson waistcoat; "or, to put it more clearly, to ask a favor is to confer a greater one."

"How very kind you are! You know that my dear brother Hilary is in the thick of very, very sad fighting. And I thought that perhaps you would not mind (as a military escort), describing exactly how you felt when first you charged the enemy."

"The deuce must be in the girl," thought

the captain; "and yet she looks so innocent. It can be only an accident. But she is too sharp to be romanced with."

"Miss Lorraine," he answered, "I belonged to the Guards, whose duty lies principally at home. I have never been in action."

"Oh, I understand; then you do not know what a sad thing real fighting is. Poor Hilary! We are most anxious about him. We have seen his name in the dispatches; and we know that he was wounded. But neither he nor Major Clumps (a brave officer in his regiment) has sent us a line since it happened."

"He was first through the breach at Badajos.* He has covered himself with glory."

"We know it," said Alice, with tears in her eyes; and for a moment she liked the captain. "But if he has covered himself with wounds, what is the good of the glory?"

"A most sensible question," Chapman answered, and fell once more to zero in the opinion of his charmer. With all the contempt that can be expressed by silence, when speech is expected, she kept on so briskly toward Bonny's castle, that her suitor (who, in spite of all martial bearing, walked in the manner of a pigeon) became hard set to keep up with her.

"The view from this spot is so lovely," he said, "I must really beg you to sit down a little. Surely we need not be in such a hurry."

"The air is chilly, and I must not loiter. My father has a bad headache to-day. That was the reason he was not at church."

"Then surely he can be in no hurry for his luncheon. I have so many things to say to you. And you really give me quite a pain in my side."

"Oh, I am so sorry! I beg your pardon. I never could have thought that I was doing that. Rest a little, and you will be better."

The complaint would have been as a joke passed over, if it had come from any body else. But she knew that the captain was not strong in his lungs, or his heart, or any thing; therefore she allowed him to sit down, while she stood and gazed back through the Ashwood lane, fringed, and arched, and dappled by the fluttering approach of spring.

"The beautiful gazing at the beautiful!" said Chapman, with his eyes so fixed as to receive his view of the landscape (if at all) by deputy. And truly his judgment was correct. For Alice, now in perfect health, with all the grace of young vigor and the charm of natural quickness, and a lovely face, and calm eyes beaming, not with the bright uncertain blue (that flashing charm of poor Hilary), but the grand ash-colored gray—the tint that deepens with the depth of life, and holds more love than any other —Alice, in a word, was something for a man to look at. The greatest man that ever was born of a woman, and knew what women are, as well as what a man is; the only one who ever combined the knowledge of both sexes; the one true poet of all ages (compared with whom all other poets are but shallow surfaces), Nature's most loving and best-loved child—even he would have looked at Alice with those large sad, loving eyes, and found her good to dwell upon.

The captain (though he bore the name of a great and grossly neglected poet) had not in him so much as half a pennyweight of poetry. He looked upon Alice as a handsome girl of good birth and good abilities, who might redeem him from his evil ways, and foster him, and make much of him. He knew that she was far above him, "in mind, and views, and all that sort of thing;" and he liked her all the more for that, because it would save him trouble.

"Do let me say a few words to you," he began, with his most seductive and insinuating glance (for he really had fine eyes, as many weak and wanton people have); "you are apt to be hard on me, Miss Lorraine, while all the time my first desire is to please, and serve, and gratify you."

"You are very kind, I am sure, Captain Chapman. I don't know what I have done to deserve it."

"Alas!" he answered with a sigh, which relieved him, because he was much pinched in, as well as a good deal out of breath, for his stays were tighter than the maiden's. "Alas! Is it possible that you have not seen the misery that you have caused me?"

"Yes, I know that I have been very rude. I have walked too fast for you. I beg your pardon, Captain Chapman. I will not do so any more."

"I did not mean that; I assure you, I didn't. I would climb the Andes or the Himalayas, only to win one smile from you."

"I fear that I should smile many times," said Alice, now smiling wickedly; "if I could only have a telescope—still, I should be so sorry for you. They are much worse than the Southdown hills."

"There, you are laughing at me again! You are so clever, Miss Lorraine; you give me no chance to say any thing."

"I am not clever, I am very stupid. And you always say more than I do."

* Upon the appearance of chapters xxxviii. to xli., we received a letter from a distinguished Peninsular officer, Major-general Sir Pons Asinorum. The general denounced us, with more vigor perhaps than courtesy, for "shamefully falsifying facts." Sir Pons himself was the first through the breach, and his brother, Sir Fitz, close after him. If Lieutenant Lorraine was there at all, he was several yards behind them. Our error was being corrected, when lo! the next post brought us six more letters from six gallant officers, each of whom had been first, and not one of them had seen the others, nor even General Asinorum, there. We immediately wrote "stet."—R. D. B.

"Well, of course — of course I do; until you come to know me. After that I always listen, because the ladies have more to say. And they say it so much better."

"Is that so?" said Alice, thinking, while the captain showed his waist, as he arose and shook himself, "it may be so; he may be right; he seems to have some very good ideas." He saw that she thought more kindly of him, and that his proper course with her was to play humility. He had never known what pure love was; he had lessened his small capacity for it by his loose and wicked life; but in spite of all that, for the first time Alice began to inspire him with it. This is a grand revolution in the mind, or the heart, of a "man of pleasure;" the result may save him even yet (if a purer nature master him) from that deadliest foe, himself. And the best (or the worst of it) is, that if a kind, and fresh, and warm, and lofty-minded girl believes herself to have gained any power of doing good in the body of some low reprobate, sweet interest, Christian hankerings, and the feminine love of paradoxes, succeed the legitimate disgust. Alice, however, was not of a weak, impulsive, and slavish nature. And she wholly disdained this Stephen Chapman.

"Now I hope that you will not hurry yourself," she said to the pensive captain; "the real hill begins as soon as we are round the corner. I must walk fast, because my father will be looking out for me. Perhaps, if you kindly are coming to our house, you would like to come more at your leisure, sir."

Stephen Chapman looked at her—not as he used to look, as if she were only a pretty girl to him—but with some new feeling, quite as if he were afraid to answer her. His dull, besotted, and dissolute manner of regarding women lay for the moment under a shock; and he wondered what he was about. And none of his stock speeches came, to help him — or to hurt him — until Alice was round the corner.

"Halloo, Chapman! what are you about? Why, you look like one of Bottler's pigs when they run about with their throats cut! Where is my niece? What have you been doing?" The rector drew up his pony sharply; and was ready to seize poor Stephen by the throat.

"You need not be in such a hurry, parson," said Captain Chapman, recovering himself. "Miss Lorraine is going up the hill a great deal faster than I can go."

"I know what a dissolute dog you are," cried the parson, smoking with indignation at having spoiled his Sunday dinner, and made a scene, for nothing. "You forced me to ride after you, sir. What do you mean by this sort of thing?"

"Mr. Hales, I have no idea what you mean. You seem to be much excited. Pray oblige me with the reason."

"The reason, indeed; when I know what you are! Two nice good girls as ever lived you have stolen out of my gallery, sir; and covered my parish with shame, sir. And are you fit to come near my niece? I have not told Sir Ronald of it, only for your father's sake; but now I will tell him, and, quiet as he is, how long do you suppose he will be in kicking you down the Coombe, sir?"

"Come, now," said Stephen, having long been proof against righteous indignation; "you must be well aware, rector, that the whole of that ancient scandal was scattered to the winds, and I emerged quite blameless."

"Indeed I know nothing of the sort. You did what money could do — however, it is some time back; and perhaps I had better have let an old story—Camerina—eh, what is it? On the other hand, if only—"

"Rector, you always mean aright, though you may be sometimes ungenerous. In your magnificent sermon to-day, what did you say? Why, you said distinctly, in a voice that came all round the pillars — there is mercy for him that repenteth."

"To be sure I did, and I meant it too; but I meant mercy up above, not in my own parish, Stephen. I can't have any mercy in my own parish."

"Let us say no more about it, sir; I am not a very young man now, and my great desire is to settle down. I now have the honor of loving your niece, as I never loved any one before. And I put it to you in a manly way, and as one of my father's most valued friends, whether you have any thing to say against it."

"You mean to say that you really want to settle down with Alice! A girl of half your age and ten times your power of life! Come, Stephen!"

"Well, sir, I know that I am not in as vigorous health as you are. You will walk me down, no doubt, when we come to shoot together on my father's land; but still, all I want is a little repose, and country life, and hunting; a little less of the clubs, and high play, and the company of the P. R., who makes us pay so hard for his friendship. I wish to leave all these bad things—once for all to shake them off — and to get a good wife to keep me straight until my dear father dies. And the moment I marry I shall start a new hunt, and cut out poor Lord Unicorn, who does not know a fox-hound from a beagle. This country is most shamefully hunted now."

"It is, my dear Stephen; it is, indeed. It puts me to the blush every time I go out. Really there is good sense in what you say. There is plenty of room for another pack; and I think I could give you some sound advice."

"I should act entirely, sir, by your opinion. Horses I understand pretty well; but as to hounds, I should never pretend to hold a candle to my uncle Hales."

"Ah, my dear boy, I could soon show you the proper way to go to work. The stamp of dog we want is something of this kind—"

The rector leaned over Maggie's neck, and took the captain by the button-hole, and fondly inditing of so good a matter, he delivered a discourse which was too learned and confidential to be reported rashly. And Stephen hearkened so well and wisely that Mr. Hales formed a better opinion than he ever before had held of him, and began to doubt whether it might not be a sensible plan in such times as these to close the ranks of the sober thinkers and knit together all well-affected, staunch, and loyal interests, by an alliance between the two chief houses of the neighborhood—the one of long lineage, and the other of broad lands; and this would be all the more needful now, if Hilary was to make a mere love-match.

But in spite of all wisdom, Mr. Hales was full of strong, warm feelings; and loving his niece as he did, and despising in his true heart Stephen Chapman, and having small faith in converted rakes, he resolved to be neutral for the present; and so rode home to his dinner.

CHAPTER XLIII.

If any man has any people who ought to care about him, and is not sure how far they exert their minds in his direction, to bring the matter to the mark, let him keep deep silence when he is known to be in danger. The test, as human nature goes, is perhaps a trifle hazardous, at any rate when tried against that existence of the wiry order which is called the masculine; but against the softer and better portion of the human race—the kinder half—whose beauty is the absence of stern reason, this bitter test (if strongly urged) is sure to fetch out something; at least, of course, if no suspicion arises of a touchstone. Wherefore now there were three persons, all of the better sex, in much discomfort about Hilary.

Of these, the first was his excellent grandmother, Lady Valeria Lorraine, whose mind (though fortified with Plowden, and even the strong Fortescue) was much amiss about his being dead, and perhaps "incremated," leaving for evidence not even circumstantial ashes. Proof of this, however invalid, would have caused her great distress—for she really loved and was proud of the youth; but the absence of proof, and the probability of its perpetual absence (for to prove a man dead is to prove a negative, according to recent philosophers), as well as the prospect of complications after the simplest solution, kept this admirable lady's ever-active mind in more activity than was good for it.

The second of the three who fretted with anxiety and fear, was Hilary's young sister Alice. Proud as she was of birth, and position, and spotless honor, and all good things, her brother's life was more precious to her than any of those worldly matters. She knew that he was rash and headlong, too good-natured, and even childish, when compared with men of the world. But she loved him all the more for that; and being herself of a stronger will, had grown (without any sense thereof) into a needful championship and vigilance for his good repute. And this, of course, endeared him more, and made her regard him as a martyr, sinned against, but sinless.

But of all these three the third was the saddest and most hard to deal with. Faith in Providence supports the sister, or even the mother of a man—whenever there is fair play for it—but it seems to have no *locus standi* in the heart of his sweetheart. That delicate young apparatus (always moving up and down, and as variable as the dew-point) is ever ready to do its best, and tells itself so, and consoles itself, and then from reason quoted wholesale, breaks into petty unassorted samples of absurdity.

In this condition, without a dream of jealousy or disloyalty, Mabel Lovejoy waited long, and wondered, hoped, despaired, and fretted, and then worked hard, and hoped again. She had no one to trust her troubles to, no cheerful and consoling voice to argue and grow angry with, and prove against it how absurd it was to speak of comfort, and yet to be imbibing comfort, even while resenting it. Her mother would not say a word, although she often longed to speak because she thought it wise and kind to let the matter die away. While Hilary was present, or at any rate in England, Mrs. Lovejoy had yielded to the romance of these young doings; but now that he was far away, and likely in every weekly journal to be returned as killed and buried, the Kentish dame, as a sensible woman, preferred the charm of a bird in the hand.

Of these there were at least half a dozen ensnared and ready to be caged for life, if Mabel would only have them; and two of them could not be persuaded that her nay meant any thing; for one possessed the mother's yea, and the other that of the father.

The suitor favored by Mrs. Lovejoy was a young physician at Maidstone, Dr. Daniel Calvert, a man of good birth and connections, and having prospects of good fortune. The grower, on the other hand, had now found out the very son-in-law he wanted—Elias Jenkins, a steady young fellow, the son of a maltster at Sevenoaks, who had bought all the barley of old Applewood Farm for forty years and upward. Elias was terribly smitten with Mabel, and suddenly found quite a vigorous joy in the planting and pruning of fruit-trees, and rode over almost every day, throughout both March and April, to take lessons, as he said, in grafting and training pears, and planting cherries, and various other branches of the gentle craft of gardening. Of course the grower could do no less than offer him dinner at every visit, in spite of Mrs. Lovejoy's frowns; and Elias, with a smiling face and blushing cheeks, would bring his chair as close as he could to Mabel's, and do his best in a hearty way to make himself agreeable. And in this he succeeded so far, that his angel did not in the least dislike him; but to think of him twice after Hilary was such an insult to all intelligence! The maiden would have liked the maltster a great deal better than she did, if only he would have dropped his practice of "popping the question" before he left every Saturday afternoon. But he knew that Sunday is a dangerous day; and as he could not well come grafting then, he thought it safer to keep a place in her thoughts until the Monday.

"Try her again, lad," the grower used to say. "Odds bobs, my boy, don't run away from her. Young gals must be watched for, and caught on the hop. If they won't say 'yes' before dinner, have at them again in the afternoon, and get them into the meadows, and then go on again after supper-time. Some take the courting kindest of a morning, and some at meal-time, and some by the moonlight."

"Well, sir, I have tried her in all sorts of ways, and she won't say 'yes' to one of them. I begin to be tired of Saturdays now. I have a great mind to try of a Friday."

"Ay!" cried the grower, looking at him as the author of a great discovery. "Sure enough now, try on Fridays—market-day, as I am a man!"

"Well, now, to think of that!" said Elias; "what a fool I must have been, to keep on so with Saturday! The mistress goes against me, I know; and that always tells up with the maidens. But I must have something settled, squire, before next malting season."

"You shall, you shall indeed, my lad; you may take my word for it. That only stands to reason. Shilly-shally is a game I hate; and no daughter of mine shall play at it. But I blame you more than her, my boy. You don't know how to manage them. Take them by the horns. There is nothing like taking them by the horns, you know."

"Yes, to be sure; if one only knew the proper way to do it, sir. But missie slips away so quick like; I never can get hold of her. And then the mistress has that fellow Calvert over here almost every Sunday."

"Aha!" cried the grower, with a knowing wink, "that is her little game, is it now? That is why she has aches and pains, and such a very sad want of tone, and failure of power in her leaders! Leave it to me, lad—that you may—I'll soon put a stop to that. A pill-grinder at Applewood Farm indeed! But I did not know you was jealous!"

"Jealous! No, no, sir; I scorn the action. But when there are two, you know, why, it makes it not half so nice for one, you know."

Squire Lovejoy, however, soon discovered that he had been a little too confident in pledging himself to keep the maltster's rival off the premises. For Mrs. Lovejoy, being a very resolute woman in a little way, at once began to ache all over, and so effectually to groan, that, instead of having the doctor once a week, she was obliged to have him at least three times. And it was not very long before the young physician's advice was sought for a still more interesting patient.

For the daughter and prime delight of the house, the bright sweet-tempered Mabel, instead of freshening with the spring, and budding with new roses, began to get pale, and thin, and listless, and to want continually to go to church, and not to care about her dinner. Her eagerness for divine service, however, could only be gratified on Sundays; for the practice of reading the prayers to the pillars twelve times a week was not yet in vogue. The novelty, therefore, of Mabel's desire made the symptom all the more alarming; and her father perceived that so strange a case called peremptorily for medical advice. But she, for a long time, did nothing but quote against himself his own opinion of the professors of the healing art; while she stoutly denied the existence on her part of any kind of malady. And so, for a while, she escaped the doctor.

Meanwhile she was fighting very bravely with deep anxiety and long suspense. And the struggle was the more forlorn, and wearisome, and low-hearted, because she must battle it out in silence, with none to sympathize, and (worse than that) with every body condemning her mutely for the conflict. Her father had a true and hearty liking for young Lorraine, preferring him greatly—so far as mere feeling went—to the maltster. But his views for his daughter were different, and he thought it high time that her folly should pass. Her mother, on the other hand, would have rejoiced to see her the wife of Hilary; but had long made up her mind that he would never return alive from Spain, and that Mabel might lose the best years of her life in waiting for a doomed soldier. Gregory Lovejoy alone was likely to side with his sister for the sake of Lorraine, the friend whom he admired so much; and Gregory had transmitted to her sweet little messages and loving words, till the date of the capture of Badajos. But this one consoler and loyal friend was far away from her all this time, having steadfastly eaten his way to the Bar, and received his lofty vocation. Thereupon Lovejoy paid five guineas for his wig, and a guinea for the box thereof, gave a frugal but pleasant "call party," and being no way ashamed of his native county, or his father's place therein, sturdily shouldered the ungrateful duties of "junior," on the home circuit. Of course he did not expect a brief until his round was trodden well; but he never failed to be in court; and his pleasant temper and obliging ways soon began to win him friends. His mother was delighted with all this; but the franklin grumbled heavily at the bags he had to fill with money, to be scattered, as he verily believed, among the senior lawyers.

Now the summer Assizes were held at Maidstone about the beginning of July; and Gregory had sent word from London, by John Shorne, that he must be there, and would spend one night at home, if his father would send a horse for him, by the time when his duties were over. His duties of the day consisted mainly in catering for the bar mess, and attending diligently thereto; and now he saw the wisdom of the rule which makes a due course of feeding essential to the legal aspirant. A hundred examinations would never have qualified him for the bar mess; whereas a long series of Temple dinners had taught him most thoroughly what to avoid.

The grower was filled with vast delight at the idea of marching into court and saying to all the best people of the town, "Pray allow me to pass, sir. My son is here somewhere, I believe. A fresh-colored barrister, if you please, ma'am, with curly hair below his wig. Ah yes, there he is! But his lordship is whispering to him, I see; I must not interrupt them." And therefore, although his time might be worth a crown an hour, ere his son's fetched a penny, he strove in vain against the temptation to go over and look at Gregory. Before breakfast he fidgeted over his fields, and was up for being down upon every one—just to let them know that this sort of talent is hereditary. His workmen winked at one another, and said (as soon as he was gone by) that he must have got out the wrong side of the bed, or else the old lady had been rating of him.

He (in the greatness of his thoughts) strode on, and from time to time worked his lips and cast sharp glances at every gate-post in the glow of imaginary speech. He could not feel that his son, on the whole, was a cleverer fellow than himself had been; and he played the traitor to knife and spade by hankering after gown and wig. "If my father," he said, "had only given me the chance I am giving Gregory, what might I be now? One of these same barons as terrify us with their javelins and gallows, and sit down with white tippets on. Or if my manners wasn't good enough for that, who could ever keep me from standing up and defying all the villains for to put me down so long as I spoke justice? And yet that might happen to be altogether wrong. I'm a great mind not to go over at all. My father was an honest man before me."

In this state of mind he sat down to breakfast, bright with reflections of Gregory's glory, yet dashed irregularly with doubts of the honesty of its origin, till, in quite his old manner, he made up his mind to keep his own counsel about the thing and ride over to the county town, leaving Applewood none the wiser. For John Shorne had orders the night before to keep his message quiet, which an old market-hand could be trusted to do; and as for the ladies, the grower was sure that they knew much less and cared much less about the Assizes than about the washing-day. So he went to his stables about nine o'clock, with enough of his Sunday raiment on to look well but awake no excitement, and taking a good horse, he trotted away with no other token behind him except that he might not be home at dinner-time, but might bring a stranger to supper, perhaps; and they ought to have something roasted.

"Pride," as a general rule, of course, "goeth before a fall;" but the father's pride in the present instance was so kindly and simple that Nature waived her favorite law and stopped Fortune from upsetting him. Although when he entered the court he did not find his son in confidential chat with the lord-chief-justice, nor even in grave deliberation with a grand solicitor, but getting the worst of a conflict with an exorbitant fish-monger; and though the townspeople were not scared as much as they should have been by the wisdom of Gregory's collected front, neither did the latter look a quarter so wise as his father; yet a turn of luck put all things right, and even did substantial good. For the grower at sight of his son was not to be stopped by any door-keeper, but pushed his way into the circle of forensic dignity, and there saluted Gregory with a kiss on the band of his horse-hair, and patted him loudly on the back, and challenging, with a quick, proud glance, the opinions of the bar and bench, exclaimed, in a good round Kentish tone,

"Well done, my boy! Hurra for Greg! Gentlemen all, I'll be dashed if my son doth not look about the wisest of all of 'ee."

Loud titters ran the horse-hair round, and more solid laughter stirred the crowd, while the officers of the court cried "Hush!" and the lord-chief-justice and his learned brother looked at the audacious grower; while he, with one hand on each shoulder of his son, gazed around and nodded graciously.

"Who is this person — this gentleman, I mean?" asked the lord-chief-justice, correcting himself through courtesy to young Lovejoy.

"My father, my lord," answered Gregory, like a man, though blushing like his sister

Mabel. "He has not seen me for a long time, my lord, and he is pleased to see me in this position."

"Ay, that I am, my lord," said the grower, making his bow with dignity. "I could not abide it at first; but his mother—ah, what would she say to see him now? Martin Lovejoy, my lord, of old Applewood Farm, very much at your lordship's service."

The judge was well pleased with this little scene, and kindly glanced at Gregory, of whom he had heard as a diligent pupil from his intimate friend, Mr. Malahide; and being a man who missed no opportunity — as his present position pretty clearly showed—he said to the gratified franklin, "Mr. Lovejoy, I shall be glad to see you, if you can spare me half an hour, after the court has risen."

These few words procured two briefs for Gregory at the next Assizes, and thus set him forth on his legal course; though the judge of course wanted — as the bar knew well—rather to receive than to give advice. For his lordship was building a mansion in Kent, and laying out large fruit-gardens, which he meant to stock with best sorts in the autumn; and it struck him that a professional grower, such as he knew Mr. Lovejoy to be, would be far more likely to advise him well, than the nurserymen who commend most abundantly whatever they have in most abundance.

When the grower had laid down the law to the judge upon the subject of fruit-trees, and invited him to come and see them in bearing as soon as time allowed of it, he set off in high spirits with his son, who had discharged his duties, but did not dine with his brethren of the wig. To do the thing in proper style a horse was hired for Gregory, and they trotted gently, enjoying the evening, along the fairest road in England. Mr. Lovejoy was not very quick of perception, and yet it struck him once or twice that his son was not very gay, and did not show much pleasure at coming home; and at last he asked him suddenly,

"What are you thinking of, Greg, my boy? All this learning is as lead on the brain, as your poor grandfather used to say. A penny for your thoughts, my lord-chief-justice."

"Well, father, I was not thinking of law-books, nor even of—well, I was thinking of nothing, except poor little Mabel."

"Ay, ay, John has told you, I suppose, how little she eats, and how pale she gets. No wonder either, with all the young fellows plaguing and pothering after her so. Between you and me, Master Gregory, I hope to see her married by the malting-time. Now, mind, she will pay a deal of heed to you now that you are a full-blown counselor: young Jenkins is the man, remember; no more about that young, dashing Lorraine."

"No, father, no more about him," said Gregory, sadly and submissively. "I wish I had never brought him here."

"No harm, my son; no harm whatever. That little fancy must be quite worn out. Elias is not overbright, as we know; but he is a steady and worthy young fellow, and will make her a capital husband."

"Well, that is the main point after all—a steadfast man who will stick to her. But you must not hurry her, father, now. That would be the very way to spoil it."

"Hark to him, hark to him!" cried the grower. "A counselor with a vengeance! The first thing he does is to counsel his father how to manage his own household!"

Gregory did his best to smile; but the sunset in his eyes showed something more like the sparkle of a tear; and then they rode on in silence.

CHAPTER XLIV.

After sunset, Mabel Lovejoy went a little way up the lane leading toward the Maidstone Road, on the chance of meeting her father. The glow of the west glanced back from the trees, and twinkled in the hedgerows, and clustered in the traveler's-joy, and here and there lay calmly waning on patches of mould that suited it. Good birds were looking for their usual roost, to hop in and out, and to talk about it, and to flap their wings and tails, until they should get sleepy. But the thrush, the latest songster now, since the riot of the nightingale, was cleaning his beak for his even-song; and a cock-robin, proud on the top of a pole, was clearing his throat, after feeding his young — the third family of the season! The bats were waiting for better light; but a great stag-beetle came out of the ivy, treading the air perpendicularly, with heavy antlers balanced.

All these things fluttered in Mabel's heart, and made her sad, yet taught her not to dwell too much in sadness. Here were all things large and good, and going on for a thousand ages, with very little difference. When the cock-robin died, and the thrush was shot, there would be quite enough to come after them. When the leaf that glanced the sunset dropped, the bud for next year would be up in its place. Even if the trees went down before the storms of winter, fine young saplings grew between them, and would be glad of their light and air. Therefore, Mabel, weary not the ever-changing world with woe.

She did not reason thus, nor even think at all about it. From time to time she looked, and listened for her father's Galloway, and the heavy content of the summer night shed gentle patience round her. As yet she had no sense of wrong, no thought of love betrayed, nor even any dream of fickleness.

Hilary was still to her the hero of all chivalry, the champion of the blameless shield, the Bayard of her life's romance. But now he lay wounded in a barbarous land, perhaps dead, with no lover to bury him. The pointed leaves of an old oak rustled, a rabbit ran away with his scut laid down, a weasel from under a root peered out, and the delicate throat of the sensitive girl quivered with bad omens—for she had not the courage of Alice Lorraine.

Through the slur of the night wind (such as it makes in July only), and the random lifting of outer leaves—too thick to be dealt with properly—and the quivering loops of dependent danglers—who really hoped that they might sleep at last—and then the fall-away of all things from their interruption to the sweetest of all sweet relapse, and the deepest depth of quietude; Mabel heard, through all of these, the lively sound of horses' feet briskly ringing on a rise of ground. For the moment some folly of fancy took her, so that she leaned against a gate, and would have been glad to get over it. She knew how unfit she was to meet him. At last he was coming, with her father, to her! She had not a thing on fit to look at. And he must have seen such girls in Spain. Oh, how cruel of him to come, and take her by surprise so! But perhaps, after all, it was herself, and not her clothes, he would care for. However, let him go on to the house—if she kept well into the gate-post—and then she might slip in and put on her dress—the buff frock he admired so; and if it was much too large in the neck, he would know for whose sake it became so.

"What! Mabel, Mab, all out here alone; and trying to hide from her own brother!"

Gregory jumped from his horse and caught her, and even in the waning light was frightened as she looked at him. Then she fell on his neck, and kissed and kissed him. Bitter as her disappointment was, it was something to have so dear a brother; and she had not seen him for so long, and he must have some news of Hilary. He felt her face, all wet with tears, turned up to him over and over again, and he felt how she trembled, and how slim she was, and he knew in a moment what it meant; and in his steadfast heart arose something that must have been a deep oath, but for much deeper sorrow. And then, like a man, he controlled it all.

"I will walk with you, darling, and lead my horse; or, father, perhaps you will take the bridle, and tell mother to be ready for us. Mab is so glad to see me that she must not be hurried over it."

"Bless my heart!" said the grower; "what a heap of gossip you chits of children always have. And nothing pleases you better than keeping your valued parents in the dark."

With this little grumble he rode on, leading Gregory's horse, and shouting back, at the corner of the lane, "Now, don't be long with your confab, children; I have scarcely had a bit to eat to-day, and I won't have my supper spoiled for you."

Gregory thought it a very bad sign that Mabel sent no little joke after her father, as she used to do. Then he threw his firm arm around her waist, and led her homeward silently. But even by his touch and step she knew that there was no good news for her.

"Oh, Gregory, what is it all about?" she cried, with one hand on his shoulder, and her soft eyes deeply imploring him. "You must have some message for me at last. It is so long since I had any. He is so kind, he would never leave me without any message all this time, unless—unless—"

"He is wounded, you know; how can he write?" asked Gregory, with some irony. "Until he was wounded, how many times did I bring you fifty thousand kisses?"

"Oh, it is not that I was thinking of, though I am sure that was very nice of him. Ah, you need not be laughing, Gregory dear, as if you would not do the same to Phyllis. But do tell me what you have heard, dear brother; I can put up with any thing better than doubt."

"Are you quite sure of that, darling Mab? Can you make up your mind for some very bad news?"

"I have not been used to it, Gregory. I—I have always been so happy. Is he dead? Only say that he is not dead?"

"No, he is not dead. Sit down a moment, under this old willow, while I fetch some water for you."

"I can not sit down till I know the worst. If he is not dead, he is dying of his wounds. Oh, my darling Hilary!"

"He is not dying; he is much better, and will soon rejoin his regiment."

"Then why did you frighten me so for nothing? Oh, how cruel it was of you! I really thought I was going to faint—a thing I have never done in my life. You bring me the best news in the world, and you spoil it by your way of telling it."

"Don't be in such a hurry, darling. I wish that was all I have to tell you. But you have plenty of pride now, haven't you?"

"I—I don't know at all, I am sure; but I suppose I am the same as other girls."

"If you thought that Lorraine was unworthy of you, you could make up your mind to forget him, I hope."

"I never could do such a thing, because I never could dream it of Hilary. He is my better in every way. From feeling myself unworthy of him I might perhaps try to do without him; but, as to forgetting him—never!"

"Not even if he forgot you, Mabel?"

"He can not do it," she answered proudly. "He has promised never to forget me. And no gentleman ever breaks a promise."

"Then Hilary Lorraine is no gentleman. He has forgotten you, and is deeply in love with a Spanish lady."

Kind and good brother as he was, he had told his bad news too abruptly in his indignation. Mabel looked up faintly at him; and was struck in the heart so that she could not speak. But the first of the tide of a sea of tears just moved beneath her eyelids.

"Now, come into supper, that's a dear," whispered Gregory, frightened by the silent springs of sorrow. "If you are not at the table, poor darling, every thing will be upside down, and every body uncomfortable." He spoke like a fool, confounding coarsely her essence and her instincts. And perhaps some little turn of contrast broke the seals of anguish. She looked up, and she smiled, to show her proper sense of duty; and then (without knowledge of what she did) she pressed her right hand to her heart, and leaned on a rail, and fell forward into a torrent of shameless weeping. She was as a little child once more, whose soul is overwhelmed with woe. And all along the hollow hedges went the voice of sobbing.

"Now do shut up," said Gregory, when he had borne it as long as a man can bear. "What is the good of it? Mabel, now, I thought you had more sense than this. After all, it may be false, you know."

"It is not false; it is what I have felt. You would not have told me, if it had been false. It has come from some dreadfully low, mean person, who spies him only too accurately."

"Now, Mabel, you are quite out of yourself. You never did say nasty things. There is nobody spying Lorraine at all. I should doubt if he were worth it. Only it is well known in the regiment (and I had it on the best authority) that he—that he—"

"That he does what? And is that all your authority? I am beginning to laugh at the whole of it."

"Then laugh, my dear Mabel. I wish that you would. It is the true way of regarding such things."

"I dare say it may be for you great men. And you think that poor women can do the same; when indeed there is nothing to laugh at. I scarcely think that you ought to suggest the idea of laughing, Gregory. The best authority, you said. Is that a thing to laugh at?"

"Well, perhaps—perhaps it was not the best authority, after all. It was only two officers of his regiment, who know my friend Capper, who lives in chambers."

"A gentleman living in chambers, indeed, to revile poor Hilary, who has been through the wall! And two officers of his regiment! Greg, I did think that you had a little more sense."

"Well, it seems to me pretty good evidence, Mabel. Would you rather have them of another regiment?"

"Certainly not. I am very glad that they were of poor Hilary's regiment; because that proves they were story-tellers. There is not an officer in his own regiment that can help being jealous of him. After the noble things he has done! How dull you must be, not to see it all! I must come to the Assizes, instead of you. Well, what a cry I have had for nothing!"

"Mabel, you are a noble girl. I am sure you deserve the noblest sweetheart."

"And I have got him," said Mabel, smiling; "and I won't let him go. And I won't believe a single word against him, until he tells me that it is true himself. Do you think that he would not have written to me, even with the stump of his left hand, and said, 'Mabel, I am tired of you; Mabel, I have seen prettier girls, and more of my own rank in life; Mabel, you must try to forget me?' When he does that, I shall cry in earnest; and there will be no more Mabel."

"Come in to supper, my pet," said Gregory. And she came in to supper, with her sweet eyes shining.

CHAPTER XLV.

Near the head of a pass of the Sierra Morena, but out of the dusty track of war, there stood a noble mansion, steadfast from and to unknown ages. The Moorish origin, here and there, was boldly manifest among Spanish, French, and Italian handiwork, both of repair and enlargement. The building must have looked queer at times, with new and incongruous elements; but the summer sun and the storms of winter had enforced among them harmony. So that now this ancient castle of the counts of Zamora was a grand and stately pile in tone, as well as height and amplitude.

The position also had been chosen well; for it stood near the line of the water-shed, commanding northward the beautiful valley of the Guadiana, and southward the plains of the Guadalquivir; so that, as the morning mists rolled off, the towers of Merida might be seen, and the high ground above Badajos; while far on the opposite sky-line flashed the gilt crosses of Cordova; and sometimes, when the distance lifted, a glimpse was afforded of the sunbeams quivering over Seville. And here, toward the latter end of August, 1812, Hilary Lorraine was a guest, and all his wishes law—save one.

The summer had been unusually hot, even for the south of Spain; and a fifth part of the British army was said to be in hospital. This may have been caused in some degree by their habits of drinking and plundering;

which even Lord Wellington declared himself unfit to cope with. To every division of his army he appointed twenty provost-marshals; whereas two hundred would not have been enough to hang these heroes punctually. The patriotic Spaniards, also, could not see why they should not have some comfort from their native land. Therefore they overran it well, with bands of fine fellows of a warlike cast, and having strong tendencies toward good things; and these were of much use to the British, not only by stopping the Frenchmen's letters, but also by living at large and gratis, so that the British, who sometimes paid, became white sheep by the side of them.

One of the fiercest of these guerrillas—or "partidas," as they called themselves—was the notorious Mina; and for lieutenant he had a man of lofty birth, and once good position, a certain Don Alcides d'Alcar, a nephew of the Count of Zamora.

This man had run through every real of a large inheritance, and had slain many gentlemen in private brawls; and his country was growing too hot to hold him, when the French invasion came. The anarchy that ensued was just the very thing to suit him; and he raised a small band of uncertain young fellows, and took to wild life in the mountains. At first they were content to rob weak foreigners without escort; but thriving thus and growing stronger, very soon they enlarged their views. And so they improved, from year to year, in every style of plunder; and being authorized by the Juntas, and favored by British generals, did harm on a large scale to their country; and when they were tired of that, to the French.

Hilary had heard from Camilla much about Alcides d'Alcar; but Claudia had never spoken of him—only blushing proudly when the patriot's name was mentioned. Camilla said that he was a man of extraordinary size and valor; enough to frighten any body, and much too large to please her. And here she glanced at Hilary softly, and dropped her eyes, in a way to show that he was of the proper size to please her—if he cared to know it. He did not care a piastre to know it; but was eager about Alcides. "Oh, then, you had better ask Claudia," Camilla replied, with a sisterly look of very subtle import; and Claudia, with her proud walk, passed, and glanced at them both disdainfully.

Now the victory of Salamanca, and his sorry absence thence, and after that the triumphant entry of the British into Madrid—although they were soon turned out again—began to work in Hilary's mind, and make him eager to rejoin. Three weeks ago he had been reported almost fit to do so, and had been ready to set forth; but Spanish ladies are full of subtlety, and Camilla stopped him. A cock of two lustres had been slain in some of the outer premises; and old Teresina stole down in the night, and behold, in the morning, the patient's wound had most evidently burst forth again. Hilary was surprised, but could not doubt the testimony of his eyes; neither could the licentiate of medicine now attending him.

But now, in the breath of the evening breeze, setting inland from the Atlantic, Lorraine was roving for the latest time in the grounds of Monte Argento. At three in the morning he must set forth, with horses provided by his host, on his journey to head-quarters. The count was known as a patriotic, wise, and wealthy noble, both of whose sons were fighting bravely in the Spanish army; and through his influence Lorraine had been left to hospitality instead of hospitals, which in truth had long been overworked. But Major Clumps had returned to his duty long ago, with a very sore heart, when he found from the Donna Camilla that "she liked him very much indeed, but could never induce herself to love him." With the sharp eye of jealousy, that brave major spied in Hilary the cause of this, and could not be brought to set down his name any more in his letters homeward, or at any rate not for a very long time.

Lorraine, in the calm of this summer evening, with the heat-clouds moving eastward, and the ripple of refreshment softly wooing the burdened air, came to a little bower, or rather a natural cove of rock and leaf, wherein (as he knew) the two fair sisters loved to watch the even-tide weaving hill and glen with shadow before the rapid twilight waned. There was something here that often brought his native Southdowns to his mind, though the foliage was so different. Instead of the rich deep gloss of the beech, the silvery stir of the aspen-tree, and the feathery droop of the graceful birch, here was the round monotony of the olive and the lemon tree, the sombre depth of the ilex, and the rugged lines of the cork-tree, relieved, it is true, just here and there by the symmetry of the silver fir, and the elegant fan of the palm. But what struck Lorraine, and always irked him under these Southern trees and skies, was the way in which the foliage cut its outline oversharply; there was none of that hovering softness, and sweetly fluctuating margin, by which a tree inspires affection as well as admiration.

Unluckily now Lorraine had neither affection nor admiration left for the innocent beauty of nature's works. His passion for Claudia was become an overwhelming and noxious power, a power that crushed for the time and scattered all his better elements. He had ceased to be light-hearted and to make the best of every thing, to love the smiles of children, and to catch a little joke and return it. He had even ceased to talk to himself, as if his conscience had let him know that he was not fit to be talked to. All the waking hours he passed, in the absence of his charmer, were devoted to the study of Spanish, and he began to despise his own English tongue. "There is no melody in it, no rhythm, no grand sonorous majesty," he used to complain; "it is, like its owners, harsh, uncouth, and countrified." After this, what can any one do but pity him for his state of mind?

Whether Claudia returned his passion—for such it was rather than true affection—was still a very doubtful point, though the most important in all the world. Generally she seemed to treat him with a pleased contempt, as if he were a pleasant boy, though several years older than herself. Her clear dark eyes were of such a depth that, though she was by no means chary of their precious glances, he had never been able to reach that inmost light which comes from the very heart. How different from somebody's—of whom he now thought less and less, and vainly strove to think no more, because of the shame that pierced him! But if this Spanish maiden really did not care about him, why did she try, as she clearly did, to conquer and subdue him? Why did she shoot such glances at him as Spanish eyes alone can shoot; why bend her graceful neck so sweetly, slope her delicate head so gently, showing the ripe, firm curve of cheek, and with careless dancings let her raven hair fall into his? Hilary could not imagine why; but poor Camilla knew too well. If ever Camilla felt for a moment the desirability of any one, Claudia (with her bolder manners, and more suddenly striking beauty, and less dignified love of conquest) might be relied upon to rush in and attract the whole attention.

Hilary found these lovely sisters in their little cove of rock, where the hot wind seldom entered through the fringe of hanging frond. They had a clever device of their own for welcoming the Atlantic breeze by means of a silken rope which lifted all the screen of fern, and creeper, and of gray rock-ivy.

Now the screen was up and the breeze flowing in, meeting a bright rill bubbling out (whose fountain was in the living rock), and the clear obscurity was lighted with forms as bright as poetry. Camilla's comely head had been laid on the bosom of her sister, as if she had made some soft appeal for mercy or indulgence there. And Claudia had been moved a little, as the glistening of her eyelids showed, and a tender gleam in her expression—the one and the only thing required to enrich her brilliant beauty. And thus, without stopping to think, she came up to Hilary, with a long, kind glance, and gave a little sigh, worth more than even that sweet glance to him.

"Alas! dear captain," she said in Spanish, which Hilary was quite pat with now; "we have been lamenting your brief departure. How shall we live when you are lost?"

"What cruelty of yourselves to think! The matter of your inquiry should be the chance of my survival."

"Well said!" she exclaimed. "You English are not so very stupid after all. Why do you not clap your hands, Camilla?"

Camilla, being commanded thus, made a weak attempt with her little palms; but her heart was down too low for any brisk concussion of flesh or air.

"I believe, Master Captain," said Claudia, throwing herself gracefully on a white bull's hide—shaped as a chair on the slopes of moss—"that you are most happy to make your escape from this long and dull imprisonment. Behold how little we have done for you, after all the brave things you have done for us!"

"Ah, no," said Camilla, gazing sadly at the "captain," who would not gaze at her; "it is true that we have done but little. Yet, señor, we meant our best."

"Your kindness to me has been wonderful, magnificent!" answered Hilary. "The days I have passed under your benevolence have been the happiest of my life."

Hereupon Camilla turned away, to hide her tenderness of tears. But Claudia had no exhibition, except a little smile, to hide.

"And will you come again?" she asked. "Will you ever think of us any more, in the scenes of your grand combats, and the fierce delight of glory?"

"Is it possible for me to forget"—began Hilary, in his noblest Spanish—"your constant care of a poor stranger, your never-fatigued attention to him, and thy—thy saving of his life? To thee I owe my life, and will at any moment render it."

This was a little too much for Camilla, who really had saved him; and being too young to know how rarely the proper person gets the praise, she gathered up her things to go.

"Darling Claudia," she exclaimed, "I can do nothing at all without my little silver spinetta. This steel thing is so rusty that it fills my work with canker. You know the danger of rusty iron, Claudia, is it not so?"

"She is cross," said Claudia, as her sister, with gentle dignity, left the cove. "What can have made her so cross to-day?"

"The saints are good to me," Hilary answered, little suspecting the truth of the case; "they grant me the chance of saying what I have long desired to say to you."

"To me, señor!" cried the maiden, displaying a tremulous glow in her long black eyes, and managing to blush divinely, and then, in the frankness of her nature, caring not to conceal a sigh. "It can not be to me, señor!"

"To you—to you, of all the worlds, of all the heavens, and all the angels!" the fervent youth fell upon his knees before his lovely idol, and seized the hand she began to press to her evidently bounding heart, and drew her toward him, and thought for the moment that she was glad to come to him. Then, in his rapture, he stroked aside her loose and deliciously fragrant hair, and waited, with all his heart intent, for the priceless glance—to tell him all. But, strongly moved as she was, no doubt, by his impassioned words and touch, and the sympathy of youthful love, she kept her oval eyelids down, as if she feared to let him see the completion of his conquest. Then, as he fain would have had her nearer, and folded in his eager arms, she gently withdrew, and turned away; but allowed him to hear one little sob, and to see tears irrepressible.

"You loveliest of all lovely beings," began Lorraine, in very decent Spanish, such as herself had taught him; "and at the same time, you best and dearest—"

"Stop, señor," she whispered, gazing sadly, and then playfully, at this prize of her eyes and slave of her lips; "I must not allow you to say so much. You will leave us to-morrow, and forget it all. What is the use of this fugitive dream?"

Hereupon the young soldier went through the usual protestations of truth, fidelity, devotion, and eternal memory; so thoroughly hurried and carried away, that he used in another tongue the words poured forth scarcely a year ago to a purer, truer, and nobler love.

"Alas!" the young donna now mimicked, in voice and attitude, some deserted one; "to how many beautiful English maidens have these very noble words been used! You cavaliers are all alike. I will say no more to you now, brave captain; the proof of truth is not in words, but in true and devoted actions. You know our proverb—'The cork is noisiest when it leaves the bottle.' If you would have me bear you in mind, you must show that you remember me."

"At the cost of my life, of my good repute, of all that I have in the world, or shall have, of every thing but my hope of you."

"I shall remember these words, my captain; and perhaps I shall put them to the test some day."

She gave him her soft and trembling hand, and he pressed it to his lips, and sought to impress a still more loving seal; but she said "Not yet, not yet, oh, beloved one!" Or whether she said "oh, enamored one!" he could not be quite certain. And before he could do or say any thing more, she had passed from his reach, and was gliding swiftly under the leafy curtain of that ever-sacred bower. "She is mine, she is mine!" cried young Lorraine, as he caught up the velvet band of her hair, and covered it with kisses, and then bestowed the same attentions on the white bull-skin where her form had lain. "The loveliest creature ever seen is mine! What can I have done to deserve her?"

While he lay in the ecstasy of his triumph, the loveliest creature ever seen stole swiftly up a rocky path, beset with myrtle and cornel-wood, and canopied with climbers. After some intricate turns, and often watching that no one followed her, she came to the door of a little hut embosomed in towering chestnut-trees. The door was open, and a man of great stature was lounging on a couch too short for his legs, and smoking a cigar of proportions more judiciously adapted to his own. Near one of his elbows stood a very heavy carbine, and a sword three-quarters of a fathom long, and by his other hand lay a great pitcher empty and rolled over.

As the young donna's footfall struck his ears, he leaped from his couch and cocked his gun; then, recognizing the sound, replaced it, and stood indolently at his door.

"At last you are come, then!" he said, with an accent decidedly of the Northern provinces (not inborn, however, but caught from comrades); "I thought that you meant to let me die of thirst. You forget that I have lost the habit of this execrable heat."

Claudia looked up at her cousin Don Alcides d'Alcar—or, as he loved to be called, "the great brigadier"—with a very different gaze from any poor Hilary could win of her. To this man alone the entire treasures of her heart were open; for him alone her glorious eyes no longer sparkled, flashed, or played with insincere allurements, but beamed and shone with depths of light, and profusion of profoundest love.

"Darling," she said, as she stood on tiptoe, and sweetly pacified him, "I have labored in vain to come sooner to you. Your commands took a long time to execute, sir. You men can scarcely understand such things. And that tiresome Camilla hung about me; I thought my occasion would never arrive. But all has gone well: he is my slave forever."

"You did not allow him to embrace you, I trust?" Before he could finish his scowl, she stopped his mouth, and re-assured him.

"Is it to be imagined? A miserable shaveling Briton!" But though she looked so indignant, she knew how near she had been to that ignominy.

"You are as clever as you are lovely," answered the brigadier, well pleased. "But I die of thirst, my beloved one. Fly swiftly to Teresina's store; for I dare not venture till the night has fallen. Would that you could manage your father as you wind those striplings round your spindle!"

For the Count of Zamora had given orders that his precious nephew should be shot, if ever found upon land of his. So Claudia took the empty pitcher, to fetch another half-skin of wine, as well as some food, for the great brigadier; and, having performed this duty, met the infatuated Hilary, for the last time, at her father's board. She wished him good-night, and good-bye, with a glance of deep meaning and kind encouragement; while the fair Camilla bent over his hand, and then departed to her chamber, with full eyes and an empty heart.

CHAPTER XLVI.

In those old times of heavy pounding, scanty food, and great hardihood, when war was not accounted yet as one of the exact sciences, and soldiers slept, in all sorts of weather, without so much as a blanket round them, much less a snug tent overhead, the duties of the different branches of the service were not quite so distinct as they are now. Lieutenant Lorraine—for the ladies had given over-rapid promotion when they called him their "brave captain"—had not rejoined his regiment long before he obtained acknowledgment of his good and gallant actions. Having proved that he could sit a horse, see distinctly at long distance, and speak the Spanish language fairly—thanks to the two young Donnas—and possessed some other accomplishments (which would now be tested by paper work) he received an appointment upon the staff, not of the Light Division, but at head-quarters, under the very keen eyes of "the hero of a hundred fights."

If the brief estimate of his compeers is of any importance to a man of powerful genius—as no doubt it must be, by its effect on his opportunities—then the Iron Duke, though crowned with good luck (as every body called each triumph of his skill and care), certainly seems to have been unlucky as to the date of his birth and work. "Providence in its infinite wisdom"—to use a phrase of the Wesleyans, who claim the great general as of kin to their own courageous founder—produced him at a time, no doubt, when he was uncommonly needful; but when (let him push his fame as he would, by victory after victory) there always was a more gigantic, because a more voracious, glory marching far in front of him. Our great hero never had the chance of terrifying the world by lopping it limb by limb and devouring it; and as real glory is the child of terror (begotten upon it by violence), the fame of Wellington could never vie with Napoleon's glory.

To him, however, this mattered little, except that it often impaired his means of discharging his duty thoroughly. His present duty was to clear the Peninsula of Frenchmen; and this he would perhaps have done in a quarter of the time it cost, if his own country had only shown due faith in his abilities. But the grandeur of his name grew slowly (as the fame of Marcellus grew, like a tree in the hidden lapse of time; and perhaps no other general ever won so many victories before his country began to dream that he could be victorious.

Now this great man was little, if at all, inferior to his mighty rival in that prime necessity of a commander—insight into his material. He made a point of learning exactly what each of his officers was fit for; and he seldom failed, in all his warfare, to put the "right man in the right place." He saw at a glance that Lieutenant Lorraine was a gallant and chivalrous young fellow, active and clever in his way, and likely to be very useful on the staff after a little training. And so many young aids had fallen lately, or were upon the sick-list, that the quartermaster-general was delighted with a recruit so intelligent and zealous as Hilary soon proved himself. And after a few lessons in his duties, he set him to work with might and main to improve his knowledge of "colloquial French."

With this Lorraine, having gift of tongues, began to grow duly familiar; and the more so perhaps because his knowledge of "epistolary English" afforded him very little pleasure just now. For all his good principles and kind feelings must have felt rude shock and shame, when he read three letters from England which reached him on the very same day at Valladolid. The first was from his uncle Struan; and after making every allowance for the rector's want of exercise in the month of August, Hilary (having perhaps a little too much exercise himself) could not help feeling that the tone was scarcely so hearty as usual. The letter was mainly as follows:

"West Lorraine, August 20th, 1812.

"My dear Nephew,—Your father and myself have not been favored with any letters from you for a period of several months. It appears to me that this is neither dutiful nor affectionate; although we know that you have been wounded, which increased our anxiety. You may have been too bad to write, and I wish to make all allowance for you. But where there is a will, there is a way. When I was at Oxford, few men perhaps in all the University felt more distaste than I did for original Latin composition. Yet every Saturday, when we went to hall to get our battel-bills—there was my essay, neatly written, and of sound Latinity."—"Come, come," cried Lorraine; "this is a little too cool, my dear uncle. How many times have I heard you boast what you used to pay your scout's son per line!"

"I can not expect any young man, of

course," continued the worthy parson, "to make such efforts for conscience' sake, as in my young days were made cheerfully. But this indolence and dislike of the pen 'furcâ expellendum est'—must be expelled with a knife and fork. Perhaps you will scarcely care to hear that your aunt and cousins are doing well. After your exploits your memory seems to have grown very short of poor folk in old England. Your birthday falling on a Sunday this year, I took occasion to allude in the course of my sermon to a mural crown, of which I remember to have heard at school. Nobody knew what I meant; but many were more affected than if they did. But, after all, it requires, to my mind, quite as much courage, and more skill, to take a dry wall properly, when nobody has been over it, than to scramble into Badajos. Alice will write to you by this post, and tell you all the gossip of the sad old house, if there is any. There seems to be nobody now with life enough to make much gossip. And all that we hear is about Captain Chapman (who means to have Alice), and about yourself.

"About you it is said, though I can not believe it, and must be ashamed of you when I do so, that you are making a fool of yourself with a Spanish lady of birth and position, but a rank, idolatrous, bigoted Papist! The Lorraines have been always sadly heterodox in religious matters, from age to age receiving every whim they came across of. They have taken to astrology, Mohammed, destiny, and the gods of Greece, and they never seem to know when to stop. The only true Church, the Church of England, never has any hold of them; and if you would marry a Papist, Hilary, it would be a judgment.

"Your father, perhaps, would be very glad of any looseness of mind and sense that might have the power to lead you astray from my ideas of honor. I have had a little explanation with him; in the course of which, as he used stronger language than I at all approve of, I ventured to remind him that from the very outset I had charged him with what I call this low intention, this design of working upon your fickle and capricious temper, to make you act dishonorably. Your poor father was much annoyed at this home-truth, and became so violent and used such unbecoming language, that I thought it the more clerical course to leave him to reflect upon it. On the following Sunday I discoursed upon the third chapter of the epistle of St. James; but there was only Alice in the Coombe pew. I saw, however, that she more than once turned away her face with shame, although I certainly did not discover any tears. It is to be hoped that she gave Sir Roland an accurate summary of my discourse; none of which (as I explained to your dear aunt after the service) was intended for my own domestic hearth. Since that time I have not had the pleasure of meeting Sir Roland Lorraine in private life.

"And now a few words as to your own conduct. Your memory is now so bad that you may have forgotten what I did for you. At a time when my parish and family were in much need of my attention, and two large coveys of quite young birds were lying every night in the corner of the Hays, I left my home in extremely hot weather, simply to be of use to you. My services may have been trifling; but at that time you did not think so. It was not my place to interfere in a matter which was for your father's decision. But I so far committed myself, that if you are fool enough and knave enough—for I never mince language, as your father does—to repudiate your engagement with a charming and sensible girl for the sake of high-flying but low-minded Papists, much of the disgrace will fall on me.

"And what are those Spanish families (descended perhaps from Don Quixote, or even Sancho Panza) to compare with Kentish land-owners, who derive their title from the good old Danes? And what are their women when they get yellow—as they always do before twenty-five—compared with an Englishwoman, who generally looks her best at forty? And not only that (for after all that is a secondary question, as a man grows wise), but is a Southern foreigner likely to make an Englishman happy? Even if she becomes converted from her image-worship (about which they are very obstinate), can she keep his house for him? Can she manage an English servant? can she order a dinner? does she even know when a bed is aired? can a gentleman dine and sleep at her house after a day's hunting, without having rheumatism, gout, and a bilious attack in the morning? All this, you will think, can be managed by deputy; and in very large places it must be so. But I have been a guest in very large places—very much finer than Coombe Lorraine, however your father may have scoffed at me; and I can only say that I would rather be the guest of an English country squire or even a parson, with a clever and active wife at the head of his table, than of a duke with a grand French cook, and a duchess who never saw a dust-pan.

"And if you should marry a Spaniard, where are you to get your grand establishment? Your father never saves a farthing, and you are even less likely to do so. And as for the lady, she of course will have nothing. 'My blood is blue because I have no breeches,' says one of their poets, feelingly; and that is the case with all of them. Whereas I have received a little hint, it does not matter how or where, that Mabel Lovejoy (who is much too good for any fickle jackanapes) is down for a nice round sum in the will of a bachelor banker at Tonbridge. Her father and mother do not know it, neither do any of her family; but I did not pass my very pleasant holiday in that town for nothing. Every one seemed to understand me, and I was thoroughly pleased with all of them.

"But I shall not be pleased at all with you, and in good truth you never shall darken my door, if you yield yourself bound hand and foot to any of those Dulcineas, or rather Delilahs. I have known a good many Spaniards, when Nelson was obliged to take them prisoners; they are a dirty, lazy lot, unfit to ride any thing but mules, and they poison the air with garlic.

"Your aunt and cousins, who have read this letter, say that I have been too hard upon you. The more they argue the more I am convinced that I have been far too lenient. So that I will only add their loves, and remain, my dear nephew, your affectionate uncle, STRUAN HALES.

"P. S.—We expect a very grand shooting season. Last year, through the drought and heat, there was not a good turnip-field in the parish. Birds were very numerous, as they always are in hot seasons, but there was no getting near them. This season the turnips are up to my knees. How I wish that you were here, instead of popping at the red legs! Through the great kindness of young Steenie Chapman I am to have free warren of all Sir Remnant's vast estates! But I like the home-shooting best; and no doubt your father will come to a proper state of mind before the first. Do not take amiss, my dear boy, whatever I may have said for your good. *Scribe cito. Responde cras.*—Your loving uncle, S. H."

All this long epistle was read by Hilary in the saddle; for he had two horses allowed him now—whenever he could get them—and now he was cantering with an order to an outpost of the advanced-guard tracking the rear of Clausel. They knew not yet what Clausel was—one of the few men who ever defied, and yet escaped from Wellington. The British staff was weak just now, though freshly recruited with Hilary, or haply the Frenchman might not have succeeded in his brilliant movement.

"He must be terribly put out," said young Lorraine, meaning neither Clausel, nor Wellington, nor Napoleon even, but his uncle Struan; "there is not a word of any paragon dog, nor the horses he has bought or chopped, nor even little Cecil. He must have had a great row with my father, and he visits it on this generation. How can he have heard of angelic Claudia, and connect her with garlic? My darling, I know what you are, though heavy-seated Britons fail to soar to such perfection! Now for Alice, I suppose. She will know how to behave, I should hope. Why, how she begins, as if I were her thirty-second cousin ten times removed! And how precious short it is! But what a beautifully clear, firm hand!"

"MY DEAR HILARY,—My father, not having any time to spare just now, and having received no letter from you which he might desire to answer, has asked me to say that we are quite well, and that we are very glad to hear that you seem to have greatly distinguished yourself. To hear this must always be, as you will feel, a pleasure and true pride to us. At the same time we have been very anxious, because you have been returned in the *Gazette* as heavily wounded. We hope, however, that it is not so, for we have been favored with a very long letter from Major Clumps of your regiment to my grandmother's dear friend, Lady de Lampnor, in which you were spoken of most highly; and since that he has not spoken of you, as he must have done, if you were wounded. Pray let us hear at once what the truth is. Uncle Struan was very rude to my father about you the other day, and used the most violent language, and preached such a sermon against himself on Sunday! But he has not been up to apologize yet; and I hear from dear Cecil that he means to tell you all about it. He is most thoroughly good, poor dear; but allowances must be made for him.

"He will tell you, of course, all the gossip of the place; which is mainly, as usual, about himself. He seems to attach so much importance to what we consider trifles. And he does the most wonderful things sometimes.

"He has taken a boy from the bottom of our hill—the boy that stole the donkey, and lived upon rags and bottles—and he has him at the rectory, every day except Sunday, to clean knives and boots. The whole of the village is quite astonished; the boy used to run for his life at the sight of dear Uncle Struan, and we can not help thinking that it is done just because we could never encourage the boy.

"Papa thinks that you are very likely to require a little cash just now, for he knows that young officers are poorly paid, even when they can get their money, which is said to be scarce with your brave army now; therefore he has placed £100 to your credit with Messrs. Shotman, for which you can draw as required; and the money will be replaced at Christmas. And grandmamma begs me to add that she is so pleased with your success in the only profession fit for a gentleman, that she sends from her own purse twenty guineas, through the hands of Messrs. Shotman. And she trusts that you will now begin to cultivate frugality.

"With these words I must now conclude, prolonging only to convey the kind love of us all, and best desires for your welfare, with which I now subscribe myself, your affectionate sister, ALICE LORRAINE.

"P.S. — DARLING BROTHER,—The above has been chiefly from that grandmamma. I have leave to write to you now myself; and the rest of this piece of paper will hold not a hundredth part of what I want to say. I am most unhappy about dear papa, and about you, and Uncle Struan and Captain Chapman, and every body. Nothing goes well; and if you fight in Spain, we fight much worse in England. Father is always thinking, and dwelling upon his thoughts, in the library. He knows that he has been hard upon you; and the better you go on, the more he worries himself about it. Because he is so thoroughly set upon being just to every one. And even concerning a certain young lady—it is not as Uncle Struan fancies. You know how headlong he is, and he can not at all understand our father. My father has a justice such as my uncle can not dream of. But dear papa doubts your knowledge of your own mind, darling Hilary. What a low idea of Uncle Struan, that you were sent to Spain to be tempted! I did not like what happened to you in Kent last summer any more than other people did. But I think that papa would despise you—and I am quite sure that I should—if you deceived any body after leading them to trust you. But of course you could not do it, darling, any more than I could.

"Now do write home a nice cheerful letter, with every word of all you do, and every thing you can think of. Papa pretends to be very quiet; but I am sure that he is always thinking of you; and he seems to grow so much older. I wish all his books were at Hanover! I would take him for a good ride every day. Good-bye, darling! If you make out this, you will deserve a crown of crosses. Uncle Struan thought that he was very learned; and he confounded the mural with the civic crown! Having earned the one, earn the other by saving us all, and your own LALLIE."

Hilary read this letter twice; and then put it by, to be read again; for some of it touched him sadly. Then he delivered the orders he bore, and made a rough sketch of the valley, and returning by another track, drew forth his third epistle. This he had feared to confront, because his conscience went against him so; for he knew that the hand was Gregory's. However, it must be met sooner or later; it was no good putting off the evil day; and so he read as follows:

"Mid. Temple, Aug. 22d, 1812.

"MY DEAR LORRAINE,—It is now many months since I heard from you, and knowing that you had been wounded, I have been very anxious about you, and wrote three several times to inquire, under date May 3d, June 7th, and July 2d. Of course none of these may have come to hand, as they were addressed to your regiment, and I do not at all understand how you manage without having any post-town. But I have heard through my friend Capper, who knows two officers of your regiment, that you were expected to return to duty in July, since which I have vainly expected to hear from you by every arrival. No one, therefore, can charge me with haste or impatience in asking, at last, for some explanation of your conduct. And this I do with a heavy heart, in consequence of some reports which have reached me from good authority."

"Confound the fellow!" cried the conscious Hilary; "how he beats about the bush! Will he never have it out and be done with it? What an abominably legal and cold-blooded style! Ah, now for it!"

"You must be aware that you have won the warmest regard, and indeed I may say the whole heart, of my sister Mabel. This was much against the wishes and intentions of her friends. She was not thrown in your way to catch the heir to a title, and a rich man's son. We knew that there would be many obstacles, and we all desired to prevent it. Even I, though carried away by my great regard for you, never approved of it. If you have a particle of your old candor left, you will confess that from first to last the engagement was of your own seeking. I knew, and my sister also knew, that your father could not be expected to like it, or allow it for a very long time to come. But we also knew that he was a man of honor and integrity, and that if he broke it off, it would be done by fair means, and not by foul. Every thing depended upon yourself. You were not a boy, but a man at least five years older than my sister; and you formed this attachment with your eyes open, and did your utmost to make it mutual."

"To be sure I did!" exclaimed the young officer, giving a swish to his innocent horse, because himself deserved it; "how could I help it? She was such a dear! How I wish I had never seen Claudia! But really, Gregory, come now, you are almost too hard upon me!"

"And not only this," continued that inexorable young barrister; "but lest there should be any doubt about your serious intentions, you induced, or at any rate you permitted, your uncle, the Rev. Struan Hales, to visit Mabel and encourage her, and assure her that all opposition would fail, if she remained true and steadfast.

"Mabel has remained true and steadfast, even to the extent of disbelieving that you can be otherwise. From day to day, and from week to week, she has been looking for a message from you, if it were only one kind word. She has felt your wound, I make bold to say, a great deal more than you have done. She has taken more pride than you can have taken in what she calls your 'glory.' She watches every morning for the man who goes for the letters, and every evening she waits and listens for a step that never comes.

"If she could only make up her mind that you had quite forgotten her, I hope that she would try to think that you were not worth grieving for. But the worst of it is that she can not bring herself to think any ill of you. And until she has it under your own hand that you are cruel and false to her, she only smiles at and despises those who think it possible.

"We must put a stop to this state of things. It is not fair that any girl should be kept in the dark and deluded so; least of all such a girl as Mabel, so gentle, and true, and tender-hearted. Therefore I must beg you at once to write to my sister or to me, and to state honestly your intentions. If your intention is to desert my sister, I ask you as a last favor to do it as rudely and roughly as possible; so that her pride may be aroused and help her to overget the blow. But if you can give any honorable explanation of your conduct, no one will be more delighted, and beg your pardon more heartily and humbly, than your former friend,

"Gregory Lovejoy."

CHAPTER XLVII.

Lorraine set spurs to his horse as soon as he got to the end of this letter. It was high time for him to gallop away from the one idea—the bitter knowledge that out of this he could not come with the conscience of a gentleman. He was right in fleeing from himself, as hard as ever he could go; for no Lorraine had been known ever to behave so shabbily. In the former days of rather low morality and high feudalism, many Lorraines might have taken fancies to pretty girls, and jilted them. But never as he had done; never approaching a pure maid as an equal, and pledging honor to her, and then dishonorably deserting her.

"I am sure I know not what to do!" he cried, in a cold sweat, while his nag was in a very hot one. "Heaven knows who my true-love is. I am almost sure that it must be Mabel; because when I think of her I get hot; and when I think of Claudia I get cold."

There may have been some sense in this; at any rate it is a question for a meteorologist. Though people who explain—as they always manage to do—every thing, might without difficulty declare that they understood the whole of it. That a young man in magnetic attitude toward two maidens widely distinct, one positive and one negative, should hop up and down, like elder-pith, would of course be accounted for by the "strange phenomena of electricity." But little was known of such things then; and every man had to confront his own acts, without any fine phraseology. And Hilary's acts had left him now in such a position—or "fix" as it is forcibly termed nowadays—that even that most inventive Arab, the Sheik of the Subterfuges, could scarcely have delivered him.

But, after all, the griefs of the body (where there is perpetual work) knock at the door of the constitution louder than those of the mind do. And not only Hilary now, but all the British army, found it hard to get any thing to eat. As for money—there was none, or next to none, among them; but this was a trifling matter to men who knew so well how to help themselves. But shoes, and clothing, and meat for dinner, and yellow soap for horny soles, and a dram of something strong at night before lying down in the hole of their hips—they felt the want of these comforts now, after spending a fortnight in Madrid. And now they were bound to march every day fifteen to twenty English miles, over very hard ground, and in scorching hot weather, after an enemy offering more than affording chance of fighting.

These things made every British bosom ready to explode with anger; and the staff was blamed, as usual, for negligence, ignorance, clumsiness, inability, and all the rest of it. These reproaches entered deeply into the bruised heart of Lorraine, and made him so zealous that his chief very often laughed while praising him. And thus in the valley of the Arlanzan, on the march toward Burgos, he became a gallant captain, with the good-will of all who knew him.

Lorraine was royally proud of this; for his nature was not self-contained. He contemplated many letters, beginning "Captain Lorraine presents his compliments to so and so;" and he even thought at one time of thus defying his uncle Struan. However, a little reflection showed him that the wisest plan was to let the rector abide a while in silence. It was out of all reason—though not, perhaps, entirely beyond precedent—that he, the least injured of all the parties, should be the loudest in complaint; and it would serve him right to learn from the hostile source of Coombe Lorraine the withering fact that his recreant nephew was a captain in the British army.

To Alice, therefore, the captain wrote at the very first opportunity, to set forth his promotion, and to thank his father and grandmother for cash. But he made no allusion to home-affairs, except to wish every body well. This letter he dispatched on the 17th of September; and then, being thoroughly stiff and weary from a week spent in the saddle, he shunned the campfires and the cooking, and slept in a tuffet of plantain-grass, to the melody of the Arlanzan.

On the following day our army, being entirely robbed of fighting by a dancing Frenchman (who kept snapping his fingers at Lord Wellington), entered in no pleasant humor into a burning city. The sun was hot enough in all conscience, roasting all wholesome Britons into a dirty Moorish color, without a poor halt and maimed soldier having to march between burning houses. A house on fire is full of interest, and has become proverbial now as an illustration of bright success. But the metaphor—whether derived or not from military privileges—proceeds on the supposition that the proper people have applied the torch. In the present case this was otherwise. The Frenchmen had fired the houses, and taken excellent care to rob them first.

Finding the heat of the town of Burgos almost past endurance, although the fire had now been quenched, Hilary strolled forth toward sunset for a little change of air. His duties, which had been so incessant, were cut short for a day or two; but to move his legs, with no horse between them, seemed at first unnatural. He passed through narrow reeking streets, where filthy people sprawled about under overlapping eaves and coignes, and then he came to the scorched, rough land, and looked back at the citadel. The garrison, now that the smoke was clearing from the houses below the steep (which they had fired for safety's sake), might be seen in the western light, training their guns upon the city, which swarmed with Spanish guerrillas.

These sons of the soil were plundering with as good a grace as if themselves had taken a hostile city; and in the enthusiasm of the moment, or from force of habit perhaps, some of them gladly lent a hand in robbing their own houses. But the British soldiers grounded arms, and looked on very grimly; for they had not carried the town by storm, and their sense of honesty prevailed. All this amused Lorraine, who watched it through his field-glass, as he sat on a rocky mound outside the city, resting himself, for his legs were stiff, and feeling quite out of his element at being his own master. But presently he saw that the French, who were very busy in the castle, were about to treat both Spaniards and Britons to a warm salute of shells; and he rose at once to give them warning, but found his legs too stiff for speed. So he threw a half-dollar to a Portuguese soldier, who was sauntering on the road below, and bade him run at his very best pace, and give notice of their danger.

But before his messenger had passed the gate, Hilary saw a Spanish chief, as in the distance he seemed to be, come swiftly out of a side street, and by rapid signals recall and place quite out of the line of fire all the plundering Spaniards. This man, as Hilary's spy-glass showed him, was of very great breadth and stature, and wore a slouch-hat with a short black feather, a green leather jerkin, and a broad, white sash; his mighty legs were encased above mid-thigh in boots of undressed hide; and he was armed with a long straight sword and dagger. Having some experience of plunderers, Hilary was surprised at the prompt obedience yielded to this guerrilla chief, until he was gratified by observing a sample of his discipline. For two of his men demurring a little to the abandonment of their prey, he knocked them down as scientifically as an English pugilist, handed their booty to others, and had them dragged by the heels round the corner. Then having his men all under cover, he stood in a calm and reflective attitude, with an immense cigar in his mouth, to see a fine group of thirsty Britons (who were drinking in the middle of the square), shot or shelled as the case might be. And when Hilary's messenger ran up in breathless haste to give the alarm, and earn his half-dollar honestly, what did that ruthless fellow do but thrust forth a long leg, trip him up, and hand him over with a grin to some brigands, who rifled his pockets and stopped his mouth. Then came what Hilary had expected, a roar, a plunge, a wreath of smoke, and nine or ten brave Englishmen lay shattered round the fountain.

"That Spaniard is a very queer ally," said Hilary, with a shudder. "He knew what was coming, and he took good care that it should not be prevented. Let me try to see his face, if my good glass will show it. I call him a bandit and nothing else. *Partidas* indeed! I call them cut-throats."

At that very moment the great guerrilla turned round to indulge in a hearty laugh, and having a panel of pitched wall behind him, presented his face (like a portrait in an ebony frame) toward Hilary. The collar of the jerkin was rolled back, and the great bull throat and neck left bare, except where a short black beard stood forth, like a spur of jet to the heavy jaws. The mouth was covered with a thick mustache; but haughty nostrils and a Roman nose, as well as deep lines of face, and fierce eyes hung with sullen eyebrows, made Hilary cry "What an ugly fellow!" as he turned his glass upon something else.

Yet this was a face such as many women dote upon and almost adore. Power is the first thing they look for in the face of a man; or at least it is the very first thing that strikes them. And "power" of that sort is headstrong will, with no regard for others. From mental power it so diverges, that very few men have embodied both; as nature has kindly provided, for the happiness of the rest of us. But Captain Lorraine, while he watched that Spaniard, knew that he must be a man of mark, though he little dreamed that his wild love Claudia utterly scorned his own comely self, in comparison with that "ugly fellow."

But for the moment the sight of that brigand, and slaughter of good English soldiers, set Hilary (who, with all his faults, was vigorously patriotic) against the whole race of Spaniards, male or female, or whatever they might be. Being driven by nature, as usual, rather with a spur than bridle, he made a strong dash at a desperate fence which for months had been puzzling him. Horses unluckily do not write, although they talk, and laugh, and think, and may tell with their eyes a great deal more than most of us who ride them. Therefore this metaphor must be dropped, for Lorraine pulled out his roll of paper, pen, and ink (which he was bound to carry), and put up his knees, all stiff and creaking, and on that desk did what he ought to have done at least three months ago. He wrote to his loving Mabel; surely better late than never.

"My darling Mabel, — I know that I have not behaved to you kindly, or even as a gentleman. Although I was not allowed to write to you, I ought to have written to your brother Gregory long ago, and I am ashamed of myself. But I am much more ashamed of the reason, and I will make no sham excuses. It is difficult to say what I want to say; but my only amends is to tell the whole truth, and I hope that you will try to allow for me.

"And the truth is this. I fell in love; not as I did with you, my darling, just because I loved you. But because—well I can not tell why, although I am trying for the very truth; I can not tell why I did it. She saved my life, and nursed me long. She was not bad-looking; but young and good.

"I hope that it is all over now. I trust in the Lord that it is so. I see that these Spaniards are cruel people, and I work night and day to forget them all. When I get any sleep, it is you that come and look upon me beautifully; and when I kick up with those plaguesome insects, the face that I see is a Spanish one. This alone shows where my heart is fixed. But you have none of those things at Old Applewood.

"And now I can say no more. I write in the midst of roaring cannon, and perhaps you will say, when you see my words, that I had better have died of my wounds, than lived to disgrace, as I have done, your

"Hilary.

"P.S.—Try to think the best of me, darling. If any body needs it, I do. Gregory wrote me such a letter that I am afraid to send you any—any thing!"

CHAPTER XLVIII.

Pessimists who love to dwell on the darker side of human nature, and find (or at any rate color) that perpetually changing object to the tone of their own dull thoughts, making our whole world no better than the chameleon of themselves; who trace every act, and word, and thought, either to very mean selfishness, or exceedingly grand destiny—according to their own pet theory—let those gloomy spirits migrate in as cheerful a manner as they can manage to the back side of the moon, the side that neither shines on earth, nor gathers any earth-shine. But even if they will not thus oblige inferior mortals, let them not come near a scene where true love dwells, and simple faith, and pleasant hours are spent in helping nature to be kind to us.

Where the rich recesses of the bosomed earth brim over with variety; where every step of man discloses some new goodness over him; and every hour of the day shows different veins of happiness; the light in sloping glances looking richer as the sun goes down, and showing with a deeper love its own good works and parentage; the children of the light presenting all their varied joy to it; some revolving, many bending, all with one accord inclining softly, sweetly, and thankfully—can any man, though of the lowest order, wander about at a time like this, with the power of the sunset over him, and walk down the alleys of trees, and think, and ponder the grand beneficence, without putting both hands into his pockets, and tapping the band of his small-clothes?

If any man could be so ungrateful to the Giver of all good things, he was not to be found in the land of Kent, but must be sought in some northern county where they grow sour gooseberries. Master Martin Lovejoy had, in the month of October, 1812, as fine a crop of pears as ever made a fountain of a tree.

For the growers did not understand the pruning of trees as we do now. They were a benighted lot altogether, proceeding only by rule of thumb, and the practice of their grandfathers, never lopping the roots of a tree, nor summer pinching, nor wiring it, nor dislocating its joints; and yet they grew as good fruit as we do! They had no right to do so; but the thing is beyond denial. Therefore one might see a pear-tree rising in its natural form, tall, and straight, and goodly, hanging its taper branches like a chandelier with lustrous weight, tier upon tier, the rich fruit glistening with the ruddy sun-streaks, or with russet veinage mellowing. Hard thereby the Golden Noble, globular and stainless, or the conical King Pippin, penciled on its orange fullness with a crimson glow, or the great bulk of Dutch codlin, oblong, ribbed and overbearing. Here was the place and the time for a man to sit in the midst of his garden, and feel that the year was not gone in vain, nor his date of life lessened fruitlessly, and looking round with right good-will, thank the Lord, and remember his father.

In such goodly mood and tenor, Master Martin Lovejoy sat, early of an October afternoon, to smoke his pipe and enjoy himself. He had finished his dinner—a plain but good one; his teeth were sound, and digestion staunch; he paid his tithes and went to church; he had not an enemy in the world, to the utmost of his knowledge; and his name was good for a thousand pounds from Canterbury to Reigate. His wheat had been fine, and his hops pretty good, his barley by no means below the mark, the cherry and strawberry season fair, and his apples and pears as you see them. Such a man would be guilty of a great mistake if he kept on the tramp perpetually. Fortune encouraged him to sit down, and set an arm-chair and a cushion for him, and mixed him a glass of Schiedam and water, with a slice of lemon, and gave him a wife to ask how his feet were, as well as a daughter to see to his slippers.

"Now you don't get on at all," he said, as he mixed Mrs. Lovejoy the least little drop, because of the wind going round to the north; "you are so abstemious, my dear soul; by-and-by you will pay out for it."

"I must be a disciplinarian, Martin," Mrs. Lovejoy replied, with a sad, sweet smile. "How ever the ladies can manage to take beer, wine, gin, bitters, and brandy, in the way they do, all of an afternoon, is beyond my comprehension."

"They get used to it," answered the grower, calmly; "and their constitution requires it. At the same time I am not saying, mind you, that some of them may not overdo it. Moderation is the golden rule; but you carry it too far, my dear."

"Better too little than too much," said Mrs. Lovejoy, sententiously. "Whatever I take, I like just to know that there is something in it, and no more. No, Martin, no—if you please, not more than the thickness of my thumb-nail. Well, now for what we were talking about. We can never go on like this, you know."

"Wife, I will tell you what it is;" here Martin Lovejoy tried to look both melancholy and stern, but failed; "we do not use our duties right; we do not work up in the position to which it has pleased God to call us. We don't make our children see that they are — bless my heart, what is the word?"

"'Oligated' is the word you mean. 'Obligated' they all of them are."

"No, no; 'bounden' is the word I mean; 'bounden' says the Catechism. They are bounden to obey, whether they like it or no, and that is the word's expression. Now is there one of them as does it?"

"I can't say there is," his wife replied, after thinking of all three of them. "Martin, no; they do their best, but you can't have them quite tied hand and foot. And I doubt whether we should love them better if we had them always to order."

"Likely not. I can not tell. They have given me no chance of trying. They do what seems best in their own eyes, and the fault of it lies with you, mother."

"Do they ever do any thing wrong, Martin Lovejoy? Do they ever disgrace you anywhere? Do they ever go about and borrow money, or trade on their name, or any thing? Surely you want to provoke me, Martin, when you begin to revile my children."

"Well," said the grower, blowing smoke, in the manner of a matrimonial man, "let us go to something else. Here is this affair of Mabel's now. How do you mean to settle it?"

"I think you should rather tell me, Martin, how you mean to settle it. She might have been settled long ago, in a good position and comfortable, if my advice had been heeded. But you are the most obstinate man in the world."

"Well, well, my dear, I don't think that you should be hard upon any one in that respect. You have set your heart upon one thing, and I upon another; and we have to deal with some one perhaps more obstinate than both of us. She takes after her good mother there."

"After her father, more likely, Martin. But she has given her promise, and she will keep it, and the time is very nearly up, you know."

"The battle of Trafalgar, yes. The 21st of October, seven years ago, as I am a man! Lord bless me, it seems but yesterday! How all the country up and wept, and how it sent our boy to sea! There never can be such a thing again; and no one would look at a drum-head Savoy!"

"Plague upon the market, Martin! I do believe you think much more of your growings than your gainings. But she fixed the day herself, because it was a battle; didn't she?"

"Yes, wife, yes. But after all, I see not so much to come of it. Supposing she gets no letter by to-morrow night, what comes of it?"

"Why, a very great deal. You men never know. She puts all her foolish ideas aside, and she does her best to be sensible."

"By the spread of my measure, oh, deary me! I thought she was bound to much more than that. She gives up him, at any rate."

"Yes, poor dear, she gives him up, and a precious cry she will make of it. Why, Martin, when you and I were young, we carried on so differently."

"What use to talk about that?" said the grower; "they all must have their romances now. Like tapping a cask of beer it is. You must let them spit out at the top a little."

"All that, of course, needs no discussion. I do not remember that, in our love-time, you expected to see me 'spit out at the top!' You grow so coarse in your ideas, Martin; the more you go growing, the coarser you get."

"Now, is there nothing to be said but that? She gives him up, and she tries to be sensible. The malting season is on, and how can Elias come and do any thing?"

"Martin, may I say one word? You keep so perpetually talking that I scarcely have a chance to breathe. We do not want that low Jenkins here. How many quarters he soaks in a week is nothing and can not be any thing to me. A tanner is more to my taste a great deal, if one must come down to the dressers. And there one might get some good ox-tails. I believe that you want to sell your daughter to get your malt for nothing."

The grower's indignation at this despicable charge was such that he rolled in his chair, like a man in a boat, and spread his sturdy legs, and said nothing, for fear of further mischief. Then he turned out his elbows, in a manner of his own, and Mrs. Lovejoy saw that she had gone too far.

"Well, well," she resumed, "perhaps not quite that. Mr. Jenkins, no doubt, is very well in his way; and he shall have fair play, so far as I am concerned. But mind, Dr. Calvert must have the same; that was our bargain, Martin. All the days of the week to be open to both, and no difference in the dinner."

"Very well, very well!" the franklin murmured, being still a little wounded about the malt. "I am sure I put up with any thing. Calvert may have her if he can cure her. I can't bear to see the poor maid so pining. It makes my heart ache many a time; but I have more faith in barley-corn than jalap; though I don't want neither of them for nothing."

"We shall see, my dear, how she will come round. The doctor prescribes carriage exercise for her. Well, how is she to get it, except in his carriage? And she can not well have his carriage, I suppose, before she marries him."

"Carriage exercise? Riding on wheels, I suppose, is what they mean by it. If riding on wheels will do her any good, she can have our yellow gig five times a week. And I want to go round the neighborhood too. There's some little bits of money owing me. I'll take her for a drive to-morrow."

"Your yellow gig! To call that a carriage! A rough sort of exercise, I doubt. Why, it jerks up, like a jack-in-a-box, at every stone you come to. If that is your idea of a carriage, Martin, pray take us all out in the dung-cart."

"The old gig was good enough for my mother; and why should my daughter be above it? They doctors and women are turning her head, worse than poor young Lorraine did. Oh, if I had Elias to prune my trees—after all I have taught him—and Lorraine to get up in the van again; I might keep out of the bankrupt court after all; I do believe I might." Here the grower fetched a long sigh through his pipe. He was going to be bankrupt every season; but never achieved that glory.

"I'm tired of that," Mrs. Lovejoy said. "You used to frighten me with it at first, whenever there came any sort of weather—a storm, or a frost, or too much sun, or too much rain, or too little of it; the Lord knows that if you have had any fruit, you have got it out of him by grumbling. And now you are longing, in a heathenish manner, to marry your daughter to two men at once! One for the night-work and one for the day. Now, will you, for once, speak your mind out truly?"

"Well, wife, there is no one that tries a man so badly as his own wife does. I am pretty well known for speaking my mind too plainly, more than too doubtfully. I can't say the same to you, as I should have to say to any body else; because you are my wife you see, and have a good right to be down upon me. And so I am forced to get away from things that ought to be argued. But about my daughter, I have a right to think my own opinion; while I leave your own to you, as a father has a right with a mother. And all I say is common sense. Our Mabel belongs to a time of life when the girls are always dreaming. And then you may say what you like to them mainly; and it makes no difference. Now she looks very pale, and she feels very queer, all through that young sort of mischief. But let her get a letter from Master Hilary—and you would see what would come over her."

"I have got it! I have got it!" cried a young voice, as if in answer, although too sudden of approach for that. "Father, here it is! Mother, here it is! Long expected, come at last! There, what do you think of that now?"

Her face was lighted with a smile of delight, and her eyes with tears of gladness, as she stood between her astonished parents, and waved in the air an open letter, fluttering less (though a breeze was blowing) than her true heart fluttered. Then she pressed the paper to her lips, and kissed it with a good smack every time; and then she laid it against her bosom, and bowed to her father and mother, as much as to say, "You may think what you like of me, I am not ashamed of it!"

The grower pushed two gray curls aside, and looked up with a grand amazement. Here was a girl, who at dinner-time even would scarcely say more than "yes," or "no;" who started when suddenly spoken to, and was obliged to clear her mind to think; who smiled now and then, when a smile was expected, and not because she had a smile—in a word, who had become a dull, careless, unnatural, cloudy, depressed, and abominably inconsistent Mabel—a cause of anxiety to her father, and of recklessness to herself—when lo, at a touch of the magic wand, here she was, as brave as ever!

The father, and the mother also, knew the old expression settled on the darling face again; the many family modes of thinking, and of looking, and of loving, and of feeling out for love, which only a father and a mother dearly know in a dear child's face. And then they looked at one another; and in spite of all small variance, the husband and the wife were one, in the matter of rejoicing.

It was not according to their schemes! and they both might still be obstinate. But by a stroke their hearts were opened—wise or foolish, right or wrong—what they might say outside reason, they really could not stop to think. They only saw that their sweet good child, for many long months a stranger to them, was come home to their hearts again. And they could have no clearer proof than this.

She took up her father's pipe, and sniffed with a lofty contempt at the sealing-wax (which was of the very lowest order), and then she snapped it off, and scraped him (with a tortoise-shell-handled knife of her own) a proper place to suck at. And while she was doing that, and most busy with one of her fingers to make a draught, she turned to her mother with her other side, as only a very quick girl could do, and tucked up some hair (which was slipping from the string, with a palpable breach of the unities) and gave her two tugs, in the very right place to make her of the latest fashion; and then let her know, with lips alone, what store she set on her opinion. And the whole of this business was done in less time than two lovers would take for their kissing!

"You have beaten me, Popsy," said Mrs. Lovejoy, fetching up an old name of the days when she was nursing this one.

"Dash me!" cried the grower, "you shall marry Old Harry, if you choose to set your heart on him."

CHAPTER XLIX.

Peradventure the eyes and the heart, as well as the boundless charity of true-love, were needed to descry what Mabel at a glance discovered, the "grand nobility" of Hilary's conduct, and the "pathetic beauty" of his self-reproach. Perhaps at first sight the justice of the latter would be a more apparent thing; but love (when it deserves the name) is a generous as well as a jealous power, especially in the tender gush of renewal and re-assurance. And Lorraine meant every word as he wrote it, and indeed for a good while afterward; so that heart took pen to heart, which is sometimes better than the wings of speech. Giving comfort thus, he also received the same from his own conscience and pure resolutions; and he felt that his good angel was, for the present, at least, come back to him. How long she would stop was another question.

And he needed her now in matters even more stirring than the hottest love-affairs. For though he had no chance of coming to the front in any of the desperate assaults on the castle of Burgos, being far away then with dispatches, he was back with his chief when the retreat began; a retreat which must have become a rout under any but the finest management. For the British army was at its worst toward the month of November, 1812. Partly from intercourse with *partidas*, partly, perhaps, from the joys of Madrid, but mainly no doubt from want of cash, the Britons were not as they had been. Even the officers dared to be most thoroughly disobedient, and to follow the route which they thought best, instead of that laid down for them. But Wellington put up with insolent ignorance, as a weaker man could not have deigned to do: he had to endure it from those above him; and he knew how to bear with it all around him; and yet to be the master. His manifold dealings with every body and every thing at this time (with nobody caring to understand him, and his own people set against him; with the whole world making little of him, because he hated flash-work; and perhaps his own mind in some doubt of its powers because they were not recognized)—these, and the wearisome uphill struggle to be honest without any money, were beginning to streak with gray the hair that had all the hard brain under it.

Here, again, was a chance for Hilary; and without thinking he worked it well. In his quick, and perhaps too sudden, way of taking impression of every one, he had stamped on his mind the abiding image of his great commander. The general knew this (as all men feel the impression they are making, as sharply almost as a butter-stamp), and of course he felt good-will toward the youth who so looked up at him. It was quite a new thing for this great captain, after all his years of conquest, to be accounted of any value; because he was not a Frenchman.

Being, however, of rigid justice, although he was no Frenchman, Lord Wellington did not lift Captain Lorraine over the heads of his compeers. He only marked him (in his own clear and most tenacious mind) as one who might be trusted for a dashing job, and deserved to have the chance of it.

And so they went into winter-quarters on the Douro and Aguada, after a great deal of fighting, far in the rear of their storms and sieges and their many victories; because the British Government paid whole millions right and left to rogues, and left its own army to live without money, and to be hanged if it stole an onion. And the only satisfaction our men had—and even in that they were generous—was to hear of the Frenchmen in Russia freezing as fast as could well be expected.

Now, while this return to the frontier and ebb of success created disgust in England and depression among our soldiers, they also bore most disastrously on the fortunes of a certain gallant and very zealous staff officer. For they brought him again into those soft meshes, whence he had well-nigh made good his escape without any serious damage; but now there was no such deliverance for him. And this was a very hard case, and he really did deserve some pity now; for he did not return of his own accord, and fall at the feet of the charmer, but in the strictest course of duty became an unwilling victim. And it happened altogether in this wise.

In the month of May, 1813, when the British commander had all things ready for that glorious campaign which drove the French over the Pyrenees, and when the British army, freshened, strengthened, and sternly redisciplined, was eager to bound forward, a sudden and sad check arose. By no means, however, a new form of hinderance, but one only too familiar, at all times and in all countries—the sinews of war were not forthcoming. The military chest was empty. The pay of the British troops was far in arrear, and so was their bounty-money; but that they were pretty well used to by this time, and, grumble as they might, they were ready to march. Not so, however, the Portuguese, who were now an important element; and even the Spanish regulars in Andalusia would do nothing until they had handled dollars.

This need of money had been well foreseen by the ubiquitous mind of Wellington; but what he had not allowed for, and what no one else would have taken into thought, so soon after Nelson's time, was the sluggishness of the British navy. Whether it were the fault of our Government, or of our admiral on the station, certain it is that the mouth of the Tagus (which was the mouth of the whole British army) was stopped for days and even weeks together by a few American privateers. And ships containing supplies for our army (whether of food, or clothing, or the even more needful British gold), if they escaped at all, could do it only by running for the dangerous bar of the Douro, or for Cadiz.

In this state of matters, the "generalissimo" sent for Captain Lorraine one day, and dispatched him on special duty.

"You know Count Zamora," said Lord Wellington, in his clear voice of precision; "and his castle in the Sierra Morena."

Hilary bowed, without a word, knowing well what his chief was pleased with.

"You also know the country well, and the passes of the Morena. Colonel Langham has orders to furnish you with the five best horses at hand, and the two most trusty men he knows of. You will go direct to Count Zamora's house, and deliver to him this letter. He will tell you what next to do. I believe that the ship containing the specie, which will be under your charge, was unable to make either Lisbon or the port of Cadiz, and ran through the Straits for Malaga. But the count will know better than I do. Remember that you are placed at his disposal, in all except one point—and that is the money. He will provide you with Spanish escort, and the Spaniards are liable for the money, through Andalusia, and the mountains, until you cross the Zujar, where a detachment from General Hill will meet you. They begged me not to send British convoy (beyond what might be needful, to authorize the delivery to them), because their own troops are in occupation.

"Never mind that; be as wide awake as if every farthing was your own, or, rather, was part of your honor. I seldom place so young a man in a position of so much trust. But the case is peculiar, and I trust you. There will be £100,000 in English gold to take care of. The Spaniards will furnish the transport, and Count Zamora will receive half of the specie, on behalf of the Junta of Seville, for the pay of the Spanish forces, and give you his receipt for it. The remainder you will place under the care of General Hill's detachment, and rejoin us as soon as possible. I have no time more. Colonel Langham will give you your passes, and smaller directions. But remember that you are in a place of trust unusual for so young an officer. Good-bye, and keep a sharp lookout."

Lord Wellington gave his hand, with a bow of the fine old type, to Hilary. And he from his proper salute recovered, and took it as one gentleman takes the courtesy of another. But as he felt that firm, and cool, and muscular hand for a moment, he knew that he was treated with extraordinary confidence; and that his future as an officer, and perhaps as a gentleman, hung on the manner in which he should acquit himself of so rare a trust. In the court-yard he found Colonel Langham, who gave him some written instructions, and his passes and credentials, as well as a good deal of sound advice, which the general had no time to give. And in another hour Hilary Lorraine was riding away in the highest spirits, thinking of Mabel and of all his luck, and little dreaming that he was galloping into the ditch of his fortunes.

Behind him rode two well-tried troopers, as thoroughly trained to their work as the best hereditary butler, gamekeeper, or even pointer. There could be found no steadier men in all the world of steadiness; one was Sergeant-major Bones, and the other was Corporal Nickles. Each of them led a spare horse by the soft, brown twist of willow-bark, steeped in tan and fish-oil, so as to make a horse think much of it. And thus they rode through the brilliant night, upon a fine old Roman road, with beautiful change, and lovely air, and nobody to challenge them. For the French army lay to the east and north, the Portuguese were far in their rear, and the Spanish forces away to the south, except a few guerrillas, who could take nothing by meddling with them. But the next day was hot, and the road grew rough, and their horses fell weary; and, haste as they might, they did not arrive at Monte Argento till after sunset of the second day.

The Count of Zamora felt some affection, as well as much gratitude, toward Lorraine, and showed it through the lofty courtesy with which he received him. And Hilary, on his part, could not help admiring the valor, and patriotism, and almost poetic dignity of this chieftain of a time gone by. For, being of a simple mind, and highly valuing eloquence, the count nearly always began with a flourish as to what he might have done for the liberation of his country if he had been younger. Having exhausted this reflection, he was wont to proceed at leisure to the military virtues of his sons. Then, if any body showed impatience, he always stopped with a lofty bow; otherwise, on he went, and the farther he went, the more he enjoyed himself. Hilary, a very polite young man, and really a kind-hearted one, had grown into the count's good graces — setting aside all gratitude—by truly believing all his exploits, and those of his father and grandfathers, and, best of all, those of his two sons, and never so much as yawning.

"You are at my orders?" said the count, with a dry smile on his fine old face. "It is well, my son; it is glorious. Our great commander has so commanded. My first order is that you come to the supper, and rest, and wear slippers for the three days to follow."

"Shall I take those instructions in writing," asked Hilary; "and under the seal of the Junta?"

"The Junta is an old woman," said his host; "she chatters, and she scolds, and she locks up the money. But enter, my son, enter, I pray you. You are at the very right moment arrived — as is your merit, or I should not be here. We have a young boar of the first nobility; and truffles are in him from the banks which you know. You shall carve him for us; you are so strong, and you Englishmen so understand sharp steel. My sons are still at the war; but my daughters —how will they be pleased to see you!"

At the smell of the innocent young roaster —for such he was in verity—light curtains rose, and light figures entered; for all Spanish ladies know well what is good. Camilla and Claudia greeted Hilary as if they had been with him all the morning, and turned their whole minds to the table at once. And Hilary, thoroughly knowing their manners, only said to himself, how well they looked!

In this he was right. The delicate grace and soft charm of Camilla set off the more brilliant and defiant beauty of young Claudia. Neither of them seemed to care in the least what any body thought of her, or whether any thought at all occurred to any body upon a subject so indifferent, distant, and theoretical. Captain Lorraine was no more to them than a friar, or pilgrim, or hermit. They were very much obliged to him for cutting up the pig; and they showed that they thought it a good pig.

Now, as it happened, these were not the tactics fitted for the moment. In an ordinary mood, Lorraine might have fallen to these fair Parthians; but knowing what danger he was running into—without any chance of avoiding it—he had made up his mind, all along the road, to be severely critical. Mabel's true affection (as shown by a letter in answer to his) had moved him; she had not hinted at any rival, or lapse of love on his part; but had told, with all her dear warm heart, the pleasure, the pride, and the love she felt. Hilary had this letter in his pocket, and it made him inclined to be critical.

Now it may, without any leze-majesty of the grand female race, be asserted that, good and kind and beautiful and purely superior as they are, they are therewith so magnanimous to men, that they abstain, for the most part, from exhibiting mere perfection. No specimen of them seems ever to occur that is entirely blameless, if submitted to rigid criticism; which, of course, they would never submit to. Therefore it was wrong of Hilary, and showed him in a despicable light, that because the young ladies would not look at him much, he looked at them with judicial eyes. And the result of his observation, over the backbone of the pig, was this:

In "physique"—a word which ought to be worse than physic to an Englishman— there was no fault of any sort to be found with either of these young ladies. They were noble examples of the best Spanish type, tall and pure, yet rich of tint, with most bewitching eyes, and classic flexure of luxuriant hair, grace in every turn and gesture, and melody in every tone. Yet even in the most expressive glance, and most enchanting smile, was there any of that simple goodness, loyalty, and comfort which were to be found in an equally lovely but less superb young woman?

Herewith the young captain began to think of his uncle Struan's advice, and even his sister's words on the matter; which from so haughty a girl—as he called her, although he knew that she was not that—had caused him at first no small surprise, and at the same time produced no small effect. And the end of it was that he gave a little squeeze to Mabel's loving letter, and said to himself that an English girl was worth a dozen Spanish ones.

On the following day the fair young donnas changed their mode of action. They vied with each other in attention to Hilary, led him through the well-known places, chattered Spanish most musically, and sang melting love-songs, lavished smiles and glances on him, and nothing was too good for him. He was greatly delighted, of course, and was bound in gratitude to flirt a little; but still, on the whole, he behaved very well. For instance, he gave no invidious preference to either of his lovely charmers; but paid as much heed to poor Camilla (whose heart was bounding with love and happiness) as he did to Claudia, who began to be in earnest now, that her sister might not conquer him. This was a dangerous turn of events for Hilary; and it was lucky for him that he was promptly called away. For his host got dispatches which compelled him to cut short hospitality; and Captain Lorraine, with great relief, set forth the next morning for Malaga. Sergeant Bones and Corporal Nickles had carried on handsomely down stairs, and were most loath to come away; but duty is always the guiding-star of the noble British corporal. Nickles and Bones, at the call of their country, cast off all domestic ties, and buckled up their belly-bands. Merrily thus they all rode on, for their horses were fresh and frolicsome, to the Spanish head-quarters near Cordova; and thence again to Malaga.

CHAPTER L.

At this particular time there was nothing so thoroughly appreciated, loved, admired, and begged, borrowed, or stolen in every corner of the Continent, as the good old English guinea. His fine old face and his jovial color made him welcome everywhere; one look at him was enough to show his purity, substance, and sterling virtue, and prove him sure to outlast in the end the flashy and upstart "Napoleon." Happily for the world, that poor, weak-colored, and adulterated coin now called the "sovereign" was not the representative of English worth at that time, otherwise Europe might have been either France or Russia for a century.

And though we are now in the mire so low—through time-servers, hucksters, and demagogues—that the voice of England is become no more than the squeak of a half-penny shoe-black, we might be glad to think of all our fathers did, at our expense, so grandly and heroically, if nations (trampled on for years, and but for England swept away) would only take it as not a mortal injury that through us they live. At any rate, many noble Spaniards in and around about Malaga condescended to come and see the unloading of the British corvette, *Cleopatra-cum-Antonio.* She was the nimblest little craft (either on or off a wind) of all ever captured from the French; and her name had been reefed into *Clipater* first, and then into "Clipper," which still holds way. And thus, in spite of all her money, she had run the gauntlet of Americans and Frenchmen, and lay on her keel discharging.

Lorraine regarded this process with his usual keen interest.

The scene was so new, and the people so strange, and their views of the world so original, that he could not have tried to step into any thing nobler and more refreshing. There was no such babel of gesticulation as in a French harbor must have been; but there was plenty of little side-play, in and out among the natives, such as a visitor loves to watch. And the dignity with which the Spaniards took the money into their charge was truly gratifying to the British mind. "They might have said 'thank you,' at any rate," thought Hilary, signing the bill of delivery, under three or four Spanish signatures. But that was no concern of his.

One hundred thousand British guineas, even when they are given away, are not to be made light of. Their weight (without heeding the iron chests wherein they were packed in Threadneedle Street) would not be so very much under a ton, and with the chests would be nearly two tons. There were ten chests, thoroughly secured and sealed, each containing ten thousand guineas, and weighing about four hundred-weight. All these were delivered by the English agent to the deputy of Count Zamora, who was accompanied by two members of the Junta of Seville, and the Alcalde of Cordova; and these great people, after no small parley, and with the aid of Spanish officers, packed all the consignment into four mule-carts, and sent them under strong escort to head-quarters near Cordova. Here the count met them, and gave a receipt to Hilary for the Spanish subsidy, which very soon went the way of all money among the Spanish soldiers. And the next day the five less lucky mules, who were dragging the pay of the

British army, went on with the five remaining chests—three in one cart and two in the other — still under Spanish escort, toward the slopes of the Sierra Morena.

Hilary, as usual, adapted himself to the tone and the humor around him. The Spanish officers took to him kindly, and so did the soldiers, and even the mules. He was in great spirits once more, and kindly and cordially satisfied with himself. His conscience had pricked him for many months concerning that affair with Claudia; but now it praised him for behaving well, and returning to due allegiance. He still had some little misgiving about his vows to the Spanish maiden; but really he did not believe that she would desire to enforce them. He was almost sure in his heart that the lovely young donna did not care for him, but had only been carried away for the moment by her own warmth and his stupid fervor. Tush! he now found himself a little too wide awake, and experienced in the ways of women, to be led astray by any of them. Claudia was a most beautiful girl, most fascinating and seductive; but now, if he only kept out of her way, as he meant most religiously to do—

"The brave and renowned young captain," said the Count of Zamora, riding up in the fork of the valley where the mountain-road divided, and one branch led to his house, "will not, of course, disdain our humble hospitality for the night."

"I fear that it can not be, dear señor," answered Lorraine, with a lift of his hat in the Spanish manner, which he had caught to perfection; "my orders are to make all speed with the treasure until I meet our detachment."

"We are responsible for the treasure," the count replied, with a smile of good-humor, and the slightest touch of haughtiness, "until you have crossed the river upon the other side of our mountains. Señor, is not that enough? We have traveled far, and the mules are weary. Even if the young captain prefers to bivouac in the open air, it is a proverb that the noble English think more of their beasts than of themselves. And behold, even now the sun is low, and there are clouds impending! The escort is under my orders as yet. If you refuse, I must exercise the authority of the Junta."

What could Hilary do but yield? He was ordered to be at the count's disposal; and thus the count disposed of him. Nevertheless he stipulated that the convoy should pursue its course, as soon as the moon had risen; for the night is better than the day for traveling, in this prime of the southern year.

So the carts were brought into a walled quadrangle of the Monte Argento; and heavy gates were barred upon them, while the mules came out of harness, and stood happily round a heap of rye. The Spanish officers, still in charge, were ready to be most convivial; and Hilary fell into their mood, with native compliance well cultivated. In a word, they all enjoyed themselves.

One alone, the star of all, the radiant, brilliant, lustrous one, the admired of all admirers, that young Claudia, was sorrowful. Hilary, in the gush of youthful spirits and promotion; in the glow of duty done and lofty standard satisfied; through all the pride of money paid by the nation he belonged to; and even the glory of saying good things in a language slightly known to him — Hilary caught from time to time those grand reproachful eyes, and felt that they quite spoiled his dinner. And he was not to get off like this.

For when he was going, in the driest manner, to order forth his carts, and march, with the full moon risen among the hills, the daintiest little note ever seen came into his hand as softly as if it were dropped by a dove too young to coo. He knew that it came from a lady of course, and in the romantic place and time his quick heart beat more quickly.

The writing was too fine for even his keen eyes by moonlight; but he managed to get to a quiet lamp, and then he read as follows: "You have forgotten your vows to me. I must have an explanation. There is no chance of it in this house. My nurse has a daughter at the 'bridge of echoes.' You know it, and you will have to cross it within a league of your journey. If I can escape I shall be on that bridge in two hours' time. You will wait for me there, if you are an English gentleman."

This letter was unsigned, but of course it could only come from Claudia. Of all those conceited young Spanish officers, who had been contradicting Lorraine, and even daring to argue with him, was there one who would not have given his right hand, his gilt spurs, or even his beard, to receive such a letter and such an appointment from the daughter of the Count of Zamora?

Hilary fancied, as he said farewell, in the cumbrous mass of shadows and the foliage of the moonlight, that Donna Camilla (who came forth with a white mantilla fluttering) made signs, as if she longed with all her heart to speak to him. But the count stood by, and the guests of the evening, and two or three mule-drivers cracking whips; and Hilary's horse turned on his tail, till the company kissed their hands to him. And thus he began to descend through trees, and rocks, and freaks of shadow-land, enjoying the freshness of summer night, and the tranquil beauty of moonlit hills. Nickles and Bones, the two English troopers, rode a little in advance of him, each of them leading a spare horse, and keeping his eyes fixed stubbornly on the treasure-carts still in the custody of the Spanish horsemen. For the

Englishmen had but little faith in the honesty of "them palavering dons," and regarded it as an affront and a folly that the treasure should be in their charge at all.

In this order they came to the river Zujar, quite a small stream here at the foot of the mountains, and forming the boundary of the count's estates. According to the compact with the Spaniards, and advices that day received, the convoy was here to be met by a squadron of horse from Hill's division, who at once would assume the charge of it, and be guided as to their line of return by Captain Lorraine's suggestions. At the ford, however, there was no sign of any British detachment, and the trumpeters sounded a flourish in vain.

Hilary felt rather puzzled by this; but his own duty could not be in doubt. He must on no account allow the treasure carts to pass the ford, and so quit Spanish custody, until placed distinctly under British protection. And this he said clearly to the Spanish colonel, who quite agreed with him on that point, and promised to halt until he got word from Lorraine to move into the water. Then Bones and Nickles were dispatched to meet and hurry the expected squadron; for the Spanish troopers were growing impatient, and their discipline was but fortuitous.

Under these circumstances young Lorraine was sure that he might, without any neglect, spare just a few minutes to do his duty elsewhere as a gentleman. He felt that he might have appeared perhaps to play fast and loose with Claudia, although in his heart he was pretty certain that she was doing that same with him. And now he intended to tell her the truth, and beg to be acquitted of that vow whose recall was more likely to gall than to grieve her.

The "bridge of echoes" was about a furlong above the ford where the convoy halted. It was an exceedingly ancient bridge, supposed to be even of Gothic date, and patched with Moorish workmanship. It stood like a pack-saddle over the torrent, which roared from the mountains under it; and it must have been of importance once, as commanding approach to the passes. For, besides two deep embrasures wherein defenders might take shelter, it had (at the south or Morena end) a heavy fortalice beetling over, with a dangerous portcullis. And the whole of it now was in bad repair, so that every flood or tempest worked it away at the top or bottom; and capable as it was of light carts or of heavy people, the officers were quite right in choosing to send the treasure by the ford below.

Hilary proved that his sword was free to leap at a touch from its scabbard, ere ever he set foot on that time-worn, shadowy, venerable, and cut-throat bridge. The precaution perhaps was a wise one. But it certainly did not at first sight exhibit any proof of true-love's confidence in the maiden he was come to meet. It showed the difference between a wise love and a wild one; and Hilary smiled as he asked himself whether he need have touched his sword in coming to meet Mabel. Then, half ashamed of himself for such very low mistrust of Claudia, he boldly walked through the crumbling gate-way, and up the steep rise of the bridge.

On the peaked crown of the old arch he stood, and looked both up and down the river. Toward the mountains there was nothing but loneliness and rugged shadow; scarred with clefts of moonlight, and at farther distance fringed with mist. And down the water and the quiet sloping of the lowlands, every thing was feeding on the comfort of the summer night; the broad delicious calm of lying under nature's womanhood, when the rage of the masculine sun is gone, and fair hesitation has followed it.

Hilary looked at all these things, but did not truly see them. He took a general idea that the view was beautiful; and he might have been glad, at another time, to stand and think about it. For the present, however, his time was short, and he must make the most of it. The British detachment might appear at the ford at any moment, and his duty would be to haste thither at once, and see to the transfer of convoy. And to make sure of this, he had begged that the Spanish trumpets might be sounded, and kept his own horse waiting for him, and grazing kindly where the grass was cold.

The shadow of the old keep and the ivy-mantled buttress fell along the roadway of the bridge, and lay in scollops there. Beyond it, every stone was clear (of facing or of parapet), and the age of each could be guessed almost, and its story and its character. Even a beetle or an earwig must have had his doings traced if an enemy were after him. But under the eaves of the lamp of night, and within all the marge of the glittering, there lay such darkness as never lies in the world where the moon is less brilliant. Hilary stood in the broad light waiting; and out of the shadow came Claudia.

"I doubted whether you would even do me the honor to meet me here," she said. "Oh, Hilary, how you are changed to me!"

"I have changed in no way, señorita, except that I know when I am loved."

"And you do not know—then you do not know—it does not become me to say it, perhaps. Your ways are so different from ours, that you would despise me if I told it all. I will not weep. No, I will not weep."

With violent self-control, she raised her magnificent eyes to prove her words; but the effort was too much for her. The great tears came, and glistened in the brilliance of the moonlight; but she would not show them, only turned away, and wished that nobody in the world should know the power of her emotions.

"Come, come!" said Hilary (for an Englishman always says "come, come," when he is taken aback), "you can not mean half of this, of course. Come, Claudia; what can have made you take such a turn? You never used to do it!"

"Ah, I may have been fickle in the days gone by. But absence—absence is the power that proves—"

"Hark! I hear a sound down the river. Horses' feet, and wheels, and clashing—"

"No; it is only the dashing of the water. I know it well. That is why this bridge is called the 'bridge of echoes.' The water makes all sorts of sounds. Look here; and I will show you."

She took his hand as she spoke, and led him away from the parapet facing the ford to the one on the upper side of the bridge, when suddenly such a faintness seized her that she was obliged to cling to him as she hung over the low and crumbling wall. And how lovely she looked in the moonlight, so pale and pure and perfect, and at the same time so intensely feminine and helpless!

"Let me fall," she murmured; "what does it matter, with no one in the world to care for me? Hilary, let me fall, I implore you."

"That would be nice gratitude to the one who nursed me, and saved my life. Señorita, sit down, I pray you. Allow me to hold you. You are in great danger."

"Oh no, oh no!" she answered faintly, as he was obliged to support her exquisite, but, alas! too sensitive figure. "Oh, I must not be embraced. Oh, Hilary, how can you do such a thing to me?"

"How can I help doing it, you mean? How very beautiful you are, Claudia!"

"What is the use of it? Alas! what is the use of it, if I am? When the only one in all the world—"

"Ah! There I heard that noise again. It is impossible that it can be the water—and I see horses, and the flash of arms."

"Oh, do not leave me! I shall fall into the torrent. For the sake of all the saints, stay one moment! How can I be found here? What infamy!—at least, at least, swear one thing."

"Fifty, if you please. But I must be gone. I may be ruined in a moment."

"And so may I. In the name of the Saviour, swear not to tell that I met you here. My father would kill me. You can not even dream—"

"I swear that no power on earth shall induce me to say a word about this scene."

"Oh, I faint, I faint! Lay me there in the shadow. No one will see me. It is the last time. Oh, how cruel, how cold, how false! how bitterly cruel you are to me!"

"Is it true," he whispered, tremulously, for he was in great excitement and hurry, and he heard the Spanish trumpets sound as he carried her toward the shadow of the keep, and there for an instant leaned over her; "is it true that you love even me, Claudia?"

"With my whole, whole—" and he thought that she glanced at the corner timidly; "oh, do not go, for one moment, darling!—with atom of my poor—"

"Heart," she was going to say, no doubt, but was spared the trouble; for down fell Hilary, stunned by a crashing blow from the dark corner; and in a moment Alcides d'Alcar had him by the throat with gigantic hands, and planted one great knee on his breast.

"Did I do it well?" whispered Claudia, recovering all her energies. "Oh, don't let him see me. He never must know it."

"Neither that nor any thing else shall he know," muttered the brigand, with a furious grasp, till poor Hilary's blue eyes started forth from their sockets. "You did it too well, my fair actress; so warmly, indeed, that I am quite jealous. The bottom of the Zujar is his marriage-couch."

"Loosen his throat, or I scream with all my power. You promised me not to hurt him. He shall not be hurt more than we can help, although he has been so faithless to me."

"Ha, ha!" laughed the great brigadier; "there is no understanding the delicate views of the females. But you shall be obeyed, beloved one. He will come to himself in about ten minutes; these Englishmen have such a thickness of head. Search him; be quick; let me have his dispatch-book. You know where your lovers keep their things."

Senseless though Hilary lay, the fair maiden kept herself out of the range of his eyes, as her nimble fingers probed him. In a moment she drew from an inner breast-pocket his private dispatch-book, and Mabel's letter. That last she stowed away for her own revenge, after glancing with great contempt at it; but the book she spread open to her lover.

"It is noble!" he cried, as the brilliant moonlight shone upon the pages. "What could be more fortunate? Here are the blank forms with the heading, and the flourish prepared for his signature. There is his metal pencil. Now write as I tell you in Spanish, but with one or two little barbarisms; such as you know him given to. 'The detachment is here. I am holding them back. They are not to cross the water. Send the two carts through, but do not come yourselves. Good-night, and many thanks to you. May we soon meet again. (Signed) Hilary Lorraine.' You know how very polite he is."

"It is written, and in his own hand most clearly. He has been my pupil, and I have been his. Poor youth, I am very sorry for him. Now let me go. Have I contented you?"

"I will tell you at the chapel to-morrow night. I shall have the cleverest and most beautiful bride in all Iberia. How can I part with you till then?"

"You will promise me not to hurt him," she whispered through his beard, as he clasped her warmly; while Hilary lay at their feet, still senseless.

"By all the saints that ever were, or will be, multiplied into all the angels! One kiss more, and then adieu, if it must be."

The active young Claudia glided away; while the great brigadier proceeded, with his usual composure, to arrange things to his liking. He lifted poor Hilary, as if he were a doll, and bound him completely with broad leather straps, which he buckled to their very tightest; and then he fixed over his mouth a scarf of the delicate wool of the mountains; and then he laid him in the shade; for he really was a most honorable man, when honor came into bearing. And though (as far as his own feelings went) he would gladly have pitched this Captain Lorraine into the rush of the Zujar, he had pledged his honor to Claudia. Therefore he only gagged and bound him, and laid him out of the moonlight; which, at the time of year, might have maddened him. After this, Don Alcides d'Alcar struck flint upon punk, and lighted a long cigar.

The whole of that country is full of fleas. The natives may say what they like; but they only damage their credit by denying it, or prove to a charitable mind their own insensibility. The older the deposit or the stratum is, the greater is the number of these active insects; and this old bridge, whether Moorish or Gothic, or even Roman (as some contended), had an antiquarian stock of them.

Therefore poor Hilary, coming to himself—as he was bound to do by-and-by—grew very uneasy, but obtained no relief, through the natural solace of scratching. He was strapped so tightly that he could only roll; and if he should be induced to roll a little injudiciously, through a gap of the parapet he must go to the bottom of the lashing water. Considering these things, he lay and listened; and though he heard many things which he disliked (and which bore a ruinous meaning to him for the rest of his young life, and all who loved him), he called his high courage to his help; and being unable to talk to himself (from the thickness of the wool between his teeth, which was a most dreadful denial to him), he thought in his inner parts, "Now, if I die, there will be no harm to say of me." He laid this to his conscience, and in contempt of all insects he rolled off to sleep.

The uncontrollable outbreak of day, in the land where the sun is paramount, came like a cataract over the mountains, and scattered all darkness with leaps of light. The winding valley and the wooded slope, the white track of water and the sombre cliffs, all sprang out of their vaporous mantle; and even the bridge of echoes looked a cheerful place to lounge on.

"A bad job surely!" said Corporal Nickles, marching with his footsteps counted, as if he were a pedometer. "Bones, us haven't searched this here ramshackle thing of a Spanish bridge. Wherever young cap'en can be, the Lord knows. At the bottom of the river, I dessay."

"Better if he never was born," replied Bones; "or leastwise now to be a dead one. Fifty thousand guineas in a sweep! All cometh of trusting them beggarly dons. Corporal, what did I say to you?"

"Like a horacle, you had foreseen it, sergeant. But we'm all right, howsomever it be. In our favor we has the hallerby."

Hilary, waking, heard all this, and he managed to sputter so through the wool, that the faithful non-commissioned officers ran to look for a wild sheep coughing.

"Is it all gone?" he asked, pretty calmly, when they had cut him free at last, but he could not stand from stiffness. "Do you mean to say that the whole is gone?"

"Captain," said Bones, with a solemn salute, which Nickles repeated as junior, "every guinea are gone, as clean as a whistle; and the Lord knows where 'em be gone to."

"Yes, your honor, every blessed guinea;" said Nickles, in confirmation. "To my mind it goes against the will of the Lord to have such a d—d lot of money."

"You are a philosopher," answered Lorraine; "it is pleasing to find such a view of the case. But as for me, I am a ruined man. No captain, nor even 'your honor,' any more."

"Your honor must keep your spirits up. It mayn't be so bad as your honor thinks," they answered, very kindly, well knowing that he was a ruined man, but saluting him all the more for it.

CHAPTER LI.

It may perhaps be said, without any painful exaggeration, that throughout the whole course of this grand war, struggle of great captains, and heroic business everywhere, few things made a deeper, sadder, and more sinister impression than the sudden disappearance of those fifty thousand guineas. On the other hand, it must not be supposed that the disappearance of guineas was rare. Far otherwise—as many people still alive can testify; and some of them perhaps with gratitude for their re-appearance in the right quarter. But these particular fifty thousand were looked out for in so many places, and had so long been the subject of hope, as a really solid installment of a shilling in the pound for heroes, that the most philosophical of these latter were inclined to use a short, strong word of distinctive nationality.

Poor Hilary felt that for this bad verb his own name must be the receptive case; and he vainly looked about for any remedy or rescue. Stiff as he was in the limbs, by reason of the straps of Don Alcides, and giddy of head from the staff of that most patriotic Spaniard, he found it for some time a little hard to reflect as calmly as he should have done. Indeed it was as much as he could do to mount his horse, who (unlike his master) had stuck to his post very steadfastly, and with sadness alike of soul and body to ride down to the fatal ford. Sergeant-major Bones and Corporal Nickles also remounted and followed the bewildered captain, keeping behind him at a proper distance for quiet interchange of opinion.

"Corporal, now," said the sergeant-major, sliding his voice from behind one hand, "what may be your sentiments as consarns this very pecooliar and most misfortunate haxident?"

"Sergeant, it would be misbehooving," replied Nickles, who was a west-country man, "as well as an onceremonious thing, for me to spake first in the matter. To you it belongeth, being the one as foretold it like a book; likewise senior hofficer."

"Corporal, you are a credit to the army. Your discretion, at your age, is wonderful. There be so few young men as remember when a man has spoken right. I am the last man in the world to desire to be overpraised, or to take to myself any sense of it. And now I wants no credit for it. To me it seems to come natteral to discern things in a sort of way that I find in nobody else a'most."

"You doos, you doos," answered Corporal Nickles. "Many's the time as I've said to myself, 'Whur can I goo to find sergeant-major, in this here trick of the henemy?' And now, sergeant, what do 'ee think of this? No fear to tell truth in spaking 'long of me."

"Corporal, I have been thinking strongly ever since us untied him. And I have been brought up in the world so much that I means to think again of it."

"Why, sergeant, you never means to say—"

"Nickles, I means just what I means. I may be right, and yet again I may be altogether wrong; as is the way of every man. 'Let me alone' is all I say. But if I was sure as you could hold your tongue, I might have something to say to you. Not of any account, you know; but still, something."

"Now, sergeant, after all the thumps us has seen and been through together, you never would behave onhandsome to me."

"Corporal Nickles, if you put it upon that footing, I can not deny you. And mind you, now, my opinion is that this is a very queer case indeed."

"Now, now, to think of that! Why, sergeant, you ought to be a general!"

"Nickles, no flattery; I am above it. Not but what I might have done so well as other people, if the will of the Lord had been so. Consarning, however, of this to-do, and a precious rumpus it will be, my opinion is that we don't know half."

Speaking thus, the sergeant nodded to the corporal impressively, and jerked his thumb toward the captain in front, and winked, and then began again.

"You see, corporal, my place is to keep both eyes wide open. There was a many things as struck me up at the old don's yonder. A carrying-on in corners, and agoing to lamps to read things, and a-winking out of young ladies' eyes, to my mind most unmilintary. But I might a' thought that was all young people, and a handsome young chap going on as they will, only for what one of they dirty devils as drives them mules have said to me."

"No, now, sergeant; never, now!"

"As true as I sit this here hoss, when us come back with the sun getting up, what did that pagan say to me? You seed him, corporal, a-running up, and you might have saved me the trouble, only you was nodding forward. 'Señor Captain,' he said to me, and the whites of his eyes was full of truth, 'the young cavalier has been too soft.' That was how I made out his country gibberish; the stuff they poor beggars are born to."

"It gooeth again the grain of my skin," Corporal Nickles answered, "to hearken them fellows chattering. But, sergeant, what did he say next?"

"Well, they may chatter, or hold their tongues, to them as can not understand them. Requireth a gift, which is a denial to most folk to understand them. And what he said, Corporal Nickles, was this—that he was coming up the river while the carts was waiting, and afore the robbery, mind you; and he seed a young woman come on to the bridge—you knows how they goes, corporal, when they expects you to look after them."

"Sergeant, I should think so."

"Well, she come on the bridge for all the world like that. Us have seen it fifty times. And she had a white handkercher on her head, or an Ishmaelitish mantle; and she were looking out for some young chap. And our young cap'en come after her. And who do you think she were? Why, one of the daughters of the old don up yonder!"

"Good heart alaive, now, Sergeant Bones, I can't a'most belave it!"

"Nickles, I tell you what was told me—

word for word; and I say no more. But knowing what the ways of the women is, as us dragoons is so forced to do, even after a marriage and family—"

"Ah, sergeant, sergeant! we tries in vain to keep inside the strick line of dooty. I does whatever a man can do; and my father were a butcher."

"Corporal, it is one of the trials which the Lord has ordered. They do look up at one so, and they puts the middle of their lips up, and then with their bodies they turns away, as if there was nothing to look at. But, Nickles, they gives you no sort of a chance to come to the bottom of them. And this is what young cap'en will found out. The good females always is found out at last; the same as my poor wife was. But here us are. We have relaxed the bonds of discipline with conversation. Corporal, eyes right, and wait orders!"

While these two trusty and veteran fellows had been discussing a subject far too deep for a whole brigade of them, and still were full of tender recollections (dashed with good escape), poor Hilary had been vainly spurring, here and there, and all about, himself not come to his clear mind yet, only hoping to know where the money was gone. Hope, however, upon that point was disappointed, as usual. The track of the heavy carts was clear in the gravel of the river, and up the rocky bank, and on the old Roman road toward Merida. And then, at the distance of about a furlong from the Zujar, the rut of the wooden wheels turned sharply into an elbow of a mountain road. Here, on the hump of a difficult rise, were marks, as if many kicks, and pricks, and even stabs, had been ministered to good mules laboring heavily. There was blood on the road, and the blue shine of friction, where hard rock encountered hard iron, and the scraping of holes in gravelly spots, and the nicks of big stones laid behind wheels to ease the tugging and afford the short relief of panting. These traces were plain, and becoming plainer as the road grew worse, for nearly a mile of the mountain-side, and then the track turned suddenly into a thicket of dark ilex, where, out of British sight and ken, the spoil had been divided.

The treasure-carts had been upset, and two of the sturdy mules, at last foundered with hard labor, lay in their blood, contented that their work was over, and that man (a greater brute than themselves) had taken all he wanted out of them. The rest had been driven or ridden on, being useful for further torment. And here on the ground were five stout coffers of good British iron; but, alas! the good British gold was flown.

At this sight Hilary stared a little; and the five chests in the morning sun glanced back at him with such a ludicrously sad expression of emptiness, that, in spite of all his trouble, the poor young captain broke into a hearty laugh. Then his horse walked up and sniffed at them, being reminded, perhaps, of his manger; and Hilary, dismounting, found a solitary guinea lying in the dust, the last of fifty thousand. The trail of coarse *esparto* bags, into which the gold had been poured from the coffers, for the sake of easier transport, was very distinct in the parts untrampled by horses, mules, or brigands. But of all the marks there was none more conspicuous than the impressions of some man's boots, larger and heavier than the rest, and appearing, over and over again, here, there, and everywhere. For a few yards up the rugged mountain, these and other foot-prints might be traced without much trouble, till suddenly they dispersed, grew fainter, and then wholly disappeared in trackless, hopeless, and (to a stranger) impenetrable forest.

"Thou honest guinea that would not be stolen!" cried poor Lorraine, as he returned and picked up the one remaining coin; "haply I shall never own another honest guinea. Forty-nine thousand nine hundred and ninety-nine prefer the ownership of rogues. Last of guineas, we will not part till gold outlives humanity!"

"Now, sir, is there any thing us can do?" cried Bones and Nickles, or one of them. "We has followed all the way up this here long hill, for want of better orders."

"No, my good fellows, there is nothing to be done. We can not follow any farther. I must go with all speed to report myself. Follow me, if you can keep up."

The sergeant nodded to the corporal—for, loyal and steadfast as they were, suspicion was at work with them; that ugly worm which, once set going, wriggles into the stoutest heart. Surely it was a queer thing of the captain not even to let them examine the spot; but order was order, and without a word they followed the young officer back to the high-road, and then, for some hours in the heat of the day, on the way toward Estremadura. At noontide they came to a bright, broad stream, known to them as the Guadalmez, a confluent of the Guadiana; and here they were challenged, to their great surprise, by a strong detachment of British hussars.

"What is your duty here?" asked Lorraine, as his uniform and face were acknowledged and saluted by sentries posted across the ford.

"To receive," cried an officer, riding through the river (for all of these people were wide awake), "Captain Lorraine and his Spanish convoy."

"I have no convoy," said Hilary, dropping his voice into very sad music. "All is lost. It is partly your fault. You were ordered to meet me at the Zujar ford."

"This is the Zujar ford," the cavalry major answered, sternly; and Hilary's heart fell from its last hope of recovering any thing.

"We haye been here these three days waiting for you," continued the major, with vehemence; "we have lost all our chance of a glorious brush; we sent you advice that we were waiting for you. And now you appear without your convoy! Captain Lorraine, what does all this mean?"

"Major, my explanation is due at headquarters rather than to you."

"And a deuced hard job you'll have to give it, or my name's not M'Rustie," the senior officer muttered, with more terseness and truth than courtesy. "I'm blessed if I'd stand in your shoes before Old Beaky, for a trifle."

Poor Hilary tried in vain to look as if he took it lightly. Even his bright and buoyant nature could not lift head against the sea of troubles all in front of him.

"I have done no harm," he kept saying to himself, when, after the few words that duty demanded, he urged his stout horse forward; and the faithful sergeant and corporal, who had shunned all inquisitive hussars, spurred vigorously after him, feeling themselves (as a Briton loves to feel himself) pregnant with mighty evidence. "What harm have I done?" asked Hilary. "I saw to every thing; I worked hard. I never quitted my post, except through duty toward a lady. Any gentleman must have done what I did. To be an officer is an adornment; to be a gentleman is a necessity."

"Have you felt altogether," said conscience to him, "the necessity of that necessity? Have you found it impossible to depart from a gentleman's first duty—good faith to those who trust in him? When you found yourself bewitched with a foreign lady, did you even let your first love know it? For months you have been playing fast and loose, not caring what misery you caused. And now you are fast in the trap of your looseness. Whatever happens serves you right."

"Whatever happens serves me right!" cried Hilary Lorraine, aloud, as he lifted his sword just a little way forth, for the last time to admire it, and into the sheath dropped a quick, hot tear. "I have done my duty as an officer badly; and far worse as a gentleman. But, Mabel, if you could see me now, I think that you would grieve for me."

He felt his heart grow warm again with the thought of his own Mabel; and in the courage of that thought he stood before Lord Wellington.

CHAPTER LII.

THE hero of a hundred fights (otherwise called "Old Beaky") had just scraped through a choking trouble on the score of money with the grasping Portuguese regency; and now, in the year 1813, he was busier than even he had ever found himself before. He had to combine, in most delicate manner and with exquisite nicety of time, the movements of columns whose number scarcely even to himself was clear; for the force of rivers unusually strong, and the doubt of bridges successively broken, and the hardship of the Tras os Montes, and the scattering of soldiers, who for want of money had to "subsist themselves"—which means to hunt far afield after cows, sheep, and hens—also the shifty and unpronounced tactics of the enemy, and a great many other disturbing elements, enough to make calculation sea-sick—a senior wrangler, or even Herr Steinitz, the Wellington of the chess-board, each in his province, might go astray, and trust at last to luck itself to cut the tangled knot for him.

It was a very grand movement, and triumphantly successful; opening up as fine a march as can be found in history, sweeping onward in victory, and closing with conquest of the Frenchmen in their own France, and nothing left to stop the advance on Paris. "Was all this luck, or was it skill?" the historian asks in wonder; and the answer, perhaps, may be found in the proverb, "Luck has a mother's love for skill."

Be that as it may, it is quite certain that Hilary, though he had shown no skill, had some little luck in the present case. For the commander-in-chief was a great deal too busy, and had all his officers too hard at work, to order, without fatal loss of time, a general court-martial now. Moreover, he had his own reasons for keeping the matter as quiet as possible for at least another fortnight. Every soldier by that time would be in march, and unable to turn his back on Brown Bess; whereas now there were some who might lawfully cast away the knapsack, if they knew that their bounty was again no better than a cloudy hope. And again, there were some ugly pot-hooks of English questions to be dealt with.

All these things passed through the rapid mind of the general, as he reined his horse, and listened calmly to poor Lorraine's over-true report. And then he fixed his keen gray eyes upon Hilary, and said shortly,

"What were you doing upon that bridge?"

"That is a question," replied Lorraine, while marveling at his own audacity, "which I am pledged by my honor, as a gentleman, not to answer."

"By your duty as an officer, in a place of special trust, you are bound to answer it."

"General, I can not. My lord, as I rather must call you now, I wish I could answer; but I can not."

"You have no suspicion who it was that stole the money, with such prearrangement?"

"I have a suspicion, but nothing more; and it makes me feel treacherous to suspect it."

"Never mind that. We have rogues to deal with. What is your suspicion?"

"My lord, I am sorry to say that again I can not, in honor, answer you."

"Captain Lorraine, I have no time to spare;"—Lord Wellington had been more than once interrupted by dispatches. "Once and for all, do you mean to give any, or no, explanation of your conduct in losing £50,000?"

"General, all my life, and the honor of my family, depend upon what I do now."

"Then go and seek advice, Lorraine," the general answered, kindly, for his heart was kind; and he had taken a liking for this young fellow, and knew a little of his family.

"I have no one to go to for advice, my lord. What is your advice to me?" With these words, Hilary looked so wretched and yet so proud from his well-bred face and beautifully-shaped blue eyes, that his general stopped from his hurry to pity him. And then he looked gently at the poor young fellow.

"This is the most irregular state of things I have ever had to deal with. You have lost a month's pay of our army, and enough to last them half a year; and you seem to think that you have done great things, and refuse all explanation. Is there any chance of recovering the money?"

"There might be, my lord, if we were not pushing so rapidly on for the Pyrenees."

"There might be, if we threw away our campaign! You have two courses before you; at least, if I choose to offer them. Will you take my advice, if I offer the choice?"

"I am only too glad to have any choice; and any thing chosen for me by you."

"Then this is just how you stand, Lorraine—if we allow the alternative. You may demand a court-martial, or you may resign your commission. On the other hand, as you know, a court-martial may at once be called upon you. What answer are you prepared to make when asked why you left your convoy?"

"I should be more stubborn to them than even your lordship has let me be to you."

"Then, Captain Lorraine, resign your commission. With my approval, it can be done."

"Resign my commission!" Lorraine exclaimed, reeling as if he had received a shot, and catching at the mane of the general's horse, without knowing what he was doing. "Oh no, I never could do that."

"Very well. I have given you my advice. You prefer your own decision; and I have other things to attend to. Captain Money will receive your sword. You are under arrest till we can form a court."

"My lord, it would break my father's heart, if he were to hear of such a thing. I suppose I had better resign my commission, if I may."

"Put that in writing, and send it to me. I will forward it to the Horse Guards, with a memorandum from myself. I am sorry to lose you, Captain Lorraine; you might have done well, if you had only proved as vigilant as you are active and gallant. But one word more—what made you stop short at the ford of a little mountain stream? I chose you as knowing the country well. You must have known that the Zujar ford was twenty miles farther on your road."

"I know all that country too well, my lord. We halted at the real Zujar ford. General Hill's detachment stopped at the ford of the Guadalmez. It is wrongly called the Zujar there. The Zujar has taken a great sweep to the east, and fallen into the Guadalmez and Guadalemar. Major M'Rustie must have been misled; and no doubt it was done on purpose. I have my information on the very best authority."

"May I ask, upon what authority? Are you pledged in honor to conceal even that?"

"No, I may tell that, I do believe," said Hilary, after one moment's thought, and with his old bright simple smile. "I had it, my lord, from the two young ladies—the daughters of the Count of Zamora."

"Aha!" cried Lord Wellington (being almost as fond of young ladies as they of him, and touched perhaps for the moment by the magic of a sweet young smile), "I begin to understand the bridge affair. But I fear that young ladies can hardly be cited as authorities on geography. Otherwise, we might make out a case against the Spanish authorities for sending our escort to the wrong place. And the Spanish escort, as you say, took that for the proper place."

"Certainly, my lord, they did. And so did the count, and every body. Is there any hope now that I may be acquitted?"

At a moment's notice from Hope that she would like to come back to her lodgings, Hilary opened his eyes so wide, and his heart so wide, and every other place that Hope is generally partial to, that the great commander (who trusted as little as possible of his work to hope) could not help smiling a quick, dry smile. And he felt some pain, as, word by word, he demolished hope in Hilary.

"The point of the thing is the money, Lorraine. And that we never could recover from the Spaniards, even if it was lost through them; for the very good reason that they have not got it. And even supposing the mistake to be theirs, and our escort to have been sent astray, you were a party to that mistake. And more than that, you were bound to see that the treasure did not cross the river until our men were there. Did you do so?"

"Oh, if I only had done that, I should not be so miserable."

"Exactly so. You neglected your duty. Take more care of your own money than you have taken of ours, Lorraine. Do as I told you. And now, good-bye."

The general, who had long been chafing at so much discourse just now, offered his hand to Lorraine, as one who was now a mere civilian.

"Is there no hope?" asked Hilary, dropping a tear into the mane of the restive horse. "Can I never be restored, my lord?"

"Never; unless the money is made good before we go into quarters again. A heavy price for a captain's commission!"

"If it is made good, my lord, will you restore me from this deep disgrace?"

"The question will be for his royal highness. But I think that, in such an extraordinary case, you may rely—at any rate, you may rely upon my good word, Lorraine."

"I thank you, my lord. The money shall be paid. Not for the sake of my commission, but for the honor of our family."

CHAPTER LIII.

THE British army now set forth on its grand career of victory, with an entirely new set of breeches. Interception of convoys, and other adverse circumstances, had kept our heroes from having any money, although they had new pockets. And the British Government, with keen insight into British nature, had insisted upon it, in the last contract, that the pockets should be all four inches wide. With this the soldiers were delighted—for all the very bravest men are boys—and they put their knuckles into their pockets, and felt what a lot of money they would hold. And though the money did not come, there was the due preparation for it. It might come any day, for all they knew; and what fools they must have looked, if their pockets would not hold it! In short, these men laid on their legs to march with empty pockets; and march they did, as history shows, all the better for not having sixpence.

Though Hilary was so heartily liked, both in his own regiment and by the staff, time (which had failed for his trial) also failed for pity of the issue. The general had desired that as little as possible should be said; and even if any one had wished to argue, the hurry and bustle would have stopped his mouth. Lorraine's old comrades were far in advance; and the staff, like a shuttle, was darting about; and the hills and the valleys were clapping their hands to the happy accompaniment of the drum.

Casting by every outward sign that he ever had been a soldier, Hilary Lorraine set forth on his sad retreat from this fine advance; afoot, and bearing on his shoulder a canvas bag on a truncheon of olive. He would not accept any knapsack, pouch, or soldier's usage of any kind. He had lost all right to that, being now but a shattered young gentleman on his way home.

However, in one way he showed good sense. By losing such a heap of the public money, he had learned to look a little better after his own; so he drew every farthing that he could get of his father's cash and his grandmother's, but scorned to accept the arrears of his pay, because he could not get them.

To a man of old, or of middle age, it has become (or it ought to become) a matter of very small account that he has thrown away his life. He has seen so many who have done the like (through indolence, pride, bad temper, reserve, timidity, or fool's confidence —into which the most timid men generally rush), that he knows himself now to be a fine example, instead of standing forth as a very unpleasant exception to the rule. And now, if he takes it all together, he finds many fellows who have done much worse, and seem all the better for it. Has he missed an appointment? They cut down the salary. Did he bang his back-door on a rising man? Well, the man, since he rose, has forgotten his hosts. Has he married a shrew? She looks after his kitchen. Remembering and reflecting thus, almost any good man must refuse to be called, in the long-run, a bigger fool than his neighbors.

But a young man is not yet late enough to know what human life is. He is sure that he sees by foresight all the things which, as they pass us, leave so little time for insight, and of which the only true view is the calm and pleasant retrospect. And then, like a high-stepping colt brought suddenly on his knees, to a sense of Macadam, he flounders about in amazement so, that if the fatal damage is not done to him, he does it.

Lorraine was not one of those who cry, as the poets of all present ages do, "Let the world stand still, because I don't get on." Nevertheless, he was greatly downcast to find his own little world so early brought to a sudden stand-still. And it seems to be sadly true that the more of versatile quickness a man has in him, the less there remains to expect of him, in the way of pith and substance. But Hilary now was in no condition to go into any philosophies. He made up his mind to walk down to the sea, and take ship at some good sea-port; and having been pleased at Malaga by the kind, quiet ways of the people, and knowing the port to be unobserved by French and American cruisers, he thought that he might as well try his luck once more in that direction.

Swift of foot as he was, and lightsome, when his heart was toward, he did not get along very fast on this penitential journey. So that it was the ninth day or the tenth, from his being turned out of the army, when he came once more to the "Bridge of Echoes," henceforth his "Bridge of Sighs" forever. Here he stopped and ate his supper, for his appetite was good again; and then he looked up and down the Zujar, and said to himself what a fool he was. For lo! where Claudia had held him trembling over a fearful abyss of torrent (as it seemed by moonlight), there now was no more than nine inches of water gliding along very pleasantly. These Spanish waters were out of his knowledge, as much as the Spanish ladies were; but though the springs might have been much higher a fortnight ago than they were now, Hilary could not help thinking that Claudia, instead of fainting on the verge, might have jumped over at any moment, without spraining her very neat ankles. And then he remembered that it was this same beautiful and romantic girl who had proved to the satisfaction of the Spanish colonel that this was the only Zujar ford, for that river merged its name where it joined the longer and larger Guadalmez. Upon this question there long had arisen a hopeful dilemma in Hilary's mind, which stated itself in this form: If this were the true Zujar ford, then surely the Spaniards, the natives of the country, were bound to apprise General Hill thereof. If this were not the Zujar ford, then the Spaniards were liable for the treasure beyond this place and as far as the true one. The latter was of course the stronger horn of the dilemma; but unluckily there arose against it a mighty monster of fact, quite strong enough to take even the Minotaur by the horns. Suppose the brave Spaniards to owe the money, it was impossible to suppose that they could pay it.

This reflection gave Hilary such a pain in his side that he straightway dropped it. And beholding the vivid summer sky beginning to darken into deeper blue, and the juts of the mountainous places preparing to throw light and shadow lengthwise, and the simmering of the sun-heat sinking into white mists laid abroad, he made up his mind to put best foot foremost, and sleep at Monte Argento. For he felt quite sure of the goodwill and sympathy of that pure hidalgo, the noble Count of Zamora; and from the young donnas he might learn something about his misadventure. He could not bring himself to believe that Claudia had been privy to the dastardly outrage upon himself. His nature was too frank and open to foster such mean ideas. Young ladies were the best and sweetest, the kindest and the largest-hearted, of created beings. So they were, and so they are; but all rules have exceptions.

Hilary, as he walked up the hill (down which he had ridden so gallantly scarcely more than a fortnight since), was touched with many thinkings. The fall of the sun (which falls and rises over us so magnanimously) had that power upon his body which it has on all things. The sun was going; he had done his work, and was tired of looking at people; mount as you might, the sun was sinking, and disdained all shadows and oblation of memorial.

Through the growth of darkness thus, and the urgency of froward trees (that could not fold their arms and go to sleep without some rustling), and all the many quiet sounds that nurse the repose of evening, Lorraine came to the heavy gates that had once secured the money. The porter knew him, and was glad to let in the young British officer whose dollars, leaping right and left, had made him many household friends. But in the hall the old steward met him, and, with many grave inclinations of his head and body, mourned that he could not receive the illustrious señor.

"There is in the castle no one now but my noble mistress, the Donna Camilla. His excellence the count is away, far from home at the wars."

"And the young Lady Claudia, where is she? I beg your pardon, steward, if I ought not to ask the question."

For the ancient steward had turned away at the sound of Donna Claudia's name; and pretending to be very deaf, began to trim a lamp or two.

"Will the Donna Camilla permit me to see her for one minute, or for two, perhaps? Her father is from home; but you, Señor Steward, know what is correct, and thus will act."

Hilary had not been so frightened at his own temerity in the deadly breach of Badajos as now when he felt himself softly slipping a brace of humble English guineas into this lofty Spaniard's palm. The steward, without knowing what he was about, except that he was trimming a very stubborn lamp, felt with his thumb that there must be a brace, and with contemptuous indignation let them slide into his pocket.

"Señor, I will do only what is right. I am of fifty years almost in this noble family. I am trusted, as I deserve. What I do is what the count himself would do. But a very sad thing has happened. We are obliged now to be most careful. The señor knows what the ladies are?"

"Señor Steward, that is the very thing that I never do know. You know them well. But, alas! I do not."

"Alas! I do," said the steward, panting, and longing to pour forth experience; but he saw some women peeping down stairs, and took the upper hand of them. "Señor, it is not worth the knowing. Our affairs are loftier. Go back, all you women, and prepare for bed. Have you not had your supper? Now, señor, in here for a minute, if you please; patience passeth all things."

But Hilary's patience itself was passed, as he waited in this little anteroom, ere the steward returned with the Donna Camilla, and, with a low bow, showed her in, and posted himself in a corner. She was dressed in pure white, which Hilary knew to be the mourning costume of the family.

The hand which the young Andalusian lady offered was cold and trembling, and her aspect and manner were timid and abashed.

"Begone!" she cried to the worthy steward, with a sudden indignation, which perhaps relieved her.

"What now shall I do?" said the steward to himself, with one hand spread upon his silver beard; "is this one also to run away?"

"Begone!" said Camilla to him once more, looking so grand that he could only go; and then quietly bolting the old gentleman out. After which she returned to Hilary.

"Señor Captain, I am very sorry to offer you any scenes of force. You have had too many from our family."

"I do not understand you, señorita. From your family I have received nothing but kindness, hospitality, and love."

"Alas, señor! and heavy blows. Our proverb is, 'Love leads to blows;' and this was our return to you. But she is of our family no more."

"I am at a loss. It is my stupidity. I do not know at all what is meant."

"In sincerity, the cavalier has no suspicion who smote down and robbed him?"

"In sincerity, the cavalier knows not; although he would be very glad to know."

"Is it possible? Oh, the dark treachery! It was my cousin who struck you down; my sister who betrayed you."

"Ah, well!" said Lorraine, in a moment seeing how she trembled for his words, and how terribly she felt the shame; "if it be so, I am still in her debt. She saved my life once, and she spared it again. Now, as you see, I am none the worse. The only loser is the British Government, which can well afford to pay."

"It is not so. The loss is ours, of honor, faith, and gratitude."

"I pray you not to take it so. Every body knows that the fault was mine. And whatever has happened only served me right."

"It served you aright for trusting us! It is too true. It is a bitter saying. My father mourns, and I mourn. She never more will be his daughter, and never more my sister."

"I pray you," said Hilary, taking her hand, as she turned away to control herself—"I pray you, Donna Camilla, to look at this little matter sensibly. I now understand the whole of it. Your sister is of very warm and strong patriotic sentiments. She felt that this money would do more good as the property of the *partidas* than as the pay of the British troops. And so she exerted herself to get it. All good Spaniards would have thought the same."

"She exerted herself to disgrace herself, and to disgrace her family. The money is not among the *partidas*, but all in the bags of her cousin Alcides, whom she has married without dispensation, and with her father's sanction forged. Can you make the best of that, señor?"

Hilary certainly could not make any thing very good out of this. And cheerful though his nature was, and tolerably magnanimous, he could not be expected to enjoy the treatment he had met with. To be knocked down and robbed, was bad enough; to be disgraced, was a great deal worse; but to be cut out by a rival, betrayed into his power, and made to pay for his wedding with trust-money belonging to poor soldiers—all this was enough to imbitter even the sweet and kind nature of young Lorraine. Therefore his face was unlike itself, as he turned it away from the young Spanish lady, being much taken up with his own troubles, and not yet ready to make light of them.

"Will you not speak to me, señor? I am not in any way guilty of this. I would have surrendered the whole of my life—"

"I pray you to pardon me," Hilary answered. "I am not accustomed to this sort of thing. Where are they now? Can I follow them?"

"Even a Spaniard could not find them. My brothers would not attempt it. Alcides knows every in and out. He has hidden his prize in the mountains of the north."

"If that is so, I can only hasten to say farewell to the Spanish land."

"To go away, and to never come back! Is it possible that you could do that?"

"It may be a bitter thing; but I must try. I am now on my way to Malaga. Being discharged from the British army, I have only to find my own way home."

"It can not be; it never can be! Our officers lose a mule's-load of money, or spend it at cards; and we keep them still, Señor Captain. You must have made some mistake. They never could discharge you."

"If there has been any mistake," said Hilary, regaining his sweet smile, with his sense of humor, "it is on their part, not on mine. Discharged I am; and the British army, as well as the Spanish cause, must do their best to get on without me."

"Saints of heaven! And you will go, and never come back any more?"

"With the help of the saints, that is my hope. What other hope is left to me?"

Camilla de Montalvan did not answer this

question with her lips, but more than answered it with her eyes. She fell back suddenly, as if with terror, into a great blue velvet chair, and her black tresses lay on her snowy arms, although her shapely neck reclined. Then with a gentle sigh, as if recovering from a troubled dream, she raised her eyes to Hilary's, and let them dwell there long enough to make him wonder where he was. And he saw that he had but to speak the word to become the owner of grace and beauty, wealth, and rank in the Spanish army, and (at least for a time) true love.

But, alas! a burned child dreads the fire. There still was a bump on Lorraine's head from the staff of Don Alcides; and Camilla's eyes were too like Claudia's to be trusted all at once. Moreover, Hilary thought of Mabel, of all her goodness, and proven trust; and Spanish ladies, though they might be queens, had no temptation for him now. And perhaps he thought—as quick men think of little things unpleasantly—"I do not want a wife whose eyes will always be deeper than my own." And so he resolved to be off as soon as it could be done politely.

Camilla, having been disappointed more than once of love's reply, clearly saw what was going on, and called her pride to the rescue. The cavalier should not say farewell to her; she would say it to the cavalier. Also, she would let him know one thing.

"If you must leave us, Captain Lorraine, and return to your native land, you will at least permit me to do what my father would have done if he were at home—to send you with escort to Malaga. The roads are dangerous. You must not go alone."

"I thank you. I am scarcely worth robbing now. I can sing in the presence of the bandit."

"You will grant me this last favor, I am sure, if I tell you one thing. It was not that wicked Claudia who drew the iron from your wound."

"It was not the Donna Claudia! To whom, then, do I owe my life?"

"Can you not, by any means, endeavor to conjecture?"

"How glad I am!" he answered, as he kissed her cold and trembling hand, "the lady to whom I owe my life is gentle, good, and truthful."

"There is no debt of life, señor. But would it have grieved you, now, if Claudia had done it? Then be assured that she did not do it. Her manner never was to do any thing good to any one. And yet how wonderful are things! Every body loved her. It is no good to be good, I fear. Pedro, you are at the door, then, are you? You have taken care to hear every thing. Go order a repast for the cavalier of the best we have, and men and horses to conduct him to Malaga. Be quick, I say, and show no hesitation." At her urgent words the steward went, yet grumbling and reluctant, and glancing over his shoulder all the way along the passage. "How that old man amuses me!" she continued, to the wondering Hilary, who had never dreamed that she could speak sharply; "ever since my sister's disgrace he thinks that his duty is to watch me. Ah! what am I to be watched for?"

"Because," said Hilary, "there is no Spaniard who would not long to steal the beautiful young donna."

"No Spaniard shall ever do that. But haste; you are in such hurry for the sunny land of Anglia."

"I do not understand the señorita. Why should I hurry to my great disgrace? I shall never hear the last of the money I have lost."

"'Tis all money, money, money, in the noble England. But the friends of the captain need not mourn; for the money was not his, nor theirs."

This grandly philosophical and most truly Spanish view of the case destroyed poor Hilary's last fond hope of any sense of a debt of honor on the part of the Montalvans. If the money lost had been Hilary's own, the Count of Zamora (all compact of chivalry and rectitude) might have discovered that he was bound to redeem his daughter's robbery. But as it stood, there was no such chance. Private honor is a mountain rill that does not always lead to any lake of public honesty. All Spaniards would bow to the will of the Lord that British guineas should slip into Spanish hands so providentially.

"We do not take such things just so," said young Lorraine, quite sadly. "I must go home and restore the money. Donna Camilla, I must say farewell."

"You will come again when you are restored? When you have proved that you did not take the money for yourself, señor, you will remember your Spanish friends?"

"I never shall forget my Spanish friends. To you I owe my life, and hold it (as long as I hold it) at your command."

"It is generously said, señor. Generosity always makes me weep. And so farewell."

CHAPTER LIV.

In all the British army—then a walking wood of British oak, without a yard of sapling—there was no bit of better stuff than the five feet and a quarter (allowing for his good game leg) of Major, by this time Colonel, Clumps. This officer knew what he had to do, and he made a point of doing it. Being short of imagination, he despised that foolish gift, and marveled over and over again at others for laughing so at nothing. That whimsical tickling of the veins of thought, which some people give so and some receive (with equal delight on either side), humor, or wit, or whatever it is, to Colonel Clumps was a vicious thing. Every thing must be either true or false. If it were true, who could laugh at the truth? If it were false, who should laugh at a falsehood?

Many a good man has reasoned thus, reducing laughter under law, and himself thenceforth abandoned by that lawless element. Colonel Clumps had always taken solid views of every thing, and the longer he lived in the world the less he felt inclined to laugh at it. But, that laughter might not be robbed of all its dues and royalties, just nature had provided that, as the colonel would not laugh at the world, the world should laugh at the colonel. He had been the subject of more bad jokes, one-sided pleasantries, and heartless hoaxes, than any other man in the army; with the usual result that now he scarcely ever believed the truth, while he still retained for the pleasure of his friends a tempting stock of his native confidence in error. So that it came to pass that when Colonel Clumps (after the battle of Vittoria, in which he had shown conspicuous valor) was told of poor Hilary's sad disgrace, he was a great deal too clever and astute to believe a single word of it.

"It is ludicrous, perfectly ludicrous!" he said, that being the strongest adjective he knew to express pure impossibility. "A gallant young fellow to be cashiered without even a court-martial! How dare you tell me such a thing, sir? I am not a man to be rough-ridden. Nobody ever has imposed on me. And the boy is almost a sort of cousin of my own. The first family in the kingdom, sir."

The colonel flew into so great a rage, twisting his white hair and stamping his lame heel, that the officer who had brought the news, being one of his own subalterns, wisely retired into doubts about it, and hinted that nobody knew the reason, and therefore that it could not be true.

"If I mention that absurd report about young Lorraine," thought Colonel Clumps, when writing to Lady de Lampnor, "I may do harm, and I can do no good, but only get myself laughed at as the victim of a stupid hoax. So I will say no more about him, except that I have not seen him lately, being so far from head-quarters, and knowing how Old Beaky is driving the Staff about." And before the brave colonel found opportunity of taking the pen in hand again, he was heavily wounded in a skirmish with the French rear-guard, and ordered home, as hereafter will perhaps appear.

It also happened that Mr. Capper's friends, those two officers who had earned so little of Mabel's gratitude by news of Hilary, were harassed and knocked about too much to find any time for writing letters. And as the *Gazette* in those days neglected the smaller concerns of the army, and became so hurried by the march of events, and the rapid sequence of battles, that the doings of junior officers slipped through its fingers until long afterward, the result was that neither Coombe Lorraine nor Old Applewood Farm received for months any news of the young staff-officer. Neither did he yet present himself at either of those homesteads. For, as the ancient saying runs, misfortunes never come alone. The ship in which Hilary sailed for England from the port of Cadiz—for he found no transport at Malaga—The *Flower of Kent*, as she was called, which appeared to him an excellent omen, was nipped in the bud of her homeward voyage. She met with a nasty French privateer to the southward of Cape Finisterre. In vain she crowded sail, and tried every known resource of seamanship; the Frenchman had the heels of her, and laid her on board at sundown. Lorraine, and two or three old soldiers, battered and going to hospital, had no idea of striking, except in the British way of doing it. But the master and the mate knew better, and stopped the hopeless conflict. So the Frenchmen sacked and scuttled the ship in the most scientific manner, and, wanting no prisoners, landed the crew on a desolate strand of Gallicia, without any money to save them.

This being their condition, it is the proper thing to leave them so; for nothing is more unwise than to ask, or rather to "institute inquiries," as to the doings of people who are much too likely to require a loan; therefore return we to the South Down hills.

The wet, ungenial, and stormy summer of 1813 was passing into a wetter, more cheerless, and most tempestuous autumn. On the northern slopes of the light-earthed hills the moss had come over the herbage, and the sweet nibble of the sheep was souring. The huddled trees (which here and there rise just to the level of the ridge, and then seem polled by the sweep of the wind-rush), the bushes also, and the gorse itself, stood, or rather stooped, beneath the burden of perpetual wet. The leaves hung down in a heavy drizzle, unable to detach themselves from the welting of the unripe stalks; the husk of the beech and the key of the ash were shriveled for want of kernels, and the clusters of the hazel-nut had no sun-varnish on them. The weakness of the summer sun (whether his face was spotted overmuch, or too immaculate), and the humor of clouds, and the tenor of winds, and even the tendency of the earth itself to devolve into eccentricity—these, and a hundred other causes, for the present state of the weather, were found, according to where they were looked for. On one point only there was no contradiction—things were not as they ought to be.

Even the rector of West Lorraine, a man of most cheerful mind, and not to be put down by any one, laying to the will of the Lord his failures, and to his own merits all good success, even the Rev. Struan Hales was scarcely a match for the weather. Sportsmen in those days did not walk in sevenfold armor for fear of a thorn, or a shower, or a cow-dab; nor skulked they for two hours in a rick, awaiting the joy of one butchering minute. Fair play for man, and dog, and gun, and fur, and feather was then the rule; and a day of sport meant a day of work, and healthful change, and fine exercise. Therefore Mr. Hales went forth with his long and heavily-loaded gun to comfort himself and refresh his mind, whatever the weather might be about upon six days out of every seven. The hounds had not begun to meet; the rivers were all in flood, of course; the air was so full of rheumatism that no man could crook his arm to write a sermon or work a concordance. Two sick old women had taken a fancy for pheasant boiled with artichoke; willy-nilly, the parson found it a momentous duty now to shoot.

And who went with him? There is no such thing as consistence of the human mind; yet well as this glorious truth was known, and bemoaned by every one for his neighbor's sake, not they, not all the parish, nor even we of the enlarged philosophy, could or can ever be brought to believe our own eyes that it was Bonny! But, in spite of all impossibility, it was; and the explanation requires relapse.

Is it within recollection that the rector once shot a boy in the hedge? The boy had climbed up into an ivied stump for purposes of his own, combining review with criticism. All critics deserve to be shot if they dare to cross the grand aims of true enterprise. They pepper, and are peppered; but they generally get the best of it. And so did this boy that was shot in the hedge. Being of a crafty order, he dropped, and howled and rolled so piteously, that poor Mr. Hales, although he had fired at a distance of more than four-score yards from the latent vagabond, cast down his gun in the horror of having slain a fellow-creature. But when he ran up and turned him over to search for the fatal injury, the boy so vigorously kicked and roared that the parson had great hopes of him. After some more rolling, a balance was struck; the boy had some blue spots under his skin, and a broad gold guinea to plaster them.

Now this boy was not our Bonny, nor fit in any way to compare with him. But uncivilized minds are very jealous; and next to our Bonny, this boy that was shot was the farthest from civilization of all the boys of the neighborhood. Therefore, of course, bitter jealousy raged betwixt him and the real outsider. Now the boy that was shot got a new pair of boots from the balance of his guinea, and a new pair of legs to his nether garments, under his mother's guidance. And to show what he was, and remove all doubts of the genuine expenditure, his father and mother combined and pricked him, with a pin in a stick, to the Sunday-school. Here Madge Hales (the second and strongest daughter of the church) laid hold of him, and converted him into right views of theology, hanging upon sound pot-hooks.

But a far greater mind than Bill Harkles could own was watching this noble experiment. Bonny had always hankered kindly after a knowledge of "pictur-books." The gifts of nature were hatching inside him, and chipped at the shell of his chickenhood. He had thrashed Bill Harkles in two fair fights, without any aid from his donkey, and he felt that Bill's mind had no right whatever to be brought up to look down on him.

This boy, therefore, being sneered at by erudite Bill Harkles, knew that his fists would be no fair answer, and retired to his cave. Here he looked over his many pickings, and proudly confessing inferior learning, refreshed himself with superior wealth. And this meditation, having sound foundation, satisfied him till the next market-day—the market-day at Steyning. Bonny had not much business here, but he always liked to look at things; and sometimes he got a good pannier of victuals, and sometimes he got nothing. For the farmers of the better sort put off their dinner till two o'clock, when the prime of the market was over, and then sat down to boiled beef and carrots in the yard of the White Horse Inn, and often did their best in that way.

Of this great "ordinary"—great, at any rate, as regards consumption—Farmer Gates, the church-warden, was by ancestral right the chairman; but for several market-days the vice-presidency had been vacant. A hot competition had raged, and all Steyning had thrilled with high commotion about the succession to the knife and fork at the bottom of the table; until it was announced, amidst general applause, that Bottler was elected. It was a proud day for this good pigman, and perhaps a still prouder one for Bonny, when the new vice-president was inducted into the Windsor chair at the foot of the long and ancient table; and it marked the turning-point in the life of more than one then present.

The vice-president's cart was in the shed close by, and on the front lade sat Bonny, sniffing the beauty of the "silver-side," and the luscious suggestions of the marrow-bone. Polly longed fiercely to be up there with him; but her mother's stern sense of decorum forbade; the pretty Miss Bottlers would be toasted after dinner; and was one to be spied in a pig-cart? No sooner was the cloth removed, than the chairman proposed, in most feeling and eloquent language, the health of his new colleague. And now it was Bottler's reply which created a grand revolution in Steyning. With graceful modesty he ascribed his present proud position, the realization of his fondest hopes, neither to his well-known integrity, industry, strict attention to business, nor even the quality of his bacon. All these things, of course, contributed; but "what was the grand element of his unparalleled success in life?" A cry of "White-stockings!" from the Bramber pig-sticker was sternly suppressed, and the man kicked out. "The grand element of his success in life was his classical education!"

Nobody knowing what was meant by this, thunders of applause ensued; until it was whispered from cup to cup that Bottler, when he was six years old, had been three months at the grammar school. He might have forgotten every word he had learned, but any one might see that it was dung dug in. So a dozen of the farmers resolved at once to have their children Latined; and Bonny in his inmost heart aspired to some education. What was the first step to golden knowledge? He put this question to himself obscurely, as he rode home on his faithful Jack, with all the marrow-bones of the great feast rattling in a bag behind him. From the case of Bill Harkles he reasoned soundly, that the first thing to do was to go and get shot.

On the following day—the month being August, or something very near it, in the year 1812 (a year behind the time we got on to), Mr. Hales, to keep his hand in, took his favorite flint-gun down, and patted it, and reprimed it. He had finished his dinner; it had been a good one; and his partner in life had been lamenting the terrible price of butcher's meat. She did not see how it could end in any thing short of a wicked rebellion, when the price of bread was put with it. And the rector had answered, with a wink to Cecil, "Order no meat for to-morrow, my dear, nor even for the next day. We shall see what we shall see." With this power of promise, he got on his legs, and stopped all who were fain to come after him. He knew every coney and coney's hole on the glebe, and on the clerk's land; and they all would now be out at grass, and must be treated gingerly. He was going to shoot for the pot, as sportsmen generally did in those days.

With visions of milky onions about to be poured on a broad and well-boiled back, the rector (after sneaking through a furzy gate) peeped down a brown trench of the steep hill-side; here he spied three little sandy juts of recent excavation, and on each of them sat a hunch-backed coney, proud of the labors of the day, and happily curling his whiskers. The rector, peering downward, saw the bulging over their large black eyes, and the prick of their delicate ears, and their gentle chewing of the grass-blade. There was no chance of a running shot, for they would pop into earth in a moment; so he tried to get two of them into a line, and then he pulled his trigger. The nearest rabbit fell dead as a stone; but the rector could scarcely believe his eyes, when through the curls of the smoke he beheld, instead of the other rabbit, a ragged boy rolling, and kicking, and hallooing!

"Am I never to shoot without shooting a boy?" cried the parson, rushing forward; "another guinea! A likely thing! I vow I will only pay a shilling this time. The sport would ruin a bishop!"

But Mr. Hales found, to his great delight, that the boy was not touched by a shot, nor even made pretense to be so. He had craftily crept through the bushes from below, and quietly lurked near the rabbits' hole, and after the shot had darted forth and thrown himself cleverly on the wounded rabbit, who otherwise must have got away to die a lingering death in his burrow. The quickness and skill of the boy, and the luck of thus bagging both rabbits, so pleased the rector that he gave him sixpence, and bade him follow to carry the game and to see more sport. Bonny had a natural turn for sport, which never could be beaten out of him; and to get it encouraged by the rector of the parish was indeed a godsend. And in his excitement at every shot he poured forth his heart about rabbits, and hares, and wood-queists, and partridges, and even pheasants.

"Why, you know more than I do!" said the rector, kindly laying his hand on the shoulder of the boy, after loading for his tenth successful shot. "How ever have you picked up all these things? The very worst poacher of the coming age, or else the best gamekeeper."

"I looks about, or we does, me and Jack together," answered Bonny, with one of his broadest and most genuine grins; and the gleam of his teeth and the twinkle of his eyes enforced the explanation.

"Come to my house in the morning, Bonny," said the rector. And that was the making of him. For the boy that cleaned the knives and boots had never conscientiously filled that sphere, though he was captain of the Bible-class. And now he had taken the measles so long that they had put him to earth the celery. Here was an opening, and Bonny seized it; and though he made very queer work at first, his native ability carried him on, till he put a fine polish on every thing. From eighteen-pence a week he rose to two-and-threepence within nine months; and to this he soon added the empty bottles, and a commission upon the grease-pot!

Even now all has not been told; for by bringing the cook good news of her sweetheart, and the parlor-maid dry sticks to light her fire, and by showing a tender interest in the chilblains of even the scullery-maid, he became such a favorite in the kitchen that the captain of the Bible-class defied him to a battle in the wash-house. The battle was fought, and victory, though long doubtful, perched at last upon the banner of brave Bonny; and with mutual esteem, and four black eyes, the heroes parted.

After this all ran smooth. The rector (who had enjoyed the conflict from his study-window, without looking off more than he could help from a sermon upon "Seek peace, and ensue it"), as soon as he had satisfied himself which of the two boys hit the straighter, went to an ancient wardrobe and examined his by-gone hunting-clothes. Here he found an old scarlet coat, made for him thirty years ago at Oxford, but now a world too small; and he sighed that he had no son to inherit it. Also a pair of old buckskin breeches, fitter for his arms than his legs just now. The moths were in both; they were growing scurfy; sentiment must give way to sense. So Bonny got coat and breeches; and the maids, with merry pinches, and screams of laughter, and consolatory kisses, adapted them. He showed all this grandeur to his donkey Jack, and Jack was in two minds about snapping at it.

This matter being cleared, and the time brought up, here we are at West Lorraine in earnest, in the month of October, 1812; long after Hilary's shocking disgrace, but before any of his own people knew it.

CHAPTER LV.

"What a lazy loon that Steenie Chapman is!" said the rector, for about the twentieth time, one fine October morning. "He knows what dreadful weather we get now, and yet he can't be here by nine o'clock! Too bad, I call it; too bad, a great deal. Send away the tea-pot, Caroline."

"But, my dear," answered Mrs. Hales, who always made the best of every one, "you forget how very bad the roads must be, after all the rain we have had. And I am sure he will want a cup of tea after riding through such flooded roads."

"Tea, indeed!" the parson muttered, as he strode in and out of the room, with his shot-belt dancing on his velveteen shooting-coat, and snapped his powder-flask impatiently; "Steenie's tea comes from the case, not the caddy. And the first gleam of sunshine I've seen for a week, after that heavy gale last night. It will rain before twelve o'clock, for a guinea. Cecil, run and see if you can find that boy Bonny. I shall start by myself, and send Bonny down the road with a message for Captain Chapman."

"The huntsman came out of the back-kitchen, Cecil, about two minutes ago," said Madge, who never missed a chance of a cut at Bonny, because he had thrashed her pet Bible-scholar; "he was routing about, with his red coat on, for scraps of yellow soap and candle-ends."

"What a story!" cried Cecil, who was Bonny's champion, being his school-mistress; "I wish your Dick was half as good a boy. He gets honester every day almost. I'll send him to you, papa, in two seconds. I suppose you'll speak to him at the side-door."

At a nod from her father, away she ran, while Madge followed slowly to help in the search; and finding that the boy had left the house, they took different paths in the garden to seek him, or overtake him on his homeward way. In a few moments, Cecil, as she passed some laurels, held up her hand to recall her sister, and crossed the grass toward her very softly, with finger on lip, and a mysterious look.

"Hush, and come here very quietly," she whispered; "I'll show you something as good as a play." Then the two girls peeped through the laurel-bush, and watched with great interest what was going on.

In an alley of the kitchen-garden sat Bonny upon an old sea-kale pot, clad in his red coat and white breeches, and deeply meditating. Before him, upon an espalier-tree, hung a tempting and beautiful apple, a scarlet pearmain, with its sleek sides glistening in the slant of the sunbeams.

"I'll lay you a shilling he steals it," Madge whispered into the ear of her sister.

"Done," replied Cecil, with her hand before her mouth.

Meanwhile Bonny was giving them the benefit of his train of reasoning. His mouth was wide open, and his eyes very bright, and his forehead a field of perplexity.

"They'se all a-grubbing in the house," he reflected; "and they an't been and offered me a bit to-day. There's ever so many more on the tree; and they locked up the scullery cupboard; and one on 'em called me a little warmint; and they tuck the key out of the beer-tap."

With all these wrongs upward, he stretched forth his hand, and pretty Cecil trembled for her shilling, shillings being very scarce with her. But the boy, without quite having touched the apple, drew back his hand; and that withdrawal perhaps was the turning-point of his life.

"He gived me all this," he said, looking at his sleeve; "and all on 'em stitched it up for me; and they lets me go in and out without watching; and twice I'se been out with him, shutting! I 'ont, I 'ont. And them bright apples seldom be worth ating of."

Sturdily he arose, and gave a kick at one of the posts of the apple-tree, and set off for the gate as hard as he could go while the virtuous vein should be uppermost.

"What a darling of honor!" cried Cecil Hales, jumping after him. "A Bayard, a Cato, an Aristides! He shall have his apple, and he shall have sixpence; and unlimited faith forever. Bonny, come back. Here's your apple for you, and sixpence; and what would you like to have best in all the world now?"

"To go out shutting with the master, miss."

"You shall do it; I will speak to papa myself. If you please, Miss Madge, pay up your shilling. Now come back, Bonny; your master wants you."

"You are a little too late for your errand, I fear," answered Margaret, pulling her purse out; "while you were pursuing this boy, I heard the sound of a grand arrival."

"So much the better!" cried Cecil, who (like her mother) always made the best of things. "Papa has been teasing his gun for an hour. Bonny, run back, and keep old Shot quiet. He will break his chain, by the noise he makes. You are as bad as he is; and you both shall go."

The rector—of all men the most hospitable, though himself so sober in the morning—revived Captain Chapman, or at least refreshed him, with brandy and bitters, after that long ride. And keenly heeding all hinderance, in his own hurry to be starting, he thought it a very bad sign for poor Alice that Stephen received no comfort from one, nor two, nor even three, large glasses.

At length they set forth, with a sickly sun shrinking back from the promise of the morning, and a vaporous glisten in the white south-east, looking as watery as the sea. "I told you so, Steenie," said the parson, who knew every sign of the weather among these hills; "we ought to have started two hours sooner. If ever we had wet jackets in our life, we shall have them to-day, bold captain."

"It will bring in the snipes," said the captain, bravely. "We are not the sort of men, I take it, to heed a little sprinkle. Tom, have you got my bladder-coat?"

"All right, your honor," his keeper replied; and "see-ho!" cried Bonny, while the dogs were ranging.

"Where, where, where?" asked the captain, dancing in a breathless flurry round a tuft of heath. "I can't see him; where is he, boy?"

"Poke her up, boy," said the rector; "surely you would not shoot the poor thing on her form!"

"Let him sit till I see him," cried the captain, cocking both his barrels; "now I am ready. Where the devil is he?"

"She can't run away," answered Bonny, "because your honor's heel be on her whiskers. Ah, there her gooth! Quick, your honor!"

And go she did in spite of his honor, and both the loads he sent after her; while the rector laughed so at the captain's plight that it was quite impossible for him to shoot. The keeper also put on an experienced grin, while Bonny flung open all the cavern of his mouth.

"Run after him, boy! Look alive!" cried the captain. "I defy him to go more than fifty yards. You must all have seen how I peppered him."

"Ay, and salted her too, I believe," said the parson; "look along the barrel of my gun, and you will see the salt still on her tail, eh, Steenie?"

As he pointed, they all saw the gallant hare at a leisurely canter crossing the valley some quarter of a mile below them.

"What!" cried the rector; "did you see that jump? What can there be to jump over there?" For Puss had made a long bound from bank to bank at a place where they could not see the bottom.

"Water, if 'e plaize, sir," answered Bonny; "a girt strame of water comed down that hollow all of a sudden this mornint; and it hath been growing stronger ever since."

"Good God!" exclaimed Mr. Hales, dropping his gun. "What is the water like, boy?"

"I never seed no water like it afore. As black as what I does your boots with, sir; but as clear—you can see every stone in it."

"Then the Lord have mercy on this poor parish, and especially to the old house of Lorraine! For the Woeburn has broken out again."

"Why, rector, you seem in a very great fright," said Captain Chapman, recovering slowly from his sad discomfiture. "What is the matter about this water? Some absurd old superstition—is not it?"

"Superstition or not," Mr. Hales answered, shortly, "I must leave you to shoot by yourself, Captain Chapman. I could not fire another shot to-day. It is more than three hundred and fifty years since this water of death was seen. In my church you may read what happened then. And not only that, but, according to tradition, its course runs directly through our village, and even through my garden. My people know nothing about it yet. It may burst upon them quite suddenly. There are many obstructions, no doubt, in its course, and many hollow places to fill up. But before many hours it will reach us. As a question of prudence, I must hasten home. Shot, come to heel this moment!"

"You are right," said the captain; "I shall do the same. Your hospitable board will excuse me to-night. I would much rather not leap the Woeburn in the dark."

With the instinct of a gentleman, he perceived that the rector, under this depression, would prefer to have no guest. Moreover, the clouds were gathering with dark menace over the hill-tops; and he was not the man—if such man there be—to find pleasure in a wet day's shooting.

"No horse has ever yet crossed the Woeburn," Mr. Hales replied, as they all turned homeward across the shoulder of the hill; "at least, if the legends about that are true. Though a hare may have leaped it to-day, to-morrow no horse will either swim or leap it."

"Bless my heart! does it rise like that? The sooner we get out of its way the better. What a pest it will be to you, rector! Why, you never will be able to come to the meet, and our opening day is next Tuesday."

"Steenie," cried the rector, imbibing hope, "it has not struck me in that light before. But it scarcely could ever be the will of the Lord to cut off a parson from his own pack!"

"Oh, don't walk so fast!" shouted Captain Chapman; "one's neck might be broken down a hill like this. Tom, let me lean on your shoulder. Boy, I'll give you sixpence to carry my gun. Tom, take the flints out, that he mayn't shoot me. Here, Uncle Struan, just sit down a minute; a minute can't make any difference, you know."

"That is true," said the rector, who was also out of breath. "Bonny, how far was the black water come? You seem to know all about it."

"Plaize, sir, it seem to be coming down a hill; and the longer I looked, the more water was a-coming."

"You little nincompoop! had it passed your own door yet—your hole, or your cave, or whatever you call it?"

"Plaize, sir, it worn't a-runnin' toward I at all. It wor makin' a hole in the ground, and kickin' a splash up in a fuzzy corner."

"My poor boy, its course is not far from your door; it may be in among your goods, and have drowned your jackass and all, by this time."

Like an arrow from a bow, away went Bonny down the headlong hill, having cast down the captain's gun, and pulled off his red coat to run the faster. The three men left behind clapped their hands to their sides and roared with laughter; at such a pace went the white buckskin breeches, through bramble, gorse, heather, over rock, sod, and chalk. "What a grand flying shot!" cried the keeper.

"Where the treasure is, there will the heart be," said the rector, as soon as he could speak. "I would give a month's tithes for a good day's rout among that boy's accumulations. He has got the most wonderful things, they say; and he keeps them on shelves, like a temple of idols. What will he do when he gets too big to go in at his own door-way? I am feeding him up with a view to that; and so are my three daughters."

"He must be a thorough young thief," said the captain. "In any other parish, he would be in prison. I scarcely know which is the softer 'Beak'—as we are called—you, or Sir Roland."

"Tom," cried the rector, "run on before us; you are young and active. Inquire where old Nanny Stilgoe lives, at the head of the village, and tell her that the flood is coming upon her; and help her to move her things, poor old soul, if she will let you help her. Tell her I sent you, and perhaps she will, although she is very hard to deal with. She has long been foretelling this break of the bourne; but the prophets are always the last to set their own affairs in order."

The keeper touched his hat, and set off. He always attended to the parson's orders more than his own master's. And Mr. Hales saw from the captain's face that he had ordered things too freely.

"Steenie, I beg your pardon," he said; "I forgot for the moment that I should have asked you before I dispatched your man like that. But I did it for your own good, because we need no longer hurry."

"Rector, I am infinitely obleeged to you. To order those men is so fatiguing. I always want some one to do it for me. And now we may go down the hill, I suppose, without snapping all our knee-caps. To go up a hill fast is a very bad thing; but to go down fast is a great deal worse, because you think you can do it."

"My dear fellow, you may take your time. I will not walk you off your legs, as that wicked niece of mine did. How are you getting on there now?"

"Well, that is a delicate question, rector. You know what ladies are, you know. But I do not see any reason to despair of calling you 'uncle' in earnest."

"Have you brought the old lady over to your side? You are sure to be right when that is done."

"She has been on my side all along, for the sake of the land. Ah, how good it is!"

"And nobody else in the field, that we know of. Then Lallie can't hold out so very much longer. Lord bless me! do you see that black line yonder?"

"To be sure! Why, it seems to be moving onward, like a great snake crawling. And it has a white head. What a wonderful thing!"

"It is our first view of the Woeburn. Would to Heaven that it were our last one! The black is the water, and the white, I suppose, is the chalky scum swept before it. It is following the old track, as lava does. It will cross the Coombe road in about five minutes. If you want to get home, you must be quick to horse. Never mind the rain:

let us run down the hill, or just stop one half minute."

They were sitting in the shelter of a chalky rock, with the sullen storm rising from the south behind them, and the drops already pattering. On the right hand and on the left, brown ridges, furzy rises, and heathery scollops overhanging slidden rubble, and the steep zigzags of the sheep, and the rounding way into nothing of the hill-tops — all of these were fading into the slaty blue of the rain-cloud. Before them spread for leagues and leagues, clear, and soft, and smiling still, the autumnal beauty of the weald-land. Tufting hamlets here and there, with darker foliage round them, elbows of some distant lane unconsciously prominent, swathes of color laid on broadly where the crops were all alike; some bold tree of many ages standing on its right to stand; and gray church-towers, far asunder, landmarks of a longer view; in the fading distance many things we can not yet make out; but hope them to be good and beauteous, calm, and large with human life.

This noble view expanded always the great heart of the rector; and he never failed to point out clearly the boundary-line of his parish. He could scarcely make up his mind to miss that opportunity even now; and was just beginning with a distant furze-rick, far to the westward under Chancton Ring, when Chapman, having heard it at least seven times, cut him short rather briskly.

"You are forgetting one thing, my dear sir. Your parish is being cut in two, while you are dwelling on the boundaries."

"Steenie, you are right. I had no idea that you had so much sense, my boy. You see how the ditches stand all full of water, so as to confuse me. A guinea for the first at the rectory gate! You ought to be handicapped. You call yourself twenty years younger, don't you?"

"Here's the guinea!" cried Chapman, as the parson set off; "two if you like; only let me come down this confounded hill considerately."

Mr. Hales found nothing yet amiss with his own premises: some people had come to borrow shovels, and wheeling-planks, and such-like; but the garden looked so fair and dry, with its pleasant slope to the east, that the master laughed at his own terrors, until he looked into the covered well, the never-failing black-diamond water, down below the tool-house. Here a great cone rose in the middle of the well, like a plume of black ostrich; and the place was alive with hollow noises.

"Dig the celery!" cried the rector. "Every man and boy, come here. I won't have my celery washed away, nor my drum-head Savoys, nor my ragged Jack. Girls, come out, every one of you. There is not a moment to lose, I tell you. I never had finer stuff in all my life; and I won't have it all washed away, I tell you. Here, you heavy-breeched Dick, what the dickens are you gaping at? I sha'n't get a thing done before dark, at this rate. Out of my way, every one of you. If you can't stir your stumps, I can."

With less avail, like consternation seized every family in West Lorraine. A river, of miraculous birth and power, was sweeping down upon all of them. There would never be any dry land any more; all the wise old women had said so. Every body expected to see black water bubbling up under his bed that night.

Meanwhile this beautiful and grand issue of the gathered hill-springs moved on its way majestically, obeying the laws it was born of. The gale of the previous night had unsealed the chamber of great waters, forcing the needful air into the duct, and opening vaults that stored the rain-fall of a hundred hills and vales. Through such a "bower of stalactite, such limpid realms and lakes enlock'd in caves," Cyrene led her weeping son,

> "Where all the rivers of the world he found,
> In separate channels gliding under-ground."

And now, as this cold resistless flood calmly reclaimed its ancient channel, swallowed up Nanny Stilgoe's well, and cut off the rector from his own church; as if to encounter its legendary bane, a poor young fellow, depressed and shattered, feeble, and wan, and heavy-hearted, was dragging his reluctant steps up the valley of the Adur. Left on the naked rocks of Spain, conquered, plundered, and half starved, Hilary Lorraine had fallen, with the usual reaction of a sanguine temperament, into low spirits and disordered health. So that when he at last made his way to Corunna, and found no British agent there, nor any one to draw supplies from, nothing but the pride of his family kept him from writing to the Count of Zamora. Of writing to England there was no chance. All communication ran through the channels of the distant and victorious army. So that he thought himself very lucky (in the present state of his health and fortunes) when the captain of an oil-ship bound for London, having lost three hands on the outward voyage, allowed him to work his passage. The fare of a landsman in feeble health was worth perhaps more than his services; but the captain was a kind-hearted man, and perceived (though he knew not who Hilary was) that he had that very common thing in those days, a "gent under a cloud" to deal with. And the gale, which had opened the Woeburn, shortened Hilary's track toward it, by forcing his ship to run for refuge into Shoreham harbor.

"How shall I go home? What shall I say? Disgraced, degraded, and broken down, a stain upon my name and race, I am not fit to enter our old doors. What will my father say to me? And proud Alice—what will her thoughts be?"

With steps growing slower at each weary drag, he crossed the bridge of Bramber, and passed beneath the ivied towers of the rivals of his ancestors, and then, avoiding Steyning town, he turned up the valley of West Lorraine. And the rain which had come on at middle-day, and soaked his sailor's slops long ago, now took him on the flank judiciously. And his heart was so low that he received it all without talking either to himself or it.

"I will go to the rectory first," he thought; "Uncle Struan is violent, but he is warm. And though he has three children of his own, he loves me much more than my father does."

With this resolution, he turned on the right down a lane that came out by the rectory. The lane broke off suddenly into black water; and a tall, robust man stood in the twilight, with a heavy spade over his shoulder. And Hilary Lorraine went up to him.

"No, no, my man; not a penny to spare!" said the rector, in anticipation; "we have a great deal too much to do with our own poor, and with this new trouble especially. The times are hard—yes, they always are; but an honest man always can get good work. Or go and fight for your country, like a man—but we can't have you in this parish."

"I have fought for my country, Uncle Struan; and this is all that has come of it."

"Good God, Hilary!" cried the rector; and for a long time he could say nothing else.

"Yes, Uncle Struan, don't you understand? Every one must have his ups and downs. I am having a long spell of downs just now."

"My dear boy, my dear boy, whatever have you done?"

"Do you mean to throw me over, Uncle Struan, as the rest of the world has beautifully done? Every thing seems to be upset. What is the meaning of this broad black stream?"

"Come into my study, and tell me all. I can let you in without sight of your aunt. The shock would be too great for her."

Hilary followed without a word. Mr. Hales led him in at the window, and warmed him, and covered him with his own dressing-gown, and watched him slowly recovering.

"Never mind the tar on your hands; it is an honest smell," he said; "my poor boy, my poor boy, what you must have been through!"

"Whatever has happened to me," answered Hilary, spreading his thin hands to the fire, "has been all of my own doing, Uncle Struan."

"You shall have a cordial; and you shall tell me all. There, I have bolted the door. I am your parson, as well as your uncle. All you say will be sacred with me. And I am sure you have done no great harm after all. We shall see what your dear aunt thinks of it."

Then Hilary, sipping a little rum-and-water, wandered through his story; not telling it brightly, as once he might have done, but hiding nothing consciously.

"Do you mean to tell me there is nothing worse than that?" asked the rector, with a sigh of great relief.

"There is nothing worse, uncle. How could it be worse?"

"And they turned you out of the army for that! How thankful I am for belonging to the Church! You are simply a martyred hero."

"Yes, they turned me out of the army for that. How could they help it?" Reasoning thus, he met his uncle's look of pity, and it was too much for him. He did what many a far greater man and braver hero has done, and will do, when the soul is moving. He burst into a hot flood of tears.

CHAPTER LVI.

Sir Roland Lorraine was almost as free from superstition as need be. To be wholly quit of that romantic element is a disadvantage still, and excepts a neighbor even now from the general neighborly sympathy. Three-score years ago, of course, that prejudice was threefold.

The swing of British judgment mainly takes magnetic repulse from whatever the French are rushing after. When they are Republican, all of us rally for throne and Constitution. When they have a Parliament, we want none. When they are pressed under empire, we are apt to be glad that it serves them right. We know them to be brave and good, lovers of honor, and sensitive; but we can not get over the line between us and them—and the rest of the world, perhaps.

Whatever might be said, or reasoned, for or against the whole of things, Sir Roland had long made up his mind to be moderate and neutral. He liked every body to speak his best (according to self-opinion), and he liked to keep out of the way of them all, and relapse into the wiser ages. He claimed his own power to think for himself, as well as the mere right of doing so. And therefore he long had been "heterodox" to earnest, right-minded people.

Never the more, however, could he shake himself free from the inborn might of hereditary leanings. The traditions of his house and race had still some power over him, a power increased by long seclusion, and the love of hearth and home. Therefore, when Trotman was cut off, on his way for his weekly paper, by a great black, gliding flood, and aghast ran up the Coombe to tell it, Sir Roland, while he smiled, felt strange misgivings creeping coldly.

Alice, a sweet and noble maiden, on the tender verge of womanhood, came to her father's side, and led him back to his favorite book-room. She saw that he was at the point of trembling; although he could still command his nerves, unless he began to think of them. Dissembling her sense of all this, she sat by the fire, and waited for him.

"My darling, we have had a very happy time," he began at last to say to her; "you and I for many years suiting one another."

"To be sure we have, father. And I mean to go on suiting you for many more years yet."

Her father saw by the fire-light the sadness in her eyes, and he put some gayety into his own, or tried.

"Lallie, you have brighter things before you—a house of your own, and society, and the grand world, and great shining."

"Excellent things, no doubt, my father; but not to be compared with you and home. Have I done any thing to vex you that you talk like this to me?"

"Let me see. Come here and show me. There are few things I enjoy so much as being vexed by you."

"There, papa, you are in a hurry to have your usual laugh at me. You shall have no material now. 'I knows what is right, and I means to do it;' as the man said to me at the turnpike-gate, when he made me pay twice over. Consider yourself, my darling father, saddled for all your life with me."

Sir Roland loved his daughter's quick bright turns of love, and loving passion, when her heart was really moved. A thousand complex moods and longings played around or pierced her then; yet all controlled, or at least concealed, by an English lady's quietude. Alice was so like himself that he always knew what she would think; and he tried his best to follow the zigzag flash of feminine feeling.

"My dear child," he said at last; "something has been too much for you. Perhaps that foolish fellow's story of this mysterious water. A gross exaggeration, doubtless. The finny tribe sticking fast by the gills in the nest of the wood-pigeon. Marry come up! Let us see these wonders. The moon is at the full to-night; and I hear no rain on the windows now. Go and fetch my crab-stick, darling."

"Oh, may I come with you, papa? Do say yes. I shall lie awake all night unless I go. The moon is sure to clear the storm off; and I will wrap up so thoroughly."

"But you can not wrap up your feet, dear child; and the roads are continually flooded now."

"Not on the chalk, papa; never on the chalk, except in the very hollow places. Besides, I will put on my new French clogs. They can't be much less than six inches thick. I shall stand among the deluge high enough for the fish to build their nests on me."

"Daughter of folly, and no child of mine, go and put your clogs on. We will go out at the eastern door, to arouse no curiosity."

As the master and his daughter passed beneath the astrologer's tower, and left the house by his private entrance, they could not help thinking of the good old prince, and his kind anxiety about them. To the best of their knowledge, the wise Agasicles had never heard of the Woeburn; or perhaps his mind had been so much engrossed with the comet that he took no heed of it. And even in his time this strange river was legendary as the Hydaspes.

After the heavy and tempestuous rain, the night was fair, as it generally is, even in the worst of weather, when the full moon rises. The long-chined hill, with its level outline stretching toward the south of east, afforded play for the glancing light of a watery and laborious moon. Long shadows, laid in dusky bars, or cast in heavy masses where the hollow land prevailed for them, and misty columns hovering and harboring over tree-clumps, and gleams of quiet light pursuing avenues of opening—all of these, at every step of deep descent, appeared to flicker like a great flag waving.

"What a very lovely night! How beautifully the clouds lie!" cried Alice, being apt to kindle rashly into poetry: "they softly put themselves in rows, and then they float toward the moon, and catch the silver of her smile—oh why do they do that, papa?"

"Because the wind is west, my dear. Take care; you are on a great flint, I fear. You are always cutting your boots out."

"No, papa, no. I have got you this time. That shows how much you attend to me. I have got my great French clogs on."

"Then how very unsafe to be looking at the moon! Lean on me steadily, if you must do that. The hill is slippery with slime on the chalk. You will skate away to the bottom, and leave me mourning."

"Oh, how I should love to skate, if ladies ever could do such a thing! I can slide very nicely, as you know, papa. Don't you think, after all this rain, we are sure to have a nice cold winter?"

"Who can tell, Lallie? I only hope not. You children, with your quick circulation, active limbs, and vigorous lungs, are always longing for frost and snow. But when they come, you get tired of them, within a week at the utmost. But in your selfish spring of life you forget all the miseries of the poor and old, or even young folk who are poor, and the children starving everywhere. And the price of all food is now most alarming."

"I am sure I meant no harm," said Alice; "one can not always think of every thing. Papa, do you know that you have lately taken to be very hard upon me?"

"Well now, every body says that of me," Sir Roland answered, thoughtfully; "I scarcely dreamed that my fault was that. But out of many mouths I am convicted. Struan Hales says it; and so does my mother. Hilary seemed to imply it also, at the time when he last was heard of. Mine own household, Trotman, Mrs. Pipkins, and that charitable Mrs. Merryjack, have combined to take the same view of me. There must be truth in it. I can not make head against such a cloud of witnesses. And now Alice joins them. What more do I want? I must revise my opinion of myself, and confess that I am a hard-hearted man."

This question Sir Roland debated with himself, in a manner which had long been growing upon him, in the gathering love of solitude. Being by nature a man with a most extraordinary love of justice, he found it hard (as such rare men do) to be perfectly sure about any thing. He always desired to look at a subject from every imaginable outside view, receding (like a lark in the clouds) from groundling consideration, yet frankly open (like a woodcock roasting) to any thing good put under him. Nobody knew him; but he did his best, when he thought of that matter, to know himself.

Now, his daughter allowed him to follow out his meditation quietly; and then she said, as they went down the hill, warily heeding each other's steps,

"Papa, I beg you particularly to pay no attention whatever to your own opinion, or any other opinion in the world, except perhaps, at least, perhaps—"

"Perhaps that of Alice."

"Quite so, papa. About my own affairs my opinion is of no value; but about yours, and the family in general, it is really—something."

"Wisest of our race, and bravest, you are rushing into the water; darling—stop; you have forgotten what we came for. We came to see the Woeburn, and here it is!"

"Is this it? And yesterday I walked across this very place! Oh, what a strange black river!"

As Alice drew suddenly back and shuddered, Sir Roland Lorraine threw his left arm round her, without a word, and looked at her. The light of the full moon fell on her face, through a cleft of jagged margins, and the shadow of a branch that had lost its leaves lay on her breast, and darkened it.

"Why, Lallie, you seem to be quite frightened," her father said, after waiting long; "look up at me, and tell me, dear."

"No, I am not at all frightened, papa, but perhaps I am a little out of spirits."

"Why?" asked Sir Roland; "you surely do not pay heed to old rhymes and silly legends. I call this a fine and most picturesque water. I only wish it were always here."

"Oh, papa, don't say that, I implore you. And I felt you shiver when you saw it first. You know what it means for our family: loss of life once, loss of property twice, and the third time the loss of honor—and with that, of course, our extinction."

"You little goose, none can lose their honor without dishonorable acts. Come, Miss Cassandra; of the present Lorraines—a very narrow residue—who is to be distinguished thus?"

"Father, you know so much more than I do; but I thought that many people were disgraced without having ever deserved it."

"Disgraced, my darling; but not dishonored. What could disgrace ever be to us? —a thing that comes and goes, according to the fickle seasons—a result of the petty human weather, as this melancholy water is of the larger influence."

"Papa, then you own that it is melancholy. That was just what I wanted you to do. You always take things so differently from every body else, that I began to think you would look upon this as a happy outburst of a desirable watering-water."

"Well done, Lallie! The command of language is an admirable gift. But the want of it leads to still finer issues. This watering-water seems inclined to go on for a long time watering."

"Of course, it must go flowing, flowing, until its time is over."

"Lallie, you have, among many other gifts, a decided turn for epigram. You scarcely could have described more tersely the tendencies of water. I firmly believe that this stream will go on flowing and flowing, until it quite stops."

"Papa, you are a great deal too bad. You must perceive that you are so, even by the moonlight. I say the most sensible things ever thought of, and out of them you make nonsense. Now let me have my turn. So please you, have you thought of bridges? How is our butcher to come, or our miller, our letters, or even our worthy beggars? We are shut off in front. Without building a boat, can I ever hear even Uncle Struan preach? Hark! I hear something like him."

"You frivolous Lallie! you are too bad. I can not permit such views of things."

"Of course, papa, I never meant it. Only please to listen."

The dark and deep stream, which now had grown to a width of some twelve yards perhaps, was gliding swiftly, but without a murmur, toward the broad and watery moon. On the right-hand side, steep scars of chalk, shedding gleams of white rays, made the hollow places darker; while on the other side, furzy tummocks, patches of brier, and tufted fallows spread the many-pointed light among their shadows justly.

"Please to listen," again said Alice, shrinking from her father, lest she might be felt to tremble. "What a plaintive, thrilling sound! It must be a good banshee, I am sure—a banshee that knows how good we are, and protests against our extinction. There it is again; and there seems to be another wail inside of it."

"A Chinese puzzle of noises, Lallie, and none of them very musical. Your ears are keener than mine, of course; but, being extinct of romance, I should say that I heard a donkey braying."

"Papa, now! papa, if it comes to that—and I said it was like Uncle Struan's voice! But I beg his pardon, quite down on my knees, if you think that it can be a donkey."

"I am saved all the trouble of thinking about it. There he is, looking hard at us!"

"Oh no, papa, he is not looking hard at us. He is looking most softly and sadly. What a darling donkey, and his nose is like a snow-drop!"

Clearly in the moonlight shone, on the opposite bank of the Woeburn, the nose of Jack, the donkey. His wailings had been coming long, and his supplications rising; he was cut off from his home, and fodder, and wholly beloved Bonny. And the wail inside a wail—as Alice had described it—was the sound of the poor boy's woe, responsive to the forlorn appeal of Jack. On the brink of the cruel dividing water they must have been for a long time striding up and down over against each other, stretching fond noses vainly forward, and outvying one another in the luxury of poetic woe.

"Don't say a word, papa," whispered Alice. "The boy can not see us here behind this bush, and we can see him beautifully in the moonlight. I want to know what he will do so much."

"I don't see what he can do except howl," Sir Roland answered, quietly; "and certainly he seems to possess remarkable powers in that way."

"Bo-hoo, hoo, hoo, hoo!" wept Bonny in confirmation of this opinion; and "eke-haw, eke-haw," from a nose of copious pathos, formed the elegiac refrain. Then, having exhausted the well of weeping, the boy became fitter for reasoning. He wiped his eyes with his scarlet sleeves, and stretched forth his arms reproachfully.

"Oh Jack, Jack, Jack, whatever have I done to you? All the crumb of the loaf you had, and the half of the very last orchard I run, and the prime of old Nanny's short-horns; and if you wasn't pleased, you might a' said so all the morning, Jack. There's none in all the world as knoweth what you and I be, but one another. And there's none as careth for either on us, only you and me, Jack. Don't 'ee, Jack, don't 'ee go and run away. If 'ee do, I'll give the thieves all as we've collected, and the folks as calls us two waggabones."

"My poor boy," said Sir Roland Lorraine, suddenly parting the bush between them, in fear of another sad boo-hoo—for Bonny had stirred his own depths, so that he was quite ready to start again—"my poor boy, you seem to be very unhappy about your donkey."

Bonny made answer to never a word. This woe belonged only to Jack and himself. They could never think of being meddled with.

"Bonny," said Alice, in her soft sweet voice, and kindly touching him, as he turned away; "do you wish to know how to recover your Jack? Would you go a long way to get him back again?"

"To the outermost end of the world, miss, if the whole of the way wor fuzz-bush. Miles and miles us have gone a'ready."

"You need not go quite to the end of the world. Instead of going up and down these banks, keep steadily up the water. In about a mile you will come to its head, if what I have heard of it is true; then keep well above it, and round the hill, and you will meet the white-nosed donkey."

"Hee-haw!" said Jack, from the opposite bank, not without a whisk of tail. Then the boy, without a word of thanks, by reason of incredulity, whistled a quick reply, and set off to test this doubtful theory.

"Observe now the bliss of possessing a donkey," Sir Roland began to meditate; "I am not at all skillful in asses, whether golden, or leaden, or wooden, or even as described by Œlian. But the contempt to which they are born proves to my mind that they do not deserve it; or otherwise how would they get it? My sentence is clumsy. My idea—if there be one—has not managed to express itself. I hear the white-nosed donkey in the distance braying at me, with an overpowering echo of contempt. I am unequal to this contest. Let me withdraw to my book-room."

"Indeed, papa, you will do nothing of the sort. You are always withdrawing to your book-room; and even I must not come in; and what good ever comes of it? You must, if you please, make up your mind to meet things very differently. And only think how long it is since we have heard of poor Hilary! There are troubles coming, overwhelming troubles, on all with the name or the love of Lorraine, as sure as I stand, my dear father, before you."

"Then I pray you to stand behind me, Alice. What an impulsive child it is! And the moolight, my darling, has had some effect, as it always has, wonderfully on such girls. You have worked yourself up, Lallie; I can see it. My pet, I must watch you carefully."

"What a mistake you make, papa! I never do any thing of the sort. You seem to regard me as any body's child, to be reasoned with, out of a window. I may be supposed to say foolish things, and to imagine all sorts of nonsense; and, of course, I can not reason, because it is not born with us. And then, when I try, I have no chance whatever; though perfect justice is my aim; and who comes lingering after me?"

"Your excellent father," Sir Roland answered, kissing away his child's excitement. "Your loving father does all this, my pet, and brings you quite home to stern reason. And now he will take you home to your home. You have caught the sad spirit of the donkey, petling; you long to go up and down this water, with some one to bewail you on the other side."

"Yes, papa, so I do. You are so clever! But I think I should go down and up, papa, if the quadruped you are thinking of went up and down."

"Now, Lallie!" he said; and he said no more. For he knew that she hinted at Stephen Chapman, and wanted to fight her own battle against him, now that she was in the humor. The father was ready to put off the conflict—as all good fathers must be—and he led his dear child up the hill, or let her lead him, peacefully.

CHAPTER LVII.

THREE days of gloom and storm ensued upon the outbreak of the water; while the old house at the head of the Coombe in happy ignorance looked down upon its hereditary foe. But dark forebodings and fine old stories agitated the loyal hearts of the domestics of the upper conclave—that ancient butler, Onesimus Binns, Mrs. Pipkins, and Mrs. Merryjack. With such uneasy feelings prevalent in the higher circle, nothing short of terror, or even panic, could be expected among the inferior dignitaries, now headed by John Trotman. This young man had long shown himself so ambitious and aggressive, even "cockroaching," as Mrs. Merryjack said, "on the most sacred rights of his betters," that the latter had really but one course left—to withdraw to their upper room, and exclude "all as didn't know how to behave theirselves."

Of these, unhappily, there were too many; and they seemed to enjoy themselves more freely after their degradation. For Trotman (though rapid of temper, perhaps, and given to prompt movements of the foot) was not at all bad (when allowed his own way), and never kicked any body who offered to be kicked. So with his dictatorship firmly established in the lesser lower regions, he became the most affable of mankind, and read all the crimes of the county to the maids, and drew forth long sighs of delicious horror, that his own brave self might console them. And now, when they heard of the sombre Woeburn, with its dismal legends, enhanced by ghastly utterances of ancient Nanny Stilgoe, and tidings brought through wailing winds of most appalling spectres, the stoutest heart was agitated with mysterious terror. At the creak of a door or the flit of a shadow, the rustle of a dry leaf or the waving of a window-blind, the hoot of an owl or even the silent creep of gloomy evening—"My goodness, Mary Ann, what was that?" or, "Polly, come closer; I hear something;" or, "Jane, do'ee look behind the plate-screen;" and then with one voice, "John, John, John, come down; that's a dear man, John!" Such was the state of the general nerve, as proved by many a special appeal from kitchen, back-kitchen, and scullery, pantry, terrible cellar, or lonesome wash-house; and the best of every thing was kept for John.

Even in the world of finer, feebler, and more foreign English; in dining-room, drawing-room, parlor, and book-room, and my lady's chamber, a mild uneasiness prevailed, and a sense of evil auspices. Lady Valeria, most of all, who carried conservatism into relapse, felt that troublous days were coming, and almost longed to depart in peace; or, at any rate, she said so. But with her keen mind and legal insight, she was bound to perceive that the authorized version of the other world is most democratic; as might be that of this world, if Christianity made Christians. Therefore her ladyship preferred to wait. Things might get better; and they could scarcely get worse. She had a good deal to see to and settle among things strictly visible, and she threatened every body with her decease, but did not prepare to make it.

Sir Roland Lorraine, on the other hand, paid little heed, of his own accord, to superstitious vanities. He found a good many instances, in classic, Persian, and Italian literature, of the outbreak of under-ground waters; and there it was always a god who caused it—either by chasing river-nymphs, or by showing the power of a horse's heels, or from benevolent motives, and a desire to water gardens. Therefore Sir Roland gathered hope. He had not invested his mind as yet in implicit faith in any thing; but rather was inclined to be tolerant, and tentative, and diffident of his own opinions. And these not being particularly strong, self-assertive, or self-important, and not being founded on any rock, but held on the briefest building-lease, their owner, leaseholder, or tenant-at-will was a very pleasant man to talk with.

That means, of course, when he could be got to talk. And less and less could he be got to talk, as the few people who had the key to his liking dropped off; and no others came. Never, even in his brightest days, had he been wont to sparkle, flash, or even glow in converse. He simply had a soft, large way of listening, and a small, dry knack of so diverting serious thought, that genial minds went roving. But now his own mind had grown more and more accustomed to go a-roving; and though, having never paid any attention to questions of science, or even to the weather (now gradually becoming one of them), he could not satisfy himself about the menacing appearance: in a very few hours he buried the portent in a still more portentous pile of books.

But Alice, though fond of reading and of meditating in her little way, was too full of youth and of healthy life to retire into the classic ages of even our English language. Her delight was rather in the writers of the day, so many of whom were making themselves the writers of all future days—Coleridge, Wordsworth, Campbell, and above all others, the "Wizard of the North," whose lays of romance and legend were a spur that raised the clear spirit of Alice.

On the third day from the Woeburn's rise, she sat in her garden-bower, absorbed in her favorite "Lady of the Lake." Her bower, though damp and mossy, and disheveled by the storms of autumn, was still a pleasant place to rest in, when the view was clear and bright. The fairest view, however, now, and the most attractive study, were not of flower, and tree, and landscape, but of face and figure—the face of Alice Lorraine, so gentle, pure, and rapt with poetic thought; and the perfect maiden form inspired by the roused nobility of the mind. The hair, in lines of flowing softness falling back, disclosed the clear tranquillity of forehead, in contrast with the quick tremor of lip and the warmth that tinted, now and then, the delicate moulding of bright young cheeks. And as the sweet face, more and more lighted up with sequent thought, and bowed with the flitting homage of a reader, genial tears for dead and buried love, and grief, and gallantry arose, and glistened in dark gray eyes, and hung like the gem that quivers in the lashes of the sun-dew.

"Plaize, Miss Halice, my leddy desireth to see you to wonst, if you plaize, miss."

Thus spake the practical, but in appearance most unpoetical, Trotman, glancing at Alice, and then at her book, with more curiosity than he durst convey. "Please to say that I will be with her as soon as I can finish some important work," she answered, speedily quenching Trotman's hope of finding out what she was reading, so as to melt the house-maids therewith at night. "Well, she always were a rum un," he muttered in his disappointment as he returned to his own little room, which he always called his "study;" "the captain will have to stand on his head to please her, or I'm mistaken. Why, a body scarce dare look at her. Sooner him than me, say I; although she is such a booty. But the old un will give her her change, I hope."

Meanwhile the young lady (unloved of Trotman, because she held fast by old Mr. Binns) put aside, with a sigh, both the poem and her own poetic dreamings, and proved that her temper, however strong, was sweet and large and well controlled, by bridling her now closed lips from any peevish exclamation. She waited a little time until the glow of her cheeks abated, and the sparkle of her eyes was tranquil, and then she put her pretty hat on (deep brown, trimmed with plumes of puce), and thinking no more of herself than that, set forth to encounter her grandmother.

By this time Alice Lorraine had grown, from a sensitive, spirited girl, into a sensitive, spirited woman. The things which she used to think and feel to be right, she was growing to know to be right; and the fleeting of doubt from her face was beginning to form the soft expression. That is to say—if it can be described, and happily it never can be—good-will, largeness of heart, rich mercy, sympathy, and quick tenderness combined with grace and refinement toward the perfection of womanly countenance.

So, whatever there was to be done, this Alice was always quite ready to do it. She had not those outlets for her active moods which young ladies have at the present day, who find or form an unknown quantity of most pressing duties. "Oh no, I have no time to marry any body," they exclaim in a breathless manner; "if I did, I must either neglect my district, or my natural history."

Poor Alice had neither district, duck-weed net, nor even microscope; and what was even worse, she had no holy priest to guide her thoughts, no texts to work in moss and sago, nor even any croquet. Whatever she did, she had to do without any rush of the feminine mind into masculine channels prepared for it, and even without any partnership of dear and good companions. So that the fight before her was to be fought out by herself alone.

This was the last quiet day of her life; the last day for thinking of little things; the last day of properly feeding her pets, her poultry, and tame hares and pigeons, self-important robins (perching upon their own impudence), and sweetly trustful turtle-doves, that have no dream of evil. She fed them all; and if it were not her last day of feeding them, it was the last time she could feed them happily, and without envying their minds.

This was that important work which she was bound to attend to before she could hurry to the side of her grandmother. That fine old lady always made a point of sending for Alice, whenever she knew her need—or rather, without knowing, needed the relief of a little explosion. Her dignity strictly barred this outlet toward those creatures of a lower creation who had the bliss of serving her. To all such people she was most forbearing, in a large and liberal style; because it must be so impossible for them at all to understand her. And for this courteous manner every woman in the place disliked her. The men, however, having slower perceptions, thought that her ladyship was quite right. They could make allowance for her—that they could; and after all, if you come to think of it, the "femmel" race was most aggravating. So they listened to what all the women had to tell; and without contradiction wisely let female opinion waste itself.

Lady Valeria Lorraine, though harassed and weakened by rheumatism and pain of the nerves (which she sternly attributed to the will of God and the weather), still sat as firmly erect as ever, and still exacted, by a glance alone, all those little attentions which she looked so worthy to receive. The farther she became removed from the rising generation the greater was the height of contempt from which she deigned to look down upon it. So that Alice used to say to her father sometimes, "I wonder whether I have any right to exist. Grandmamma seems to think it so impertinent of me." "One thing is certain," Sir Roland answered, with a quiet smile at his favorite; "and that is, that you can not exist without impertinence, my dear."

This fine old lady was dressed with her usual taste and elaboration; no clumsy chits would she have to help her during the three hours occupied by what she termed, not inaptly, her "devotions." She wore a maroon-colored velvet gown of the softest and richest fabric, trimmed, not too profusely, with exquisite point-lace; while her cap, of the same lace with dove-colored ribbon, at the same time set off and was surpassed by the beauty of her snow-white hair. Among many other small crotchets, she held that brilliants did not suit a very old lady; and she wore no jewels, except a hoop of magnificent pearls with a turquoise setting, to preserve her ancient wedding-ring. And now, as her grandchild entered quietly, she was a little displeased at delay, and feigned to hear no entrance.

"Here I am, grandmamma, if you please," said Alice, after three most graceful courtesies, which she was always commanded to make, and made with much private amusement; "will you please to look round, grandmamma, and tell me what you want of me?"

"I could scarcely have dreamed," answered Lady Valeria, slowly turning toward her grandchild, and smiling with superior dignity, "that any member of our family would use the very words of the clown in the ring. But, perhaps, as I always try to think, you are more to be pitied than condemned. Partly through your own fault, and partly through peculiar circumstances, you have lost those advantages which a young lady of our house is entitled to. You have never been at court; you have seen no society; you have never even been in London!"

"Alas! it is all too true, grandmamma. But how often have you told me that I never must hope, in this degenerate age, to find any good model to imitate! And you have always discouraged me, by presenting yourself as the only one for me to follow."

"You are quite right," said the ancient lady, failing to observe the turn of thought, as Alice was certain that she would do, else scarcely would she have ventured it; "but you do not make the most of even that advantage. You can read and write, perhaps better than you ought, or better than used to be thought at all needful; but you can not come into a room, or make a tolerable courtesy; and you spend all your time with dogs and poets and barrows of manure and little birds!"

"Now really, madam, you are too hard upon me. I may have had a barrow-load of poets; but more than a month ago, you gave orders that I was not to have one bit more of manure."

"Certainly I did, and high time it was. A young gentlewoman to dabble in worms, and stable-stuff, and filthiness! However, I did not send for you to speak about such little matters. What I have to say is for your own good; and I will trouble you not to be playing with your hands, but just to listen to me."

"I beg your pardon," said Alice, gently; "I did not know I was moving my hands. I will listen without doing that any more."

"Now, my dear child," began Lady Valeria, being softened by the dutiful manner and sweet submission of the girl, "whatever we do is for your own good. You are not yet old enough to judge what things may profit, and what may hurt you. Even I, who had been brought up in a wholly superior manner, could not at your age have thought of any thing. I was ready to be led by wiser people; although I had seen a good deal of the world. And you, who have seen nothing, must be only too glad to do the same. You know quite well, what has long been settled, between your dear father and myself, about what is to be done with you."

"To be done with me!" exclaimed poor Alice, despite her resolve to hold her tongue. "To be done with me! As if I were just a bundle of rags, to be got rid of!"

"Prouder and handsomer girls than you," answered Lady Valeria, quietly—for she loved to provoke her grandchild, partly because it was so hard to do—"have become bundles of rags by indulging just such a temper as yours is. You will now have the goodness to listen to me, without any vulgar excitement. Your marriage with Captain Chapman has for a very long time been agreed upon. It is high time now to appoint the day. Sir Remnant Chapman has done me the honor of a visit on that subject. He is certainly a man of the true old kind; though his birth is comparatively recent. I was pleased with him; and I have pledged myself to the marriage within three months from this day."

"It can not be! it shall not be! You may bury me, but not marry me. Who gave you the right to sell me? And who made me to be sold? You selfish, cold-hearted—no, I beg your pardon. I know not what I am saying."

"You may well fall away, child, and cower like that, when you have dared to use such dreadful words. No; you may come to yourself, as you please. I am not going to give you any volatile salts, or ring and make a scene of it. That is just what you would like; and to be petted afterward. I hope you have not hurt yourself so much as you have hurt me, perhaps, by your violent want of self-control. I am not an old woman—as you were going to call me—but an elderly lady. And I have lived indeed to be too old, when any one descended from me has so little good blood in her as to call her grandmother an old woman!"

"I am very, very sorry," said Alice, with catches of breath, as she spoke, and afraid to trust herself yet to rise from the chair, into which she had fallen; "I used no such words, that I can remember. But I spoke very rudely, I must confess. I scarcely know what I am to do when I hear such dreadful things, unless I bite my tongue off."

"I quite agree with you. And I believe it is the very best thing all young people can do. But I strive to make every allowance for you, because you have been so very badly brought up. Now come to this window, child, and look out. Tut, tut—tears indeed! What are young girls made of now? White sugar in a wet tea-cup. Now, if the result of your violence allows you to see any thing at all, perhaps you will tell me what that black line is among the rough ground at the bottom of the hill. To me it is perfectly clear, although I am such a very old woman."

"Why, of course, it is the Woeburn, madam. It has been there for three days."

"You know what it means; and you calmly tell me that!"

"I know that it means harm, of course. But I really could not help its coming. And it has not done any harm as yet."

"No, Alice, it waits its due time, of course. Three months is its time, I believe, for running before it destroys the family. Your marriage affords the only chance of retrieving the fortunes of this house, so as to defy disasters. Three months, therefore, is the longest time to which we can possibly defer it. How many times have we weakly allowed you to slip out of any certain day. But now we have settled that you must be Mrs. Chapman by the 15th of January at the latest."

"Oh, grandmamma, to think that I ever should live to be called Mrs. Chapman!"

"The name is a very good one, Alice, though it may not sound very romantic. But poor Sir Remnant, I fear, is unlikely to last for a great time longer. He seemed so bent, and his sight so bad, and requiring so much refreshment! And then, of course, you would be Lady Chapman, if you care about such trifles."

"It is a piteous prospect, madam. And I think Captain Chapman must be older than his father. You know the old picture, 'The Downhill of Life;' the excellent and affectionate couple descending so nicely hand in hand. Well, I should illustrate that at once. I should have to lead my—no, I won't call him husband—but my tottering partner down the hill, whenever we came to see you and papa. Oh, that would be so interesting!"

"You silly child, you might do much worse than that. Lady de Lampnor has promised most kindly to see to your outfit in London. But I can not talk of that at present. There, now you may go. I have told you all."

"Thank you, grandmamma. But, if you please, I have not told you all, nor half. It need not, however, take very long. It is just this. No power on earth shall ever compel me to marry Stephen Chapman; unless, indeed, it were so to happen—"

"You disobedient and defiant creature—unless what should happen?"

"Unless the existence, and even the honor, of the Lorraines required it. But of that I see no possibility at all. At present it seems to be nothing more than a small and ignominious scheme. More and more I despise and dislike that heroic officer. I will not be sacrificed for nothing; and I have not the smallest intention of being the purchase-money for old acres."

"After that, I shall leave you to your father," answered Lady Valeria, growing tired. "It may amuse you to talk so largely, and perhaps for the moment relieves you. But your small self-will and your childish fancies can not be always gratified. However, I will ask you one thing. If the honor, and even the life of Lorraine, can be shown to you to require it, will you sacrifice your noble self?"

"I will," answered Alice, with brave eyes flashing, and looking tall and noble. "If the honor of the Lorraines depend upon me, I will give myself and my life for it."

CHAPTER LVIII.

Hilary was so weak and weary, and so seriously ill, when at last he reached the rectory, that his uncle and aunt would not hear of his coming down stairs for a couple of days at least. They saw that his best chance of escaping some long and perhaps fatal malady was to be found in rest and quietude, nursing, and kindly feeding. And the worst of it was that, whatever they did, they could not bring him to feed a quarter so kindly as he ought to do. The rector said, "Confound the fellow!" And Mrs. Hales shook her head, and cried "Poor dear!" as dish after dish, and dainty little plate, came out of his room untasted.

And now, on the morning of that same day on which Alice thus had pledged herself (being the third from her brother's arrival, of which she was wholly ignorant), the rector of West Lorraine arose, and girded himself, and ate his breakfast with no small excitement. He had received a new clerical vestment of the loftiest symbolism, and he hoped to exhibit it at the head of a very long procession.

"About poor Hilary? What am I to do?" asked Mrs. Hales, coming into the lobby, to see her good husband array himself. "All sorts of things may happen while you are away."

"Now, Caroline, how can you ask such a question? Feed, feed, feed; that's the line of treatment. And above all things, lock up your medicine-chest. He wants no squills, or scammony, or even your patent electuary—of all things the most abominable; though I am most ungrateful to call it so, for I owe to it half my burial-fees. He wants no murderous doctor's stuff; he wants a good breakfast—that's what he wants."

"But, my dear, you forget," answered good Mrs. Hales, who kept a small wardrobe of bottles and pills, gallipots, powders, and little square scales; "you are quite overlooking the state of his tongue. He has not eaten the size of my little finger. Why? Why, because of the fur on his tongue!"

"Bless the boy's tongue, and yours too!" cried the rector. "I should not care twopence about his tongue, if he only used his teeth properly."

"Ah, Struan, Struan! those who have never known what ache or pain is can not hope to understand the system. I know exactly how to treat him—a course of gentle drastics first, and then three days of my electuary, and then cardamomum, exhibited with liquor potassa. Doctoring has always been in my dear mother's family; and when your time comes to be ill and weak, how often you will thank Providence!"

"I thank the Lord for all things," said the parson, who was often of a religious turn; "but I must be brought very low indeed ere I thank him for your electuary."

"Put on your new hunting-coat, my dear. There it hangs, and I know that you are dying to exhibit it. The vanity of men surpasses even the love of women. There, there! You never will learn how to put a coat on. Just come to the hall-chair for me to pull it up. You are so unreasonably tall, that you never can get your coat up at the neck. Now, will you have it done, or will you go as you are, and look a regular figure in the saddle? You call it a 'bottle-green!' I call it a green, without the bottle."

"Caroline, sometimes you are most provoking. It is not your nature; but you try to do it. The cloth is of quite an invisible green, as the man in London told me—manufactured on purpose for ecclesiastics; though hundreds of parsons, God knows, go after the hounds in the good old scarlet. If you say any more, I will order a scarlet, and keep West Grinstead in countenance. They always do it in the west of England. In invisible green I am a hypocrite."

"Now don't excite yourself, Struan, or you won't enjoy your opening day at all. And I am sure that the green is as bright as can be; and you look very well—very well, indeed. Though I don't quite see how you can button it. Perhaps it is meant for a button-hook, or a leather thong over your stomach, dear."

"It is meant to fit me, Mrs. Hales; and it fits me to a nicety. It could not fit better; and it will be too easy when we have had a few hard runs. Where are my daughters? They know a good fit; and they know how to put a thing on my shoulders. Carry, Madge, and Cecil, come to the rescue of your father. Your father is baited, worse than any badger. Come all of you; don't stop a minute, or get perverted by your mother. Now, in simple truth, what do you say to this, my dears? Each speak her own opinion."

"It suits you most beautifully, papa."

"Papa, I think that I never saw you look a quarter so well before."

"My dear father, if there are any ladies, mamma will have reason to be jealous. But I fear that I see the back-seam starting."

"You clever little Cecil, I am afraid that it is. I feel a relief in front—ahem!—I mean an uncomfortable looseness in the chest. I told the fellow forty-eight inches at least. He has scamped the cloth, the London rascal! However, we can spare it from round the waist, as soon as our poor Cobble can see to it. But for to-day—ah yes, well thought of! My darling, go and get some of your green purse-silk. You are so handy. You can herring-bone it, so as to last for the day at least. Your mother will show you how to do it. Madge, tell Bonny to run and tell Robert not to bring the mare yet for a quarter of an hour. Now, ladies, I am at your mercy."

"Now, papa dear," asked Cecil, as she stitched away at the seam of her father's burly back, "if poor Cousin Hilary should get up and want to go out, what are we to do?"

"How can you even put such a question? Even for our opening day, I would not dream of leaving the house, if I thought that you could be so stupid as to let that poor boy out. I would not have him seen in the parish, and I would not have his own people see him, even for the brush of the Fox-coombe fox, who is older than the hills, they say, and no hound dare go near him. One of you must be always handy; and if he gets restless, turn the key on him. Nothing can be simpler."

With his bottle-green coat, now warranted to last (unless he overbuttoned it), the rector kissed his dear wife and daughters; and then universal good wishes, applauses, and kissings of hand set him forth on his way, with a bright smile spread upon his healthy face.

"Now mind we are left in charge," said Madge. "You are his doctor, of course, mamma; but we are to be his constables. I hope to goodness that he will eat by-and-by. It makes me miserable to see him. And the trouble we have had to keep the servants from knowing who he is, mamma!"

"My dear, your father has ordered it so. For my part, I can not see why there should be so much mystery about it. But he always knows better than we do, of course."

"Surely, mamma," suggested Cecil, "it would be a dreadful shock to the family to receive poor Hilary in such a condition, just after the appearance of that horrid water. They would put the two things together, and believe it the beginning of great calamities."

"Now, my dear child," answered Mrs. Hales, who loved to speak a word in season, "let not us, who are Christians, hearken to such superstitious vanities. Trust in the Lord, and all will be well. He holdeth in the hollow of his hands the earth and all that therein is; yea, and the waters that be under the earth. Now run up and see whether your poor cousin has eaten that morsel of anchovy toast. And tell him that I am going to prepare his draught, but he must not take the pills until half-past eleven."

"Oh, mamma dear, you'll drive him out of the house. Poor fellow, how I do pity him!"

Now Hilary certainly deserved this pity—not for his bodily ailments only, and the cruel fate which had placed him at the mercy of the medicine-chest, but more especially for the low and feverish condition of his heart and mind. Brooding perpetually on his disgrace, and attributing to himself more blame than his folly and failure demanded, he lost the refreshment of dreamless sleep, which his jaded body called out for. No rest could he find in the comforting words of his uncle and aunt and cousins: he knew that they were meant for comfort, and such knowledge vexes, or at least it irritates a man until the broader time of life when things are taken as they are meant, and any good word is welcome.

He was not, however, so very far gone as to swallow his dear aunt's boluses. He allowed his pillow to take his pills; and his good-natured cousins let him swallow them, as much as a juggler swallows swords. "I can't take them while you are looking," he said; "when you come in again you will find them gone."

Now one of the girls—it was never known which, because all three denied it—stupidly let the sick cousin know that the master of the house was absent. Hilary paid no special heed at the moment when he heard it; but after a while he began to perceive (as behooved a blockaded soldier) that here was his chance for a sally. And he told them so, after his gravy-beef and a raw egg beaten up with sherry.

"How cunning you are now!" said Cecil, who liked and admired him very deeply. "But you are not quite equal, Master Captain, to female ingenuity. The Spanish ladies must have taught you that, if half that I hear is true of them. Now you need not look so wretched, because I know nothing about them. Only this I know, that out of this house you are not allowed to go, without—oh, what do you call it?—a pass, or a watch-word, or a countersign, or something or other from papa himself. So you may just as well lie down, or mamma will come up with a powder for you."

"The will of the Lord be done," said Hilary; "but, Cecil, you are getting very pretty, and you need not take away my breeches."

"I am sorry to do it, Cousin Hilary; but I know quite well what I am about. And none of your military ways of going on can mislead me as to your character. You want to be off. We are quite aware of it. You can scarcely put two feet to the ground."

"Oh dear, how many ought I to be able to put?"

"You know best—at least four, I should hope. But you are not equal to argument. And we are all particularly ordered to keep you from what is too much for you. Now I shall take away these things—whatever they are called, I have no idea; but I do what I am told to do. And after this you will take that glass of the red wine, declared to be wonderful; and then you will shut both your eyes, if you please, till my father comes home from his hunting."

The lively girl departed with a bow of light defiance, carrying away her father's small-clothes (which had been left for Hilary), and locking the door of his bedroom with a decisive turn of a heavy key. "Mother, you may go to sleep," she said, as she ran down into the drawing-room: "I defy him to go, if he were Jack Sheppard; he has got no breeches to go in."

"Cecil, you are almost too clever! How your father will laugh, to be sure!" And the excellent lady began her nap.

As the afternoon wore away Hilary grew more and more impatient of his long confinement. Not only that he pined for the open air—as, of course, he must do, after living so long with the free sky for his canopy—but also that he felt most miserable at being so near the old house on the hill, yet doubtful of his reception there. More than once he rang the bell; but the old nurse, who alone of the servants was allowed to enter, would do no more than scold or coax him, and quietly lock him in again. So at last he got out of bed and feebly made his way to the window, and thence beheld betwixt him and the grassy mounds of the church-yard that swift black stream which had so surprised him on the night of his arrival.

Since then he had persuaded himself, or allowed others to persuade him, that the water had been a vision only of his weak and excited brain. But now he saw it clearly, calmly, and in a very few moments knew what it was, and of what dark import.

"How can I have let them keep me here?" he exclaimed, with indignation. "My father and sister must believe me dead, while I play at this miserable hide-and-seek. Perhaps they will think that I had better have been dead; but, at any rate, they shall know the truth."

With these words he took up his sailor-clothes, which the vigilant Cecil had overlooked, and which had been left in his room for fear of setting the servants talking; and he dressed himself as well as he could, and tried to look clean and tidy. But do what he might he could only cut a poor and sorry figure; and looking in the glass, he was frightened at his wan and worn appearance. Then, knowing the habits of the house, and wishing to avoid excitement, he waited until the two elder daughters were gone down to the village for their gossip, and Cecil was seeing the potatoes dug, and Mrs. Hales sleeping over Fisher or Patrick, while the cook was just putting the dinner down; and then, without trying the door at all, he quietly descended from the window, with the help of a stack-pipe and a spurry pear-tree.

So feeble was he now that this slight exertion made him turn faint, and sick and giddy, and he was obliged to sit down and rest under a shrub, into which he had staggered. But after a while, he found himself getting a little better, and pulling up one of the dahlia-stakes, to help himself along with, he made his way to the gate; and there being cut off from the proper road, followed the leave of the land and the water along the valley upward.

Alice Lorraine had permitted herself not quite to lose her temper, but still to get a little worried by her grandmother's exhortations. Of all living beings, she felt herself to be one of the very most reasonable; and whenever she began to doubt it, she knew there was something wrong with her. Her favorite cure for this state of mind was a free and independent ride over the hills and far away. She hated to have a groom behind her, watching her, and perhaps criticising the movements of her figure. But as it was scarcely the proper thing for Miss Lorraine to be scouring the country, like a yeoman's daughter, she always had to start with a trusty groom; but she generally managed to get rid of him.

And now, having vainly coaxed her father to come for a breezy canter, Alice set forth about four o'clock for an hour of rapid air to clear, invigorate, and enliven her. Whatever she did, or failed of doing (when her grandmother was too much for her), she always looked graceful and bright and kind. But she never looked better than when she was sitting, beautifully straight, on her favorite mare, skimming the sward of the hills, or bowing her head in some tangled covert. This day she allowed the groom to chase her (like the black care that sits behind) until she had taken free burst of the hills, and longed to see things quietly. And then she sent him, in the kindest manner, to a very old woman at Lower Chancton, to ask whether she had been frightened; and when he had turned the corner of a difficult plantation Alice took her course for that which she had made up her mind to do.

According to the ancient stories, no fair-blooded creatures (such as man, or horse, cow, dog, or pigeon) would ever put lip to the accursed stream; whereas all foul things, polecats, foxes, fitches, badgers, ravens, and the like, were drawn by it, as by a loadstone, and made a feasting-place of it. So Alice resolved that her darling "Elfrida" should be compelled to pant with thirst, and then should have the fairest offer of the water of the Woeburn. And of this intent she was so full that she paid no heed to the "dressing-bell," clanging over the lonely hill, nor even to her pet mare's sense of dinner; but took a short cut of her own knowledge down a lonely bostall to the channel of new waters.

The stream had risen greatly ever since the day before yesterday, and now in full volume swept on grandly toward the river Adur. Any one who might chance to see it for the first time, and without any impression, or even idea concerning it, could scarcely fail to observe how it differed from ordinary waters. Not only through its pellucid blackness, and the swaying of long grass under it (whose every stalk, and sheath, and awn, and even empty glume, was clear, as they quivered, wavered, severed, and spread, or sheafed themselves together again, and hustled in their common immersion), not only in this, and the absence of any water-plants along its margin, was the stream peculiar, but also in its force and flow. It did not lip, or lap, or ripple, or gurgle, or wimple, or even murmur, as all well-meaning rivers do; but swept on in one even sweep, with a face as smooth as the best plate-glass, and the silent slide of night-fall.

Now the truth of the good old saying was made evident to Alice that one can take a horse to water, but a score can not make him drink unless he is so minded. It was not an easy thing to get Elfrida to go near the water. She started away with flashing eyes, pricked ears, and snorting nostrils; and nothing but her perfect faith in Alice would have made her come nigh. But as for drinking, or even wetting her nose in that black liquid — might the horse-fiend seize her if she dreamed of doing a thing so dark and unholy!

"You shall, you shall, you wicked little witch!" cried Alice, who was often obstinate. "I mean to drink it; and you shall drink it; and we won't have any superstition." She leaped off lightly, with her skirt tucked up, and taking the mare by the cheek-piece of the bridle, drew her forward. "Come along, come along, you shall drink. If you don't, I'll pour it up your nostrils, Frida; somehow or other, you shall swallow it. You know I won't have any nonsense, don't you?"

The beautiful filly, with great eyes partly defiant and partly suppliant, drew back her straight nose and blowing nostrils and the glistening curve of the foamy lip. Not even a hair of her muzzle should touch the face of the accursed water.

"Very well, then, you shall have it thus," cried Alice, with her curved palm brimming with the unpopular liquid; when suddenly a shadow fell on the shadowy brilliance before her—a shadow distinct from her own and Elfrida's, and cast farther into the wavering.

"Who are you?" cried Alice, turning sharply round; "and what business have you on my father's land?" She was in the greatest fright at the sudden appearance of a foreign sailor, and the place so lonely and beyond all help; but without thinking twice she put a brave face on her terror.

"Who am I?" said Hilary, trying to get up a sprightly laugh. "Well, I think you must have seen me once or twice in the course of your long life, Miss Lorraine."

"Oh, Hilary, Hilary, Hilary!"

She threw herself into his arms with a jump, relying upon his accustomed strength, and without any thought of the difference. He tottered backward, and must have fallen, but for the trunk of a pollard ash. And seeing how it was, she again cried out, "Oh, Hilary, Hilary, Hilary!"

"That is my name," he answered, after kissing her in a timid manner; "but not my nature; at the present moment I am not so very hilarious."

"Why, you are not fit to walk, or talk, or even to look like a hero. You are the bravest fellow that ever was born. Oh, how proud we are of you! My darling, what is the matter? Why, you look as if you did not know me! Help, help, help! He is going to die. Oh, for God's sake, help!"

Poor Hilary, after looking wildly around, and trying in vain to command his mouth, fell suddenly back, convulsed, distorted, writhing, foaming, and wallowing in the depths of epilepsy. Sky, hill, and tree swung to and fro across his strained and starting eyes, and then whirled round like a spinning-wheel, with radiating sparks and spots. Then all fell into abyss of darkness down a bottomless pit, into utter and awful loss of every thing.

The vigor of youth had fought against this robbery of humanity so long and hard that Alice, the only spectator of the conflict, began to recover from shriek and wailing by the time that her brother fell into the black insensibility. The ground sloped so that if she had not been there the unfortunate youth must have rolled into the Woeburn, and so ended. But being a prompt and active girl, she had saved him from this, at any rate. She had had the wit also to save his tongue by slipping a glove between his teeth; which scarcely a girl in a hundred who saw such a thing for the first time would have done. And now, though her face was bathed in tears, and her hands almost as tremulous as if themselves convulsed, she filled her low-crowned riding-hat with water from the river, and sprinkled his forehead gently, and released his neck from cumbrance. And then she gazed into his thin, pale features, and listened for the beating of his heart.

This was so low that she could not hear or even feel it anywhere. "Oh, how can I get him home?" she cried. "Oh, my only brother, my only brother!" In fright and misery she leaped upon a crest of chalk, to seek around for any one to help her; and suddenly she espied her groom against the sky-line a long way off, galloping up the ridge from Chancton. In hope that one of the many echoes of the cliffs might aid her, she shrieked with all her power, and tore a white kerchief from under her riding-habit, and put it on her whip and waved it. And presently she had the joy of seeing the horse's head turned toward her. The rider had not caught her voice, but had descried some white thing fluttering between him and the sombre stripe which he was watching earnestly.

This groom was a strong and hearty man, and the father of seven children. He made the best of the case, and ventured to comfort his young mistress. And then he laid Hilary upon Elfrida, the docile and soft-stepper; and making him fast with his own bridle, and other quick contrivances, he tethered his own horse to a tree, and leading the mare, set off with Alice, walking carefully, and supporting the head of her senseless brother. So came this hero, after all his exploits, back to the home of his fathers.

CHAPTER LIX.

"WHAT can I do? Oh, how can I escape?" cried Alice to herself one morning, toward the end of the dreary November; "one month out of three is gone already, and the chain of my misery tightens round me. No, don't come near me, any of you birds; you will have to do without me soon; and you had better begin to practice. Ah me! you can make your own nests, and choose your mates; how I envy you! Well, then, if you must be fed, you must. Why should I be so selfish?" With tears in her eyes, she went to her bower and got her little basket of moss, well known to every cock-robin and thrush and blackbird dwelling on the premises. At the bottom were stored, in happy ignorance of the fate before them, all the delicacies of the season—the food of woodland song, the stimulants of aërial melody. Here were wood-lice, beetles, earwigs, caterpillars, slugs, and nymphs, well-girt brandlings, and the offspring of the tightly buckled wasp, together with the luscious mealworm, and the peculiarly delicious grub of the cock-chafer—all as fresh as a West-end salmon, and savoring sweetly of moss and milk—no wonder the beaks of the birds began to water at the mere sight of that basket.

"You have had enough now for to-day," said Alice; "it is useless to put all your heads on one side, and pretend that you are just beginning. I know all your tricks quite well by this time. No, not even you, you Methusalem of a Bob, can have any more—or at least, not much."

For this robin (her old pet of all, and through whose powers of interpretation the rest had become so intimate) made a point of perching upon her collar and nibbling at her ear whenever he felt himself neglected. "There is no friend like an old friend," was his motto; and his poll was gray and his beak quite blunted with the cares of age, and his large black eyes were fading. "Methusalem, come and help yourself," said Alice, relenting, softly; "you will not have the chance much longer."

Now as soon as the birds, with a chirp and a jerk, and one or two futile hops, had realized the stern fact that there was no more for them, and then had made off to their divers business (but all with an eye to come back again), Alice, with a smiling sigh—if there can be such a mixture—left her pets, and set off alone to have a good walk and talk and think. The birds, being guilty of "cupboard love," were content to remain in their trees and digest; and as many of them as were in voice expressed their gratitude brilliantly. But out of the cover they would not budge; they hated to be ruffled up under their tails: and they knew what the wind on the Downs was.

"I shall march off straight for Chancton Ring," said Alice Lorraine, most resolutely. "How thankful I am to be able to walk! and poor Hilary—ah, how selfish of me to contrast my state with his!"

Briskly she mounted the crest of the coombe, and passed to the open upland, the long chine of hill which trends to its highest prominence at Chancton Ring—a landmark for many a league around. Crossing the trench of the Celtic camp—a very small obstruction now—which loosely girds the ancient trees, Alice entered the venerable throng of weather-beaten and fantastic trunks. These are of no great size, and shed no impress of hushed awe, as do the mossy ramparts and columnar majesty of New Forest beech-trees. Yet, from their countless and furious struggles with the winds in their might in the wild midnight, and from their contempt of aid or pity in their bitter loneliness, they enforce the respect and the interest of any who sit beneath them.

At the foot of one of the largest trees, the perplexed and disconsolate Alice rested on a lowly mound, which held (if faith was in tradition) the bones of her famous ancestor, the astrologer Agasicles. The tree which overhung his grave, perhaps as a sapling had served to rest without obstructing his telescope; and the boughs, whose murmurings soothed his sleep, had been little twigs too limp for him to hang his Samian cloak on. Now his descendant in the ninth or tenth generation—whichever it was—had always been endowed with due (but mainly rare) respect for those who must have gone before her. She could not perceive that they must have been fools, because many things had happened since they died; and she was not even aware that they must have been rogues to beget such a set of rogues.

Therefore she had veneration for the remains that lay beneath her (mouldering in no ugly coffin, but in swaddling-clothes committed like an infant into the mother's bosom), and the young woman dwelt, as all mortals must, on death, when duly put to them. The everlasting sorrow of the moving winds was in the trees, and the rustling of the sad, sear leaf, and creaking of the lichened bough. And above their little bustle and small fuss about themselves, the large, sonorous stir was heard of Weymouth pines and Scottish firs swaying in the distance slowly, like the murmur of the sea. Even the waving of yellow grass-blades (where the trees allowed them), and the ruffling of tufted briers, and of thorny thickets, shone and sounded melancholy with a farewell voice and gaze.

In the midst of all this autumn Alice felt her spirits fall. She knew that they were low before, and she was here to enlarge and lift them, with the breadth of boundless prospect and the height of the breezy hill. But fog and cloud came down the weald, and gray encroachment creeping, and on the hill-tops lay heavy sense of desolation. And Alice being at heart in union with the things around her (although she tried to be so brave), began to be weighed down, and lonesome, sad, and wondering, and afeard. From time to time she glanced between the uncouth pillars of the trees, to try to be sure of no man being in among them hiding. And every time when she saw no one, she was so glad that she need not look again—and then she looked again.

"It is quite early," she said to herself; "nothing—not even three o'clock. I get into the stupidest, fearfullest ways from such continual nursing. How I wish poor Hilary was here! One hour of this fine breeze and cheerful scene— My goodness, what was that!"

The cracking of a twig, without any sign of what had cracked it, the rustle of trodden leaves; but no one, in and out the graves of leafage, visible to trample them. And then the sound of something waving, and a sharp snap as of metal, and a shout into the distant valley.

"It is the astrologer," thought Alice. "Oh, why did I laugh at him? He has felt me sitting upon his skull. He is waving his cloak, and snapping his casket. He has had me in view for his victim always, and now he is shouting for me."

In confirmation of this opinion, a tall gray form, with one arm thrown up, and a long cloak hanging gracefully, came suddenly gliding between the trees. The maiden, whose brain had been overwrought, tried to spring up with her usual vigor; but the power failed her. She fell back against the sepulchral trunk and did not faint, but seemed for the moment very much disposed thereto.

When she was perfectly sure of herself, and rid of all presence of spectres, she found a strong arm behind her head, and somebody leaning over her. And she laid both hands before her face, without meaning any rudeness, having never been used to be handled at all, except by her brother or father.

"I beg your pardon most humbly, madam. But I was afraid of your knocking yourself."

"Sir, I thank you. I was very foolish. But now I am quite well again."

"Will you take my hand to get up? I am sure I was scared as much as you were."

"Now, if I could only believe that," said Alice, "my self-respect would soon return; for you do not seem likely to be frightened very easily."

She was blushing already, and now her confusion deepened, with the consciousness that the stranger might suppose her to be admiring his manly figure; of which, of course, she had not been thinking, even for one moment.

"I ought not to be so," he answered, in the simplest manner possible; "but I had a sun-stroke in America, fifteen months ago or so; and since that I have been good for nothing. May I tell you who I am?"

"Oh yes, I should like so much to know." Alice was surprised at herself as she spoke; but the stranger's unusually simple yet most courteous manner led her on.

"I am one Joyce Aylmer, not very well known; though at one time I hoped to become so. A major in his Majesty's service"—here he lifted his hat and bowed—"but on the sick-list ever since we fought the Americans at Fort Detroit."

"Oh, Major Aylmer, I have often heard of you, and how you fell into a sad brain-fever, through saving the life of a poor little child. My uncle, Mr. Hales, knows you, I believe, and has known your father for many years."

"That is so. And I am almost sure that I must be talking to Miss Lorraine, the daughter of Sir Roland Lorraine, whom my father has often wished to know."

"Yes. And perhaps you know my brother, who has served in the Peninsula, and is now lying very ill at home."

"I am sorry indeed to hear that of him. I know him, of course, by reputation, as the hero of Badajos; but I think I was ordered across the Atlantic before he joined; or, at any rate, I never met him that I know of—though I shall hope to do so soon. May I see you across this lonely hill? Having frightened you so, I may claim the right to prevent any others from doing it."

Alice would have declined the escort of any other stranger; but she had heard such noble stories of this Major Aylmer, and felt such pity for a brave career baffled by its own bravery (which in some degree resembled her poor brother's fortunes), that she gave him one of her soft bright smiles, such a smile as he never had received before. Therefore he set down his broad sketch-book, and the case of pencils, and went to the rim of the Ring that looks toward the vale of Sussex; and there he shouted, to countermand the groom, who had been waiting for him at the farm-house far below.

"I am ordered to ride about," he said, as he returned to Alice, "and to be out-of-doors all day — a very pleasant medicine. And so, for something to do, I have taken up my old trick of drawing; because I must not follow hounds. I would not talk so about myself, except to show you how it was that you did not hear me moving."

"How soon it gets dark on the top of these hills!" cried Alice, most unscientifically. "I always believe that they feel it sooner because they see the sun go down."

"That seems to me to be a fine idea," Joyce Aylmer answered, faithfully. And his mind was in a loose condition of reason all the way to Coombe Lorraine.

CHAPTER LX.

Sir Remnant Chapman, in his dry old fashion, was a strongly determined man. He knew the bitter strait of Coombe Lorraine for ready money; and from his father, Sir Barker Chapman (a notorious usurer), he had inherited the gift of spinning a disk into a globe. But, like most of the men who labor thus to turn their guineas, he could be very liberal with them for the advancement of his family; and though the Chapmans had gradually acquired such a length of rent-roll, their pedigree was comparatively short among their Norman neighbors. Nothing would cure that local defect more speedily and permanently than a wedlock with Lorraine; and father and son were now eager tenfold by reason of Hilary's illness. They had made up their minds that he must die within a few months; and then Alice, of course, would be the heiress of Coombe Lorraine. But the marriage must be accomplished first, before the mourning stopped it. Then Hilary would drop off out of the way; and after Sir Roland's time was passed, and the properties had been united, there ought not to be any very great trouble, with plenty of money to back the claim, in awakening the dormant earldom of Lorraine, and enhancing its glory with a Chapman.

To secure all this success at once they set forth in their yellow coach one fine November morning. They knew that Sir Roland was fretting and pining (although too proud to speak of it) at his son's disgrace, and the crippled and fettered fortunes of the family. Even apart from poor Hilary's illness, and perhaps fatal despondency, the head of the house of Lorraine would have felt (with his ancient pride and chivalry) that a stain must lie on his name until the money was made good again. And now the last who could prolong male heritage unbroken—of which the Lorraines were especially proud—was likely to go to a world that does not heed direct succession — except from the sinful Adam—for the want of fifty thousand pounds.

Cut and clipped and cleft with fissures of adjacent owners, the once broad lands of Lorraine were now reduced, for the good of the neighbors. But even in those evil days, when long war had lowered every thing, the residue of the estates would have been for that sum good security, being worth about twice the money. This, however, was of no avail; because, by the deed of settlement (made in the time of the late Sir Roger, under the Lady Valeria), nothing could be bound beyond life interest while Alice was living, and under age. This point had been settled hopelessly by reference to the highest and deepest legal authority of the age, Sir Glanvil Malahide, K.C. Sir Glanvil was not at all the man to stultify his own doings. He had been instructed to tie tight; and he was pleased to show now how tight he had tied, after his own remonstrance. "I am of opinion," wrote this great lawyer (after drawing his pen through the indorsement of a fifty-guinea fee on the case), "that under the indentures Lease and Release, dated August 5th and 6th, 1799, the estates comprised therein are assured to uses precluding any possibility of valid title being made until Alice Lorraine is of age or deceased." There was a good deal more, of course; but that was the gist of the matter.

Having learned from the rector how these things stood, the captain devised a clever stroke, by which he could render the escape of Alice almost an impossibility. For by this contrivance he could make Sir Roland most desirous of the match, who up to the present, though well aware of the many substantial advantages offered, had always listened to his daughter's pleading, and promised not to hurry her. The captain's plan was very simple, as all great ideas are; the honor of the family was to be redeemed by the sacrifice of Alice. For, among other points, it had been arranged, upon the treaty of marriage, that fifty thousand pounds should be settled on Alice, for her separate use, with the usual powers of appointment.

Now the captain's excellent idea was that on his wedding-day this sum should be paid in hard cash to Sir Roland and Hilary, as trustees for Alice; and they, by deed of even date, should charge that sum on the Lorraine estate—"*valeat quantum*," as the lawyers say; for they could only bind their own interests. The solicitors would be directed to waive the obvious objections, which might lead to mischief, or might not, according to circumstances. Thus the flaw of title, which would be fatal to any cold-blooded mortgage, might well be turned to good use, when stopped by a snug little family arrangement.

Sir Remnant, with inherited instinct, saw the blot of this conception. "It comes to this," he said, as soon as ever he was told of it, "that you get the Lorraine property saddled with a loss of fifty thousand pounds, which has gone to the scoundrelly Government! The Government rob us all they can. In a sensible point of view, young Lorraine is the first sensible man of his family. He has stolen fifty thousand pounds, which the Government stole from us tax-payers. As for paying it back again—an idiot might think of it! It makes me kick; and that always hurts me."

Nevertheless, he was brought round (when he had kicked his passion out), as most of the obstinate old men are, to the plans and aims of the younger ones. Steenie was a fool—they all were fools—there was scarcely any sense left in any body but himself, and the boy who stole all that money, and was dying for fear of being prosecuted. Sir Remnant could not bring himself to believe a word of the story, except as himself had shaped it. Thus he worked himself up, with his want of faith, to believe that poor Hilary had got the money buried somewhere on the Downs, and would dig it up like a mole, as soon as the stir of the moment was over. If so, there could be no loss after all; only it would have been very much better to make no fuss about the money stolen.

Revolving these things in his mind, and regretting the good old times when any one (if at all in a good position) might have stolen fifty thousand pounds without any trumpery scandal, this baronet of the fine old school prepared to listen, in a quiet way, to any plans that would come home again. And he thought that this plan of his son would do so, either in money or in kind. Yet having formed some misty sketch of the character of Sir Roland, each of these Chapmans wished the other to begin the overture.

It would have been pleasant for any body, quite outside of danger, to watch the great yellow coach of the captain, laboring up the chalky road, the best approach to Coombe Lorraine, now that the Steyning road was stopped for all who could not walk a tree by the outburst of the water. All the roads were drenched just now; and wet chalk is a most slippery thing, especially when it has taken blue stripes from the rubbing of soft iron, the "drag" of some heavy wagon sliding down the steep with a clank and jerk. Sir Remnant had very little faith in his son's most expensive gift of driving; and he jerked out his bad head at every corner in anxiety for his good body and soul. The wicked, however, are protected always; and thus this venturesome baronet was fetched out of his coach, with much applause and a little touch of gout about him such as he would not stop to groan at.

Sir Roland Lorraine was not glad to see them, and did not feign to be so. He wanted to be left alone just now, with such a number of things to think of. He perceived that they were come to hurry him about a thing he was not ripe with. Knowing his daughter's steadfast nature, and his mother's stubborn stuff, in the calm of his heart he had hoped good things. To balance one against the other in psychological counterpoise—as all good English writers of the present day express it—or, as our rude granddads said, "to let them fight it out between them."

"Over your books again, Lorraine! Well, well, I can understand all that. I was pretty nigh taking to such things myself, after I put my knee-cap out. Steenie is a wonderful scholar now. I believe a' can construe Homer!"

"That depends on the mood I am in," said the captain, modestly; "sometimes I can make out a very nice piece."

"Well, that is more than any man can say in the county that I know of, except, of course, one or two new parsons, and Sir Roland here, and some ragamuffins that come about teaching their stuff in lodgings. Lorraine, now, after all, how are you? How do you get through these bad times?"

Sir Roland Lorraine, for the third time now, shook hands with Sir Remnant Chapman. Not from any outburst of hospitality on his part, but because the other would have it so. A strong opinion had newly set in that all good Britons were bound to shake hands; that dirty and cold-blooded Frenchmen bowed at a distance homicidally; and therefore that wholesome Englishmen must squeeze one another's knuckles to the utmost; and that idea is not yet extinct.

"And how is her ladyship?" asked Sir Remnant, striking his gold-headed stick on the floor very firmly at the mere thought of her. "Do you think she will see her most humble servant? Gadzooks, sir, she is of the true old sort."

"I was amazed the last time you were here," Sir Roland answered, smiling, "to find how thoroughly you and my mother seemed to understand each other. I am sure that if she is well enough to see any body she will see you. Meanwhile, will you take something?"

"Now that is not the way to put it. Of course I will take something. I like to see the glasses all brought in, and then the cupboards opened, and then the young women all going about, with hot and cold water, and sugar-tongs."

"We will try to do those little things aright," the host answered very quietly, "by the time of your re-appearance. Trotman is come to say that my mother will do herself the honor of receiving you."

"Steenie, you stop here," shouted Sir Remnant, getting up briskly, and setting his eyebrows, eyes, and knees for business. "Steenie, you are a boy as yet, and court ladies prefer the society of men. No, no; I can pick up my cane myself. Just you sit down quietly, Steenie, and entertain Sir Roland till I come back."

Sir Remnant, though somewhat of a bear by nature, prided himself on his courtly manners, when occasion called for them. "Gadzooks, sir," he used to say, "nurse my vittels, if I can't make a leg with the very best of them!" And he carried his stick in a manner to prove that he must have kissed hands, or toes, or something.

Entering Lady Valeria's drawing-room in his daintiest manner, the old reprobate (as he called himself, sometimes with pride, and sometimes with terror, according as his spirits were up or down) made a slow and deep obeisance, then kissed the tips of his fingers, and waved them, and, seeing a smile on the lady's face, ventured to lay his poor hand on his heart.

"Oh, Sir Remnant, you are too gallant!" said the lady, who in good truth despised him, and hated him also as the owner of great broad stripes of the land of Lorraine. "We never get such manners now—never since the court was broken up; and things that it would not become me at all to hint at are encouraged."

"You are right, my lady; you are right all over. Gadzooks—ahem, I beg your ladyship's pardon."

"By no means, Sir Remnant. The gentlemen always, in the best society, were allowed to say those little things. And I missed them sadly when I came down here."

"Madam, my admiration of you increases with every word you speak. From what I hear of the mock court now (as you and I might call it), and my son has been hand-in-glove for years with the P. R., indeed the whole number of their royal highnesses—in short, I can not tell your ladyship. Things are very bad, very bad indeed." And Sir Remnant made a grimace, as if his own whole life had been purity.

"I fear that it is too true," the lady answered, looking straight at him. "We find things always growing worse, as we ourselves grow wiser. But come now, and sit in this chair, and tell me, if you please, Sir Remnant, how the poor things are getting on—your captain and my poor grandchild."

"Well, madam, I need not tell a lady of your high breeding and experience the maids of the present day are not at all the same thing as they used to be. But, thank the Lord, they get on, on the whole, as well as can be expected. But Sir Roland will not help us; and the young maid flies and flickers, and don't seem to come to know her own mind. You know, my lady, the Lord in heaven scarce knows what to make of them. They will have this, and they won't have that; and they hates to look at any thing but their swinging-glasses."

"Oh, sir, you have not been at court for nothing. You have come to a very sad view of the ladies. But they deserve a great deal more than that. If you were to hear what even I, at this great distance, know of them—but I will say no more; it is always best, and charitable, not to speak of them. So let us go back, if you please, Sir Remnant; I have my own ways of considering things. Indeed, I am obliged to have them, in a manner now scarcely understood. But I hear a noise—is it a mouse, or a rat, do you think?"

It was neither mouse nor rat; as Lady Valeria knew quite well. It was simply poor Sir Remnant tapping on the floor with his walking-stick; which of course he had no right to do, while the lady was addressing him.

"It sounds like a very little mouse," he said; "or perhaps it was the death-tick. It often comes in these old rooms, when any of the people are going to die."

The old gentleman had not been at court for nothing (as the old lady had told him); he knew how timid and superstitious were the brave women of the fine old time.

"Now, sir, are you sure that you never made a tap?" asked Lady Valeria, anxiously.

"Not a quarter of a tap, as I hope to be saved," the old reprobate answered, below his breath. "I pay no heed to nonsense; but a thing of this sort must mean something."

"There have been a great many signs of late," said the old lady, after listening, with her keener ear brought round, and the misty lace of her beautiful cap quivering like a spider's web; "there seem to have been a great many signs of bad things coming, in their proper time."

"They will come before we are ready, madam; old Scratch waits for no invitation. But they say that the death-tick runs before him, and keeps time with his cloven heel."

"Oh Lord, Sir Remnant, how dreadfully you talk! I beg you to spare me; I have had no sleep since I was told of that horrible water, and of my poor grandson. Poor Hilary! He has done great things, and spent no money of his own; and indeed he had none of his own to spend; and having denied himself so, is it right that he should be disgraced, and break his heart because he could not help losing a little money that was not at all his own? And he had taken a town worth ten times as much. Now, truly speaking, is it fair of them?"

"Certainly not, madam; pox upon them! It is the scurviest thing ever heard of."

"And you must remember, sir, if you please, that from his childhood upward, indeed ever since he could move on two legs, he always lost every sixpence put by kind people into his pockets. I gave him a guinea on his very fifth birthday, and in the afternoon what do you think he showed me? A filthy old tobacco-pipe, and nothing else—no change whatever. And his pride was more than he could set forth; though he always was a chatterer. Now, if such a thing as that could only be properly put at the Horse Guards by some one of good position, surely, Sir Remnant, they would make allowance; they would see that it was his nature; at least they would have done so in my time."

"Of course they would, of course, my lady. But things have been growing, from year to year, to such a pitch of"—here Sir Remnant took advantage of the lady's courtly indulgence toward bad language—"that—that—they seem to want almost, gadzooks, they want to treat men almost all alike!"

"They never can do that, good sir. They never could be such fools as to try it. And bad as they may be, they must be aware that my grandson has done no harm to them. Why, the money he lost was not theirs at all; it was all for the pay of the common soldiers. It comes out of every body's pocket, and it goes into nobody's. And to my mind it serves them all perfectly right. Who is that general—I forget his name, an Irishman, if I remember aright—who is he, or of what family, that he should put a Lorraine to look after dirty money? The heir of all the Lorraines to be put to do a cashier's business!"

"Heaven save me from such a proud woman as this!" thought poor Sir Remnant Chapman; "if Alice is like her, the Lord have pity on our unlucky Steenie! He won't dare have his nip of brandy, even in a corner!"

"And now, poor dear, he is very ill indeed," continued the ancient lady, recovering from the indignation which had even wrinkled her firm and smooth forehead; "he has pledged his honor to make good the money; and my son also thinks that the dignity of our family demands it, though to me it seems quite a ridiculous thing; and you of course will agree with me. And the doctors say that he has something on his mind; and if he can not be relieved of it he must die, poor boy. And then what becomes of the name of Lorraine, that has been here for nearly eight hundred years?"

"It becomes extinct, of course, my lady," answered Sir Remnant, as calmly as if the revolution of the earth need not be stopped; "but it might be revived in the female line, by royal license, hereafter."

"That would be of very little use. Why, even your grandson might be a Lorraine! Is that what you were thinking of?"

"No, no, no! Of course not, my lady. Nothing could be farther from my thoughts." The old baronet vainly endeavored, as he spoke, to meet the suspicious gaze of the lady's still penetrating and bright eyes.

"We are not so particular about the spindle," she resumed, with some condescension; "but in the sword-line we must be represented duly; and we never could be supplanted by a Chapman."

"Gadzooks, madam, are the Chapmans dirt? But in order to show how you wrong us, my lady, I will tell you what I am come to propose."

Herewith he looked very impressive, and leaned both hands on his stick, as if inditing of an excellent matter. And thus he set forth his scheme, which bore at first sight a fair and magnanimous face; as if all that large sum of money were given, or without security trusted, for no other purpose, except to save a life precious to both families. The old lady listened with prudent reserve, yet an inward sense of relief, and even a faint, suspicious gratitude. She was too old now to digest very freely any generous sentiment. Blessed are they who, crossing the limit of human years, can carry with them faith in worn humanity.

CHAPTER LXI.

Of all trite proverbs no truer there is in the affairs of men (perhaps because in the kingdom of the clouds so untrue) than this venerable saying, "it never rains, but what it pours." The Chapmans had come with a storm of cash to wash away Hilary's obstructions; and now on that very same day there appeared a smaller, but more kindly cloud, to drop its little fatness.

Just when Sir Roland had managed to get rid (at the expense of poor Alice, perhaps) of that tedious half-born Stephen Chapman, the indefatigable Trotman came, with his volatile particles uppermost. "If you please, sir," he said, "I can't stop un at all. He saith as he will see you."

"Well, if he will, he must, of course. But who is this man of such resolute mind?"

"If you please, sir, I never have seed un from Adam. And I showed un the wrong way, to get a little time."

"Then go now and show him the right way, John. I am always ready to see any one."

Sir Roland knew well that this was not true. He had said it without thinking; and with his pure love of truth he began to condemn himself for saying it. He knew that he liked no strangers now, nor even any ordinary friends; and he was always sorry to hear that any one made demand to see him. Before he could repent of his repentance the door was opened, and in walked a man of moderate stature, sturdy frame, and honest, ruddy, and determined face, well shaven betwixt gray whiskers. Sir Roland had never been wont to take much heed of the human countenance; therefore he was surprised to find himself rushing to a rash conclusion: "An honest man, if ever there was one; also a very kind one."

The grower came forward, without any sign of humility, awkwardness, sense of difference, or that which is lowest of all—intense and shallow self-assertion. He knew that he was not of Sir Roland's rank, and he had no idea of defying it; he was simply a man, come to speak to a man, for the love of those dependent on him, in the largeness of humanity. At the same time, he was a little afraid of going too far with any thing. He made a bow (by no means graceful, but of a tidy English sort, when the back always wants to go back again), and then, as true Englishmen generally do, he waited to be spoken to.

"I am very sorry," Sir Roland said, "that you have had trouble in finding me. We generally manage to get on well; but sometimes things go crooked. Will you come and sit down here, and tell me why you are come to see me?"

Martin Lovejoy made another bow, of pattern less like a tenter-hook. He had come with a will to be roughly received; and lo, there was nothing but smoothness. Full as he was of his errand, and the largest views of every thing, he had made up his mind to say something fierce; and here was no opportunity. For he took it for granted in his simple way, that Sir Roland knew thoroughly well who he was.

"I am come to see you, Sir Roland Lorraine," he began, with a slightly quivering voice, after declining the offered chair; "not to press myself upon you, but only for the sake of my daughter."

"Indeed!" the other answered, beginning to suspect; "are you, then, the father of that young lady—"

"I am the father of Mabel Lovejoy. And sorry I should be to be her father, if—if—I mean, sir, if she was any body else's daughter. But being as it is, she is my own dear child; and no man has a better one. And if any one says that she threw herself at the feet of your son for the sake of his name, Sir Roland, that man is a liar."

"My good sir, I know it. I never supposed that your daughter did any thing of the kind. I have heard that the fault was my son's altogether."

"Then why have you never said a word to say so? Why did you leave us, like so many dogs, to come when you might whistle? Because we are beneath you in the world, is your son to do a great wrong to my daughter, while you sit up here on the top of your hill as if you had never heard of us? Is this all the honor that comes of high birth? Then I thank the Almighty that we are not high-born."

The grower struck his ash-stick with disdain upon the rich Turkey-carpet, and turned his broad back on Sir Roland Lorraine; not out of rudeness (as the latter thought), but to hide the tears that came and spoiled the righteous sparkle of his eyes. The baronet perhaps had never felt so small and self-condemned before. He had not been so blind and narrow-minded as to forget through the past two years that every question has two sides. He had often felt that the Kentish homestead had a grievance against the South Down castle; but with his contemplative ease, and hatred of any disturbance, he had left the case mainly to right itself; persuading himself at last that he must have done all that could be expected in making that promise to Struan Hales. But now all the fallacy of such ideas was scattered by a father's honest wrath. And he was not a man who would argue down the rights of another, when he saw them.

"You are right, Mr. Lovejoy," he said at last; "I have not behaved at all well to you. I will make no excuses, but tell you fairly that I am sorry for my conduct, now that you put it so plainly. And whatever I can do shall be done to make amends to your daughter."

"Amends means money, from one rank to another. Would you dare to offer me money, sir?"

"Certainly not; it is the very last thing I ever should dream of doing. Not to mention the scarcity of cash—just now, in such a case money is an insult."

"I should think so—I should think so. What money would ever pay for our Mabel? If you had only seen her once, you could never have been angry with your son. Although I was; although I was—until I heard how ill he is. But bless you, sir, they will do these things—and there is no stopping them. It puts one into a passion with them, until one begins to remember. But now, sir, I have heard all sorts of things. Is it true that Master Hilary lies very ill abed, for want of money?"

"You put it very shortly; but it comes to that. He has lost a large sum of the public money, and we can not very well replace it."

"Then you should a' come to me. I'll cure all that trouble in a jiffy," said the grower, tugging heavily at something well inside his waistcoat; "there, that's a very tidy lump of money, and no call to be ashamed of it, in the way you high folk look at things—because us never made it. Not a farden of it ever saw Covent Garden; all come straight without any trade whatever! He can't a' lost all that, anyhow."

Martin Lovejoy, with broad-tipped fingers, and nails not altogether exempt from chewing, was working away as he spoke at a bag such as wheat is sampled in, and tied with whip-cord round the neck. Sir Roland Lorraine, without saying a word, looked on, and smiled softly with quiet surprise.

"No patience—I haven't no patience with counting, since I broke my finger, sir—seventeen, eighteen, nineteen, no—well it must be right, and I've reckoned amiss; our Mab reckoned every penny—no longer than yesterday morning—twenty thousand pounds it must be, according to the ticket. There is one lot a-missing; oh, here it is, in among my fingers, I do believe! What slippery rubbish these bank-notes be! Will you please now to score them all up, Sir Roland?"

"Mr. Lovejoy, why should I do that? It can not matter what the quantity is. The meaning is what I am thinking of."

"Well, sir, and the meaning is just this: My daughter Mabel hath had a fortune left her by her godfather, the famous banker Lightgold, over to the town of Tonbridge. No doubt you have heard of him, Sir Roland, and of his death six months agone. Well, no, I forget; it is so far away. I be so used to home that I always speak as if I was at home. And they made me trustee for her—that they did; showing confidence in my nature almost on the part of the laiyers, sir, do you think? At least I took it in that way."

"It was kind of you so to take it. They have no confidence in any body's nature, whenever they can help it."

"So I have heard, sir. I have heard that same, and in my small way proved it. But will you be pleased just to count the money?"

"I must be worse than the lawyers if I did. Your daughter Mabel must be the best, and kindest-hearted, and most loving—"

"Of course, of course," cried the grower, as if that point wanted no establishing; "but business is business, Sir Roland Lorraine. I am my daughter's trustee, do you see, and bound to be sure that her money goes right. And it is a good bit of money, mind you; more than I could earn in all my life."

"Will you tell me exactly what she said? I should like to hear her very words. I beg you to sit down. Are you afraid that I shall run off with the trust-funds?"

"You are like your son—I'll be dashed if you aren't. Excuse me, Sir Roland, for making so free—but that was just his way of turning things; a sort of a something in a funny manner that won the heart of my poor maid. None of our people know how to do it, except of course our Mabel. Mabel can do it, answer for answer, with any that come provoking her. But she hathn't shown the spirit for it now ever since—the Lord knows what was the name of the town Master Hilary took. That signifies nothing, neither here nor there; only it showeth how they do take on."

"Yes, Mr. Lovejoy, I see all that. But what was it your good daughter said?"

"She is always saying something, sir—something or other; except now and then, when her mind perhaps is too much for it. But about this money-bag she said—is that what you ask, Sir Roland? Well, sir, what she said was this. They had told me a deal, you must understand, about investing in good securities, meaning their own blessed pockets, no doubt. But they found me too old a bird for that. 'Down with the money!' says I, the same as John Shorne might in the market. They wouldn't. They wouldn't. Not a bit of it, till I put another laiyer at them—my own son, sir, if you please, a counselor on our circuit; and he brought them to book in no time, and he laid down the law to me pretty strong about my being answerable. So, as soon as I got it, I said to her, 'Mabel, how am I to lodge it for you, to fetch proper interest, until you come of age?' But the young silly burst out crying, and she said, 'What good can it ever be to me? Take it all, father, take every penny, and see if it will do any good to him.' And no peace could I have, till at last I set off. And there it is, Sir Roland. But I am thinking that, the money in no way belonging to me, I am bound to ask you to make a receipt, or give me your note of hand for it, or something as you think proper, just to disappoint the laiyers."

"You shall have my receipt," said Sir Roland Lorraine, with his eyes beginning to glisten. "Meanwhile place all the money in the bag, and tie it up securely."

The grower fetched a quiet little sigh, and allowed the corners of his mouth to drop, as he did what he was told to do. It had cost him many a hard fight with Mabel, and many a sulky puff of pipe, to be sent on such an errand. Money is money; and a man who makes it with so much anxiety, chance of season, and cheating from the middle-men, as a fruit-grower has to struggle through—such a man wants to know the reason why he should let it go all of a head. However,

Martin Lovejoy was one of the "noblest works of God," an honest man—though an honest woman is even yet more noble, if value goes by rarity—and he knew that the money was his daughter's own, to do what she pleased with, in a twelvemonth's time, when she would be a spinster of majority.

"I have written my receipt," said Sir Roland, breaking in on Master Lovejoy's sad retrospect at the bag of money. "Read it, and tell me if I have been too cold."

It is a thing quite unaccountable, haply (and yet there must be some cause for it), that some men who allow no tone of voice, no pressure of hand, to betray emotion, yet can not take pen without doing it, and letting the fount of heart break open from the sealed reserve of eye. No other explanation can be offered for this note of hand from Sir Roland Lorraine. The grower put on his specks, and then he took them off and wiped them; and then, as the shadow of the hill came over, he found it hard to read any thing. The truth was that he had read every word, but had no idea of being overcome. And the note, so hard to read, was as follows:

"MABEL,—I have done you much injustice. And I hope that I may live long enough to show what now I think of you. Your perfect faith and love are more than any one can have deserved of you, and least of all my son, who has fallen into all his sad distress by wandering away from you. Your money, of course, I can not accept; but your good-will I value more than I have power to tell you. If you would come and see Hilary, I think it would do him more good than a hundred doctors. Sometimes he seems pretty well; and again he is fit for little or nothing. I know that he longs to see you, Mabel; and having so wronged you, I ask you humbly to come, and let us do you justice. ROLAND LORRAINE."

CHAPTER LXII.

IT did not occur to Sir Roland Lorraine (as he shook Martin Lovejoy's hand, and showed him forth on his way to meet the Reigate coach at Pyecombe) that Mabel's rich legacy might be supposed to have changed his own views concerning her. Whether her portion was to be twenty thousand pounds or twenty pence made very little difference to him; but what made all the difference was the greatness of her faith and love.

The grower was a man who judged a man very much by eyesight. He had found out ever so many rogues by means of that "keen Kentish look," for which the Sidneys, and some other old families, were famous. And having well applied this to Sir Roland, he had no longer any doubt of him. And yet, with his shrewd common sense, he was not sorry to button up his coat with the money once more inside it in the sample-bag which had sampled so much love, and trust, and loyalty. Money is not so light to come by as great landlords might suppose; and for a girl to be known to have it is the best of all strings to her bow. So Master Lovejoy grasped his staff; and it would have been a hard job for even the famous Black Robin, the highwayman of the time, to have wrested the trust-fund from him.

Covering the ground at an active pace, and crossing the Woeburn by a tree-bridge (rudely set up where the old one had been), he strode through West Lorraine and Steyning, and over the hills to Pyecombe corner, where he took the Reigate coach; and he slept that night at Reigate.

Meanwhile the Chapmans gathered their forces for perfect conquest of Alice. Father and son had quite agreed that the final stroke of victory might best be made by occupying the commanding fortress Valeria. They knew that this stronghold was only too ready, for the sake of the land below it, to surrender at discretion; and the guns thereof being turned on the castle, the whole must lie at their mercy.

Yet there were two points which these besiegers had not the perception to value duly, and seize to their own advantage. One was the character of Sir Roland; the other was the English courage and Norman spirit of Alice. "It is all at our mercy now," they thought; "we have only to hammer away; and the hammer of gold is too heavy for any thing." They did not put it so clearly as that—for people of that sort do not put their views to themselves very clearly; still, if they had looked inside their ideas, they would have found them so.

"Steenie, let me see him first," said Sir Remnant, meeting his son, by appointment, at the sun-dial in the eastern walk (which for half the year possessed a sinecure office, and an easy berth even through the other half). "Steenie, you will make a muddle; you have been at your flask again."

"Well, what can I do? That girl is enough to roll any body over. I wish I had never seen her—oh, I wish I had never seen her! She dis-dis-dis—"

"Dislikes you, Steenie! She can never do that. Of all I have settled with, none have said it. They are only too fond of you, Steenie; just as they were of your father before you. And now you are straight, and going on so well! After all you have done for the women, Steenie, no girl can dislike you."

"That is the very thing I try to think. And I know that it ought to be so, if only from proper jealousy. But she never seems to care when I talk of girls; and she looks at me so that I scarcely dare speak; and it scarcely makes any difference at all what girls have been in love with me!"

"Have you had the sense to tell her of any of the royal family?"

"Of course I did. I mentioned two or three, with good foundation. But she never inquired who they were, and nothing seems to touch her. I think I must give it up, after all. I never cared for any girl before. And it does seem so hard, after more than a score of them, when one is in downright earnest at last, not to be able to get a chance of the only one I ever lov-lov-loved!"

"Steenie, you are a mere ass," said Sir Remnant; "you always are, when you get too much—which you ought to keep for dinner-time. I have settled every thing for you up stairs, so that it must come right, if only you can hold your tongue and wait. I have them all under my thumb; and nothing but your rotten fuss about the young maid can make us one day later. Her time is fixed. And whether she dislikes—"

"Dis-dis-dis—what I meant to say was—despises."

"Pish and tush, fiddlemaree! A young girl to despise a man! I had better marry her myself, I trow, if that is all you are fit for. Now just go away; go down the hill; go and see old Hales; go anywhere for a couple of hours, while I see Lorraine. Only first give me your honor for this, that you will not touch one more drop of drink until you come back for the dinner-time."

"You are always at me about that now. And I have had almost less than nothing. And even that drop I should not have had, if Alice had not upset me so."

"Well, you may have needed it. I will say no more. We will upset her pretty well by-and-by, the obstinate, haughty fagot! But, Steenie, you will give me your honor —not another drop, except water. You always keep your honor, Steenie."

"Yes, sir, I do. And I will give it. But I must not go near either Alice or Hales. She does so upset me that I must have a drop. And I defy any body to call upon Hales without having two or three good glasses. Oh, I know what I'll do; and I need not cross that infernal black water to do it. I'll call upon the boy at the bottom of the hill, and play at pitch-guineas with him. They say that he rolls every night in money."

"Then, Steenie, go and take a lesson from him. All you do with the money is to roll it away — ducks and drakes, and dipping yourself. I would not have stuck to this matter so much, except that I know it for your last chance. Your last chance, Steenie, is to have a wife, with sense and power to steer you. It is worth all the money we are going to pay, even if it never come back again, which I will take deuced good care it does. You know you are my son, my boy."

"Well, I suppose I can't be any body's else; you carried on very much as I do."

"And when my time is over, Steenie—if you haven't drunk yourself to death before me—you will say that you had a good kind father, who would go to the devil to save you."

"Really, sir, you were down upon me for having had a sentimental drop. But I think I may return the compliment."

"Go down the hill, Steenie—go down the hill. It seems to be all that you are fit for. And do try to put your neckcloth tidy before you come back to dinner."

Sir Remnant Chapman returned to the house, with a heavy sigh from his withered breast. He had not the goodness in him which is needed to understand the value of a noble maiden, or even of any good girl, taken as against man's selfishness. But in his little way, he thought of the bonds of matrimony as a check upon his son's poor rambling life; and he knew that a lady was wanted in his house; and his great ambition was to see, at last, a legitimate grandson. "If he comes of the breed of Lorraine," he exclaimed, "I will settle one hundred thousand pounds the very day he is born on him."

With this in his head, he came back to try his measures with Sir Roland. He knew that he must not work at all as he had done with Lady Valeria, but put it all strictly as a matter of business, with no obligation on either side; but as if there were "landed security" for the purchase-money of Alice. And he managed all this so well, that Sir Roland, proud and high-minded as he was, saw nothing improper in an arrangement by which Alice would become an incumbent on the Lorraine estates for the purpose of vindicating the honor of Lorraine, and saving, perhaps, the male heir thereof. Accordingly the matter was referred to the lawyers, who put it in hand, with the understanding that the trustees of the marriage settlement would waive all defects, and accept as good a mortgage as could be made by deed of even date to secure the fifty thousand pounds.

Sir Roland had long been unwilling to give his favorite Alice to such a man as Captain Chapman seemed to be. Although, through his own retiring and rather unsociable habits, he was not aware of the loose, unprincipled doings of the fellow, he could not but perceive the want of solid stuff about him, of any power for good, or even respectable powers of evil. But he first tried to think, and then began to believe, that his daughter would cure these defects, and take a new pride and delight in doing so. He knew what a spirited girl she was; and he thought it a likely thing enough that she would do better with a weak, fond husband, than with one of superior mind, who might fail to be polite to her. And he could not help seeing that Steenie was now entirely devoted to her. Perpetual snubbings and supreme disdain made little difference to Steenie. He knew that he must win in the end, and then his turn might come, perhaps; and in half an hour after his worst set-down he was up again on the arm of Cognac.

Alice Lorraine, with that gift of waiting for destiny, which the best women have, allowed the whole thing to go on, as if she perceived there was no hope for it. She made no touching appeals to her father, nor frantic prayers to her grandmother; she let the time slip on and on, and the people say what they liked to her. She would give her life for her brother's life, and the honor of the family; but firmly was she resolved to be never the wife of Stephen Chapman.

The more she saw of this man the more deeply and utterly she despised him. She could not explain to her father or even herself why so she loathed him. She did not know that it was the native shrinking of the good from evil, of the lofty from the low, the brave from the coward, the clean from the unclean. All this she was too young to think of, too maidenly to dwell upon. But she felt, perhaps, an unformed thought, an unpronounced suggestion, that death was a fitter husband for a pure girl than a rake-hell.

Meanwhile Hilary, upon whom she waited with unwearying love and care, was beginning to rally from his sad disorder and incipient decline. The doctors, who had shaken their heads about him, now began to smile, and say that under skillful treatment youth and good constitution did wonders; that "really they had seldom met with clearer premonitory indications of phthisis pulmonum, complicated by cardiac and hypochondriac atony, and aggravated by symptomatic congestion of the cerebellum; but proper remedial agents had been instrumental in counteracting all organic cachexy, and now all the principles of sound hygiene imperatively demanded quietude." In plain English, he was better, but must not be worried. Therefore he was not even told of the arrangement about his sister. Alice used to come and sit by his bed, or sofa, or easy-chair, as he grew a little stronger, and talk light nonsense to him, as if her heart was above all cloud and care. If he alluded to any trouble she turned it at once to ridicule; and when he spoke of his indistinct remembrance of the Woeburn, she made him laugh till his heart grew fat, by her mimicry of Nanny Stilgoe, whom she could do to the very life. "How gay you are, Lallie; I never saw such a girl!" he exclaimed, with the gratitude which arises from liberated levity. "You do her with the stick so well! Do her again with the stick, dear Lallie." His mind was a little childish now, from long lassitude of indoor life, which is enough to weaken and depress the finest mind that ever came from heaven, and hankers for sight of its birthplace. In a word, Alice Lorraine was bestowing whatever of mirth or fun she had left (in the face of the coming conflict), all the liveliness of her life, and revolt of bright youth against misery, to make her poor brother laugh a little, and begin to look like himself again.

CHAPTER LXIII.

Hilary's luck was beginning to turn; for in a few days he received a grand addition to his stock of comforts, and wholesome encouragement to get well. For after the grower's return to his home, and recovery from hard Sussex air (which upset him for two days and three nights, "from the want of any fruitiness about it"), a solemn council was called and held in the state apartment of Applewood Farm. There were no less than five personages present, all ready to entertain and maintain fundamentally opposite opinions. Mr. Martin Lovejoy, M.G., Mrs. Martin Lovejoy, Counselor Gregory Lovejoy (brought down upon special retainer), Miss Phyllis Catherow, and Lieutenant Charles Lovejoy, R.N. Poor Mabel was not allowed to be present, for fear she should cry, and disturb strong minds, and corrode all bright honor with mercy. The grower thought that Master John Shorne, as the London representative of the house, was entitled to be admitted; but no one else saw it in that light, and so the counsel of a Kentish crust was lost.

The question before the meeting was, Whether without lese-majesty of the ancient Lovejoy family, and in consistence with maiden dignity, and the laws of Covent Garden, Mabel Lovejoy might accept the invitation of Coombe Lorraine? A great deal was said upon either side, but no one convinced or converted, till the master said, "You may all talk as you like, but I will have my own way, mind."

Mrs. Lovejoy and Gregory were against accepting any thing. A letter written on the spur of the moment was not the proper overture; neither ought Mabel to go at last, because they might happen to want her. But the father said, and the sailor also, and sweet Cousin Phyllis, that if she was wanted she ought to go, dispensing with small formality, especially if she should want to go.

She did want to go, and go she did, backed up by kind opinions; and her father being busy with his pears and hops (which were poor and late this wet season), the fine young sailor, now adrift on shore—while his ship was refitting at Chatham—made sail, with his sister in convoy, for the old roadstead of the South Downs. Gregory (who had refused to go, for reasons best known to himself, but sensible and sound ones) wished them good luck, and returned to his chambers in the Middle Temple.

Now there is no time to set forth how these two themselves set forth: the sailor with all the high spirit of the sea when it overruns the land; the spinster inclined to be meditative, tranquil, and deep of eye and heart, yet compelled to come out of herself and smile, and then let herself come into her smile. It is a way all kind-hearted girls have when they know that they ought to be grave, and truly intend to be so, yet can not put a chain on the pop-gun pellets of young age, health, and innocence.

Enough that they arrived quite safely at the old house in the Coombe, with the sailor of course in a flurry of ambition to navigate his father's horse whenever he looked between his ears. The inborn resemblance between ships and horses has been perceived, and must have been perceived, long before Homer, or even Job, began to consider the subject; and it still holds good, and deserves to be treated by the most eloquent man of the age, retiring into silence.

Mr. Hales had claimed the right of introducing his favorite Mabel to his brother-in-law, Sir Roland. For amity now reigned again between the Coombe and the rectory; the little quarrel of the year before had long since been adjusted, and the parson was as ready to contribute his valuable opinion upon any subject as he was when we began with him. One might almost say even more so; for the longer a good man lives with a wife and three daughters to receive the law from him, and a parish to accept his divinity, the less hesitation he has in admitting the extent of his own capacities. Nevertheless he took very good care to keep out of Lady Valeria's way.

"Bless my heart! you look better than ever," said the rector to the blushing Mabel, as her pretty figure descended into his strong arms at the great house door. "Give me a kiss—that's a hearty lass. I shall always insist upon it. What! trembling lips! That will never do. A little more Danish courage, if you please. You know I am the Danish champion. And here is the royal Dane of course, or a Dane in the Royal Navy, which does quite as well, or better. Charlie, my boy, I want no introduction. You are a fisherman — that is enough, or too much, if your sister's words are true. You can catch trout when I can't."

"No sir, never. I never should dare. But Mabel always makes me a wonder."

"Well, perhaps we shall try some day, the Church against the Navy; and Mabel to bring us the luncheon. Well said, well said! I have made her smile; and that is worth a deal of trying. She remembers the goose, and the stuffing, and how she took in the clerk from Sussex. I don't believe she made a bit of it."

"I did, I did! How can you say such things? I can make better stuffing than that to-morrow. I was not at all at my best then."

"You are at your best now," he replied, having purposely moved her mettle. "Come in with that color and those sparkling eyes, and you will conquer every one."

"I want to conquer no one," she answered, with female privilege of last word; "I only came to see poor Hilary."

The rector, with the fine gallantry and deference of old-fashioned days, led the beautiful and good girl, and presented her to Sir Roland. She was anxious to put her hair a little back before being looked at; but the impetuous parson wisely would not let her trim herself. She could not look better than she did; so coy, and soft, and bashful, resolved to be by no means timid, but afraid that she could not contrive to be brave.

Sir Roland Lorraine came forward gently, and took her hand and kissed her. He felt in his heart that he had been hard upon this very pretty maiden, imputing petty ambition to her which one glance of her true dear eyes disproved to his mind forever. She was come to see Hilary; nothing more. Her whole heart was on Hilary. She had much admiration of Sir Roland, as her clear eyes told him. But she had more than admiration for some one on another floor.

"You want to go up stairs, my dear," Sir Roland said, with the usual pathos of all critical moments; "you would like to take off your things, and so on, before you see poor Hilary."

"Of course, she must touch herself up," cried the rector; "what do you know about young women? Roland, where is Mrs. Pipkins?"

"I told her to be not so very far off; but she is boiling down bullace-plums, or something of the highest national importance. We could not tell when this dear child would come, or we might have received her better."

"Oh, I am so glad! You can not receive me, you could not receive me, better. And now that you have called me your dear child, I shall always love you. I did not think that you would do it. And I came for nothing of the kind — I only came for Hilary."

"Oh, we quite understand that we are nobodies," answered Sir Roland, smiling; "you shall go to him directly. But you must not be frightened by his appearance. He has been a good deal knocked about, and fallen into sad trouble; but we all hope that now he is getting better, and the sight of you will be better than a hundred doctors to him. But you must not stay very long, of course, and you must keep him very quiet. But I need not tell you—I see that you have a natural gift of nursing."

"All who have the gift of cookery have the gift of nursing," exclaimed Mr. Hales, "because 'omne majus continet in se minus.' Ah, Roland, you think nothing of my learning. If only you knew how I am pervaded with Latin, and with logic!"

These elderly gentlemen chattered thus because they were gentlemen. They saw that poor Mabel longed to have their attention nicely withdrawn from her; and without showing what they saw they nicely thus withdrew it. Then Alice, having heard of Miss Lovejoy's arrival, came down and was good to her, and their hearts were speedily drawn together by their common anxiety. Alice thought Mabel the prettiest girl she ever had seen anywhere; and Mabel thought Alice the loveliest lady that could exist out of a picture.

What passed between Mabel and Hilary may better be imagined, doubtless, than put into clumsy words.

CHAPTER LXIV.

THE darkness of the hardest winter of the present century—so far as three-fourths of its span enable us to estimate—was gathering over the South Down hills, and all hills and valleys of England. There may have been severer cold, by fits and starts, before and since; but the special character of this winter was the consistent low temperature. There may have been some fiercer winters, whose traditions still abide, and terrify us beyond range of test and fair thermometer. But within the range of trusty records there has been no frost to equal that which began on Christmas-day, 1813.

Seven weeks it lasted, and then broke up and then began again, and lingered; so that in hilly parts the snow-drifts chilled not only the lap of May but the rosy skirt of June. That winter was remarkable, not only for perpetual frost, but for continual snow-fall; so that no man of the most legal mind could tell when he was trespassing. Hedges and ditches were all alike, and hollow places were made high; and hundreds of men fell into drifts; and some few saved their lives by building frozen snow to roof them, and cuddling their knees and chins together in a pure white home, having heard the famous and true history of Elizabeth Woodcock.

But now, before this style of things set in in bitter earnest, nobody on the South Down hills could tell what to make of the weather. For twenty years the shepherds had not seen things look so strange like. There was no telling their marks, or places, or the manners of the sheep. A sulky gray mist crawled along the ground, even when the sky was clear. In the morning every blade, and point, and little spike of attraction, and serrate edge (without any intention of ever sawing any thing), and drooping sheath of something which had vainly tried to ripen, and umbellate awning of the stalks that had discharged their seed, were one and all alike incrusted with a little filmy down. Sometimes it looked like the cotton-grass that grows in boggy places; and sometimes like the "American blight," so common now on apple-trees; and sometimes more like gossamer, or the track of flying spiders. The shepherds had never seen this before; neither had the sheep—the woolly sages of the weather. The sheep turned up their soft black eyes with wonder toward the heavens—the heavens where every sheep may hope to walk, in the form of a fleecy cloud, when men have had his legs of mutton.

It is needless to say that this long warning (without which no great frost arrives) was wholly neglected by every man. The sheep, the cattle, and the pigs foresaw it, and the birds took wing to fly from it; the fish of the rivers went into the mud, and the fish of the sea to deep water. The slug and the cockroach, the rat and the wholesome toad, came home to their snuggeries; and every wire-worm and young grub bored deeper down than he meant to do. Only the human race straggled about, without any perception of any thing.

In this condition of the gloomy air, and just when frost was hovering in the gray clouds before striking, Alice Lorraine came into her father's book-room on the Christmas-eve. There was no sign of any merry Christmas in the shadowed house, nor any young delighted hands to work at decoration. Mabel was gone, after a longer visit than had ever been intended; and Alice (who had sojourned in London, under lofty auspices) had not been long enough yet at home to be sure again that it was her home. Upon her return she had enjoyed the escort of a mighty warrior, no less a hero than Colonel Clumps, the nephew of her hostess. The colonel had been sadly hacked about in a skirmish soon after Vittoria, when pressing too hotly on the French rear-guard. He had lost not only his right arm, but a portion of his one sound leg; and instead of saying his prayers every morning, he sat for an hour on the edge of the bed and devoted all his theological knowledge to the execration of the clumsy bullet, which could not even select his weak point for attack. This choler of his made much against the recovery of what was left of him, and the doctors thought that country air might mitigate his state of mind, and at the same time brace his body, which sadly wanted bracing. Therefore it had been arranged that he should go for a month to Coombe Lorraine, posting all the way, of course, and having the fair Alice to wait on him—which is the usual meaning of escort.

At the date of this journey the colonel's two daughters were still away at a boarding-school; but they were to come and spend the Christmas with his aunt in London, and then accompany her into Sussex, and perhaps appear as brides-maids. Meanwhile their father was making himself a leading power at Coombe Lorraine. He naturally entered into strict alliance with his aunt's friend, Lady Valeria, and sternly impressed upon every body the necessity of the impending marriage. "What earthly objection can there be?" he argued with Mrs. Pipkins, now Alice's only partisan, except old Mr. Binns, the butler; "even if Captain Chapman is rather lazy and a little too fond of his wine-glass, both points are in her favor, ma'am. She will manage him like a top, of course. And as for looking up to him, that's all nonsense. If she did, he would have to look down upon her: and that's what the women can't bear, of course. How would you like it now, Mrs. Pipkins? Tut, tut, tut, now don't tell me! I am a little too old to be taken in. I only wish one of my good daughters had fifty thousand pounds thrown at her, with twenty thousand pounds a year to follow."

"But perhaps, sir, your young ladies is not quite so particular, and romantic like, as our poor dear Miss Alice."

"I should hope not. I'd romantic them. Bread-and-water is the thing for young hussies who don't know on which side their bread is buttered. But I don't believe a bit of it. It's all sham, and girlish make-believe. In her heart she is as ready as he is."

Almost every body said the same thing; and all the credit the poor girl got for her scorn of a golden niddering was to be looked upon as a coy piece of affectation and thanklessness. All this she was well aware of. Evil opinion is a thing to which we are alive at once, though good opinion is well content to impress itself on the coffin. Alice (who otherwise rather liked his stolid and upright nature) thought that Colonel Clumps had no business to form opinion upon her affairs, or, at any rate, none to express it. But the colonel always did form opinions, and felt himself bound to express them.

"I live in this house," he said, when Alice hinted at some such phantasy; "and the affairs of this house are my concern. If I am not to think about the very things around me, I had better have been cut in two, than made into three pieces." He waved the stalk of his arm, and stamped the stump of the foot of his better leg with such a noise and gaze of wrath that the maiden felt he must be in the right. And so perhaps he may have been. At any rate, he got his way, as a veteran colonel ought to do.

With every body he had his way. Being unable to fight any more, he had come to look so ferocious, and his battered and shattered body so fiercely backed up the charge of his aspect, that none without vast reserve of courage could help being scattered before him. Even Sir Roland Lorraine (so calm, and of an infinitely higher mind), by reason perhaps of that gave way, and let the maimed veteran storm his home. But Alice rebelled against all this.

"Now, father," she said on that Christmas-eve, when the house was chilled with the coming cold, and the unshedden snow hung over it, and every sheep and cow and crow and shivering bird down to the willow-wren was hieing in search of shelter, "father, I have not many words to say to you; but, such as they are, I must say them."

Sir Roland Lorraine, being struck by her quite unwonted voice and manner, rose from his chair of meditation, left his thoughts about things which never can be thought out by mankind, and came to meet what a man should think of foremost—his child, his woman child.

"Lallie, my dear," he said very gently, and kindly looking at her sad, wild eyes, whose difference from their natural softness touched him with some terror—"Lallie, now what has made you look like this?"

"Papa, I did not mean to look at all out of my usual look. I beg you pardon, if indeed I do. I know that all such things are very small in your way of regarding things. But still, papa—but still, papa, you might let me say something."

"Have I ever refused you, Alice, the right to say almost every thing?"

"No, that you have never done, of course. But what I want to say now is something more than I generally want to say. Of course, it can not matter to you, papa; but to me it makes all the difference."

"My dear, you are growing sarcastic. All that matters to you matters a great deal more to me, of course. You know what you have always been to me."

"I do, papa. And that is why I find it so very hard to believe that you can be now so hard with me. I do not see what I can have done to make you so different to me. Girls like me are fond of saying very impudent things sometimes; and they seem to be taken lightly. But they are not forgiven as they are meant. Have I done any thing at all to vex you in that way, papa?"

"How can you be so foolish, Lallie? You talk as if I were a girl myself. You never do a thing to vex me."

"Then why do you do a thing to kill me? It must come to that, and you know it must. I am not very good, nor in any way grand, and I don't want to say what might seem harsh. But, papa, I think I may say this—you will never see me Stephen Chapman's wife."

"Well, Lallie, it is mainly your own doing. I did not wish to urge it, until it seemed to become inevitable. You encouraged him so in the summer, that we can not now draw back honorably."

"Father, I encouraged him!"

"Yes. Your grandmother tells me so. I was very busy at that time; and you were away continually. And whenever I wanted you, I always heard, 'Miss Alice is with Captain Chapman.'"

"How utterly untrue! But, oh papa, now, you got jealous! Do say that you got jealous; and then I will forgive you every thing."

"My dear, there was nothing to be jealous of. I thought that you were taking nicely to the plan laid out for you."

"The plan that will lay me out, papa. But will you tell me one thing?"

"Yes, my dear child, a hundred things, if you will only ask them quietly."

"I am not making any noise, papa; it is only that my collar touched my throat. But what I want to know is this. If any thing should happen to me, as they say; if I should drop out of every body's way, could the money be got that you are all so steadfastly set upon getting? Could the honor of the family be set up, and poor Hilary yet restored, and well, and the Lorraines go on forever? Why don't you answer me, papa? My question is a very simple one. What I have a right to ask is this—am I, for some inscrutable reason (which I have had nothing to do with), the stumbling-block—the fatal obstacle to the honor and the life of the family?"

"Alice, I never knew you talk like this, and I never saw you look so. Why, your cheeks are perfectly burning! Come here, and let me feel them."

"Thank you, papa; they will do very well. But will you just answer my question? Am I the fatal—am I the death-blow to the honor and life of our lineage?"

Sir Roland Lorraine was by no means pleased with this curt mode of putting things. He greatly preferred, at his time of life, the rounding off and softening of affairs that are too dramatic. He loved his beautiful daughter more than any thing else on the face of the earth; he knew how noble her nature was, and he often thought that she took a more lofty view of the world than human nature in the end would justify. But still he must not give way to that.

"Alice," he said, "I can scarcely see why you should so disturb yourself. There are many things always to be thought of—more than one has time for."

"To be sure, papa, I know all that; and I hate to see you worried. But I think that you might try to tell me whether I am right or not."

"My darling, you are never wrong. Only things appear to you in a stronger light than they do to me; of course, because you are younger and get into a hurry about many things that ought to be more dwelt upon. It is true that your life is interposed, through the command of your grandmother and the subtlety of the lawyers, between poor Hilary and the money that might have been raised to save him."

"That is true, papa; now, is it? I believe every word that you say, but I never believe one word of my grandmother's."

"You shocking child! Yes, it is true enough. But after all, it comes to nothing. Of the law I know nothing, I am thankful to say; but from Sir Glanvil Malahide I understand, through some questions which your grandmother laid before him, that the money can only be got—either through this family arrangement, or else by waiting till you, as a spinster, attain the age of twenty-one—which would be nearly two years too late."

"But, papa, if I were to die?"

"Lallie, why are you so vexatious? If you were to die, the whole of the race might end—so far as I care."

"My father, you say that to make me love you more than I do already, which is a hopeless attempt on your part. Now you need not think that I am jealous; it is the last thing I could dream of. But ever since Mabel Lovejoy appeared, I have not been what I used to be, either with you or with Hilary. In the case of poor Hilary, I must of course expect it, and put up with it. But I can not see, for a moment, why I ought to be cut out with you, papa."

"What foolish jealousy, Alice! Shall I tell you why I like and admire Mabel so much? But as for comparing her with you—"

"But, papa, why do you like and admire her so deeply?"

"You jealous child, I did not say 'deeply.' But I like her because she is so gentle, so glad to do what she is told, so full of self-sacrifice and self-devotion."

"While I am harsh and disobedient, self-seeking and devoted to self. No doubt she would marry according to order. Though I dreamed that I heard of a certain maltster, who had the paternal sanction. 'Veni, vidi, vici,' appears to be her motto. Even grandmamma is vanquished by her, or by her legacy. She says that she courtesies much better than I do. She is welcome to that distinction. I am not at all sure that the prime end and object of woman's life is to courtesy.

But I see exactly how I am placed. I will never trouble you any more, papa."

With these words Alice Lorraine arose and kissed her father's forehead gently, and turned away, not to worry him with the long sigh of expiring hope. She had still three weeks to make up her mind, or rather to wait with her mind made up. And three weeks still is a long spell of time for the young to anticipate misery.

"You are quite unlike yourself, my child," Sir Roland said with perfect truth; "you surprise me very much to-day. I am sure that you do not mean a quarter of what you are saying."

"You are right, papa. I do not mean even a tenth part of my spitefulness. I will try to be more like Mabel Lovejoy, who really is so good and nice. It is quite a mistake to suppose that I could ever be jealous of her. She is a dear, kind-hearted girl, and the very wife for Hilary. But I think that she differs a little from me."

"It is no matter of opinion, Alice. Mabel differs from you as widely as you differ from your cousin Cecil. I begin to incline to an old opinion (which I came across the other day), that much more variety is to be found in the weaker than in the stronger sex. Regard it thus—"

"Excuse me, father. I have no courage for regarding any thing. You can look at things in fifty lights, and I in one shadow only. Good-bye, darling. Perhaps I shall never speak to you again as I have to-night. But I hope you will remember that I meant it for the best."

CHAPTER LXV.

According to all the best accounts, that long and heavy frost began with the clearing of the sky upon Christmas-day. At least it was so in the south of England, though probably two or three days earlier in the northern counties. A great frost always advances slowly, creeping from higher latitudes. If the cold begins in London sooner than it does in Edinburgh, it very seldom lasts out the week; and if it comes on with a violent wind, its time is generally shorter. It does seem strange, but it is quite true, that many people, even well informed, attribute to this severity of cold the destruction of the great French army during its retreat from Moscow, and the ruin of Napoleon. They know the date of the ghastly carnage of the Beresina and elsewhere, which happened more than a year ere this; but they seem to forget that each winter belongs to the opening, and not to the closing year. Passing all such matters, it is enough to say that Christmas-day, 1813, was unusually bright and pleasant. The lowering sky and chill gray mist of the last three weeks at length had yielded to the gallant assault of the bright-speared sun. That excellent knight was pricking merrily over the range of the South Down hills; his path was strown with sparkling trinkets from the casket of the clouds; the brisk air moved before him, and he was glad to see his way again. But behind him and before him lay the ambush of the "snow-blink" to catch him at night, when he should go down, and to stop him of his view in the morning. However, for the time he looked very well; and as no one had seen him for ever so long, nobody cross-questioned him.

Mr. Struan Hales was famous for his sermon on Christmas-day. For five-and-twenty years he had made it his grand sermon of the year. He struck no strokes of enthusiasm—which nobody dreamed of doing then, except the very low Dissenters—still he had always a strong idea that he ought to preach above the average. And he never failed to do so—partly through inspiration of other divines, but mainly by summing up all the sins of his parish, and then forgiving them.

The parish listened with apathy to the wisdom and eloquence of great men (who said what they had to say in English—a lost art for nearly two centuries), and then the parish pricked up all its ears to hear of its own doings. The rector preached the first part of his sermon in a sing-song manner, with a good seesaw. But when he came down to his parish bounds, and traced his own people's trespasses, he changed his voice altogether, so that the deafest old sinner could hear him. It was the treat of all the year to know what the parson was down upon; and, to be sure, who had done it. Then, being of a charitable kind, and loving while he chastened, the rector always let them go, with a blessing which sounded as rich as a grace for every body's Christmas dinner. Every body went out of church happy and contented. They had enough to talk about for a week; and they all must have earned the good-will of the Lord by going to church on a week-day. But the rector always waited for his two church-wardens to come into the vestry, and shake hands and praise his sermon. And, not to be behindhand, Farmer Gates and Mr. Botler (now come from Steyning to West Lorraine, and immediately appointed, in right of the number of pigs killed weekly, junior church-warden)—these two men of excellent presence and of accomplished manners got in under the vestry arch, and congratulated the rector.

Alice Lorraine was not at church. Every body had missed her in her usual niche between two dark marble records of some of her ancestors. There she used to sit, and be set off by their fine antiquity; but she did not go to church that day, as her father could not take her.

West Lorraine church had been honored that day by the attendance of several people entitled to as handsome monuments as could be found inside it. For instance, there was Sir Remnant Chapman (for whom even an epitaph must strain its elastic charity); Stephen, his son—who had spent his harm without having much to show for it; Colonel Clumps, who would rise and fight, if the resurrection restored his legs; a squire of high degree (a distant and vague cousin of the true Lorraines), who wanted to know what was going on, having great hopes through the Woeburn, but sworn to stick (whatever might happen) to his own surname, Bloggs; and last, and best of all, Joyce Aylmer, Viscount Aylmer's only son, of a true old English family, but not a very wealthy one.

"A merry Christmas to you all!" cried Mr. Hales, as they stood in the porch. "A merry Christmas, gentlemen! But, my certy, we shall have a queer one. How keen the air is getting!"

They all shook hands with the parson and thanked him, after the good old fashion, "for his learned and edifying discourse;" and they asked what he meant about the weather; but he was too deep to tell them. Even he had been wrong upon that matter, and was now too wise to commit himself. Then Cecil, who followed her father of course, made the proper courtesies as the men made bows to her; and Major Aylmer's horse was brought, and a carriage for the rest of them.

"Are you coming with us, rector? We dine early," said Sir Remnant, with a hungry squeak. "You can't have another service, can you? God knows, you have done enough for one day."

"Enough to satisfy you at any rate," the rector answered, smiling; "but I should have my house about my ears if I dined outside of it on a Christmas-day. Plain and wholesome and juicy fare, sir—none of your foreign poisons. Well, good-bye, gentlemen; I shall hope to see all of you again to-morrow, if the snow is not too deep." The rector knew that a very little snow would be quite enough to stop them, on the morning of the morrow—the Sunday.

"Snow, indeed! No sign of snow," Sir Remnant answered sharply: he had an inborn dislike of snow, and he wanted to be at home on the Monday. "But I say, missie, remember one thing. Tuesday fortnight is the day. Have all your fallals ready. Blushing brides-maids—ah! fine creatures! I shall claim a score of busses, mind. Don't you wish it was your own turn, eh?"

The old rogue, with a hearty smack, blew a kiss to Cecil Hales, who blushed and shivered, and then tried to smile, for fear of losing her locket; for it had been whispered that Sir Remnant Chapman had ordered a ten-guinea locket in London for each of the six brides-maids. So checking the pert reply which trembled on the tip of her tongue, she made them a pretty courtesy as they drove away.

"Now, did you observe, papa," she asked, as she took her father's arm, intending to gossip with him all up the street, "how terribly pale Major Aylmer turned when he heard about the brides-maids? I thought he was going to drop, as they say he used to do when he first came home from America. I am sure I was right, papa; I am sure I was, in what I told you the other day."

"Nonsense! fiddlestick! romantic flummery! You girls are never content without rivalry, jealousy, love, and despair."

"You may laugh as much as you like; but it makes no difference to me, papa. I tell you that Major Aylmer has lost his heart to Alice a great deal worse than he lost his head in America."

"Well, then, he must live with no head and no heart. He can't have Alice. He has got no money; even if it were possible to change the bridegroom at the door of the church."

"I will tell you what proves it beyond all dispute. You know how that wretched little Captain Chapman looks up when he hates any one, and thinks he has made a hit of it. There—like that; only I can't do it until I get much uglier. He often does it to me, you know. And then he patted his wonderful waistcoat."

"Now, Cecil, what spiteful things girls are! It is quite impossible that he can hate you."

"I am thankful to say that he does, papa, or perhaps you might have sold me to him. If ever any girl was sold, Alice is both bought and sold. And Sir Roland can not love her, as she used to think, or he would have had nothing to do with it. It must be fearfully bitter for her. And to marry a man who is tipsy every night, and tremulous every morning. Oh papa, papa!"

"My dear, you exaggerate horribly. You have always disliked poor Steenie; perhaps that is why he looks up to you. We must hope for the best; we must hope for the best. Why, bless my heart, if every man was to have the whole of his doings raked up, I should never want the marriage register!"

"Oh, but papa, if we could only manage to change the man, you know! The other is so different, so kind, and noble, and grand, and simple! If any man in all the world is worthy to marry dear Alice it is Major Aylmer."

"The man might be changed, but not the money," said the rector, rather shortly; and his daughter knew from the tone of his voice that she must quit the subject; the truth being (as she was well aware) that her father was growing a little ashamed of his own share in the business.

CHAPTER LXVI.

Dark weather and dark fortune do not always come together. Indeed the spirit of the British race, and the cheer flowing from high spirit, seem to be most forward in the worst conditions of the weather. Something to battle with, something to talk about, something to make the father more than usually welcome, and the hearth more bright and warm to him, and something also which enlarges by arousing charity, and spreads a man's interior comfort into general good-will — bitter weather, at the proper season, is not wholly bitterness.

But when half a dozen gentlemen, who care not a fig for one another, hate books (as they hated their horn-books), scorn all indoor pursuits but gambling, gormandizing, and drinking, and find little scope for pursuing these — when a number of these are snowed up together and can not see out of the windows—to express it daintily, there is likely to be much malediction.

And this is exactly what fell upon them, for more than a week, at Coombe Lorraine. They made a most excellent dinner on Christmas-day, about three o'clock, as they all declared; and, in spite of the shortness of the days, they saw their way till the wine came. They were surprised at this, so far as any of them noticed any thing; for, of course, no glance of the setting sun came near the old house in the winter. And they thought it a sign of fine hunting weather, and so they went on about it; whereas it was really one of the things scarcely ever seen down here, but common in the Arctic regions, the catch and the recast, and the dispersion of all vague light downward, by unmeasurable depth of gathering snow vapor.

The snow began about seven o'clock, when the influence of the sun was lost; and for three days and three nights it snowed, without taking or giving breathing-time. It came down, without any wind, or unfair attempt at drifting. The meaning of the sky was to snow and no more, and let the wind wait his time afterward. There was no such thing as any spying between the flakes at any time. The flakes were not so very large, but they came as close together as the sand pouring down in an hour-glass. They never danced up and down, like gnats or motes, as common snow-flakes do, but one on the back of another fell, expecting millions after them. And if any man looked up to see that gravelly infinitude of pelting spots, which swarms all the air in a snow-storm, he might just as well have shut both eyes, before it was done by snow-flakes.

All the visitors, except the colonel, were to have left on Monday morning, but only one of them durst attempt the trackless waste of white between the South Down Coombe and their distant homes. For although no drifting had begun as yet, some forty hours of heavy fall had spread a blinding cover over road and ditch, and bog and bank, and none might descry any sign-post, house, tree, or hill, or other landmark, at the distance of a hundred yards through the snow, still coming down as heavily as ever. Therefore every body thought Major Aylmer almost mad when he ordered his horse for the long ride home in the midst of such terrible weather.

"I don't think I ought to let you go," his host said, as the horse came round, as white already as a counterpane. 'Alice, where is your persuasive voice? Surely you might beg Major Aylmer to see what another day will bring."

"Another day would only make it worse," Joyce Aylmer replied, with a glance at Alice, which she perfectly understood. "I might be snowed up for a week, Sir Roland, with my father the whole time fidgeting. And after all, what is this compared to the storms we had in America?"

"Oh, but you were much stronger then. You would not be here were it not so."

"I scarcely know. I shall soon rejoin if I get on so famously as this. But I am keeping you in the cold so long, and Miss Lorraine in a chilly draught. Good-bye once more. Can I leave any message for you at the rectory?"

In another second the thick snow hid him and his floundering horse as they headed toward the borstall, for as yet there was only a foot-bridge thrown over the course of the Woeburn, and horsemen or carriages northward bound were obliged to go southward first, and then turn to the right on the high land, and thus circumvent the stream; even as Alice, quickly thinking, had enabled poor Bonny to recover his Jack.

Alice went back, with a sigh, to her own little room to sit and think a while. She knew that she had seen the last of a man whom she could well have loved, and who loved her (as she knew somehow) much too well already. Feeling that this could do no good, but only harm to both of them, he had made up his mind to go ere any mischief should arise from it. He had no idea how vastly Alice scorned poor Steenie Chapman, otherwise even his duty toward his host might perhaps have failed him. However, he had acted wisely, and she would think no more of him.

This resolution was hard to keep when she heard a little later in the day that the major had sent back his groom, after making believe to take him. The groom brought a message from his master begging quarters for him for a day or two on the plea that his horse had broken down; but Alice felt sure that he had been sent back, because Major Aylmer would not expose him to the risk which he meant himself to face. For she knew it to be more than twenty miles (having studied the map on the subject) from Coombe Lorraine to Stoke-Aylmer; and all in the teeth of a bitter wind now just beginning to crawl and wail as only a snowy wind can do.

The rest of the gentlemen plagued the house. It was hard to say which was the worst of them—Sir Remnant (who went to the lower regions to make the acquaintance of the kitchen-maids), or Colonel Clumps (who sat on a sideboard, and fought all his battles over again with a park of profane artillery), or Squire Bloggs (who bit his nails, and heavily demanded beer all day), or Steenie, who scorned beer altogether, and being repulsed by Onesimus Binns, at last got into Trotman's "study," and ordered some bottles up, and got on well. He sent for his groom, and he sent for his horn (which he had not wind enough to blow), and altogether he carried on so with a greasy pack of cards and a dozen grimy tumblers, that while the women, being strictly sober, looked down on his affability, the men said that they had known much worse.

For a week Sir Roland Lorraine was compelled to endure this wearing worry—tenfold wearisome as it was to a man of his peculiar nature. He had always been shy of inviting guests; but when they were once inside his door, the hospitality of his race and position revived within him. All in the house was at their service, including the master himself, so far as old habits can be varied. But now he was almost like the whelk who admits the little crab for company, and is no more the master of his own door. No man in all England longed that the roads might look like roads again more heartily and sadly than the hospitable Sir Roland.

With brooms of every sort and shape, and shovels, and even pickaxes, all the neighborhood turned out, as soon as ever a man could manage to open his own cottage-door. For three days it had been no good to try to do any thing but look on; but the very first moment the sky left off, every body living under it began to recover courage. The boys came first in a joyful manner, sinking over their brace-buttons in the shallow places, and then the girls came, and were puzzled by the manner of their dress, till they made up their minds to be boys for a time.

And after these came out their mother for the sake of scolding them; and then the father could do no less than stand on his threshold with pipe in mouth, and look up wisely at the sky, and advise every body to wait a bit. And thus a great many people managed to get out of their houses; and it was observed, not only then, but also for many years to come, how great the mercy of the Lord was. Having seen fit to send such a storm, he chose for it, not a Wednesday night, nor a Thursday night, nor a Friday night, but a Saturday night, when he knew, in his wisdom, that every man had got his wages, and had filled his bread-pan.

As for the roads, they were blocked entirely against both wheels and horses until a violent wind arose from the east, and winnowed fiercely. Sweeping along all the bend of the hill, and swaying the laden copses, it tore up the snow in squally spasms, and cast white blindness everywhere. Three days the snow had defied the wind, and for three days now the wind had its way. Vexed mortals could do nothing more than shelter themselves in their impotence, and hope, as they shivered and sniffed at their pots, that the Lord would repent of his anger. It was already perceived, and where people could get together they did not hide it, that Mr. Bottler must go up, and Farmer Gates come down a peg. For although the sheep were folded well, and mainly fetched into the hollows, as soon as the drift began, it was known that the very precaution would murder them. For sheep have a foolish trick of crowding into the lee of the fold, just where the drift must be the deepest. But pigs are as clever as their mother, dirt—which always gets over every thing. So Farmer Gates lost three hundred sheep, while Bottler did not lose a pig, but saved (and exalted the price of) his bacon.

When the snow, on the wings of the wind, began to pierce the windows of Coombe Lorraine (for in such case no putty will keep it out), and every ancient timber creaked with cold disgust of shrinking, and the "drawing" of all the fire-places was more to the door than the chimney, and the chimneys drew submissive moans to the howling of the tempest, and chilly rustles and frosty taps sounded outside the walls and in—from all these things the young lady of the house gained some hope and comfort. Surely in such weather no one could ever think of a wedding; nobody could come or go; it would take a week to dig out the church, and another week to get to it. Blow, blow, thou east wind, blow, and bury rather than marry us.

But the east wind (after three days of blowing, and mixing snow of earth and sky) suddenly fell with a hollow sound, like the "convolutions of a shell," into deep silence. Clear deep silence settled on the storm of drifted billows. As the wind left them, so they stopped until the summer rose under them; for spring there was none in that terrible year, and no breath of summer until it broke forth. And now set in the long steadfast frost, which stopped the Thames and Severn, the Trent and Tweed, and all the other rivers of Great Britain. From the source to the mouth a man might cross them without feeling water under him.

Alas for poor Alice! The roads of the weald (being mainly unhedged at that time) were opened as if by "Sesame." The hill-roads were choked many fathoms deep wherever they lay in shelter; but the furious wind had swept the flat roads clear, as with a besom. Their brown tract might be traced for miles, frozen as hard as an oaken plank, except where a slight depression, or a sudden bend, or a farmer's wall, had kept the white wave from shoaling. So, as soon as a passage had been dug through the borstall, and down the dell to the westward, the Chapmans were free to come and go with their gaudy coach as usual.

Alice took this turn of matters with all the calmness of despair. It was nothing but a childish thing to long for a few days' reprieve, which could not help her much, and might destroy all the good of her sacrifice. In one way or the other, she must go; standing so terribly across the welfare of all that was dear to her, and seeming (as she told herself) to have no one now to whom she was dear. With no one to admire or aid her, no one even to feel for her, she had to meet the saddest doom that can befall proud woman—wedlock with an abject.

CHAPTER LXVII.

And now there was but one day left; Monday was come, and on the morrow Alice was to be Mrs. Stephen Chapman.

"You call yourself an unlucky fellow," said Colonel Clumps, to Hilary, who was leaning back in his easy-chair; "but I call you the luckiest dog in the world. What other man in the British army could have lost fifty thousand guineas, escaped court-martial, and had a good furlough, made it all snug with his sweetheart (after gallivanting to his heart's content), and then got the chance to get back again under Old Beaky, and march into Paris? I tell you they will march into Paris, sir. What is there to stop them?"

"But, colonel, you forget that I can scarcely march across the room as yet. And even if I could, there is much to be done before I get back again. Our fellows may go into winter-quarters, and then the general's promise drops; or even without that, he may fail with the Duke of York, who loves him not."

"Stuff and rubbish, my dear boy! You pay the money—that's all you've got to do. No fear of their refusing it. Of course it will all be kept very quiet; and we shall find in the very next 'Gazette' some such paragraph as this: 'Captain Lorraine, of the Head-quarter Staff, who has long been absent on sick-leave, is now on his way to rejoin, and will resume his duties upon the Staff.'"

"Come now, colonel, you are too bad," cried Hilary, blushing with pleasure, "they never could put me on the Staff again. It is impossible that they could have the impudence."

"Don't tell me. Why, they had the impudence never to put me on it! They have impudence enough for any thing. You set to and get strong, that is all. Are you going to your sister's wedding to-morrow?"

"I will tell you a secret. I mean to go, though I am under strict orders not to go. What do I care for the weather? Tush! I have settled it all very cleverly. You will see me there when you least expect it. Lallie has behaved very badly to me; so has every body else about it. Am I never to be told any thing? She seems to be in a great hurry about it. Desperately in love, no doubt, though from what I remember of Stephen Chapman I am a little surprised at her taste; but of course—"

"Of course, of course, one must never say a word about young ladies' fancies. There was a young lady in Spain—to be sure there are a great many young ladies in Spain—"

The colonel dropped the subject in the clumsiest manner possible. He was under medical orders not to say a word that might stir up Hilary; and yet from the time he came into the room he had done nothing else but stir him up. Colonel Clumps was about the last man in the world that ought to stump in at any sick man's door. "Dash it, there I am again!" he used to say, as he began to let out something, and stopped short, and jammed his lips up, and set his wooden apparatus down. Therefore he had not been allowed to pay many visits to Hilary, otherwise the latter must soon have discovered the nature of the arrangement pending to retrieve his fortunes. At present he thought that the money was to be raised by a simple mortgage, of which he vowed, in his sanguine manner, that he would soon relieve the estates, by getting an appointment in India, as soon as he had captured Paris. Mabel of course would go with him, and be a great lady, and make his curries. He was never tired of this idea, and was talking of it to Colonel Clumps, who had seen some Indian service, when a gentle knock at the door was heard, and a soft voice said, "May I come in?" As Alice entered, the battered warrior arose and made a most ingenious bow, quite of his own invention. Necessity is the mother of that useful being; and the colonel having no leg to stand upon, and only one arm to balance with, was in a position of extreme necessity. Of late he had almost begun to repent of serving under Lady Valeria; the beauty and calm resignation of Alice had made their way into his brave old heart; and the more he saw of Captain Chapman the more he looked down on that feather-bed soldier.

"Good-bye, my lad. Keep your pecker up," he said, beginning with his thick bamboo to beat a retreat; for Hilary was not allowed two visitors; "we'll march into Paris yet, brave boys, with Colonel Clumps at the head of the column. Don't be misled by appearances, Alice; the colonel has got good work in him yet. His sword is only gone to be sharpened, ma'am; and then he'll throw away this d—d bamboo."

In his spirited flourish, the colonel slipped, not yet being master of his wooden leg, and down he must have come, without the young lady's arm as well as the aid of the slighted staff. Alice, in spite of all her misery, could not help a little laugh, as the colonel, recovering his balance, strutted carefully down the passage.

"What a merry girl you are!" cried Hilary, who was a little vexed at having his martial council routed. "You seem to me to be always laughing when there is nothing to laugh at."

"That shows a low sense of humor," she answered, "or else an excess of high spirits. Perhaps in my case the two combine. But I am sorry if I disturbed you."

"I am not quite so easily disturbed. I am as well as I ever was. It is enough to make one ill to be coddled up in this kind of way."

"My dear brother, you are to be released as soon as the weather changes. At present nobody ventures out who is not going to be married."

"Of that I can judge from the window, Lallie; and even from my water-jugs. But how is your very grand wedding to be? I have seen a score of men shoveling. You seem to be in such a hurry, dear."

"Perhaps not. Let us talk of something else. Do you really think, without any nonsense, that all your good repute and welfare depend on the payment of the money which you lost?"

"How can you ask me such a stupid question? I never could lift up my head again; but it is not myself, not at all for myself —it is what will be said of the family, Alice. And I do not see how the raising of the money can interfere at all with you."

"No, no, of course not," she said, and then she turned away and looked out of the window, reflecting that Hilary was right enough. Neither loss nor gain of money could long interfere at all with her.

"Good-bye, darling," she said, at last, forgiving his sick petulance, and putting back his curly hair, and kissing his white forehead; "good-bye, darling; I must not stay; I always seem to excite you so. You will not think me unkind, I am sure; but you may not see me again for ever—oh, ever so long; I have so much to do before I am ready for—my wedding."

Hilary allowed himself to be kissed with brotherly resignation; and then he called merrily after her, "Now Lallie, mind, you must look your best. You are going to make a grand match, you know. Don't be astonished if you see me there. Why don't you answer?"

She would not look round, because of the expression of her face, which she could not conceal in a moment. "I am not at all sure," said the brother wisely, as the sister shut the door and fled, "that the man who marries Alice won't almost have caught a Tartar. She is very sweet-tempered; but the good Lord knows that she is determined also. Now Mabel is quite another sort of girl," etc., etc.—reflections which he may be left to reflect.

Alice Lorraine, having none to advise with, and being in her firm heart set to do the right thing without flinching, through dark days and through weary nights had been striving to make sure what was the one right thing to do. It was plain that the honor of her race must be saved at her expense. By reason of things she had no hand in, it had come to pass that her poor self stood in every body's way. Her poor self was full of life, and natural fun, and mind perhaps a little above the average. No other self in the world could find it harder to go out of the world; to be a self no more peradventure, but a wandering something. To lose the sight and touch and feeling of the light and life and love; not to have the influence even of the weather on them; to lie in a hollow place, forgotten, cast aside, and dreaded; never more to have or wish for power to say yes or no.

This was all that lay before her if she acted truly. As to marrying a man she scorned—she must scorn herself ere she thought of it. She knew that she was nothing very great; and her little importance was much pulled down by the want of any one to love her; but her purity was her own inborn right, and nobody should sell or buy it.

"I will go to my father once more," she thought; "he can not refuse to see me. I will not threaten—that would be low. But if he cares at all to look, he will know from my face what I mean to do. He used, if I had the smallest pain, he used to know it in a moment. But now he cares not for a pain that seems to take my life away. Perhaps it is my own fault; perhaps I have been too proud to put it so. I have put it defiantly, and not begged. I will beg, I will beg; on my knees I will beg, I will cry, as I never cried before, oh, father, father, father!"

Perhaps if she had won this chance, she might even yet have vanquished; for her last reflection was true enough. She had been too defiant, and positive in her strength of will toward her father. She had never tried the power of tears and prayers, and a pet child's eloquence. And her father, no doubt, had felt this change in her attitude toward him, and had therefore believed more readily his mother's repeated assertions, that nothing stood in the way of a most desirable arrangement except the coyness of a spirited girl, whose fancy was not taken.

But the luckless girl lost all the chances of a last appeal, through a simple and rather prosaic affair. Her father was not to be found in his book-room; and hurrying on in search of him, she heard the most melancholy drone, almost worse than the sad east wind. Her prophetic soul told her what it was, and that she had a right to be present. So she knocked at the door of a stern, cold room, and being told to enter, entered. There she saw seven people sitting, and looking very miserable; for the bitter cold had not been routed by the new-made fire. One was reading a tremendous document, five were pretending to listen, and one was listening very keenly. The reader was a lawyer's clerk; three of the mock listeners were his principal, and the men of the other side; the other two were Sir Roland Lorraine and Captain Stephen Chapman. The real listener was Sir Remnant, who pricked up his ears at every sentence. Upon the table lay another great deed, or rather a double one, lease and release—the mortgage of all the Lorraine estates, invalid without her signature, which she was too young to give.

Alice Lorraine knew what all this meant. It was the charter of her slavery, or rather the warrant of her death. She bowed to them all, and left the room with "And the said, and the said—doth hereby, doth hereby—" buzzing in her helpless brain.

Now followed a thing which forever settled and sealed her determination. Steenie, on the eve of his wedding-day, really felt that he ought to do something toward conciliating his bride. He really loved (so far as his nature was capable of honest love) this proud and most lovable maiden, who was to belong to him to-morrow. And his father had said to him, as they came over to go through the legal ceremony, "Nurse my vittels, now Steenie, for God's sake, try to be a man a bit. The mistake you make with the girl is the way you keep your distance from her. Why, they draw up their figures, and screw up their mouths, on purpose to make you run after them. I have seen such a lot of it; and so have you. All girls are alike, as you ought to know now. Why can't you treat her properly?"

The unfortunate Steenie took this advice, and he took (which was worse) a great draught of brandy. And so, when the lawyer's drone had driven him thoroughly out of his patience, at the sight of Alice he slipped out and followed her down the passage. She despised him too much to run away, as he had hoped that she would do. She heard his weak step, and weaker breath, and stopped, and faced him quietly.

CHAPTER LXVIII.

STANDING in a dark gray corner of the old stone passage, below a faded and exiled portrait of some ancestor of hers, Alice looked so calm and noble, that Steenie (although he "had his grog on board," with his daily bill of lading) found it harder than he expected to follow his father's counsel. In twenty-four hours he would have this lovely creature at his mercy; and then he would tame her, and make her love him, and perhaps even try to keep to her. For he really did love this poor girl in a way that quite surprised him; and he could not help thinking that if she knew it, by Jove, she must be grateful!

"Alice, dear Alice, sweet Alice!" he said, as at every approach she shrank farther away; "lovely Alice, what have I done, that you will not yield me one beautiful smile? You know how very well I have behaved. I have not even pleaded for one kiss. And considering all that is between us—"

"Considering the distance there is between us, you have shown your judgment."

"You do not understand me at all. What I meant was entirely different. There should be no difference between us. Why should there be? Why should there be? In a few hours more we shall both be alike; flesh of one flesh, and bone of one bone. I am not quite sure that I have got it right. But I am not far out, at any rate."

"Your diffidence is your one good point. You are very far out when you overcome it. Have the kindness to keep at a proper distance, and hear what I have to say. I believe that you mean well, Stephen Chapman; so far as you have any meaning left. I believe that you even mean well by me; and, in your weak manner, like me. But if you had gone all round the world, you could not have found one to suit you less. I used to think that I was humble; as of course I ought to be; but when I search into myself, I find the proudest of the proud. Nothing but great misery could have led me to this knowledge. I speak to you now for the last time, Stephen; and I never meant to speak as I do. But I believe that, in your little way, you like me, and I can not bear to be thought too hard."

Here Alice burst into bitter crying at the thought of the name she might leave behind.

"What shall I do? Whatever can I do?" cried Stephen, not being such a very hard fellow, any more than the rest of us, but feeling himself unworthy even to touch her pocket-handkerchief.

"You have nothing to do, I should hope, indeed," answered Alice, recovering dignity; "I am very glad that, whatever happens, you may blame other people. Please to remember that I said that. And good-bye, Captain Chapman."

"Good-bye, till dinner-time, my darling—well, then, good-bye, Miss Lorraine."

"At any rate I am glad," she thought, as she hastened to her room, "that, even to him, I have said my last as kindly as I could manage it."

When she entered her room, it was three o'clock, and the day already waning; though the snow from hill and valley, and the rime of quiet frost, spread the flat pervading whiteness of the cold and hazy light. Alice looked out, and thought a little; and the scene was by no means cheering. The eastern side of the steep straight coombe (up which clomb the main road to the house) lay thirty or forty feet deep in snow, being filled by the drift that swept over its crest, for nearly the breadth of the coombe itself. But under the western rampart still a dark-brown path was open, where the wind, leaping over the eastern scarp, had whirled the snow up the western. And here, through her own pet garden, fell a direct path down to the Woeburn.

She had long been ready to believe that here her young and lively life must end. Down this steep and narrow way she had gazed, or glanced, or peeped (according to the measure of her courage), ever since the Woeburn rose, and she was sure what it meant for her. Now looking at it, with her mind made up, and her courage steadfast, she could not help perceiving that she had a great deal to be thankful for. Her life had been very bright and happy, and it had been long enough. She had learned to love all pleasant creatures, and to make them love her. She had found out that nature has tenfold more of kindness than of cruelty; and that of her kindness all the best and dearest ends in death. Painless death, the honest and the peaceful end of earthly things; noble death, that settles all things, scarcely leaving other life (its brief exception) time to mourn.

All this lay clear and bright before her, now that the golden mist of hope was scattered by stern certainty. Many times she had been confused by weak desires to escape her duty, and foolish hankerings after things that were but childish trifles. About her bridal dress, for instance, she had been much inclined to think. Of course, she never meant to wear it; still, she knew that the London people meant to charge to a long extreme; and she thought that she ought to try it on once more ere ever it was rashly paid for. She truly cared, no more than can be helped by any woman, whether it set her off or not; but she knew that it must be paid for, and she wanted to know if the Frenchwoman had caught any idea of her figure.

To settle this question, she locked the door, and then very carefully changed her dress. Being the tidiest of the tidy, and as neat as an old maid in her habits, she left not a pin, nor a hair on the cloth, nor even a brush set crooked. Then being in bridal perfection, and as lovely a bride as was ever seen, without one atom of conceit, she knew that she was purely beautiful. She stood before the glass, and sadly gazed at all her beauty. There she saw the large sweet forehead (calm and clear as ever), the deep desire of loving eyes for some one to believe in, the bright lips even now relaxing into a sadly playful smile, the oval symmetry of chastened face, in soft relief against the complex curves and waves of rebellious hair. To any man who could have won her love, what a pet, what a treasure she might have been, what a pearl beyond all price—or, as she simply said to herself, what a dear good wife! It was worse than useless to think of that; but, being of a practical turn of mind, she did not see why she should put on her lovely white satin and let no one see it.

Therefore she rung for her maid, who stared, and cried, "Oh, laws, miss! what a booty you do look!" and then, of course, wanted to put in a pin, and to trim a bow here, and to stroke a plait there. "It is waste of time," said Alice. Then she told her to send Mrs. Pipkins up; and the good housekeeper came and kissed her beautiful pet, as she always called her (maintaining the rights of the nursery days), and then began some of the very poor jokes supposed to suit such occasions.

"Pippy," said Alice, that the old endearment might cure the pain of the sudden check, "you must not talk so; I can not bear it. Now just tell papa, not yet, but when the dinner is going in, give him this message—say with my love that I beg him to excuse me from coming in to dinner, because I have other things to see to. And mind, Pippy, one thing: I have many arrangements to make before I go away; and if my door should be locked to-night nobody is to disturb me. I can trust you to see to that, I know. And now say 'good-bye' to me, Pippy, dear; I may not see you again, you know. Let me kiss you as I used to do, when I was a dear good little child, and used to coax for sugar-plums."

As soon as her kind old friend was gone, Alice made fast her door again, and took off her bridal dress, and put on a plain white frock of small value; and then she knelt down at the side of her bed, and said her usual evening prayers. Although she made no pretense to any vehement power of piety, in the depth of heart and mind she nourished love of God, and faith in him. She believed that he gives us earthly life, to be rendered innocently back to him, not in cowardly escape from trouble, but when honor and love demand it. In the ignorance common to us all she prayed.

Then, when all the house was quiet, except for the sound of plates and dishes (greasily going into deep baskets, one on the head of another), Alice Lorraine, having gathered her long hair into a Laconian knot, put her favorite garden-hat on, and made the tie firm under her firm chin. She looked round her favorite room once more, and nodded farewell to every thing, and went to seek death with a firmer step than a bride's toward a bridegroom.

Attired in pure white she walked through a scene of bridal beauty. Every tree was overcast with crystal lace and jewelry; common bushes and ignominious shrubs stood up like sceptres; weeping branches shone like plumes of ostrich turned to diamond. And on the ground wave after wave of snow-drift, like a stormy tide driven by tempestuous wind, and bound in its cresting wrath by frost.

Although there was now no breath of wind, Alice knew from the glittering whiteness that it must be very cold. She saw her pretty bower like a pillow under bed-clothes; and on the clear brown walk she scattered crumbs for the poor old robin as soon as he should get up in the morning. Then for fear of giving way, she gathered up her dress and ran. She had no overwhelming sense of fate, necessity, or Até—the powers that drove fair maids of Greece to offer themselves for others. She simply desired to do her duty, to save the honor of her race, and her pure self from defilement.

The Woeburn was running as well as ever, quite untouched by any frost, and stretched at its length like a great black leech who puts out his head for suction. Gliding through great piles of snow, it looked sable as Cocytus, with long curls of white vapor hovering where the cold air lay on it. The stars were beginning to sparkle now; and a young moon gazing over Chancton Ring avouched the calm depth of heaven.

Then Alice came forward, commended her soul to God in good Christian manner, and without a fear, or tear, or sigh, committed her body to the Deathbourne.

CHAPTER LXIX.

It seems to be almost a settled point in the affairs of every body (except perhaps Prince Bismarck) that nothing shall come to pass exactly according to arrangement. The best and noblest of mankind can do no more than plan discreetly, firmly act, and humbly wait the pleasure of a just, beneficent, and all-seeing Power.

For instance, Mr. Bottler had designed for at least three weeks to slay a large styful of fat pigs. But from day to day he had been forced to defer the operation. The frost was so intense that this good Azraël of the grunters had no faith in the efficacy of his ministrations. Not indeed as regarded his power to dismiss them to a happier world. In any kind of weather he could stick a pig; the knife they could not very well decline, when skillfully suggested; but they might, and very often did, break all the laws of hospitality, by sternly refusing to accept his salt. And the object of a pig's creation is triple (setting aside his head, and heels, and other small appurtenances)—fresh pork, pickled pork, and bacon; and the greatest of these three is bacon.

Now what was West Lorraine to do, and even the town of Steyning? Cart-loads of mutton came into the market, from the death in the snow of so many sheep; which (as the general public reasoned) must have made the meat beautifully white; and a great many laborers got a good feed, who had almost forgotten the taste of meat; and it did them good and kept them warm. But the "best families" would not have this; they liked their mutton to have "interviewed" the butcher in a constitutional manner; and not being sure how to prove this point, they would not look at any mutton at all, till lamb came out of snow-drift. This being so, what was now to be done? Many people said, "Live on bread, and so on, red herrings, and ship-chandler's stores, and whatever else the Lord may send." Fifty good women came up through the snow to learn the rector's opinion; and all he could say was, "Boil down your bones."

This produced such a desperate run upon the bank of poor Bonny, which really was a bank—of marrow-bones, put by in the summer to season—that Jack was at work almost all the day long, and got thoroughly up to the tricks of the snow, and entirely learned how to tread it. Bonny's poor hands were so chapped by the cold, that he slurred all the polish of the rector's boots; and Mr. Hales said that he had better grease them; which cut the boy deeper than any chap.

Superior people, however, could not think of relying upon Bonny's bones; their money was ready, and they would pay for good meat what it was worth—and no more. Now a thoroughly honest man grows uneasy at the thought of getting more than he ought to get. It is pleasant to cheat the public; but the pleasure soaks down through the conscience, leaving tuberculous affection there, or bacteria; or at any rate some microscopic affliction. Bottler felt all these visitations; and in spite of all demand, he could not bring himself to do any more than treble the price of pig-meat.

"It does weigh so light this weather!

Only take it in your hand," he was bound to tell every body, for their own sakes; "now you might scarcely think it—but what with one thing and another, that pig have cost me two-and-threepence a pound, and I sell him at one-and-ninepence."

"Oh, Mr. Bottler, what a shame of you!"

"True, as you stand there, my dear! You might not believe it, from any one but me; till you marry, and go into business. Ah, and a very bad business it is. Starvation to every body, unless they was bred and born to it; and even then only a crust of bread!" Mr. Church-warden Bottler, however, did not look at all as if he sustained existence on a crust of bread. His stockings, whiter than the snow-drifts round him, showed very substantial bulge of leg; and his blue baize apron did like duty for that part of the human being which is so fatal to the race of pigs. And the soft smile, without which he never spoke, arose and subsided in no gaunt cheeks, and flickered in the channels of no paltry chin. In a word, Mr. Bottler was quite fat enough to kill.

"Polly," he said to his favorite child, as soon as he had finished his Monday dinner, "you have been a good child through this very bad weather; and dad means to give you a rare treat to-night. Not consarning the easing of the pigs," he continued, in answer to her usual nod, and employing his regular euphemism; "there will be a many pigs to be eased, to satisfy the neighborhood, and shut off the rogue to Bramber. But you shall see, Polly; you shall see something as will astonish you."

Bottler put on his brown leather apron, and gently performed his spiriting.

And without any nonsense, Polly saw a lovely scene soon afterward. For her father had made up his mind to do a thing which would greatly exalt his renown, and quench that little rogue at Bramber. In spite of the weather he would kill pigs; and in spite of the weather he would pickle them. He had five nice porkers and four bacon pigs, as ready as pigs can be for killing. They seemed to him daily to reproach him for their unduly prolonged existence. They could not lay on any fat in this weather, but relapsed for want of carving.

For Bottler in the morning had done this—which could not have occurred to any but a very superior mind. In his new premises facing the lane, a short way below Nanny Stillgoe's cottage, he had a little yard, well away from all thatch, and abutting on nothing but his scalding-house. This yard was square, and inclosed by a wall of the chalky flints that break so black, and bind so well into mortar.

Of course the whole place was still snowed up; but Master Bottler soon cured that. He went to the parish school, which was to have opened after the Christmas holidays on this 10th of January; but the school-master vowed that, in such weather, he would warm no boy's educational part, unless the parish first warmed his own. And the parish replied that he might do that for himself; not a knob of coal should he have; it was quite beginning at the wrong end to warm him first. His answer was to bolt the school-door, and sit down with a pipe and a little kettle.

The circumspect church-warden had anticipated this state of siege; for he knew that every boy in the parish (who would have run like the devil if the door was open) knowing the door to be bolted would spend the whole day in kicking at it. And here he found them, Bonny at the head, as a boy of rising intellect, and Captain Dick of the Bible corps, and the boy who had been shot in the hedge, and many other less distinguished boys, furiously raging together because robbed of their right to a flogging.

"Come along, my lads," said Bottler, knowing how to manage boys; "you may kick all day, and wear out your shoes. I've got a job for fifty of you, and a penny a piece for all as works well."

Not to be too long, these boys all followed Church-warden Bottler; and he led them to his little yard, and there he fitted every one of them up with something or other to work with. Some had brooms and some had shovels, some had spades and some had mops, one or two worked with old frying-pans, and Bonny had a worn-out warming-pan. All the boys who had got into breeches were to have twopence apiece; and the rest, who were still stitched up at the middle, might earn a penny a head if they worked hard.

Not one of them shirked his work. They worked as boys alone ever do work, throwing all their activity into it. And taking the big with the little ones, it cost Mr. Bottler four shillings and fourpence to get some hundred cubic yards of snow cleared out so thoroughly that if a boy wanted to pelt a boy, he must go outside for his snowball. Mr. Bottler smiled calmly as he paid them; well he knew what an area of hunger he was spreading for his good pork, by means of this army of work-boys. Then he showed the boys the pigs still living, and patted their shoulders, and smacked his lips with a relish that found an echo at more than forty hearths that evening. "Ah, won't they come up rare?" he said; "ay, and go down rarer still," replied Bonny, already beginning to stand in high esteem for jocosity, which he did his very best to earn.

All boys other than Bonny departed with lips overflowing with love of pork into little icicles. Then Mr. Bottler went to his cart-shed, and came back with his largest tarpaulin. He spread and fixed this in a clever manner over the middle of his little yard, leaving about ten feet clear all round between the edge of it and the wall. This being done, he invited Bonny to dinner, and enjoyed his converse, and afterward pledged himself to Polly, as heretofore recorded. Later in the day many squeaks were heard; while Bonny worked hard at the furze-rick.

All things are judged always by their results. Be it enough, then, to chronicle these. West Lorraine, Wiston, and Steyning itself pronounced with one voice on the following day that a thing had been done on the bank of the Woeburn that verily vanquished the Woeburn itself. As Hercules conquered the Acheloüs, and the great Pelides hacked up by the roots both Simois and Scamander, so Bottler (a greater hero than even Nestor himself could call to mind, to snub inferior pig-stickers)—Bottler aroused his valor, and scotched and slew that Python—the Woeburn.

It is not enough to speak of such doings in this casual sort of way. Bottler's deeds are now passing into the era of romance, which always precedes the age of history. Out of romance they all emerge with a tail of attestation; and if any body lays hold of this, and clearly sees what to do with it, his story becomes history, and himself a great historian. But lo! here are the data for any historian of duly combative enthusiasm to work out what Bottler did.

He let Bonny work—as all heroes permit—a great deal harder than he worked himself. He calmly looked on, and smoked his pipe; and knowing quite well how the pigs would act (according to bulk and constitution) in the question of cooling down, he kept his father's watch in hand, and at proper periods eased them. Meanwhile Bonny labored for his life, and by the time all the pigs were ready for posthumous toilet, their dressing-room was warm and waiting for them. A porker may come home to his positive degree—pork—in less than no time; but the value of his dedication of himself—in the manner of a young curate—to the service of humanity, depends very much upon how he is treated.

The pork-trade at this time of writing is so active, that every body—however small his operations are—should strive to give it a wholesome check rather than further impetus. And for that reason the doings of Bottler—fully as they deserve description—shall not have a bit of it.

CHAPTER LXX.

AGAIN, another thing will show how heavily and wearily all people that on earth do dwell plod and plod their little way, and are but where they came from. Three young people, all well wrapped up, and ready to face any thing, set out from Old Applewood Farm on the very day next after Twelfth-day. They meant with one accord to be at Coombe Lorraine by the Saturday night, all being summoned upon church-service. There was not one of them that could be dispensed with—according to the last advices—and they felt their extreme responsibility when the grower locked them out of the great white gate.

"Now don't make fools of yourselves," he shouted; "you won't be there quite so soon as you think." They laughed him to scorn; but even before they got to Tonbridge a snow-storm came behind them, and quite smothered all their shoulders up, and grizzled the roots of the whiskers of the only one who had any. This was Counselor Gregory, and the other two laughed at him, and vowed that his wig must have slipped down there, and then flicked him with pocket-handkerchiefs.

Counselor Gregory took no heed. He was wonderfully staid and sapient now; and the day when he had played at darts—if cross-examination could have fetched it up—would have been to his expanded mind a painful remembrance of All-fools' Day. He stuck to his circuit, and cultivated the art of circuitous language. And being a sound and diligent lawyer, of good face and temper, he was able already to pay a clerk, who carried his bag and cleaned his boots.

But any client who had seen him now driving two spirited horses actually in tandem process, and sitting as if he were on the King's Bench, would have met him at the gate with a *quo warranto* if not a *quousque tandem?* He was well aware of this; his conscience told him that a firm of attorneys abode in the chief street of Tonbridge, and in spite of the snow either partner or clerk would almost be sure to be out at the door. He would not have been the grower's son if he had tried to circumvent them; so he drove by their door, and the senior partner took off his hat to Mabel, and said that Gregory was a most rising young man.

Mabel sat in the middle, of course, with a brother on either side to break the cold wind, and keep off the snow. She laughed at the weather at first; but soon the weather had the laugh of her. According to their own ideas, they were to put up for the night at the fine old inn at Horsham, and make their way thence to Coombe Lorraine in time for dinner on the Saturday. For Mabel, of course, was to be a brides-maid—the rector's three daughters and the colonel's two completing the necessary six. But it soon became clear that the grower knew more about roads and weather than the counselor and the sailor did. By the time these eager travelers passed Penshurst and the home of the Sidneys, the road was some eight or nine inches deep with soft new-fallen snow. They had wisely set forth with a two-wheeled carriage, strong and not easily knocked out of gear—no other, in fact, than the old yellow gig disdained by Mrs. Lovejoy. For the look of it they cared not one jot; any thing was good enough for such weather; and a couple of handsome and powerful horses would carry off a great deal worse than that, even if they had thought of it. But they never gave one thought to the matter. Except that the counselor was a little tamed by "the law and its ramifications," they all took after their father about the *esse* vs. the *videri*. Nevertheless, they all got snowed up for the Friday night at East Grinstead, instead of getting on to Horsham.

For the farther they got away from home the more they managed to lose their way. The hedges and the ditches were all as one, the guide-posts were buried long ago; instead of the proper finger and thumb, great fists and bellies of drift now and then stuck out to stop the traveler. "No thoroughfare here" in great letters of ivy—the ivy that hangs in such deep relief, as if itself relieved by snow—and "Trespassers beware" from an alder, perhaps overhanging a swamp, where, if the snow-crust were once cut through, a poor man could only toss up his arms, and go down and be no more heard of.

And now that another heavy storm was at it (black behind them, and white in front), the horses asked for nothing better than to be left to find their way. They threw up their forelocks, and jerked their noses, and rattled their rings, and expressed their ribs, and fingered away at the snow with their feet; meaning that their own heads were the best, if they could only have them. So the counselor let them have their heads, for the evening dusk was gathering; and the leader turned round to the wheeler, and they had many words about it. And then they struck off at a merry trot, having both been down that road before, and supped well at the end of it. Foreseeing the like delight, with this keen weather to enhance it, they put their feet out at a tidy stretch, scuffling one another's snowballs; and by the time of candle-lighting, landed their three inferior bipeds at the "Green Man," at East Grinstead.

On the following day they were still worse off, for although it did not snow again, they got into an unknown country without any landmarks; and the cold growing more and more severe, they resolved to follow the Brighton road, if ever they should find it. But the Brighton coaches were taken off, and the road so entirely stopped that they must have crossed without perceiving it. And both the nags growing very tired, and their own eyes dazed with so much white, they had made up their minds to build themselves a snow-house like the Esquimaux, when the sailor spied something in the distance, tall and white against the setting sun, which proved to be Horsham spire. With difficulty they reached the town by starlight, and all pretty well frost-bitten; and there they were obliged to spend the Sunday, not only for their horses' sakes, but equally for their own poor selves.

To finish a bitter and tedious journey, they started from Horsham on the Monday morning, as soon as the frozen-out sun appeared; and although the traveling was wonderfully bad, they fetched to West Grinstead by twelve o'clock, and found good provender for man and beast. After an hour's halt, and a peck of beans to keep the cold out of the horses' stomachs, and a glass of cherry-brandy to do the like for their own, and a visit to the blacksmith (to fetch up the cogs of the shoes, and repair the springs), all set off again in the best of spirits, and vowing never to be beaten. But, labor as they might, the sun had set ere they got to Steyning; and under the slide of the hills, of course, they found the drift grow deeper; so that by the time they were come to the long loose street of West Lorraine, almost every soul therein, having regard to the weather, was tucked up snugly under the counterpane. With the weary leader stooping chin to knee to rub off icicles, and the powerful wheeler tramping sedately with his withers down and his crupper up, these three bold travelers, Gregory, Mabel, and Charles Lovejoy, sitting abreast in the yellow gig, passed silently through the deep silence of snow; and not even a boy beheld them, until they came to a place where red light streamed from an opening upon the lane, and cast on the snow the shadow of a tall man leaning on a gate. Inside the gate was a square of bright embers, and a man in white stockings uncommonly busy.

"Oh, Gregory, stop for a moment," cried Mabel; "how beautifully warm it looks! Oh, how I wish I was a pig!"

They drew up in the ruddy light, and turned their frosted faces, frozen cloaks, and numb hands toward it. And the leader turned round on his traces and cheered up his poor nose with gazing; for warmth, as well as light, came forth in clouds upon the shivering air.

"What a wonderful man!" exclaimed Mabel again. "We have nobody like him in all our parish. He looks very good-natured. Oh, do let us go in and warm ourselves."

"And get our noses frozen off directly we came out. No, thank you," said Gregory, "we will drive on. Get up, Spangler, will you, then?"

He flipped the leader with his frozen lash, and the tall man leaning upon the gate (as if he were short of employment) turned round and looked at them, and bade the busy man a very good evening, and came out into the snow, as if he were glad of any wheel-track. At the turn of the lane they lost sight of him, slowly as they plowed their way, and in another minute a very extraordinary thing befell them.

"Hark!" cried Mabel, as they came to a bank, where once the road might have gone straight on, but now turned sharply to the right, being broken by a broad black water. "I am quite sure I heard something."

"The frost is singing in your ears," said Charlie; "that is what it always does at sea. Or a blessed cold owl is hooting. Greg, what do you say?"

"I will offer my opinion," replied the counselor, "when I have sufficient data."

"And when you get your fee indorsed. There it is again! Now did you hear it?" And she stood up between her two brothers, and stayed herself, in the mighty jerks of road, with a hand on the shoulder of each of them. They listened, and doubted her keener ears, and gave her a pull to come back again. "What a child it is!" said the counselor; "she always loses her wits when she gets within miles of that blessed Hilary."

"Is that all you know about it—now, after all the mischief you have made! You have done your worst to part us."

Though still quite a junior counsel, Gregory had been long enough called to the Bar to understand that women must not be cited to the bar of reason. Their opinions deserve the most perfect respect, because they are inspired; and no good woman ever changes them.

At any rate, Mabel was right this time. Before they could say a word, or look round, they not only heard but saw a boy riding and raving furiously, on the other side of the water. He was coming down the course of the stream toward them as fast as his donkey could flounder, and slide, and tear along over the snow-drifts. And at the top of his voice he was shouting,

"A swan, a swan, a girt white swan! The bootiful leddy have turned into a girt swan! Oh, I never!"

"Are you mad, you young fool? Just get back from the water!" cried Gregory Lovejoy, sternly; for as Bonny pulled up, the horses, weary as they were, jumped round in affright at Jack's white nose and great ears jerking in a shady place. "Get back from the water, or we shall all be in it!" For the wheeler having caught the leader's scare, was backing right into the Woeburn, and Mabel could not help a little scream; till the sailor sprang cleverly over the wheel, and seized the shaft-horse by the head.

"There she cometh! there she cometh!" shouted Bonny all the while; "oh, whatever shall I do?"

"I see it! I see it!" cried Mabel, leaning over the rail of the gig, and gazing up the dark stream steadfastly; "oh, what can it be? It is all white. And it hangs upon the water so. It must be some one floating drowned!"

Charlie, the sailor, without a word, ran to a bulge of the bank, as he saw the white thing coming nearer, looked at it for an instant with all his eyes, then flung off his coat and plunged into the water, as if for a little pleasant swim. He had no idea of the power of the current; but if he had known all about it, he would have gone headforemost all the same. For he saw in mid-channel the form of a woman, helpless, senseless, at the mercy of the water; and that was quite enough for him.

From his childhood up he had been a swimmer, and was quite at his ease in rough water, and therefore despised this sliding smoothness. But before he had taken three strokes he felt that he had mistaken his enemy. Instead of swimming up the stream (which looked very easy to do from the bank), he could not even hold his own with arms and legs against it, but was quietly washed down by the force bearing into the cups of his shoulders. But, in spite of the volume of torrent, he felt as comfortable as could be; for the water was by some twenty degrees warmer than the frosty air.

"Cut the traces!" he managed to shout, as his brother and sister hung over the bank.

"What does he mean?" asked Gregory.

"Take my little knife," said Mabel; "it cuts like a razor; but my hands shake."

"I see, I see," nodded the counselor, and he cut the long traces of the leader, and knotted them together. Meanwhile Charlie let both feet sink, and stood edgewise in the rapid current, treading water quietly. Of course he was carried down stream as he did it; but slowly (compared with a floating body). And he found that the movement was much less rapid at three or four feet from the surface. Before he had time to think of this, or fairly fetch his balance, the white thing he was waiting for came gliding in the blackness toward him. He flung out his arms at once, and cast his feet back, and made toward it. In the gliding hurry, and the flit of light, it passed him so far that he said "Good-bye," and then (perhaps from the attraction of bodies) it seemed for a second to stop, and the hand he cast forth laid hold of something. His own head went under water, and he swallowed a good mouthful; but he stuck to what he had got hold of, as behooves an Englishman. Then he heard great shouting upon dry land, and it made him hold the tighter. "Bravo, my noble fellow!" He heard; he was getting a little tired; but encouragement is every thing. "Catch it! catch it! lay hold! lay hold!" he heard in several voices, and he saw the splash of the traces thrown, but had no chance to lay hold of them. The power of the black stream swept him on, and he vainly strove for either bank, unless he would let loose his grasp, and he would rather drown with it than do that.

Now who saved him and his precious salvage? A poor, despised, and yet clever boy, whose only name was Bonny. When Gregory Lovejoy had lashed the Woeburn with his traces vainly, and Mabel had fixed her shawl to the end of them, and the tall man who followed the gig had dropped into the water quietly, and Bottler (disturbed by the shouting) had left his pigs and shone conspicuous—not one of them could have done a bit of good, if it had not been for Bonny. From no great valor on the part of the boy, but from a quick-witted suggestion.

His suggestion had to cross the water, as many good suggestions have to do; and but for Bottler's knowledge of his voice, nobody would have noticed it.

"Ye'll nab 'em down to bridge," he cried; "hurn down to bridge, and ye'll nab 'em. Tell un not to faight so."

"Let yoursen go with the strame," shouted Bottler to the gallant Charlie: "no use faighting for the bank. There's a tree as crosseth down below; and us'll pull 'ee both out, when 'a gets there."

Charlie had his head well up, and saw the wisdom of this counsel. He knew by long battle that he could do nothing against the tenor of the Woeburn, and the man who had leaped in to help him, brave and strong as he was, could only follow as the water listed. The water went at one set pace, and swimmers only floated. And now it was a breathless race for the people on the dry land to gain the long tree that spanned the Woeburn, ere its victims were carried under. And but for sailor Lovejoy's skill, and presence of mind, in seeking downward, and paddling more than swimming, the swift stream would have been first at the bridge; and then no other chance for them.

As it was, the runners were just in time, with scarcely a second to spare for it. Three men knelt on the trunk of the tree, while Mabel knelt in the snow and prayed. The merciless stream was a fathom below them; But they hung the staunch traces in two broad loops, made good at each end in a fork of bough, and they showed him where they were by flipping the surface of the water.

Clinging to his helpless burden still, and doing his best to support it, the young sailor managed to grasp the leather; but his strength was spent and he could not rise, and all things swam around him; the snowy banks, the eager faces, the white form he held, and the swift black current—all like a vision swept through his brain, and might sweep on forever. His wits were gone, and he must have followed, and been swept away to another world, if a powerful swimmer had not dashed up in full command of all faculties. The tall man, whom nobody had heeded in the rush and hurry, came down the black gorge with his head well up, and the speed and strength of an osprey. He seized the broad traces with such a grasp that the timber above them trembled, and he bore himself up with his chest to the stream, and tearing off his neck-cloth, fastened first the drowned white figure, and then poor Charlie, to the loop of the strap, and saw them drawn up together; then gathering all his remaining powers, he struck for the bank, and gained it.

"Hurra!" shouted Bottler; and every one present, Mabel included, joined the shout.

"Be quick! be quick! It is no time for words," cried the tall man, shaking his dress on the snow; "let me have the lady; you bring the fine fellow as quickly as possible to Bottler's yard. Bottler, just show us the shortest way."

"To be sure, sir," Mr. Bottler answered; "but, major, you can not carry her, and the drops are freezing on you."

"Do as I told you. Run in front of me; and just show the shortest road."

"Dash my stockings!" cried Master Bottler, "they won't be worth looking at tomorrow. And all through the snow, I've a kept un white. And I an't got any more clean ones."

However, he took a short cut to his yard; while Aylmer, with the lady in his arms, and her head hanging over his shoulder, followed so fast, that the good pig-sticker could scarcely keep in front of him. "Never mind me," cried brave Charlie, reviving; "I am as right as ever. Mabel, go on and help; though I fear it is too late to do any good."

"Whoever it is, it is dead as a stone," said the counselor, wiping the wet from his sleeves; "it fell away from me like an empty bag; you might have spared your ducking, Charlie. But it must have been a lovely young woman."

"Dead or alive, I have done my duty. But don't you know who it is? Oh, Mabel!"

"How could I see her face?" said Mabel; "the men would not let me touch her. And about here I know no one."

"Yes, you do. You know Alice Lorraine. It is poor Sir Roland's daughter."

CHAPTER LXXI.

While these things were going on down in the valley, a nice little argument was raging in the dining-room of the old house on the hill. By reason of the bitter weather, Mr. Binns and John Trotman had brought in two large three-winged screens of ancient poikolo-dædal canvas. Upon them was depicted every bird that flies, and fish that swims, and beast that walks on the face of the earth, besides many that never did any thing of that sort. And betwixt them and a roaring fire sat six good gentlemen, taking their wine in the noble manner of the period.

Under the wings of one great screen Sir Roland Lorraine, and Colonel Clumps, and Parson Hales were sitting. In the other, encamped Sir Remnant Chapman, Stephen his son, and Mr. John Ducksbill, a fundamentally trusty solicitor, to see to the deeds in the morning.

The state of the weather brought about all this. It would have been better for the bridegroom to come with a dash of horses in the morning, stir up the church, and the law, and the people, and scatter a pound's worth of halfpence. But after so long an experience of the cold white mood of the weather, common sense told every body that if a thing was to be done at all, all who were to do it must be kept pretty well together.

But, alas! even when the weather makes every body cry "alas!" it is worse than the battles of the wind and snow, for six male members of the human race to look at one another with the fire in their front, and the deuce of a cold draught in their backs, and wine without stint at their elbows, and dwell wholly together in harmony. And the most exciting of all subjects unluckily had been started—or rather might be said "inevitably." Six gentlemen could not in any reason be hoped to sit over their wine, without getting into the subject of the ladies.

This is a thing to be always treated with a deep reserve and confidential hint of something that must not go beyond a hint. Every man thinks, with his glass in his hand, that he knows a vast deal more about women than any woman's son before him. Opinions at once begin to clash. Every man speaks from his own experience; which, upon so grand a matter, is as the claw of a lobster grasping at a whale—the largest of the mammals.

"Rector, I tell you," repeated Sir Remnant, with an angry ring of his wine-glass, "that you know less than nothing about it, sir. All the more to your credit, of course, of course. A parson must stick to his cloth and his gown, and keep himself clear of the petticoats."

"But, my dear sir, my own three daughters—"

"You may have got thirty daughters, without knowing any thing at all about them."

"But, my good sir, my wife, at least—come now, is that no experience?"

"You may have got sixty wives, sir, and be as much in the dark as ever. Ducksbill, you know; come now, Ducksbill, give us your experience."

"Sir Remnant, I am inclined to think that, upon the whole, your view of the question is the one that would be sustained. Though the subject has so many ramifications, that possibly his Reverence—"

"Knows nothing at all about it. Gadzooks, sir, less than nothing. I tell you they have no will of their own, any more than they have any judgment. A man with a hap'orth of brains may do exactly what he likes with them. Colonel, you know it; come, colonel, now, after all your battles—"

"My battles were not fought among the women," said Colonel Clumps, most dryly.

"Hear, hear!" cried the rector, smacking his fat leg, in the joy of a new alliance.

"Very well, sir," said Sir Remnant, with his wrath diverted from the parson to the soldier; "you mean, I suppose, that my battles have been fought among the women only?"

"I said nothing of the sort. I know nothing of your battles. You alluded to mine, and I spoke my mind." Colonel Clumps had been vexed by Sir Remnant's words. He had long had a brother officer's widow in his mind; and ever since he had been under-fitted with a piece of box-wood, his feelings were hurt whenever women were run down in his presence.

"Chapman, I think," said Sir Roland Lorraine, to assuage the rising storm, "that we might as well leave these little points (which have been in debate for some centuries) for future centuries to settle at their perfect leisure. Mr. Ducksbill, the wine is with you. Struan, you are not getting on at all. My son has been in Portugal, and he says that these olives are the right ones."

All the other gentlemen took the hint, and dropped the pugnacious subject; but Sir Remnant was such a tough old tyrant that there was no diverting him. He took a mighty pinch of snuff, rapped the corner of his box, and began again.

"Why, look you, Lorraine, at that girl of yours, as nice a girl as ever lived, and well brought up by her grandmother. A clever girl too—I'll be dashed if she isn't. She has said many things that have made me laugh; and it takes a good joke to do that, I can tell you. But no will of her own—no judgment—no what I may call decision."

"I am sorry to hear it," said Sir Roland, dryly; "I thought that my daughter had plenty of all those."

"Of course you did. All men think that until they find their mistake out. Nurse my vittels if there is any one thing a woman should know her own mind about, it would be her own marriage. But gadzooks, gentlemen, Miss Lorraine over and over again declared that she would not have our Steenie; and to-morrow morning she will have him, as merry as a grig, sir!"

"Now, father," began Captain Chapman; but as he spoke the screens were parted; and Trotman stood there, in all the importance of a great news-bearer.

"What do you mean, sir?" cried Colonel Clumps, whose sedentary arrangements were suddenly disturbed; "by Gad, sir, if I only had my bamboo!"

"If you plaize, sir," said Trotman, looking only at his master; "there be very bad news indeed. Miss Halice have a-drownded herself in the Woeburn; and her corpse be at Bottler the pigman's, dead."

"Good God!" cried the rector; and the men either started to their feet, or fell back on their chairs, according to their constitutions. Sir Roland alone sat as firm as a rock.

"Upon what authority, au-thor-i-ty—" Sir Roland neither finished that sentence, nor began another. His face became livid; his under-jaw fell; he rolled on his side, and lay there. As if by a hand direct from heaven, he was struck with palsy.

CHAPTER LXXII.

As soon as the master of the house had been taken to his bedroom, and a groom sent off at full gallop for the nearest doctor, Mr. Hales went up to Stephen Chapman, who was crying in a corner, and hauled him forth, and took his hand, and patted him on the shoulder. "Come, my good fellow," he said, "you must not allow yourself to be so overcome; the thing may be greatly exaggerated; every thing always is, you know. I never believe more than half of a story; and I generally find that twice too much."

"Oh, but I did so love—love—love her. It does seem too hard upon me. Oh, parson, I feel as if I should die almost. When the doctor comes, let him see me first. He can not do any good to Sir Roland; and Sir Roland is old, and he has always been good; but I have been a very bad man always—"

"Bad or good, be a man of some sort—not a whining baby," said the rector. "Put on your hat, and come out with me, if you have got a bit of pluck in you. I am going down to see my poor niece, at once."

"Oh, I could not do it! I could never do it! How can you ask me to do such a thing? And in such weather as this is!"

"Very well," Mr. Hales replied, buttoning up the collar of his coat; "I have no son, Stephen Chapman; and I am in holy orders, and therefore canonically debarred from the use of unclerical language; but if I had a son like you, dash me if I would not kick him from my house-door to my mixen!" Having thus relieved his mind, the rector went to the main front passage, and chose for himself a most strenuous staff, and then he pulled the wire of the front-door bell, that the door might be fastened behind him. And before any of the scared servants came up, he thought of something. "Who is it? oh, Mrs. Merryjack; is it?"

"Yes, sir; please, sir, the men are all away, and the house-maid's too frightened to come up the stairs."

"You are a good woman. Where is Mrs. Pipkins?"

"She hath fetched up her great jar of leeches, sir; and she is trying them with poor master. Lord bless you, you might every bit as well put horse-radish on him!"

"And better, Merryjack—better, I believe. Now you are a sensible and clever woman."

"No, sir. Oh, Lord, sir, I was never told that! though some folk may a' said so."

"They were right, every time they said it, ma'am. And no one has said it more often than I have. Now, Mrs. Merryjack—"

"Yes, sir; yes, sir. Any thing you tells me, sir."

"It is only this; I am going, as fast as I can, to Church-warden Bottler's. I shall take the short cut, and cross the water. You can not do that; it would not be safe for a woman, in the dark, to attempt it. But just do this: order the light close carriage as soon as possible. The horses are roughed, to go to church to-morrow. Get inside it, with your warmest cloak on, and blankets, and shawls, and any thing else you can think of, and tell the man to drive for his life to Bottler's. Women will be wanted there, for one thing or the other."

"Yes, sir; to be sure, sir. We are always wanted. Oh's me, the poor, young dear!"

The rector set off by a path to the right, passing eastward of the coombe, and leading, as well as might be, to the tree that crossed the water. It was a rough and dreary road; and none but a veteran sportsman could, in that state of the weather, have followed it. But Mr. Hales knew every yard of the hill, and when he could trust the drift, and where it would have been death to venture. And though the moon had set long ere this, the sky was bright, and the sparkle of the stars was spread, as in a concave mirror, by the radiance of the snow.

At Bottler's gate Mr. Hales was rudely repulsed, until they looked at him. Gregory and Bonny were on guard, with a great tarpaulin behind them; each of them having a broom in hand, ready to be thrust into any body's face. A great glow of light was in the air, and by it their eyes shone—whether it were with ferocity, or whether it were with tenderness.

"I am her own uncle—I must go in. I stand in the place of her father."

Bonny, of course, knew his master, and opened the paling-gate to let him in. And there Mr. Hales beheld a thing such as he never had seen before. Every sign of the singeing or dressing of pigs had been done away with. The embers of fuel, all round the gray walls, had given their warmth, and lay quivering. The gray flints, bedded in lime behind them, were of a dull and sulky red; the ground all over the court-yard steamed, as the blow of the frost rose out of it, and the cover spread overhead reflected genial warmth and comfort.

Near the middle of the yard, on a mattress, lay the form of poor Alice, infolded in warm blankets, and Mrs. Bottler's best counterpane. That kind and good woman, with Mabel's help, had removed the wet and freezing clothes, when Major Aylmer had laid his burden in Mrs. Bottler's parlor. The only hope that the fleeting spirit might remain, or return, was to be found in warmth, or rather strong heat, applied at once; and therefore (with the major's advice and aid) clever use had been made of Mr. Bottler's great preparations. It is needless to say that the pigman (who had now galloped off to Steyning for a doctor) would, if left to himself, have settled matters very speedily, by hanging the poor girl up head downward, to drain off the water she had swallowed. But now, under Major Aylmer's care, every thing had been done as well as a doctor could have managed it. The body was laid with the head well up, and partly inclined on the right side, so that the feeble flutter of the heart—if any should arise—might not be hindered. The slender feet, so white and beautifully arched, were laid on a brown stone jar of hot water; and the little helpless palms were chafed by the rough hands of Mrs. Bottler. Mabel also spread light friction, with a quick and glancing touch, over the cold heart, frozen breast, and chill relapse of every thing. And from time to time she endeavored to inspire the gentle rise and fall of breath.

The major came forward and took the hand of his friend, the rector, silently. "Is there any hope?" whispered Mr. Hales.

"Less and less. It is now two hours since we began trying to restore her. I was nearly drowned myself, some years ago, and lay for an hour insensible. Every minute that passes now lessens the chance. But this young lady is wonderfully clever."

"I only do what you tell me," said Mabel, looking up, without leaving off her persevering efforts.

"Flying in the face of the Almighty, I call it," cried Mrs. Bottler, who was very tired, and ought to have had equal share of the praise. "Poor dear! we had better let her bide till the doctor cometh, or the crowner."

"Not till a doctor declares her dead," said Major Aylmer, quietly; "I am delighted that you are come, Mr. Hales. You are a great re-enforcement. I have longed to try my own hand, but—but you can; you are her uncle. Perhaps you have not seen a case like this. Will you act under my directions?"

"With all my heart," replied the rector, pulling off his coat, and pitching it down anywhere. "Oh my dear, my pretty dear, I do believe you will know my touch. Go out of the way, Mrs. Bottler, now—go and make some soup, ma'am. Mabel and I, Mabel and I, when we get together, I do believe we could make a flock of sheep out of a row of flints. Now, sir, what am I to do?"

Whatever he was told, he did with such a will, that presently Mabel looked up, and exclaimed with breathless delight, "Oh, I feel a little throb—I did feel a little flutter of the heart—I am almost sure I did."

"My dear girl, rub away," answered the rector; "that is right, major, is not it?"

"I believe so. Now is the critical time. A relapse—and all is over."

"There shall be no relapse," cried the rector, working away with his shirt-sleeves up, and his ruddy face glowing in the fire-light; "please God, there shall be no relapse; the bravest and the noblest maid in the world shall not go out of it. Do you know me, my darling? You ought to know your kind uncle Struan."

Purely white, and beautiful as a piece of the noblest sculpture, Alice lay before them. Her bashful virgin beauty was (even in the shade of death) respected with pure reverence. The light of the embers (which alone could save her mouldering ash of life) showed the perfect outline, and the absence of the living gift, which makes it more than outline. Mabel's face, intense with vital energy and quick resolve, shone and glowed in contrast with the apathy and dull whiteness over which she bent so eagerly. Now, even while she gazed, the dim absorption of white cheeks and forehead slowly passed and changed its dullness (like a hydrophane immersed) into glancing and reflecting play of tender light and life. Rigid lines, set lineaments, fixed curves, and stubborn vacancy, began to yield a little and a little, and then more and more, to the soft return of life, and the sense of being alive again.

There is no power of describing it. Those who have been through it can not tell what happened to them. Only this we know, that we were dead and now we live again. And by the law of nature (which we under-crept so narrowly) we are driven to the opposite extreme of violent vitality.

Softly as an opening flower, and with no more knowledge of the windy world around us, eyelids, fair as Cytherea's, raised their fringe, and fell again. Then a long deep sigh of anguish (quite uncertain where it was, but resolved to have utterance) arose from rich pure depth of breast, and left the kind heart lighter.

"Darling," cried Mabel; "do you know me? Open your eyes again, and tell me."

Alice opened her eyes again; but she could not manage to say any thing. And she did not seem to know any one. Then the doctor pulled up at the paling-gate, skipped in, felt pulse, or felt for it, and forthwith ordered stimulants.

"Put her to bed in a very warm room. The carriage is here with the blankets. But on no account must she go home. Mrs. Bottler will give up her best room. Let Mrs. Merryjack sit up all night. She is a cook, she can keep a good fire up. Let her try to roast her young mistress. Only keep the air well moving. I see that you have a first-rate nurse—this pretty young lady—excuse me, ma'am. Well, I shall be back in a couple of hours. I have a worse case to see to."

He meant Sir Roland; but would not tell them. He had met the groom from Coombe Lorraine; and he knew how the power of life has dropped from a score of years to three-score.

CHAPTER LXXIII.

In this present state of things, and difficulty everywhere, the one thing most difficult of all is to imagine greater goodness than that of Mr. Bottler. He had a depression that could not be covered by a five-pound note to begin with, in the value of the pig-meat he was dressing scientifically, when he had to turn it all out to be frozen, and take in poor Alice to thaw instead. Of that he thought nothing, less than nothing—he said so; and he tried to feel it. But take it as you will, it is something. A man's family may be getting lighter, as they begin to maintain themselves; but the man himself wants more maintenance, after all his exertions with them; and the wife of his old bosom lacks more nourishment than the bride of his young one. More money goes out, as more money comes in.

And not only that, but professional pride grows stronger as a man grows older and more thoroughly up to his business, especially if a lot of junior fellows, like the man at Bramber, rush in, and invent new things, and boast of work that we know to be clumsy. If any man in England was proud of the manner in which he turned out his pork, that man was Church-warden Bottler. Yet disappointment combined with loss could not quench his accustomed smile, or plow one wrinkle in his snowy hose, as he quitted his cart on the following morning, and made his best duty and bow to Alice.

Alice, still looking very pale and frail, was lying on the couch in the pigman's drawing-room; while Mabel, who had been with her all the night, sat on a chair by her pillow. Alice had spoken, with tears in her eyes, of the wonderful kindness of every one. Her mind was in utter confusion yet as to any thing that had befallen her; except that she had some sense of having done some desperate deed, which had caused more trouble than she was worthy of. Her pride and courage were far away. Her spirit had been so near the higher realms where human flesh is not, that it was delighted to get back, and substantially ashamed of itself.

"What will my dear father say? And what will other people think? I seem to have considered nothing; and I can consider nothing now."

"Darling, don't try to consider," Mabel answered softly; "you have considered far too much; and what good ever comes of it?"

"None," she answered; "less than none. Consider the lilies that consider not. Oh, my head is going round again."

It was the roundness of her head which had saved her life in the long dark water. Any long head must have fallen back and yielded up the ghost; but her purely spherical head, with the garden hat fixed tightly round it, floated well on a rapid stream, with air and natural hair resisting any water-logging. And thus the Woeburn had borne her for a mile, and vainly endeavored to drown her.

"Oh, why does not my father come?" she cried, as soon as she could clear her mind; "he always used to come at once, and be in such a hurry, even if I got the nettle-rash. He must have made his mind up now to care no more about me. And when he has once made up his mind, he is stern—stern—stern. He never will forgive me. My own father will despise me. Where now, where is somebody?"

"You are getting to be foolish again," said Mabel, much as it grieved her to speak thus; "your father can not come at the very first moment you call for him. He is full of lawyers' business, and allowances must be made for him. Now you are so clever, and you have inherited from the Normans such a quick perception. Take this thing; and tell me, Alice, what it can be meant for."

From the place of honor in the middle of the mantel-piece, Mabel Lovejoy took down a tool which had been dwelling on her active mind ever since the night before. She understood taps, she had knowledge of cogs, she could enter into intricate wards of keys, and was fond of letter-padlocks; but now she had something which combined them all; and she could not make head or tail of it.

"I thought that I knew every metal that grows," she said, as Alice opened her languid hand for such a trifle; "I always do our forks and spoons, and even mother's tea-pots. But I never beheld any metal of such a color as this has got before. Can you tell me what this metal is?"

"I ought to know something, but I know nothing," Alice answered, wearily; "my father is acknowledged to be full of learning. Every minute I expect him."

"No doubt he will tell us, when he comes. But I am so impatient. And it looks like the key of some wonderful lock, that nothing else would open. May I ask what it is? Come, at least say that."

"It will give me the greatest delight to know," said Alice, with a yawn, "what the thing is; because it will please you, darling. And it certainly does look curious."

Upon this question Mrs. Bottler, like a good wife, referred them to her more learned husband, who came in now from his morning drive, scraping off the frozen snow, and accompanied, of course, by Polly.

"Polly's doll, that's what we call it," he said; "the little maid took such a liking to it that Bonny was forced to give it her. Where the boy got it, the Lord only knows. The Lord hath given him the gift of finding a'most every thing. He hath it both in his eyes and hands. I believe that boy'd die Lord Mayor of London, if he'd only come out of his hole in the hill."

"But can not we see him, Mr. Bottler?" asked Mabel. "When he is finding these things, does he lose himself?"

"Not he, miss!" replied the man of bacon. "He knows where he is, go where he will. You can hear him a-whistling down the lane now. He knoweth when I've a been easing of the pigs, sharper than my own steel do. Chittlings, or skirt, or milt, or trimmings—oh, he's the boy for a rare pig's fry—it don't matter what the weather is. I'd as lief dine with him as at home a'most."

"Oh! let me go and see him at the door," cried Mabel; "I am so fond of clever boys." So out she ran without waiting for leave, and presently ran back again. "Oh, what a nice boy!" she exclaimed to Alice; "so very polite; and he has got such eyes! But I am sadly afraid he'll be impudent when he grows much older."

"Aha, miss, aha, miss! you are right enough there," observed Mr. Bottler, with a crafty grin. "He an't overbashful already perhaps."

"And where do you think he found this most extraordinary instrument? At Shoreham, drawn up by the nets from the sea! And they said that it must have been dropped from a ship, many and many a year ago, when Shoreham was a place for foreign traffic. And he is almost sure that it must be a key of some very strange old-fashioned lock."

"Then you may depend upon it that it is a key, and nothing else," said Bottler, with his fine soft smile. "That boy Bonny hath been about so much among odds, and ends, and rakings, that he knoweth a bit about every thing."

"An old-fashioned key from the sea at Shoreham? Let me think of something," said Alice Lorraine, leaning back on her pillow, with her head still full of the Woeburn. "I seem to remember something, and then I am not at all sure what it is. Oh! when is my father coming?"

"Your father hath sent orders, Miss Alice," said Bottler, coming back with a good bold lie, "that you must go up to the house, if you please. He hath so much to see to with them Chapman lot, that he must not leave home nohow. The coach is a-coming for you now just."

"Very well," answered Alice, "I will do as I am told. I always mean to do as I am told henceforth. But will you lend me Polly's doll?"

"Lord bless you, miss, I daren't do it for my life. Polly would have the house down. She'm the strangest child as you ever did see, until you knows how to manage her. Her requireth to be taken the right side up. Now, if I say 'Poll' to her, her won't do nothing; but if I say 'Polly dear'—why, there she is!"

Alice was too weak and worn to follow this great question up. But Mabel was as wide awake as ever, although she had been up all night. "Now, Mr. Bottler, just do this: Go and say, 'Polly dear, will you lend your doll to the pretty lady, till it comes back covered with sugar-plums?'" Mr. Bottler promised that he would do this; and by the time Alice was ready to go, square Polly, with a very broad gait, came up and placed her doll, without a word, in the hands of Alice, and then ran away, and could never stop sobbing, until her father put the horse in on purpose, and got her between his legs in the cart. "Where are you going?" cried Mrs. Bottler. "We will drive to the end of the world," he answered; "I'm blowed if I think there'll be any gate to pay between this and that, by the look of things. Polly, hold on by my knees."

CHAPTER LXXIV.

In the old house and good household, warmth of opinion and heat of expression abounded now about every thing. Pages might be taken up with saying what even one man thought, and tens of pages would not contain the half of what one woman said. Enough, that when poor Alice was brought back through the snow-drifts quietly, every movable person in the house was at the door. Every body loved her and every body admired her; but now, with a pendulous conscience. Also, with much fear about themselves; as the household of Admetus gazed at the pale return of Alcestis.

Alice, being still so weak, and quite unfit for any thing, was frightened at their faces, and drew back and sunk with faintness.

"Sillies," cried Mabel, jumping out, with Polly's doll inside her muff; "naturals, or whatever you are, just come and do your duty."

They still hung away, and not one of them would help poor Alice across her own father's threshold, until a great scatter of snow flew about, and a black horse was reined up hotly.

"You zanies!" cried the rector, "you cowardly fools! You never come to church, or you would know what to do. You skulking hounds, are you afraid of your own master's daughter? I have got my big whip. By the Lord, you shall have it! Out of my parish I'll set to and kick every dastardly son of a cook of you!"

"Where is my father?" said Alice faintly; "I hoped that he would have come for me."

At the sound of her voice they began to perceive that she was not the ghost of the Woeburn; and the rector's strong championship cast at once the broad and sevenfold shield of the Church over the maiden's skeary deed. "Oh, Uncle Struan," she whispered, hanging upon his arm as he led her in; "have I committed a great crime? Will my father be ashamed of me?"

"He should rather be ashamed of himself, I think," he answered, for the present declining the subject, which he meant to have out with her some day; "but, my dear, he is not quite well; that is why he does not come to see you. And, indeed, he does not know—I mean he is not at all certain how you are. Trotman, open that door, sir, this moment."

The parson rather carried than led his niece into a sitting-room, and set her by a bright fire, and left Mabel Lovejoy to attend to her; while he himself hurried away to hear the last account of Sir Roland, and to consult the doctor as to the admittance of poor Alice. But in the passage he met Colonel Clumps, heavily stamping to and fro, with even more than wonted energy.

"Upon my life and soul, master parson, I must get out of this house!" he cried; "slashing work, sir, horrible slashing! I had better be under old Beaky again. I came here to quiet my system, sir, and zounds, sir, they make every hair stand up."

"Why, colonel, what is the matter now? Surely, a man of war, like you—"

"Yes, sir, a man of war I am; but not a man of suicide, and paralysis, and precipices, and concussions of the brain, sir—battle, and murder, and sudden death—why, my own brain is in a concussion, sir!"

"So it appears," said the rector, dryly. "But surely, colonel, you can tell us what the news is?"

"The news is just this, sir," cried the colonel, stamping, "the two Chapmans were upset in their coach last night down a precipice, and both killed as dead as stones, sir. They sent for the doctor; that's proof of it; our doctor has had to be off for his life. No man ever sends for the doctor until he is dead."

"There is some truth in that," replied Mr. Hales; "but I won't believe it quite yet, at any rate. No doubt they have been upset. I said so as soon as I heard they were gone, particularly with their postilions drunk. And I dare say they are a good deal knocked about. But snow is a fine thing to ease a fall. Whatever has happened, they brought on themselves, by their panic and selfish cowardice."

"Ay, they ran like rats from a sinking ship when they saw poor Sir Roland's condition. Alice had frightened them pretty well; but the other affair quite settled them. Sad as it was, I could scarcely help laughing."

"A sad disappointment for your nice girls, colonel. Instead of a gay wedding, a house of death."

"And for your pretty daughters, rector, too. However, we must not think of that. You have taken in the two Lovejoys, I hear."

"Gregory and Charlie? Yes, poor fellows. They were thoroughly scared last night, and of course Bottler had no room for them. That Charlie is a grand fellow, and fit to follow in the wake of Nelson. He was frozen all over as stiff as a rick just thatched, and what did he say to me? He said, 'I shall get into the snow and sleep. I won't wet Mother Bottler's floor.'"

"Well done! well said! There is nothing in the world to equal English pluck, sir, when you come across the true breed of it. Ah, if those d—d fellows had left me my leg, I would have whistled about my arm, sir. But the worst of the whole is this, supposing that I am grossly insulted, sir, how can I do what a Briton is bound to do—how can I kick—you know what I mean, sir?"

"Come, colonel, if you can manage to spin round like that, you need not despair of compassing the national salute. But here we are at Sir Roland's door. Are we allowed to go in? or what are the orders of the doctor?"

"Oh yes; he is quite unconscious. You might fire off a cannon close to his ear, without his starting a hair's-breadth. He will be so for three days, the doctor thinks; and then he will awake, and live or die, according as the will of the Lord is."

"Most of us do that," answered the parson; "but what shall I say to his daughter?"

"Leave her to me. I will take her a message, sir. I have been hoaxed so in the army that now I can hoax any one."

"I believe you are right. She will listen to you a great deal more than she would to me. Moreover, I want to be off as soon as I have seen poor Sir Roland. I shall ride on and ask how the Chapmans are. I don't believe they are dead; they are far too tough. What a blessing it is to have you here, colonel, with the house in such a state! How is that confounded old woman, who lies at the bottom of all this mischief?"

"Lady Valeria Lorraine," said the colonel,

rather stiffly, "is as well as can be expected, sir. She has been to see her son Sir Roland, and her grandson Hilary. My opinion is that this brave girl inherits her spirit from her grandmother. Whatever happens, I am sure of one thing, she ought to be the mother of heroes, sir; not the wife of Steenie Chapman."

"Ah's me!" cried the rector, "it will take a brave man to marry her, after what she has done."

"Stuff and nonsense," answered the colonel; "a good man will value her all the more, and scorn the opinion of the county, sir."

The rector, in his own stout heart, was much of the same persuasion; but it would not do for him to say so yet. So, after a glance at Sir Roland's wan and death-like features, he rode forth, with a sigh, to look after the Chapmans.

CHAPTER LXXV.

A GRAND physician, being called from London, pronounced that Sir Roland's case was one of asthenic apoplexy, rather than of pure paralysis. He gave the proper directions, praised the local practitioners, hoped for the best, took his fifty guineas with promptitude, and departed. If there were any weight on the mind, it must be cast aside at once, as soon as the mind should have sense of it. For this a little effort might be allowed, "such as the making of a will, or so forth, or good-bye to children; for on the first return of sense, some activity was good for it. But after that, repose, dear sir; insist on repose and good nourishing food. No phlebotomy—no, that is quite a mistake; an anachronism, a barbarism, in such a case as this is. It is anæmia with our poor friend, and vascular inaction. No arterial plethorism; quite the opposite, in fact. You have perfectly diagnosed the case. How it will end I can not say, any more than you can."

One more there was, one miserable heart, perpetually vexed and torn, that could not tell how things would end, if even they ended anyhow. Alice Lorraine could not be kept from going to her father's bed, and she was not strong enough yet to bear the view of the wreck before her.

"It is my doing—my doing!" she cried; "oh, what a wicked thing I must have done, to be punished so bitterly as this!"

"If you please, miss, to go away with your excitement," said the old nurse, who was watching him. "You promised to behave yourself, and this is how you do it! Us never can tell what they hears, or what they don't; when they lies with their ears pricked up so."

"Nurse, I will go away," said Alice; "I always do more harm than good."

The only comfort she now could get flowed from the warm bright heart of Mabel. Every body else gave signs of being a little or much afraid of her. And what is more dreadful for any kind heart than for other hearts to dread it? She knew that she had done a desperate thing; and she felt that every body had good reason for shrinking away from her large deep eyes. She tried to keep up her courage, in spite of all that was whispered about her; and truly speaking, her whole heart vested in her father and her brother.

Mabel watched the whole of this, and did her best to help it. But, sweet and good girl as she was, and in her way very noble, she belonged to a stratum of womanhood distinct from that of Alice. She would never have jumped into the river. She would simply have defied them to take her to church. She would have cried, "Here I am, and I won't marry any man, unless I love him. I don't love this man; and I won't have him. Now do your worst, every one of you." A sensible way of regarding the thing, in a family not too chivalrous.

On the third day Sir Roland moved his eyes and feebly raised one elbow. Alice sat there at his side, as now she was almost always sitting. "Oh, father," she cried, "if you would only give one little sign that you know me. Just to move your darling hand, or just to give me one little glance. Or if I have no right to that—"

"Go away, miss; leave the room, if you please. My orders was very particular to have nobody near him, when he first begins to take notice to any thing."

Alice, with a deep sigh, obeyed the orders of the cross old dame; and when the doctor came she received her reward in his approval. It was pitiful to see how humble this poor girl was now become. The accident to the Chapmans, her father's "stroke," poor Hilary's ruin, the lowering of the family for years, had all been attributed to her "wicked sin," by Lady Valeria, whose wrath was boundless at the overthrow of all her plans.

"What good have you done? What good have you done by such a heinous outrage? You have disgraced yourself forever. Who will ever look at you now?"

"Every body, I am afraid, madam," Alice answered with a blush.

"You know what I mean, as well as I do. Even if you were drowned, I believe, you would catch at the words of your betters."

"Drowning people catch at straws," she answered, with a shudder of memory.

"And you could not even drown yourself. You were too clumsy to do even that."

"Well, madam," said Alice, with a smile almost resembling that of better times, "surely even you will admit that I did my best toward it."

"Ah, you flighty child, leave my room, and go and finish killing your father."

Now when the doctor came and saw the slight revival of his patient, he hurried in search of Miss Lorraine, toward whom he had taken a liking. After he had given his opinion of the case, and comforted her until she cried, he said, "Now you must come and see him. And if you can think of any thing likely to amuse him, or set his mind in motion—any interesting remembrance or suggestion of mild surprise, it will be the very best thing possible."

"But surely, to see me again will sufficiently astonish him."

"It is not likely. In most of these cases perfect oblivion is the rule as to the occurrence that stimulated the predisposition to these attacks. Sir Roland will not have the smallest idea that—that any thing has happened to you."

And so it proved. When Alice came to her father's side, he looked at her exactly as he used to do, except that his glance was weak and wavering, and full of desire to comfort her. The doctor had told her to look cheerful, and even gay, and she did her best. Sir Rowland had lost all power of speech, but his hearing was as good as ever; and being ordered to take turtle-soup, he was propped up on a bank of pillows, and doing his best to execute medical directions.

"Oh, my darling, darling," cried Alice, after a little while, being left to feed her father delicately: "I have got such a surprise for you! You will say you were never so astonished in all the course of your life before."

She knew how her father would have answered if he had been at all himself. He would have lifted his eyebrows, and aroused her dutiful combativeness with some of that little personal play which passes between near relatives who love and understand each other. As it was, he could only nod, to show his anxiety for some surprise. And then Alice did a thing which, under any other circumstances, would have been most inconsistent in her. In the drawer of his looking-glass she found his best-beloved snuff-box, and she put one little pinch between his limp forefinger and white thumb, and raised them toward the proper part, and trusted to nature to do the rest. A pleasant light shone forth his eyes; and she felt that she had earned a kiss. Betwixt a smile and a tear, she took it; and then, for fear of a chill, she tucked him up, and sat quietly by him. She had learned, as we learn in our syntax, what "vacuis committere venis."

When he had slept for two or three hours, with Alice hushing the sound of her breath, he was seized with sudden activity. His body had been greatly strengthened by the most nourishing of all food, and now his mind began to aim at like increase of movement.

"What do you think I have got to show you?" said Alice, perceiving this condition. "Nothing less, I do believe, than the key of the fine old Astrologer's case! Of course, I can only guess, because you have got it locked away, papa. But from the metal looking just the same, and the shape of it, and the seven corners, and its being found at Shoreham, in the sea, where Memel was said to have lost it, I do think it must be that very same key. And I found it, papa—well I found it under rather peculiar circumstances. Now may I go and try? There can be no harm, if it turns out to be pure fancy."

Her father nodded, and pointed to a drawer where he kept his important keys, as Alice of course was well aware. And in five minutes Alice came back again, with the strange old case in one hand and Polly's queer doll in the other. Mabel lingered in the passage, not being sure that she ought to come in, though Alice tried to fetch her. Then Alice set the case, or cushion, upon her father's bedside table, and with a firm hand pushed the key down, and endeavored to turn it. Not a little would any thing yield or budge, although it was clear to the dullest eye that lock and key belonged together.

"It is the key, papa," cried Alice. "It fits to a hair; but it won't turn. This queer old thing goes round and round, instead of staying quiet, and waiting to be unlocked justly. I suppose my hands are too weak. Oh there! Provoking thing, it goes round again. I know how I could manage it, if I may, my darling father. In the Astrologer's room I saw a tremendous vise, fit to take any thing. I have inherited some of his turn for tools and mechanism, though of course in a most degenerate degree. Now may I go up? I shall have no fear whatever, if Mabel comes with me."

Winning mute assent, she ran for the key of that room, and took Mabel with her; and soon they had that obstinate case set fast in a vise, whose screw had not been turned for more than two centuries. The bottom of the cone was hard and solid, and bedded itself in the old oak slabs. "Now turn, Mabel, turn; the key is warped; or we might apply more force," said Alice. They did not know that it had been crooked by the jaws of Jack, the donkey. Even so it would not yield, until they passed an ancient chisel through its loop and worked away. Then with a thin and sulky screech the cogs began to move, and the upper half of the case to slide aside.

"Oh! I am so frightened, Alice!" cried Mabel, drawing back her hands. "And the room is so cold! It seems so unholy! It feels like witchcraft! And all his old tools looking at us!"

"Witch, or wizard, or necromancer, I am not going to leave off now," answered Alice the resolute. "You may run away, if you like. But I mean to get to the bottom of this, if I—if I can, at least."

She was going to say, "if I die for it." But she had been so close to Death quite lately that she feared to take his name in vain.

"How slowly it moves! How it does resist!" cried Mabel, returning to the charge. "I thought I was pretty strong—well, it ought to be worth something for all this work."

"It is fire-proof! It is lined with asbestus!" Alice answered eagerly. "Oh! there must be an enormous lot of gold."

"There can't be," said Mabel; "why, a thousand guineas is more than you or I could carry. And you carried this easily in one hand."

"Don't talk so!" cried Alice; "but work away. I am desperately anxious."

"As for me, I am positively dying of curiosity. Lend me your pocket-handkerchief, dear. I am cutting my hands to pieces."

"Here it comes, I do believe. Well, what an extraordinary thing!"

The dome of the cone had yielded sulkily to the vigor and perseverance of two beautiful young ladies. It had slidden horizontally, the key of course sliding with it, upon a strong rack of metal, which had been purposely made to go stiffly; and now that the cover had passed the cogs, it was lifted off quite easily. All this was the handiwork of the man, the simple-minded Eastern sage, who loved the shepherds and the sheep; and whose fine spirit would have now rejoiced to see the result of good workmanship.

The two fair girls poured hair together, with forehead close to forehead, when the round substantial case lay coverless before them. A disk of yellow parchment was spread flat on the top of every thing, with its edges crenelled into the asbestus lining. Hours and perhaps days of care had been spent by clever brain and hands, to keep the air and dust out.

"Who shall lift it?" asked Mabel, panting. "I am almost afraid to move."

"I will lift it, of course," said Alice; "I am his descendant; and he foresaw that I should do it."

She took from the lathe a little narrow tool for turning ivory (which had touched no hand since the Prince's), and she delicately loosened up the parchment and examined it. It was covered with the finest manuscript, in concentric rings, beginning with half an inch of diameter; but she could not interpret a word of that. Below it shone a thick flossy layer of the finest mountain wool, and under that the soft spun amber of the richest native silk.

"Now, Alice, do you mean to stop all night?" cried Mabel; "see how the light is fading!"

The light was fading, and spreading also, in a way that reminded Alice (although the season and the weather were so entirely different) of her visit to that room, two and a half long years ago, alone among the shadows. The white light, with the snow-gleam in it, favored any inborn light in every thing else that was beautiful.

Alice, with the gentlest touch of the fairy-gifts of her fingers, raised the last gossamer of the silk, and drew back, and sighed with wonder. Mabel (always prompt to take the barb and shaft of every thing) leaned over, and looked in, and at once enlarged her eyes and lovely mouth in purest stupefaction.

Before and between these two most lovely specimens of the human race lay the most beautiful and more lasting proofs of what nature used to do, before the production of women. Alice and Mabel, with the light in their eyes, and the flush in their fair cheeks quivering, felt that their beauty was below contempt—except in the opinion of stupid men—if compared with what they were looking at.

Of all the colors cast by nature on the world, as lavishly as Shakspeare threw his jewels forth, of all the tints of sun and heaven in flower, sea, and rainbow, there was not one that did not glance, or gleam, or glow, or lie in ambush, and then suddenly flash forth, and blush, and then fall back again. None of them waited to be looked at, all were in perpetual play; they had been immured for centuries, and when the glad light broke upon them, forth they danced like meteors. And then, as if all quick with life, they began to weave their crossing rays, and cast their tints through one another, like the hurtling of the Aurora. And to back their fitful brilliance, in among them lay and spread a soft, delicious, milky-way of bashful white serenity.

"It is terrible witchcraft!" cried dazzled Mabel.

"No," said Alice; "it is the noblest casket ever seen of precious opals, and of pearls. You shall carry them to my father."

"Indeed, I will not," said the generous Mabel; "you have earned, and you shall offer them."

CHAPTER LXXVI.

Beauty having due perception and affection for itself, it is natural that young ladies should be much attached to jewels. It does not, however, follow that they know any thing about them, any more than they always do about other objects of their attachment. Nevertheless they always want to know the money-value.

"I should say they were worth a thousand pounds, if they are worth a penny," said Mabel, sagely shaking her head, and looking wonderfully learned.

"A thousand!" cried Alice. "Ten thousand, you mean. Now put it all back as we found it."

"Oh, one more glance, one more good look, before other people see them! Oh! let the light fall sideways."

Mabel, in her admiration, danced all round the Astrologer's room, whisking the dust from the wheel of his lathe, and scattering quaint rare tools about, while Alice, calmly smiling at her, repacked the case, silk, wool, and parchment, and giving her friend the cover to carry, led the way toward her father's room.

Sir Roland Lorraine was so amazed that for the moment the mind resumed command of the body; the needful effort was made; and he "spake with his tongue" once more, though feebly and inarticulately.

"Father, darling, that is worth more to me," cried Alice, throwing her arms around him, "than all the jewels that ever were made from the first year of the world to this. Oh, I could never, never live without hearing your dear voice!"

It was long, however, before Sir Roland recovered mind and spirit so as to attempt a rendering of the provident sage's document. The writing was so small that a powerful lens was wanted for it; the language, moreover, was Latin, and the contractions crabbed to the last degree. And crammed as it was with terms of art, an interpreter might fairly doubt whether his harder task was to make out what the words were, or what they meant. But omitting some quite unintelligible parts, it seemed to be somewhat as follows:

"O descendant of mine in far-off ages, neither be thou carried away by desire of riches, neither suppose thine ancestor to have been so carried! I bid thee rather to hold thy money in the place of nothing, and to be taught that it is a work of royal amplitude, and most worthy of the noblest princes, to conquer the obstinacy of nature by human skill and fortitude. Laboring much I have accomplished little; seeking many things I have found some; it is not just that I should be forgotten, or mingled with those of my time and rank who live by violence, and do nothing for the benefit of humanity.

"Among many other things which I have by patience and learning conquested, the one the most likely of all to lead to wealth is of a simple kind. To wit, as Glaucus of Chios (following up the art of Celmis and Damnameneus) discovered the κόλλησις of iron, so have I discovered that of jewels—the opal, and perhaps the ruby. As regards the opal, I am certain; as regards the ruby, I have still some difficulties to conquer. All who know the opal can, with very clear vision, perceive that its lustre and versatile radiance flows from innumerable lamins, united by fusion in the endless flux of years. Having discovered how to solve the opal with a caustic liquor"—here followed chemical marks, which none but a learned chemist could understand—"and how to recompose it, I have spent twelve months in Hungary collecting a full medimnus of small opals of the purest quality. After many trials and a great waste of material, I have accomplished things undreamed by Baccius, Evax, or Leonardus; I have produced the priceless opal, cast to mould, and of purest water, from the size of an avellan-nut to that of a small castane. Larger I would not make them, knowing the incredulity of mankind, who take for false all things more than twice the size of their own experience.

"Alas! it is allowed to no man, great works having been carried through, to see what will become of them. These gems of inestimable value, polished by their own liquescence, and coherent as the rainbow, demand, so far as I yet can judge, at least a hundred years of darkness and of cavernous seclusion, such as nature and the gods require for all perfect work. And when the air is first let in, it must be very slowly done, otherwise all might fall abroad, as though I had never touched them. For this, with the vigilance of a great philosopher, I have provided.

"Now farewell, whether descended from me, or whether (if the fates will) alien. A philosopher who has penetrated, and, under the yoke, led nature, is the last of all men to speak proudly, or record his own great deeds. That he leaves for inferior and less tranquil minds, as are those of the poets. Only do not thou sell these gems for little, if thou sell them. The smallest of them is larger and finer than that of the Senator Nonius, or that which is called 'Troy burning,' from the propugnacled flash of its movement. Be not misled by jewelers. Rogues they are, and imitators, and perpetually striving to make gain disgracefully. Hearken thou not to one word of these; but keep these jewels, if thou canst. If narrow matters counsel sale, then go to the king of thy country, or great nobles, who will not wrong thee. And be sure that thou keep them well advised that neither in skill of hand nor in learning should they attempt to vie with Agasicles the Carian."

CHAPTER LXXVII.

LONG ere the writing of the diffident sage had been thus interpreted, the casket, or rather its contents (being intrusted to the wary hands of the counselor on his return to London), had passed the severest test and been pronounced of enormous value. The great philosopher had not deigned to say a word about the pearls, whether produced or amalgamated by his skill, or whether they were heirlooms in his ancient family. The jewelers said that they were Cingalese and of the rarest quality, and for these alone one large house (holding a commission from a nobleman) offered fifteen and then twenty, and finally twenty-five thousand pounds. But Sir Roland had resolved not to part with these, but divide them between his daughter and future daughter-in-law, if he could raise the required sum without them. In this no difficulty was found. Though opals were not in fashion just then (and indeed they are even now undervalued through a stupid superstition), six of the smaller gems were sold for sixty-five thousand pounds, and now their owners would not accept double that price.

Lady Valeria right quickly discarded her terror of that casket, and very quietly appropriated the magnificent central gem. It was the cover, with its spiral coils of metal, which had frightened her ladyship. The strongest-minded ladies are, as a general rule, the most obstinate in their dread of what has injured them. The Earl of Thanet, this lady's father, had been a great lover of the honey-bee, and among his other experiments he had a small metal hive, which his daughter upset, with results which need not trouble us so much as they troubled the lady. And although so much smaller, the Astrologer's case strangely resembled that deadly hive.

When Hilary's sin had been purged, and himself (at certainly a somewhat heavy figure) allowed to draw his sword again, he soon regained all his former strength and health, and perhaps a little more than his former share of wisdom. But he did not march into Paris, as Colonel Clumps had once predicted; or at least not in that memorable year 1814. But in July of the following year, he certainly put in an appearance there under the immortal Wellington, who had been truly pleased to have him under his command, but never on his staff again. And Hilary Lorraine, at Waterloo, had shown most clearly (through the thick of the smoke) that if the duke had erred about his discretion, he had made no mistake about his valor.

And it was, of course, tenfold more valorous of him to carry on as he did there, when he called to mind that he had at home a lovely wife, of the name of Mabel, and a baby of the name of Roger. Because he had taken advantage of the piping time of peace —when all the "crowned heads" were in England — to put on his own head that "crown of glory" (richer than mural or civic) whereof the wise man speaks the more warmly, because he had so many of them. In June, 1814, Hilary and Mabel were made one, under junction of the good rector; and nature, objecting to this depopulating fusion of her integrals, had sternly recouped her arithmetic by appeal to the multiplication-table.

At Waterloo, Hilary worked his right arm much harder than he worked it through the rest of his life; because there he lost it. When the French cuirassiers made their grand third charge upon the British artillery, to change the fortune, or meet their fate, Lorraine, with his troop of the Dasher hussars, now commanded by Colonel Aylmer, was in front of the rest of the regiment. The spirit of these men was up; they had been a long while held in that day, and they could not see any reason why they should not have their turn at it. Man and horse were of one accord, needing no spur, neither heeding bridle. As straight as hounds in full view, they flew; and Hilary flew in front of them. In the crush and crash, he got rolled over, dismounted, and left slashing wildly in a storm of horses. An enormous cuirassier made at him with a sword of monstrous length. Their eyes met, and they knew each other—the robber and the robbed; the crafty plotter and the simple one; the victor and the victim.

Alcides cried in Spanish, "Thou art at thy latest gasp; I have no orders now from my precious wife—receive this, and no more of thee!" With rowels deep in the flank of his horse, he made horrible swoop at Hilary, spent of strength and able only to present a feeble guard. Hilary's blade spun round and round, and his right arm flew off at the elbow; and the crash was descending upon his poor head, when a stern reply met Alcides. Through the joints of his harness Joyce Aylmer's sword went in, and drank his life-blood. His horse dashed on; and he lay on the plain, like the felled trunk of a poison-tree—that plain where lay so many nobler, and so few meaner, than himself. Having run through the whole of the stolen money, he had donned the French cuirass, and left his wife and infant child to starve.

When the times of slaughter passed, and nature began to be aware again that she has other manure than bloodshed; when even the cows could low without fear of telling where they rubbed their ribs, and mares could lick their foals unwept on; and hills and valleys began again to listen to the voice of quiet waters (drowned no more in the din of the drum); and every thing in our dear country was most wonderfully dear, something happened at this period not to be passed over. Parenthetically it may be said —and deserves no more than parenthesis— that neither of the Chapmans had been killed (as mendacious fame reported), only knocked on the head, and legs, and stomach, and other convenient places. It repented them, in deep holes, of the day when they tried to drag Alice down into their pit.

But now there is just time to say that it must have been broad August, when the fields were growing white for harvest, after the swath of Waterloo, ere Colonel Aylmer durst bring forth what he nursed in his heart for Alice. His words were short and simple, though he did not mean to make them so. But he found her in old Chancton Ring, where first he had beholden her; and so much came across him, that he never took his hat off, but just whispered underneath it. The whisper went under a prettier hat, where it long had been expected; and if a feather waved at all it only was a white one.

"Are you not afraid of me?" asked Alice Lorraine, with a tremulous glance, enough to terrify any one.

"That I am, to the last degree. I never shall get over it."

"That augurs well," she replied with a smile—such a smile as no one else could give; "but I mean more than that; I mean your fear of what the world will say of me."

"Of that I am infinitely more afraid. It will vex me so to hear forever, 'What has he done to deserve such a wife?'"

"Then what he has done is simply this," cried Alice, looking nobly; "he has saved her life and her brother's; and her heart is his, if he cares for it."

CHAPTER LXXVIII.

It takes but little time to tell what happened to the rest of them. Sir Roland Lorraine had the pleasure of seeing two tribes of grandchildren round him, who routed him out of his book-room, and scattered his unwholesome tendencies wholesale. If he shocked society in his middle age, society had revenge in the end, and pursued him, like the Eumenides. The difference was this, however, that here were truly well-meaning ones, not called so by timorous truckling. And another point of distinction might be found in the style of their legs and bodies. Also, they had no "stony glare," but the brightest of all young eyes, that shine like a flower filled with morning dew.

These little men and women played at hide-and-seek, and made rich echo in the Woeburn channel. Forsooth, that fearful stream (like other fateful rivers), beaten by Vulcanian fires of Bottler—or, as some people said (who knew not Bottler), by the power of the long dry frost—retired into the bowels of the earth, and never means to come forth again. But before leaving off, it did one good thing—it drowned old Nanny Stilgoe. "Prophet of ill, never yet to me spakest thou thing lucksome"—this was the sentiment of that river when disappointed of Alice. Old Nanny ran out of her door the next day, with a stick, at a boy who cast snow-balls, and she slipped on some ice, and in she went; and many people tried to rake her out, but she would not be laid hold of. Her prophecies of evil fell like lead on her head, and sunk her, and the parish was fiercely divided whether she ought to have Christian burial. But rector Hales let them talk as they liked, and shunned disceptation about it. He made up his own mind what to do (which of all things is the foremost); so he buried old Nanny, and paid for it all, and set up her tombstone, whereon the sculptor, with visions of his own date prolonged, set down her figure at 110.

The passing of time is one of those things that most astonish every one. For instance, no one would ever believe, except with a hand upon either temple, that Applewood Farm is now carried on, and all the growing business done, by a sturdy and highly enlightened young fellow whose name is Struan Lovejoy. He owes his origin to a heavy cold, caught by his father (the present highly respected Admiral Sir Charles Lovejoy), through the freezing of his naval trowsers, and the coddling which of course ensued. Charlie's heart lay open through all the stages of catarrh, and he knew (though he could not well speak about it) whose initials were done in hair on the handkerchief under his pillow. In short, no sooner did his nose begin to resume its duty in the system, and his eyes to cease from running, than he took Cecil Hales by the hand, and said that he had something to say to her. And he said it well; as sailors do. And she could not deny that it might mean something, if ever they could maintain themselves.

This is what all young people say; some with a little, and some with less, discretion upon the subject. The helm of all the question hangs upon the man's own stern-post. There is no time to talk of that. Charlie married Cecil; and they had a son called "Struan."

Struan Lovejoy took the turn for gardening and for growing, which had failed the Lovejoy race in the middle generation. Gout descends, and so does growing, with a skip of one step of mankind; and you can not make the wrong generation lay heel on spade, or toe in slipper.

But most of us can make some men feel—however small our circle is—that there is room for them inside it. That we scorn hypocritical love of mean humanity; but love the noble specimens—when we get them. That we know how short our time is, and attempt to do a little forward for the slowly rolling age. In a word, that, taking things altogether, they are pretty nearly as good as could have been hoped for, even sixty years ago.

But it is quite a few years back, to wit in 1861, when the great leading case upon rights of way—"Lovejoy *vs.* Shatterlocks"—was tried for the ninth and final time. Chief-justice Sir Gregory Lovejoy, through feelings of delicacy, left the bench, and would not even allow his wife—our Phyllis Catherow—to be called. But Major-general Sir Hilary Lorraine marched into the witness-box; and so vividly did he call to mind what had passed (and what had been stopped) at the white gate, and where the key was kept half a century agone, that the defendant had no leg to stand upon. Mabel (who heard all his evidence, with a grandchild Mabel's hand in hers) vowed that he made a confusion of keys, and was thinking of the gate where she came to meet him. And when he had time for more reflection he could not contradict her.

Now what says Bonny? He sits on his hill. He sees his life before him. Though he does not know that for finding that key he is to have one thousand pounds invested already, and to accumulate, until he settles down. In fullness of time he will cast away the unsalable portion of his rags, and wed square Polly Bottler. Their hearts are as one; they only wait for parental assent, and the band or ban—whichever may be the proper word—shouted thrice by the rector, defiant of the world to forbid those two. They are not ready yet to be joined together; but they are polishing their fire-irons.

Meanwhile Bonny may be seen to sit in one of those wonderful nicks of the hills, which seem to be elbowed by nature and padded, to tempt her restless mankind to rest. For here the curve of the slope is so snug that only pleasant airs find entry, with the flowery tales they bring, and the grass is of the greenest, and the peep into the lowland distance of the most refreshing blue. Lulled on a bank, here Bonny sits, not quite so fair as the fairy-queen (who perhaps is watching him unseen), but picturesque enough for the age, and provided with a donkey worthy of Titania's purest love. Jack is gazing with deep interest at an image of himself, cleverly shaped by his master on the green with snowy outline of chalky flints. Here are set forth his long tail, white nose, and ears as long and rich as the emblem of fair Ceres. He sniffs at his nose, and he treads on his toes, and not being able to explain away all things, he falls to and grazes from his own stomach.

But what is Bonny doing here, instead of attending to his rags and bones? Well, he ought to be, but he certainly is not, attending to the rector's sheep. To wit, Mr. Hales, growing stiff in the saddle, betakes himself freely to saddles of mutton; and has paid, and is paying, his three daughters' portions after the manner of the patriarchs. But leaving the flock to their own devices (for which, an he were satirical, he might quote his master as precedent), Bonny opens his capacious mouth, and the fresh air of the downs rings richly with a simple

SOUTHDOWN SONG.

1.

When the sheep are on the hill,
  In the early summer day,
They may wander at their will,
  While I go myself astray.

Chorus (sustained by sheep and Jack).

We may wander at our will,
  While you go to sleep or play!

2.

If the May wind hath an edge
  Rather winterly and cold,
I shall sit beneath a hedge,
  While they wander o'er the wold.

Chorus (by the same performers).

There you sit beneath a hedge
  Singing like a minstrel bold!

3.

Should ill-natured people say
  That I loiter or do ill,
Pick a hole in me they may—
  When they see me through the hill.

Chorus.

When they catch you at your play,
  Whip you merrily they will.

4.

Playful creatures grow not old;
  Play is healthy nature's pledge.
'Tis the dull heart gives the hold
  For the point of trouble's wedge.

Chorus.

These reflections are as old
  As the saws of rush and sedge.

5.

Frisky lambkins in the grass,
  Mint and pepper if they spy,
Do they weep, and cry "alas!"
  Nay, but whisk their tails on high.

Chorus.

Weep indeed, and cry "alas!"
  Sooner you than we, or I!

6.

Look how soon the shadows pass!
  How the sun hath chased the gloom!
If our life is but as grass,
  Grass is where the flowers bloom.

Chorus.

If our life is in the grass,
  Many flowers we consume.

And so may we leave them singing.

THE END.

Novels are sweets. All people with healthy literary appetites love them—almost all women; a vast number of clever, hard-headed men. Judges, bishops, chancellors, mathematicians, are notorious novel readers, as well as young boys and sweet girls, and their kind, tender mothers.—THACKERAY.

Harper's Select Library of Fiction rarely includes a work which has not a decided charm, either from the clearness of the story, the significance of the theme, or the charm of the execution; so that on setting out upon a journey, or providing for the recreation of a solitary evening, one is wise and safe in procuring the later numbers of this attractive series.—*Boston Transcript.*

A COMPLETE LIST OF NOVELS

PUBLISHED BY

HARPER & BROTHERS, NEW YORK.

☞ *For full titles and description, see* HARPER'S CATALOGUE, *which will be sent by mail on receipt of ten cents.*

The Novels in this List, except where otherwise designated, are in Octavo, pamphlet form. The Duodecimo Novels are bound in Cloth, unless otherwise specified.

	PRICE
AGUILAR'S Home Influence..........12mo	$1 00
The Mother's Recompense..............	75
AINSWORTH'S Crichton..............12mo	1 50
ALAMANCE	50
ANDERSEN'S (Hans Christian) The Improvisatore..........................	50
Only a Fiddler and O.T...............	50
ANNE Furness..........................	75
BACHELOR of the Albany...........12mo	1 50
BAKER'S The New Timothy...........12mo	1 50
Inside: a Chronicle of Secession. Ills..	1 25
Cloth	1 75
BANIM'S The Smuggler...............12mo	1 50
BELIAL................................	50
BELL'S (Miss) Julia Howard.............	50
BENEATH the Wheels....................	50
BENEDICT'S John Worthington's Name...	1 00
Cloth	1 50
Miss Dorothy's Charge................	1 00
Cloth	1 50
Miss Van Kortland....................	1 00
Cloth	1 50
Mr. Vaughan's Heir....................	1 00
Cloth	1 50
My Daughter Elinor...................	1 00
Cloth	1 50
BLACK'S A Daughter of Heth............	50
A Princess of Thule..................	75
In Silk Attire.......................	50
Kilmeny..............................	50
Love or Marriage?....................	50
The Maid of Killeena, and Other Stories.	50
The Monarch of Mincing Lane. Ill's.	50
The Strange Adventures of a Phaeton.	75
BLACKMORE'S Cradock Nowell..........	75
The Maid of Sker.....................	75
Alice Lorraine. (*In Press.*)	
Lorna Doone..........................	75
BLACKWELL'S (Mrs. A. B.) The Island Neighbors. Illustrated............	75
BORROW'S Lavengro.....................	75
Romany Rye...........................	75

	PRICE
BRADDON'S (Miss) Aurora Floyd........	$ 75
A Strange World......................	75
Birds of Prey. Illustrated............	75
Bound to John Company. Illustrated.	75
Charlotte's Inheritance...............	50
Dead Sea Fruit. Illustrations.........	50
Eleanor's Victory.....................	75
Fenton's Quest. Illustrated..........	50
John Marchmont's Legacy............	75
Lost for Love. Illustrated.............	75
Publicans and Sinners................	75
Strangers and Pilgrims. Illustrated.	75
Taken at the Flood....................	75
The Lovels of Arden. Illustrated.....	75
To the Bitter End. Illustrated.........	75
BREACH of Promise.....................	50
BREMER'S (Miss) Brothers and Sisters.....	50
New Sketches of Every-Day Life.......	50
Nina..................................	50
The H. Family.........................	50
The Home..............................	50
The Midnight Sun......................	25
The Neighbors.........................	50
The Parsonage of Mora.................	25
The President's Daughters.............	25
BRONTË'S (Charlotte) Jane Eyre.........	75
Illustrated. 12mo	1 50
Shirley...............................	1 00
Illustrated. 12mo	1 50
Villette..............................	75
Illustrated. 12mo	1 50
The Professor. Illustrated.......12mo	1 50
(Anna) The Tenant of Wildfell Hall. Illustrated. 12mo	1 50
(Emily) Wuthering Heights. Illustrated. 12mo	1 50
BROOKS'S Sooner or Later. Illustrated....	1 50
Cloth	2 00
The Gordian Knot.....................	50
The Silver Cord. Illustrated....	1 50
Cloth	2 00

PRICE

BROUGHAM'S Albert Lunel.............$ 75
BRUNTON'S (Mary) Self-Control......... 75
BULWER'S Alice......................... 50
A Strange Story. Illustrated......... 1 00
12mo 1 25
Devereux........................... 50
Ernest Maltravers..................... 50
Eugene Aram.......................... 50
Godolphin........................... 50
12mo 1 50
Harold, the Last of the Saxon Kings.... 1 00
Kenelm Chillingly..................... 75
12mo 1 25
Leila.............................. 50
12mo 1 00
Lucretia............................ 75
My Novel........................... 1 50
2 vols. 12mo 2 50
Night and Morning.................... 75
Paul Clifford......................... 50
Pelham............................. 75
Rienzi.............................. 75
The Caxtons......................... 75
12mo 1 25
The Disowned........................ 75
The Last Days of Pompeii............. 50
The Last of the Barons............... 1 00
The Pilgrims of the Rhine............. 25
The Parisians. Illustrated........... 1 00
12mo 1 50
What will He do with it?............. 1 50
Cloth 2 00
Zanoni............................. 50
BULWER'S (Robert—"Owen Meredith")
The Ring of Amasis...........12mo 1 50
BURBURY'S (Mrs.) Florence Sackville..... 75
BURNEY'S (Miss) Evelina...........12mo 1 00
CAMPBELL'S (Miss) Self-Devotion....... 50
CAPRON'S (Miss) Helen Lincoln......12mo 1 50
CARLEN'S (Miss) Ivar; or, The Skjuts-Boy. 50
The Brothers' Bet..................... 25
The Lover's Stratagem................ 50
CASTE. By the Author of "Colonel Dacre." 50
CASTLETON'S Salem..................12mo 1 25
CHARLES Auchester.................... 75
CHURCH'S (Mrs. Ross) Her Lord and Master............................. 50
The Prey of the Gods................. 30
CITIZEN of Prague.................... 1 00
CLARKE'S The Beauclercs, Father and Son. 50
COLLINS'S (Mortimer) The Vivian Romance. 50
COLLINS'S (Wilkie) Armadale. Illustrated. 1 00
Antonina........................... 50
Man and Wife. Illustrated........... 1 00
No Name. Illustrated................ 1 00
Poor Miss Finch. Illustrated......... 1 00
The Law and the Lady. Illustrated.... 75
The Moonstone. Illustrated.......... 1 00
The New Magdalen................... 50
The Woman in White. Illustrated.... 1 00
COLLINS'S (Wilkie) Illustrated Library Edition.............12mo, per vol. 1 50

Antonina.	Poor Miss Finch.
Armadale.	The Dead Secret.
Basil.	The Moonstone.
Hide-and-Seek.	The New Magdalen.
Man and Wife.	The Woman in White.
No Name.	My Miscellanies.
After Dark, and Other Stories.	Queen of Hearts.
	The Law and the Lady.

PRICE

COLONEL Dacre. By the Author of "Caste."$ 50
CONSTANCE Lyndsay.................. 50
COOKE'S Henry St. John............12mo 1 50
Leather Stocking and Silk........12mo 1 50
CORNWALLIS'S Pilgrims of Fashion.12mo 1 00
CRAIK'S (Mrs. D. M.). *See Miss Mulock.*
(Miss G. M.) Mildred................. 50
Sylvia's Choice...................... 50
CUNNINGHAM'S Lord Roldan........... 1 50
CURTIS'S Trumps. Illustrated......12mo 2 00
D'ARBOUVILLE'S Tales.............12mo 1 50
D'ISRAELI'S The Young Duke.......12mo 1 50
D'ORSAY'S (Countess) Clouded Happiness. 50
DANGEROUS Guest, A.................. 50
DE BEAUVOIR'S Safia.................. 50
DE FOREST'S Miss Ravenel's Conversion from Secession to Loyalty....12mo 1 50
DE MILLE'S Cord and Creese. Illustrated. 75
Cloth 1 25
The American Baron. Illustrated..... 1 00
Cloth 1 50
The Cryptogram. Illustrated.......... 1 50
Cloth 2 00
The Dodge Club. Illustrated......... 75
Cloth 1 25
The Living Link. Illustrated.............. 1 00
Cloth 1 50
DE VIGNY'S Cinq Mars................. 50
DENISON'S (Mrs.) Home Pictures....12mo 1 50
DICKENS'S Novels. Illustrated.
Oliver Twist........................ 50
Cloth 1 00
Martin Chuzzlewit.................... 1 00
Cloth 1 50
The Old Curiosity Shop............... 75
Cloth 1 25
David Copperfield.................... 1 00
Cloth 1 50
Dombey and Son..................... 1 00
Cloth 1 50
Nicholas Nickleby.................... 1 00
Cloth 1 50
Bleak House........................ 1 00
Cloth 1 50
Pickwick Papers..................... 1 00
Cloth 1 50
Little Dorrit........................ 1 00
Cloth 1 50
Barnaby Rudge...................... 1 00
Cloth 1 50
A Tale of Two Cities.................. 50
Cloth 1 00
Our Mutual Friend. (*In Press.*)
Great Expectations. (*In Press.*)
Christmas Stories. (*In Press.*)
Bleak House. Illustrated..2 vols., 12mo 3 00
Hard Times......................... 50
12mo 1 25
Mrs. Lirriper's Legacy................ 10
The Mystery of Edwin Drood. Ill's.... 25
DRAYTON........................12mo 1 50
DRURY'S (Miss A. H.) Eastbury:.....12mo 1 50
Misrepresentation.................... 1 00
DUMAS'S (Alex.) Amaury................ 50
Ascanio............................ 75
Chevalier d'Harmental................ 50
DUPUY'S (Miss E. A.) Country Neighborhood 50
The Huguenot Exiles...........12mo 1 25

PRICE

EDGEWORTH'S (Miss) Novels. Engravings.........10 vols., 12mo, per vol. $1 50
Vol. I. Castle Rackrent; Essay on Irish Bulls; Essay on Self-Justification; The Prussian Vase; The Good Aunt.
Vol. II. Angelina; The Good French Governess; Mademoiselle Panache; The Knapsack; Lame Jervis; The Will; Out of Debt, Out of Danger; The Limerick Gloves; The Lottery; Rosanna.
Vol. III. Murad the Unlucky; The Manufacturers; Ennui; The Contrast; The Grateful Negro; To-morrow; The Dun.
Vol. IV. Manœuvring; Almeria; Vivian.
Vol. V. The Absentee; Madame de Fleury; Emily de Boulanges; The Modern Griselda. [Vol. VI. Belinda.
Vol. VII. Leonora; Letters on Female Education; Patronage.
Vol. VIII. Patronage; Comic Dramas.
Vol. IX. Harrington; Thoughts on Bores; Ormond. [Vol. X. Helen.
Frank.....................2 vols. 18mo 1 50
Harry and Lucy..........2 vols. 18mo 3 00
Moral Tales..............2 vols. 18mo 1 50
Popular Tales............2 vols. 18mo 1 50
Rosamond..........................12mo 1 50
EDWARDS'S (Amelia B.) Barbara's History. 75
Debenham's Vow. Illustrated......... 75
Half a Million of Money.............. 75
Hand and Glove..................... 50
Miss Carew.......................... 50
My Brother's Wife.................. 50
The Ladder of Life.................. 50
(M. B.) Kitty......................... 50
EILOART'S (Mrs.) Curate's Discipline..... 50
From Thistles—Grapes?............. 50
The Love that Lived................. 50
ELIOT'S (George) Novels.
Adam Bede. Illustrated.........12mo 1 00
Felix Holt, the Radical.................. 75
Illustrated. 12mo 1 00
Middlemarch.......................... 1 50
Cloth 2 00
2 vols. 12mo 3 50
Romola. Illustrated.................. 1 00
Cloth 1 50
Scenes of Clerical Life and Silas Marner.
Illustrated. 12mo 1 00
The Mill on the Floss................... 75
Illustrated. 12mo 1 00
ELLIS'S (Mrs.) Home.................12mo 1 50
Look to the End....................... 50
Chapters on Wives...............12mo 1 50
ESTELLE Russell......................... 75
FALKENBURG........................... 75
FARJEON'S Blade-o'-Grass. Illustrations. 35
At the Sign of the Silver Flagon....... 40
Bread-and-Cheese and Kisses. Ill's.... 35
Golden Grain. Illustrated............ 35
Grif.. 40
Cloth 90
Jessie Trim................................ 50
Joshua Marvel............................ 40
Cloth 90
London's Heart. Illustrated.......... 1 00
Cloth 1 50
Love's Victory. (*In Press.*).
The King of No-Land. Illustrated.... 25

FEMALE Minister, The...................$ 50
FENN'S Ship Ahoy! Illustrated............ 40
The Treasure Hunters..................... 40
FERRIER'S (Miss) Marriage............... 50
FIELDING'S Amelia.................12mo 1 50
Tom Jones................2 vols, 12mo 2 75
FIRST Friendship, A...................... 50
FIVE Hundred Pounds Reward........... 50
FLAGG'S A Good Investment. Illustrated. 50
FRANCILLON'S The Earl's Dene......... 50
FREYTAG'S Debit and Credit........12mo 1 50
FULLOM'S Daughter of Night............ 50
GARIBALDI'S Rule of the Monk......... 50
GASKELL'S (Mrs.) Cranford..........12mo 1 25
Dark Night's Work, A................ 50
Mary Barton.......................... 50
Moorland Cottage................18mo 75
My Lady Ludlow...................... 25
North and South...................... 50
Right at Last, &c................12mo 1 50
Sylvia's Lovers........................ 75
Cousin Phillis.......................... 25
Wives and Daughters. Illustrations... 1 00
Cloth 1 50
GIBBON'S For Lack of Gold.............. 50
For the King.......................... 50
In Honor Bound........................ 50
Robin Gray............................ 50
GILBERT Rugge......................... 1 00
GODDARD'S (Julia) Baffled.............. 75
GODWIN'S Caleb Williams.....16mo, Paper 37
Cloth 1 00
GOLDSMITH'S Vicar of Wakefield. 18mo, Cloth 75
GOLD Worshipers........................ 50
GORE'S (Mrs.) Peers and Parvenus....... 50
The Banker's Wife.................... 50
The Birthright.......................... 25
The Queen of Denmark............... 50
The Royal Favorite.................... 50
GRATTAN'S Chance Light Medley....... 50
GREEN Hand, The....................... 75
GREENWOOD'S True History of a Little Ragamuffin......................... 50
GREY'S (Mrs.) The Bosom Friend.......... 50
The Gambler's Wife.................. 50
The Young Husband.................. 50
GWYNNE'S The School for Fathers...12mo 1 25
HAKLANDER'S Clara...............12mo 1 50
HALL'S (Mrs. S. C.) Midsummer Eve....... 50
Tales of Woman's Trials............... 75
The Whiteboy.......................... 50
HAMILTON'S Cyril Thornton........12mo 1 50
HAMLEY'S Lady Lee's Widowhood....... 50
HANNAY'S (D.) Ned Allen............... 50
(J.) Singleton Fontenoy............... 50
HARDY'S (Lady) Daisy Nichol............ 50
HAVERS'S (Dora) Jack's Sister............. 75
HAY'S (Mary Cecil) Old Myddelton's Money. 50
HEIR Expectant, The...................... 50
HIDDEN Sin, The......................... 1 00
Cloth 1 50
HOEY'S (Mrs.) A Golden Sorrow.......... 50
The Blossoming of an Aloe............ 50
HOFLAND'S (Mrs.) Daniel Dennison...... 50
The Czarina........................... 50
The Unloved One...................... 50
HOPE'S Anastasius..................12mo 1 50
HOWITT'S (Mary) The Author's Daughter. 25
Who Shall be Greatest?......18mo, Cloth 75
The Heir of Wast Wayland.......12mo 1 50
(Wm.) Jack of the Mill.............. 25

	PRICE
HUBBACK'S Wife's Sister	$ 50
HUGO'S Ninety-Three	25
12mo	1 75
The Toilers of the Sea. Illustrated	75
Cloth	1 50
HUNGERFORD'S The Old Plantation. 12mo.	1 50
HUNT'S The Foster Brother	50
INCHBALD'S (Mrs.) A Simple Story	50
IN Duty Bound. Illustrated	50
ISABEL. 18mo, Cloth	75
JAMES'S Leonora d'Orco	50
The Old Dominion	50
Ticonderoga	50
A Life of Vicissitudes	50
Agnes Sorel	50
Pequinillo	50
Aims and Obstacles	50
The Fate	50
The Commissioner	1 00
Henry Smeaton	50
The Old Oak Chest	50
The Woodman	75
The Forgery	50
Thirty Years Since	75
A Whim and its Consequences	50
Gowrie; or, The King's Plot	50
Sir Theodore Broughton	50
The Last of the Fairies	25
The Convict	50
Margaret Graham	25
Russell	50
The Castle of Ehrenstein	50
Beauchamp	75
Heidelberg	50
The Step-Mother	1 25
The Smuggler	75
Agincourt	50
Arrah Neil	50
Rose d'Albret	50
Arabella Stuart	50
The False Heir	50
Forest Days	50
The Club Book. 12mo	1 50
De L'Orme. 12mo	1 50
The Gentleman of the Old School. 12mo	1 50
The Gipsy. 12mo	1 50
Henry of Guise. 12mo	1 50
Henry Masterton. 12mo	1 50
The Jacquerie. 12mo	1 50
Morley Ernstein. 12mo	1 50
One in a Thousand. 12mo	1 50
Philip Augustus. 12mo	1 50
Attila. 12mo	1 50
Corse de Lion. 12mo	1 50
The Ancient Régime. 12mo	1 50
The Man at Arms. 12mo	1 50
Charles Tyrrel. 12mo	1 50
The Robber. 12mo	1 50
Richilieu. 12mo	1 50
The Huguenot. 12mo	1 50
The King's Highway. 12mo	1 50
The String of Pearls. 12mo	1 25
Mary of Burgundy. 12mo	1 50
Darnley. 12mo	1 50
John Marston Hall. 12mo	1 50
The Desultory Man. 12mo	1 50
JEAFFRESON'S Isabel. 12mo	1 50
Live it Down	1 00
Lottie Darling	75
Not Dead Yet	1 25
Cloth	1 75
Olive Blake's Good Work	75
JESSIE'S Flirtations	$ 50
JERROLD'S Chronicles of Clovernook	25
JEWSBURY'S (Miss) Adopted Child. 16mo.	1 00
Constance Herbert	50
Zoe	50
JILT, The	50
JOHNSON'S (Miss) A Sack of Gold	50
Joseph the Jew	50
KATHLEEN	50
KINGSLEY'S (Chas.) Alton Locke. 12mo	1 50
Yeast. 12mo	1 50
(Henry) Hetty	25
Stretton	40
KNORRING'S The Peasant and his Landlord. 12mo	1 50
KNOWLES'S Fortescue	1 00
LAJETCHNIKOFF'S The Heretic	50
LAMARTINE'S Genevieve. 12mo, Paper	25
Raphael. 12mo	1 25
Stone Mason of St. Point. 12mo	1 25
LAWRENCE'S (Geo. A.) Anteros	50
Brakespeare	50
Breaking a Butterfly	35
Guy Livingstone. 12mo	1 50
Hagarene	75
Maurice Dering	50
Sans Merci	50
Sword and Gown	25
LEE'S (Holme) Annis Warleigh's Fortunes.	75
Kathie Brande. 12mo	1 50
Mr. Wynyard's Ward	50
Sylvan Holt's Daughter. 12mo	1 50
LE FANU'S All in the Dark	50
A Lost Name	50
Guy Deverell	50
The Tenants of Malory	50
Uncle Silas	75
LE SAGE'S Gil Blas. 12mo	1 50
LEVER'S A Day's Ride	50
Bramleighs of Bishop's Folly	50
Barrington	75
Daltons	1 50
Dodd Family Abroad	1 25
Gerald Fitzgerald	50
Glencore and his Fortunes	50
Lord Kilgobbin. Illustrated	1 00
Cloth	1 50
Luttrell of Arran	1 00
Cloth	1 50
Martins of Cro' Martin	1 25
Maurice Tiernay	1 00
One of Them	75
Roland Cashel. Engravings	1 25
Sir Brook Fosbrooke	50
Sir Jasper Carew	75
That Boy of Norcott's. Illustrated	25
Tony Butler	1 00
Cloth	1 50
LEWES'S Three Sisters and Three Fortunes.	75
LILY. 12mo	1 25
LINTON'S (Mrs.) Lizzie Lorton of Greyrigg.	75
Sowing the Wind	50
LIVONIAN Tales	25
LOCKHART'S Fair to See	75
McCARTHY'S My Enemy's Daughter. Ill's.	75
The Waterdale Neighbors	50
McINTOSH'S (Miss) Conquest and Self-Conquest. 18mo, Cloth	75
The Cousins. 18mo, Cloth	75
Praise and Principle. 18mo, Cloth	75
Woman an Enigma. 18mo, Cloth	75

PRICE

MABEL'S Progress........................$ 50
MABERLY'S (Mrs.) Lady and the Priest.. 50
Leontine............................ 50
MACDONALD'S Alec Forbes............ 75
Annals of a Quiet Neighborhood..12mo 1 75
Guild Court.......................... 50
MACKENZIE'S (Henry) Novels......12mo 1 50
MACQUOID'S (Mrs.) Patty............. 50
Too Soon........................... 50
MAID of Honor, The.................. 50
MAID of Orleans, The................. 75
MARGARET Denzil's History.......... 75
MARGARET'S Engagement............. 50
MARLITT'S Countess Gisela............ 25
MARRYAT'S (Capt.) Children of New Forest..........................12mo 1 25
Japhet in Search of a Father.....12mo 1 25
Little Savage....................12mo 1 25
MARSH'S (Mrs.) Adelaide Lindsay........ 50
Angela..........................12mo 1 50
Aubrey.............................. 75
Castle Avon 50
Emilia Wyndham..................... 75
Evelyn Marston...................... 50
Father Darcy........................ 75
Heiress of Haughton................. 50
Lettice Arnold....................... 25
Mordaunt Hall....................... 50
Norman's Bridge..................... 50
Ravenscliffe 50
Rose of Ashurst...................... 50
Time, the Avenger................... 50
Triumphs of Time 75
Wilmingtons 50
MARTINEAU'S (Harriet) The Hour and the Man............................ 50
MATURIN'S Bianca.................12mo 1 25
MEINHOLD'S Sidonia the Sorceress....... 1 00
MELVILLE'S Mardi ....2 vols. 12mo 3 00
Moby-Dick.......................12mo 1 75
Omoo...........................12mo 1 50
Pierre...........................12mo 1 50
Redburn 12mo 1 50
Typee 12mo 1 50
Whitejacket.....................12mo 1 50
MEREDITH'S Evan Harrington......12mo 1 50
MILMAN'S Arthur Conway............... 50
The Wayside Cross................... 25
MORE'S (Hannah) Complete Works. Engravings..........1 vol. 8vo, Sheep 3 00
2 vols. 8vo, Cloth 4 00
Sheep 5 00
The Same................7 vols. 12mo 8 75
MORLEY'S (Susan) Aileen Ferrers......... 50
MOTHER'S Trials, A................12mo 1 25
MOULTON'S My Third Book 12mo 1 25
MUHLBACH'S Bernthal 50
MULOCK'S (Miss) My Mother and I. Ill's. 50
12mo 1 50
A Brave Lady. Illustrated.............. 1 00
Cloth 1 50
12mo 1 50
The Woman's Kingdom. Illustrated.... 1 00
Cloth 1 50
12mo 1 50
A Hero, &c.........................12mo 1 25
A Life for a Life 50
12mo 1 50
Agatha's Husband........................ 50
12mo 1 50
MULOCK'S (Miss) Avillion, and Other Tales.$1 25
Christian's Mistake..................12mo 1 50
A Noble Life 12mo 1 50
Hannah. Illustrated..................... 50
12mo 1 50
Head of the Family...................... 75
12mo 1 50
John Halifax, Gentleman................. 75
Illustrated. 12mo 1 50
Mistress and Maid........................ 50
12mo 1 50
Nothing New.............................. 50
Ogilvies 50
12mo 1 50
Olive....................................... 50
12mo 1 50
A French Country Family. Translated. Illustrations.........................12mo 1 50
Motherless. Translated. Ill's....12mo 1 50
Unkind Word and Other Stories...12mo 1 50
Two Marriages......................12mo 1 50
MURRAY'S The Prairie Bird................. 1 00
MY Husband's Crime. Illustrated.......... 75
MY Uncle the Curate........................ 50
NABOB at Home, The........................ 50
NATURE'S Nobleman........................ 50
NEALE'S The Lost Ship...................... 75
NICHOLS'S The Sanctuary. Ill's......12mo 1 50
NORA and Archibald Lee.................... 50
NORTON'S Stuart of Dunleath.............. 50
OLIPHANT'S (Mrs.) Agnes................... 75
Athelings................................... 75
Brownlows 37
Chronicles of Carlingford.................. 1 25
Cloth 1 75
Days of My Life.......................12mo 1 50
For Love and Life.......................... 75
Innocent. Illustrated....................... 75
John: a Love Story......................... 50
Katie Stewart............................... 25
The House on the Moor...........12mo 1 50
The Laird of Norlaw...............12mo 1 50
The Last of the Mortimers.........12mo 1 50
Lucy Crofton.........................12mo 1 50
Madonna Mary............................. 50
Miss Majoribanks.......................... 50
Ombra....................................... 75
The Perpetual Curate...................... 1 00
Cloth 1 50
Quiet Heart................................. 25
Son of the Soil.............................. 1 00
Cloth 1 50
Squire Arden................................ 75
The Story of Valentine; and his Brother. 75
The Minister's Wife......................... 75
PAYN'S (Jas.) At Her Mercy................. 50
A Woman's Vengeance..................... 50
Best of Husbands........................... 50
Beggar on Horseback....................... 35
Bred in the Bone........................... 50
Carlyon's Year.............................. 25
Cecil's Tryst................................ 50
Found Dead................................. 50
Gwendoline's Harvest....................... 25
Murphy's Master........................... 25
One of the Family.......................... 25
Won—Not Wooed........................... 50
PICKERINGS (Miss) The Grandfather...... 50
The Grumbler 50
POINT of Honor, A......................... 50

PRICE

POLLARD'S (Eliza F.) Hope Deferred......$ 50
PONSONBY'S (Lady) Discipline of Life.... 50
Mary Lindsay.................................. 50
Pride and Irresolution..................... 50
PROFESSOR'S Lady............................ 25
RACHEL'S Secret............................... 75
RAYMOND'S Heroine 50
READE'S (Charles) Hard Cash. Ill's....... 50
Cloth 1 00
A Simpleton 50
Cloth 1 00
Griffith Gaunt. Illustrations............ 25
It is Never Too Late to Mend............ 50
Love Me Little, Love Me Long.......... 50
12mo 1 00
Foul Play....................................... 25
White Lies..................................... 50
Peg Woffington and Other Tales......... 50
Put Yourself in His Place. Illustrations. 75
Cloth 1 25
12mo 1 00
A Terrible Temptation. Illustrated.... 50
12mo 75
The Cloister and the Hearth.............. 50
The Wandering Heir. Illustrations.... 25
Cloth 60
RECOLLECTIONS of Eton. Illustrated.... 50
REGENT'S Daughter.......................... 50
RIDDELL'S (Mrs. J. H.) Maxwell Drewitt. 75
Phemie Keller.................................. 50
Race for Wealth.............................. 75
A Life's Assize 50
ROBINSON'S (F. W.) For Her Sake. Ill's. 75
A Bridge of Glass............................ 50
Carry's Confession........................... 75
Christie's Faith.........................12mo 1 75
Her Face was Her Fortune............... 50
Little Kate Kirby. Illustrations....... 75
Mattie: a Stray............................... 75
No Man's Friend 75
Poor Humanity............................... 50
Second-Cousin Sarah. Illustrations..... 75
Stern Necessity.............................. 50
True to Herself.............................. 50
A Girl's Romance, and Other Stories.... 50
ROMANCE and its Hero, The..........12mo 1 25
ROWCROFT'S The Bush Ranger............ 50
SACRISTAN'S Household, The. Illustrated. 75
SAFELY Married............................... 50
SALA'S Quite Alone........................... 75
SAUNDERS'S Abel Drake's Wife.......... 75
Bound to the Wheel........................ 75
Hirell... 50
Martin Pole.................................... 50
SEDGWICK'S (Miss) Hope Leslie. 2 vols. 12mo 3 00
The Linwoods...................2 vols. 12mo 3 00
Live and Let Live...........18mo, Cloth 75
Married or Single?..........2 vols. 12mo 3 00
Means and Ends..............18mo, Cloth 75
Poor Rich Man and Rich Poor Man....
18mo, Cloth 75
Stories for Young Persons...18mo, Cloth 75
Tales of Glauber Spa...............12mo 1 50
Wilton Harvey and Other Tales...18mo,
Cloth 75
SEDGWICK'S (Mrs.) Walter Thornley. 12mo 1 50
SELF... 75
SEWELL'S (Miss) Amy Herbert............ 50

PRICE

SHERWOOD'S (Mrs.) Henry Milner. 2 vols.
12mo. $3 00
Lady of the Manor........4 vols. 12mo 6 00
Roxobel..............3 vols. 18mo, Cloth 2 25
Fairchild Family......................12mo 1 50
John Marten...........................12mo 1 50
SHERWOOD'S (Mrs.) Works. Engravings.
16 Vols., 12mo, Cloth, per vol. 1 50

The Volumes sold separately or in sets.

Vol. I. The History of Henry Milner, Parts I., II., and III.

Vol. II. Fairchild Family; Orphans of Normandy; The Latter Days, &c.

Vol. III. Little Henry and his Bearer; Lucy and her Dhaye; Memoirs of Sergeant Dale, his Daughter, and the Orphan Mary; Susan Gray; Lucy Clare; Theophilus and Sophia; Abdallah, the Merchant of Bagdad.

Vol. IV. The Indian Pilgrim; The Broken Hyacinth; the Babes in the Wood of the New World; Catherine Seward; The Little Beggars, &c.

Vol. V. The Infant's Progress; The Flowers of the Forest; Ermina, &c.

Vol. VI. The Governess; The Little Momiere; The Stranger at Home; Pere la Chaise; English Mary; My Uncle Timothy.

Vol. VII. The Nun; Intimate Friends; My Aunt Kate; Emeline; Obedience; The Gipsy Babes; The Basket-maker; The Butterfly, &c.

Vol. VIII. Victoria; Arzoomund; The Birth-Day Present; The Errand Boy; The Orphan Boy; The Two Sisters; Julian Percival; Edward Mansfield; The Infirmary; The Young Forester; Bitter Sweet; Common Errors, &c.

Vol. IX., X., XI., and XII. The Lady of the Manor.

Vol. XIII. The Mail-Coach; My Three Uncles; The Old Lady's Complaint; The Shepherd's Fountain; The Hours of Infancy; Economy; Old Things and New Things; The Swiss Cottage; The Infant's Grave; The Father's Eye; Dudley Castle; The Blessed Family; Caroline Mordaunt, &c.

Vol. XIV. The Monk of Cimies; The Rosary, or Rosee of Montreux; The Roman Baths; Saint Hospice; The Violet Leaf; The Convent of St. Clair.

Vol. XV. The History of Henry Milner, Part IV.; Sabbaths on the Continent; The Idler.

Vol. XVI. John Marten.

SINCLAIR'S (Miss) Sir Edward Graham... 1 00
SMITH'S (Horace) Adam Brown............ 50
Arthur Arundel.............................. 50
Love and Mesmerism........................ 75
SMOLLETT'S Humphrey Clinker......12mo 1 50
SPINDLER'S The Jew......................... 75
STANDISH the Puritan.................12mo 1 50
STEELE'S So Runs the World Away........ 50
STONE EDGE.................................... 25

PRICE
SUE'S Arthur.................................$ 75
Commander of Malta...................... 50
De Rohan.................................. 50
TABOR'S (Eliza) Hope Meredith............ 50
Jeanie's Quiet Life..................... 50
Meta's Faith............................ 50
St. Olave's.............................. 75
The Blue Ribbon......................... 50
TALBOT'S Through Fire and Water. Ill's. 25
TALES from the German.................. 50
TEFFT'S The Shoulder Knot...........12mo 1 50
TEMME'S Anna Hammer.................... 50
THACKERAY'S (Miss) Complete Works.... 1 25
Illustrations. Cloth 1 75
Old Kensington. Illustrations.......... 1 00
Village on the Cliff...................... 25
THACKERAY'S (W. M.) Novels.
Vanity Fair. Illustrations............... 50
Cloth 1 00
Library Edition, 3 vols., Crown 8vo 7 50
Pendennis. Illustrations................ 75
12mo 1 25
2 vols. 8vo Cloth 2 00
The Virginians. Illustrations........... 75
Cloth 1 25
The Newcomes. Illustrations............ 75
Cloth 1 25
The Adventures of Philip. Illustrations. 50
Cloth 1 00
Henry Esmond and Lovel the Widower.
Illustrations............................ 75
Denis Duval. Illustrations.............. 50
Great Hoggarty Diamond................ 25
THOMAS'S (Miss Annie) Called to Account. 50
A Passion in Tatters..................... 75
Denis Donne.............................. 50
False Colors.............................. 50
"'He Cometh Not,' She Said"......... 50
Maud Mohan.............................. 25
On Guard.................................. 50
Only Herself.............................. 50
Played Out................................ 75
Playing for High Stakes. Illustrations 25
The Dower House......................... 50
Theo Leigh................................ 50
The Two Widows......................... 50
Walter Goring............................ 75
(Miss Martha M.) Life's Lesson....12mo 1 50
THOMPSON'S (Mrs.) Lady of Milan........ 75
TIECK'S The Elves......................... 50
TOM Brown's School Days. By An Old Boy.
Illustrated............................... 50
TOM Brown at Oxford. Illustrations....... 75
The two in One Volume 1 50
TROLLOPE'S (Anthony) The Belton Estate 50
The Bertrams.......................12mo 1 50
Brown, Jones, and Robinson............ 50
Can You Forgive Her?.................. 1 50
Cloth 2 00
Castle Richmond....................12mo 1 50
Claverings. Illustrations............... 50
Cloth 1 00
Doctor Thorne......................12mo 1 50
Popular Edition 75
Framley Parsonage. Illustrations..12mo 1 75
Harry Heathcote of Gangoil............ 25
He Knew He was Right.................. 1 00
Cloth 1 50
The Golden Lion of Granpere. Ill's... 75
Cloth 1 25

TROLLOPE'S (Anthony) Lady Anna.......$ 50
Last Chronicle of Barset................ 1 50
Cloth 2 00
Miss Mackenzie........................... 50
Phineas Finn............................ 1 25
Cloth 1 75
Phineas Redux........................... 1 25
Cloth 1 75
The Eustace Diamonds.................. 1 25
Cloth 1 75
Orley Farm. Illustrations.............. 1 50
Cloth 2 00
Rachel Ray............................... 50
Ralph the Heir. Illustrations.......... 1 25
Cloth 1 75
Sir Harry Hotspur of Humblethwaite.
Engravings............................ 50
The Small House at Allington. Ill's.... 1 50
Cloth 2 00
The Three Clerks...................12mo 1 50
The Vicar of Bullhampton. Illustrations. 1 25
Cloth 1 75
The Warden and Barchester Towers.
In one volume........................ 75
The Way we Live Now. (*In Press.*)
(Mrs.) Petticoat Government............ 50
(T. A.) Lindisfarn Chase................ 1 50
Cloth 2 00
A Siren.................................... 50
Durnton Abbey........................... 50
Diamond Cut Diamond.............12mo 1 25
TUTOR'S Ward, The....................... 50
TWO Families, The....................12mo 1 50
TYTLER'S (Sarah) The Huguenot Family.
12mo 1 50
UNDER Foot. Illustrated................. 50
UNDER the Ban........................... 1 25
Cloth 1 75
VERONICA................................ 50
WARBURTON'S Darien..................... 50
Reginald Hastings........................ 50
WARREN'S Diary of a Physician....3 vols.
16mo, Cloth 2 25
Now and Then.......................12mo 1 25
WARD'S Chatsworth....................... 50
De Vere.............................12mo 1 50
WEALTH and Worth...........18mo, Cloth 75
WHAT'S to be Done?...........18mo, Cloth 75
WHEAT and Tares......................12mo 1 25
WHICH is the Heroine?.................... 50
WHITE Slave, The........................ 1 00
WHITE'S Circe............................ 50
WILKINSON'S (Miss) Hands not Hearts... 50
WILLIAMS'S The Luttrells................ 50
WILLS'S Notice to Quit................... 50
The Wife's Evidence..................... 50
WISE'S Captain Brand. Illustrations...... 1 50
Cloth 2 00
WOOD'S (Mrs. Henry) Danesbury House.
12mo 1 25
WYOMING................................. 50
YATES'S Black Sheep...................... 50
Kissing the Rod........................ 75
Land at Last............................ 50
Wrecked in Port......................... 50
Dr. Wainwright's Patient................ 50
ZSCHOKKE'S Veronica.................... 50

Harper's Catalogue.

The attention of gentlemen, in town or country, designing to form Libraries or enrich their Literary Collections, is respectfully invited to Harper's Catalogue, which will be found to comprise a large proportion of the standard and most esteemed works in English and Classical Literature—COMPREHENDING OVER THREE THOUSAND VOLUMES—which are offered, in most instances, at less than one-half the cost of similar productions in England.

To Librarians and others connected with Colleges, Schools, &c., who may not have access to a trustworthy guide in forming the true estimate of literary productions, it is believed this Catalogue will prove especially valuable for reference.

To prevent disappointment, it is suggested that, whenever books can not be obtained through any bookseller or local agent, applications with remittance should be addressed direct to Harper & Brothers, which will receive prompt attention.

Sent by mail on receipt of Ten Cents.

Address HARPER & BROTHERS,
FRANKLIN SQUARE, NEW YORK.

www.ingramcontent.com/pod-product-compliance
Lightning Source LLC
LaVergne TN
LVHW011203110826
845150LV00006B/1305

* 9 7 8 1 4 2 5 5 1 8 1 1 0 *